L. KOSSUTH

Austria, Frontispiece.

AUSTRIA

ITS

RISE AND PRESENT POWER

BY

JOHN S. C. ABBOTT

WITH A SUPPLEMENTARY CHAPTER OF RECENT EVENTS

By WILFRED C. LAY, Ph.D.

ILLUSTRATED

WILDSIDE PRESS

PREFACE.

THE annals of the world contain no other such narrative as that of Italy. Legendary Rome, the frenzied strife with Carthage, the wild career of Hannibal, the lifelong struggles of Pompey and Cæsar, the culmination of the empire into universal sovereignty, the rise of Christianity, the crumbling temples of Paganism, the sweep of Moslem armies, the surging billows of barbaric invasion, the fall of imperial Rome, the gloom and chaos of the dark ages, the struggle of the great monarchies of Europe to grasp the fragments of the empire, the amazing campaigns of Napoleon I., the triumph of the allies, the new dismemberment of Italy, the campaigns of Magenta and Solferino, and the recent re-establishment of Rome as the capital of re-united Italy, — all these conspire in furnishing historical records, which, in interest and instruction, are without a parallel.

The materials from which to gather information upon these points are inexhaustible. Those upon which the author has mainly relied are the works of Niebuhr, Arnold, Schmidt, Livy, Tacitus, Plutarch, Guicciardini, Sforzozi, Botta, Luigi Bosri, Sismondi, Percival, Spaulding, Gibbon, Robertson, Thiers, Alison, Julie de Marguerites, together with reviews and encyclopædias upon important characters and events. The author has spared no pains to attain all possible accuracy, having devoted to the most important events here recorded the studies of many years. Where there has been discrepancy of authorities, he has adopted that statement, which, after the most careful consideration, has appeared to him best authenticated.

It is affecting to observe in the history of Germany, through what woes humanity has passed in attaining even its present position of civilization. It is to be hoped that the human family may never again suffer what it has already endured. We shall be indeed insane if we do not gain some wisdom from the struggles and the calamities of those who have gone before us. The narrative of the career of the Austrian Empire, must, by contrast, excite emotions of gratitude in every American bosom. Our lines have fallen to us in pleasant places ; we have a goodly heritage.

It is the author's intention soon to issue, as the second of this series, the History of the Empire of Russia.

JOHN S. C. ABBOTT.

BRUNSWICK, Maine, 1859.

CONTENTS.

CHAPTER I.
RHODOLPH OF HAPSBURG.
FROM 1232 TO 1291.

CHAPTER II.
REIGNS OF ALBERT I., FREDERIC, ALBERT AND OTHO.
FROM 1291 TO 1347.

CHAPTER III.
RHODOLPH II., ALBERT IV. AND ALBERT V.
FROM 1339 TO 1437.

1*

CHAPTER VIII.

CHARLES V. AND THE REFORMATION.

From 1531 to 1552.

CHAPTER IX.

CHARLES V. AND THE TURKISH WARS

From 1552 to 1555.

CHAPTER X.

FERDINAND I. — HIS WARS AND INTRIGUES.

From 1555 to 1562.

CHAPTER XI.
DEATH OF FERDINAND I.—ACCESSION OF MAXIMILIAN II.
FROM 1562 TO 1576.

CHAPTER XII.
CHARACTER OF MAXIMILIAN.—SUCCESSION OF RHODOLPH III.
FROM 1576 TO 1604.

CHAPTER XIII.
RHODOLPH III. AND MATTHIAS.
FROM 1604 TO 1609.

CHAPTER XIV.
RHODOLPH III. AND MATTHIAS.
FROM 1609 TO 1612.

CHAPTER XV.
MATTHIAS.
FROM 1612 TO 1619.

CHAPTER XVI.
FERDINAND II.
FROM 1619 TO 1621.

CHAPTER XVII.
FERDINAND II.
FROM 1621 TO 1629.

CHAPTER XXV.

CHARLES VI. AND THE TURKISH WAR RENEWED.

From 1735 to 1789.

CHAPTER XXVI.

MARIA THERESA.

From 1789 to 1741.

CHAPTER XXVII.

MARIA THERESA.

From 1741 to 1743.

CHAPTER XXVIII.

MARIA THERESA.

From 1743 to 1748.

CHAPTER XXIX.
MARIA THERESA.
FROM 1748 TO 1759.

CHAPTER XXX.
MARIA THERESA.
FROM 1759 TO 1780.

CHAPTER XXXI.
JOSEPH II. AND LEOPOLD II.
FROM 1780 TO 1792.

LIST OF ILLUSTRATIONS

AUSTRIA

THE EMPIRE OF AUSTRIA.

CHAPTER I

RHODOLPH OF HAPSBURG.

HAWK'S CASTLE.—ALBERT, COUNT OF HAPSBURG.—RHODOLPH OF HAPSBURG.—HIS MARRIAGE AND ESTATES.—EXCOMMUNICATION AND ITS RESULTS.—HIS PRINCIPLES OF HONOR.—A CONFEDERACY OF BARONS.—THEIR ROUTE.—RHODOLPH'S ELECTION AS EMPEROR OF GERMANY.—THE BISHOP'S WARNING.—DISSATISFACTION AT THE RESULT OF THE ELECTION.—ADVANTAGES ACCRUING FROM THE POSSESSION OF AN INTERESTING FAMILY.—CONQUEST.—OTTOCAR ACKNOWLEDGES THE EMPEROR; YET BREAKS HIS OATH OF ALLEGIANCE.—GATHERING CLOUDS.—WONDERFUL ESCAPE.—VICTORY OF RHODOLPH.—HIS REFORMS.

IN the small canton of Aargau, in Switzerland, on a rocky bluff of the Wulpelsberg, there still remains an old baronial castle, called Hapsburg, or Hawk's Castle. It was reared in the eleventh century, and was occupied by a succession of warlike barons, who have left nothing to distinguish themselves from the feudal lords whose castles, at that period, frowned upon almost every eminence of Europe. In the year 1232 this castle was occupied by Albert, fourth Count of Hapsburg. He had acquired some little reputation for military prowess, the only reputation any one could acquire in that dark age, and became ambitious of winning new laurels in the war with the infidels in the holy land. Religious fanaticism and military ambition were then the two great powers which ruled the human soul.

With the usual display of semi-barbaric pomp, Albert made arrangements to leave his castle to engage in the perilous holy war against the Saracens, from which few ever returned. A few years were employed in the necessary preparations. At the sound of the bugle the portcullis was raised, the draw-

1*

bridge spanned the moat, and Albert, at the head of thirty steel-clad warriors, with nodding plumes, and banners unfurled, emerged from the castle, and proceeded to the neighboring convent of Mari. His wife, Hedwige, and their three sons, Rhodolph, Albert and Hartman, accompanied him to the chapel where the ecclesiastics awaited his arrival. A multitude of vassals crowded around to witness the imposing ceremonies of the church, as the banners were blessed and the knights, after having received the sacrament of the Lord's Supper, were commended to the protection of God. Albert felt the solemnity of the hour, and in solemn tones gave his farewell address to his children.

"My sons," said the steel-clad warrior, "cultivate truth and piety; give no ear to evil counselors, never engage in unnecessary war, but when you are involved in war be strong and brave. Love peace even better than your own personal interests. Remember that the counts of Hapsburg did not attain their heights of reputation and glory by fraud, insolence or selfishness, but by courage and devotion to the public weal. As long as you follow their footsteps, you will not only retain, but augment, the possessions and dignities of your illustrious ancestors."

The tears and sobs of his wife and family interrupted him while he uttered these parting words. The bugles then sounded. The knights mounted their horses; the clatter of hoofs was heard, and the glittering cavalcade soon disappeared in the forest. Albert had left his ancestral castle, never to return. He had but just arrived in Palestine, when he was taken sick at Askalon, and died in the year 1240.

Rhodolph, his eldest son, was twenty-two years of age at the time of his father's death. Frederic II., one of the most renowned monarchs of the middle ages, was then Emperor of that conglomeration of heterogeneous States called Germany. Each of these States had its own independent ruler and laws, but they were all held together by a common bond for mutual

protection, and some one illustrious sovereign was chosen as
Emperor of Germany, to preside over their common affairs.
The Emperor of Germany, having influence over all these
States, was consequently, in position, the great man of the
age.

Albert, Count of Hapsburg, had been one of the favorite
captains of Frederic II. in the numerous wars which desolated
Europe in that dark age. He was often at court, and the emperor even condescended to present his son Rhodolph at the
font for baptism. As the child grew, he was trained to all
athletic feats, riding ungovernable horses, throwing the jave-
lin, wrestling, running, and fencing. He early gave indications of surprising mental and bodily vigor, and, at an age
when most lads are considered merely children, he accompanied his father to the camp and to the court. Upon the
death of his father, Rhodolph inherited the ancestral castle,
and the moderate possessions of a Swiss baron. He was surrounded by barons of far greater wealth and power than himself, and his proud spirit was roused, in disregard of his father's
counsels, to aggrandize his fortunes by force of arms, the only
way then by which wealth and power could be attained. He
exhausted his revenues by maintaining a princely establishment, organized a well-selected band of his vassals into a military corps, which he drilled to a state of perfect discipline,
and then commenced a series of incursions upon his neighbors.
From some feeble barons he won territory, thus extending his
domains; from others he extorted money, thus enabling him
to reward his troops, and to add to their number by engaging
fearless spirits in his service wherever he could find them.

In the year 1245, Rhodolph strengthened himself still
more by an advantageous marriage with Gertrude, the beautiful daughter of the Count of Hohenberg. With his bride he
received as her dowry the castle of Oeltingen, and very considerable territorial possessions. Thus in five years Rhodolph,
by that species of robbery which was then called heroic ad-

vent ire, and by a fortunate marriage, had more than doubled
his hereditary inheritance. The charms of his bride, and the
care of his estates seem for a few years to have arrested the
progress of his ambition; for we can find no further notice of
him among the ancient chronicles for eight years. But, with
almost all men, love is an ephemeral passion, which is eventually vanquished by other powers of the soul. Ambition slumbered for a little time, but was soon roused anew, invigorated
by repose.

In 1253 .we find Rhodolph heading a foray of steel-clad
knights, with their banded followers, in a midnight attack
upon the city of Basle. They break over all the defenses,
sweep all opposition before them, and in the fury of the fight,
either by accident or as a necessity of war, sacrilegiously set
fire to a nunnery. For this crime Rhodolph was excommunicated by the pope. Excommunication was then no farce.
There were few who dared to serve a prince upon whom the
denunciations of the Church had fallen. It was a stunning
blow, from which few men could recover. Rhodolph, instead
of sinking in despair, endeavored, by new acts of obedience
and devotion to the Church, to obtain the revocation of the
sentence.

In the region now called Prussia, there was then a barbaric
pagan race, against whom the pope had published a crusade.
Into this war the excommunicated Rhodolph plunged with all
the impetuosity of his nature; he resolved to work out abso-
lution, by converting, with all the potency of fire and sword,
the barbarians to the Church. His penitence and zeal seem to
have been accepted, for we soon find him on good terms again
with the pope. He now sought to have a hand in every quarrel, far and near. Wherever the sounds of war are raised,
the shout of Rhodolph is heard urging to the strife. In every
hot and fiery foray, the steed of Rhodolph is rearing and
plunging, and his saber strokes fall in ringing blows upon
cuirass and helmet. He efficiently aided the city of Stras-

bourg in their war against their bishop, and received from them in gratitude extensive territories, while at the same time they reared a monument to his name, portions of which still exist. His younger brother died, leaving an only daughter, Anne, with a large inheritance. Rhodolph, as her guardian, came into possession of the counties of Kyburg, Lentzburg and Baden, and other scattered domains.

This rapidly-increasing wealth and power, did but increase his energy and his spirit of encroachment. And yet he adopted principles of honor which were far from common in that age of barbaric violence. He would never stoop to ordinary robbery, or harass peasants and helpless travelers, as was constantly done by the turbulent barons around him. His warfare was against the castle, never against the cottage. He met in arms the panoplied knight, never the timid and crouching peasant. He swept the roads of the banditti by which they were infested, and often espoused the cause of citizens and freemen against the turbulent barons and haughty prelates. He thus gained a wide-spread reputation for justice, as well as for prowess, and the name of Rhodolph of Hapsburg was ascending fast into renown. Every post of authority then required the agency of a military arm. The feeble cantons would seek the protection of a powerful chief; the citizens of a wealthy town, ever liable to be robbed by bishop or baron, looked around for some warrior who had invincible troops at his command for their protection. Thus Rhodolph of Hapsburg was chosen chief of the mountaineers of Uri, Schweitz and Underwalden; and all their trained bands were ready, when his bugle note echoed through their defiles, to follow him unquestioning, and to do his bidding. The citizens of Zurich chose Rhodolph of Hapsburg as their prefect or mayor; and whenever his banner was unfurled in their streets, all the troops of the city were at his command.

The neighboring barons, alarmed at this rapid aggrandizement of Rhodolph, formed an alliance to crush him. The

mountaineers heard his bugle call, and rushed to his aid.
Zurich opened her gates, and her marshaled troops hastened
to his banner.   From Hapsburg, and Rheinfelden, and Suabia, and Brisgau, and we know not how many other of the
territorial possessions of the count, the vassals rushed to the
aid of their lord.   They met in one of the valleys of Zurich.
The battle was short, and the confederated barons were put
to utter flight.   Some took refuge in the strong castle of
Balder, upon a rocky cliff washed by the Albis.   Rhodolph
selected thirty horsemen and thirty footmen.

"Will you follow me," said he, "in an enterprise where
the honor will be equal to the peril ?"

A universal shout of assent was the response.   Concealing
the footmen in a thicket, he, at the head of thirty horsemen,
rode boldly to the gates of the castle, bidding defiance, with
all the utterances and gesticulations of contempt, to the whole
garrison.   Those on the ramparts, stung by the insult, rushed
out to chastise so impudent a challenge.   The footmen rose
from their ambush, and assailants and assailed rushed pell
mell in at the open gates of the castle.   The garrison were cut
down or taken captive, and the fortress demolished.   Another
party had fled to the castle of Uttleberg.   By an ingenious
stratagem, this castle was also taken.   Success succeeded success with such rapidity, that the confederate barons, struck
with consternation, exclaimed,

"All opposition is fruitless.   Rhodolph of Hapsburg is invincible."

They consequently dissolved the alliance, and sought peace
on terms which vastly augmented the power of the conqueror.

Basle now incurred the displeasure of Rhodolph.   He led
his armies to the gates of the city, and extorted satisfaction.
The Bishop of Basle, a haughty prelate of great military power,
and who could summon many barons to his aid, ventured to
make arrogant demands of this warrior flushed with victory.
The palace and vast possessions of the bishop were upon the

other side of the unbridged Rhine, and the bishop imagined that he could easily prevent the passage of the river. But Rhodolph speedily constructed a bridge of boats, put to flight the troops which opposed his passage, drove the peasants of the bishop everywhere before him, and burned their cottages and their fields of grain. The bishop, appalled, sued for a truce, that they might negotiate terms of peace. Rhodolph consented, and encamped his followers.

He was asleep in his tent, when a messenger entered at midnight, awoke him, and informed him that he was elected Emperor of Germany. The previous emperor, Richard, had died two years before, and after an interregnum of two years of almost unparalleled anarchy, the electors had just met, and, almost to their own surprise, through the fluctuations and combinations of political intrigue, had chosen Rhodolph of Hapsburg as his successor. Rhodolph himself was so much astonished at the announcement, that for some time he could not be persuaded that the intelligence was correct.

To wage war against the Emperor of Germany, who could lead almost countless thousands into the field, was a very different affair from measuring strength with the comparatively feeble Count of Hapsburg. The news of his election flew rapidly. Basle threw open her gates, and the citizens, with illuminations, shouts, and the ringing of bells, greeted the new emperor. The bishop was so chagrined at the elevation of his foe, that he smote his forehead, and, looking to heaven, profanely said,

"Great God, take care of your throne, or Rhodolph of Hapsburg will take it from you!"

Rhodolph was now fifty-five years of age. Alphonso, King of Castile, and Ottocar, King of Bohemia, had both been candidates for the imperial crown. Exasperated by the unexpected election of Rhodolph, they both refused to acknowledge his election, and sent ambassadors with rich presents to the pope to win him also to their side. Rhodolph, justly appre-

B

ciating the power of the pope, sent him a letter couched in those terms which would be most palatable to the pontiff.

"Turning all my thoughts to Him," he wrote, " under whose authority we live, and placing all my expectations on you alone, I fall down before the feet of your Holiness, beseeching you, with the most earnest supplication, to favor me with your accustomed kindness in my present undertaking; and that you will deign, by your mediation with the Most High, to support my cause. That I may be enabled to perform what is most acceptable to God and to His holy Church, may it graciously please your Holiness to crown me with the imperial diadem; for I trust I am both able and willing to undertake and accomplish whatever you and the holy Church shall think proper to impose upon me."

Gregory X. was a humane and sagacious man, influenced by a profound zeal for the peace of Europe and the propagation of the Christian faith. Gregory received the ambassadors of Rhodolph graciously, extorted from them whatever concessions he desired on the part of the emperor, and pledged his support.

Ottocar, King of Bohemia, still remained firm, and even malignant, in his hostility, utterly refusing to recognize the emperor, or to perform any of those acts of fealty which were his due. He declared the electoral diet to have been illegally convened, and the election to have been the result of fraud, and that a man who had been excommunicated for burning a convent, was totally unfit to wear the imperial crown. The diet met at Augsburg, and irritated by the contumacy of Ottocar, sent a command to him to recognize the authority of the emperor, pronouncing upon him the ban of the empire should he refuse. Ottocar dismissed the ambassadors with defiance and contempt from his palace at Prague, saying,

" Tell Rhodolph that he may rule over the territories of the empire, but he shall have no dominion over mine. It is a disgrace to Germany, that a petty count of Hapsburg should have been preferred to so many powerful sovereigns."

War, and a fearful one, was now inevitable. Ottocar was a veteran soldier, a man of great intrepidity and energy, and his pride was thoroughly roused. By a long series of aggressions he had become the most powerful prince in Europe, and he could lead the most powerful armies into the field. His dominions extended from the confines of Bavaria to Raab in Hungary, and from the Adriatic to the shores of the Baltic. The hereditary domains of the Count of Hapsburg were comparatively insignificant, and were remotely situated at the foot of the Alps, spreading through the defiles of Alsace and Suabia. As emperor, Rhodolph could call the armies of the Germanic princes into the field; but these princes moved reluctantly, unless roused by some question of great moment to them all. And when these heterogeneous troops of the empire were assembled, there was but a slender bond of union between them.

But Rhodolph possessed mental resources equal to the emergence. As cautious as he was bold, as sagacious in council as he was impetuous in action, he calmly, and with great foresight and deliberation, prepared for the strife. To a monarch in such a time of need, a family of brave sons and beautiful daughters, is an inestimable blessing. Rhodolph secured the Duke of Sclavonia by making him the happy husband of one of his daughters. His son Albert married Elizabeth, daughter of the Count of Tyrol, and thus that powerful and noble family was secured. Henry of Bavaria he intimidated, and by force of arms compelled him to lead his troops to the standard of the emperor; and then, to secure his fidelity, gave his daughter Hedwige to Henry's son Otho, in marriage, promising to his daughter as a dowry a portion of Austria, which was then a feeble duchy upon the Danube, but little larger than the State of Massachusetts.

Ottocar was but little aware of the tremendous energies

of the foe he had aroused.   Regarding Rhodolph almost with contempt, he had by no means made the arrangements which his peril demanded, and was in consternation when he heard that Rhodolph, in alliance with Henry of Bavaria, had already entered Austria, taken possession of several fortresses, and, at the head of a force of a thousand horsemen, was carrying all before him, and was triumphantly marching upon Vienna. Rhodolph had so admirably matured his plans, that his advance seemed rather a festive journey than a contested conquest.   With the utmost haste Ottocar urged his troops down through the defiles of the Bohemian mountains, hoping to save the capital.   But Rhodolph was at Vienna before him, where he was joined by others of his allies, who were to meet him at that rendezvous.   Vienna, the capital, was a fortress of great strength.   Upon this frontier post Charlemagne had established a strong body of troops under a commander who was called a margrave ; and for some centuries this city, commanding the Danube, had been deemed one of the strongest defenses of the empire against Mohammedan invasion.   Vienna, unable to resist, capitulated.   The army of Ottocar had been so driven in their long and difficult march, that, exhausted and perishing for want of provisions, they began to mutiny. The pope had excommunicated Ottocar, and the terrors of the curse of the pope, were driving captains and nobles from his service.   The proud spirit of Ottocar, after a terrible struggle, was utterly crushed, and he humbly sued for peace.   The terms were hard for a haughty spirit to bear.   The conquered king was compelled to renounce all claim to Austria and several other adjoining provinces, Styria, Carinthia, Carniola and Windischmark ; to take the oath of allegiance to the emperor, and publicly to do him homage as his vassal lord.   To cement this compulsory friendship, Rhodolph, who was rich in daughters, having six to proffer as bribes, gave one, with an abundant dowry in silver, to a son of Ottocar.

The day was appointed for the king, in the presence of the

whole army, to do homage to the emperor as his liege lord. It was the 25th of November, 1276. With a large escort of Bohemian nobles, Ottocar crossed the Danube, and was received by the emperor in the presence of many of the leading princes of the empire. The whole army was drawn up to witness the spectacle. With a dejected countenance, and with indications, which he could not conceal, of a crushed and broken spirit, Ottocar renounced these valuable provinces, and kneeling before the emperor, performed the humiliating ceremony of feudal homage. The pope in consequence withdrew his sentence of excommunication, and Ottocar returned to his mutilated kingdom, a humbler and a wiser man.

Rhodolph now took possession of the adjacent provinces which had been ceded to him, and, uniting them, placed them under the government of Louis of Bavaria, son of his firm ally Henry, the King of Bavaria. Bavaria bounded Austria on the west, and thus the father and the son would be in easy coöperation. He then established his three sons, Albert, Hartmann, and Rhodolph, in different parts of these provinces, and, with his queen, fixed his residence at Vienna.

Such was the nucleus of the Austrian empire, and such the commencement of the powerful monarchy which for so many generations has exerted so important a control over the affairs of Europe. Ottocar, however, though he left Rhodolph with the strongest protestations of friendship, returned to Prague consumed by the most torturing fires of humiliation and chagrin. His wife, a haughty woman, who was incapable of listening to the voice of judgment when her passions were inflamed, could not conceive it possible that a petty count of Hapsburg could vanquish her renowned husband in the field. And when she heard that Ottocar had actually done fealty to Rhodolph, and had surrendered to him valuable provinces of the kingdom, no bridle could be put upon her woman's tongue. She almost stung her husband to madness with taunts and reproaches.

Thus influenced by the pride of his queen, Cunegunda, Ot. tocar violated his oath, refused to execute the treaty, impris oned in a convent the daughter whom Rhodolph had given to his son, and sent a defiant and insulting letter to the emperor. Rhodolph returned a dignified answer and prepared for war. Ottocar, now better understanding the power of his foe, made the most formidable preparations for the strife, and soon took the field with an army which he supposed would certainly triumph over any force which Rhodolph could raise. He even succeeded in drawing Henry of Bavaria into an alliance; and many of the German princes, whom he could not win to his standard, he bribed to neutrality. Numerous chieftains, lured to his camp by confidence of victory, crowded around him with their followers, from Poland, Bulgaria, Pomerania, Magdeburg, and from the barbaric shores of the Baltic. Many of the fierce nobles of Hungary had also joined the standard of Ottocar.

Thus suddenly clouds gathered around Rhodolph, and many of his friends despaired of his cause. He appealed to the princes of the German empire, and but few responded to his call. His sons-in-law, the Electors of Palatine and of Saxony, ventured not to aid him in an emergence when defeat seemed almost certain, and where all who shared in the defeat would be utterly ruined. In June, 1275, Ottocar marched from Prague, met his allies at the appointed rendezvous, and threading the defiles of the Bohemian mountains, approached the frontiers of Austria. Rhodolph was seriously alarmed for it was evident that the chances of war were against him He could not conceal the restlessness and agitation of his spirit as he impatiently awaited the arrival of troops whom he summoned, but who disappointed his hopes.

"I have not one," he sadly exclaimed, "in whom I can confide, or on whose advice I can depend."

The citizens of Vienna perceiving that Rhodolph was abandoned by his German allies, and that they could present no effectual resistance to so powerful an army as was approaching, and terrified in view of a siege, and the capture of the city by storm, urged a capitulation, and even begged permission to choose a new sovereign, that they might not be involved in the ruin impending over Rhodolph. This address roused Rhodolph from his despondency, and inspired him with the energies of despair. He had succeeded in obtaining a few troops from his provinces in Switzerland. The Bishop of Basle, who had now become his confessor, came to his aid, at the head of a hundred horsemen, and a body of expert slingers. Rhodolph, though earnestly advised not to undertake a battle with such desperate odds, marched from Vienna to meet the foe.

Rapidy traversing the southern banks of the Danube to Hamburg, he crossed the river and advanced to Marcheck, on the banks of the Morava. He was joined by some troops from Styria and Carinthia, and by a strong force led by the King of Hungary. Emboldened by these accessions, though still far inferior in strength to Ottocar, he pressed on till the two armies faced each other on the plains of Murchfield. It was the 26th of August, 1278.

At this moment some traitors deserting the camp of Ottocar, repaired to the camp of Rhodolph and proposed to assassinate the Bohemian king. Rhodolph spurned the infamous offer, and embraced the opportunity of seeking terms of reconciliation by apprising Ottocar of his danger. But the king, confident in his own strength, and despising the weakness of Rhodolph, deemed the story a fabrication and refused to listen to any overtures. Without delay he drew up his army in the form of a crescent, so as almost to envelop the feeble band before him, and made a simultaneous attack upon the center and upon both flanks. A terrific battle ensued, in which one party fought, animated by undoubting confidence, and the other impelled by despair. The strife was long and bloody. The tide of victory repeatedly ebbed and flowed. Ottocar had offered a large reward to any of his followers who would bring to him Rhodolph, dead or alive.

A number of knights of great strength and bravery, con federated to achieve this feat. It was a point of honor to be effected at every hazard. Disregarding all the other perils of the battle, they watched their opportunity, and then in a united swoop, on their steel-clad chargers, fell upon the emperor. His feeble guard was instantly cut down. Rhodolph was a man of herculean power, and he fought like a lion at bay. One after another of his assailants he struck from his horse, when a Thuringian knight, of almost fabulous stature and strength, thrust his spear through the horse of the emperor, and both steed and rider fell to the ground. Rhodolph, encumbered by his heavy coat of mail, and entangled in the housings of his saddle, was unable to rise. He crouched upon the ground, holding his helmet over him, while saber strokes and pike thrusts rang upon cuirass and buckler like blows upon an anvil. A corps of reserve spurred to his aid, and the emperor was rescued, and the bold assailants who had penetrated the very center of his army were slain.

The tide of victory now set strongly in favor of Rhodolph, for "the race is not always to the swift, nor the battle to the strong." The troops of Bohemia were soon everywhere put to rout. The ground was covered with the dead. Ottocar, astounded at his discomfiture, and perhaps fearing the tongue of his wife more than the sabers of his foes, turned his back upon his flying army, and spurred his horse into the thickest of his pursuers. He was soon dismounted and slain. Fourteen thousand of his troops perished on that disastrous day. The body of Ottocar, mutilated with seventeen wounds, was carried to Vienna, and, after being exposed to the people, was buried with regal honors.

Rhodolph, vastly enriched by the plunder of the camp, and having no enemy to encounter, took possession of Moravia, and triumphantly marched into Bohemia. All was con

sternation there. The queen Cunegunda, who had brought
these disasters upon the kingdom, had no influence. Her
only son was but eight years of age. The turbulent nobles,
jealous of each other, had no recognized leader. The queen,
humiliated and despairing, implored the clemency of the conqueror, and offered to place her infant son and the kingdom
of Bohemia under his protection. Rhodolph was generous in
this hour of victory. As the result of arbitration, it was
agreed that he should hold Moravia for five years, that its
revenues might indemnify him for the expenses of the war.
The young prince, Wenceslaus, was acknowledged king, and
during his minority the regency was assigned to Otho, margrave or military commander of Brundenburg. Then ensued
some politic matrimonial alliances. Wenceslaus, the boy king,
was affianced to Judith, one of the daughters of Rhodolph.
The princess Agnes, daughter of Cunegunda, was to become
the bride of Rhodolph's second son. These matters being
all satisfactorily settled, Rhodolph returned in triumph to
Vienna.

The emperor now devoted his energies to the consolida-
tion of these Austrian provinces. They were four in number,
Austria, Styria, Carinthia and Carniola. All united, they
made but a feeble kingdom, for they did not equal, in extent of
territory, several of the States of the American Union. Each
of these provinces had its independent government, and its
local laws and customs. They were held together by the simple bond of an arbitrary monarch, who claimed, and exercised
as he could, supreme control over them all. Under his wise and
energetic administration, the affairs of the wide-spread empire
were prosperous, and his own Austria advanced rapidly in
order, civilization and power. The numerous nobles, turbulent, unprincipled and essentially robbers, had been in the habit
of issuing from their castles at the head of banditti bands, and
ravaging the country with incessant incursions. It required
great boldness in Rhodolph to brave the wrath of these united

nobles. He did it fearlessly, issuing the decree that there should be no fortresses in his States which were not necessary for the public defense. The whole country was spotted with castles, apparently impregnable in all the strength of stone and iron, the secure refuge of high-born nobles. In one year seventy of these turreted bulwarks of oppression were torn down; and twenty-nine of the highest nobles, who had ventured upon insurrection, were put to death. An earnest petition was presented to him in behalf of the condemned insurgents.

"Do not," said the king, "interfere in favor of robbers they are not nobles, but accursed robbers, who oppress the poor, and break the public peace. True nobility is faithful and just, offends no one, and commits no injury."

CHAPTER II.

RHODOLPH of Hapsburg was one of the most remarkable men of his own or of any age, and many anecdotes
illustrative of his character, and of the rude times in which he
lived, have been transmitted to us. The Thuringian knight
who speared the emperor's horse in the bloody fight of Murchfield, was rescued by Rhodolph from those who would cut
him down.

"I have witnessed," said the emperor, "his intrepidity,
and never could forgive myself if so courageous a knight
should be put to death."

During the war with Ottocar, on one occasion the army
were nearly perishing of thirst. A flagon of water was
brought to him. He declined it, saying,

"I can not drink alone, nor can I divide so small a quantity
among all. I do not thirst for myself, but for the whole army."

By earnest endeavor he obtained the perfect control of his
passions, naturally very violent. "I have often," said he,
" repented of being passionate, but never of being mild and
humane."

One of his captains expressed dissatisfaction at a **rich gift** the emperor made to a literary man who presented him a manuscript describing the wars of the Romans.

" My good friend," Rhodolph replied, " be contented that men of learning praise our actions, and thereby inspire us with additional courage in war. I wish I could employ more time in reading, and could expend some of that money on learned men which I must throw away on so many illiterate knights."

One cold morning at Metz, in the year 1288, he walked out dressed as usual in the plainest garb. He strolled into a baker's shop, as if to warm himself. The baker's termagant wife said to him, all unconscious who he was,

" Soldiers have no business to come into poor women's houses."

" True," the emperor replied, " but do not be angry, my good woman; I am an old soldier who have spent all my fortune in the service of that rascal Rhodolph, and he suffers me to want, notwithstanding all his fine promises."

" Good enough for you," said the woman ; " a man who will serve such a fellow, who is laying waste the whole earth, deserves nothing better."

She then, in her spite, threw a pail of water on the fire, which, filling the room with smoke and ashes, drove the emperor into the street.

Rhodolph, having returned to his lodgings, sent a rich present to the old woman, from the emperor who had warmed himself at her fire that morning, and at the dinner-table told the story with great glee to his companions. The woman, terrified, hastened to the emperor to implore mercy. He ordered her to be admitted to the dining-room, and promised to forgive her if she would repeat to the company all her abusive epithets, not omitting one. She did it faithfully, to the infinite merriment of the festive group.

So far as we can now judge, and making due allowance

for the darkness of the age in which he lived, Rhodolph appears to have been, in the latter part of his life, a sincere, if not an enlightened Christian. He was devout in prayer, and punctual in attending the services of the Church. The humble and faithful ministers of religion he esteemed and protected, while he was ever ready to chastise the insolence of those haughty prelates who disgraced their religious professions by arrogance and splendor.

At last the infirmities of age pressed heavily upon him. When seventy-three years old, knowing that he could not have much longer to live, he assembled the congress of electors at Frankfort, and urged them to choose his then only surviving son Albert as his successor on the imperial throne. The diet, however, refused to choose a successor until after the death of the emperor. Rhodolph was bitterly disappointed, for he understood this postponement as a positive refusal to gratify him in this respect. Saddened in spirit, and feeble in body, he undertook a journey, by slow stages, to his hereditary dominions in Switzerland. He then returned to Austria, where he died on the 15th of July, 1291, in the seventy-third year of his age.

Albert, who resided at Vienna, succeeded his father in authority over the Austrian and Swiss provinces. But he was a man stern, unconciliating and domineering. The nobles hated him, and hoped to drive him back to the Swiss cantons from which his father had come. One great occasion of discontent was, that he employed about his person, and in important posts, Swiss instead of Austrian nobles. They demanded the dismission of these foreign favorites, which so exasperated Albert that he clung to them still more tenaciously and exclusively.

The nobles now organized a very formidable conspiracy, and offered to neighboring powers, as bribes for their aid, portions of Austria. Austria proper was divided by the river Ens into two parts called Upper and Lower Austria. Lower

Austria was offered to Bohemia; Styria to the Duke of Ba
varia; Upper Austria to the Archbishop of Saltzburg; Car
niola to the Counts of Guntz; and thus all the provinces were
portioned out to the conquerors. At the same time the citizens of Vienna, provoked by the haughtiness of Albert, rose
in insurrection. With the energy which characterized his
father, Albert met these emergencies. Summoning immediately an army from Switzerland, he shut up all the avenues
to the city, which was not in the slightest degree prepared
for a siege, and speedily starved the inhabitants into submission. Punishing severely the insurgents, he strengthened his
post at Vienna, and confirmed his power. Then, marching
rapidly upon the nobles, before they had time to receive that
foreign aid which had been secretly promised them, and securing all the important fortresses, which were now not many
in number, he so overawed them, and so vigilantly watched
every movement, that there was no opportunity to rise and
combine. The Styrian nobles, being remote, made an effort
at insurrection. Albert, though it was in the depth of winter,
plowed through the snows of the mountains, and plunging unexpectedly among them, routed them with great slaughter.

While he was thus conquering discontent by the sword, and
silencing murmurs beneath the tramp of iron hoofs, the diet
was assembling at Frankfort to choose a new chief for the
Germanic empire. Albert was confident of being raised to
the vacant dignity. The splendor of his talents all admitted.
Four of the electors were closely allied to him by marriage,
and he arrogantly felt that he was almost entitled to the office
as the son of his renowned father. But the electors feared his
ambitious and despotic disposition, and chose Adolphus of
Nassau to succeed to the imperial throne.

Albert was mortified and enraged by this disappointment,
and expressed his determination to oppose the election; but
the troubles in his own domains prevented him from putting
this threat into immediate execution. His better judgment

soon taught him the policy of acquiescing in the election, and he sullenly received the investiture of his fiefs from the hands of the Emperor Adolphus. Still Albert, struggling against unpopularity and continued insurrection, kept his eye fixed eagerly upon the imperial crown. With great tact he conspired to form a confederacy for the deposition of Adolphus.

Wenceslaus, the young King of Bohemia, was now of age, and preparations were made for his coronation with great splendor at Prague. Four of the electors were present on this occasion, which was in June, 1297. Albert conferred with them respecting his plans, and secured their coöperation. The electors more willingly lent their aid since they were exceedingly displeased with some of the measures of Adolphus for the aggrandizement of his own family. Albert with secrecy and vigor pushed his plans, and when the diet met the same year at Metz, a long list of grievances was drawn up against Adolphus. He was summoned to answer to these charges. The proud emperor refused to appear before the bar of the diet as a culprit. The diet then deposed Adolphus and elected Albert II. to the imperial throne, on the 23d of June, 1298.

The two rival emperors made vigorous preparations to settle the dispute with the sword, and the German States arrayed themselves, some on one side and some on the other. The two armies met at Gelheim on the 2d of July, led by the rival sovereigns. In the thickest of the fight Adolphus spurred his horse through the opposing ranks, bearing down all opposition, till he faced Albert, who was issuing orders and animating his troops by voice and gesture.

"Yield," shouted Adolphus, aiming a saber stroke at the head of his foe, "your life and your crown."

"Let God decide," Albert replied, as he parried the blow, and thrust his lance into the unprotected face of Adolphus. At that moment the horse of Adolphus fell, and he himself was instantly slain. Albert remained the decisive victor on this bloody field. The diet of electors was again summoned, and he was now chosen unanimously emperor. He was soon crowned with great splendor at Aix-la-Chapelle.

Still Albert sat on an uneasy throne. The pope, indignant that the electors should presume to depose one emperor and choose another without his consent, refused to confirm the election of Albert, and loudly inveighed him as the murderer of Adolphus. Albert, with characteristic impulsiveness, declared that he was emperor by choice of the electors and not by ratification of the pope, and defiantly spurned the opposition of the pontiff. Considering himself firmly seated on the throne, he refused to pay the bribes of tolls, privileges, territories, etc., which he had so freely offered to the electors. Thus exasperated, the electors, the pope, and the King of Bohemia, conspired to drive Albert from the throne. Their secret plans were so well laid, and they were so secure of success, that the Elector of Mentz tauntingly and boastingly said to Albert, " I need only sound my hunting-horn and a new emperor will appear."

Albert, however, succeeded by sagacity and energy, in dispelling this storm which for a time threatened his entire destruction. By making concessions to the pope, he finally won him to cordial friendship, and by the sword vanquish ing some and intimidating others, he broke up the league His most formidable foe was his brother-in-law, Wenceslaus, King of Bohemia. Albert's sister, Judith, the wife of Wenceslaus, had for some years prevented a rupture between them, but she now being dead, both monarchs decided to refer their difficulties to the arbitration of the sword. While their armies were marching, Wenceslaus was suddenly taken sick and died, in June, 1305. His son, but seventeen years of age, weak in body and in mind, at once yielded to all the demands of his imperial uncle. Hardly a year, however, had elapsed ere this young prince, Wenceslaus III, was assassinated, leaving no issue.

Albert immediately resolved to transfer the crown of Bo

hemia to his own family, and thus to annex the powerful king
dom of Bohemia to his own limited Austrian territories. Bo
hemia added to the Austrian provinces, would constitute quite
a noble kingdom. The crown was considered elective, though
in fact the eldest son was almost always chosen during the
lifetime of his father. The death of Wenceslaus, childless,
opened the throne to other claimants. No one could more
imperiously demand the scepter than Albert. He did demand
it for his son Rhodolph in tones which were heard and obeyed.
The States assembled at Prague on the 1st of April, 1306.
Albert, surrounded by a magnificent retinue, conducted his
son to Prague, and to confirm his authority married him to
the widow of Wenceslaus, a second wife. Rhodolph also,
about a year before, had buried Blanche, his first wife. Albert
was exceedingly elated, for the acquisition of Bohemia was an
accession to the power of his family which doubled their territory, and more than doubled their wealth and resources.

A mild government would have conciliated the Bohemians,
but such a course was not consonant with the character of the
imperious and despotic Albert. He urged his son to measures of arbitrary power which exasperated the nobles, and led
to a speedy revolt against his authority. Rhodolph and the
nobles were soon in the field with their contending armies,
when Rhodolph suddenly died from the fatigues of the camp,
aged but twenty-two years, having held the throne of Bohemia less than a year.

Albert, grievously disappointed, now demanded that his
second son, Frederic, should receive the crown. As soon as
his name was mentioned to the States, the assembly with great
unanimity exclaimed, "We will not again have an Austrian
king." This led to a tumult. Swords were drawn, and two
of the partisans of Albert were slain. Henry, Duke of Carinthia, was then almost unanimously chosen king. But the
haughty Albert was not to be thus easily thwarted in his plans.
He declared that his son Frederic was King of Bohemia, and

raising an army, he exerted all the influence and military power which his position as emperor gave him, to enforce his claim.

But affairs in Switzerland for a season arrested the atten-tion of Albert, and diverted his armies from the invasion of Bohemia. Switzerland was then divided into small sovereign-ties, of various names, there being no less than fifty counts, one hundred and fifty barons, and one thousand noble families. Both Rhodolph and Albert had greatly increased, by annexa-tion, the territory and the power of the house of Hapsburg. By purchase, intimidation, war, and diplomacy, Albert had for some time been making such rapid encroachments, that a general insurrection was secretly planned to resist his power. All Switzerland seemed to unite as with one accord. Albert was rejoiced at this insurrection, for, confident of superior power, he doubted not his ability speedily to quell it, and it would afford him the most favorable pretext for still greater aggrandizement. Albert hastened to his domain at Hapsburg, where he was assassinated by conspirators led by his own nephew, whom he was defrauding of his estates.

Frederic and Leopold, the two oldest surviving sons of Albert, avenged their father's death by pursuing the conspira tors until they all suffered the penalty of their crimes. With ferocity characteristic of the age, they punished mercilessly the families and adherents of the assassins. Their castles were demolished, their estates confiscated, their domestics and men at arms massacred, and their wives and children driven out into the world to beg or to starve. Sixty-three of the retain-ers of Lord Balne, one of the conspirators, though entirely innocent of the crime, and solemnly protesting their uncon-sciousness of any plot, were beheaded in one day. Though but four persons took part in the assassination, and it was not known that any others were implicated in the deed, it is estimated that more than a thousand persons suffered death through the fury of the avengers. Agnes, one of the daugh-ters of Albert, endeavored with her own hands to strangle the infant child of the Lord of Eschenback, when the soldiers, moved by its piteous cries, with difficulty rescued it from her hands.

Elizabeth, the widow of Albert, with her implacable fanatic daughter Agnes, erected a magnificent convent on the spot at Königsburg, where the emperor was assassinated, and there in cloistered gloom they passed the remainder of their lives. It was an age of superstition, and yet there were some who comprehended and appreciated the pure morality of the gospel of Christ.

"Woman," said an aged hermit to Agnes, "God is not served by shedding innocent blood, and by rearing convents from the plunder of families. He is served by compassion only, and by the forgiveness of injuries."

Frederic, Albert's oldest son, now assumed the government of the Austrian provinces. From his uncommon personal attractions he was called Frederic the Handsome. His character was in conformity with his person, for to the most chivalrous bravery he added the most feminine amiability and mildness. He was a candidate for the imperial throne, and would probably have been elected but for the unpopularity of his despotic father. The diet met, and on the 27th of November, 1308, the choice fell unanimously upon Henry, Count of Luxemburg.

This election deprived Frederic of his hopes of uniting Bohemia to Austria, for the new emperor placed his son John upon the Bohemian throne, and was prepared to maintain him there by all the power of the empire. In accomplishing this, there was a short conflict with Henry of Carinthia, but he was speedily driven out of the kingdom.

Frederic, however, found a little solace in his disappointment, by attaching to Austria the dominions he had wrested from the lords he had beheaded as assassins of his father. In the midst of these scenes of ambition, intrigue and violence, the Emperor Henry fell sick and died, in the fifty-second year of his age. This unexpected event opened again to Frederic the prospect of the imperial crown, and all his friends, in the now very numerous branches of the family, spared neither money nor the arts of diplomacy in the endeavor to secure the coveted dignity for him. A year elapsed after the death of Henry before the diet was assembled. During that time all the German States were in intense agitation canvassing the claims of the several candidates. The prize of an imperial crown was one which many grasped at, and every little court was agitated by the question. The day of election, October 9th, 1314, arrived. There were two hostile parties in the field, one in favor of Frederic of Austria, the other in favor of Louis of Bavaria. The two parties met in different cities, the Austrians at Saxenhausen, and the Bavarians at Frankfort. There were, however, but four electors at Saxenhausen, while there were five at Frankfort, the ancient place of election. Each party unanimously chose its candidate. Louis, of Bavaria, receiving five votes, while Frederic received but four, was unquestionably the legitimate emperor. Most of the imperial cities acknowledged him. Frankfort sung his triumph, and he was crowned with all the ancient ceremonials of pomp at Aix-la-Chapelle.

But Frederic and his party were not ready to yield, and all over Germany there was the mustering of armies. For two years the hostile forces were marching and countermarching with the usual vicissitudes of war. The tide of devastation and blood swept now over one State, and now over another, until at length the two armies met, in all their concentrated strength, at Muhldorf, near Munich, for a decisive battle. Louis of Bavaria rode proudly at the head of thirty thousand foot, and fifteen hundred steel-clad horsemen. Frederic of Austria, the handsomest man of his age, towering above all his retinue, was ostentatiously arrayed in the most splendid armor art could furnish, emblazoned with the Austrian eagle and his helmet was surmounted by a crown of gold.

As he thus led the ranks of twenty-two thousand footmen, and seven thousand horse, all eyes followed him, and all hearts throbbed with confidence of victory. From early dawn, till night darkened the field, the horrid strife raged. In those days gunpowder was unknown, and the ringing of battle-axes on helmet and cuirass, the strokes of sabers and the clash of spears, shouts of onset, and the shrieks of the wounded, as sixty thousand men fought hand to hand on one small field, rose like the clamor from battling demons in the infernal world. Hour after hour of carnage passed, and still no one could tell on whose banners victory would alight. The gloom of night was darkening over the exhausted combatants, when the winding of the bugle was heard in the rear of the Austrians, and a band of four hundred Bavarian horsemen came plunging down an eminence into the disordered ranks of Frederic. The hour of dismay, which decides a battle, had come. A scene of awful carnage ensued as the routed Austrians, fleeing in every direction, were pursued and massacred. Frederic himself was struck from his horse, and as he fell, stunned by the blow, he was captured, disarmed and carried to the presence of his rival Louis.

The spirit of Frederic was crushed by the awful, the irretrievable defeat, and he appeared before his conqueror speechless in the extremity of his woe. Louis had the pride of magnanimity and endeavored to console his captive.

"The battle is not lost by your fault," said he. "The Bavarians have experienced to their cost that you are a valiant prince; but Providence has decided the battle. Though I am happy to see you as my guest, I sympathize with you in your sorrow, and will do what I can to alleviate it."

For three years the unhappy Frederic remained a prisoner of Louis of Bavaria, held in close confinement in the castle at Trausnitz. At the end of that time the emperor, alarmed at the efforts which the friends of Frederic were making to combine several Powers to take up arms for his relief, visited his prisoner, and in a personal interview proposed terms of recon ciliation. The terms, under the circumstances, were consid ered generous, but a proud spirit needed the discipline of three years' imprisonment before it could yield to such demands.

It was the 13th of March, 1325, when this singular inter- view between Louis the emperor, and Frederic his captive, took place at Trausnitz. Frederic promised upon oath that in exchange for his freedom he would renounce all claim to the imperial throne; restore all the districts and castles he had wrested from the empire; give up all the documents relative to his election as emperor; join with all his family in- fluence to support Louis against any and every adversary, and give his daughter in marriage to Stephen the son of Louis. He also promised that in case he should fail in the fulfillment of any one of these stipulations, he would return to his cap- tivity.

Frederic fully intended a faithful compliance with these requisitions. But no sooner was he liberated than his fiery brother Leopold, who presided over the Swiss estates, and who was a man of great capacity and military energy, refused per- emptorily to fulfill the articles which related to him, and made vigorous preparations to urge the war which he had already, with many allies, commenced against the Emperor Louis. The pope also, who had become inimical to Louis, declared that Frederic was absolved from the agreement at Trausnitz, as it was extorted by force, and, with all the authority of the head of the Church, exhorted Frederic to reassert his claim to the imperial crown.

Amidst such scenes of fraud and violence, it is refreshing to record an act of real honor. Frederic, notwithstanding the entreaties of the pope and the remonstrances of his friends, declared that, be the consequences what they might, he never would violate his pledge; and finding that he could not fulfill the articles of the agreement, he returned to Bavaria and sur- rendered himself a prisoner to the emperor. It is seldom that

history has the privilege of recording so noble an act. Louis
of Bavaria fortunately had a soul capable of appreciating the
magnanimity of his captive. He received him with courtesy
and with almost fraternal kindness. In the words of a contemporary historian, " They ate at the same table and slept in
the same bed ;" and, most extraordinary of all, when Louis
was subsequently called to a distant part of his dominions to
quell an insurrection, he intrusted the government of Bavaria,
during his absence, to Frederic.

Frederic's impetuous and ungovernable brother Leopold,
was unwearied in his endeavors to combine armies against the
emperor, and war raged without cessation. At length Louis,
harassed by these endless insurrections and coalitions against
him, and admiring the magnanimity of Frederic, entered into
a new alliance, offering terms exceedingly honorable on his
part. He agreed that he and Frederic should rule conjointly
as emperors of Germany, in perfect equality of power and dignity, alternately taking the precedence.

With this arrangement Leopold was satisfied, but unfortunately, just at that time, his impetuous spirit, exhausted by
disappointment and chagrin, yielded to death. He died at
Strasbourg on the 28th of February, 1326. The pope and
several of the electors refused to accede to this arrangement,
and thus the hopes of the unhappy Frederic were again
blighted, for Louis, who had consented to this accommodation
for the sake of peace, was not willing to enforce it through
the tumult of war. Frederic was, however, liberated from
captivity, and he returned to Austria a dejected, broken-hearted
man. He pined away for a few months in languor, being
rarely known to smile, and died at the castle of Gullenstein on
the 13th of January, 1330. His widow, Isabella, the daughter
of the King of Arragon, became blind from excessive grief,
and soon followed her husband to the tomb.

As Frederic left no son, the Austrian dominions fell to his
two brothers, Albert III. and Otho. Albert, by marriage

added the valuable county of Ferret in Alsace to the dominions of the house of Austria. The two brothers reigned with such wonderful harmony, that no indications can be seen of separate administrations. They renounced all claim to the imperial throne, notwithstanding the efforts of the pope to the contrary, and thus secured friendship with the Emperor Louis. There were now three prominent families dominant in Germany. Around these great families, who had gradually, by marriage and military encroachments, attained their supremacy, the others of all degrees rallied as vassals, seeking protection and contributing strength. The house of Bavaria, reigning over that powerful kingdom and in possession of the imperial throne, ranked first. Then came the house of Luxembourg, possessing the wide-spread and opulent realms of Bohemia. The house of Austria had now vast possessions, but these were widely scattered ; some provinces on the banks of the Danube and others in Switzerland, spreading through the defiles of the Alps.

John of Bohemia was an overbearing man, and feeling quite impregnable in his northern realms beyond the mountains, assumed such a dictatorial air as to rouse the ire of the princes of Austria and Bavaria. These two houses consequently entered into an intimate alliance for mutual security. The Duke of Carinthia, who was uncle to Albert and Otho, died, leaving only a daughter, Margaret. This dukedom, about the size of the State of Massachusetts, a wild and mountainous region, was deemed very important as the key to Italy. John of Bohemia, anxious to obtain it, had engaged the hand of Margaret for his son, then but eight years of age. It was a question in dispute whether the dukedom could descend to a female, and Albert and Otho claimed it as the heirs of their uncle. Louis, the emperor, supported the claims of Austria, and thus Carinthia became attached to this growing power.

John, enraged, formed a confederacy with the kings of Hungary and Poland, and some minor princes, and invaded Aus tria. For some time they swept all opposition before them. But the Austrian troops and those of the empire checked them at Landau. Here they entered into an agreement without a battle, by which Austria was permitted to retain Carinthia, she making important concessions to Bohemia. In February, 1339, Otho died, and Albert was invested with the sole administration of affairs. The old King of Bohemia possessed vehemence of character which neither age nor the total blindness with which he had become afflicted could repress. He traversed the empire, and even went to France, organizing a powerful confederacy against the emperor. The pope, Clement VI., who had always been inimical to Louis of Bavaria, influenced by John of Bohemia, deposed and excommunicated Louis, and ordered a new meeting of the diet of electors, which chose Charles, eldest son of the Bohemian monarch, and heir to that crown, emperor.

The deposed Louis fought bravely for the crown thus torn from his brow. Albert of Austria aided him with all his energies. Their united armies, threading the defiles of the Bohemian mountains, penetrated the very heart of the kingdom, when, in the midst of success, the deposed Emperor Louis fell dead from a stroke of apoplexy, in the year 1347. This event left Charles of Bohemia in undisputed possession of the imperial crown. Albert immediately recognized his claim, effected reconciliation, and becoming the friend and the ally of the emperor, pressed on cautiously but securely, year after year, in his policy of annexation. But storms of war incessantly howled around his domains until he died, a crippled paralytic, on the 16th of August, 1358.

CHAPTER III.

RHODOLPH II., ALBERT IV. AND ALBERT V.

FROM 1339 TO 1437.

RHODOLPH II.—MARRIAGE OF JOHN TO MARGARET.—INTRIGUING FOR THE TYROL.—DEATH OF RHODOLPH.—ACCESSION OF POWER TO AUSTRIA.—DIVIDING THE EMPIRE.—DELIGHT OF THE EMPEROR CHARLES.—LEOPOLD.—HIS AMBITION AND SUCCESSES.—HEDWIGE, QUEEN OF POLAND.—"THE COURSE OF TRUE LOVE NEVER DID RUN SMOOTH."—UNHAPPY MARRIAGE OF HEDWIGE.—HEROISM OF ARNOLD OF WINKELREID.—DEATH OF LEOPOLD.—DEATH OF ALBERT IV.—ACCESSION OF ALBERT V.—ATTEMPTS OF SIGISMOND TO BEQUEATH TO ALBERT V. HUNGARY AND BOHEMIA.

RHODOLPH II., the eldest son of Albert III., when but nineteen years of age succeeded his father in the government of the Austrian States. He had been very thoroughly educated in all the civil and military knowledge of the times. He was closely allied with the Emperor Charles IV. of Bohemia, having married his daughter Catherine. His character and manhood had been very early developed. When he was in his seventeenth year his father had found it necessary to visit his Swiss estates, then embroiled in the fiercest war, and had left him in charge of the Austrian provinces. He soon after was intrusted with the whole care of the Hapsburg dominions in Switzerland. In this responsible post he developed wonderful administrative skill, encouraging industry, repressing disorder, and by constructing roads and bridges, opening facilities for intercourse and trade.

Upon the death of his father, Rhodolph removed to Vienna, and being now the monarch of powerful realms on the Danube and among the Alps, he established a court rivaling the most magnificent establishments of the age.

Just west of Austria and south of Bavaria was the magnifi

cent dukedom of Tyrol, containing some sixteen thousand square miles, or about twice the size of the State of Massachusetts. It was a country almost unrivaled in the grandeur of its scenery, and contained nearly a million of inhabitants. This State, lying equally convenient to both Austria and Bavaria, by both of these kingdoms had for many years been regarded with a wistful eye. The manner in which Austria secured the prize is a story well worth telling, as illustrative of the intrigues of those times.

It will be remembered that John, the arrogant King of Bohemia, engaged for his son the hand of Margaret, the only daughter of the Duke of Carinthia. Tyrol also was one of the possessions of this powerful duke. Henry, having no son, had obtained from the emperor a decree that these possessions should descend, in default of male issue, to his daughter. But for this decision the sovereignty of these States would descend to the male heirs, Albert and Otho of Austria, nephews of Henry. They of course disputed the legality of the decree, and, aided by the Emperor Louis of Bavaria, obtained Carinthia, relinquishing for a time their claim to Tyrol. The emperor hoped to secure that golden prize for his hereditary estates of Bavaria.

When John, the son of the King of Bohemia, was but seventeen years of age, and a puny, weakly child, he was hurriedly married to Margaret, then twenty-two. Margaret, a sanguine, energetic woman, despised her baby husband, and he, very naturally, impotently hated her. She at length fled from him, and escaping from Bohemia, threw herself under the protection of Louis. The emperor joyfully welcomed her to his court, and promised to grant her a divorce, by virtue of his imperial power, if she would marry his son Louis. The compliant princess readily acceded to this plan, and the divorce was announced and the nuptials solemnized in February, 1342

The King of Bohemia was as much exasperated as the King of Bavaria was elated by this event, for the one felt that he had lost the Tyrol, and the other that he had gained it. It was this successful intrigue which cost Louis of Bavaria his imperial crown; for the blood of the King of Bohemia was roused. Burning with vengeance, he traversed Europe almost with the zeal and eloquence of Peter the Hermit, to organize a coalition against the emperor, and succeeded in inducing the pope, always hostile to Louis, to depose and excommunicate him. This marriage was also declared by the pope unlawful, and the son, Meinhard, eventually born to them, was branded as illegitimate.

While matters were in this state, as years glided on, Rhodolph succeeded in winning the favor of the pontiff, and induced him to legitimate Meinhard, that this young heir of Tyrol might marry the Austrian princess Margaret, sister of Rhodolph. Meinhard and his wife Margaret ere long died, leaving Margaret of Tyrol, a widow in advancing years, with no direct heirs. By the marriage contract of her son Meinhard with Margaret of Austria, she promised that should there be failure of issue, Tyrol should revert to Austria. On the other hand, Bavaria claimed the territory in virtue of the marriage of Margaret with Louis of Bavaria.

Rhodolph was so apprehensive that Bavaria might make an immediate move to obtain the coveted territory by force of arms, that he hastened across the mountains, though in the depth of winter, obtained from Margaret an immediate possession of Tyrol, and persuaded her to accompany him, an honored guest, to his capital, which he had embellished with unusual splendor for her entertainment.

Rhodolph had married the daughter of Charles, King of Bohemia, the emperor, but unfortunately at this juncture, Rhodolph, united with the kings of Hungary and Poland, was at war with the Bavarian king. Catherine his wife, however, undertook to effect a reconciliation between her husband and her father. She secured an interview between them, and the emperor, the hereditary rival of his powerful neighbor the

King of Bavaria, confirmed Margaret's gift, invested Rhodolph with the Tyrol, and pledged the arm of the empire to maintain this settlement. Thus Austria gained Tyrol, the country of romance and of song, interesting, perhaps, above all other portions of Europe in its natural scenery, and invaluable from its location as the gateway of Italy. Bavaria made a show of armed opposition to this magnificent accession to the power of Austria, but soon found it in vain to assail Rhodolph sustained by Margaret of Tyrol, and by the energies of the empire.

Rhodolph was an antiquarian of eccentric character, ever poring over musty records and hunting up decayed titles. He was fond of attaching to his signature the names of all the innumerable offices he held over the conglomerated States of his realm. He was Rhodolph, Margrave of Baden, Vicar of Upper Bavaria, Lord of Hapsburg, Arch Huntsman of the Empire, Archduke Palatine, etc., etc. His ostentation provoked even the jealousy of his father, the emperor, and he was ordered to lay aside these numerous titles and the arrogant armorial bearings he was attaching to his seals. His desire to aggrandize his family burned with a quenchless flame. Hoping to extend his influence in Italy, he negotiated a matrimonial alliance for his brother with an Italian princess. As he crossed the Alps to attend the nuptials, he was seized with an inflammatory fever, and died the 27th of July, 1365, but twenty-six years of age, and leaving no issue.

His brother Albert, a young man but seventeen years of age, succeeded Rhodolph. Just as he assumed the government, Margaret of Tyrol died, and the King of Bavaria, thinking this a favorable moment to renew his claims for the Tyrol, vigorously invaded the country with a strong army. Albert immediately applied to the emperor for assistance. Three years were employed in fightings and diplomacy, when Bavaria, in consideration of a large sum of money and sundry other concessions, renounced all pretensions to Tyrol, and left the rich prize henceforth undisputed in the hands of Austria. Thus the diminutive margrave of Austria, which was at first but a mere military post on the Danube, had grown by rapid accretions in one century to be almost equal in extent of territory to the kingdoms of Bavaria and of Bohemia. This grandeur instead of satisfying the Austrian princes, did but increase their ambition.

The Austrian territories, though widely scattered, were declared, both by family compact and by imperial decree, to be indivisible. Albert had a brother, Leopold, two years younger than himself, of exceedingly restless and ambitious spirit, while Albert was inactive, and a lover of ease and repose. Leopold was sent to Switzerland, and intrusted with the administration of those provinces. But his imperious spirit so dominated over his elder but pliant brother, that he extorted from him a compact, by which the realm was divided, Albert remaining in possession of the Austrian provinces of the Danube, and Leopold having exclusive dominion over those in Switzerland; while the magnificent new acquisition, the Tyrol, lying between the two countries, bounding Switzerland on the east, and Austria on the west, was shared between them.

Nothing can more clearly show the moderate qualities of Albert than that he should have assented to such a plan. He did, however, with easy good nature, assent to it, and the two brothers applied to the Emperor Charles to ratify the division by his imperial sanction. Charles, who for some time had been very jealous of the rapid encroachments of Austria, rubbed his hands with delight.

"We have long," said he, "labored in vain to humble the house of Austria, and now the dukes of Austria have humbled themselves."

Leopold the First inherited all the ambition and energy of the house of Hapsburg, and was ever watching with an eagle eye to extend his dominions, and to magnify his power. By money, war, and diplomacy, in a few years he obtained Fri burg and the little town of Basle; attached to his dominions the counties of Feldkirch, Pludenz, Surgans and the Rienthal, which he wrested from the feeble counts who held them, and obtained the baillages of Upper and Lower Suabia, and the towns of Augsburg and Gingen. But a bitter disappointment was now encountered by this ambitious prince.

Louis, the renowned King of Hungary and Poland, had two daughters, Maria and Hedwige, but no sons. To Maria he promised the crown of Hungary as her portion, and among the many claimants for her hand, and the glittering crown she held in it, Sigismond, son of the Emperor Charles, King of Bohemia, received the prize. Leopold, whose heart throbbed in view of so splendid an alliance, was overjoyed when he secured the pledge of the hand of Hedwige, with the crown of Poland, for William, his eldest son. Hedwige was one of the most beautiful and accomplished princesses of the age. William was also a young man of great elegance of person, and of such rare fascination of character, that he had acquired the epithet of William the Delightful. His chivalrous bearing had been trained and polished amidst the splendors of his uncle's court of Vienna. Hedwige, as the affianced bride of William, was invited from the more barbaric pomp of the Hungarian court, to improve her education by the aid of the refinements of Vienna. William and Hedwige no sooner met than they loved one another, as young hearts, even in the palace, will sometimes love, as well as in the cottage. In brilliant festivities and moonlight excursions the young lovers passed a few happy months, when Hedwige was called home by the final sickness of her father. Louis died, and Hedwige was immediately crowned Queen of Poland, receiving the most enthusiastic greetings of her subjects.

Bordering on Poland there was a grand duchy of immense extent, Lithuania, embracing sixty thousand square miles. The Grand Duke Jaghellon was a burly Northman, not more than half civilized, whose character was as jagged as his name.

This pagan proposed to the Polish nobles that he should marry Hedwige, and thus unite the grand duchy of Lithuania with the kingdom of Poland; promising in that event to renounce paganism, and embrace Christianity. The beautiful and accomplished Hedwige was horror-struck at the proposal, and declared that never would she marry any one but William.

But the Polish nobles, dazzled by the prospect of this magnificent accession to the kingdom of Poland, and the bishops, even more powerful than the nobles, elated with the vision of such an acquisition for the Church, resolved that the young and fatherless maiden, who had no one to defend her cause, should yield, and that she should become the bride of Jaghellon. They declared that it was ridiculous to think that the interests of a mighty kingdom, and the enlargement of the Church, were to yield to the caprices of a love-sick girl.

In the meantime William, all unconscious of the disappointment which awaited him, was hastening to Cracow, with a splendid retinue, and the richest presents Austrian art could fabricate, to receive his bride. The nobles, however, a semi-barbaric set of men, surrounded him upon his arrival, refused to allow him any interview with Hedwige, threatened him with personal violence, and drove him out of the kingdom. Poor Hedwige was in anguish. She wept, vowed deathless fidelity to William, and expressed utter detestation of the pagan duke, until, at last, worn out and broken-hearted, she, in despair, surrendered herself into the arms of Jaghellon. Jaghellon was baptized by the name of Ladislaus, and Lithuania was annexed to Poland.

The loss of the crown of Poland was to Leopold a grievous affliction; at the same time his armies, engaged in sundry measures of aggrandizement, encountered serious reverses. Leopold, the father of William, by these events was plunged into the deepest dejection. No effort of his friends could lift the weight of his gloom. In a retired apartment of one of his castles he sat silent and woful, apparently incapacitated for any exertion whatever, either bodily or mental. The affairs of his realm were neglected, and his bailiffs and feudal chiefs, 'eft with irresponsible power, were guilty of such acts of extortion and tyranny, that, in the province of Suabia the barons combined, and a fierce insurrection broke out. Forty important towns united in the confederacy, and secured the co-operation of Strasburg, Mentz and other large cities on the Rhine. Other of the Swiss provinces were on the eve of joining this alarming confederacy against Leopold, their Austrian ruler. As Vienna for some generations had been the seat of the Hapsburg family, from whence governors were sent to these provinces of Helvetia, as Switzerland was then called, the Swiss began to regard their rulers as foreigners, and even Leopold found it necessary to strengthen himself with Austrian troops.

This formidable league roused Leopold from his torpor, and he awoke like the waking of the lion. He was immediately on the march with four thousand horsemen, and fourteen hundred foot, while all through the defiles of the Alps bugle blasts echoed, summoning detachments from various cantons under their bold barons, to hasten to the aid of the insurgents. On the evening of the 9th of July, 1396, the glittering host of Leopold appeared on an eminence overlooking the city of Sempach and the beautiful lake on whose border it stands. The horses were fatigued by their long and hurried march, and the crags and ravines, covered with forest, were impracticable for the evolutions of cavalry. The impetuous Leopold, impatient of delay, resolved upon an immediate attack, notwithstanding the exhaustion of his troops, and though a few hours of delay would bring strong reinforcements to his camp. He dismounted his horsemen, and formed his whole force in solid phalanx. It was an imposing spectacle, as six thousand men, covered from head to foot with blazing armor, presenting a front of shields like a wall of burnished steel, bristling with innumerable pikes and spears, moved with slow, majestic tread down upon the city.

The confederate Swiss, conscious that the hour of vengeance had come, in which they must conquer or be miserably slain, marched forth to meet the foe, emboldened only by despair. But few of the confederates were in armor. They were furnished with such weapons as men grasp when despotism rouses them to insurrection, rusty battle-axes, pikes and halberts, and two-handed swords, which their ancestors, in descending into the grave, had left behind them. They drew up in the form of a solid wedge, to pierce the thick concentric wall of steel, apparently as impenetrable as the cliffs of the mountains. Thus the two bodies silently and sternly approached each other. It was a terrific hour; for every man knew that one or the other of those hosts must perish utterly. For some time the battle raged, while the confederates could make no impression whatever upon their steel-clad foes, and sixty of them fell pierced by spears before one of their assailants had been even wounded.

Despair was fast settling upon their hearts, when Arnold of Winkelreid, a knight of Underwalden, rushed from the ranks of the confederates, exclaiming—

"I will open a passage into the line; protect, dear countrymen, my wife and children."

He threw himself upon the bristling spears. A score pierced his body; grasping them with the tenacity of death, he bore them to the earth as he fell. His comrades, emulating his spirit of self-sacrifice, rushed over his bleeding body, and forced their way through the gate thus opened into the line. The whole unwieldy mass was thrown into confusion. The steel-clad warriors, exhausted before the battle commenced, and encumbered with their heavy armor, could but feebly resist their nimble assailants, who outnumbering them and overpowering them, cut them down in fearful havoc. It soon became a general slaughter, and not less than two thousand of the followers of Leopold were stretched lifeless upon the ground. Many were taken prisoners, and a few, mounting their horses, effected an escape among the wild glens of the Alps.

In this awful hour Leopold developed magnanimity and heroism worthy of his name. Before the battle commenced, his friends urged him to take care of his own person.

"God forbid," said he, "that I should endeavor to save my own life and leave you to die! I will share your fate, and, with you, will either conquer or perish."

When all was in confusion, and his followers were falling like autumn leaves around him, he was urged to put spurs to his horse, and, accompanied by his body-guard, to escape.

"I would rather die honorably," said Leopold, "than live with dishonor."

Just at this moment his standard-bearer was struck down by a rush of the confederates. As he fell he cried out, "Help, Austria, help!" Leopold frantically sprang to his aid, grasped the banner from his dying hand, and waving it, plunged into the midst of the foe, with saber strokes hewing a path before him. He was soon lost in the tumult and the carnage of the battle. His body was afterward found, covered with wounds, in the midst of heaps of the dead.

Thus perished the ambitious and turbulent Leopold the 1st, after a stormy and unhappy life of thirty-six years, and a reign of constant encroachment and war of twenty years. Life to him was a dark and somber tempest. Ever dissatisfied with what he had attained, and grasping at more, he could never enjoy the present, and he finally died that death of violence to which his ambition had consigned so many thousands. Leopold, the second son of the duke, who was but fifteen years of age, succeeded his father, in the dominion of the Swiss estates; and after a desultory warfare of a few months, was successful in negotiating a peace, or rather an armed truce, with the successful insurgents.

In the meantime, Albert, at Vienna, apparently happy in being relieved of all care of the Swiss provinces, was devoting himself to the arts of peace. He reared new buildings, encouraged learning, repressed all disorders, and cultivated friendly relations with the neighboring powers. His life was as a summer's day—serene and bright. He and his family were happy, and his realms in prosperity. He died at his rural residence at Laxendorf, two miles out from Vienna, on the 29th of August, 1395. All Austria mourned his death. Thousands gathered at his burial, exclaiming, " We have lost our friend, our father!" He was a studious, peace-loving, warm-hearted man, devoted to his family and his friends, fond of books and the society of the learned, and enjoying the cultivation of his garden with his own hands. He left, at his death, an only son, Albert, sixteen years of age.

William, the eldest son of Leopold, had been brought up in the court of Vienna. He was a young man of fascinating character and easily won all hearts. After his bitter disappointment in Poland he returned to Vienna, and now, upon the death of his uncle Albert, he claimed the reins of government as the oldest member of the family. His cousin Albert, of course, resisted this claim, demanding that he himself should enter upon the post which his father had occupied. A violent dissension ensued which resulted in an agreement that they should administer the government of the Austrian States, jointly, during their lives, and that then the government should be vested in the eldest surviving member of the family.

Having effected this arrangement, quite to the satisfaction of both parties, Albert, who inherited much of the studious thoughtful turn of mind of his father, set out on a pilgrimage to the holy land, leaving the government during his absence in the hands of William. After wanderings and adventures so full of romance as to entitle him to the appellation of the " Wonder of the World," he returned to Vienna. He married a daughter of the Duke of Holland, and settled down to a monkish life. He entered a monastery of Carthusian monks, and took an active part in all their discipline and devotions No one was more punctual than he at matins and vespers. ot more devout in confessions, prayers, genuflexions and the divine service in the choir. Regarding himself as one of the fraternity, he called himself brother Albert, and left William untrammeled in the cares of state. His life was short, for he died the 14th of September, 1404, in the twenty-seventh year of his age, leaving a son Albert, seven years old. William, who married a daughter of the King of Naples, survived him but two years, when he died childless.

A boy nine years old now claimed the inheritance of the Austrian estates; but the haughty dukes of the Swiss branch of the house were not disposed to yield to his claims. Leopold II., who after the battle of Sempach succeeded his father in the Swiss estates, assumed the guardianship of Albert, and the administration of Austria, till the young duke should be of age. But Leopold had two brothers who also inherited their father's energy and ambition. Ernest ruled over Styria, Carinthia and Carniola. Frederic governed the Tyrol.

Leopold II. repaired to Vienna to assume the administration; his two brothers claimed the right of sharing it with him. Confusion, strife and anarchy ensued. Ernest, a very determined and violent man, succeeded in compelling his brother to give him a share of the government, and in the midst of incessant quarrels, which often led to bloody conflicts, each of the two brothers strove to wrest as much as possible from Austria before young Albert should be of age. The nobles availed themselves of this anarchy to renew their expeditions of plunder. Unhappy Austria for several years was a scene of devastation and misery. In the year 1411, Leopold II. died without issue. The young Albert had now attained his fifteenth year.

The emperor declared Albert of age, and he assumed the

government as Albert V. His subjects, weary of disorder
and of the strife of the nobles, welcomed him with enthusiasm. With sagacity and self-denial above his years, the young
prince devoted himself to business, relinquishing all pursuits
of pleasure. Fortunately, during his minority he had honor
able and able teachers who stored his mind with useful knowledge, and fortified him with principles of integrity. The
change from the most desolating anarchy to prosperity and
peace was almost instantaneous. Albert had the judgment
to surround himself with able advisers. Salutary laws were
enacted; justice impartially administered; the country was
swept of the banditti which infested it, and while all the
States around were involved in the miseries of war, the song
of the contented husbandman, and the music of the artisan's
tools were heard through the fields and in the towns of happy
Austria.

Sigismond, second son of the Emperor Charles IV., King
of Bohemia, was now emperor. It will be remembered that
by marrying Mary, the eldest daughter of Louis, King of Hungary and Poland, he received Hungary as the dower of his
bride. By intrigue he also succeeded in deposing his effemi-
nate and dissolute brother, Wenceslaus, from the throne of
Bohemia, and succeeded, by a new election, in placing the
crown upon his own brow. Thus Sigismond wielded a three-
fold scepter. He was Emperor of Germany, and King of
Hungary and of Bohemia.

Albert married the only daughter of Sigismond, ana a very
strong affection sprung up between the imperial father and his
son-in-law. They often visited each other, and coöperated
very cordially in measures of state. The wife of Sigismond
was a worthless woman, described by an Austrian historian as
"one who believed in neither God, angel nor devil; neither
in heaven nor hell." Sigismond had set his heart upon be-
queathing to Albert the crowns of both Hungary and Bohemia, which magnificent accessions to the Austrian domains

would elevate that power to be one of the first in Europe. But Barbara, his queen, wished to convey these crowns to the son of the pagan Jaghellon, who had received the crown of Poland as the dowry of his reluctant bride, Hedwige. Sigismond, provoked by her intrigues for the accomplishment of this object, and detesting her for her licentiousness, put her under arrest. Sigismond was sixty-three years of age, in very feeble health, and daily expecting to die.

He summoned a general convention of the nobles of Hungary and Bohemia to meet him at Znaim in Moravia, near the frontiers of Austria, and sent for Albert and his daughter to hasten to that place. The infirm emperor, traveling by slow stages, succeeded in reaching Znaim. He immediately summoned the nobles to his presence, and introducing to them Albert and Elizabeth, thus affectingly addressed them :

" Loving friends, you know that since the commencement of my reign I have employed my utmost exertions to maintain public tranquillity. Now, as I am about to die, my last act must be consistent with my former actions. At this moment my only anxiety arises from a desire to prevent dissension and bloodshed after my decease. It is praiseworthy in a prince to govern well ; but it is not less praiseworthy to provide a successor who shall govern better than himself. This fame I now seek, not from ambition, but from love to my subjects. You all know Albert, Duke of Austria, to whom in preference to all other princes I gave my daughter in marriage, and whom I adopted as my son. You know that he possesses experience and every virtue becoming a prince. He found Austria in a state of disorder, and he has restored it to tranquillity. He is now of an age in which judgment and experience attain their perfection, and he is sovereign of Austria, which, lying between Hungary and Bohemia, forms a connecting link between the two kingdoms.

" I recommend him to you as my successor. I leave you a king, pious, honorable, wise and brave. I give him my

kingdom. or rather I give him to my kingdoms, to whom I can
give or wish nothing better.   Truly you belong to him in con
sideration of his wife, the hereditary princess of Hungary and
Bohemia.   Again I repeat that I do not act thus solely from
love to Albert and my daughter, but from a desire in my last
moments to promote the true welfare of my people.   Happy
are those who are subject to Albert.   I am confident he is no
less beloved by you than by me, and that even without my
exhortations you would unanimously give him your votes.   But
I beseech you by these tears, comfort my soul, which is de-
parting to God, by confirming my choice and fulfilling my
will."

The emperor was so overcome with emotion that he could
with difficulty pronounce these last words.   All were deeply
moved ; some wept aloud ; others, seizing the hand of the emperor and bathing it in tears, vowed allegiance to Albert, and
declared that while he lived they would recognize no other
sovereign.

The very next day, November, 1437, Sigismond died.   Albert and Elizabeth accompanied his remains to Hungary.   The
Hungarian diet of barons unanimously ratified the wishes of
the late king in accepting Albert as his successor.   He then
hastened to Bohemia, and, notwithstanding a few outbursts
of disaffection, was received with great demonstrations of joy
by the citizens of Prague, and was crowned in the cathedral.

CHAPTER IV.

ALBERT, LADISLAUS AND FREDERIC.

THE kingdom of Bohemia thus attached to the duchies of Austria contained a population of some three millions and embraced twenty thousand square miles of territory, being about three times as large as the State of Massachusetts. Hungary was a still more magnificent realm in extent of territory, being nearly five times as large as Bohemia, but inhabited by about the same number of people, widely dispersed. In addition to this sudden and vast accession of power, Albert was chosen Emperor of Germany. This distinguished sovereign displayed as much wisdom and address in administering the affairs of the empire, as in governing his own kingdoms.

The Turks were at this time becoming the terror of Christendom. Originating in a small tribe between the Caspian Sea and the Euxine, they had with bloody cimeters overrun all Asia Minor, and, crossing the Hellespont, had intrenched themselves firmly on the shores of Europe. Crowding on in victorious hosts, armed with the most terrible fanaticism, they had already obtained possession of Bulgaria, Servia, and Bosnia, eastern dependencies of Hungary, and all Europe was trembling in view of their prowess, their ferocity and their apparently exhaustless legions.

Sigismond, beholding the crescent of the Moslem floating over the castles of eastern Hungary, became alarmed for the kingdom, and sent ambassadors from court to court to form a crusade against the invaders. He was eminently successful, and an army of one hundred thousand men was soon collected, composed of the flower of the European nobility. The republics of Venice and Genoa united to supply a fleet. With this powerful armament Sigismond, in person, commenced his march to Constantinople, which city the Turks were besieging, to meet the fleet there. The Turkish sultan himself gathered his troops and advanced to meet Sigismond. The Christian troops were utterly routed, and nearly all put to the sword. The emperor with difficulty escaped. In the confusion of the awful scene of carnage he threw himself unperceived into a small boat, and paddling down the Danube, as its flood swept through an almost uninhabited wilderness, he reached the Black Sea, where he was so fortunate as to find a portion of the fleet, and thus, by a long circuit, he eventually reached his home.

Bajazet, the sultan, returned exultant from this great victory, and resumed the siege of Constantinople, which ere long fell into the hands of the Turks. Amurath, who was sultan at the time of the death of Sigismond, thought the moment propitious for extending his conquests. He immediately, with his legions, overran Servia, a principality nearly the size of the State of Virginia, and containing a million of inhabitants. George, Prince of Servia, retreating before the merciless followers of the false prophet, threw himself with a strong garrison into the fortress of Semendria, and sent an imploring message to Albert for assistance. Servia was separated from Hungary only by the Danube, and it was a matter of infinite moment to Albert that the Turk should not get possession of that province, from which he could make constant forays into Hungary.

Albert hastily collected an army and marched to the banks of the Danube just in time to witness the capture of Semendria and the massacre of its garrison. All Hungary was now in terror. The Turks in overwhelming numbers were firmly intrenched upon the banks of the Danube, and were preparing to cross the river and to supplant the cross with the crescent on all the plains of Hungary. The Hungarian nobles, in crowds, flocked to the standard of Albert, who made herculean exertions to meet and roll back the threatened tide of invasion. Exhausted by unremitting toil, he was taken sick and suddenly died, on a small island of the Danube, on the 17th of October, 1439, in the forty-third year of his age. The death of such a prince, heroic and magnanimous, loving the arts of peace, and yet capable of wielding the energies of war, was an apparent calamity to Europe.

Albert left two daughters, but his queen Elizabeth was expecting, in a few months, to give birth to another child. Every thing was thus involved in confusion, and for a time intrigue and violence ran riot. There were many diverse parties, the rush of armed bands, skirmishes and battles, and all the great matters of state were involved in an inextricable labyrinth of confusion. The queen gave birth to a son, who was baptized by the name of Ladislaus. Elizabeth, anxious to secure the crown of Hungary for her infant, had him solemnly crowned at Alba Regia, by the Archbishop of Gran when the child was but four months old.

But a powerful party arose, opposed to the claims of the infant, and strove by force of arms to place upon the throne Uladislaus, King of Poland and Lithuania, and son of the pagan Jaghellon and the unhappy Hedwige. For two years war between the rival parties desolated the kingdom, when Elizabeth died. Uladislaus now redoubled his endeavors, and finally succeeded in driving the unconscious infant from his hereditary domain, and established himself firmly on the throne of Hungary.

The infant prince was taken to Bohemia. There also he encountered violent opposition. "A child," said his opponents, "can not govern. It will be long before Ladislaus will be capable of assuming the reins of government. Let us choose another sovereign, and when Ladislaus has attained the age of twenty-four we shall see whether he deserves the crown."

This very sensible advice was adopted, and thirteen electors were appointed to choose a sovereign. Their choice fell upon Albert of Bavaria. But he, with a spirit of magnanimity very rare in that age, declared that the crown, of right, belonged to Ladislaus, and that he would not take it from him. They then chose Frederic, Duke of Styria, who, upon the death of Albert, had been chosen emperor. Frederic, incited by the example of Albert, also declined, saying, "I will not rob my relation of his right." But anxious for the peace of the empire, he recommended that they should choose some illustrious Bohemian, to whom they should intrust the regency until Ladislaus became of age, offering himself to assume the guardianship of the young prince.

This judicious advice was accepted, and the Bohemian nobles chose the infant Ladislaus their king. They, however, appointed two regents instead of one. The regents quarreled and headed two hostile parties. Anarchy and civil war desolated the kingdom, with fluctuations of success and discomfiture attending the movements of either party. Thus several years of violence and blood passed on. One of the regents, George Podiebrad, drove his opponent from the realm and assumed regal authority. To legitimate its usurped power he summoned a diet at Pilgram, in 1447, and submitted the following question:

"Is it advantageous to the kingdom that Ladislaus should retain the crown, or would it not be more beneficial to choose a monarch acquainted with our language and customs, and in spired with love of our country?"

Warm opposition to this measure arose, and the nobles voted themselves loyal to Ladislaus. While these events were passing in Bohemia, scenes of similar violence were transpiring in Hungary. After a long series of convulsions, and Uladislaus, the Polish king, who had attained the crown of Hungary, having been slain in a battle with the Turks, a diet of Hungarian nobles was assembled and they also declared the young Ladislaus to be their king. They consequently wrote to the Emperor Frederic, Duke of Styria, who had assumed the guardianship of the prince, requesting that he might be sent to Hungary. Ladislaus Posthumous, so-called in consequence of his birth after the death of his father, was then but six years of age.

The Austrian States were also in a condition of similar confusion, rival aspirants grasping at power, feuds agitating every province, and all moderate men anxious for that repose which could only be found by uniting in the claims of Ladislaus for the crown. Thus Austria, Bohemia and Hungary, so singularly and harmoniously united under Albert V., so suddenly dissevered and scattered by the death of Albert, were now, after years of turmoil, all reuniting under the child Ladislaus.

Frederic, however, the faithful guardian of the young prince, was devoting the utmost care to his education, and refused to accede to the urgent and reiterated requests to send the young monarch to his realms. When Ladislaus was about ten years of age the Emperor Frederic visited the pope at Rome, and took Ladislaus in his glittering suite. The precocious child here astonished the learned men of the court, by delivering an oration in Latin before the consistory, and by giving many other indications of originality and vigor of mind far above his years. The pope became much attached to the youthful sovereign of three such important realms, and as

Frederic was about to visit Naples, Ladislaus remained a guest in the imperial palace.

Deputies from the three nations repaired to Rome to urge the pope to restore to them their young sovereign. Failing in this, they endeavored to induce Ladislaus to escape with them. This plan also was discovered and foiled. The nobles were much irritated by these disappointments, and they resolved to rescue him by force of arms. All over Hungary, Bohemia and Austria there was a general rising of the nobles, nationalities being merged in the common cause, and all hearts united and throbbing with a common desire. An army of sixteen thousand men was raised. Frederic, alarmed by these formidable preparations for war, surrendered Ladislaus and he was conveyed in triumph to Vienna. A numerous assemblage of the nobles of the three nations was convened, and it was settled that the young king, during his minority, should remain at Vienna, under the care of his maternal uncle, Count Cilli, who, in the meantime, was to administer the government of Austria. George Podiebrad was intrusted with the regency of Bohemia; and John Hunniades was appointed regent of Hungary.

Ladislaus was now thirteen years of age. The most learned men of the age were appointed as his teachers, and he pursued his studies with great vigor. Count Cilli, however, an ambitious and able man, soon gained almost unlimited control over the mind of his young ward, and became so arrogant and dictatorial, filling every important office with his own especial friends, and removing those who displeased him, that general discontent was excited and conspiracy was formed against him. Cilli was driven from Vienna with insults and threats, and the conspirators placed the regency in the hands of a select number of their adherents.

While affairs were in this condition, John Hunniades, as regent, was administering the government of Hungary with great vigor and sagacity. He was acquiring so much renown that Count Cilli regarded him with a very jealous eye, and excited the suspicions of the young king that Hunniades was seeking for himself the sovereignty of Hungary. Cilli endeavored to lure Hunniades to Vienna, that he might seize his person, but the sagacious warrior was too wily to be thus entrapped.

The Turks were now in the full tide of victory. They had conquered Constantinople, fortified both sides of the Bosporus and the Hellespont, overrun Greece and planted themselves firmly and impregnably on the shores of Europe. Mahomet II. was sultan, succeeding his father Amurath. He raised an army of two hundred thousand men, who were all inspired with that intense fanatic ferocity with which the Moslem then regarded the Christian. Marching resistlessly through Bulgaria and Servia, he contemplated the immediate conquest of Hungary, the bulwark of Europe. He advanced to the banks of the Danube and laid siege to Belgrade, a very important and strongly fortified town at the point where the Save enters the great central river of eastern Europe.

Such an army, flushed with victory and inspired with all the energies of fanaticism, appalled the European powers. Ladislaus was but a boy, studious and scholarly in his tastes, having developed but little physical energy and no executive vigor. He was very handsome, very refined in his tastes and courteous in his address, and he cultivated with great care the golden ringlets which clustered around his shoulders. At the time of this rearful invasion Ladislaus was on a visit to Buda, one of the capitals of Hungary, on the Danube, but about three hundred miles above Belgrade. The young monarch, with his favorite, Cilli, fled ingloriously to Vienna, leaving Hunniades to breast as he could the Turkish hosts. But Hunniades was, fortunately, equal to the emergence.

A Franciscan monk, John Capistrun, endowed with the eloquence of Peter the Hermit, traversed Germany, displaying the cross and rousing Christians to defend Europe from the

infidels. He soon collected a motley mass of forty thousand
men, rustics, priests, students, soldiers, unarmed, undisciplined,
a rabble rout, who followed him to the rendezvous where Hunniades had succeeded in collecting a large force of the bold
barons and steel-clad warriors of Hungary. The experienced
chief gladly received this heterogeneous mass, and soon armed
them, brought them into the ranks and subjected them to
the severe discipline of military drill.

At the head of this band, which was inspired with zeal
equal to that of the Turk, the brave Hunniades, in a fleet of
boats, descended the Danube. The river in front of Belgrade
was covered with the flotilla of the Turks. The wall in many
places was broken down, and at other points in the wall they
had obtained a foothold, and the crescent was proudly unfurled to the breeze. The feeble garrison, worn out with toil
and perishing with famine, were in the last stages of despair.
Hunniades came down upon the Turkish flotilla like an inundation; both parties fought with almost unprecedented ferocity,
but the Christians drove every thing before them, sinking, dispersing, and capturing the boats, which were by no means prepared for so sudden and terrible an assault. The immense reinforcement, with arms and provisions, thus entered the city, and
securing the navigation of the Danube and the Save, opened
the way for continued supplies. The immense hosts of the
Mohammedans now girdled the city in a semicircle on the
land side. Their tents, gorgeously embellished and surmounted
with the crescent, glittered in the rays of the sun as far as the
eye could extend. Squadrons of steel-clad horsemen swept
the field, while bands of the besiegers pressed the city with
out intermission, night and day.

Mohammed, irritated by this unexpected accession of
strength to the besieged, in his passion ordered an immediate
and simultaneous attack upon the town by his whole force
The battle was long and bloody, both parties struggling with
utter desperation. The Turks were repulsed. After one of

the longest continuous conflicts recorded in history, lasting all one night, and all the following day until the going down of the sun, the Turks, leaving thirty thousand of their dead beneath the ramparts of the city, and taking with them the sultan desperately wounded, struck their tents in the darkness of the night and retreated.

Great was the exultation in Hungary, in Germany and all over Europe. But this joy was speedily clouded by the intelligence that Hunniades, the deliverer of Europe from Moslem invasion, exhausted with toil, had been seized by a fever and had died. It is said that the young King Ladislaus rejoiced in his death, for he was greatly annoyed in having a subject attain such a degree of splendor as to cast his own name into insignificance. Hunniades left two sons, Ladislaus and Matthias. The king and Cilli manifested the meanest jealousy in reference to these young men, and fearful that the renown of their father, which had inspired pride and gratitude in every Hungarian heart, might give them power, they did every thing they could to humiliate and depress them. The king lured them both to Buda, where he perfidiously beheaded the eldest, Ladislaus, for wounding Cilli, in defending himself from an attack which the implacable count had made upon him, and he also threw the younger son, Matthias, into a prison.

The widow of Hunniades, the heroic mother of these children, with a spirit worthy of the wife of her renowned husband, called the nobles to her aid. They rallied in great numbers, roused to indignation. The inglorious king, terrified by the storm he had raised, released Matthias, and fled from Buda to Vienna, pursued by the execrations and menaces of the Hungarians.

He soon after repaired to Prague, in Bohemia, to solemnize his marriage with Magdalen, daughter of Charles VII., King of France. He had just reached the city, and was making preparations for his marriage in unusual splendor, when he was attacked by a malignant disease, supposed to be the plague and died after a sickness of but thirty-six hours. The unhappy king, who, through the stormy scenes of his short life, had developed no grandeur of soul, was oppressed with the awfulness of passing to the final judgment. In the ordinances of the Church he sought to find solace for a sinful and a troubled spirit. Having received the sacrament of the Lord's Supper, with dying lips he commenced repeating the Lord's prayer. He had just uttered the words " deliver us from evil," when his spirit took its flight to the judgment seat of Christ.

Frederic, the emperor, Duke of Styria, was now the oldest lineal descendant of Rhodolph of Hapsburg, founder of the house of Austria. The imperial dignity had now degenerated into almost an empty title. The Germanic empire consisted of a few large sovereignties and a conglomeration of petty dukedoms, principalities, and States of various names, very loosely held together, in their heterogeneous and independent rulers and governments, by one nominal sovereign upon whom the jealous States were willing to confer but little real power. A writer at that time, Æneas Sylvius, addressing the Germans, says:

" Although you acknowledge the emperor for your king and master, he possesses but a precarious sovereignty; he has no power; you only obey him when you choose; and you are seldom inclined to obey. You are all desirous to be free; neither the princes nor the States render to him what is due. He has no revenue, no treasure. Hence you are involved in endless contests and daily wars. Hence also rapine, murder, conflagrations, and a thousand evils which arise from divided authority."

Upon the death of Ladislaus there was a great rush and grasping for the vacant thrones of Bohemia and Hungary, and for possession of the rich dukedoms of Austria. After a long conflict the Austrian estates were divided into three portions. Frederic, the emperor, took Upper Austria; his brother Albert, who had succeeded to the Swiss estates, took Lower

Austria; Sigismond, Albert's nephew, a man of great energy of character, took Carinthia. The three occupied the palace in Vienna in joint residence.

The energetic regent, George Podiebrad, by adroit diplomacy succeeded, after an arduous contest, in obtaining the election by the Bohemian nobles to the throne of Bohemia. The very day he was chosen he was inaugurated at Prague, and though rival candidates united with the pope to depose him, he maintained his position against them all.

Frederic, the emperor, had been quite sanguine in the hopes of obtaining the crown of Bohemia. Bitterly disappointed there, he at first made a show of hostile resistance; but thinking better of the matter, he concluded to acquiesce in the elevation of Podiebrad, to secure amicable relations with him, and to seek his aid in promotion of his efforts to obtain the crown of Hungary. Here again the emperor failed. The nobles assembled in great strength at Buda, and elected unanimously Matthias, the only surviving son of the heroic Hunniades, whose memory was embalmed in the hearts of all the Hungarians. The boy then, for he was but a boy, and was styled contemptuously by the disappointed Frederic the boy king, entered into an alliance with Podiebrad for mutual protection, and engaged the hand of his daughter in marriage. Thus was the great kingdom of Austria, but recently so powerful in the union of all the Austrian States with Bohemia and Hungary, again divided and disintegrated. The emperor, in his vexation, foolishly sent an army of five thousand men into Hungary, insanely hoping to take the crown by force of arms, but he was soon compelled to relinquish the hopeless enterprise.

And now Frederic and Albert began to quarrel at Vienna. The emperor was arrogant and domineering. Albert was irritable and jealous. First came angry words; then the enlisting of partisans, and then all the miseries of fierce and determined civil war. The capital was divided into hostile factions, and the whole country was ravaged by the sweep of armies. The populace of Vienna, espousing the cause of Albert, rose in insurrection, pillaged the houses of the adherents of Frederic, drove Frederic, with his wife and infant child, into the citadel, and invested the fortress. Albert placed himself at the head of the insurgents and conducted the siege. The emperor, though he had but two hundred men in the garrison, held out valiantly. But famine would soon have compelled him to capitulate, had not the King of Bohemia, with a force of thirteen thousand men, marched to his aid. Podiebrad relieved the emperor, and secured a verbal reconciliation between the two angry brothers, which lasted until the Bohemian forces had returned to their country, when the feud burst out anew and with increased violence. The emperor procured the ban of the empire against his brother, and the pope excommunicated him. Still Albert fought fiercely, and the strife raged without intermission until Albert suddenly died on the 4th of December, 1463.

The Turks, who, during all these years, had been making predatory excursions along the frontiers of Hungary, now, in three strong bands of ten thousand each, overran Servia and Bosnia, and spread their devastations even into the heart of Illyria, as far as the metropolitan city of Laybach. The ravages of fire and sword marked their progress. They burnt every village, every solitary cottage, and the inhabitants were indiscriminately slain. Frederic, the emperor, a man of but little energy, was at his country residence at Lintz, apparently more anxious, writes a contemporary, "to shield his plants from frost, than to defend his domains against these barbarians."

The bold barons of Carniola, however, rallied their vassals, raised an army of twenty thousand men, and drove the Turks back to the Bosphorus. But the invaders, during their unimpeded march, had slain six thousand Christians, and they carried back with them eight thousand captives.

Again, a few years after, the Turks, with a still larger army, rushed through the defiles of the Illyrian mountains, upon the plains of Carinthia. Their march was like the flow of volcanic fire. They left behind them utter desolation, smouldering hearth-stones and fields crimsoned with blood. At length they retired of their own accord, dragging after them twenty thousand captives. During a period of twenty-seven years, under the imbecile reign of Frederic, the very heart of Europe was twelve times scourged by the inroads of these savages. No tongue can tell the woes which were inflicted upon humanity. Existence, to the masses of the people, in that day, must indeed have been a curse. Ground to the very lowest depths of poverty by the exactions of ecclesiastics and nobles, in rags, starving, with no social or intellectual joys, they might indeed have envied the beasts of the field.

The conduct of Frederic seems to be marked with increasing treachery and perfidy. Jealous of the growing power of George Podiebrad, he instigated Matthias, King of Hungary, to make war upon Bohemia, promising Matthias the Bohemian crown. Infamously the King of Hungary accepted the bribe, and raising a powerful army, invaded Bohemia, to wrest the crown from his father-in-law. His armies were pressing on so victoriously, in conjunction with those of Frederic, that the emperor was now alarmed lest Matthias, uniting the crowns of Hungary and Bohemia, should become too powerful. He therefore not only abandoned him, but stirred up an insurrection among the Hungarian nobles, which compelled Matthias to abandon Bohemia and return home.

Matthias, having quelled the insurrection, was so enraged with the emperor, that he declared war against him, and immediately invaded Austria. The emperor was now so distrusted that he could not find a single ally. Austria alone, was no match for Hungary. Matthias overran all Lower Austria, took all the fortresses upon the Danube, and invested

Vienna. The emperor fled in dismay to Lintz, and was obliged to purchase an ignominious peace by an immense sum of money, all of which was of course to be extorted by taxes on the miserable and starving peasantry.

Poland, Bohemia and the Turks, now all pounced upon Hungary, and Frederic, deeming this a providential indication that Hungary could not enforce the fulfillment of the treaty, refused to pay the money. Matthias, greatly exasper ated, made the best terms he could with Poland, and again led his armies in Austria. For four years the warfare raged fiercely, when all Lower Austria, including the capital, was in the hands of Matthias, and the emperor was driven from his hereditary domains ; and, accompanied by a few followers, he wandered a fugitive from city to city, from convent to convent, seeking aid from all, but finding none.

CHAPTER V.

WANDERINGS OF THE EMPEROR FREDERIC.—PROPOSED ALLIANCE WITH THE DUKE OF
BURGUNDY.—MUTUAL DISTRUST.—MARRIAGE OF MARY.—THE AGE OF CHIVALRY.—
THE MOTIVE INDUCING THE LORD OF PRAUNSTEIN TO DECLARE WAR.—DEATH OF
FREDERIC II.—THE EMPEROR'S SECRET.—DESIGNS OF THE TURKS.—DEATH OF MA-
HOMET II.—FIRST ESTABLISHMENT OF STANDING ARMIES.—USE OF GUNPOWDER.—
ENERGY OF MAXIMILIAN.—FRENCH AGGRESSIONS.—THE LEAGUE TO EXPEL THE
FRENCH.—DISAPPOINTMENTS OF MAXIMILIAN.—BRIBING THE POPE.—INVASION OF
ITALY.—CAPTURE AND RECAPTURE.—THE CHEVALIER DE BAYARD.

ADVERSITY only developed more fully the weak and
ignoble character of Frederic. He wandered about, recognized Emperor of Germany, but a fugitive from his own
Austrian estates, occasionally encountering pity, but never
sympathy or respect. Matthias professed his readiness to surrender Austria back to Frederic so soon as he would fulfill the
treaty by paying the stipulated money. Frederic was accompanied in his wanderings by his son Maximilian, a remarkably
elegant lad, fourteen years of age. They came to the court
of the powerful Duke of Burgundy. The dukedom extended
over wide realms, populous and opulent, and the duke had the
power of a sovereign but not the regal title. He was ambitious of elevating his dukedom into a kingdom and of being
crowned king; and he agreed to give his only daughter and
heiress, Mary, a beautiful and accomplished girl, to the emper-
or's son Maximilian, if Frederic would confer upon his estates
the regal dignity and crown him king. The bargain was
made, and Maximilian and Mary both were delighted, for they
regarded each other with all the warmth of young lovers.
Mary, heiress to the dukedom of Burgundy, was a prize which

any monarch might covet; and half the princes of Europe were striving for her hand.

But now came a new difficulty. Neither the emperor nor duke had the slightest confidence in each other. The King of France, who had hoped to obtain the hand of Mary for his son the dauphin, caused the suspicion to be whispered into the ear of Frederic that the Duke of Burgundy sought the kingly crown only as the first step to the imperial crown; and that so soon as the dukedom was elevated into a kingdom, Charles, the Duke of Burgundy, would avail himself of his increased power, to dethrone Frederic and grasp the crown of Germany. This was probably all true. Charles, fully understanding the perfidious nature of Frederic, did not dare to solemnize the marriage until he first should be crowned. Frederic, on the other hand, did not dare to crown the duke until the marriage was solemnized, for he had no confidence that the duke, after having attained the regal dignity, would fulfill his pledge.

Charles was for hurrying the coronation, Frederic for pushing the marriage. A magnificent throne was erected in the cathedral at Treves, and preparations were making on the grandest scale for the coronation solemnities, when Frederic, who did not like to tell the duke plumply to his face that he was fearful of being cheated, extricated himself from his embarrassment by feigning important business which called him suddenly to Cologne. A scene of petty and disgraceful intrigues ensued between the exasperated duke and emperor, and there were the marching and the countermarching of hostile bands and the usual miseries of war, until the death of Duke Charles at the battle of Nancy on the 5th of January, 1477.

The King of France now made a desperate endeavor to obtain the hand of Mary for his son. One of the novel acts of this imperial courtship, was to send an army into Burgundy, which wrested a large portion of Mary's dominions from her, which the king, Louis XI., refused to surrender unless Mary would marry his son. Many of her nobles urged the claims of France. But love in the heart of Mary was stronger than political expediency, and more persuasive than the entreaties of her nobles. To relieve herself from importunity, she was hurriedly married, three months after the death of her father, by proxy to Maximilian.

In August the young prince, but eighteen years of age, with a splendid retinue, made his public entry into Ghent. His commanding person and the elegance of his manners, attracted universal admiration. His subjects rallied with enthusiasm around him, and, guided by his prowess, in a continued warfare of five years, drove the invading French from their territories. But death, the goal to which every one tends, was suddenly and unexpectedly reached by Mary. She died the 7th of August, 1479, leaving two infant children, Philip and Margaret.

The Emperor Frederic also succeeded, by diplomatic cunning, in convening the diet of electors and choosing Maximilian as his successor to the imperial throne. Frederic and Maximilian now united in the endeavor to recover Austria from the King of Hungary. The German princes, however, notwithstanding the summons of the emperor, refused to take any part in the private quarrels of Austria, and thus the battle would have to be fought between the troops of Maximilian and of Matthias. Maximilian prudently decided that it would be better to purchase the redemption of the territory with money than with blood. The affair was in negotiation when Matthias was taken sick and died the 15th of July, 1490. He left no heir, and the Hungarian nobles chose Ladislaus, King of Bohemia, to succeed him. Maximilian had been confident of obtaining the crown of Hungary. Exasperated by the disappointment, he relinquished all idea of purchasing his patrimonial estates, but making a sudden rush with his troops upon the Hungarians, he drove them out of Austria, and pursued them far over the frontiers of Hungary. Ladislaus, the new

King of Hungary, now listened to terms of peace. A singu- lar treaty was made. The Bohemian king was to retain the crown of Hungary, officiating as reigning monarch, while Maxi- milian was to have the *title* of King of Hungary. Ladislaus relinquished all claim to the Austrian territories, and paid a large sum of money as indemnity for the war.

Thus Austria again comes into independent existence, to watch amidst the tumult and strife of Europe for opportuni ties to enlarge her territories and increase her power. Maxi- milian was a prince, energetic and brave, who would not allow any opportunity to escape him. In those dark days of vio- lence and of blood, every petty quarrel was settled by the sword. All over Germany the clash of steel against steel was ever resounding. Not only kings and dukes engaged in wars, but the most insignificant baron would gather his few retain- ers around him and declare formal war against the occupant of the adjacent castle. The spirit of chivalry, so called, was so rampant that private individuals would send a challenge to the emperor. Contemporary writers record many curious specimens of these declarations of war. The Lord of Praun- stein declared war against the city of Frankfort, because a young lady of that city refused to dance with his uncle at a ball.

Frederic was now suffering from the infirmities of age. Surrendering the administration of affairs, both in Austria and over the estates of the empire, to Maximilian, he retired, with his wife and three young daughters, to Lintz, where he de- voted himself, at the close of his long and turbulent reign, to the peaceful pursuits of rural life. A cancerous affection of the leg rendered it necessary for him to submit to the ampu- tation of the limb. He submitted to the painful operation with the greatest fortitude, and taking up his severed limb, with his accustomed phlegm remarked to those standing by,

" What difference is there between an emperor and a peas- ant ? Or rather, is not a sound peasant better than a sick em-

peror? Yet I hope to enjoy the greatest good which can hap-
pen to man—a happy exit from this transitory life."

The shock of a second amputation, which from the vitiated
state of his blood seemed necessary, was too great for his enfeebled frame to bear. He died August 19th, 1493, seventy-
eight years of age, and after a reign of fifty-three years. He
was what would be called, in these days, an ultra temper-
ance man, never drinking even wine, and expressing ever the
strongest abhorrence of alcoholic drinks, calling them the
parent of all vices. He seems to have anticipated the future
greatness of Austria; for he had imprinted upon all his books,
engraved upon his plate and carved into the walls of his palace a mysterious species of anagram composed of the five vow-
els, A, E, I, O, U.

The significance of this great secret no one could obtain
from him. It of course excited great curiosity, as it everywhere met the eye of the public. After his death the riddle
was solved by finding among his papers the following interpretation—

Austri Est Imperare   Orbi   Universo.
Austria Is To govern The world Universal.

Maximilian, in the prime of manhood, energetic, ambitious,
and invested with the imperial dignity, now assumed the government of the Austrian States. The prospect of greatness
was brilliant before Maximilian. The crowns of Bohemia
and Hungary were united in the person of Ladislaus, who
was without children. As Maximilian already enjoyed the
title of King of Hungary, no one enjoyed so good a chance
as he of securing both of those crowns so soon as they should
fall from the brow of Ladislaus.

Europe was still trembling before the threatening cimeter
of the Turk. Mahomet II., having annihilated the Greek empire, and consolidated his vast power, and checked in his
career by the warlike barons of Hungary, now cast a lustful
eye across the Adriatic to the shores of Italy. He crossed the

sea, landed a powerful army and established twenty thousand men, strongly garrisoned, at Otranto, and supplied with pro. visions for a year. All Italy was in consternation, for a pas sage was now open directly from Turkey to Naples and Rome. Mahomet boasted that he would soon feed his horse on the altar of St. Peter's. The pope, Sextus IV., in dismay, was about abandoning Rome, and as there was no hope of uniting the discordant States of Italy in any effectual resist-ance, it seemed inevitable that Italy, like Greece, would soon become a Turkish province. And where then could it be hoped that the ravages of the Turks would be arrested ?

In this crisis, so alarming, Providence interposed, and the sudden death of Mahomet, in the vigor of his pride and am-bition, averted the danger. Bajazet II. succeeded to the Moslem throne, an indolent and imbecile sultan. Insurrec-tion in his own dominions exhausted all his feeble energies. The Neapolitans, encouraged, raised an army, recovered Otranto, and drove the Turks out of Italy. Troubles in the Turkish dominions now gave Christendom a short respite, as all the strength of the sultan was required to subjugate insur-gent Circassia and Egypt.

Though the Emperor of Germany was esteemed the first sovereign in Europe, and, on state occasions, was served by kings and electors, he had in reality but little power. The kings who formed his retinue on occasions of ceremonial pomp, were often vastly his superiors in wealth and power. Frequently he possessed no territory of his own, not even a castle, but depended upon the uncertain aids reluctantly granted by the diet.

Gunpowder was now coming into use as one of the most efficient engines of destruction, and was working great changes in the science of war. It became necessary to have troops drilled to the use of cannon and muskets. The baron could no longer summon his vassals, at the moment, to abandon the plow, and seize pike and saber for battle, where the strong arm only was needed. Disciplined troops were needed, who could sweep the field with well-aimed bullets, and crumble walls with shot and shells. This led to the establishment of standing armies, and gave the great powers an immense ad-vantage over their weaker neighbors. The invention of printing, also, which began to be operative about the middle of the fifteenth century, rapidly changed, by the diffusion of intelligence, the state of society, hitherto so barbarous. The learned men of Greece, driven from their country by the Turkish invasion, were scattered over Europe, and contrib-uted not a little to the extension of the love of letters. The discovery of the mariner's compass and improvements in nautical astronomy, also opened new sources of knowledge and of wealth, and the human mind all over Europe com-menced a new start in the career of civilization. Men of let-ters began to share in those honors which heretofore had belonged exclusively to men of war; and the arts of peace began to claim consideration with those who had been accus-tomed to respect only the science of destruction.

Maximilian was at Innspruck when he received intelli-gence of the death of his father. He commenced his reign with an act of rigor which was characteristic of his whole career. A horde of Turks had penetrated Styria and Car-niola, laying every thing waste before them as far as Carniola. Maximilian, sounding the alarm, inspired his countrymen with the same energy which animated his own breast. Fifteen thousand men rallied at the blast of his bugles. Instead of intrusting the command of them to his generals, he placed himself at their head, and made so fierce an onset upon the invaders, that they precipitately fled. Maximilian returned at the head of his troops triumphant to Vienna, where he was received with acclamations such as had seldom resounded in the metropolis. He was hailed as the deliverer of his coun-try, and at once rose to the highest position in the esteem and affection of the Austrians.

Maximilian had encountered innumerable difficulties in Burgundy, and was not unwilling to escape from the vexa- tions and cares of that distant dukedom, by surrendering its government to his son Philip, who was now sixteen years of age, and whom the Burgundians claimed to be their ruler as the heir of Mary. The Swiss estates were also sundered from Austrian dominion, and, uniting with the Swiss confederacy, were no longer subject to the house of Hapsburg. Thus Maximilian had the Austrian estates upon the Danube only, as the nucleus of the empire he was ambitious of establish- ing.

Conscious of his power, and rejoicing in the imperial title, he had no idea of playing an obscure part on the conspicuous stage of European affairs. With an eagle eye he watched the condition of the empire, and no less eagerly did he fix his eye upon the movements of those great southern powers, now be- coming consolidated into kingdoms and empires, and mar- shaling armies which threatened again to bring all Europe under a dominion as wide and despotic as that of Rome.

Charles VIII., King of France, crossed the Alps with an army of twenty-two thousand men, in the highest state of dis- cipline, and armed with all the modern enginery of war. With ease he subjugated Tuscany, and in a triumphant march through Pisa and Siena, entered Rome as a conqueror. It was the 31st of December, 1394, when Charles, by torchlight, at the head of his exultant troops, entered the eternal city. The pope threw himself into the castle of St. Angelo, but was soon compelled to capitulate and to resign all his fortresses to the conqueror. Charles then continued his march to Naples, which he reached on the 22d of February. He overran and subjugated the whole kingdom, and, having consolidated his conquest, entered Naples on a white steed, beneath imperial banners, and arrogantly assumed the title of King of Naples, Sicily and Jerusalem Alphonso, King of Naples, in despair, abdicated in favor of his son, Ferdinand; and Ferdinand, unable to oppose any effectual resistance, abandoned his kingdom to the conqueror, and fled to the island of Ischia.

These alarming aggressions on the part of France, already very powerful, excited general consternation throughout Europe. Maximilian, as emperor, was highly incensed, and roused all his energies to check the progress of so dangerous a rival. The Austrian States alone could by no means cope with the kingdom of France. Maximilian sent agents to the pope, to the Dukes of Milan and Florence, and to the King of Arragon, and formed a secret league to expel the French from Italy, and restore Ferdinand to Naples. It was understood that the strength of France was such, that this enterprise could only be achieved through a long war, and that the allies must continue united to prevent France, when once expelled from Italy, from renewing her aggressions. The league was to continue twenty-two years. The pope was to furnish six thousand men, and the other Italian States twelve thousand. Maximilian promised to furnish nine thousand. Venice granted the troops of the emperor a free passage through her dominions.

These important first steps being thus taken secretly and securely, the emperor summoned a diet of Germany to enlist the States of the empire in the enterprise. This was the most difficult task, and yet nothing could be accomplished without the coöperation of Germany. But the Germanic States, loosely held together, jealous of each other, each grasping solely at its own aggrandizement, reluctantly delegating any power to the emperor, were slow to promise coöperation in any general enterprise, and having promised, were still slower to perform. The emperor had no power to enforce the fulfillment of agreements, and could only supplicate. During the long reign of Frederic the imperial dignity had lapsed more and more into an empty title; and Maximilian had an arduous task before him in securing even respectful attention to his demands. He was fully aware of the difficulties, and made arrangements accordingly

The memorable diet was summoned at Worms, on the 26th of May, 1496. The emperor had succeeded, by great exertion, in assembling a more numerous concourse of the princes and nobles of the empire than had ever met on a similar occasion. He presided in person, and in a long and earnest address endeavored to rouse the empire to a sense of its own dignity and its own high mission as the regulator of the affairs of Europe. He spoke earnestly of their duty to combine and chastise the insolence of the Turks; but waiving that for the present moment, he unfolded to them the danger to which Europe was immediately and imminently exposed by the encroachments of France. To add to the force of his words, he introduced ambassadors from the King of Naples, who informed the assembly of the conquests of the French, of their haughty bearing, and implored the aid of the diet to repel the invaders. The Duke of Milan was then presented, and, as a member of the empire, he implored as a favor and claimed as a right, the armies of the empire for the salvation of his duchy. And then the legate of the pope, in the robes of the Church, and speaking in the name of the Holy Father to his children, pathetically described the indignities to which the pope had been exposed, driven from his palace, bombarded in the fortress to which he had retreated, compelled to capitulate and leave his kingdom in the hands of the enemy; he expatiated upon the impiety of the French troops, the sacrilegious horrors of which they had been guilty, and in tones of eloquence hardly surpassed by Peter the Hermit, strove to rouse them to a crusade for the rescue of the pope and his sacred possessions.

Maximilian had now exhausted all his powers of persuasion. He had done apparently enough to rouse every heart to intensest action. But the diet listened coldly to all these appeals, and then in substance replied,

"We admit the necessity of checking the incursions of the Turks; we admit that it is important to check the progress of the French. But our first duty is to secure peace in Germany. The States of the empire are embroiled in incessant wars with each other. All attempts to prevent these private wars between the States of the empire have hitherto failed. Before we can vote money and men for any foreign enterprise whatever, we must secure internal tranquillity. This can only be done by establishing a supreme tribunal, supported by a power which can enforce its decisions."

These views were so manifestly judicious, that Maximilian assented to them, and, anxious to lose no time in raising troops to expel the French from Italy, he set immediately about the organization of an imperial tribunal to regulate the internal affairs of the empire. A court was created called the Imperial Chamber. It was composed of a president and sixteen judges, half of whom were taken from the army, and half from the class of scholars. To secure impartiality, the judges held their office for life. A majority of suffrages decided a question, and in case of a tie, the president gave a casting vote. The emperor reserved the right of deciding certain questions himself. This court gradually became one of the most important and salutary institutions of the German empire.

By the 7th of August these important measures were arranged. Maximilian had made great concessions of his imperial dignity in transferring so much of his nominal power to the Imperial Chamber, and he was now sanguine that the States would vote him the supplies which were needed to expel the French from Italy, or, in more honest words, to win for the empire in Italy that ascendency which France had attained. But bitter indeed was his disappointment. After long deliberation and vexatious delays, the diet voted a ridiculous sum, less than one hundred and fifty thousand dollars, to raise an army " sufficient to check the progress of the French." One third of this sum Maximilian was to raise from his Austrian States ; the remaining two thirds he was permitted to obtain by a loan. Four years were to be allowed for raising the money, and the emperor, as a condition for the reception of even this miserable boon, was required to pledge his word of honor that at the expiration of the four years he would raise no more. And even these hundred and fifty thousand dollars were to be intrusted to seven treasurers, to be administered according to their discretion. One only of these treasurers was to be chosen by the emperor, and the other six by the diet.

Deeply chagrined by this result, Maximilian was able to raise only three thousand men, instead of the nine thousand which he had promised the league. Charles VIII., informed of the formidable coalition combining against him, and not aware of the feeble resources of the emperor, apprehensive that the armies of Germany, marching down and uniting with the roused States of Italy, might cut off his retreat and overwhelm him, decided that the " better part of courage is discretion ;" and he accordingly abandoned his conquests, recrossed the Apennines, fought his backward path through Italy, and returned to France. He, however, left behind him six thousand men strongly intrenched, to await his return with a new and more powerful armament.

Maximilian now resolved chivalrously to throw himself into Italy, and endeavor to rouse the Italians themselves to resist the threatened invasion, trusting that the diet of Germany, when they should see him struggling against the hosts of France, would send troops to his aid. With five hundred horse, and about a thousand foot soldiers, he crossed the Alps. Here he learned that for some unknown reason Charles had postponed his expedition. Recoiling from the ridicule attending a quixotic and useless adventure, he hunted around for some time to find some heroic achievement which would redeem his name from reproach, when, thwarted in every thing, he returned to Austria, chagrined and humiliated.

Thus frustrated in all his attempts to gain ascendency in Italy, Maximilian turned his eyes to the Swiss estates of the

house of Hapsburg, now sundered from the Austrian territories. He made a vigorous effort, first by diplomacy, then
by force of arms, to regain them. Here again he was frustrated, and was compelled to enter into a capitulation by
which he acknowledged the independence of the Helvetic
States, and their permanent severance from Austrian juris-
diction.

In April, 1498, Charles VIII. died, and Louis XII. succeeded him on the throne of France. Louis immediately
made preparations for a new invasion of Italy. In those
miserable days of violence and blood, almost any prince was
ready to embark in war under anybody's banner, where there
was the least prospect of personal aggrandizement. The
question of right or wrong, seemed seldom to enter any one's
mind. Louis fixed his eyes upon the duchy of Milan as the
richest and most available prize within his grasp. Conscious
that he would meet with much opposition, he looked around
for allies.

"If you will aid me," he said to Pope Alexander VI., " 1
will assist you in your war against the Duke of Romagna. I
will give your son, Cæsar Borgia,* a pension of two thousand
dollars a year, will confer upon him an important command
in my army, and will procure for him a marriage with a princess of the royal house of Navarre."

The holy father could not resist this bribe, and eagerly
joined the robber king in his foray. To Venice Louis said—

" If you will unite with me, I will assist you in annexing
to your domains the city of Cremona, and the Ghiaradadda."
Lured by such hopes of plunder, Venice was as eager as the
pope to take a share in the piratic expedition. Louis then
sent to the court of Turin, and offered them large sums of
money and increased territory, if they would allow him a free

---

* Cæsar Borgia, who has filled the world with the renown of his infamy,
was the illegitimate son of Alexander VI., and of a Roman lady named
Vanozza.

passage across the Alps.   Turin bowed obsequiously, and grasped at the easy bargain.   To Florence he said, "If you raise a hand to assist the Duke of Milan, I will crush you.   If you remain quiet, I will leave you unharmed."   Florence, overawed, remained as meek as a lamb.   The diplomacy being thus successfully closed, an army of twenty-two thousand men was put in vigorous motion in July, 1499.   They crossed the Alps, fought a few battles, in which, with overpowering num-bers, they easily conquered their opposers, and in twenty days were in possession of Milan.   The Duke Ludovico with diffi-culty escaped.   With a few followers he threaded the defiles of the Tyrolese mountains, and hastened to Innspruck, the capital of Tyrol, where Maximilian then was, to whom he con-veyed the first tidings of his disaster.   Louis XII. followed after his triumphant army, and on the 6th of October made a triumphal entry into the captured city, and was inaugurated Duke of Milan.

Maximilian promised assistance, but could raise neither money nor men.   Ludovico, however, succeeded in hiring fif-teen hundred Burgundian horsemen, and eight thousand Swiss mercenaries—for in those ages of ignorance and crime all, men were ready, for pay, to fight in any cause—and emerging from the mountains upon the plains of Milan, found all his former subjects disgusted with the French, and eager to rally under his banners.   His army increased at every step.   He fell fiercely upon the invaders, routed them everywhere, drove them from the duchy, and recovered his country and his capital as rapidly as he had lost them.   One fortress only the French maintained.   The intrepid Chevalier De Bayard, *the knight without fear and without reproach*, threw himself into the citadel of Novarra, and held out against all the efforts of Ludovico, awaiting the succor which he was sure would come from his powerful sovereign the King of France.

CHAPTER VI.

MAXIMILIAN I.

FROM 1500 TO 1519.

LOUIS XII., stung by the disgrace of his speedy expulsion from Milan, immediately raised another army of five thousand horse and fifteen thousand foot to recover his lost plunder. He also sent to Switzerland to hire troops, and without difficulty engaged ten thousand men to meet, on the plains of Milan, the six thousand of their brethren whom Ludovico had hired, to hew each other to pieces for the miserable pittance of a few pennies a day. But Louis XII. was as great in diplomacy as in war. He sent secret emissaries to the Swiss in the camp of Ludovico, offering them larger wages if they would abandon the service of Ludovico and return home. They promptly closed the bargain, unfurled the banner of mutiny, and informed the Duke of Milan that they could not, in conscience, fight against their own brethren. The duke was in despair. He plead even with tears that they would not abandon him. All was in vain. They not only commenced their march home, but basely betrayed the duke to the French. He was taken prisoner by Louis, carried to France and for five years was kept in rigorous confinement in the strong fortresses of the kingdom. Afterward, through the intercession of Maxi-milian, he was allowed a little more freedom. He was, how-ever, kept in captivity until he died in the year 1510. Ludo-vico merits no commiseration. He was as perfidious and un principled as any of his assailants could be.

The reconquest of Milan by Louis, and the capture of Lu-dovico, alarmed Maximilian and roused him to new efforts. He again summoned the States of the empire and implored their coöperation to resist the aggressions of France. But he was as unsuccessful as in his previous endeavors. Louis watched anxiously the movements of the German diet, and finding that he had nothing to fear from the troops of the em-pire, having secured the investiture of Milan, prepared for the invasion of Naples. The venal pope was easily bought over. Even Ferdinand, the King of Arragon, was induced to loan his connivance to a plan for robbing a near relative of his crown, by the promise of sharing in the spoil. A treaty of partition was entered into by the two robber kings, by which Ferdinand of Arragon was to receive Calabria and Apulia, and the King of France the remaining States of the Neapolitan kingdom. The pope was confidentially informed of this secret plot, which was arranged at Grenada, and promised the plunderers his benediction, in consideration of the abundant reward promised to him.

The doom of the King of Naples was now sealed. All un-conscious that his own relative, Ferdinand of Arragon, was conspiring against him, he appealed to Ferdinand for aid against the King of France. The perfidious king considered this as quite a providential interposition in his favor. He affected great zeal for the King of Naples, sent a powerful army into his kingdom, and stationed his troops in the important for-tresses. The infamous fraud was now accomplished. Frederic of Naples, to his dismay, found that he had been placing his empire in the hands of his enemies instead of friends; at the same time the troops of Louis arrived at Rome, where they were cordially received; and the pope immediately, on the 25th of June, 1501, issued a bull deposing Frederic from his kingdom, and, by virtue of that spiritual authority which he derived from the Apostle Peter, invested Louis and Ferdinand with the dominions of Frederic. Few men are more to be commiserated than a crownless king. Frederic, in his despair, threw himself upon the clemency of Louis. He was taken to France and was there fed and clothed by the royal bounty.

Maximilian impatiently watched the events from his home in Austria, and burned with the desire to take a more active part in these stirring scenes. Despairing, however, to rouse the German States to any effectual intervention in the affairs of southern Europe, he now endeavored to rouse the enthusiasm of the German nobles against the Turks. In this, by appealing to superstition, he was somewhat successful He addressed the following circular letter to the German States:

"A stone, weighing two hundred pounds, recently fell from heaven, near the army under my command in Upper Alsace, and I caused it, as a fatal warning from God to men, to be hung up in the neighboring church of Encisheim. In vain I myself explained to all Christian kings the signification of this mysterious stone. The Almighty punished the neglect of this warning with a dreadful scourge, from which thousands have suffered death, or pains worse than death. But since this punishment of the abominable sins of men has produced no effect, God has imprinted in a miraculous manner the sign of the cross, and the instruments of our Lord's passion in dark and bloody colors, on the bodies and garments of thousands. The appearance of these signs in Germany, in particular, does not indeed denote that the Germans have been peculiarly distinguished in guilt, but rather that they should set the example to the rest of the world, by being the first to undertake a crusade against the infidels."

For a time Maximilian seemed quite encouraged, for quite
a wave of religious enthusiasm seemed to roll over Europe.
All the energies of the pope were apparently enlisted, and he
raised, through all the domains of the Church, large sums ot
money for the holy enterprise of driving the invading infidels
out of Europe. England and France both proffered their co-
operation, and England, opening her inexhaustible purse, presented a subsidy of ten thousand pounds. The German nobles
rallied in large numbers under the banner of the cross. But
disappointment seemed to be the doom of the emperor. The
King of France sent no aid. The pope, iniquitously squandered all the money he had raised upon his infamous, dissolute
son, Cæsar Borgia. And the emperor himself was drawn into
a war with Bavaria, to settle the right of succession between
two rival claimants. The settlement of the question devolved
upon Maximilian as emperor, and his dignity was involved in
securing respect for his decision. Thus the whole gorgeous
plan of a war against the Turks, such as Europe had never
beheld, vanished into thin air, and Maximilian was found at the
head of fourteen thousand infantry, and twelve thousand horse,
engaged in a quarrel in the heart of Germany. In this war
Maximilian was successful, and he rewarded himself by annexing to Austria several small provinces, the sum total of which
quite enlarged his small domains.

By this time the kings of France and Spain were fiercely
fighting over their conquest of Naples and Sicily, each striving to grasp the lion's share. Maximilian thought his interests
would be promoted by aiding the Spaniards, and he accordingly sent three thousand men to Trieste, where they embarked, and sailing down the Adriatic, united with the Span
ish troops. The French were driven out of Italy. There then
ensued, for several years, wars and intrigues in which France,
Spain, Italy and Austria were involved ; all alike selfish and
grasping. Armies were ever moving to and fro, and the
people of Europe, by the victories of kings and nobles, were

kept in a condition of misery. No one seemed ever to think of their rights or their happiness.

Various circumstances had exasperated Maximilian very much against the Venetians. All the powers of Europe were then ready to combine against any other power whatever, if there was a chance of obtaining any share in the division of the plunder. Maximilian found no difficulty in secretly form ing one of the most formidable leagues history had then recorded, the celebrated league of Cambray. No sympathy need be wasted upon the Venetians, the victims of this coalition, for they had rendered themselves universally detestable by their arrogance, rapacity, perfidy and pride. France joined the coalition, and, in view of her power, was to receive a lion's share of the prey—the provinces of Brescia, Bergamo, Cremona, and the Ghiradadda. The King of Arragon was to send ships and troops, and receive his pay in the maritime towns on the shores of the Adriatic. The pope, Julius II., the most grasping, perfidious and selfish of them all, demanded Ravenna, Cervia, Faenza, Rimini, Immola and Cesena. His exorbitant claims were assented to, as it was infinitely important that the piratic expedition should be sanctioned by the blessing of the Church. Maximilian was to receive, in addition to some territories which Venice had wrested from him, Roveredo, Verona, Padua, Vicenza, Trevigi, and the Friuli. As Maximilian was bound by a truce with Venice, and as in those days of chivalry some little regard was to be paid to one's word of honor, Maximilian was only to march at the summons of the pope, which no true son of the Church, under any cir cumstances, was at liberty to disobey. Sundry other minor dukes and princes were engaged in the plot, who were also to receive a proportionate share of the spoil.

After these arrangements were all completed, the holy father, with characteristic infamy, made private overtures to the Venetians, revealing to them the whole plot, and offering to withdraw from the confederacy and thwart all its plans, if

Venice would pay more as the reward of perfidy than Rome could hope to acquire by force of arms. The haughty republic rejected the infamous proposal, and prepared for a desperate defense.

All the powers of the confederacy were now collecting their troops. But Maximilian was dependent upon the German diet for his ability to fulfill his part of the contract. He assembled the diet at Worms on the 21st of April, 1509, presented to them the plan of the league, and solicited their sup ort. The diet refused to coöperate, and hardly affecting even the forms of respect, couched its refusal in terms of stinging rebuke.

"We are tired," they said, "of these innumerable calls for troops and money. We can not support the burden of these frequent diets, involving the expense of long journeys, and we are weary of expeditions and wars. If the emperor enters into treaties with France and the pope without consulting us, it is his concern and not ours, and we are not bound to aid him to fulfill his agreement. And even if we were to vote the succors which are now asked of us, we should only be involved in embarrassment and disgrace, as we have been by the previous enterprises of the emperor."

Such, in brief, was the response of the diet. It drew from the emperor a long defense of his conduct, which he called an "Apology," and which is considered one of the most curious and characteristic documents of those days. He made no attempt to conceal his vexation, but assailed them in strong language of reproach.

"I have concluded a treaty with my allies," he wrote, "in conformity to the dictates of conscience and duty, and for the honor, glory and happiness of the empire and of Christendom. The negotiation could not be postponed, and if I had convoked a diet to demand the advice of the States, the treaty would never have been concluded. I was under the necessity of concealing the project of the combined powers, that we might fall on the Venetians at once and unexpectedly, which could not have been effected in the midst of public deliberations and endless discussions; and I have, I trust, clearly proved, both in my public and my private communications, the advantage which is likely to result from this union. If the aids hitherto granted by diets have produced nothing but disgrace and dishonor, I am not to blame, but the States who acted so scandalously in granting their succors with so much reluctance and delay. As for myself, I have, on the contrary, exposed my treasure, my countries, my subjects and my life, while the generality of the German States have remained in dishonorable tranquillity at home. I have more reason to complain of you than you of me; for you have constantly refused me your approbation and assistance; and even when you have granted succors, you have rendered them fruitless by the scantiness and tardiness of your supplies, and compelled me to dissipate my own revenues, and injure my own subjects."

Of course these bitter recriminations accomplished nothing in changing the action of the diet, and Maximilian was thrown upon the Austrian States alone for supplies. Louis of France, at the head of seventeen thousand troops, crossed the Alps. The pope fulminated a bull of excommunication against the Venetians, and sent an army of ten thousand men. The Duke of Ferrara and the Marquis of Mantua sent their contingents. Maximilian, by great exertions, sent a few battalions through the mountains of the Tyrol, and was preparing to follow with stronger forces. Province after province fell before the resistless invaders, and Venice would have fallen irretrievably had not the conquerors began to quarrel among themselves. The pope, in secret treaty, was endeavoring to secure his private interests, regardless of the interests of the allies. Louis, from some pique, withdrew his forces, and abandoned Maximilian in the hour of peril, and the emperor, shackled by want of money, and having but a feeble force, was quite unable to make progress alone against the Venetian troops.

It does not seem to be the will of Providence that the plots of unprincipled men, even against men as bad as themselves, should be more than transiently prosperous. Maximilian, thus again utterly thwarted in one of his most magnificent plans, covered with disgrace, and irritated almost beyond endurance, after attempting in vain to negotiate a truce with the Venetians, was compelled to retreat across the Alps, inveighing bitterly against the perfidious refusal to fulfill a perfidious agreement.

The holy father, Julius II., outwitted all his accomplices. He secured from Venice very valuable accessions of territory, and then, recalling his ecclesiastical denunciations, united with Venice to drive the *barbarians*, as he affectionately called his French and German allies, out of Italy. Maximilian returned to Austria as in a funeral march, ventured to summon another diet, told them how shamefully he had been treated by France, Venice and the pope, and again implored them to do something to help him. Perseverance is surely the most efficient of virtues. Incredible as it may seem, the emperor now obtained some little success. The diet, indignant at the conduct of the pope, and alarmed at so formidable a union as that between the papal States and Venice, voted a succor of six thousand infantry and eighteen hundred horse. This encouraged the emperor, and forgetting his quarrel with Louis XII. of France, in the stronger passion of personal aggrandizement which influenced him, he entered into another alliance with Louis against the pope and Venice, and then made a still stronger and a religious appeal to Germany for aid. A certain class of politicians in all countries and in all ages, have occasionally expressed great solicitude for the reputation of religion.

"The power and government of the pope," the emperor proclaimed, "which ought to be an example to the faithful, present, on the contrary, nothing but trouble and disorder. The enormous sums daily extorted from Germany, are perverted to the purposes of luxury or worldly views, instead of being employed for the service of God, or against the infidels. As Emperor of Germany, as advocate and protector of the Christian Church, it is my duty to examine into such irregularities, and exert all my efforts for the glory of God and the advantage of the empire; and as there is an evident necessity to reëstablish due order and decency, both in the ecclesiastical and temporal state, I have resolved to call a general council, without which nothing permanent can be effected."

It is said that Maximilian was now so confident of success, that he had decided to divide Italy between himself and France. He was to take Venice and the States of the Church, and France was to have the rest. Pope Julius was to be deposed, and to be succeeded by Pope Maximilian. The following letter from Maximilian to his daughter, reveals his ambitious views at the time. It is dated the 18th of September, 1511.

"To-morrow I shall send the Bishop of Guzk to the pope at Rome, to conclude an agreement with him that I may be appointed his coadjutor, and on his death succeed to the papacy, and become a priest, and afterwards a saint, that you may be bound to worship me, of which I shall be very proud. I have written on this subject to the King of Arragon, intreating him to favor my undertaking, and he has promised me his assistance, provided I resign my imperial crown to my grandson Charles, which I am very ready to do. The people and nobles of Rome have offered to support me against the French and Spanish party. They can muster twenty thousand combatants, and have sent me word that they are inclined to favor my scheme of being pope, and will not consent to have either a Frenchman, a Spaniard or a Venetian.

"I have already began to sound the cardinals, and, for that purpose, two or three hundred thousand ducats would be of great service to me, as their partiality to me is very great. The King of Arragon has ordered his ambassadors to assure me that he will command the Spanish cardinals to favor my pretensions to the papacy. I intreat you to keep this matter secret for the present, though I am afraid it will soon be known, for it is impossible to carry on a business secretly for which it is necessary to gain over so many persons, and to have so much money. Adieu. Written with the hand of your dear father Maximilian, future pope. The pope's fever has increased, and he can not live long."

It is painful to follow out the windings of intrigue and the labyrinths of guile, where selfishness seemed to actuate every heart, and where all alike seem destitute of any principle of Christian integrity. Bad as the world is now, and selfish as political aspirants are now, humanity has made immense progress since that dark age of superstition, fraud and violence. After many victories and many defeats, after innumerable fluctuations of guile, Maximilian accepted a bribe, and withdrew his forces, and the King of France was summoned home by the invasion of his own territories by the King of Arragon and Henry VIII. of England, who, for a suitable consideration, had been induced to join Venice and the pope. At the end of this long campaign of diplomacy, perfidy and blood, in which misery had rioted through ten thousand cottages, whose inhabitants the warriors regarded no more than the occupants of the ant-hills they trampled beneath their feet, it was found that no one had gained any thing but toil and disappointment.

On the 21st of February, 1513, Pope Julius II. died, and the cardinals, rejecting all the overtures of the emperor, elected John of Medici pope, who assumed the name of Leo X. The new pontiff was but thirty-six years of age, a man of brilliant talents, and devoted to the pursuit of letters. Inspired by boundless ambition, he wished to signalize his reign by the magnificence of his court and the grandeur of his achievements.

Thus far nothing but disaster seemed to attend the enterprises of Maximilian; but now the tide suddenly turned and

rolled in upon him billows of prosperity. It will be remembered that Maximilian married, for his first wife, Mary, the
daughter of the Duke of Burgundy. Their son Philip married Joanna, daughter of Ferdinand and Isabella, whose marriage, uniting the kingdoms of Castile and Arragon, created
the splendid kingdom of Spain. Philip died young, leaving a
son, Charles, and Joanna, an insane wife, to watch his grave
through weary years of woe. Upon the death of Ferdinand,
in January, 1516, Charles, the grandson of Maximilian, became
undisputed heir to the whole monarchy of Spain; then, perhaps, the grandest power in Europe, including Naples, Sicily
and Navarre. This magnificent inheritance, coming so directly into the family, and into the line of succession, invested
Maximilian and the house of Austria with new dignity.

It was now an object of intense solicitude with Maximilian,
to secure the reversion of the crowns of Hungary and Bohemia, which were both upon the brow of Ladislaus, to his
own family. With this object in view, and to render assurance doubly sure, he succeeded in negotiating a marriage
between two children of Ladislaus, a son and a daughter, and
two of his own grand-children. This was a far pleasanter
mode of acquiring territory and family aggrandizement than
by the sword. In celebration of the betrothals, Ladislaus and
his brother Sigismond, King of Poland, visited Vienna, where
Ladislaus was so delighted with the magnificent hospitality
of his reception, that he even urged upon the emperor, who
was then a widower, fifty-eight years of age, that he should
marry another of his daughters, though she had but attained
her thirteenth year. The emperor declined the honor, jocu-
larly remarking—

"There is no method more pleasant to kill an old man,
than to marry him to a young bride."

The German empire was then divided into ten districts, or
circles, as they were then called, each of which was responsible for the maintenance of peace among its own members

These districts were, Austria, Burgundy, the Upper Rhine, the Lower Rhine, Franconia, Bavaria, Suabia, Westphalia, Upper Saxony and Lower Saxony. The affairs of each district were to be regulated by a court of a few nobles, called a diet. The emperor devoted especial attention to the improvement of his own estate of Austria, which he subdivided into two districts, and these into still smaller districts. Over all, for the settlement of all important points of dispute, he established a tribunal called the Aulic Council, which subsequently exerted a powerful influence over the affairs of Austria.

One more final effort Maximilian made to rouse Germany to combine to drive the Turks out of Europe. Though the benighted masses looked up with much reverence to the pontiff, the princes and the nobles regarded him only as a *power*, wielding, in addition to the military arm, the potent energies of superstition. A diet was convened. The pope's legate appeared, and sustained the eloquent appeal of the emperor with the paternal commands of the holy father. But the press was now becoming a power in Europe, diffusing intelligence and giving freedom to thought and expression. The diet, after listening patiently to the arguments of the emperor and the requests of the pontiff, dryly replied—

"We think that Christianity has more to fear from the pope than from the Turks. Much as we may dread the ravages of the infidel, they can hardly drain Christendom more effectually than it is now drained by the exactions of the Church."

It was at Augsburg in July, 1518, that the diet ventured thus boldly to speak. This was one year after Luther had nailed upon the church door in Wittemberg, his ninety-five propositions, which had roused all Germany to scrutinize the abominable corruptions of the papal church. This bold language of the diet, influenced by the still bolder language of the intrepid monk, alarmed Leo X., and on the 7th of August he issued his summons commanding Luther to repair to Rome to answer for heresy. Maximilian, who had been foiled in his own attempt to attain the chair of St. Peter, who had seen so much of the infamous career of Julius and Alexander, as to lose all his reverence for the sacred character of the popes, and who regarded Leo X. merely as a successful rival who had thwarted his own plans, espoused, with cautious development, but with true interest, the cause of the reformer. And now came the great war of the Reformation, agitating Germany in every quarter, and rousing the lethargic intellect of the nations as nothing else could rouse it. Maximilian, with characteristic fickleness, or rather, with characteristic pliancy before every breeze of self-interest, was now on the one side, now on the other, and now, nobody knew where, until his career was terminated by sudden and fatal sickness.

The emperor was at Innspruck, all overwhelmed with his cares and his plans of ambition, when he was seized with a slight fever. Hoping to be benefited by a change of air, he set out to travel by slow stages to one of his castles among the mountains of Upper Austria. The disease, however, rapidly increased, and it was soon evident that death was approaching. The peculiarities of his character were never more strikingly developed than in these last solemn hours. Being told by his physicians that he had not long to live and that he must now prepare for the final judgment, he calmly replied, "I have long ago made that preparation. Had I not done so, it would be too late now."

For four years he had been conscious of declining health, and had always carried with him, wherever he traveled, an oaken coffin, with his shroud and other requisites for his funeral. With very minute directions he settled all his worldly affairs, and gave the most particular instructions respecting his funeral. Changing his linen, he strictly enjoined that his shirt should not be removed after his death, for his fastidious modesty was shocked by the idea of the exposure of his body, even after the soul had taken its flight.

He ordered his hair, after his death, to be cut off, all his teeth to be extracted, pounded to powder and publicly burned in the chapel of his palace. For one day his remains were to be exposed to the public, as a lesson of mortality. They were then to be placed in a sack filled with quicklime. The sack was to be enveloped in folds of silk and satin, and then placed in the oaken coffin which had been so long awaiting his remains. The coffin was then to be deposited under the altar of the chapel of his palace at Neustadt, in such a position that the officiating priest should ever trample over his head and heart. The king expressed the hope that this humiliation of his body would, in some degree, be accepted by the Deity in atonement for the sins of his soul. How universal the instinct that sin needs an atonement!

Having finished these directions the emperor observed that some of his attendants were in tears. "Do you weep," said he, "because you see a mortal die? Such tears become women rather than men." The emperor was now dying. As the ecclesiastics repeated the prayers of the Church, the emperor gave the responses until his voice failed, and then continued to give tokens of recognition and of faith, by making the sign of the cross. At three o'clock in the morning of the 11th of January, 1519, the Emperor Maximilian breathed his last. He was then in the sixtieth year of his age.

Maximilian is justly considered one of the most renowned of the descendants of Rhodolph of Hapsburg. It is saying but little for his moral integrity, to affirm that he was one of the best of the rulers of his age. According to his ideas of religion, he was a religious man. According to his ideas of honesty and of honor, he was both an honest and an honorable man. According to his idea of what is called *moral conduct*, he was irreproachable, being addicted to no *ungenteel* vices, or any sins which would be condemned by his associates. His ambition was not to secure for himself ease or luxury, but to extend his imperial power, and to aggrandize his family.

For these objects he passed his life, ever tossed upon the billows of toil and trouble. In industry and perseverance, he has rarely been surpassed.

Notwithstanding the innumerable interruptions and cares attendant upon his station, he still found time, one can hardly imagine when, to become a proficient in all the learning of the day. He wrote and spoke four languages readily, Latin, French, German and Italian. Few men have possessed more persuasive powers of eloquence. All the arts and sciences he warmly patronized, and men of letters of every class found in him a protector. But history must truthfully declare that there was no perfidy of which he would not be guilty, and no meanness to which he would not stoop, if he could only extend his hereditary domains and add to his family renown.

CHAPTER VII.

CHARLES V. AND THE REFORMATION.

CHARLES V. OF SPAIN.—HIS ELECTION AS EMPEROR OF GERMANY.—HIS CORONATION.—
THE FIRST CONSTITUTION.—PROGRESS OF THE REFORMATION.—THE POPE'S BULL
AGAINST LUTHER.—HIS CONTEMPT FOR HIS HOLINESS.—THE DIET AT WORMS.—
FREDERIC'S OBJECTION TO THE CONDEMNATION OF LUTHER BY THE DIET.—HE OB-
TAINS FOR LUTHER THE RIGHT OF DEFENSE.—LUTHER'S TRIUMPHAL MARCH TO THE
TRIBUNAL.—CHARLES URGED TO VIOLATE HIS SAFE CONDUCT.—LUTHER'S PATMOS.—
MARRIAGE OF SISTER CATHARINE BORA TO LUTHER.—TERRIBLE INSURRECTION.—THE
HOLY LEAGUE.—THE PROTEST OF SPIRES.—CONFESSION OF AUGSBURG.—THE TWO
CONFESSIONS.—COMPULSORY MEASURES.

CHARLES V. of Spain, as the nearest male heir, inherited
from Maximilian the Austrian States. He was the grandson of the late emperor, son of Philip and of Joanna, daughter
of Ferdinand and Isabella, and was born on the 24th of February, 1500. He had been carefully educated in the learning
and accomplishments of the age, and particularly in the arts
of war. At the death of his grandfather, Ferdinand, Charles,
though but sixteen years of age, assumed the title of King of
Spain, and though strongly opposed for a time, he grasped
firmly and held securely the reins of government.

Joanna, his mother, was legally the sovereign, both by the
laws of united Castile and Arragon, and by the testaments of
Isabella and Ferdinand. But she was insane, and was sunk in
such depths of melancholy as to be almost unconscious of the
scenes which were transpiring around her. Two years had
elapsed between the accession of Charles V. to the throne of
Spain and the death of his grandfather, Maximilian. The
young king, with wonderful energy of character, had, during

that time, established himself very firmly on the throne. Upon the death of Maximilian many claimants rose for the imperial throne. Henry VIII. of England and Francis of France, were prominent among the competitors. For six months all the arts of diplomacy were exhausted by the various candidates, and Charles of Spain won the prize. On the 28th of June, 1519, he was unanimously elected Emperor of Germany. The youthful sovereign, who was but nineteen years of age, was at Barcelona when he received the first intelligence of his election. He had sufficient strength of character to avoid the slightest appearance of exultation, but received the announcement with dignity and gravity far above his years.

The Spaniards were exceedingly excited and alarmed by the news. They feared that their young sovereign, of whom they had already begun to be proud, would leave Spain to establish his court in the German empire, and they should thus be left, as a distant province, to the government of a viceroy. The king was consequently flooded with petitions, from all parts of his dominions, not to accept the imperial crown. But Charles was as ambitious as his grandfather, Maximilian, whose foresight and maneuvering had set in train those influences which had elevated him to the imperial dignity.

Soon a solemn embassy arrived, and, with the customary pomp, proffered to Charles the crown which so many had coveted. Charles accepted the office, and made immediate preparations, notwithstanding the increasing clamor of his subjects, to go to Germany for his coronation. Intrusting the government of Spain during his absence to officers in whom he reposed confidence, he embarked on shipboard, and landing first at Dover in England, made a visit of four days to Henry VIII. He then continued his voyage to the Netherlands; proceeding thence to Aix-la-Chapelle, he was crowned on the 20th of October, 1520, with magnificence far surpassing that of any of his predecessors. Thus Charles V., when but twenty years of age, was the King of Spain and the crowned

Emperor of Germany. It is a great mistake to suppose that youthful precocity is one of the innovations of modern times.

In the changes of the political kaleidoscope, Austria had now become a part of Spain, or rather a prince of Austrian descent, a lineal heir of the house of Hapsburg, had inherited the dominion of Spain, the most extensive monarchy, in its continental domains and its colonial possessions, then upon the globe. The Germanic confederation at this time made a decided step in advance. Hitherto the emperors, when crowned, had made a sort of verbal promise to administer the government in accordance with the laws and customs of the several states. They were, however, apprehensive that the new emperor, availing himself of the vast power which he possessed independently of the imperial crown, might, by gradual encroachments, defraud them of their rights. A sort of constitution was accordingly drawn up, consisting of thirty-six articles, defining quite minutely the laws, customs and privileges of the empire, which constitution Charles was required to sign before his coronation.

Charles presided in person over his first diet which he had convened at Worms on the 6th of January, 1521. The theological and political war of the Reformation was now agitating all Germany, and raging with the utmost violence. Luther had torn the vail from the corruptions of papacy, and was exhibiting to astonished Europe the enormous aggression and the unbridled licentiousness of pontifical power. Letter succeeded letter, and pamphlet pamphlet, and they fell upon the decaying hierarchy like shot and shell upon the walls of a fortress already crumbling and tottering through age.

On the 15th of July, 1520, three months before the coronation of Charles V., the pope issued his world-renowned bull against the intrepid monk. He condemned Luther as a heretic, forbade the reading of his writings, excommunicated him if he did not retract within sixty days, and all princes and states were commanded, under pain of incurring the same censure, to seize his person and punish him and his adherents. Many were overawed by these menaces of the holy father, who held the keys of heaven and of hell. The fate of Luther was considered sealed. His works were publicly burned in several cities.

Luther, undaunted, replied with blow for blow. He declared the pope to be antichrist, renounced all obedience to him, detailed with scathing severity the conduct of corrupt pontiffs, and called upon the whole nation to renounce all allegiance to the scandalous court of Rome. To cap the climax of his contempt and defiance, he, on the 10th of December, 1520, not two months after the crowning of Charles V., led his admiring followers, the professors and students of the university of Wittemberg, in procession to the eastern gate of the city, where, in the presence of a vast concourse, he committed the papal bull to the flames, exclaiming, in the words of Ezekiel, " Because thou hast troubled the Holy One of God, let eternal fire consume thee." This dauntless spirit of the reformer inspired his disciples throughout Germany with new courage, and in many other cities the pope's bull of excommunication was burned with expressions of indignation and contempt.

Such was the state of this great religious controversy when Charles V. held his first diet at Worms. The pope, wielding all the energies of religious fanaticism, and with immense temporal revenues at his disposal, with ecclesiastics, officers of his spiritual court, scattered all over Europe, who exercised almost a supernatural power over the minds of the benighted masses, was still perhaps the most formidable power in Europe. The new emperor, with immense schemes of ambition opening before his youthful and ardent mind, and with no principles of heartfelt piety to incline him to seek and love the truth, as a matter of course sought the favor of the imperial pontiff, and was not at all disposed to espouse the cause of the obscure monk.

Charles, therefore, received courteously the legates of the pontiff at the diet, gave them a friendly hearing as they inveighed against the heresy of Luther, and proposed that the diet should also condemn the reformer. Fortunately for Luther he was a subject of the electorate of Saxony, and neither pope nor emperor could touch him but through the elector. Frederic, the Duke of Saxony, one of the electors of the empire, governed a territory of nearly fifteen thousand square miles, more than twice as large as the State of Massachusetts, and containing nearly three millions of inhabitants. The duchy has since passed through many changes and dismemberments, but in the early part of the sixteenth century the Elector of Saxony was one of the most powerful princes of the German empire. Frederic was not disposed to surrender his subject untried and uncondemned to the discipline of the Roman pontiff. He accordingly objected to this summary condemnation of Luther, and declared that before judgment was pronounced, the accused should be heard in his own defense. Charles, who was by no means aware how extensively the opinions of Luther had been circulated and received, was surprised to find many nobles, each emboldened by the rest, rise in the diet and denounce, in terms of ever-increasing severity, the exactions and the arrogance of the court of Rome.

Notwithstanding the remonstrances of the pope's legates, the emperor found it necessary to yield to the demands of the diet, and to allow Luther the privilege of being heard, though he avowed to the friends of the pope that Luther should not be permitted to make any defense, but should only have an opportunity to confess his heresy and implore forgiveness. Worms, where the diet was in session, on the west banks of the Rhine, was not within the territories of the Elector of Saxony, and consequently the emperor, in sending a summons to Luther to present himself before the diet, sent, also, a safe conduct. With alacrity the bold reformer obeyed the summons. From Wittemberg, where Luther was both professor in the univer sity and also pastor of a church, to Worms, was a distance of nearly three hundred miles. But the journey of the reformer through all of this long road was almost like a triumphal procession. Crowds gathered everywhere to behold the man who had dared to bid defiance to the terrors of that spiritual power before which the haughtiest monarchs had trembled. The people had read the writings of Luther, and justly regarded him as the advocate of civil and religious liberty. The nobles, who had often been humiliated by the arrogance of the pontiff, admired a man who was bringing a new power into the field for their disenthrallment.

When Luther had arrived within three miles of Worms, accompanied by a few friends and the imperial herald who had summoned him, he was met by a procession of two thousand persons, who had come from the city to form his escort. Some friends in the city sent him a warning that he could not rely upon the protection of his *safe conduct*, that he would probably be perfidiously arrested, and they intreated him to retire immediately again to Saxony. Luther made the memorable reply,

"I will go to Worms, if as many devils meet me there as there are tiles upon the roofs of the houses."

The emperor was astonished to find that greater crowds were assembled, and greater enthusiasm was displayed in witnessing the entrance of the monk of Wittemberg, than had greeted the imperial entrance to the city.

It was indeed an august assemblage before which Luther was arrayed. The emperor himself presided, sustained by his brother, the Archduke Ferdinand. Six electors, twenty-four dukes, seven margraves, thirty bishops and prelates, and an uncounted number of princes, counts, lords and ambassadors filled the spacious hall. It was the 18th of April, 1521. His speech, fearless, dignified, eloquent, unanswerable, occupied two hours. He closed with the noble words,

"Let me be refuted and convinced by the testimony of the Scriptures or by the clearest arguments; otherwise I can not and will not recant; for it is neither safe nor expedient to act against conscience. Here I take my stand. I can do no otherwise, so help me God, Amen."

In this sublime moral conflict Luther came off the undisputed conqueror. The legates of the pope, exasperated at his triumph, intreated the emperor to arrest him, in defiance of his word of honor pledged for his safety. Charles rejected the infamous proposal with disdain. Still he was greatly annoyed at so serious a schism in the Church, which threatened to alienate from him the patronage of the pope. It was evident that Luther was too strongly intrenched in the hearts of the Germans, for the youthful emperor, whose crown was not yet warm upon his brow, and who was almost a stranger in Germany, to undertake to crush him. To appease the pope he drew up an apologetic declaration, in which he said, in terms which do not honor his memory,

"Descended as I am from the Christian emperors of Germany, the Catholic kings of Spain, and from the archdukes of Austria and the Dukes of Burgundy, all of whom have preserved, to the last moment of their lives, their fidelity to the Church, and have always been the defenders and protectors of the Catholic faith, its decrees, ceremonies and usages, I have been, am still, and will ever be devoted to those Christian doctrines, and the constitution of the Church which they have left to me as a sacred inheritance. And as it is evident that a simple monk has advanced opinions contrary to the sentiments of all Christians, past and present, I am firmly determined to wipe away the reproach which a toleration of such errors would cast on Germany, and to employ all my powers and resources, my body, my blood, my life, and even my soul, in checking the progress of this sacrilegious doctrine. I will not, therefore, permit Luther to enter into any further explanation, and will instantly dismiss and afterward treat him as a heretic. But I can not violate my safe conduct, but will cause him to be conducted safely back to Wittemberg."

The emperor now attempted to accomplish by intrigue that which he could not attain by authority of force. He held a private interview with the reformer, and endeavored, by all those arts at the disposal of an emperor, to influence Luther to a recantation. Failing utterly in this, he delayed further operations for a month, until many of the diet, including the Elector of Saxony and other powerful friends of Luther, had retired. He then, having carefully retained those who would be obsequious to his will, caused a decree to be enacted, as it were the unanimous sentiment of the diet, that Luther was a heretic; confirmed the sentence of the pope, and pronounced the ban of the empire against all who should countenance or protect him.

But Luther, on the 26th of May, had left Worms on his return to Wittemberg. When he had passed over about half the distance, his friend and admirer, Frederic of Saxony, conscious of the imminent peril which hung over the intrepid monk, sent a troop of masked horsemen who seized him and conveyed him to the castle of Wartburg, where Frederic kept him safely concealed for nine months, not allowing even his friends to know the place of his concealment. Luther, acquiescing in the prudence of this measure, called this retreat his Patmos, and devoted himself most assiduously to the study of the Scriptures, and commenced his most admirable translation of the Bible into the German language, a work which has contributed vastly more than all others to disseminate the principles of the Reformation throughout Germany.

It will be remembered that Maximilian's son Ferdinand, who was brother to Charles V., had married Anne, daughter of Ladislaus, King of Hungary and Bohemia. Disturbances in Spain rendered it necessary for the emperor to leave Germany, and for eight years his attention was almost constantly occupied by wars and intrigues in southern Europe. Ferdinand was invested with the government of the Austrian States. In the year 1521, Leo X. died, and Adrian, who seems to have been truly a conscientious Christian man, assumed the tiara He saw the deep corruptions of the Church, confessed them openly, mourned over them and declared that the Church needed a thorough reformation.

This admission, of course, wonderfully strengthened the Lutheran party. The diet, meeting soon after, drew up a list of a hundred grievances, which they intreated the pope to reform, declaring that Germany could no longer endure them. They declared that Luther had opened the eyes of the people to these corruptions, and that they would not suffer the edicts of the diet of Worms to be enforced. Ferdinand of Austria, entering into the views of his brother, was anxious to arrest the progress of the new ideas, now spreading with great rapidity, and he entered—instructed by a legate, Campegio, from the pope—into an engagement with the Duke of Bavaria, and most of the German bishops, to carry the edict of Worms into effect.

Frederic, the Elector of Saxony, died in 1525, but he was succeeded by his brother John the Constant, who cordially embraced and publicly avowed the doctrines of the Reforma tion; and Luther, in July of this year, gave the last signa proof of his entire emancipation from the superstitions of the papacy by marrying Catharine Bora, a noble lady who, having espoused his views, had left the nunnery where she had been an inmate. It is impossible for one now to conceive the impression which was produced in Catholic Europe by the marriage of a priest and a nun.

Many of the German princes now followed the example of John of Saxony, and openly avowed their faith in the Lu theran doctrines. In the Austrian States, notwithstanding all Ferdinand's efforts to the contrary, the new faith steadily spread, commanding the assent of the most virtuous and the most intelligent. Many of the nobles avowed themselves Lutherans, as did even some of the professors in the university at Vienna. The vital questions at issue, taking hold, as they did, of the deepest emotions of the soul and the daily habits of life, roused the general mind to the most intense activity. The bitterest hostility sprung up between the two parties, and many persons, without piety and without judgment, threw off the superstitions of the papacy, only to adopt other superstitions equally revolting.   The sect of Anabaptists rose, abjuring all civil as well as all religious authority, claiming to be the elect of God, advocating a community of goods and of wives, and discarding all restraint.   They roused the ignorant peasantry, and easily showed them that they were suffering as much injustice from feudal lords as from papal bishops.   It was the breaking out of the French Revolution on a small scale.   Germany was desolated by infuriate bands, demolishing alike the castles of the nobles and the palaces of the bishops, and sparing neither age nor sex in their indiscriminate slaughter.

The insurrection was so terrible, that both Lutherans and papists united to quell it ; and so fierce were these fanatics, that a hundred thousand perished on fields of blood before the rebellion was quelled.   These outrages were, of course, by the Catholics regarded as the legitimate results of the new doctrines, and it surely can not be denied that they sprung from them.   The fire which glows on the hearth may consume the dwelling.   But Luther and his friends assailed the Anabaptists with every weapon they could wield.   The Catholics formed powerful combinations to arrest the spread of evangelical views.   The reformers organized combinations equally powerful to diffuse those opinions, which they were sure involved the welfare of the world.

Charles V., having somewhat allayed the troubles which harassed him in southern Europe, now turned his attention to Germany, and resolved, with a strong hand, to suppress the religious agitation.   In a letter to the German States he very peremptorily announced his determination, declaring that he would exterminate the errors of Luther, exhorting them to resist all attacks against the ancient usages of the Church, and expressing to each of the Catholic princes his earnest approval of their conduct.

Germany was now threatened with civil war. The Catholics demanded the enforcement of the edict of Worms. The reformers demanded perfect toleration—that every man should enjoy freedom of opinion and of worship. A new war in Italy perhaps prevented this appeal to arms, as Charles V. found himself involved in new difficulties which engrossed all his energies. Ferdinand found the Austrian States so divided by this controversy, that it became necessary for him to assume some degree of impartiality, and to submit to something like toleration. A new pope, Clement VII., succeeded the short reign of Adrian, and all the ambition, intrigue and corruption which had hitherto marked the course of the court of Rome, resumed their sway. The pope formed the celebrated Holy League to arrest the progress of the new opinions; and this led all the princes of the empire, who had espoused the Lutheran doctrines, more openly and cordially to combine in self-defense. In every country in Europe the doctrines of the reformer spread rapidly, and the papal throne was shaken to its base.

Charles V., whose arms were successful in southern Europe, and whose power was daily increasing, was still very desirous of restoring quiet to Europe by reëstablishing the supremacy of the papal Church, and crushing out dissent. He accordingly convened another diet at Spires, the capital of Rhenish Bavaria, on the 15th of March, 1529. As the emperor was detained in Italy, his brother Ferdinand presided. The diet was of course divided, but the majority passed very stringent resolutions against the Reformation. It was enacted that the edict of Worms should be enforced; that the mass should be reëstablished wherever it had been abolished; and that preachers should promulgate no new doctrines. The minority entered their protest. They urged that the mass had been clearly proved to be contrary to the Word of God ; that the Scriptures were the only certain rule of life ; and declared their resolution to maintain the truths of the Old and New Testaments, regardless of traditions. This *Protest* was sustained by powerful names—John, Elector of Saxony ; George, Margrave of Brandenburg ; two Dukes of Brunswick ; the Landgrave of Hesse Cassel ; the Prince of Anhalt, and fourteen imperial cities, to which were soon added ten more. Nothing can more decisively show than this the wonderful progress which the Reformation in so short a time had made. From this Protest the reformers received the name of Protestants, which they have since retained.

The emperor, flushed with success, now resolved, with new energy, to assail the principles of the Reformation. Leaving Spain he went to Italy, and met the pope, Clement VII., at Bologna, in February, 1530. The pope and the emperor held many long and private interviews. What they said no one knows. But Charles V., who was eminently a sagacious man, became convinced that the difficulty had become far too serious to be easily healed, that men of such power had embraced the Lutheran doctrines that it was expedient to change the tone of menace into one of respect and conciliation. He accordingly issued a call for another diet to meet in April, 1530, at the city of Augsburg in Bavaria.

" I have convened," he wrote, " this assembly to consider the difference of opinion on the subject of religion. It is my intention to hear both parties with candor and charity, to examine their respective arguments, to correct and reform what requires to be corrected and reformed, that the truth being known, and harmony established, there may, in future, be only one pure and simple faith, and, as all are disciples of the same Jesus, all may form one and the same Church."

These fair words, however, only excited the suspicions of the Protestants, which suspicions subsequent events proved to be well founded. The emperor entered Augsburg in great state, and immediately assumed a dictatorial air, requiring the diet to attend high mass with him, and to take part in the procession of the host.

"I will rather," said the Marquis of Brandenburg to the emperor, "instantly offer my head to the executioner, than renounce the gospel and approve idolatry, Christ did not institute the sacrament of the Lord's Supper to be carried in pomp through the streets, nor to be adored by the people. He said, 'Take, eat;' but never said, 'Put this sacrament into a vase, carry it publicly in triumph, and let the people prostrate themselves before it.'"

The Protestants, availing themselves of the emperor's declaration that it was his intention to hear the sentiments of all, drew up a confession of their faith, which they presented to the emperor in German and in Latin. This celebrated creed is known in history as the *Confession of Augsburg.* The emperor was quite embarrassed by this document, as he was well aware of the argumentative powers of the reformers, and feared that the document, attaining celebrity, and being read eagerly all over the empire, would only multiply converts to their views. At first he refused to allow it to be read. But finding that this only created commotion which would add celebrity to the confession, he adjourned the diet to a small chapel where but two hundred could be convened. When the Chancellor of Saxony rose to read the confession, the emperor commanded that he should read the Latin copy, a language which but few of the Germans understood.

"Sire," said the chancellor, "we are now on German ground. I trust that your majesty will not order the apology of our faith, which ought to be made as public as possible, to be read in a language not understood by the Germans."

The emperor was compelled to yield to so reasonable a request. The adjacent apartments, and the court-yard of the palace, were all filled with an eager crowd. The chancellor read the creed in a voice so clear and loud that the whole multitude could hear. The emperor was very uneasy, and at the close of the reading, which occupied two hours, took both the Latin and the German copies, and requested that the confession should not be published without his consent. Luther and Melancthon drew up this celebrated document. Melancthon was an exceedingly mild and amiable man, and such a lover of peace that he would perhaps do a little violence to his own conscience in the attempt to conciliate those from whom he was constrained to differ. Luther, on the contrary, was a man of great force, decision and fearlessness, who would speak the truth in the plainest terms, without softening a phrase to conciliate either friend or foe. The Confession of Augsburg being the joint production of both Melancthon and Luther, did not *exactly* suit either. It was a little too uncompromising for Melancthon, a little too pliant and yielding for Luther. Melancthon soon after took the confession and changed it to bring it into more entire accordance with his spirit. Hence a division which, in oblivion of its origin, has continued to the present day. Those who adhered to the original document which was presented to the emperor, were called Lutherans; those who adopted the confession as softened by Melancthon, were called German Reformed.

The emperor now threw off the mask, and carrying with him the majority of the diet, issued a decree of intolerance and menace, in which he declared that all the ceremonies, doctrines and usages of the papal church, without exception, were to be reëstablished, married priests deposed, suppressed convents restored, and every innovation, of whatever kind, to be revoked. All who opposed this decree were to be exposed to the ban of the empire, with all its pains and penalties.

This was indeed an appalling measure. Recantation or war was the only alternative. Charles, being still much occupied by the affairs of his vast kingdom of Spain, with all its ambitions and wars, needed a coadjutor in the government of Germany, as serious trouble was evidently near at hard. He

F

therefore proposed the election of his brother Ferdinand as coadjutor with him in administering the affairs of Germany. Ferdinand, who had recently united to the Austrian territories the crowns of Hungary and Bohemia, was consequently chosen, on the 5th of January, 1531, King of the Romans. Charles was determined to enforce his decrees, and both parties now prepared for war.

CHAPTER VIII.

CHARLES V. AND THE REFORMATION.

FROM 1531 TO 1552.

DETERMINATION TO CRUSH PROTESTANTISM.—INCURSION OF THE TURKS.—VALOR OF THE PROTESTANTS.—PREPARATIONS FOR RENEWED HOSTILITIES.—AUGMENTATION OF THE PROTESTANT FORCES.—THE COUNCIL OF TRENT.—MUTUAL CONSTERNATION.—DEFEAT OF THE PROTESTANT ARMY.—UNLOOKED FOR SUCCOR.—REVOLT IN THE EMPEROR'S ARMY.—THE FLUCTUATIONS OF FORTUNE.—IGNOBLE REVENGE.—CAPTURE OF WITTEMBERG.—PROTESTANTISM APPARENTLY CRUSHED.—PLOT AGAINST CHARLES.—MAURICE OF SAXONY.—A CHANGE OF SCENE.—THE BITER BIT.—THE EMPEROR HUMBLED.—HIS FLIGHT.—HIS DETERMINED WILL.

THE intolerant decrees of the diet of Augsburg, and the evident determination of the emperor unrelentingly to enforce them, spread the greatest alarm among the Protestants. They immediately assembled at Smalkalde in December, 1530, and entered into a league for mutual protection. The emperor was resolved to crush the Protestants. The Protestants were resolved not to be crushed. The sword of the Catholics was drawn for the assault—the sword of the reformers for defense. Civil war was just bursting forth in all its horrors, when the Turks, with an army three hundred thousand strong, like ravening wolves rushed into Hungar' This danger was appalling. The Turks in their bloody march had, as yet, encountered no effectual resistance ; though they had experienced temporary checks, their progress had been on the whole resistless, and wherever they had planted their feet they had established themselves firmly. Originating as a small tribe on the shores of the Caspian, they had spread over all Asia Minor, had crossed the Bosphorus, captured Constantinople, and had brought all Greece under their sway. They were still pressing on, flushed with victory. Christian

Europe was trembling before them. And now an army of. three hundred thousand had crossed the Danube, sweeping all opposition before them, and were spreading terror and destruction through Hungary. The capture of that immense kingdom seemed to leave all Europe defenseless.

The emperor and his Catholic friends were fearfully alarmed. Here was a danger more to be dreaded than even the doctrines of Luther. All the energies of Christendom were requisite to repel this invasion. The emperor was compelled to appeal to the Protestant princes to coöperate in this great emergence. But they had more to fear from the fiery persecution of the papal church than from the cimeter of the infidel, and they refused any coöperation with the emperor so long as the menaces of the Augsburg decrees were suspended over them. The emperor wished the Protestants to help him drive out the Turks, that then, relieved from that danger, he might turn all his energies against the Protestants.

After various negotiations it was agreed, as a temporary arrangement, that there should be a truce of the Catholic persecution until another general council should be called, and that until then the Protestants should be allowed freedom of conscience and of worship. The German States now turned their whole force against the Turks. The Protestants contributed to the war with energy which amazed the Catholics. They even trebled the contingents which they had agreed to furnish, and marched to the assault with the greatest intrepidity. The Turks were driven from Hungary, and then the emperor, in violation of his pledge, recommenced proceeding against the Protestants. But it was the worst moment the infatuated emperor could have selected. The Protestants, already armed and marshaled, were not at all disposed to lie down to be trodden upon by their foes. They renewed their confederacy, drove the emperor's Austrian troops out of the territories of Wirtemberg, which they had seized, and restored the duchy to the Protestant duke, Ulric. Civil war had now commenced. But the Protestants were strong, determined, and had proved their valor in the recent war with the Turks. The more moderate of the papal party, foreseeing a strife which might be interminable, interposed, and succeeded in effecting a compromise which again secured transient peace.

Charles, however, had not yet abandoned his design to compel the Protestants to return to the papal church. He was merely temporizing till he could bring such an array of the papal powers against the reformers that they could present no successful resistance. With this intention he entered into a secret treaty with the powerful King of France, in which Francis agreed to concentrate all the forces of his kingdom to crush the Lutheran doctrines. He then succeeded in concluding a truce with the Turks for five years. He was now prepared to act with decision against the reformed religion.

But while Charles had been marshaling his party the Protestants had been rapidly increasing. Eloquent preachers, able writers, had everywhere proclaimed the corruptions of the papacy and urged a pure gospel. These corruptions were so palpable that they could not bear the light. The most intelligent and conscientious, all over Europe, were rapidly embracing the new doctrines. These new doctrines embraced and involved principles of civil as well as religious liberty. The Bible is the most formidable book which was ever penned against aristocratic usurpation. God is the universal Father. All men are brothers. The despots of that day regarded the controversy as one which, in the end, involved the stability of their thrones. " Give us light," the Protestants said. " Give us darkness," responded the papacy, " or the submissive masses will rise and overthrow despotic thrones as well as idolatrous altars."

Several of the ablest and most powerful of the bishops who, in that day of darkness, had been groping in the dark, now that light had come into the world, rejoiced in that light, and enthusiastically espoused the truth. The emperor was quite appalled when he learned that the Archbishop of Cologne, who was also one of the electors of the empire, had joined the reformers; for, in addition to the vast influence of his name, this conversion gave the Protestants a majority in the electoral diet, so many of the German princes had already adopted the opinions of Luther. The Protestants, encouraged by the rapidity with which their doctrines were spreading, were not at all disposed to humble themselves before their opponents, but with their hands upon the hilts of their swords, declared that they would not bow their necks to intolerance.

It was indeed a formidable power which the emperor was now about to marshal against the Protestants. He had France, Spain, all the roused energies of the pope and his extended dominions, and all the Catholic States of the empire. But Protestantism, which had overrun Germany, had pervaded Switzerland and France, and was daily on the increase. The pope and the more zealous papists were impatient and indignant that the emperor did not press his measures with more vigor. But the sagacious Charles more clearly saw the difficulties to be surmounted than they did, and while no less determined in his resolves, was more prudent and wary in his measures.

With the consent of the pope he summoned a general council to meet at Trent on the confines of his own Austrian territories, where he could easily have every thing under his own control. He did every thing in his power, in the meantime to promote division among the Protestants, by trying to enter into private negotiations with the Protestant princes. He had the effrontery to urge the Protestants to send their livines to the council of Trent, and agreed to abide by its decisions, even when that council was summoned by the pope, and was to be so organized as to secure an overwhelming majority to the papists. The Protestants, of course, rejected so silly a proposition, and refused to recognize the decrees of such a council as of any binding authority.

In preparation for enforcing the decrees which he intended to have enacted by the council of Trent, Charles obtained from the pope thirteen thousand troops, and five hundred thousand ducats (one million one hundred thousand dollars). He raised one army in the Low Countries to march upon Germany. He gathered another army in his hereditary States of Austria. His brother Ferdinand, as King of Hungary and Bohemia, raised a large army in each of those dominions. The King of France mustered his legions, and boasted of the condign punishment to which he would consign the heretics. The pope issued a decree offering the entire pardon of all sins to those who should engage in this holy war for the extirpation of the doctrines of the reformers.

The Protestants were for a moment in consternation in view of the gatherings of so portentous a storm. The emperor, by false professions and affected clemency, had so deceived them that they were quite unprepared for so formidable an attack. They soon, however, saw that their only salvation depended upon a vigorous defense, and they marshaled their forces for war. With promptness and energy which even astonished themselves, they speedily raised an army which, on the junction of its several corps, amounted to eighty thousand men. In its intelligence, valor, discipline and equipments, it was probably the best army which had ever been assembled in the States of Germany. Resolutely they marched under Schartlin, one of the most experienced generals of the age, toward Ratisbon, where the emperor was holding a diet.

Charles V. was as much alarmed by this unexpected apparition, as the Protestants had been alarmed by the preparations of the emperor. He had supposed that his force was so resistless that the Protestants would see at once the hopelessness of resistance, and would yield without a struggle. The emperor had a guard of but eight thousand troops at Ratisbon. The Duke of Bavaria, in whose dominions he was, was wavering, and the papal troops had not commenced their march. But there was not a moment to be lost. The emperor himself might be surrounded and taken captive. He retired precipitately about thirty miles south to the strong fortress of Landshut, where he could hold out until he received succor from his Austrian territories, which were very near, and also from the pope.

Charles soon received powerful reinforcements from Austria, from the pope, and from his Spanish kingdom. With these he marched some forty miles west to Ingolstadt and intrenched himself beneath its massive walls. Here he waited for further reinforcements, and then commencing the offensive, marched up the Danube, taking possession of the cities on either bank. And now the marshaled forces of the emperor began to crowd the Protestants on all sides. The army became bewildered, and instead of keeping together, separated to repel the attack at different points. This caused the ruin of the Protestant army. The dissevered fragments were speedily dispersed. The emperor triumphantly entered the Protestant cities of Ulm and Augsburg, Strasbourg and Frankfort, compelled them to accept humiliating conditions, to surrender their artillery and military stores, and to pay enormous fines. The Archbishop of Cologne was deposed from his dignities. The emperor had thrown his foes upon the ground and bound them.

All the Protestant princes but two were vanquished, the Elector of Saxony and the Landgrave of Hesse. It was evident that they must soon yield to the overwhelming force of the emperor. It was a day of disaster, in which no gleam of light seemed to dawn upon the Protestant cause. But in that gloomy hour we see again the illustration of that sentiment, that "the race is not always to the swift nor the battle to the strong." Unthinking infidelity says sarcastically, "Providence always helps the heavy battalions." But Providence often brings to the discomfited, in their despair, reinforcements all unlooked for.

There were in the army of Ferdinand, gathered from the Austrian territories by the force of military conscription, many troops more or less influenced by the reformed religion. They were dissatisfied with this warfare against their brothers, and their dissatisfaction increased to murmurs and then to revolt. Thus encouraged, the Protestant nobles in Bohemia rose against Ferdinand their king, and the victorious Ferdinand suddenly found his strong battalions melting away, and his banners on the retreat.

The other powers of Europe began to look with alarm upon the vast ascendency which Charles V. was attaining over Europe. His exacting and aggressive spirit assumed a more menacing aspect than the doctrines of Luther. The King of France, Francis I., with the characteristic perfidy of the times, meeting cunning with cunning, formed a secret league against his ally, combining, in that league, the English ministry who governed during the minority of Edward VI., and also the coöperation of the illustrious Gustavus Vasa, the powerful King of Sweden, who was then strongly inclined to that faith of the reformers which he afterwards openly avowed. Even the pope, who had always felt a little jealous of the power of the emperor, thought that as the Protestants were now put down it might be well to check the ambition of Charles V. a little, and he accordingly ordered all his troops to return to Italy. The holy father, Paul III., even sent money to the Protestant Elector of Saxony, to enable him to resist the emperor, and sent ambassadors to the Turks, to induce them to break the truce and make war upon Christendom, that the emperor might be thus embarrassed.

Charles thus found himself, in the midst of his victories, suddenly at a stand. He could no longer carry on offensive operations, but was compelled to prepare for defense against the attacks with which he was threatened on every side.

Again, the kaleidoscope of political combination received

a jar, and all was changed. The King of France died. This so embarrassed the affairs of the confederation which Francis had organized with so much toil and care, that Charles availed himself of it to make a sudden and vigorous march against the Elector of Saxony. He entered his territories with an army of thirty-three thousand men, and swept all opposition before him. In a final and desperate battle the troops of the elector were cut to pieces, and the elector himself, surrounded on all sides, sorely wounded in the face and covered with blood, was taken prisoner. Charles disgraced his character by the exhibition of a very ignoble spirit of revenge. The captive elector, as he was led into the presence of his conqueror, said—

"Most powerful and gracious emperor, the fortune of war has now rendered me your prisoner, and I hope to be treated—"

Here the emperor indignantly interrupted him, saying—

"I am *now* your gracious emperor! Lately you could only vouchsafe me the title of Charles of Ghent!"

Then turning abruptly upon his heel, he consigned his prisoner to the custody of one of the Spanish generals. The emperor marched immediately to Wittemberg, which was distant but a few miles. It was a well fortified town, and was resolutely defended by Isabella, the wife of the elector. The emperor, maddened by the resistance, summoned a court martial, and sentenced the elector to instant death unless he ordered the surrender of the fortress. He at first refused, and prepared to die. But the tears of his wife and his family conquered his resolution, and the city was surrendered. The emperor took from his captive the electoral dignity, and extorted from him the most cruel concessions as the ransom for his life. Without a murmur he surrendered wealth, power and rank, but neither entreaties nor menaces could induce him in a single point to abjure his Christian faith.

Charles now entered Wittemberg in triumph. The great

reformer had just died. The emperor visited the grave of Luther, and when urged to dishonor his remains, replied—

" I war not with the dead, but with the living. Let him repose in peace ; he is already before his Judge."

The Landgrave of Hesse Cassel, now the only member of the Protestant league remaining in arms, was in a condition utterly hopeless, and was compelled to make an unconditional submission.

The landgrave, ruined in fortune, and crushed in spirit, was led a captive into the imperial camp at Halle, in Saxony, the 19th of June, 1547. He knelt before the throne, and made an humble confession of his crime in resisting the emperor ; he resigned himself and all his dominions to the clemency of his sovereign. As he rose to kiss the hand of the emperor, Charles turned contemptuously from him and ordered him to be conveyed to one of the apartments of the palace as a prisoner. Most ignobly the emperor led his two illustrious captives, the Elector of Saxony and the Landgrave of Hesse Cassel, as captives from city to city, exhibiting them as proofs of his triumph, and as a warning to all others to avoid their fate. Very strong jealousies had now sprung up between the emperor and the pope, and they could not cooperate. The emperor, consequently, undertook to settle the religious differences himself. He caused twenty-six articles to be drawn up as the basis of pacification, which he wished both the Catholics and the Protestants to sign. The pope was indignant, and the Catholics were disgusted with this interference of the emperor in the faith of the Church, a matter which in their view belonged exclusively to the pope and the councils which he might convene.

The emperor, however, resolutely persevered in the endeavor to compel the Protestants to subscribe to his articles, and punished severely those who refused to do so. In his Burgundian provinces he endeavored to establish the inquisition, that all heresy might be nipped in the bud. In his zeal he

quite outstripped the pope. As Julius III. had now ascended
the pontifical throne, Charles, fearful that he might be too
liberal in his policy towards the reformers, and might make
too many concessions, extorted from him the promise that
he would not introduce any reformation in the Church without consulting him and obtaining his consent. Thus the pope
himself became but one of the dependents of Charles V.,
and all the corruptions of the Church were sustained by the
imperial arm. He then, through the submissive pope, summoned a council of Catholic divines to meet at Trent. He
had arranged in his own mind the decrees which they were
to issue, and had entered into a treaty with the new King of
France, Henry II., by which the French monarch agreed,
with all the military force of his kingdom, to maintain the
decrees of the council of Trent, whatever they might be.

The emperor had now apparently attained all his ends.
He had crushed the Protestant league, vanquished the Protestant princes, subjected the pope to his will, arranged religious matters according to his views, and had now assembled
a subservient council to ratify and confirm all he had done.
But with this success he had become arrogant, implacable
and cruel. His friends had become alienated and his enemies
exasperated. Even the most rigorous Catholics were alarmed
at his assumptions, and the pope was humiliated by his
haughty bearing.

Charles assembled a diet of the States of the empire at
Augsburg, the 26th of July, 1550. He entered the city with
the pomp and the pride of a conqueror, and with such an array
of military force as to awe the States into compliance with his
wishes. He then demanded of all the States of the empire an
agreement that they would enforce in all their dominions the
decrees of the council of Trent, which council was soon to be
convened. There is sublimity in the energy with which this
monarch moved, step by step, toward the accomplishment of
his plans. He seemed to leave no chance for failure. The

members of the diet were as obsequious as spaniels to their imperious master, and watched his countenance to learn when they were to say yes, and when no.

In one thing only he failed. He wished to have his son Philip elected as his successor on the imperial throne. His brother Ferdinand opposed him in this ambitious plan, and thus emboldened the diet to declare that while the emperor was living it was illegal to choose his successor, as it tended to render the imperial crown hereditary. The emperor, sagacious as he was domineering, waived the prosecution of his plan for the present, preparing to resume it when he had punished and paralyzed those who opposed.

The emperor had deposed Frederic the Elector of Saxony, and placed over his dominons, Maurice, a nephew of the deposed elector. Maurice had married a daughter of the Landgrave of Hesse Cassel. He was a man of commanding abilities, and as shrewd, sagacious and ambitious as the emperor himself. He had been strongly inclined to the Lutheran doctrines, but had been bought over to espouse the cause of Charles V. by the brilliant offer of the territories of Saxony. Maurice, as he saw blow after blow falling upon his former friends; one prince after another ejected from his estates, Protestantism crushed, and finally his own uncle and his wife's father led about to grace the triumph of the conqueror; as he saw the vast power to which the emperor had attained, and that the liberties of the German empire were in entire subjection to his will, his pride was wounded, his patriotism aroused, and his Protestant sympathies revived. Maurice, meeting Charles V. on the field of intrigue, was Greek meeting Greek.

Maurice now began with great guile and profound sagacity to plot against the despotic emperor. Two circumstances essentially aided him. Charles coveted the dukedoms of Parma and Placentia in Italy, and the Duke Ottavia had been deposed. He rallied his subjects and succeeded in uniting France

on his side, for Henry II. was alarmed at the encroachments
the emperor was making in Italy. A very fierce war instantly
blazed forth, the Duke of Parma and Henry II. on one side,
the pope and the emperor on the other. At the same time
the Turks, under the leadership of the Sultan Solyman himself, were organizing a formidable force for the invasion of
Hungary, which invasion would require all the energies of
Ferdinand, with all the forces he could raise in Austria, Hungary and Bohemia to repel.

Next to Hungary and Bohemia, Saxony was perhaps the
most powerful State of the Germanic confederacy. The emperor placed full reliance upon Maurice, and the Protestants
in their despair would have thought of him as the very last to
come to their aid ; for he had marched vigorously in the armies of the emperor to crush the Protestants, and was occupying the territories of their most able and steadfast friend. Secretly, Maurice made proposals to all the leading Protestant
princes of the empire, and having made every thing ready for
an outbreak, he entered into a treaty with the King of France,
who promised large subsidies and an efficient military force.

Maurice conducted these intrigues with such consummate
skill that the emperor had not the slightest suspicion of the
storm which was gathering. Every thing being matured, early in April, 1552, Maurice suddenly appeared before the gates
of Augsburg with an army of twenty-five thousand men. At
the same time he issued a declaration that he had taken up
arms to prevent the destruction of the Protestant religion, to
defend the liberties of Germany which the emperor had infringed, and to rescue his relatives from their long and unjust
imprisonment. The King of France and other princes issued
similar declarations. The smothered disaffection with the em
peror instantly blazed forth all over the German empire. The
cause of Maurice was extremely popular. The Protestants in
a mass, and many others, flocked to his standard. As by magic
and in a day, all was changed. The imperial towns Augsburg

Nuremberg and others, threw open their gates joyfully to Maurice. Whole provinces rushed to his standard. He was everywhere received as the guardian of civil and religious liberty. The ejected Protestant rulers and magistrates were reinstated, the Protestant churches opened, the Protestant preachers restored. In one month the Protestant party was predominant in the German empire, and the Catholic party either neutral or secretly favoring one who was humbling that haughty emperor whom even the Catholics had begun to fear. The prelates who were assembling at Trent, alarmed by so sudden and astounding a revolution, dissolved the assembly and hastened to their homes.

The emperor was at Innspruck seated in his arm chair, with his limbs bandaged in flannel, enfeebled and suffering from a severe attack of the gout, when the intelligence of this sudden and overwhelming reverse reached him. He was astonished and utterly confounded. In weakness and pain, unable to leave his couch, with his treasury exhausted, his armies widely scattered, and so pressed by their foes that they could not be concentrated from their wide dispersion, there was nothing left for him but to endeavor to beguile Maurice into a truce. But Maurice was as much at home in all the arts of cunning as the emperor, and instead of being beguiled, contrived to entrap his antagonist. This was a new and a very salutary experience for Charles. It is a very novel sensation for a successful rogue to be the dupe of roguery.

Maurice pressed on, his army gathering force at every step. He entered the Tyrol, swept through all its valleys, took possession of all its castles and its sublime fastnesses, and the blasts of his bugles reverberated among the cliffs of the Alps, ever sounding the charge and announcing victory, never signaling a defeat. The emperor was reduced to the terrible humiliation of saving himself from capture only by flight. The emperor could hardly credit his senses when told that his conquering foes were within two days' march of Innspruck, and that a squadron of horse might at any hour appear and cut off his retreat. It was in the night when these appalling tidings were brought to him. The tortures of the gout would not allow him to mount on horseback, neither could he bear the jolting in a carriage over the rough roads. It was a dark and stormy night, the 20th of May, 1552. The rain fell in torrents, and the wind howled through the fir-trees and around the crags of the Alps. Some attendants wrapped the monarch in blankets, took him out into the court-yard of the palace, and placed him in a litter. Attendants led the way with lanterns, and thus, through the inundated and storm-swept defiles of the mountains, they fled with their helpless sovereign through the long hours of the tempestuous night, not daring to stop one moment lest they should hear behind them the clatter of the iron hoofs of their pursuers. What a change for one short month to produce! What a comment upon earthly grandeur! It is well for man in the hour of most exultant prosperity to be humble. He knows not how soon he may fall. Instructive indeed is the apostrophe of Cardinal Wolsey, illustrated as the truth he utters is by almost every page of history :

> " This is the state of man; to-day he puts forth
> The tender leaves of hope, to-morrow blossoms,
> The third day comes a frost, a killing frost;
> And when he thinks, good easy man, full surely
> His greatness is a ripening—nips his root,
> And then he falls as I do."

The fugitive emperor did not venture to stop for refreshment or repose until he had reached the strong town of Villach in Carinthia, nearly one hundred and fifty miles west of Innspruck. The troops of Maurice soon entered the city which the emperor had abandoned, and the imperial palace was surrendered to pillage. Heroic courage, indomitable perseverance always commands respect. These are great and noble qualities, though they may be exerted in a bad cause

The will of Charles was unconquerable. In these hours of disaster, tortured with pain, driven from his palace, deserted by his allies, impoverished, and borne upon his litter in hu miliating flight before his foes, he was just as determined to enforce his plans as in the most brilliant hour of victory.

He sent his brother Ferdinand and other ambassadors to Passau to meet Maurice, and mediate for a settlement of the difficulties. Maurice now had no need of diplomacy. His de- mands were simple and reasonable. They were, that the em- peror should liberate his father-in-law from captivity, tolerate the Protestant religion, and grant to the German States their accustomed liberty. But the emperor would not yield a sin- gle point. Though his brother Ferdinand urged him to yield, though his Catholic ambassadors intreated him to yield, though they declared that if he did not they should be compelled to abandon his cause and make the best terms for themselves with the conqueror that they could, still nothing could bend his inflexible will, and the armies, after the lull of a few days, were again in motion. The despotism of the emperor we ab- hor ; but his indomitable perseverance and unconquerable en- ergy are worthy of all admiration and imitation. Had they but been exerted in a good cause !

CHAPTER IX.

CHARLES V. AND THE TURKISH WARS.

FROM 1552 TO 1555.

THE Turks, animated by this civil war which was raging in
Germany, were pressing their march upon Hungary with
great vigor, and the troops of Ferdinand were retiring discomfited before the invader. Henry of France and the Duke
of Parma were also achieving victories in Italy endangering
the whole power of the emperor over those States. Ferdinand, appalled by the prospect of the loss of Hungary, im-
ploringly besought the emperor to listen to terms of reconciliation. The Catholic princes, terrified in view of the progress
of the infidel, foreseeing the entire subjection of Europe to
the arms of the Moslem unless Christendom could combine in
self-defense, joined their voices with that of Ferdinand so earnestly and in such impassioned tones, that the emperor finally,
though very reluctantly, gave his assent to the celebrated
treaty of Passau, on the 2d of August, 1552. By this pacification the captives were released, freedom of conscience and of
worship was established, and the Protestant troops, being disbanded, were at liberty to enter into the service of Ferdinand
to repel the Turks. Within six months a diet was to be as

sembled to attempt an amicable adjustment of all civil and religious difficulties.

The intrepid Maurice immediately marched, accompanied
by many of the Protestant princes, and at the head of a powerful army, to repel the Mohammedan armies. Charles, relieved from his German troubles, gathered his strength to
wreak revenge upon the King of France. But fortune seemed
to have deserted him. Defeat and disgrace accompanied his
march. Having penetrated the French province of Lorraine,
he laid siege to Metz. After losing thirty thousand men beneath its walls, he was compelled, in the depth of winter, to
raise the siege and retreat. His armies were everywhere
routed; the Turks menaced the shores of Italy; the pope became his inveterate enemy, and joined France against him.
Maurice was struck by a bullet, and fell on the field of battle.
The electorate of Saxony passed into the hands of Augustus,
a brother of Maurice, while the former elector, Ferdinand, who
shortly after died, received some slight indemnification.

Such was the state of affairs when the promised diet was
summoned at Passau. It met on the 5th of February, 1555.
The emperor was confined with the gout at Brussels, and his
brother Ferdinand presided. It was a propitious hour for
the Protestants. Charles was sick, dejected and in adversity.
The better portion of the Catholics were disgusted with the
intolerance of the emperor, intolerance which even the more
conscientious popes could not countenance. Ferdinand was
fully aware that he could not defend his own kingdom of Hungary from the Turks without the intervention of Protestant
arms. He was, therefore, warmly in favor of conciliation.

The world was not yet sufficiently enlightened to comprehend the beauty of a true toleration, entire freedom of conscience
and of worship. After long and very exciting debates—after
being again and again at the point of grasping their arms
anew--they finally agreed that the Protestants should enjoy
the free exercise of their religion wherever Protestantism had

been established and recognized by the Confession of Augsburg. That in all other places Protestant princes might prohibit the Catholic religion in their States, and Catholic princes prohibit the Protestant religion. But in each case the ejected party was at liberty to sell their property and move without molestation to some State where their religion was dominant. In the free cities of the empire, where both religions were established, both were to be tolerated.

Thus far, and no further, had the spirit of toleration made progress in the middle of the sixteenth century.

Such was the basis of the pacification. Neither party was satisfied. Each felt that it had surrendered far too much to the other; and there was subsequently much disagreement respecting the interpretation of some of the most important articles. The pope, Paul IV., was indignant that such toleration had been granted to the Protestants, and threatened the emperor and his brother Ferdinand of Austria with excommunication if they did not declare these decrees null and void throughout their dominions. At the same time he entered into correspondence with Henry II. of France to form a new holy league for the defense of the papal church against the inroads of heresy.

And now occurred one of the most extraordinary events which history has recorded. Charles V., who had been the most enterprising and ambitious prince in Europe, and the most insatiable in his thirst for power, became the victim of the most extreme despondency. Harassed by the perplexities which pressed in upon him from his widely-extended realms, annoyed by the undutiful and haughty conduct of his son, who was endeavoring to wrest authority from his father by taking advantage of all his misfortunes, and perhaps inheriting a melancholy temperament from his mother, who died in the glooms of insanity, and, more than all, mortified and wounded by so sudden and so vast a reverse of fortune, in which all his plans seemed to have failed—thus oppressed, humbled, despondent.

he retired in disgust to his room, indulged in the most fretful temper, admitted none but his sister and a few confidential servants to his presence, and so entirely neglected all business as to pass nine months without signing a single paper.

While the emperor was in this melancholy state, his insane mother, who had lingered for years in delirious gloom, died on the 4th of April, 1555. It will be remembered that Charles had inherited valuable estates in the Low Countries from his marriage with the daughter of the Duke of Burgundy. Having resolved to abdicate all his power and titles in favor of his son, he convened the States of the Low Countries at Brussels on the 25th of October, 1555. Charles was then but fifty-five years of age, and should have been in the strength of vigorous manhood. But he was prematurely old, worn down with care, toil and disappointment. He attended the assembly accompanied by his son Philip. Tottering beneath infirmities, he leaned upon the shoulders of a friend for support, and addressed the assembly in a long and somewhat boastful speech, enumerating all the acts of his administration, his endeavors, his long and weary journeys, his sleepless care, his wars, and, above all, his victories. In conclusion he said:

" While my health enabled me to perform my duty, I cheerfully bore the burden ; but as my constitution is now broken by an incurable distemper, and my infirmities admonish me to retire, the happiness of my people affects me more than the ambition of reigning. Instead of a decrepid old man, tottering on the brink of the grave, I transfer your allegiance to a sovereign in the prime of life, vigilant, sagacious, active and enterprising. With respect to myself, if I have committed any error in the course of a long administration, forgive and impute it to my weakness, not to my intention. I shall ever retain a grateful sense of your fidelity and attachment, and your welfare shall be the great object of my prayers to Almighty God, to whom I now consecrate the remainder of my days."

Then turning to his son Philip, he said :

" And you, my son, let the grateful recollection of this day redouble your care and affection for your people.   Othei sovereigns may rejoice in having given birth to their sons and in leaving their States to them after their death.   But I am anxious to enjoy, during my life, the double satisfaction of feeling that you are indebted to me both for your birth and power.   Few monarchs will follow my example, and in the lapse of ages I have scarcely found one whom I myself would imitate.   The resolution, therefore, which I have taken, and which I now carry into execution, will be justified only by your proving yourself worthy of it.   And you will alone render yourself worthy of the extraordinary confidence which I now repose in you by a zealous protection of your religion, and by maintaining the purity of the Catholic faith, and by governing with justice and moderation.   And may you, if ever you are desirous of retiring like myself to the tranquillity of private life, enjoy the inexpressible happiness of having such a son, that you may resign your crown to him with the same satisfaction as I now deliver mine to you."

The emperor was here entirely overcome by emotion, and embracing Philip, sank exhausted into his chair.   The affecting scene moved all the audience to tears.   Soon after this, with the same formalities the emperor resigned the crown of Spain to his son, reserving to himself, of all his dignities and vast revenues, only a pension of about twenty thousand dollars a year.   For some months he remained in the Low Countries, and then returned to Spain to seek an asylum in a convent there.

When in the pride of his power he once, while journeying in Spain, came upon the convent of St. Justus in Estramadura, situated in a lovely vale, secluded from all the bustle of life.   The massive pile was embosomed among the hills ; forests spread widely around, and a beautiful rivulet murmured by its walls.   As the emperor gazed upon the enchanting scene

of solitude and silence he exclaimed, " Behold a lovely retreat
for another Diocletian !"

The picture of the convent of St. Justus had ever remained
in his mind, and perhaps had influenced him, when overwhelmed with care, to seek its peaceful retirement. Embark-
ing in a ship for Spain, he landed at Loredo on the 28th of
September, 1556. As soon as his feet touched the soil of his
native land he prostrated himself to the earth, kissed the
ground, and said,

"Naked came I into the world, and naked I return to
thee, thou common mother of mankind. To thee I dedicate
my body, as the only return I can make for all the benefits
conferred on me."

Then kneeling, and holding the crucifix before him, with
tears streaming from his eyes, and all unmindful of the attendants who were around, he breathed a fervent prayer of
gratitude for the past, and commended himself to God for the
future. By slow and easy stages, as he was very infirm, he
journeyed to the vale of Estramadura, near Placentia, and
entered upon his silent, monastic life.

His apartments consisted of six small cells. The stone
walls were whitewashed, and the rooms furnished with the
utmost frugality. Within the walls of the convent, and com-
municating with the chapel, there was a small garden, which
the emperor had tastefully arranged with shrubbery and
flowers. Here Charles passed the brief remainder of his days.
He amused himself with laboring in the garden with his own
hands. He regularly attended worship in the chapel twice
every day, and took part in the service, manifestly with the
greatest sincerity and devotion.

The emperor had not a cultivated mind, and was not fond
of either literary or scientific pursuits. To beguile the hours
he amused himself with tools, carving toys for children, and
ingenious puppets and automata to astonish the peasants. For
a time he was very happy in his new employment. After so

stormy a life, the perfect repose and freedom from care which he enjoyed in the convent, seemed to him the perfection of bliss. But soon the novelty wore away, and his constitutional despondency returned with accumulated power.

His dejection now assumed the form of religious melan-choly. He began to devote every moment of his time to de-votional reading and prayer, esteeming all amusements and all employments sinful which interfered with his spiritual ex-ercises. He expressed to the Bishop of Toledo his determina-tion to devote, for the rest of his days, every moment to the service of God. With the utmost scrupulousness he carried out this plan. He practiced rigid fasts, and conformed to all the austerity of convent discipline. He renounced his pen-sion, and sitting at the abstemious table with the monks, de-clined seeing any other company than that of the world-renouncing priests and friars around him. He scourged him-self with the most cruel severity, till his back was lacerated with the whip. He whole soul seemed to crave suffering, in expiation for his sins. His ingenuity was tasked to devise new methods of mortification and humiliation. Ambition had ever been the ruling passion of his soul, and now he was am-bitious to suffer more, and to abuse himself more than any other mortal had ever done.

Goaded by this impulse, he at last devised the scheme of solemnizing his own funeral. All the melancholy arrange-ments for his burial were made; the coffin provided; the em-peror reclined upon his bed as dead; he was wrapped in his shroud, and placed in his coffin. The monks, and all the in-mates of the convent attended in mourning; the bells tolled; requiems were chanted by the choir; the funeral service was read, and then the emperor, as if dead, was placed in the tomb of the chapel, and the congregation retired. The mon-arch, after remaining some time in his coffin to impress him-self with the sense of what it is to die, and be buried, rose from his tomb, kneeled before the altar for some time in wor ship, and then returned to his cell to pass the night in deep meditation and prayer.

The shock and the chill of this solemn scene were too much for the old monarch's feeble frame and weakened mind. He was seized with a fever, and in a few days breathed his last, in the 59th year of his age. He had spent a little over three years in the convent. The life of Charles V. was a 'sad one. Through all his days he was consumed by unsatisfied ambition, and he seldom enjoyed an hour of contentment. To his son he said—

"I leave you a heavy burden ; for, since my shoulders have borne it, I have not passed one day exempt from disquietude."

Indeed it would seem that there could have been but little happiness for anybody in those dark days of feudal oppression and of incessant wars. Ambition, intrigue, duplicity, reigned over the lives of princes and nobles, while the masses of the people were ever trampled down by oppressive lords and contending armies. Europe was a field of fire and blood. The cimeter of the Turk spared neither mother, maiden nor babe. Cities and villages were mercilessly burned, cottages set in flames, fields of grain destroyed, and whole populations carried into slavery, where they miserably died. And the ravages of Christian warfare, duke against duke, baron against baron, king against king, were hardly less cruel and desolating. Balls from opposing batteries regard not the helpless ones in their range. Charging squadrons must trample down with iron hoof all who are in their way. The wail of misery rose from every portion of Europe. The world has surely made some progress since that day.

There was but very little that was loveable in the character of Charles, and he seems to have had but very few friends. So intense and earnest was he in the prosecution of the plans of grandeur which engrossed his soul, that he was seldom known to smile. He had many of the attributes of greatness indomitable energy and perseverance, untiring industry, comprehensive grasp of thought and capability of superintending the minutest details. He had, also, a certain fanatic conscientiousness about him, like that which actuated Saul of Tarsus, when, holding the garments of those who stoned the martyr, he "verily thought that he was doing God service."

Many anecdotes are told illustrative of certain estimable traits in his character. When a boy, like other boys, he was not fond of study, and being very self-willed, he would not yield to the entreaties of his tutors. He consequently had but an imperfect education, which may in part account for his excessive illiberality, and for many of his stupendous follies. The mind, enlarged by liberal culture, is ever tolerant. He afterwards regretted exceedingly this neglect of his early studies. At Genoa, on some public occasion, he was addressed in a Latin oration, not one word of which he understood.

"I now feel," he said, "the justice of my preceptor Adrian's remonstrances, who frequently used to predict that I should be punished for the thoughtlessness of my youth."

He was fond of the society of learned men, and treated them with great respect. Some of the nobles complained that the emperor treated the celebrated historian, Guicciardini, with much more respect than he did them. He replied—

"I can, by a word, create a hundred nobles; but God alone can create a Guicciardini."

He greatly admired the genius of Titian, and considered him one of the most resplendent ornaments of his empire. He knew full well that Titian would be remembered long after thousands of the proudest grandees of his empire had sunk into oblivion. He loved to go into the studio of the illustrious painter, and watch the creations of beauty as they rose beneath his pencil. One day Titian accidentally dropped

THE QUAY, VIENNA

his brush. The emperor picked it up, and, presenting it to
the artist, said gracefully—

"Titian is worthy of being served by an emperor."

Charles V. never, apparently, inspired the glow of affection, or an emotion of enthusiasm in any bosom. He accomplished some reforms in the German empire, and the only
interest his name now excites is the interest necessarily involved in the sublime drama of his long and eventful reign.

It is now necessary to retrace our steps for a few years,
that we may note the vicissitudes of Austria, while the empire was passing through the scenes we have narrated.

Ferdinand I., the brother of Charles V., who was left alone
in the government of Austria, was the second son of Philip
the Handsome and Joanna of Spain. His birth was illustrious,
the Emperor Maximilian being his paternal grandfather, and
Ferdinand and Isabella being his grandparents on his mother's
side. He was born in Spain, March 10, 1503, and received a
respectable education. His manners were courteous and winning, and he was so much more popular than Charles as quite
to excite the jealousy of his imperious and imperial spirit.
Charles, upon attaining the throne, ceded to his brother the
Austrian territories, which then consisted of four small provinces, Austria, Styria, Carinthia and Carniola, with the Tyrol.

Ferdinand married Ann, princess of Hungary and Bohemia.
The death of his wife's brother Louis made her the heiress of
those two crowns, and thus secured to Ferdinand the magnificent dowry of the kingdoms of Hungary and Bohemia. But
possession of the scepter of those realms was by no means a
sinecure. The Turkish power, which had been for many years
increasing with the most alarming rapidity and had now acquired appalling strength, kept Hungary, and even the Austrian States, in constant and terrible alarm.

The Turks, sweeping over Persia, Arabia, Egypt, Syria,
all Asia Minor, crossing the straits and inundating Greece,
fierce and semi-savage, with just civilization enough to organ-

ize and guide with skill their wolf-like ferocity, were now pressing Europe in Spain, in Italy, and were crowding, in wave after wave of invasion, up the valley of the Danube. They had created a navy which was able to cope with the most powerful fleets of Europe, and island after island of the Mediterranean was yielding to their sway.

In 1520, Solyman, called the Magnificent, overran Bosnia, and advancing to the Danube, besieged and captured Belgrade, which strong fortress was considered the only reliable barrier against his encroachments. At the same time his fleet took possession of the island of Rhodes. After some slight reverses, which the Turks considered merely embarrassments, they resumed their aggressions, and Solyman, in 1525, again crossing the Danube, entered Hungary with an army of two hundred thousand men. Louis, who was then King of Hungary, brother of the wife of Ferdinand, was able to raise an army of but thirty thousand to meet him. With more courage than discretion, leading this feeble band, he advanced to resist the foe. They met on the plains of Mohatz. The Turks made short work of it. In a few hours, with their cimeters they hewed down nearly the whole Christian army. The remnant escaped as lambs from wolves. The king, in his heavy armor, spurred his horse into a stream to cross in his flight. In attempting to ascend the bank, the noble charger, who had borne his master bravely through the flood, fell back upon his rider, and the dead body of the king was afterward picked up by the Turks, covered with the mud of the morass. All Hungary would now have fallen into the hands of the Turks had not Solyman been recalled by a rebellion in one of his own provinces.

It was this event which placed the crowns of Bohemia and Hungary on the brow of Ferdinand, and by annexing those two kingdoms to the Austrian States, elevated Austria to be one of the first powers in Europe. Ferdinand, thus strengthened sent ambassadors to Constantinople to demand the restitu

tion of Belgrade and other important towns which the Turks
still held in Hungary.

"Belgrade!" exclaimed the haughty sultan, when he heard
the demand. "Go tell your master that I am collecting troops
and preparing for my expedition. I will suspend at my neck
the keys of my Hungarian fortresses, and will bring them to
that plain of Mohatz where Louis, by the aid of Providence,
found defeat and a grave. Let Ferdinand meet and conquer
me, and take them, after severing my head from my body!
But if I find him not there, I will seek him at Buda or follow
him to Vienna."

Soon after this Solyman crossed the Danube with three
hundred thousand men, and advancing to Mohatz, encamped
for several days upon the plain, with all possible display oi
Oriental pomp and magnificence. Thus proudly he threw
down the gauntlet of defiance. But there was no champion
there to take it up. Striking his tents, and spreading his banners to the breeze, in unimpeded march he ascended the Danube two hundred miles from Belgrade to the city of Pest.
And here his martial bands made hill and vale reverberate the
bugle blasts of victory. Pest, the ancient capital of Hungary,
rich in all the wealth of those days, with a population of some
sixty thousand, was situated on the left bank of the river.
Upon the opposite shore, connected by a fine bridge three
quarters of a mile in width, was the beautiful and opulent city
of Buda. In possession of these two maritime towns, then
perhaps the most important in Hungary, the Turks rioted for
a few days in luxury and all abominable outrage and indulgence, and then, leaving a strong garrison to hold the fortresses, they continued their march. Pressing resistlessly onward some hundred miles further, taking all the towns by the
way, on both sides of the Danube, they came to the city of
Raab.

It seems incredible that there could have been such an un
obstructed march of the Turks, through the very heart oi

Hungary. But the Emperor Charles V. was at that time in Italy, all engrossed in the fiercest warfare there. Throughout the German empire the Catholics and the Protestants were engaged in a conflict which absorbed all other thoughts. And the Protestants resolutely refused to assist in repelling the Turks while the sword of Catholic vengeance was suspended over them. From Raab the invading army advanced some hundred miles further to the very walls of Vienna. Ferdinand, conscious of his inability to meet the foe in the open field, was concentrating all his available strength to defend his capital.

At Cremnitz the Turks met with the first serious show of resistance. The fortress was strong, and the garrison, inspired by the indomitable energy and courage of their commandant, Nicholas, Count of Salm, for a month repelled every assault of the foe. Day after day and night after night the incessant bombardment continued; the walls were crumbled by the storm of shot; column after column of the Turks rushed to the assault, but all in vain. The sultan, disappointed and enraged, made one last desperate effort, but his strong columns, thinned, mangled and bleeding, were compelled to retire in utter discomfiture.

Winter was now approaching. Reinforcements were also hastening from Vienna, from Bohemia, and from other parts of the German empire. Solyman, having devastated the country around him, and being all unprepared for the storms of winter, was compelled to retire. He struck his tents, and slowly and sullenly descended the Danube, wreaking diabolical vengeance upon the helpless peasants, killing, burning and destroying. Leaving a strong garrison to hold what remained of Buda and Pest, he carried thousands with him into captivity, where, after years of woe, they passed into the grave.

> " 'Tis terrible to rouse the lion,
>   Dreadful to cross the tiger's path;
> But the most terrible of terrors,
>   Is man himself in his wild wrath."

Solyman spent two years in making preparation for another march to Vienna, resolved to wipe out the disgrace of his last defeat by capturing all the Austrian States, and of then spreading the terror of his arms far and wide through the empire of Germany. The energy with which he acted may be inferred from one well authenticated anecdote illustrative of his character. He had ordered a bridge to be constructed across the Drave. The engineer who had been sent to accomplish the task, after a careful survey, reported that a bridge could not be constructed at that point. Solyman sent him a linen cord with this message :

"The sultan, thy master, commands thee, without consideration of the difficulties, to complete the bridge over the Drave. If thou doest it not, on his arrival he will have thee strangled with this cord."

With a large army, thoroughly drilled, and equipped with all the enginery of war, the sultan commenced his campaign. His force was so stupendous and so incumbered with the necessary baggage and heavy artillery, that it required a march of sixty days to pass from Constantinople to Belgrade. Ferdinand, in inexpressible alarm, sent ambassadors to Solyman, hoping to avert the storm by conciliation and concessions. This indication of weakness but increased the arrogance of the Turk.

He embarked his artillery on the Danube in a flotilla of three thousand vessels. Then crossing the Save, which at Belgrade flows into the Danube, he left the great central river of Europe on his right, and marching almost due west through Sclavonia, approached the frontiers of Styria, one of the most important provinces of the Austrian kingdom, by the shortest route. Still it was a long march of some two hundred miles Among the defiles of the Illyrian mountains, through which he was compelled to pass in his advance to Vienna, he came upon the little fortress of Guntz, garrisoned only by eight hundred men. Solyman expected to sweep this slight annoyance

away as he would brush a fly from his face. He sent his ad
vance guard to demolish the impudent obstacle; then, sur
prised by the resistance, he pushed forward a few more battalions; then, enraged at the unexpected strength developed
he ordered to the attack what he deemed an overwhelming
force; and then, in astonishment and fury, impelled against
the fortress the combined strength of his whole army. But
the little crag stood, like a rock opposing the flooding tide.
The waves of war rolled on and dashed against impenetrable
and immovable granite, and were scattered back in bloody
spray. The fortress commanded the pass, and swept it clean
with an unintermitted storm of shot and balls. For twenty-
eight days the fortress resisted the whole force of the Turkish army, and prevented it from advancing a mile. This
check gave the terrified inhabitants of Vienna, and of the surrounding region, time to unite for the defense of the capital.
The Protestants and the Catholics having settled their difficulties by the pacification of Ratisbon, as we have before narrated, combined all their energies; the pope sent his choicest
troops; all the ardent young men of the German empire,
from the ocean to the Alps, rushed to the banners of the cross,
and one hundred and thirty thousand men, including thirty
thousand mounted horsemen, were speedily gathered within
and around the walls of Vienna.

Thus thwarted in his plans, Solyman found himself compelled to retreat ingloriously, by the same path through which
he had advanced. Thus Christendom was relieved of this terrible menace. Though the Turks were still in possession of
Hungary, the allied troops of the empire strangely dispersed
without attempting to regain the kingdom from their domination.

CHAPTER X.

FERDINAND I.—HIS WARS AND INTRIGUES

FROM 1555 TO 1562.

John of Tapoli.—The Instability of Compacts.—The Sultan's Demands.—A Reign of War.—Powers and Duties of the Monarchs of Bohemia.—The Diet.—The King's Desire to crush Protestantism.—The Entrance to Prague.—Terror of the Inhabitants.—The King's Conditions.—The bloody Diet.—Disciplinary Measures.—The establishment of the Order of Jesuits.—Abdication of Charles V. in favor of Ferdinand.—Power of the Pope.—Paul IV.—A quiet but powerful Blow.—The Progress of the Reformers.—Attempts to reconcile the Protestants.—The unsuccessful Assembly.

DURING all the wars with the Turks, a Transylvanian count, John of Tapoli, was disputing Ferdinand's right to the throne of Hungary and claiming it for himself. He even entered into negotiations with the Turks, and coöperated with Solyman in his invasion of Hungary, having the promise of the sultan that he should be appointed king of the realm as soon as it was brought in subjection to Turkey. The Turks had now possession of Hungary, and the sultan invested John of Tapoli with the sovereignty of the kingdom, in the presence of a brilliant assemblage of the officers of his army and of the Hungarian nobles.

The last discomfiture and retreat of Solyman encouraged Ferdinand to redoubled exertions to reconquer Hungary from the combined forces of the Turks and his Transylvanian rival. Several years passed away in desultory, indecisive warfare, while John held his throne as tributary king to the sultan. At last Ferdinand, finding that he could not resist their united strength, and John becoming annoyed by the exactions of his Turkish master, they agreed to a compromise, by which John, who was aged, childless and infirm, was to remain king of all that part of Hungary which he held until he died; and the whole kingdom was then to revert to Ferdinand and his heirs. But it was agreed that should John marry and have a son, that son should be viceroy, or, as the title then was, *univode*, of his father's hereditary domain of *Transylvania*, having no control over any portion of Hungary proper.

Somewhat to the disappointment of Ferdinand, the old monarch immediately married a young bride. A son was born to them, and in fourteen days after his birth the father died of a stroke of apoplexy. The child was entitled to the viceroyship of Transylvania, while all the rest of Hungary was to pass unincumbered to Ferdinand. But Isabella, the ambitious young mother, who had married the decrepit monarch that she might enjoy wealth and station, had no intention that her babe should be less of a king than his father was. She was the daughter of Sigismond, King of Poland, and relying upon the support of her regal father she claimed the crown of Hungary for her boy, in defiance of the solemn compact. In that age of chivalry a young and beautiful woman could easily find defenders whatever might be her claims. Isabella soon rallied around her banner many Hungarian nobles, and a large number of adventurous knights from Poland.

Under her influence a large party of nobles met, chose the babe their king, and crowned him, under the name of Stephen, with a great display of military and religious pomp. They then conveyed him and his mother to the strong castle of Buda and dispatched an embassy to the sultan at Constantinople, avowing homage to him, as their feudal lord, and imploring his immediate and vigorous support.

Ferdinand, thus defrauded, and conscious of his inability to rescue the crown from the united forces of the Hungarian partisans of Stephen, and from the Turks, condescended also to send a message to the sultan, offering to hold the crown as his fief and to pay to the Porte the same tribute which John had paid, if the sultan would support his claim. The imperious

Turk, knowing that he could depose the baby king at his pleasure, insultingly rejected the proposals which Ferdinand had humiliated himself in advancing. He returned in answer, that he demanded, as the price of peace, not only that Ferdinand should renounce all claim whatever to the crown of Hungary, but that he should also acknowledge the Austrian territories as under vassalage to the Turkish empire, and pay tribute accordingly.

Ferdinand, at the same time that he sent his embassy to Constantinople, without waiting for a reply dispatched an army into Hungary, which reached Buda and besieged Isabella and her son in the citadel.

He pressed the siege with such vigor that Isabella must have surrendered had not an army of Turks come to her rescue. The Austrian troops were defeated and dispersed. The sultan himself soon followed with a still larger army, took possession of the city, secured the person of the queen and the infant prince, and placed a garrison of ten thousand janissaries in the citadel. The Turkish troops spread in all directions, establishing themselves in towns, castles, fortresses, and setting at defiance all Ferdinand's efforts to dislodge them. These events occurred during the reign of the Emperor Charles V. The resources of Ferdinand had become so exhausted that he was compelled, while affairs were in this state, in the year 1545, ten years before the abdication of the emperor, to implore of Solyman a suspension of arms.

The haughty sultan reluctantly consented to a truce of five years upon condition that Ferdinand would pay him an annual tribute of about sixty thousand dollars, and become feudatory of the Porte. To these humiliating conditions Ferdinand felt compelled to assent. Solyman, thus relieved from any trouble on the part of Ferdinand, compelled the queen to renounce to himself all right which either she or her son had to the throne. And now for many years we have nothing but a weary record of intrigues, assassinations, wars and woes

Miserable Hungary was but a field of blood.   There were three parties, Ferdinand, Stephen and Solyman, all alike ready to be guilty of any inhumanity or to perpetrate any perfidy in the accomplishment of their plans.   Ferdinand with his armies held one portion of Hungary, Solyman another, and Stephen, with his strong partisans another.   Bombardment succeeded bombardment ; cities and provinces were now overrun by one set of troops and now by another ; the billows of war surged to and fro incessantly, and the wail of the widow and the cry of the orphan ascended by day and by night to the ear of God.

In 1556 the Turks again invested Stephen with the government of that large portion of Hungary which they held, including Transylvania.   Ferdinand still was in possession of several important fortresses, and of several of the western districts of Hungary bordering on the Austrian States.   Isabella, annoyed by her subjection to the Turks, made propositions to Ferdinand for a reconciliation, and a truce was agreed upon which gave the land rest for a few years.

While these storms were sweeping over Hungary, events of scarcely less importance were transpiring in Bohemia.   This kingdom was an elective monarchy, and usually upon the death of a king the fiercest strife ensued as to who should be his successor.   The elected monarch, on receiving the crown, was obliged to recognize the sovereignty of the people as having chosen him for their ruler, and he promised to govern according to the ancient constitution of the kingdom.   The monarch, however, generally found no difficulty in surrounding himself with such strong supporters as to secure the election of his son or heir, and frequently he had his successor chosen before his death.   Thus the monarchy, though nominally elective, was in its practical operation essentially hereditary.

The authority of the crown was quite limited.   The monarch was only intrusted with so much power as the proud nobles were willing to surrender to one of their number whom

they appointed chief, whose superiority they reluctantly acknowledged, and against whom they were very frequently involved in wars.   In those days the *people* had hardly a recognized existence.   The nobles met in a congress called a diet,
and authorized their elected chief, the king, to impose taxes,
raise troops, declare war and institute laws according to their
will.   These diets were differently composed under different
reigns, and privileged cities were sometimes authorized to send
deputies whom they selected from the most illustrious of their
citizens.   The king usually convoked the diets ; but in those
stormy times of feuds, conspiracies and wars, there was hardly
any general rule.   The nobles, displeased at some act of the
king, would themselves, through some one or more of their
number, summon a diet and organize resistance.   The numbers attending such an irregular body were of course very various.   There appear to have been diets of the empire composed of not more than half a dozen individuals, and others
where as many hundreds were assembled.   Sometimes the
meetings were peaceful, and again tumultuous with the clashing of arms.

   In Bohemia the conflict between the Catholics and the reformers had raged with peculiar acrimony, and the reformers
in that kingdom had become a very numerous and influential
body.   Ferdinand was anxious to check the progress of the
Reformation, and he exerted all the power he could command
to defend and maintain Catholic supremacy.   For ten years
Ferdinand was absent from Bohemia, all his energies being
absorbed by the Hungarian war.   He was anxious to weaken
the power of the nobles in Bohemia.   There was ever, in those
days, either an open or a smothered conflict between the king
and the nobles, the monarch striving to grasp more power,
the nobles striving to keep him in subjection to them.   Ferdinand attempted to disarm the nobles by sending for all the
artillery of the kingdom, professing that he needed it to carry
on his war with the Turks.   But the wary nobles held on to

their artillery.   He then was guilty of the folly of hunting up some old exploded compacts, in virtue of which he declared that Bohemia was not an elective but a hereditary monarchy, and that he, as hereditary sovereign, held the throne for himself and his heirs.

This announcement spread a flame of indignation through all the castles of Bohemia.   The nobles rallied, called a diet, passed strong resolutions, organized an army, and adopted measures for vigorous resistance.   But Ferdinand was prepared for all these demonstrations.   His Hungarian truce enabled him to march a strong army on Bohemia.   The party in power has always numerous supporters from those who, being in office, will lose their dignities by revolution.   The king summoned all the well affected to repair to his standards, threatening condign punishment to all who did not give this proof of loyalty.   Nobles and knights in great numbers flocked to his encampment.   With menacing steps his battalions strode on, and triumphantly entered Prague, the capital city, situated in the very heart of the kingdom.

The indignation in the city was great, but the king was too strong to be resisted, and he speedily quelled all movements of tumult.   Prague, situated upon the steep and craggy banks of the Moldau, spanning the stream, and with its antique dwellings rising tier above tier upon the heights, is one of the most grand and imposing capitals of Europe.   About one hundred and twenty thousand inhabitants crowd its narrow streets and massive edifices.   Castles, fortresses, somber convents and the Gothic palaces of the old Bohemian monarchs, occupying every picturesque locality, as gray with age as the eternal crags upon which they stand, and exhibiting every fantastic variety of architecture, present an almost unrivaled aspect of beauty and of grandeur.   The Palace on the Hill alone is larger than the imperial palace at Vienna, containing over four hundred apartments, some of them being rooms of magnificent dimensions.   The cathedral within the precincts of this

palace occupied more than one hundred and fifty years in its
erection.

Ferdinand, with the iron energy and determined will of an
enraged, successful despot, stationed his troops at the gates,
the bridges and at every commanding position, and thus took
military possession of the city. The inhabitants, overawed and
helpless, were in a state of terror. The emperor summoned
six hundred of the most influential of the citizens to his palace, including all who possessed rank or office or wealth.
Tremblingly they came. As soon as they had entered, the
gates were closed and guarded, and they were all made prisoners. The king then, seated upon his throne, in his royal
robes, and with his armed officers around him, ordered the
captives like culprits to be led before him. Sternly he charged
them with treason, and demanded what excuse they had to
offer. They were powerless, and their only hope was in self-
abasement. One, speaking in the name of the rest, said :

" We will not presume to enter into any defense of our
conduct with our king and master. We cast ourselves upon
his royal mercy."

They then all simultaneously threw themselves upon their
knees, imploring his pardon. The king allowed them to remain for some time in that posture, that he might enjoy their
humiliation. He then ordered his officers to conduct them
into the hall of justice, and detain them there until he had
decided respecting their punishment. For some hours they
were kept in this state of suspense. He then informed them,
that out of his great clemency he had decided to pardon them
on the following conditions.

They were to surrender all their constitutional privileges,
whatever they were, into the hands of the king, and be satisfied with whatever privileges he might condescend to confer
upon them. They were to bring all their artillery, muskets
and ammunition to the palace, and surrender them to his
officers ; all the revenues of the city, together with a tax upon

malt and beer, were to be paid into his hands for his disposal
and all their vassals, and their property of every kind, they
were to resign to the king and to his heirs, whom they were
to acknowledge as the *hereditary* successors to the throne of
Bohemia. Upon these conditions the king promised to spare
the rebellious city, and to pardon all the offenders, excepting
a few of the most prominent, whom he was determined to
punish with such severity as to prove an effectual warning to
all others.

The prisoners were terrified into the immediate ratification
of these hard terms. They were then all released, excepting
forty, who were reserved for more rigorous punishment. In
the same manner the king sent a summons to all the towns
of the kingdom; and by the same terrors the same terms were
extorted. All the rural nobles, who had manifested a spirit
of resistance, were also summoned before a court of justice for
trial. Some fled the kingdom. Their estates were confiscated to Ferdinand, and they were sentenced to death should
they ever return. Many others were deprived of their possessions. Twenty-six were thrown into prison, and two condemned to public execution.

The king, having thus struck all the discontented with terror,
summoned a diet to meet in his palace at Prague. They met
the 22d of August, 1547. A vast assemblage was convened,
as no one who was summoned dared to stay away. The king,
wishing to give an intimation to the diet of what they were
to expect should they oppose his wishes, commenced the session by publicly hanging four of the most illustrious of his
captives. One of these, high judge of the kingdom, was in
the seventieth year of his age. The Bloody Diet, as it has
since been called, was opened, and Ferdinand found all as
pliant as he could wish. The royal discipline had effected
wonders. The slightest intimation of Ferdinand was accepted
with eagerness.

The execrable tyrant wished to impress the whole king-

dom with a salutary dread of incurring his paternal displeasure. He brought out the forty prisoners who still remained
in their dungeons. Eight of the most distinguished men of
the kingdom were led to three of the principal cities, in each
of which, in the public square, they were ignominiously and
cruelly whipped on the bare back. Before each flagellation
the executioner proclaimed—

"These men are punished because they are traitors, and
because they excited the people against their *hereditary*
master."

They then, with eight others, their property being confiscated, in utter beggary, were driven as vagabonds from the
kingdom. The rest, after being impoverished by fines, were
restored to liberty. Ferdinand adopted vigorous measures
to establish his despotic power. Considering the Protestant
religion as peculiarly hostile to despotism, in the encouragement it afforded to education, to the elevation of the masses,
and to the diffusion of those principles of fraternal equality
which Christ enjoined ; and considering the Catholic religion
as the great bulwark of kingly power, by the intolerance of
the Church teaching the benighted multitudes subjection to
civil intolerance, Ferdinand, with unceasing vigilance, and
with melancholy success, endeavored to eradicate the Lutheran doctrines from the kingdom. He established the most
rigorous censorship of the press, and would allow no foreign
work, unexamined, to enter the realm. He established in
Bohemia the fanatic order of the Jesuits, and intrusted to
them the education of the young.

It is often impossible to reconcile the inconsistencies of the
human heart. Ferdinand, while guilty of such atrocities, affected, on some points, the most scrupulous punctilios of honor.
The clearly-defined privileges which had been promised the
Protestants, he would not infringe in the least. They were
permitted to give their children Protestant teachers, and to
conduct worship in their own way. He effected his object of

changing Bohemia from an elective to a hereditary monarchy, and thus there was established in Bohemia the renowned doctrine of regal legitimacy; of the *divine right* of kings to govern. With such a bloody hand was the doctrine of the sovereignty, not of the *people*, but of the *nobles*, overthrown in Bohemia. The nobles are not much to be commiserated, for they trampled upon the people as mercilessly as the king did upon them. It is merely another illustration of the old and melancholy story of the strong devouring the weak: the owl takes the wren; the eagle the owl.

Bohemia, thus brought in subjection to a single mind, and shackled in its spirit of free enterprise, began rapidly to exhibit symptoms of decline and decay. It was a great revolution, accomplished by cunning and energy, and maintained by the terrors of confiscation, exile and death.

The Emperor Charles V., it will be remembered, had attempted in vain to obtain the reversion of the imperial crown for his son Philip at his own death. The crown of Spain was his hereditary possession, and that he could transmit to his son. But the crown of the empire was elective. Charles V. was so anxious to secure the imperial dignity for his son, that he retained the crown of the empire for some months after abdicating that of Spain, still hoping to influence the electors in their choice. But there were so many obstacles in the way of the recognition of the young Philip as emperor, that Charles, anxious to retain the dignity in the family, reluctantly yielded to the intrigues of his brother Ferdinand, who had now become so powerful that he could perhaps triumph over any little irregularity in the succession and silence murmurs.

Consequently, Charles, nine months after the abdication. of the thrones of the Low Countries and of Spain, tried the experiment of abdicating the *elective* crown of the empire in favor of Ferdinand. It was in many respects such an act as if the President of the United States should abdicate in favor of some one of his own choice. The emperor had, however, a semblance of right to place the scepter in the hands of whom he would during his lifetime. But, upon the death of the emperor, would his appointee still hold his power, or would the crown at that moment be considered as falling from his brow? It was the 7th of August, 1556, when the emperor abdicated the throne of the empire in behalf of his brother Ferdinand. It was a new event in history, without a precedent, and the matter was long and earnestly discussed throughout the German States. Notwithstanding all Ferdinand's energy, sagacity and despotic power, two years elapsed before he could secure the acknowledgment of his title, by the German States, and obtain a proclamation of his imperial state.

The pope had thus far had such an amazing control over the conscience, or rather the superstition of Europe, that the choice of the electors was ever subject to the ratification of the holy father. It was necessary for the emperor elect to journey to Rome, and be personally crowned by the hands of the pope, before he could be considered in legal possession of the imperial title and of a right to the occupancy of the throne. Julius II., under peculiar circumstances, allowed Maximilian to assume the title of *emperor elect* while he postponed his visit to Rome for coronation; but the want of the papal sanction, by the imposition of the crown upon his brow by those *sacred hands*, thwarted Maximilian in some of his most fondly-cherished measures.

Paul IV. was now pontiff, an old man, jealous of his prerogatives, intolerant in the extreme, and cherishing the most exorbitant sense of his spiritual power. He execrated the Protestants, and was indignant with Ferdinand that he had shown them any mercy at all. But Ferdinand, conscious of the importance of a papal coronation, sent a very obsequious embassy to Rome, announcing his appointment as emperor, and imploring the benediction of the holy father and the reception of the crown from his hands. The haughty and dis dainful reply of the pope was characteristic of the times and of the man. It was in brief, as follows:

"The Emperor Charles has behaved like a madman; and his acts are no more to be respected than the ravings of insanity. Charles V. received the imperial crown from the head of the Church; in abdicating, that crown could only return to the sacred hands which conferred it. The nomination of Ferdinand as his successor we pronounce to be null and void. The alleged ratification of the electors is a mockery, dishonored and vitiated as it is by the votes of electors polluted with heresy. We therefore command Ferdinand to relinquish all claim to the imperial crown."

The irascible old pontiff, buried beneath the senseless pomps of the Vatican, was not at all aware of the change which Protestant preaching and writing had effected in the public mind of Germany. Italy was still slumbering in the gloom of the dark ages; but light was beginning to dawn upon the hills of the empire. One half of the population of the German empire would rally only the more enthusiastically around Ferdinand, if he would repel all papal assumptions with defiance and contempt. Ferdinand was the wiser and the better informed man of the two. He conducted with dignity and firmness which make us almost forget his crimes. A diet was summoned, and it was quietly decreed that a *papal coronation was no longer necessary.* That one short line was the heaviest blow the papal throne had yet received. From it, it never recovered and never can recover.

Paul IV. was astounded at such effrontery, and as soon as he had recovered a little from his astonishment, alarmed in view of such a declaration of independence, he took counsel of discretion, and humiliating as it was, made advances for a reconciliation. Ferdinand was also anxious to be on good terms with the pope. While negotiations were pending, Paul died, his death being perhaps hastened by chagrin. Pius IV. succeeded him, and pressed still more earnestly overtures for rec onciliation. Ferdinand, through his ambassador, expressed his willingness to pledge the accustomed *devotion* and *reverence* to the head of the Church, omitting the word *obedience.* But the pope was anxious, above all things, to have that emphatic word *obey* introduced into the ritual of subjection, and after employing all the arts of diplomacy and cajolery, carried his point. Ferdinand, with duplicity which was not honorable, let the word remain, saying that it was not his act, but that of his ambassador. The pope affected satisfaction with the formal acknowledgment of his power, while Ferdinand ever after refused to recognize his authority. Thus terminated the long dependence, running through ages of darkness and delusion, of the German emperors upon the Roman see.

Ferdinand did not trouble himself to receive the crown from the pope, and since his day the emperors of Germany have no longer been exposed to the expense and the trouble of a journey to Rome for their coronation. Though Ferdinand was strongly attached to the tenets of the papal church, and would gladly have eradicated Protestantism from his domains, he was compelled to treat the Protestants with some degree of consideration, as he needed the aid of their arms in the wars in which he was incessantly involved with the Turks. He even made great efforts to introduce some measure of conciliation which should reconcile the two parties, and thus reunite his realms under one system of doctrine and of worship.

Still Protestantism was making rapid strides all over Europe. It had become the dominant religion in Denmark and Sweden, and, by the accession of Elizabeth to the throne of England, was firmly established in that important kingdom. In France also the reformed religion had made extensive inroads, gathering to its defense many of the noblest spirits, in rank and intellect, in the realm. The terrors of the inquisition had thus far prevented the truth from making much progress in Spain and Portugal.

With the idea of promoting reconciliation, Ferdinand

adopted a measure which contributed greatly to his popular ity with the Protestants. He united with France and Spain in urging Pius IV., a mild and pliant pontiff, to convene a council in Germany to heal the religious feud. He drew up a memorial, which was published and widely scattered, declaring that the Protestants had become far too powerful to be treated with outrage or contempt; that there were undeniable wrongs in the Church which needed to be reformed; and that no harm could accrue from permitting the clergy to marry, and to administer both bread and wine to the communicants in the Lord's Supper. It was a doctrine of the Church of Rome, that the laity could receive the bread only; the wine was reserved for the officiating priest.

This memorial of Ferdinand, drawn up with much distinctness and great force of argument, was very grateful to the Protestants, but very displeasing to the court of Rome. These conflicts raged for several years without any decisive results. The efforts of Ferdinand to please both parties, as usual, pleased neither. By the Protestants he was regarded as a persecutor and intolerant; while the Catholics accused him of lukewarmness, of conniving at heresy and of dishonoring the Church by demanding of her concessions derogatory to her authority and her dignity.

Ferdinand, finding that the Church clung with deathly tenacity to its corruptions, assumed himself quite the attitude of a reformer. A memorable council had been assembled at Trent on the 15th of January, 1562. Ferdinand urged the council to exhort the pope to examine if there was not room for some reform in his own person, state or court. "Because," said he, "the only true method to obtain authority for the reformation of others, is to begin by amending oneself." He commented upon the manifest impropriety of scandalous indulgences; of selling the sacred offices of the Church to the highest bidder, regardless of character; of extorting fees for the administration of the sacrament of the Lord's Supper; of

offering prayers and performing the services of public devo
tion in a language which the people could not understand; and
other similar and most palpable abuses. Even the kings of
France and Spain united with the emperor in these remonstrances.

It is difficult now to conceive of the astonishment and indignation with which the pope and his adherents received
these very reasonable suggestions, coming not from the Protestants but from the most staunch advocates of the papacy.
The see of Rome, corrupt to its very core, would yield nothing. The more senseless and abominable any of its corruptions were, the more tenaciously did pope and cardinals cling
to them. At last the emperor, in despair of seeing any thing
accomplished, requested that the assembly might be dissolved,
saying, "Nothing good can be expected, even if it continue
its sittings for a hundred years."

CHAPTER XI.

DEATH OF FERDINAND I.—ACCESSION OF MAXIMILIAN II.

FROM 1562 TO 1576.

THE COUNCIL OF TRENT.—SPREAD OF THE REFORMATION.—FERDINAND'S ATTEMPT TO IN-
FLUENCE THE POPE.—HIS ARGUMENTS AGAINST CELIBACY.—STUBBORNNESS OF THE
POPE.—MAXIMILIAN II.—DISPLEASURE OF FERDINAND.—MOTIVES FOR NOT ABJUR-
ING THE CATHOLIC FAITH.—RELIGIOUS STRIFE IN EUROPE.—MAXIMILIAN'S ADDRESS
TO CHARLES IX.—MUTUAL TOLERATION.—ROMANTIC PASTIME OF WAR.—HEROISM
OF NICHOLAS, COUNT OF ZRINI.—ACCESSION OF POWER TO AUSTRIA.—ACCESSION OF
RHODOLPH III.—DEATH OF MAXIMILIAN.

THIS celebrated council of Trent, which was called with the hope that by a spirit of concession and reform the religious dissensions which agitated Europe might be adjusted, declared, in the very bravado of papal intolerance, the very worst abuses of the Church to be essential articles of faith, which could only be renounced at the peril of eternal condemnation, and thus presented an insuperable barrier to any reconciliation between the Catholics and the Protestants. Ferdinand was disappointed, and yet did not venture to break with the pope by withholding his assent from the decrees which were enacted.

The Lutheran doctrines had spread widely through Ferdinand's hereditary States of Austria. Several of the professors in the university at Vienna had embraced those views; and quite a number of the most powerful and opulent of the territorial lords even maintained Protestant chaplains at their castles. The majority of the inhabitants of the Austrian States had, in the course of a few years, become Protestants. Though Ferdinand did every thing he dared to do to check their progress, forbidding the circulation of Luther's translation of the

Bible, and throwing all the obstacles he could in the way of Protestant worship, he was compelled to grant them very considerable toleration, and to overlook the infraction of his decrees, that he might secure their aid to repel the Turks. Providence seemed to overrule the Moslem invasion for the protection of the Protestant faith. Notwithstanding all the efforts of Ferdinand, the reformers gained ground in Austria as in other parts of Germany.

The two articles upon which the Protestants at this time placed most stress were the right of the clergy to marry and the administration of the communion under both kinds, as it was called ; that is, that the communicants should partake of both the bread and the wine. Ferdinand, having failed entirely in inducing the council to submit to any reform, opened direct communication with the pope to obtain for his subjects indulgence in respect to these two articles. In advocacy of this measure he wrote :

" In Bohemia no persuasion, no argument, no violence, not even arms and war, have succeeded in abolishing the use of the cup as well as the bread in the sacrament. In fact the Church itself permitted it, although the popes revoked it by a breach of the conditions on which it was granted. In the other States, Hungary, Austria, Silesia, Styria, Carinthia, Carniola, Bavaria and other parts of Germany, many desire with ardor the same indulgence. If this concession is granted they may be reunited to the Church, but if refused they will be driven into the party of the Protestants. So many of the priests have been degraded by their diocesans for administering the sacrament in both kinds, that the country is almost deprived of priests. Hence children die or grow up to maturity without baptism ; and men and women, of all ages and of all ranks, live like the brutes, in the grossest ignorance of God and of religion."

In reference to the marriage of the clergy he wrote : " If a permission to the clergy to marry can not be granted, may

H

not married men of learning and probity be ordained, according to the custom of the eastern church ; or married priests
be tolerated for a time, provided they act according to the
Catholic and Christian faith ?   And it may be justly asked
whether such concessions would not be far preferable to tol-
erating, as has unfortunately been done, fornication and concubinage ?   I can not avoid adding, what is a common observation, that priests who live in concubinage are guilty of
greater sin than those who are married ; for the last only
transgress a law which is capable of being changed, whereas
the first sin against a divine law, which is capable of neither
change nor dispensation."

The pope, pressed with all the importunity which Ferdinand could urge, reluctantly consented to the administration
of the cup to the laity, but resolutely refused to tolerate the
marriage of the clergy.   Ferdinand was excessively annoyed
by the stubbornness of the court of Rome in its refusal to
submit to the most reasonable reform, thus rendering it impossible for him to allay the religious dissensions which were still
spreading and increasing in acrimony.   His disappointment
was so great that it is said to have thrown him into the fever
of which he died on the 25th of July, 1564.

For several ages the archdukes of Austria had been endeavoring to unite the Austrian States with Hungary and Bohemia under one monarchy.   The union had been temporarily
effected once or twice, but Ferdinand accomplished the permanent union, and may thus be considered as the founder of
the Austrian monarchy essentially as it now exists.   As Archduke of Austria, he inherited the Austrian duchies.   By his
marriage with Anne, daughter of Ladislaus, King of Hungary
and Bohemia, he secured those crowns, which he made hereditary in his family.   He left three sons.   The eldest, Maximilian, inherited the archduchy of Austria and the crowns of
Bohemia and Hungary, of course inheriting, with Hungary
prospective war with the Turks.   The second son, Ferdinand

had, as his legacy, the government and the revenues of the Tyrol. The third son, Charles, received Styria. There were nine daughters left, three of whom took the vail and the rest formed illustrious marriages.

Ferdinand appears to have been a sincere Catholic, though he saw the great corruptions of the Church and earnestly desired reform. As he advanced in years he became more tolerant and gentle, and had his wise counsels been pursued Europe would have escaped inexpressible woes. Still he clung to the Church, unwisely seeking unity of faith and discipline, which can hardly be attained in this world, rather than toleration with allowed diversity.

Maximilian II. was thirty-seven years of age on his accession to the throne. Although he was educated in the court of Spain, which was the most bigoted and intolerant in Europe, yet he developed a character remarkable for mildness, affability and tolerance. He was indebted for these attractive traits to his tutor, a man of enlarged and cultivated mind, and who had, like most men of his character at that time, a strong leaning towards Protestantism. These principles took so firm a hold of his youthful mind that they could never be eradicated. As he advanced in life he became more and more interested in the Protestant faith. He received a clergyman of the reformed religion as his chaplain and private secretary, and partook of the sacrament of the Lord's Supper, from his hands, in both kinds. Even while remaining in the Spanish court he entered into a correspondence with several of the most influential advocates of the Protestant faith. Returning to Austria from Spain, he attended public worship in the chapels of the Protestants, and communed with them in the sacrament of the Lord's Supper. When some of his friends warned him that by pursuing such a course he could never hope to obtain the imperial crown of Germany, he replied:

"I will sacrifice all worldly interests for the sake of my salvation."

His father, the Emperor Ferdinand, was so much displeased with his son's advocacy of the Protestant faith, that after many angry remonstrances he threatened to disinherit him if he did not renounce all connection with the reformers. But Maximilian, true to his conscience, would not allow the apprehension of the loss of a crown to induce him to swerve from his faith. Fully expecting to be thus cast off and banished from the kingdom, he wrote to the Protestant elector Palatine:

"I have so deeply offended my father by maintaining a Lutheran preacher in my service, that I am apprehensive of being expelled as a fugitive, and hope to find an asylum in your court."

The Catholics of course looked with apprehension to the accession of Maximilian to the throne, while the Protestants anticipated the event with great hope. There were, however, many considerations of vast moment influencing Maximilian not to separate himself, in form, from the Catholic church. Philip, his cousin, King of Spain, was childless, and should he die without issue, Ferdinand would inherit that magnificent throne, which he could not hope to ascend, as an avowed Protestant, without a long and bloody war. It had been the most earnest dying injunction of his father that he should not abjure the Catholic faith. His wife was a very zealous Catholic, as was also each one of his brothers. There were very many who remained in the Catholic church whose sympathies were with the reformers—who hoped to promote reformation in the Church without leaving it. Influenced by such considerations, Maximilian made a public confession of the Catholic faith, received his father's confessor, and maintained, in his court, the usages of the papal church. He was, however, the kind friend of the Protestants, ever seeking to shield them from persecution, claiming for them a liberal toleration, and seeking, in all ways, to promote fraternal religious feeling throughout his domains.

The prudence of Maximilian wonderfully allayed the bit-

terness of religious strife in Germany, while other portions of
Europe were desolated with the fiercest warfare between the
Catholics and Protestants.   In France, in particular, the conflict raged with merciless fury.   It was on August 24th, 1572,
but a few years after Maximilian ascended the throne, when
the Catholics of France perpetrated the Massacre of St. Bartholomew, perhaps the most atrocious crime recorded in history.   The Catholics and Protestants in France were nearly
equally divided in numbers, wealth and rank.   The papal
party, finding it impossible to crush their foes by force of
arms, resolved to exterminate them by a simultaneous massacre.   They feigned toleration and reconciliation.   The court
of Paris invited all the leading Protestants of the kingdom to
the metropolis to celebrate the nuptials of Henry, the young
King of Navarre, with Margaret, sister of Charles IX., the
reigning monarch.   Secret orders were dispatched all over
the kingdom, for the conspirators, secretly armed, at a given
signal, by midnight, to rise upon the Protestants, men,
women and children, and utterly exterminate them.   " Let
not one remain alive," said the King of France, " to tell the
story."

The deed was nearly accomplished.   The king himself,
from a window of the Louvre, fired upon his Protestant
subjects, as they fled in dismay through the streets.   In a
few hours eighty thousand of the Protestants were mangled
corpses.   Protestantism in France has never recovered from
this blow.   Maximilian openly expressed his execration of
this deed, though the pope ordered Te Deums to be chanted
at Rome in exultation over the crime.   Not long after this
horrible slaughter, Charles IX. died in mental torment.   Henry
of Valois, brother of the deceased king, succeeded to the
throne.   He was at that time King of Poland.   Returning to
France, through Vienna, he had an interview with Maximilian, who addressed him in those memorable words which have
often been quoted to the honor of the Austrian sovereign:

"There is no crime greater in princes," said Maximilian, "than to tyrannize over the consciences of their subjects. By shedding the blood of heretics, far from honoring the common Father of all, they incur the divine vengeance; and while they aspire, by such means, to crowns in heaven, they justly expose themselves to the loss of their earthly kingdoms."

Under the peaceful and humane reign of Ferdinand, Germany was kept in a general state of tranquillity, while storms of war and woe were sweeping over almost all other parts of Europe. During all his reign, Maximilian II. was unwearied in his endeavors to promote harmony between the two great religious parties, by trying, on the one hand, to induce the pope to make reasonable concessions, and, on the other hand, to induce the Protestants to moderate their demands. His first great endeavor was to induce the pope to consent to the marriage of the clergy. In this he failed entirely. He then tried to form a basis of mutual agreement, upon which the two parties could unite. His father had attempted this plan, and found it utterly impracticable. Maximilian attempted it, with just as little success. It has been attempted a thousand times since, and has always failed. Good men are ever rising who mourn the divisions in the Christian Church, and strive to form some plan of union, where all true Christians can meet and fraternize, and forget their minor differences. Alas! for poor human nature, there is but little prospect that this plan can ever be accomplished. There will be always those who can not discriminate between essential and non-essential differences of opinion. Maximilian at last fell back simply upon the doctrine of a liberal toleration, and in maintaining this he was eminently successful.

At one time the Turks were crowding him very hard in Hungary. A special effort was requisite to raise troops to repel them. Maximilian summoned a diet, and appealed to the assembled nobles for supplies of men and money. In Austria proper, Protestantism was now in the decided ascendency. The nobles took advantage of the emperor's wants to reply—

"We are ready to march to the assistance of our sov·ereign, to repel the Turks from Hungary, if the Jesuits are first expelled from our territories."

The answer of the king was characteristic of his policy and of his career. "I have convened you," he said, "to give me contributions, not remonstrances. I wish you to help me expel the Turks, not the Jesuits."

From many a prince this reply would have excited exasperation. But Maximilian had established such a character for impartiality and probity, that the rebuke was received with applause rather than with murmurs, and the Protestants, with affectionate zeal, rallied around his standard. So great was the influence of the king, that toleration, as one of the virtues of the court, became the fashion, and the Catholics and Protestants vied with each other in the manifestation of mutual forbearance and good will. They met on equal terms in the palace of the monarch, shared alike in his confidence and his favors, and coöperated cordially in the festivities of the banqueting room, and in the toils of the camp. We love to dwell upon the first beautiful specimen of toleration which the world has seen in any court. It is the more beautiful, and the more wonderful, as having occurred in a dark age of bigotry, intolerance and persecution. And let us be sufficiently candid to confess, that it was professedly a Roman Catholic monarch, a member of the papal church, to whom the world is indebted for this first recognition of true mental freedom. It can not be denied that Maximilian II. was in advance of the avowed Protestants of his day.

Pope Pius V. was a bigot, inflexible, overbearing; and he determined, with a bloody hand, to crush all dissent. From his throne in the Vatican he cast an eagle eye to Germany, and was alarmed and indignant at the innovations which Max·imilian was permitting. In all haste he dispatched a legate to remonstrate strongly against such liberality. Maximilian received the legate, Cardinal Commendon, with courtesy, but for a time firmly refused to change his policy in obedience to the exactions of the pope. The pope brought to bear upon him all the influence of the Spanish court. He was threatened with war by all the papal forces, sustained by the then immense power of the Spanish monarchy. For a time Maximilian was in great perplexity, and finally yielded to the pope so far as to promise not to permit any further innovations than those which he had already allowed, and not to extend his principles of toleration into any of his States where they had not as yet been introduced. Thus, while he did not retract any concessions he had made, he promised to stop where he was, and proceed no further.

Maximilian was so deeply impressed with the calamities of war, that he even sent an embassy to the Turks, offering to continue to pay the tribute which they had exacted of his father, as the price of a continued armistice. But Solyman, having made large preparations for the renewed invasion of Hungary, and sanguine of success, haughtily rejected the offer, and renewed hostilities.

Nearly all of the eastern and southern portions of Hungary were already in the hands of the Turks. Maximilian held a few important towns and strong fortresses on the western frontier. Not feeling strong enough to attempt to repel the Turks from the portion they already held, he strengthened his garrisons, and raising an army of eighty thousand men, of which he assumed the command, he entered Hungary and marched down the Danube about sixty miles to Raab, to await the foe and act on the defensive. Solyman rendezvoused an immense army at Belgrade, and commenced his march up the Danube.

"Old as I am," said he to his troops, "I am determined to chastise the house of Austria, or to perish in the attempt beneath the walls of Vienna."

It was beautiful spring weather, and the swelling buds and

hourly increasing verdure, decorated the fields with loveliness.
For several days the Turks marched along the right bank of
the Danube, through green fields, and beneath a sunny sky,
encountering no foe. War seemed but as the pastime of a
festive day, as gay banners floated in the breeze, groups of
horsemen, gorgeously caparisoned, pranced along, and the tur-
baned multitude, in brilliant uniform, with jokes, and laugh-
ter and songs, leisurely ascended the majestic stream. A fleet
of boats filled the whole body of the river, impelled by sails
when the wind favored, or, when the winds were adverse,
driven by the strong arms of the rowers against the gentle
tide. Each night the white tents were spread, and a city for
a hundred thousand inhabitants rose as by magic, with its
grassy streets, its squares, its busy population, its music, its
splendor, blazing in all the regalia of war. As by magic the
city rose in the rays of the declining sun. As by magic it disappeared in the early dawn of the morning, and the mighty
hosts moved on.

A few days thus passed, when Solyman approached the fortified town of Zigeth, near the confluence of the Drave and the
Danube. Nicholas, Count of Zrini, was intrusted with the
defense of this place, and he fulfilled his trust with heroism
and valor which has immortalized both his name and the fortress which he defended. Zrini had a garrison of but three
thousand men. An army of nearly a hundred thousand were
marching upon him. Zrini collected his troops, and took a
solemn oath, in the presence of all, that, true to God, to his
Christian faith, and his country, he never would surrender the
town to the Turks, but with his life. He then required each
soldier individually to take the same oath to his captain. All
the captains then, in the presence of the assembled troops,
took the same oath to him.

The Turks soon arrived and commenced an unceasing bombardment day and night. The little garrison vigorously responded. The besieged made frequent sallies, spiking the guns

of the besiegers, and again retiring behind their works. But their overpowering foes advanced, inch by inch, till they got possession of what was called the "old city." The besieged retiring to the "new city," resumed the defense with unabated ardor. The storm of war raged incessantly for many days, and the new city was reduced to a smoldering heap of fire and ashes. The Turks, with incredible labor, raised immense mounds of earth and stone, on the summits of which they planted their batteries, where they could throw their shot, with unobstructed aim, into every part of the city. Roads were constructed across the marsh, and the swarming multitudes, in defiance of all the efforts of the heroic little garrison, filled up the ditch, and were just on the rush to take the place by a general assault, when Zrini abandoned the new city to flames, and threw himself into the citadel. His force was now reduced to about a thousand men. Day after day the storm of war blazed with demoniac fury around the citadel. Mines were dug, and, as by volcanic explosions, bastions, with men and guns, were blown high into the air. The indomitable Hungarians made many sallies, cutting down the gunners and spiking the guns, but they were always driven back with heavy loss. Repeated demands for capitulation were sent in and as repeatedly rejected. For a week seven assaults were made daily upon the citadel by the Turks, but they were always repulsed. At length the outer citadel was entirely demolished. Then the heroic band retired to the inner works. They were now without ammunition or provisions, and the Turks, exasperated by such a defense, were almost gnashing their teeth with rage. The old sultan, Solyman, actually died from the intensity of his vexation and wrath. The death of the sultan was concealed from the Turkish troops, and a general assault was arranged upon the inner works. The hour had now come when they must surrender or die, for the citadel was all battered into a pile of smoldering ruins, and there were no ramparts capable of checking the progress of the foe. Zrini as sembled his little band, now counting but six hundred, and said,

"Remember your oath. We must die in the flames, or perish with hunger, or go forth to meet the foe. Let us die like men. Follow me, and do as I do."

They made a simultaneous rush from their defenses into the thickest of the enemy. For a few moments there was a scene of wildest uproar and confusion, and the brave defenders were all silent in death. The Turks with shouts of triumph now rushed into the citadel. But Zrini had fired trains leading to the subterranean vaults of powder, and when the ruins were covered with the conquerors, a sullen roar ran beneath the ground and the whole citadel, men, horses, rocks and artillery were thrown into the air, and fell a commingled mass of ruin, fire and blood. A more heroic defense history has not recorded. Twenty thousand Turks perished in this siege. The body of Zrini was found in the midst of the mangled dead. His head was cut off and, affixed to a pole, was raised as a trophy before the tent of the deceased sultan.

The death of Solyman, and the delay which this desperate siege had caused, embarrassed all the plans of the invaders, and they resolved upon a retreat. The troops were consequently withdrawn from Hungary, and returned to Constantinople.

Maximilian, behind his intrenchments at Raab, did not dare to march to the succor of the beleaguered garrison, for overpowering numbers would immediately have destroyed him had he appeared in the open field. But upon the withdrawal of the Turks he disbanded his army, after having replenished his garrisons, and returned to Vienna. Selim succeeded Solyman, and Maximilian sent an embassy to Constantinople to offer terms of peace. At the same time, to add weight to his negotiations, he collected a large army, and made the most vigorous preparations for the prosecution of the war.

Selim, just commencing his reign, anxious to consolidate his power, and embarrassed by insurrection in his own realms, was glad to conclude an armistice on terms highly favorable to Maximilian. John Sigismond, who had been crowned by the Turks, as their tributary King of Hungary, was to retain Transylvania. The Turks were to hold the country generally between Transylvania and the river Teiss, while Ferdinand was to have the remainder, extending many hundred miles from the Teiss to Austria. The Prince of Transylvania was compelled, though very reluctantly, to assent to this treaty. He engaged not to assume the title of King of Hungary, except in correspondence with the Turks. The emperor promised him one of his nieces in marriage, and in return it was agreed that should John Sigismond die without male issue, Transylvania should revert to the crown of Hungary.

Soon after this treaty, John Sigismond died, before his marriage with the emperor's niece, and Transylvania was again united to Hungary and came under the sway of Maximilian. This event formed quite an accession to the power of the Austrian monarch, as he now held all of Hungary save the southern and central portion where the Turks had garrisoned the fortresses. The pope, the King of Spain, and the Venetians, now sent united ambassadors to the emperor urging him to summon the armies of the empire and drive the Turks entirely out of Hungary. Cardinal Commendon assured the emperor, in the name of the holy father of the Church, that it was no sin to violate any compact with the infidel. Maximilian nobly replied,

"The faith of treaties ought to be considered as inviolable, and a Christian can never be justified in breaking an oath."

Maximilian never enjoyed vigorous health, and being anxious to secure the tranquillity of his extended realms after his death, he had his eldest son, Rhodolph, in a diet at Presburg, crowned King of Hungary. Rhodolph at once entered upon the government of his realm as viceroy during the life of his father. Thus he would have all the reins of government in his hands, and, at the death of the emperor, there would be no apparent change.

It will be remembered that Ferdinand had, by violence and treachery, wrested from the Bohemians the privilege of electing their sovereign, and had thus converted Bohemia into an hereditary monarchy. Maximilian, with characteristic prudence, wished to maintain the hereditary right thus established, while at the same time he wished to avoid wounding the prejudices of those who had surrendered the right of suffrage only to fraud and the sword. He accordingly convoked a diet at Prague. The nobles were assembled in large numbers, and the occasion was invested with unusual solemnity. The emperor himself introduced to them his son, and recommended him to them as their future sovereign. The nobles were much gratified by so unexpected a concession, and with enthusiasm accepted their new king. The emperor had thus wisely secured for his son the crowns of Hungary and Bohemia.

Having succeeded in these two important measures, Maximilian set about the more difficult enterprise of securing for his son his succession upon the imperial throne. This was a difficult matter in the strong rivalry which then existed between the Catholics and the Protestants. With caution and conciliation, encountering and overturning innumerable obstacles, Maximilian proceeded, until having, as he supposed, a fair chance of success, he summoned the diet of electors at Ratisbon. But here new difficulties arose. The Protestants were jealous of their constantly-imperiled privileges, and wished to surround them with additional safeguards. The Catholics, on the contrary, stimulated by the court of Rome, wished to withdraw the toleration already granted, and to pursue the Protestant faith with new rigor. The meeting of the diet was long and stormy, and again they were upon the point of a violent dissolution. But the wisdom, moderation and perseverance of Maximilian finally prevailed, and his suc

cess was entire. Rhodolph III. was unanimously chosen to
succeed him upon the imperial throne, and was crowned at
Ratisbon on the 1st of November, 1575.

Poland was strictly an elective monarchy. The tumultuous nobles had established a law prohibiting the election of
a successor during the lifetime of the monarch. Their last
king had been the reckless, chivalrous Henry, Duke of Anjou,
brother of Charles IX. of France. Charles IX. having died
without issue, Henry succeeded him upon the throne of France,
and abdicated the crown of the semi-barbaric wilds of Poland.
The nobles were about to assemble for the election. There
were many influential candidates. Maximilian was anxious to
obtain the crown for his son Ernest. Much to the surprise of
Maximilian, he himself was chosen king. Protestantism had
gained the ascendency in Poland, and a large majority of the
nobles united upon Maximilian. The electors honored both
themselves and the emperor in assigning, as the reason for
their choice, that the emperor had conciliated the contending
factions of the Christian world, and had acquired more glory
by his pacific policy than other princes had acquired in the
exploits of war.

There were curious conditions at that time assigned to the
occupancy of the throne of Poland. The elected monarch,
before receiving the crown, was required to give his pledge
that he would reside two years uninterruptedly in the kingdom, and that then he would not leave without the consent
of the nobles. He was also required to construct four fortresses at his own expense, and to pay all the debts of the last
monarch, however heavy they might be, including the arrears
of the troops. He was also to maintain a sort of guard of
honor, consisting of ten thousand Polish horsemen.

In addition to the embarrassment which these conditions
presented, there were many indications of jealousy on the part
of other powers, in view of the wonderful aggrandizement of
Austria. Encouraged by the emperor's delay and by the hos

ility of other powers, a minority of the nobles chose Stephen Bathori, a Transylvanian prince, King of Poland; and to strengthen his title, married him to Anne, sister to Sigismond Augustus, the King of Poland who preceded the Duke of Anjou. Maximilian thus aroused, signed the articles of agreement, and the two rival monarchs prepared for war. The kingdoms of Europe were arraying themselves, some on the one side and some on the other, and there was the prospect of a long, desperate and bloody strife, when death stilled the tumult.

Maximilian had long been declining. On the 12th of October, 1576, he breathed his last at Ratisbon. He apparently died the death of the Christian, tranquilly surrendering his spirit to his Saviour. He died in the fiftieth year of his age and the twelfth of his reign. He had lived, for those dark days, eminently the life of the righteous, and his end was peace.

> " So fades the summer cloud away,
>   So sinks the gale when storms are o'er
> So gently shuts the eye of day,
>   So dies a wave along the shore.'

CHAPTER XII.

CHARACTER OF MAXIMILIAN II.—SUCCESSION OF RHODOLPH III.

FROM 1576 TO 1604.

CHARACTER OF MAXIMILIAN.—HIS ACCOMPLISHMENTS.—HIS WIFE.—FATE OF HIS CHILDREN.—RHODOLPH III.—THE LIBERTY OF WORSHIP.—MEANS OF EMANCIPATION.— RHODOLPH'S ATTEMPTS AGAINST PROTESTANTISM.—DECLARATION OF A HIGHER LAW. —THEOLOGICAL DIFFERENCES.—THE CONFEDERACY AT HEILBRUN.—THE GREGORIAN CALENDAR.—INTOLERANCE IN BOHEMIA.—THE TRAP OF THE MONKS.—INVASION OF THE TURKS.—THEIR DEFEAT.—COALITION WITH SIGISMOND.—SALE OF TRANSYLVANIA.—RULE OF BASTA.—THE EMPIRE CAPTURED AND RECAPTURED.—DEVASTATION OF THE COUNTRY.—TREATMENT OF STEPHEN BOTSKOI.

IT is indeed refreshing, in the midst of the long list of selfish and ambitious sovereigns who have disgraced the thrones of Europe, to meet with such a prince as Maximilian, a gentleman, a philosopher, a philanthropist and a Christian. Henry of Valois, on his return from Poland to France, visited Maximilian at Vienna. Henry was considered one of the most polished men of his age. He remarked in his palace at Paris that in all his travels he had never met a more accomplished gentleman than the Emperor Maximilian. Similar is the testimony of all his contemporaries. With all alike, at all times, and under all circumstances, he was courteous and affable. His amiability shone as conspicuously at home as abroad, and he was invariably the kind husband, the tender father, the indulgent master and the faithful friend.

In early life he had vigorously prosecuted his studies, and thus possessed the invaluable blessing of a highly cultivated mind. Fond of the languages, he not only wrote and conversed in the Latin tongue with fluency and elegance, but was quite at home in all the languages of his extensive domains.

Notwithstanding the immense cares devolving upon the ruler of so extended an empire, he appropriated a portion of time every day to devotional reading and prayer; and his hours were methodically arranged for business, recreation and repose. The most humble subject found easy access to his person, and always obtained a patient hearing. When he was chosen King of Poland, some ambassadors from Bohemia voluntarily went to Poland to testify to the virtues of their king. It was a heartfelt tribute, such as few sovereigns have ever received.

"We Bohemians," said they, "are as happy under his government as if he were our father. Our privileges, laws, rights, liberties and usages are protected and defended. Not less just than wise, he confers the offices and dignities of the kingdom only on natives of rank, and is not influenced by favor or artifice. He introduces no innovations contrary to our immunities; and when the great expenses which he incurs for the good of Christendom render contributions necessary, he levies them without violence, and with the approbation of the States. But what may be almost considered a miracle is, the prudence and impartiality of his conduct toward persons of a different faith, always recommending union, concord, peace, toleration and mutual regard. He listens even to the meanest of his subjects, readily receives their petitions and renders impartial justice to all."

Not an act of injustice sullied his reign, and during his administration nearly all Germany, with the exception of Hungary, enjoyed almost uninterrupted tranquillity. Catholics and Protestants unite in his praises, and have conferred upon him the surname of the Delight of Mankind. His wife Mary was the daughter of Charles V. She was an accomplished, exemplary woman, entirely devoted to the Catholic faith. For this devotion, notwithstanding the tolerant spirit of her husband, she was warmly extolled by the Catholics. Gregory XIII. called her the firm column of the Catholic faith, and Pius V pronounced her worthy of being worshiped. After the death of her husband she returned to Spain, to the bigoted court of her bigoted brother Philip. Upon reaching Madrid she developed the spirit which dishonored her, in expressing great joy that she was once more in a country where no heretic was tolerated. Soon after she entered a nunnery where she remained seven years until her death.

It is interesting briefly to trace out the history of the children of this royal family. It certainly will not tend to make one any more discontented to move in a humbler sphere. Maximilian left three daughters and five sons.

Anne, the eldest daughter, was engaged to her cousin, Don Carlos, only son of her uncle Philip, King of Spain. As he was consequently heir to the Spanish throne, this was a brilliant match. History thus records the person and character of Don Carlos. He was sickly and one of his legs was shorter than the other. His temper was not only violent, but furious, breaking over all restraints, and the malignant passions were those alone which governed him. He always slept with two naked swords under his pillow, two loaded pistols, and several loaded guns, with a chest of fire-arms at the side of his bed. He formed a conspiracy to murder his father. He was arrested and imprisoned. Choking with rage, he called for a fire and threw himself into the flames, hoping to suffocate himself. Being rescued, he attempted to starve himself. Failing in this, he tried to choke himself by swallowing a diamond. He threw off his clothes, and went naked and barefoot on the stone floor, hoping to engender some fatal disease. For eleven days he took no food but ice. At length the wretched man died, and thus Anne lost her lover. But Philip, the father of Don Carlos, and own uncle of Anne, concluded to take her for himself. She lived a few years as Queen of Spain, and died four years after the death of her father, Maximilian.

Elizabeth, the second daughter, was beautiful. At sixteen years of age she married Charles IX., King of France, who was then twenty years old. Charles IX. ascended the throne when but ten years of age, under the regency of his infamous mother, Catherine de Medici, perhaps the most demoniac female earth has known. Under her tutelage, her boy, equally impotent in body and in mind, became as pitiable a creature as ever disgraced a throne. The only energy he ever showed was in shooting the Protestants from a window of the Louvre in the horrible Massacre of St. Bartholomew, which he planned at the instigation of his fiend-like mother. A few wretched years the youthful queen lived with the monster, when his death released her from that bondage. She then returned to Vienna, a young and childless widow, but twenty years of age. She built and endowed the splendid monastery of St. Mary de Angelis, and having seen enough of the pomp of the world, shut herself up from the world in the imprisonment of its cloisters, where she recounted her beads for nineteen years, until she died in 1592.

Margaret, the youngest daughter, after her father's death, accompanied her mother to Spain. Her sister Anne soon after died, and Philip II., her morose and debauched husband, having already buried four wives, and no one can tell how many guilty favorites, sought the hand of his young and fresh niece. But Margaret wisely preferred the gloom of the cloister to the Babylonish glare of the palace. She rejected the polluted and withered hand, and in solitude and silence, as a hooded nun, she remained immured in her cell for fifty-seven years. Then her pure spirit passed from a joyless life on earth, we trust, to a happy home in heaven.

Rhodolph, the eldest son, succeeded his father, and in the subsequent pages we shall record his career.

Ernest, the second son, was a mild, bashful young man, of a temperament so singularly melancholy that he was rarely known to smile. His brother Rhodolph gave him the appointment of Governor of Hungary. He passed quietly down the stream of time until he was forty-two years of age, when he died of the stone, a disease which had long tortured him with excruciating pargs.

Matthias, the third son, became a restless, turbulent man, whose deeds we shall have occasion to record in connection with his brother Rhodolph, whom he sternly and successfully opposed.

Maximilian, the fourth son, when thirty years of age was elected King of Poland. An opposition party chose John, son of the King of Sweden. The rival candidates appealed to the cruel arbitration of the sword. In a decisive battle Maximilian's troops were defeated, and he was taken prisoner. He was only released upon his giving the pledge that he renounced all his right to the throne. He rambled about, now governing a province, and now fighting the Turks, until he died unmarried, sixty years of age.

Albert, the youngest son, was destined to the Church. He was sent to Spain, and under the patronage of his royal uncle he soon rose to exalted ecclesiastical dignities. He, however, eventually renounced these for more alluring temporal honors. Surrendering his cardinal's hat, and archiepiscopal robes, he espoused Isabella, daughter of Philip, and from the governorship of Portugal was promoted to the sovereignty of the Netherlands. Here he encountered only opposition and war. After a stormy and unsuccessful life, in which he was thwarted in all his plans, he died childless.

From this digression let us return to Rhodolph III., the heir to the titles and the sovereignties of his father the emperor. It was indeed a splendid inheritance which fell to his lot. He was the sole possessor of the archduchy of Austria, King of Bohemia and of Hungary, and Emperor of Germany. He was but twenty-five years of age when he entered upon the undisputed possession of all these dignities. His natural disposition was mild and amiable, his education had been carefully attended to, his moral character was good, a rare virtue in those days, and he had already evinced much industry, en-

erg} and talents for business. His father had left the finances
and the internal administration of all his realms in good condition ; his moderation had greatly mitigated the religious
animosities which disturbed other portions of Europe, and all
obstacles to a peaceful and prosperous reign seemed to have
been removed.

But all these prospects were blighted by the religious bigotry which had gained a firm hold of the mind of the young
emperor. When he was but twelve years of age he was sent
to Madrid to be educated. Philip II., of Spain, Rhodolph's
uncle, had an only daughter, and no son, and there seemed to
be no prospect that his queen would give birth to another
child. Philip consequently thought of adopting Rhodolph as
his successor to the Spanish throne, and of marrying him to
his daughter. In the court of Spain where the Jesuits held
supreme sway, and where Rhodolph was intrusted to their
guidance, the superstitious sentiments which he had imbibed
from his mother were still more deeply rooted. The Jesuits
found Rhodolph a docile pupil; and never on earth have there
been found a set of men who, more thoroughly than the Jesuits, have understood the art of educating the mind to subjection. Rhodolph was instructed in all the petty arts of
intrigue and dissimulation, and was brought into entire subserviency to the Spanish court. Thus educated, Rhodolph
received the crown.

He commenced his reign with the desperate resolve to
crush out Protestantism, either by force or guile, and to bring
back.his realms to the papal church. Even the toleration of
Maximilian, in those dark days, did not allow freedom of
worship to any but the nobles. The wealthy and emancipated
citizens. of Vienna, and other royal cities, could not establish
a church of their own ; they could only, under protection of
the nobles, attend the churches which the nobles sustained.
In other words, the people were slaves, who were hardly
thought of in any state arrangements. The nobles were

merely the slaveholders. As there was not difference of color to mark the difference between the slaveholder and the slaves or vassals, many in the cities, who had in various ways achieved their emancipation, had become wealthy and instructed, and were slowly claiming some few rights. The country nobles could assemble their vassals in the churches where they had obtained toleration. In some few cases some of the citizens of the large towns, who had obtained emancipation from some feudal oppressions, had certain defined political privileges granted them. But, in general, the nobles or slaveholders, some having more, and some having less wealth and power, were all whom even Maximilian thought of including in his acts of toleration. A learned man in the universities, or a wealthy man in the walks of commerce, was compelled to find shelter under the protection of some powerful noble. There were nobles of all ranks, from the dukes, who could bring twenty thousand armed men into the field, down to the most petty, impoverished baron, who had perhaps not half a dozen vassals.

Rhodolph's first measure was to prevent the *burghers*, as they were called, who were those who had in various ways obtained emancipation from vassal service, and in the large cities had acquired energy, wealth and an air of independence, from attending Protestant worship. The nobles were very jealous of their privileges, and were prompt to combine whenever they thought them infringed. Fearful of rousing the nobles, Rhodolph issued a decree, confirming the toleration which his father had granted the nobles, but forbidding the burghers from attending Protestant worship. This was very adroitly done, as it did not interfere with the vassals of the rural nobles on their estates; and these burghers were freed men, over whom the nobles could claim no authority. At the same time Rhodolph silenced three of the most eloquent and influential of the Protestant ministers, under the plea that they assailed the Catholic church with too much viru-

lence ; and he also forbade any one thenceforward to officiate
as a Protestant clergyman without a license from him. These
were very decisive acts, and yet very adroit ones, as they
did not directly interfere with any of the immunities of the
nobles.

The Protestants were, however, much alarmed by these
measures, as indicative of the intolerant policy of the new
king. The preachers met together to consult. They corre-
sponded with foreign universities respecting the proper course
to pursue ; and the Protestant nobles met to confer upon the
posture of affairs. As the result of their conferences, they
issued a remonstrance, declaring that they could not yield to
such an infringement of the rights of conscience, and that
" they were bound to obey God rather than man."

Rhodolph was pleased with this resistance, as it afforded
him some excuse for striking a still heavier blow. He declared the remonstrants guilty of rebellion. As a punishment,
he banished several Protestant ministers, and utterly forbade
the exercise of any Protestant worship whatever, in any of
the royal towns, including Vienna itself. He communicated
with the leading Catholics in the Church and in the State,
urging them to act with energy, concert and unanimity. He
removed the Protestants from office, and supplied their places
with Catholics. He forbade any license to preach or aca-
demical degree, or professorship in the universities from being
conferred upon any one who did not sign the formulary of
the Catholic faith. He ordered a new catechism to be drawn
up for universal use in the schools, that there should be no
more Protestant education of children ; he allowed no town
to choose any officer without his approbation, and he refused
to ratify any choice which did not fall upon a Catholic. No
person was to be admitted to the rights of burghership, until
he had taken an oath of submission to the Catholic priest-
hood. These high-handed measures led to the outbreak of a
few insurrections, which the emperor crushed with iron rigor

In the course of a few years, by the vigorous and unrelenting prosecution of these measures, Rhodolph gave the Catholics the ascendency in all his realms.

While the Catholics were all united, the Protestants were shamefully divided upon the most trivial points of discipline, or upon abstruse questions in philosophy above the reach of mortal minds. It was as true then, as in the days of our Saviour, that "the children of this world are wiser in their generation than the children of light." Henry IV., of France, who had not then embraced the Catholic faith, was anxious to unite the two great parties of Lutherans and Calvinists, who were as hostile to each other as they were to the Catholics. He sent an ambassador to Germany to urge their union. He entreated them to call a general synod, suggesting, that as they differed only on the single point of the Lord's Supper, it would be easy for them to form some basis of fraternal and harmonious action.

The Catholic church received the doctrine, so called, of *transubstantiation ;* that is, the bread and wine, used in the Lord's Supper, is converted into the actual body and blood of Jesus Christ, that it is no longer bread and wine, but real flesh and blood ; and none the less so, because it does not appear such to our senses. Luther renounced the doctrine of transubstantiation, and adopted, in its stead, what he called *consubstantiation ;* that is, that after the consecration of the elements, the body and blood of Christ are substantially *present with* (cum et sub,) with and under, the substance of the bread and wine. Calvin taught that the bread and wine represented the real body and blood of Christ, and that the body and blood were *spiritually present* in the sacrament. It is a deplorable exhibition of the weakness of good men, that the Lutherans and the Calvinists should have wasted their energies in contending together upon such a point. But we moderns have no right to boast. Precisely the same spirit is manifested now, and denominations differ and strive together upon questions which the human mind can never settle. The spirit which then animated the two parties may be inferred from the reply of the Lutherans.

" The partisans of Calvin," they wrote, " have accumulated such numberless errors in regard to the person of Christ, the communication of His merits and the dignity of human nature : have given such forced explanations of the Scriptures, and adopted so many blasphemies, that the question of the Lord's Supper, far from being the principal, has become the least point of difference.   An outward union, merely for worldly purposes, in which each party is suffered to maintain its peculiar tenets, can neither be agreeable to God nor useful to the Church.   These considerations induced us to insert into the formulary of concord a condemnation of the Calvinistical errors; and to declare our public decision that false principles should not be covered with the semblance of exterior union, and tolerated under pretense of the right of private judgment, but that all should submit to the Word of God, as the only rule to which their faith and instructions should be conformable."

They, in conclusion, very politely informed King Henry IV. himself, that if he wished to unite with them, he must sign their creed.   This was sincerity, honesty, but it was the sincerity and honesty of minds but partially disinthralled from the bigotry of the dark ages.   While the Protestants were thus unhappily disunited, the pope coöperated with the emperor, and wheeled all his mighty forces into the line to recover the ground which the papal church had lost.   Several of the more enlightened of the Protestant princes, seeing all their efforts paralyzed by disunion, endeavored to heal the schism.   But the Lutheran leaders would not listen to the Calvinists, nor the Calvinists to the Lutherans, and the masses, as usual, blindly followed their leaders.

Several of the Calvinist princes and nobles, the Lutherans refusing to meet with them, united in a confederacy at Heil-

I

brun, and drew up a long list of grievances, declaring that, until they were redressed, they should withhold the succors which the emperor had solicited to repel the Turks. Most of these grievances were very serious, sufficiently so to rouse men to almost any desperation of resistance. But it would be amusing, were it not humiliating, to find among them the complaint that the pope had changed the calendar from the Julian to the Gregorian.

By the Julian calendar, or Old Style as it was called, the solar year was estimated at three hundred and sixty-five days and six hours; but it exceeds this by about eleven minutes. As no allowance was made for these minutes, which amount to a day in about one hundred and thirty years, the current year had, in process of ages, advanced ten days beyond the real time. Thus the vernal equinox, which really took place on the 10th of March, was assigned in the calendar to the 21st. To rectify this important error the New Style, or Gregorian calendar, was introduced, so called from Pope Gregory XII. Ten days were dropped after the 4th of October, 1582, and the 5th was called the 15th. This reform of the calendar, correct and necessary as it was, was for a long time adopted only by the Catholic princes, so hostile were the Protestants to any thing whatever which originated from the pope. In their list of grievances they mentioned this most salutary reform as one, stating that the pope and the Jesuits presumed even to change the order of times and years.

This confederacy of the Calvinists, unaided by the Lutherans, accomplished nothing; but still, as year after year the disaffection increased, their numbers gradually increased also, until, on the 12th of February, 1603, at Heidelberg they entered into quite a formidable alliance, offensive and defensive.

Rhodolph, encouraged by success, pressed his measure of intolerance with renovated vigor. Having quite effectually abolished the Protestant worship in the States of Austria, he turned his attention to Bohemia, where, under the mild gov ernment of his father, the Protestants had enjoyed a degree of liberty of conscience hardly known in any other part of Europe. The realm was startled by the promulgation of a decree forbidding both Calvinists and Lutherans from holding any meetings for divine worship, and declaring them incapacitated from holding any official employment whatever. At the same time he abolished all their schools, and either closed all their churches, or placed in them Catholic preachers. These same decrees were also promulgated and these same measures adopted in Hungary. And still the Protestants, insanely quarreling among themselves upon the most abstruse points of theological philosophy, chose rather to be devoured piecemeal by their great enemy than to combine in self-defense.

The emperor now turned from his own dominions of Austria, Hungary and Bohemia, where he reigned in undisputed sway, to other States of the empire, which were governed by their own independent rulers and laws, and where the power of the emperor was shadowy and limited. He began with the city of Aix-la-Chapelle, in a Prussian province on the Lower Rhine; sent an army there, took possession of the town, expelled the Protestants from the magistracy, driving some of them into exile, inflicting heavy fines upon others, and abolishing entirely the exercise of the Protestant religion.

He then turned to Donauworth, an important city of Bavaria, upon the Upper Danube. This was a Protestant city, having within its walls but few Catholics. There was in the city one Catholic religious establishment, a Benedictine abbey. The friars enjoyed unlimited freedom of conscience and worship within their own walls, but were not permitted to occupy the streets with their processions, performing the forms and ceremonies of the Catholic church. The Catholics, encouraged by the emperor, sent out a procession from the walls of the abbey, with torches, banners, relics and all the pageants of Catholic worship. The magistrates stopped the procession, took away their banners and sent them back to

the abbey, and then suffered the procession to proceed. Soon
after the friars got up another procession on a funeral occa
sion. The magistrates, apprehensive that this was a trap to
excite them to some opposition which would render it plausi
ble for the emperor to interfere, suffered the procession to
proceed unmolested. In a few days the monks repeated the
experiment. The populace had now become excited, and there
were threats of violence. The magistrates, fearful of the consequences, did every thing in their power to soothe the people, and urged them, by earnest proclamation, to abstain from
all tumult. For some time the procession, displaying all the
hated pomp of papal worship, paraded the streets undisturbed.
But at length the populace became ungovernable, attacked the
monks, demolished their pageants and pelted them with mire
back into the convent.

This was enough. The emperor published the ban of the
empire, and sent the Duke of Bavaria with an army to execute
the decree. Resistance was hopeless. The troops took possession of the town, abolished the Protestant religion, and delivered the churches to the Catholics.

The Protestants now saw that there was no hope for them
but in union. Thus driven together by an outward pressure
which was every day growing more menacing and severe, the
chiefs of the Protestant party met at Aschhausen and established a confederacy to continue for ten years. Thus united,
they drew up a list of grievances, and sent an embassy to present their demands to the emperor. And now came a very
serious turn in the fortunes of Rhodolph. Notwithstanding
the armistice which had been concluded with the Turks by
Rhodolph, a predatory warfare continued to rage along the
borders. Neither the emperor nor the sultan, had they wished
it, could prevent fiery spirits, garrisoned in fortresses frowning
at each other, from meeting occasionally in hostile encounter.
And both parties were willing that their soldiers should have
enough to do to keep up their courage and their warlike spirit

Aggression succeeding aggression, sometimes on one side and sometimes on the other, the sultan at last, in a moment of exasperation, resolved to break the truce.

A large army of Turks invaded Croatia, took several fortresses, and marching up the valley of the Save, were opening before them a route into the heart of the Austrian States. The emperor hastily gathered an army to oppose them. They met before Siseck, at the confluence of the Kulpa and the Save. The Turks were totally defeated, with the loss of twelve thousand men. Exasperated by the defeat, the sultan roused his energies anew, and war again raged in all its horrors. The advantage was with the Turks, and they gradually forced their way up the valley of the Danube, taking fortress after fortress, till they were in possession of the important town of Raab, within a hundred miles of Vienna.

Sigismond, the waivode or governor of Transylvania, an energetic, high-spirited man, had, by his arms, brought the provinces of Wallachia and Moldavia under subjection to him. Having attained such power, he was galled at the idea of holding his government under the protection of the Turks. He accordingly abandoned the sultan, and entered into a coalition with the emperor. The united armies fell furiously upon the Turks, and drove them back to Constantinople.

The sultan, himself a man of exceedingly ferocious character, was thoroughly aroused by this disgrace. He raised an immense army, placed himself at its head, and in 1596 again invaded Hungary. He drove the Austrians everywhere before him, and but for the lateness of the season would have bombarded Vienna. Sigismond, in the hour of victory, sold Transylvania to Rhodolph for the governorship of some provinces in Silesia, and a large annual pension. There was some fighting before the question was fully settled in favor of the emperor, and then he placed the purchased and the conquered province under the government of the imperial general Basta.

The rule of Basta was so despotic that the Transylvanians

rose in revolt, and under an intrepid chief, Moses Tzekeli, appealed to the Turks for aid. The Turks were rejoiced again to
find the Christians divided, and hastened to avail themselves of
the coöperation of the disaffected. The Austrians were driven
from Transylvania, and the Turks aided in crowning Tzekeli
Prince of Transylvania, under the protection of the Porte.
The Austrians, however, soon returned in greater force, killed
Tzekeli in the confusion of battle, and reconquered the country. During all this time wretched Hungary was ravaged
with incessant wars between the Turks and Austrians. Army
after army swept to and fro over the smoldering cities and
desolated plains. Neither party gained any decisive advantage, while Hungary was exposed to misery which no pen can
describe. Cities were bombarded, now by the Austrians and
now by the Turks, villages were burned, harvests trodden
down, every thing eatable was consumed. Outrages were
perpetrated upon the helpless population by the ferocious
Turks which can not be told.

The Hungarians lost all confidence in Rhodolph. The bigoted emperor was so much engaged in the attempt to extirpate what he called heresy from his realms, that he neglected
to send armies sufficiently strong to protect Hungary from
these ravages. He could have done this without much difficulty; but absorbed in his hostility to Protestantism, he merely sent sufficient troops to Hungary to keep the country in a
constant state of warfare. He filled every important governmental post in Hungary with Catholics and foreigners. To all
the complaints of the Hungarians he turned a deaf ear; and
his own Austrian troops frequently rivaled the Turks in devastation and pillage. At the same time he issued the most
intolerant edicts, depriving the Protestants of all their rights,
and endeavoring to force the Roman Catholic religion upon
the community.

He allowed, and even encouraged, his rapacious generals
to insult and defraud the Protestant Hungarian nobles, seiz

ing their castles, confiscating their estates and driving them into exile. This oppression at last became unendurable. The people were driven to despair. One of the most illustrious nobles of Hungary, a magnate of great wealth and distinction, Stephen Botskoi, repaired to Prague to inform the emperor ot the deplorable state of Hungary and to seek redress. He was treated with the utmost indignity; was detained for hours in the ante-chamber of the emperor, where he encountered the most cutting insults from the minions of the court. The indignation of the high-spirited noble was roused to the highest pitch. And when, on his return to Hungary, he found his estates plundered and devastated by order of the imperial governor, he was all ready to head an insurrection.

CHAPTER XIII.

RHODOLPH III. AND MATTHIAS.

FROM 1604 TO 1609.

STEPHEN BOTSKOI issued a spirited manifesto to his countrymen, urging them to seek by force of arms that redress which they could obtain in no other way. The Hungarians flocked in crowds to his standard. Many soldiers deserted from the service of the emperor and joined the insurrection. Botskoi soon found himself in possession of a force sufficiently powerful to meet the Austrian troops in the field. The two hostile armies soon met in the vicinity of Cassau. The imperial troops were defeated with great slaughter, and the city of Cassau fell into the hands of Botskoi; soon his victorious troops took several other important fortresses. The inhabitants of Transylvania, encouraged by the success of Botskoi, and detesting the imperial rule, also in great numbers crowded his ranks and intreated him to march into Transylvania. He promptly obeyed their summons. The misery of the Transylvanians was, if possible, still greater than that of the Hungarians. Their country presented but a wide expanse of ruin and starvation. Every aspect of comfort and industry was obliterated. The famishing inhabitants were compelled to use the most disgusting animals for food; and when these were

gone, in many cases they went to the grave-yard, in the frenzied torments of hunger, and devoured the decaying bodies of
the dead.   Pestilence followed in the train of these woes, and
the land was filled with the dying and the dead.

The Turks marched to the aid of Botskoi to expel the Austrians.   Even the sway of the Mussulman was preferable to
that of the bigoted Rhodolph.   Hungary, Transylvania and
Turkey united, and the detested Austrians were driven out of
Transylvania, and Botskoi, at the head of his victorious army,
and hailed by thousands as the deliverer of Transylvania, was
inaugurated prince of the province.   He then returned to
Hungary, where an immense Turkish army received him, in
the plains of Rahoz, with regal honors.   Here a throne was
erected.   The banners of the majestic host fluttered in the
breeze, and musical bands filled the air with their triumphal
strains as the regal diadem was placed upon the brow of Botskoi, and he was proclaimed King of Hungary.   The Sultan
Achment sent, with his congratulations to the victorious noble, a saber of exquisite temper and finish, and a gorgeous
standard.   The grand vizier himself placed the royal diadem
upon his brow.

Botskoi was a nobleman in every sense of the word.   He
thought it best publicly to accept these honors in gratitude to
the sultan for his friendship and aid, and also to encourage and
embolden the Hungarians to retain what they had already acquired.   He knew that there were bloody battles still before
them, for the emperor would doubtless redouble his efforts to
regain his Hungarian possessions.   At the same time Botskoi,
in the spirit of true patriotism, was not willing even to appear
to have usurped the government through the energies of the
sword.   He therefore declared that he should not claim the
crown unless he should be freely elected by the nobles ; and
that he accepted these honors simply as tokens of the confidence of the allied army, and as a means of strengthening
their power to resist the emperor.

The campaign was now urged with great vigor, and nearly all of Hungary was conquered. Such was the first great disaster which the intolerance and folly of Rhodolph brought upon him. The Turks and the Hungarians were now good friends, cordially coöperating. A few more battles would place them in possession of the whole of Hungary, and then, in their alliance they could defy all the power of the emperor, and penetrate even the very heart of his hereditary dominions of Austria. Rhodolph, in this sudden peril, knew not where to look for aid. The Protestants, who constituted one half of the physical force, not only of Bohemia and of the Austrian States, but of all Germany, had been insulted and oppressed beyond all hope of reconciliation. They dreaded the papal emperor more than the Mohammedan sultan. They were ready to hail Botskoi as their deliverer from intolerable despotism, and to swell the ranks of his army. Botskoi was a Protestant, and the sympathies of the Protestants all over Germany were with him. Elated by his advance, the Protestants withheld all contributions from the emperor, and began to form combinations in favor of the Protestant chief. Rhodolph was astonished at this sudden reverse, and quite in dismay. He had no resource but to implore the aid of the Spanish court.

Rhodolph was as superstitious as he was bigoted and cruel. Through the mysteries of alchymy he had been taught to believe that his life would be endangered by one of his own blood. The idea haunted him by night and by day; he was to be assassinated, and by a near relative. He was afraid to marry lest his own child might prove his destined murderer. He was afraid to have his brothers marry lest it might be a nephew who was to perpetrate the deed. He did not dare to attend church, or to appear any where in public without taking the greatest precautions against any possibility of attack. The galleries of his palace were so arranged with windows in the

roof, that he could pass from one apartment to another shel
tered by impenetrable walls.

This terror, which pursued him every hour, palsied his en·
ergies ; and while the Turks were drawing nearer to his capi
tal, and Hungary had broken from his sway, and insurrection
was breaking out in all parts of his dominions, he secluded
himself in the most retired apartments of his palace at Prague,
haunted by visions of terror, as miserable himself as he had
already made millions of his subjects.   He devoted himself to
the study of the mystic sciences of astrology and alchymy·
He became irritable, morose, and melancholy even to madness.   Foreign ambassadors could not get admission to his
presence.   His religion, consisting entirely in ecclesiastical rit·
uals and papal dogmas, not in Christian morals, could not
dissuade him from the most degrading sensual vice.   Low
born mistresses, whom he was continually changing, became
his only companions, and thus sunk in sin, shame and misery,
he virtually abandoned his ruined realms to their fate.

Rhodolph had received the empire from the hands of his
noble father in a state of the very highest prosperity.   In
thirty years, by shameful misgovernment, he had carried it to
the brink of ruin.   Rhodolph's third brother, Matthias, was
now forty-nine years of age.   He had been educated by the
illustrious Busbequias, whose mind had been liberalized by
study in the most celebrated universities of Flanders, France
and Italy.   His teacher had passed many years as an ambassador in the court of the sultan, and thus had been able to give
his pupil a very intimate acquaintance with the resources, the
military tactics, the manners and customs of the Turks.   He
excelled in military exercises, and was passionately devoted to
the art of war.   In all respects he was the reverse of his
brother—energetic, frank, impulsive.   The two brothers, so
dissimilar, had no ideas in common, and were always involved
in bickerings.

The Netherlands had risen in revolt against the infamous

Philip II. of Spain.   They chose the intrepid and warlike Matthias as their leader.   With alacrity he assumed the perilous
post.   The rivalry of the chiefs thwarted his plans, and he resigned his post and returned to Austria, where his brother, the
emperor, refused even to see him, probably fearing assassination.   Matthias took up his residence at Lintz, where he lived
for some time in obscurity and penury.   His imperial brother
would neither give him help nor employment.   The restless
prince fretted like a tiger in his cage.

In 1595 Rhodolph's second brother, Ernest, died childless,
and thus Matthias became heir presumptive to the crown of
Austria.   From that time Rhodolph made a change, and intrusted him with high offices.   Still the brothers were no
nearer to each other in affection.   Rhodolph dreaded the ambition and was jealous of the rising power of his brother.
He no longer dared to treat him ignominiously, lest his brother
should be provoked to some desperate act of retaliation.   On
the other hand, Matthias despised the weakness and superstition of Rhodolph.   The increasing troubles in the realm and
the utter inefficiency of Rhodolph, convinced Matthias that
the day was near when he must thrust Rhodolph from the
throne he disgraced, and take his seat upon it, or the splendid
hereditary domains which had descended to them from their
ancestors would pass from their hands forever.

With this object in view, he did all he could to conciliate
the Catholics, while he attempted to secure the Protestants by
promising to return to the principles of toleration established
by his father, Maximilian.   Matthias rapidly increased in popularity, and as rapidly Rhodolph was sinking into disgrace.
Catholics and Protestants saw alike that the ruin of Austria
was impending, and that apparently there was no hope but in
the deposition of Rhodolph and the enthronement of Matthias.

It was not difficult to accomplish this revolution, and yet
it required energy, secrecy and an extended combination.
Even the weakest reigning monarch has power in his hands

which can only be wrested from him by both strength and
skill. Matthias first gained over to his plan his younger
brother, Maximilian, and two of his cousins, princes of the
Styrian line. They entered into a secret agreement, by which
they declared that in consequence of the incapacity of Rhodolph, he was to be considered as deposed by the will of
Providence, and that Matthias was entitled to the sovereignty
as head of the house of Austria. Matthias then gained, by
the varied arts of diplomatic bargaining, the promised support
of several other princes. He purchased the coöperation of Botskoi by surrendering to him the whole of Transylvania, and all
of Hungary to the river Theiss, which, including Transylvania,
constitutes one half of the majestic kingdom. Matthias agreed
to grant general toleration to all Protestants, both Lutherans
and Calvinists, and also to render them equally eligible with
the Catholics to all offices of emolument and honor. Both
parties then agreed to unite against the Turks if they refused
to accede to honorable terms of peace. The sultan, conscious
that such a union would be more than he could successfully
oppose, listened to the conditions of peace when they afterwards made them, as he had never condescended to listen before. It is indicative of the power which the Turks had at
that day attained, that a truce with the sultan for twenty
years, allowing each party to retain possession of the territories which they then held, was purchased by paying a sum
outright, amounting to two hundred thousand dollars. The
annual tribute, however, was no longer to be paid, and thus
Christendom was released from the degradation of vassalage
to the Turk.

Rhodolph, who had long looked with a suspicious eye upon
Matthias, watching him very narrowly, began now to see indications of the plot. He therefore, aided by the counsel and
the energy of the King of Spain, who was implacable in his
hostility to Matthias, resolved to make his cousin Ferdinand,
a Styrian prince, his heir to succeed him upon the throne

He conferred upon Ferdinand exalted dignities; appointed him to preside in his stead at a diet at Ratisbon, and issued a proclamation full of most bitter recriminations against Matthias.

Matters had now come to such a pass that Matthias was compelled either to bow in humble submission to his brother, or by force of arms to execute his purposes. With such an alternative he was not a man long to delay his decision. Still he advanced in his plans, though firmly, with great circumspection. To gain the Protestants was to gain one half of the physical power of united Austria, and more than one half of its energy and intelligence. He appointed a rendezvous for his troops at Znaim in Moravia, and while Rhodolph was timidly secluding himself in his palace at Prague, Matthias left Vienna with ten thousand men, and marched to meet them. He was received by the troops assembled at Znaim with enthusiasm. Having thus collected an army of twenty-five thousand men, he entered Bohemia. On the 10th of May, 1608, he reached Craslau, within sixty miles of Prague. Great multitudes now crowded around him and openly espoused his cause. He now declared openly and to all, that it was his intention to depose his brother and claim for himself the government of Hungary, Austria and Bohemia.

He then urged his battalions onward, and pressed with rapid march towards Prague. Rhodolph was now roused to some degree of energy. He summoned all his supporters to rally around him. It was a late hour for such a call, but the Catholic nobles generally, all over the kingdom, were instantly in motion. Many Protestant nobles also attended the assembly, hoping to extort from the emperor some measures of toleration. The emperor was so frightened that he was ready to promise almost any thing. He even crept from his secluded apartments and presided over the meeting in person. The Protestant nobles drew up a paper demanding the same toleration which Maximilian had granted, with the additional permis sion to build churches and to have their own burying-grounds. With this paper, to which five or six hundred signatures were attached, they went to the palace, demanded admission to the emperor, and required him immediately to give his assent to them. It was not necessary for them to add any threat, for the emperor knew that there was an Austrian and Hungarian army within a few hours' march.

While matters were in this state, commissioners from Matthias arrived to inform the king that he must cede the crown to his brother and retire into the Tyrol. The emperor, in terror, inquired, " What shall I do ?" The Protestants demanded an immediate declaration, either that he would or would not grant their request. His friends told him that resistance was unavailing, and that he must come to an accommodation. Still the emperor had now thirty-six thousand troops in and around Prague. They were, however, inspired with no enthusiasm for his person, and it was quite doubtful whether they would fight. A few skirmishes took place between the advance guards with such results as to increase Rhodolph's alarm.

He consequently sent envoys to his brother. They met at Liebau, and after a negotiation of four days they made a partial compromise, by which Rhodolph ceded to Matthias, without reservation, Hungary, Austria and Moravia. Matthias was also declared to be the successor to the crown of Bohemia should Rhodolph die without issue male, and Matthias was immediately to assume the title of " appointed King of Bohemia." The crown and scepter of Hungary were surrendered to Matthias. He received them with great pomp at the head of his army, and then leading his triumphant battalions out of Bohemia, he returned to Vienna and entered the city with all the military parade of a returning conqueror.

Matthias had now gained his great object, but he was not at all inclined to fulfill his promises. He assembled the nobles of Austria, to receive from them their oaths of allegiance. But the Protestants, taught caution by long experience, wished first to see the decree of toleration which he had promised. Many of the Protestants, at a distance from the capital, not waiting for the issuing of the decree, but relying upon his promise, reëstablished their worship, and the Lord of Inzendorf threw open his chapel to the citizens of the town. But Matthias was now disposed to play the despot. He arrested the Lord of Inzendorf, and closed his church. He demanded of all the lords, Protestant as well as Catholic, an unconditional oath of allegiance, giving vague promises, that perhaps at some future time he would promulgate a decree of toleration, but declaring that he was not bound to do so, on the miserable quibble that, as he had received from Rhodolph a hereditary title, he was not bound to grant any thing but what he had received.

The Protestants were alarmed and exasperated. They grasped their arms; they retired in a body from Vienna to Hern; threw garrisons and provisions into several important fortresses; ordered a levy of every fifth man; sent to Hungary and Moravia to rally their friends there, and with amazing energy and celerity formed a league for the defense of their faith. Matthias was now alarmed. He had not anticipated such energetic action, and he hastened to Presburg, the capital of Hungary, to secure, if possible, a firm seat upon the throne. A large force of richly caparisoned troops followed him, and he entered the capital with splendor, which he hoped would dazzle the Hungarians. The regal crown and regalia, studded with priceless jewels, which belonged to Hungary, he took with him, with great parade. Hungary had been deprived of these treasures, which were the pride of the nation, for seventy years. But the Protestant nobles were not to be cajoled with such tinsel. They remained firm in their demands, and refused to accept him as their sovereign until the promised toleration was granted. Their claims were very distinct and intelligible, demanding full toleration for both Calvinists and Lutherans, and equal eligibility for Protestants

with Catholics, to all governmental offices; none but native
Hungarians were to be placed in office; the king was to reside
in Hungary, and when necessarily absent, was to intrust the
government to a regent, chosen jointly by the king and the
nobles; Jesuits were not to be admitted into the kingdom;
no foreign troops were to be admitted, unless there was war
with the Turks, and the king was not to declare war without
the consent of the nobles.

Matthias was very reluctant to sign such conditions, for he
was very jealous of his newly-acquired power as a sovereign
But a refusal would have exposed him to a civil war, with such
forces arrayed against him as to render the result at least
doubtful. The Austrian States were already in open insurrection. The emissaries of Rhodolph were busy, fanning the
flames of discontent, and making great promises to those who
would restore Rhodolph to the throne. Intolerant and odious
as Rhodolph had been, his great reverses excited sympathy,
and many were disposed to regard Matthias but as a usurper.
Thus influenced, Matthias not only signed all the conditions,
but was also constrained to carry them into immediate execution. These conditions being fulfilled, the nobles met on the
19th of November, 1606, and elected Matthias king, and inaugurated him with the customary forms.

Matthias now returned to Vienna, to quell the insurrection
in the Austrian States. The two countries were so entirely
independent of each other, though now under the same ruler,
that he had no fear that his Hungarian subjects would interfere at all in the internal administration of Austria. Matthias
was resolved to make up for the concessions he had granted
the Hungarians, by ruling with more despotic sway in Austria.
The pope proffered him his aid. The powerful bishops of
Passau and Vienna assured him of efficient support, and encouraged the adoption of energetic measures. Thus strengthened Matthias, who was so pliant and humble in Hungary,
assumed the most haughty airs of the sovereign in Austria.

He peremptorily ordered the Protestants to be silent, and to cease their murmurings, or he would visit them with the most exemplary punishment.

North-east of the duchy of Austria, and lying between the kingdoms of Hungary and Bohemia, was the province of Moravia. This territory was about the size of the State of Massachusetts, and its chief noble, or governor, held the title of margrave, or marquis. Hence the province, which belonged to the Austrian empire, was called the margraviate of Moravia. It contained a population of a little over a million. The nobles of Moravia immediately made common cause with those of Austria, for they knew that they must share the same fate. Matthias was again alarmed, and brought to terms. On the 16th of March, 1609, he signed a capitulation, which restored to all the Austrian provinces all the toleration which they had enjoyed under Maximilian II. The nobles then, of all the States of Austria, took the oath of allegiance to Matthias.

The ambitious monarch, having thus far succeeded, looked with a covetous eye towards Transylvania. That majestic province, on the eastern borders of Hungary, being three times the size of Massachusetts, and containing a population of about two millions, would prove a splendid addition to the Hungarian kingdom. While Matthias was secretly encouraging what in modern times and republican parlance is called a fillibustering expedition, for the sake of annexing Transylvania to the area of Hungary, a new object of ambition, and one still more alluring, opened before him.

The Protestants in Bohemia were quite excited when they heard of the great privileges which their brethren in Hungary, and in the Austrian provinces had extorted from Matthias. This rendered them more restless under the intolerable burdens imposed upon them. Soon after the armies of Matthias had withdrawn from Bohemia, Rhodolph, according to his promise, summoned a diet to deliberate upon the state of affairs. The Protestants, who despised Rhodolph, attended th diet, resolved to demand reform, and, if necessary, to seek it by force of arms. They at once assumed a bold front, and refused to discuss any civil affairs whatever, until the freedom of religious worship, which they had enjoyed under Maximilian, was restored to them. But Rhodolph, infatuated, and under the baleful influence of the Jesuits, refused to listen to their appeal.

Matthias, informed of this state of affairs, saw that there was a fine opportunity for him to place himself at the head of the Protestants, who constituted not only a majority in Bohemia, but were also a majority in the diet. He therefore sent his emissaries among them to encourage them with assurances of his sympathy and aid. The diet which Rhodolph had summoned, separated without coming to other result than rousing thoroughly the spirit of the Protestants. They boldly called another diet to meet in May, in the city of Prague itself, under the very shadow of the palace of Rhodolph, and sent deputies to Matthias, and to the Protestant princes generally of the German empire, soliciting their support. Rhodolph issued a proclamation forbidding them to meet. Regardless of this injunction they met, at the appointed time and place, opened the meeting with imposing ceremonies, and made quiet preparation to repel force with force. These preparations were so effectually made that upon an alarm being given that the troops of Rhodolph were approaching to disperse the assembly, in less than an hour twelve hundred mounted knights and more than ten thousand foot soldiers surrounded their hall as a guard.

This was a very broad hint to the emperor, and it surprisingly enlightened him. He began to bow and to apologize, and to asseverate upon his word of honor that he meant to do what was right, and from denunciations, he passed by a single step to cajolery and fawning. It was, however, only his intention to gain time till he could secure the coöperation of the pope, and other Catholic princes. The Protestants, however, were not to be thus deluded. As unmindful of his protestations as they had been of his menaces, they proceeded esolutely in establishing an energetic organization for the defense of their civil and religious rights. They decreed the levying of an army, and appointed three of the most distinguished nobles as generals. The decree was hardly passed before it was carried into execution, and an army of three thousand foot soldiers, and two thousand horsemen was assembled as by magic, and their numbers were daily increasing.

Rhodolph, still cloistered in his palace, looked with amazement upon this' rising storm. He had no longer energy for any decisive action. With mulish obstinaey he would concede nothing, neither had he force of character to marsha. any decisive resistance. But at last he saw that the hand of Matthias was also in the movement; that his ambitious, unrelenting brother was coöperating with his foes, and would inevitably hurl him from the throne of Bohemia, as he had already done from the kingdom of Hungary and from the dukedom of Austria. He was panic-stricken by this sudden revelation, and in the utmost haste issued a decree, dated July 5th, 1609, granting to the Protestants full toleration of religious worship, and every other right they had demanded. The despotic old king became all of a sudden as docile and pliant as a child. He assured his faithful and well-beloved Protestant subjects that they might worship God in their own chapels without any molestation; that they might build churches; that they might establish schools for their children; that their clergy might meet in ecclesiastical councils; that they might choose chiefs, who should be confirmed by the sovereign, to watch over their religious privileges and to guard against any infringement of this edict; and finally, all ordinances contrary to this act of free and full toleration, which might hereafter be issued, either by the present sovereign or any of his successors, were declared null and void.

The Protestants behaved nobly in this hour of bloodless triumph. Their demands were reasonable and honorable, and they sought no infringement whatever of the rights of others. Their brethren of Silesia had aided them in this great achieve-ment. The duchy of Silesia was then dependent upon Bohe-mia, and was just north of Moldavia. It contained a popula-tion of about a million and a half, scattered over a territory of about fifteen thousand square miles. The Protestants de-manded that the Silesians should share in the decree. "Most certainly," replied the amiable Rhodolph. An act of general amnesty for all political offenses was then passed, and peace was restored to Germany.

Never was more forcibly seen, than on this occasion, the power of the higher classes over the masses of the people. In fact, popular tumults, disgraceful mobs, are almost invariably excited by the higher classes, who push the mob on while they themselves keep in the background. It was now for the in-terest of the leaders, both Catholic and Protestant, that there should be peace, and the populace immediately imbibed that spirit. The Protestant chapel stood by the side of the Romish cathedral, and the congregations mingled freely in courtesy and kindness, as they passed to and from their places of worship. Mu-tual forbearance and good will seemed at once to be restored.

And now the several cities of the German empire, where religious freedom had been crushed by the emperor, began to throng his palace with remonstrants and demands. They, uni-ted, resolved at every hazard to attain the privileges which their brethren in Bohemia and Austria had secured. The Prince of Anhalt, an able and intrepid man, was dispatched to Prague with a list of grievances. In very plain language he inveighed against the government of the emperor, and de-manded for Donauworth and other cities of the German empire, the civil and religious freedom of which Rhodolph had de-prived them ; declaring, without any softening of expression, that if the emperor did not peacefully grant their requests, they would seek redress by force of arms. The humiliated and dishonored emperor tried to pacify the prince by vague promises and honeyed words, to which the prince replied in language which at once informed the emperor that the time for dalliance had passed.

"I fear," said the Prince of Anhalt, in words which sovereigns are not accustomed to hear, "that this answer will rather tend to prolong the dispute than to tranquillize the united princes. I am bound in duty to represent to your imperial ..ajesty the dangerous flame which I now see bursting forth in Germany. Your counselors are ill adapted to extinguish this rising flame—those counselors who have brought you into such imminent danger, and who have nearly destroyed public confidence, credit and prosperity throughout your dominions. I must likewise exhort your imperial majesty to take all important affairs into consideration yourself, intreating you to recollect the example of Julius Cæsar, who, had he not neglected to read the note presented to him as he was going to the capitol, would not have received the twenty wounds which caused his death."

This last remark threw the emperor into a paroxysm of terror. He had long been trembling from the apprehension of assassination. This allusion to Julius Cæsar he considered an intimation that his hour was at hand. His terror was so great that Prince Anhalt had to assure him, again and again, that he intended no such menace, and that he was not aware that any conspiracy was thought of any where, for his death. The emperor was, however, so alarmed that he promised any thing and every thing. He doubtless intended to fulfill his promise, but subsequent troubles arose which absorbed all his remaining feeble energies, and obliterated past engagements from his mind.

Matthias was watching all the events with the intensest eagerness, as affording a brilliant prospect to him, to obtain the crown of Bohemia, and the scepter of the empire. This ambition consumed his days and his nights, verifying the ad age, "uneasy lies the head which wears a crown."

CHAPTER XIV.

RHODOLPH III. AND MATTHIAS.

FROM 1609 TO 1612.

DIFFICULTIES AS TO THE SUCCESSION.—HOSTILITY OF HENRY IV. TO THE HOUSE OF AUS-
TRIA.—ASSASSINATION OF HENRY IV.—SIMILARITY IN SULLY'S AND NAPOLEON'S
PLANS.—EXULTATION OF THE CATHOLICS.—THE BROTHERS' COMPACT.—HOW RHO-
DOLPH KEPT IT.—SEIZURE OF PRAGUE.—RHODOLPH A PRISONER.—THE KING'S AB-
DICATION.—CONDITIONS ATTACHED TO THE CROWN.—RAGE OF RHODOLPH.—MATTHIAS
ELECTED KING.—THE EMPEROR'S RESIDENCE.—REJOICINGS OF THE PROTESTANTS.—
REPLY OF THE AMBASSADORS.—THE NUREMBURG DIET.—THE UNKINDEST CUT OF
ALL.—RHODOLPH'S HUMILIATION AND DEATH.

AND now suddenly arose another question which threatened to involve all Europe in war. The Duke of Cleves,
Juliers, and Berg died without issue. This splendid duchy,
or rather combination of duchies, spread over a territory of
several thousand square miles, and was inhabited by over a
million of inhabitants. There were many claimants to the
succession, and the question was so singularly intricate and
involved, that there were many who seemed to have an equal
right to the possession. The emperor, by virtue of his imperial authority, issued an edict, putting the territory in sequestration, till the question should be decided by the proper
tribunals, and, in the meantime, placing the territory in the
hands of one of his own family as administrator.

This act, together with the known wishes of Spain to prevent so important a region, lying near the Netherlands, from
falling into the hands of the Protestants, immediately changed
the character of the dispute into a religious contest, and, as
by magic, all Europe wheeled into line on the one side or the
other. Every other question was lost sight of, in the all-

absorbing one, Shall the duchy fall into the hands of the Pro.
estants or the Catholics ?

Henry IV. of France zealously espoused the cause of the
Protestants. He was very hostile to the house of Austria for
the assistance it had lent to that celebrated league which for so
many years had deluged France in blood, and kept Henry IV.
from the throne ; and he was particularly anxious to humble
that proud power. Though Henry IV., after fighting for
many years the battles of Protestantism, had, from motives
of policy, avowed the Romish faith, he could never forget his
mother's instructions, his early predilections and his old friends
and supporters, the Protestants ; and his sympathies were always with them. Henry IV., as sagacious and energetic as
he was ambitious, saw that he could never expect a more favorable moment to strike the house of Austria than the one
then presented. The Emperor Rhodolph was weak, and
universally unpopular, not only with his own subjects, but
throughout Germany. The Protestants were all inimical to
him, and he was involved in desperate antagonism with his
energetic brother Matthias. Still he was a formidable foe, as,
in a war involving religious questions, he could rally around
him all the Catholic powers of Europe.

Henry IV., preparatory to pouring his troops into the
German empire, entered into secret negotiations with England, Denmark, Switzerland, Venice, whom he easily purchased with offers of plunder, and with the Protestant princes
of minor power on the continent. There were not a few, indifferent upon religious matters, who were ready to engage in
any enterprise which would humble Spain and Austria. Henry
collected a large force on the frontiers of Germany, and, with
ample materials of war, was prepared, at a given signal, to
burst into the territory of the empire.

The Catholics watched these movements with alarm, and
began also to organize. Rhodolph, who, from his position as
emperor, should have been their leader, was a wretched by

pochondriac, trembling before imaginary terrors, a prey to the most gloomy superstitions, and still concealed in the secret chambers of his palace. He was a burden to his party, and was regarded by them with contempt. Matthias was watching him, as the tiger watches its prey. To human eyes it would appear that the destiny of the house of Austria was sealed. Just at that critical point, one of those unexpected events occurred, which so often rise to thwart the deepest laid schemes of man.

On the 14th of May, 1610, Henry IV. left the Louvre in his carriage to visit his prime minister, the illustrious Sully, who was sick. The city was thronged with the multitudes assembled to witness the triumphant entry of the queen, who had just been crowned. It was a beautiful spring morning, and the king sat in his carriage with several of his nobles, the windows of his carriage being drawn up. Just as the carriage was turning up from the rue St. Honore into the rue Ferronnerie, the passage was found blocked up by two carts. The moment the carriage stopped, a man sprung from the crowd upon one of the spokes of the wheel, and grasping a part of the coach with his right hand, with his left plunged a dagger to the hilt into the heart of Henry IV. Instantly withdrawing it, he repeated the blow, and with nervous strength again penetrated the heart. The king dropped dead into the arms of his friends, the blood gushing from the wound and from his mouth. The wretched assassin, a fanatic monk, Francis Ravaillac, was immediately seized by the guard. With difficulty they protected him from being torn in pieces by the populace. He was reserved for a more terrible fate, and was subsequently put to death by the most frightful tortures human ingenuity could devise.

The poniard of the assassin changed the fate of Europe. Henry IV. had formed one of the grandest plans which ever entered the human mind. Though it is not at all probable that he could have executed it, the attempt, with the immense means he had at his disposal, and with his energy as a warrior and diplomatist, would doubtless have entirely altered the aspect of human affairs.   There was very much in his plan to secure the approval of all those enlightened men who were mourning over the incessant and cruel wars with which Europe was ever desolated.   His intention was to reconstruct Europe into fifteen States, as nearly uniform in size and power as possible.   These States were, according to their own choice, to be monarchical or republican, and were to be associated on a plan somewhat resembling that of the United States of North America.   In each State the majority were to decide which religion, whether Protestant or Catholic, should be established.   The Catholics were all to leave the Protestant States, and assemble in their own.   In like manner the Protestants were to abandon the Catholic kingdoms.   This was the very highest point to which the spirit of toleration had then attained.   All Pagans and Mohammedans were to be driven out of Europe into Asia.   A civil tribunal was to be organized to settle all national difficulties, so that there should be no more war.   There was to be a standing army belonging to the confederacy, to preserve the peace, and enforce its decrees, consisting of two hundred and seventy thousand infantry, fifty thousand cavalry, two hundred cannon, and one hundred and twenty ships of war.

This plan was by no means so chimerical as at first glance it might seem to be.   The sagacious Sully examined it in all its details, and gave it his cordial support.   The coöperation of two or three of the leading powers would have invested the plan with sufficient moral and physical support to render its success even probable.   But the single poniard of the monk Ravaillac arrested it all.

The Emperor Napoleon I. had formed essentially the same plan, with the same humane desire to put an end to interminable wars; but he had adopted far nobler principles of toleration.

"One of my great plans," said he at St. Helena, "was the rejoining, the concentration of those same geographical nations which have been disunited and parcelled out by revolution and policy.   There are dispersed in Europe upwards of thirty millions of French, fifteen millions of Spaniards, fifteen millions of Italians, and thirty millions of Germans.   It was my intention to incorporate these several people each into one nation.   It would have been a noble thing to have advanced into posterity with such a train, and attended by the blessings of future ages. I felt myself worthy of this glory.

"After this summary simplification, it would have been possible to indulge the chimera of the *beau ideal* of civilization.   In this state of things there would have been some chance of establishing in every country a unity of codes, of principles, of opinions, of sentiments, views and interests. Then perhaps, by the help of the universal diffusion of knowledge, one might have thought of attempting in the great human family the application of the American Congress, or the Amphictyons of Greece.   What a perspective of power, grandeur, happiness and prosperity would thus have appeared.

"The concentration of thirty or forty millions of Frenchmen was completed and perfected.   That of fifteen millions of Spaniards was nearly accomplished.   Because I did not subdue the Spaniards, it will henceforth be argued that they were invincible, for nothing is more common than to convert accident into principle.   But the fact is that they were actually conquered, and, at the very moment when they escaped me, the Cortes of Cadiz were secretly in treaty with me.   They were not delivered either by their own resistance or by the efforts of the English, but by the reverses which I sustained at different points, and, above all, by the error I committed in transferring my whole forces to the distance of three thousand miles from them.   Had it not been for this, the Spanish government would have been shortly consolidated the public mind would have been tranquilized, and hostile parties

would have been rallied together. Three or four years would
have restored the Spaniards to profound peace and brilliant
prosperity. They would have become a compact nation, and
I should have well deserved their gratitude, for I should have
saved them from the tyranny by which they are now oppressed,
and the terrible agitations which await them.

" With regard to the fifteen millions of Italians, their concentration was already far advanced ; it only wanted maturity.
The people were daily becoming more firmly established in
the unity of principles and legislation, and also in the unity of
thought and feeling—that certain and infallible cement of human thought and concentration. The union of Piedmont to
France, and the junction of Parma, Tuscany and Rome, were,
in my mind, only temporary measures, intended merely to
guarantee and promote the national education of the Italians.
The portions of Italy that were united to France, though that
union might have been regarded as the result of invasion on
our part, were, in spite of their Italian patriotism, the very
places that continued most attached to us.

" All the south of Europe, therefore, would soon have been
rendered compact in point of locality, views, opinions, sentiments and interests. In this state of things, what would have
been the weight of all the nations of the North ? What human efforts could have broken through so strong a barrier ?
The concentration of the Germans must have been effected
more gradually, and therefore I had done no more than sim-
plify their monstrous complication. Not that they were unprepared for concentralization ; on the contrary, they were
too well prepared for it, and they might have blindly risen in
reaction against us before they had comprehended our designs. How happens it that no German prince has yet formed
a just notion of the spirit of his nation, and turned it to good
account ? Certainly if Heaven had made me a prince of Germany, amid the critical events of our times I should infallibly
have governed the thirty millions of Germans combined ; and,

from what I know of them, I think I may venture to affirm that if they had once elected and proclaimed me they would not have forsaken me, and I should never have been at St. Helena.

" At all events," the emperor continued, after a moment's pause, " this concentration will be brought about sooner or later by the very force of events. The impulse is given, and I think that since my fall and the destruction of my system, no grand equilibrium can possibly be established in Europe except by the concentration and confederation of the principal nations. The sovereign who in the first great conflict shall sincerely embrace the cause of the people, will find himself at the head of Europe, and may attempt whatever he pleases."

Thus similar were the plans of these two most illustrious men. But from this digression let us return to the affairs of Austria. With the death of Henry IV., fell the stupendous plan which his genius conceived, and which his genius alone could execute. The Protestants, all over Europe, regarded his death as a terrible blow. Still they did not despair of securing the contested duchy for a Protestant prince. The fall of Henry IV. raised from the Catholics a shout of exultation, and they redoubled their zeal.

The various princes of the house of Austria, brothers, uncles, cousins, holding important posts all over the empire, were much alarmed in view of the peril to which the family ascending was exposed by the feebleness of Rhodolph. They held a private family conference, and decided that the interests of all required that there should be reconciliation between Matthias and Rhodolph ; or that, in their divided state, they would fall victims to their numerous foes. The brothers agreed to an outward reconciliation ; but there was not the slightest mitigation of the rancor which filled their hearts. Matthias, however, consented to acknowledge the superiority of his brother, the emperor, to honor him as the head of the family, and to hold his possessions as fiefs of Rhodolph intrusted to him by favor. Rhodolph, while hating Matthias, and watching for an opportunity to crush him, promised to regard him hereafter as a brother and a friend.

And now Rhodolph developed unexpected energy, mingled with treachery and disgraceful duplicity. He secretly and treacherously invited the Archduke Leopold, who was also Bishop of Passau and Strasbourg, and one of the most bigoted of the warrior ecclesiastics of the papal church, to invade, with an army of sixteen thousand men, Rhodolph's own kingdom of Bohemia, under the plea that the wages of the soldiers had not been paid. It was his object, by thus introducing an army of Roman Catholics into his kingdom, and betraying into their hands several strong fortresses, then to place himself at their head, rally the Catholics of Bohemia around him, annul all the edicts of toleration, crush the Protestants, and then to march to the punishment of Matthias.

The troops, in accordance with their treacherous plan, burst into Upper Austria, where the emperor had provided that there should be no force to oppose them. They spread themselves over the country, robbing the Protestants and destroying their property with the most wanton cruelty. Crossing the Danube they continued their march and entered Bohemia. Still Rhodolph kept quiet in his palace, sending no force to oppose, but on the contrary contriving that towns and fortresses, left defenseless, should fall easily into their hands. Bohemia was in a terrible state of agitation. Wherever the invading army appeared, it wreaked dire vengeance upon the Protestants. The leaders of the Protestants hurriedly ran together, and, suspicious of treachery, sent an earnest appeal to the king.

The infamous emperor, not yet ready to lay aside the vail, called Heaven to witness that the irruption was made without his knowledge, and advised vigorous measures to repel the foe, while he carefully thwarted the execution of any such measures. At the same time he issued a proclamation to Leopold, commanding him to retire. Leopold understood all this be-

forehand, and smiling, pressed on. Aided by the treason of
the king, they reached Prague, seized one of the gates massacred the guard, and took possession of the capital. The
emperor now came forward and disclosed his plans. The foreign troops, holding Prague and many other of the most important towns and fortresses in the kingdom, took the oath of
allegiance to Rhodolph as their sovereign, and he placed in
their hands five pieces of heavy artillery, which were planted
in battery on an eminence which commanded the town. A
part of Bohemia rallied around the king in support of these
atrocious measures.

But all the Protestants, and all who had any sympat! y with
the Protestants, were exasperated to the highest pitch. They
immediately dispatched messengers to Matthias and t. their
friends in Moravia, imploring aid. Matthias immediately start-
ed eight thousand Hungarians on the march. As they entered Bohemia with rapid steps and pushed their way toward
Prague they were joined every hour by Protestant levies pouring in from all quarters. So rapidly did their ranks increase
that Leopold's troops, not daring to await their arrival, in a
panic, fled by night. They were pursued on their retreat, attacked, and put to flight with the loss of two thousand men.
The ecclesiastical duke, in shame and confusion, slunk away to
his episcopal castle of Passau.

The contemptible Rhodolph now first proposed terms of
reconciliation, and then implored the clemency of his indignant conquerors. They turned from the overtures of the perjured monarch with disdain, burst into the city of Prague,
surrounded every avenue to the palace, and took Rhodolph a
prisoner. Soon Matthias arrived, mounted in regal splendor,
at the head of a gorgeous retinue. The army received him
with thunders of acclaim. Rhodolph, a captive in his palace,
heard the explosion of artillery, the ringing of bells and the
shouts of the populace, welcoming his dreaded and detested
rival to the capital. It was the 20th of March, 1611.

The nobles commanded Rhodolph to summon a diet. The humiliated, degraded, helpless emperor knew full well what this signified, but dared not disobey. He summoned a diet. It was immediately convened. Rhodolph sent in a message, saying,

"Since, on account of my advanced age, I am no longer capable of supporting the weight of government, I hereby abdicate the throne, and earnestly desire that my brother Matthias may be crowned without delay."

The diet were disposed very promptly to gratify the king in his expressed wishes. But there arose some very formidable difficulties. The German princes, who were attached to the cause which Rhodolph had so cordially espoused, and who foresaw that his fall threatened the ascendency of Protestantism throughout the empire, sent their ambassadors to the Bohemian nobles with the menace of the vengeance of the empire, if they proceeded to the deposition of Rhodolph and to the inauguration of Matthias, whom they stigmatized as an usurper. This unexpected interposition reanimated the hopes of Rhodolph, and he instantly found such renovation of youth and strength as to feel quite able to bear the burden of the crown a little longer; and consequently, notwithstanding his abdication, through his friends, all the most accomplished mechanism of diplomacy, with its menaces, its bribes, and its artifice were employed to thwart the movements of Matthias and his friends.

There was still another very great difficulty. Matthias was very ambitious, and wished to be a sovereign, with sovereign power. He was very reluctant to surrender the least portion of those prerogatives which his regal ancestors had grasped. But the nobles deemed this a favorable opportunity to regain their lost power. They were disposed to make a hard bargain with Matthias. They demanded—1st, that the throne should no longer be hereditary, but elective; 2d, that the nobles should be permitted to meet in a diet, or congress, to deliberate upon public affairs whenever and wherever they pleased ; 3d, that all financial and military affairs should be left in their hands ; 4th, that although the king might appoint all the great officers of state, they might remove any of them at pleasure; 5th, that it should be the privilege of the nobles to form all foreign alliances ; 6th, that they were to be empowered to form an armed force by their own authority.

Matthias hesitated in giving his assent to such demands, which seemed to reduce him to a cipher, conferring upon him only the shadow of a crown. Rhodolph, however, who was eager to make any concessions, had his agents busy through the diet, with assurances that the emperor would grant all these concessions. But Rhodolph had fallen too low to rise again. The diet spurned all his offers, and chose Matthias, though he postponed his decision upon these articles until he could convene a future and more general diet. Rhodolph had eagerly caught at the hope of regaining his crown. As his messengers returned to him in the palace with the tidings of their defeat, he was overwhelmed with indignation, shame and despair. In a paroxysm of agony he threw up his window, and looking out upon the city, exclaimed,

" O Prague, unthankful Prague, who hast been so highly elevated by me ; now thou spurnest at thy benefactor. May the curse and vengeance of God fall upon thee and all Bohemia."

The 23d of May was appointed for the coronation. The nobles drew up a paper, which they required Rhodolph to sign, absolving his subjects from their oath of allegiance to him. The degraded king writhed in helpless indignation, for he was a captive. With the foolish petulance of a spoiled child, as he affixed his signature in almost an illegible scrawl, he dashed blots of ink upon the paper, and then, tearing the pen to pieces, threw it upon the floor, and trampled it beneath his feet.

It was still apprehended that the adherents of Rhodolph

might make some armed demonstration in his favor. As a precaution against this, the city was filled with troops, the gates closed, and carefully guarded. The nobles met in the great hall of the palace. It was called a meeting of the States, for it included the higher nobles, the higher clergy, and a few citizens, as representatives of certain privileged cities. The forced abdication of Rhodolph was first read. It was as follows:—

"In conformity with the humble request of the States of our kingdom, we graciously declare the three estates, as well as all the inhabitants of all ranks and conditions, free from all subjection, duty and obligation; and we release them from their oath of allegiance, which they have taken to us as their king, with a view to prevent all future dissensions and confusion. We do this for the greater security and advantage of the whole kingdom of Bohemia, over which we have ruled six-and-thirty years, where we have almost always resided, and which, during our administration, has been maintained in peace, and increased in riches and splendor. We accordingly, in virtue of this present voluntary resignation, and after due reflection, do, from this day, release our subjects from all duty and obligation."

Matthias was then chosen king, in accordance with all the ancient customs of the hereditary monarchy of Bohemia. The States immediately proceeded to his coronation. Every effort was made to dazzle the multitude with the splendors of the coronation, and to throw a halo of glory around the event, not merely as the accession of a new monarch to the throne, but as the introduction of a great reform in reinstating the nation in its pristine rights.

While the capital was resounding with these rejoicings, Rhodolph had retired to a villa at some distance from the city, in a secluded glen among the mountains, that he might close his ears against the hateful sounds. The next day Matthias, fraternally or maliciously, for it is not easy to judge which

motive actuated him, sent a stinging message of assumed gratitude to his brother, thanking him for relinquishing in his
brother's favor his throne and his palaces, and expressing the
hope that they might still live together in fraternal confidence
and affection.

Matthias and the States consulted their own honor rather
than Rhodolph's merits, in treating him with great magnanimity. Though Rhodolph had lost, one by one, all his own
hereditary or acquired territories, Austria, Hungary, Bohemia,
he still retained the imperial crown of Germany. This gave
him rank and certain official honors, with but little real power.
The emperor, who was also a powerful sovereign in his own
right, could marshal his own forces to establish his decrees.
But the emperor, who had no treasury or army of his own,
was powerless indeed.

The emperor was permitted to occupy one of the palaces
at Prague. He received an annual pension of nearly a million of dollars; and the territories and revenues of four lord-
ships were conferred upon him.   Matthias having consolidated his government, and appointed the great officers of
his kingdom, left Prague without having any interview with
his brother, and returned to his central capital at Vienna,
where he married Anne, daughter of his uncle Ferdinand
of Tyrol.

The Protestants all over the German empire hailed these
events with public rejoicing. Rhodolph had been their implacable foe. He was now disarmed and incapable of doing
them any serious injury. Matthias was professedly their
friend, had been placed in power mainly as their sovereign,
and was now invested with such power, as sovereign of the collected realms of Austria, that he could effectually protect them
from persecution. This success emboldened them to unite in
a strong, wide-spread confederacy for the protection of their
rights. The Protestant nobles and princes, with the most distinguished of their clergy from all parts of the German em

pire, held a congress at Rothenburg. This great assembly, in
the number, splendor and dignity of its attendants, vied with
regal diets. Many of the most illustrious princes of the empire were there in person, with imposing retinues. The emperor and Matthias both deemed it expedient to send ambassadors to the meeting. The congress at Rothenburg was one
of the most memorable movements of the Protestant party.
They drew up minute regulations for the government of their
confederacy, established a system of taxation among themselves, made efficient arrangements for the levying of troops,
established arsenals and magazines, and strongly garrisoned a
fortress, to be the nucleus of their gathering should they at
any time be compelled to appeal to arms.

Rhodolph, through his ambassadors, appeared before this
resplendent assembly the mean and miserable sycophant he
ever was in days of disaster. He was so silly as to try to win
them again to his cause. He coaxed and made the most liberal promises, but all in vain. Their reply was indignant and
decisive, yet dignified.

" We have too long," they replied, " been duped by spe-
cious and deceitful promises. We now demand actions, not
words. Let the emperor show us by the acts of his administration that his spirit is changed, and then, and then only,
can we confide in him."

Matthias was still apprehensive that the emperor might
rally the Catholic forces of Germany, and in union with the
pope and the formidable power of the Spanish court, make an
attempt to recover his Bohemian throne. It was manifest that
with any energy of character, Rhodolph might combine Catho
lic Europe, and inundate the plains of Germany with blood.
While it was very important, therefore, that Matthias should
do every thing he could to avoid exasperating the Catholics,
it was essential to his cause that he should rally around him
the sympathies of the Protestants.

The ambassadors of Matthias respectfully announced to the

congress the events which had transpired in Bohemia in the transference of the crown, and solicited the support of the congress. The Protestant princes received this communication with satisfaction, promised their support in case it should be needed, and, conscious of the danger of provoking Rhodolph to any desperate efforts to rouse the Catholics, recommended that he should be treated with brotherly kindness, and, at the same time, watched with a vigilant eye.

Rhodolph, disappointed here, summoned an electoral meeting of the empire, to be held at Nuremburg on the 14th of December, 1711. He hoped that a majority of the electors would be his friends. Before this body he presented a very pathetic account of his grievances, delineating in most melancholy colors the sorrows which attend fallen grandeur. He detailed his privations and necessities, the straits to which he was reduced by poverty, his utter inability to maintain a state befitting the imperial dignity, and implored them, with the eloquence of a Neapolitan mendicant, to grant him a suitable establishment, and not to abandon him, in his old age, to penury and dishonor.

The reply of the electors to the dispirited, degraded, downtrodden old monarch was the unkindest cut of all. Much as Rhodolph is to be execrated and despised, one can hardly refrain from an emotion of sympathy in view of this new blow which fell upon him. A deputation sent from the electoral college met him in his palace at Prague. Mercilessly they recapitulated most of the complaints which the Protestants had brought against him, declined rendering him any pecuniary relief, and requested him to nominate some one to be chosen as his successor on the imperial throne.

"The emperor," said the delegation in conclusion, "is himself the principal author of his own distresses and misfortunes. The contempt into which he has fallen and the disgrace which, through him, is reflected upon the empire, is derived from his own indolence and his obstinacy in following perverse counsels.

He might have escaped all these calamities if, instead of resigning himself to corrupt and interested ministers, he had followed the salutary counsels of the electors."

They closed this overwhelming announcement by demanding the immediate assembling of a diet to elect an emperor to succeed him on the throne of Germany. Rhodolph, not yet quite sufficiently humiliated to officiate as his own executioner, though he promised to summon a diet, evaded the fulfillment of his promise. The electors, not disposed to dally with him at all, called the assembly by their own authority to meet on the 31st of May.

This seemed to be the finishing blow. Rhodolph, now sixty years of age, enfeebled and emaciated by disease and melancholy, threw himself upon his bed to die. Death, so often invoked in vain by the miserable, came to his aid. He welcomed its approach. To those around his bed he remarked,

"When a youth, I experienced the most exquisite pleasure in returning from Spain to my native country. How much more joyful ought I to be when I am about to be delivered from the calamities of human nature, and transferred to a heavenly country where there is no change of time, and where no sorrow can enter!"

In the tomb let him be forgotten.

CHAPTER XV.

MATTHIAS.

FROM 1612 TO 1619.

UPON the death of Rhodolph, Matthias promptly offered himself as a candidate for the imperial crown. But the Catholics, suspicious of Matthias, in consequence of his connection with the Protestants, centered upon the Archduke Albert, sovereign of the Netherlands, as their candidate. Many of the Protestants, also, jealous of the vast power Matthias was attaining, and not having full confidence in his integrity, offered their suffrages to Maximilian, the younger brother of Matthias. But notwithstanding this want of unanimity, political intrigue removed all difficulties and Matthias was unanimously elected Emperor of Germany.

The new emperor was a man of renown. His wonderful achievements had arrested the attention of Europe, and it was expected that in his hands the administration of the empire would be conducted with almost unprecedented skill and vigor. But clouds and storms immediately began to lower around the throne. Matthias had no spirit of toleration in his heart, and every tolerant act he had assented to, had been extorted from him. He was, by nature, a despot, and most reluctantly, for the sake of grasping the reins of power, he had relinquished

a few of the royal prerogatives. He had thus far evaded many
of the claims which had been made upon him, and which he
had partially promised to grant, and now, being both king and
emperor, he was disposed to grasp all power, both secular and
religious, which he could attain.

Matthias's first endeavor was to recover Transylvania. This
province had fallen into the hands of Gabriel Bethlehem, who
was under the protection of the Turks. Matthias, thinking
that a war with the infidel would be popular, summoned a
diet and solicited succors to drive the Turks from Moldavia
and Wallachia, where they had recently established themselves.
The Protestants, however, presented a list of grievances which
they wished to have redressed before they listened to his request. The Catholics, on the other hand, presented a list of
their grievances, which consisted, mainly, in privileges granted
the Protestants, which they also demanded to have redressed
before they could vote any supplies to the emperor. These
demands were so diametrically hostile to each other, that there
could be no reconciliation. After an angry debate the diet
broke up in confusion, having accomplished nothing.

Matthias, disappointed in this endeavor, now applied to the
several States of his widely extended Austrian domains—to
his own subjects. A general assembly was convened at Lintz.
Matthias proposed his plans, urging the impolicy of allowing
the Turks to retain the conquered provinces, and to remain in
the ascendency in Transylvania. But here again Matthias was
disappointed. The Bohemian Protestants were indignant in
view of some restrictions upon their worship, imposed by the
emperor to please the Catholics. The Hungarians, weary of
the miseries of war, were disposed on any terms to seek peace
with the Turks. The Austrians had already expended an immense amount of blood and money on the battle-fields of Hungary, and urged the emperor to send an ambassador to treat
for peace. Matthias was excessively annoyed in being thus
thwarted in all his plans.

Just at this time a Turkish envoy arrived at Vienna, proposing a truce for twenty years. The Turks had never before condescended to send an embassage to a Christian power. This afforded Matthias an honorable pretext for abandoning his warlike plan, and the truce was agreed to.

The incessant conflict between the Catholics and Protestants allowed Germany no repose. A sincere toleration, such as existed during the reign of Maximilian I., established fraternal feelings between the contending parties. But it required ages of suffering and peculiar combination of circumstances, to lead the king and the nobles to a cordial consent to that toleration. But the bigotry of Rhodolph and the trickery of Matthias, had so exasperated the parties, and rendered them so suspicious of each other, that the emperor, even had he been so disposed, could not, but by very slow and gradual steps, have secured reconciliation. Rnodolph had put what was called the ban of the empire upon the Protestant city of Aix-la-Chapelle, removing the Protestants from the magistracy, and banishing their chiefs from the city. When Rhodolph was sinking into disgrace and had lost his power, the Protestants, being in the majority, took up arms, reëlected their magistracy, and expelled the Jesuits from the city. The Catholics now appealed to Matthias, and he insanely revived the ban against the Protestants, and commissioned Albert, Archduke of Cologne, a bigoted Catholic, to march with an army to Aix-la-Chapelle and enforce its execution.

Opposite Cologne, on the Rhine, the Protestants, in the days of bitter persecution, had established the town of Mulheim. Several of the neighboring Protestant princes defended with their arms the refugees who settled there from all parts of Germany. The town was strongly fortified, and here the Protestants, with arms in their hands, maintained perfect freedom of religious worship. The city grew rapidly and became one of the most important fortresses upon the river. The Catholics, jealous of its growing power, appealed to the em-

peror. He issued a decree ordering the Protestants to demolish every fortification of the place within thirty days; and to
put up no more buildings whatever.

These decrees were both enforced by the aid of a Spanish
army of thirty thousand men, which, having executed the ban,
descended the river and captured several others of the most
important of the Protestant towns. Of course all Germany
was in a ferment. Everywhere was heard the clashing of
arms, and every thing indicated the immediate outburst of civil
war. Matthias was in great perplexity, and his health rapidly failed beneath the burden of care and sorrow. All the
thoughts of Matthias were now turned to the retaining of the
triple crown of Bohemia, Hungary and the empire, in the
family. Matthias was old, sick and childless. Maximilian, his
next brother, was fifty-nine years of age and unmarried. The
next brother, Albert, was fifty-eight, and without children.
Neither of the brothers could consequently receive the crowns
with any hope of retaining them in the family. Matthias
turned to his cousin Ferdinand, head of the Styrian branch of
the family, as the nearest relative who was likely to continue
the succession. In accordance with the custom which had
grown up, Matthias wished to nominate his successor, and
have him recognized and crowned before his death, so that im
mediately upon his death the new sovereign, already crowned,
could enter upon the government without any interregnum.

The brothers, appreciating the importance of retaining the
crown in the family, and conscious that all the united influence they then possessed was essential to securing that result, assented to the plan, and coöperated in the nomination
of Ferdinand. All the arts of diplomatic intrigue were called
into requisition to attain these important ends. The Bo·
hemian crown was now electoral; and it was necessary to
persuade the electors to choose Ferdinand, one of the most
intolerant Catholics who ever swayed a scepter. The crown
of Hungary was nominally hereditary. But the turbulen

nobles, ever armed, and strong in their fortresses, would accept no monarch whom they did not approve. To secure
also the electoral vote for Emperor of Germany, while parties were so divided and so bitterly hostile to each other, required the most adroit application of bribes and menaces.

Matthias made his first movement in Bohemia. Having
adopted previous measures to gain the support of the prin
cipal nobles, he summoned a diet at Prague, which he attended in person, accompanied by Ferdinand. In a brief
speech he thus addressed them.

"As I and my brothers," said the king, " are without children, I deem it necessary, for the advantage of Bohemia,
and to prevent future contests, that my cousin Ferdinand
should be proclaimed and crowned king. I therefore request
you to fix a day for the confirmation of this appointment."

Some of the leading Protestants opposed this, on the
ground of the known intolerance of Ferdinand. But the
majority, either won over by the arts of Matthias, or dread-
ing civil war, accepted Ferdinand. He was crowned on the
10th of June, 1616, he promising not to interfere with the
government during the lifetime of Matthias. The emperor
now turned to Hungary, and, by the adoption of the same
measures, secured the same results. The nobles accepted
Ferdinand, and he was solemnly crowned at Presburg.

Ferdinand was Archduke of Styria, a province of Austria
embracing a little more than eight thousand square miles,
being about the size of the State of Massachusetts, and containing about a million of inhabitants. He was educated by
the Jesuits after the strictest manner of their religion. He
became so thoroughly imbued with the spirit of his monastic
education, that he was anxious to assume the cowl of the
monk, and enter the order of the Jesuits. His devotion to
the papal church assumed the aspect of the most inflexible
intolerance towards all dissent. In the administration of the
government of his own duchy, he had given free swing to

his bigotry. Marshaling his troops, he had driven all the Protestant preachers from his domains. He had made a pilgrimage to Rome, to receive the benediction of the pope, and another to Loretto, where, prostrating himself before the miraculous image, he vowed never to cease his exertions until he had extirpated all heresy from his territories. He often declared that he would beg his bread from door to door, submit to every insult, to every calamity, sacrifice even life itself, rather than suffer the true Church to be injured. Ferdinand was no time-server—no hypocrite. He was a genuine bigot, sincere and conscientious. Animated by this spirit, although two thirds of the inhabitants of Styria were Protestants, he banished all their preachers, professors and schoolmasters; closed their clurches, seminaries and schools; even tore down the churches and school-houses; multiplied papal institutions, and called in teachers and preachers from other States.

Matthias and Ferdinand now seemed jointly to reign, and the Protestants were soon alarmed by indications that a new spirit was animating the councils of the sovereign. The most inflexible Catholics were received as the friends and advisers of the king. The Jesuits loudly exulted, declaring that heresy was no longer to be tolerated. Banishments and confiscations were talked of, and the alarm of the Protestants became intense and universal: they looked forward to the commencement of the reign of Ferdinand with terror.

As was to be expected, such wrongs and perils called out an avenger. Matthew Henry, Count of Thurn, was one of the most illustrious and wealthy of the Bohemian nobles. He had long been a warm advocate of the doctrines of the Reformation; and having, in the wars with the Turks, acquired a great reputation for military capacity and courage, and being also a man of great powers of eloquence, and of exceedingly popular manners, he had become quite the idol of the Protestant party. He had zealously opposed the election of Ferdinand to the throne of Bohemia, and had thus increased that

jealousy and dislike with which both Matthias and Ferdinand
had previously regarded so formidable an opponent.   He was,
in consequence, very summarily deprived of some very important dignities. This roused his impetuous spirit, and caused
the Protestants more confidingly to rally around him as a
martyr to their cause.

The Count of Thurn, as prudent as he was bold, as deliberate as he was energetic, aware of the fearful hazard of entering into hostilities with the sovereign who was at the
same time king of all the Austrian realms, and Emperor of
Germany, conferred with the leading Protestant princes, and
organized a confederacy so strong that all the energies of
the empire could with difficulty crush it.   They were not disposed to make any aggressive movements, but to defend their
rights if assailed.   The inhabitants of a town in the vicinity
of Prague began to erect a church for Protestant worship.
The Roman Catholic bishop, who presided over that diocese,
forbade them to proceed.   They plead a royal edict, which
authorized them to erect the church, and continued their
work, regardless of the prohibition. Count Thurn encouraged
them to persevere, promising them ample support.   The
bishop appealed to the Emperor Matthias. He also issued
his prohibition; but aware of the strength of the Protestants,
did not venture to attempt to enforce it by arms.   Ferdinand, however, was not disposed to yield to this spirit, and
by his influence obtained an order, demanding the immediate
surrender of the church to the Catholics, or its entire demolition. The bishop attempted its destruction by an armed
force, but the Protestants defended their property, and sent
a committee to Matthias, petitioning for a revocation of the
mandate. These deputies were seized and imprisoned by the
king, and an imperial force was sent to the town, Brunau, to
take possession of the church. From so small a beginning
rose the Thirty Years' War.

Count Thurn immediately summoned a convention of six

delegates from each of the districts, called circles in Bohemia. The delegates met at Prague on the 16th of March, 1618. An immense concourse of Protestants from all parts of the surrounding country accompanied the delegates to the capital. Count Thurn was a man of surpassing eloquence, and seemed to control at will all the passions of the human heart. In the boldest strains of eloquence he addressed the assembly, and roused them to the most enthusiastic resolve to defend at all hazards their civil and religious rights. They unanimously passed a resolve that the demolition of the church and the suspension of the Protestant worship were violations of the royal edict, and they drew up a petition to the emperor demanding the redress of this grievance, and the liberation of the imprisoned deputies from Brunau. The meeting then adjourned, to be reassembled soon to hear the reply of the emperor.

As the delegates and the multitudes who accompanied them returned to their homes, they spread everywhere the impression produced upon their minds by the glowing eloquence of Count Thurn. The Protestant mind was roused to the highest pitch by the truthful representation, that the court had adopted a deliberate plan for the utter extirpation of Protestant worship throughout Bohemia, and that foreign troops were to be brought in to execute this decree. These convictions were strengthened and the alarm increased by the defiant reply which Matthias sent back from his palace in Vienna to his Bohemian subjects. He accused the delegates of treason and of circulating false and slanderous reports, and declared that they should be punished according to their deserts. He forbade them to meet again, or to interfere in any way with the affairs of Brunau, stating that at his leisure he would repair to Prague and attend to the business himself.

The king could not have framed an answer better calculated to exasperate the people, and rouse them to the most determined resistance. Count Thurn, regardless of the pro hibition, called the delegates together and read to them the answer, which the king had not addressed to them but to the council of regency. He then addressed them again in those impassioned strains which he had ever at command, and roused them almost to fury against those Catholic lords who had dictated this answer to the king and obtained his signature.

The next day the nobles met again. They came to the place of meeting thoroughly armed and surrounded by their retainers, prepared to repel force by force. Count Thurn now wished to lead them to some act of hostility so decisive that they would be irrecoverably committed. The king's council of regency was then assembled in the palace of Prague. The regency consisted of seven Catholics and three Protestants. For some unknown reason the Protestant lords were not present on this occasion. Three of the members of the regency, Slavata and Martinetz and the burgrave of Prague, were peculiarly obnoxious on account of the implacable spirit with which they had ever persecuted the reformers. These lords were the especial friends of Ferdinand and had great influence with Matthias, and it was not doubted that they had framed the answer which the emperor had returned. Incited by Count Thurn, several of the most resolute of the delegates, led by the count, proceeded to the palace, and burst into the room where the regency was in session.

Their leader, addressing Slavata, Martinetz, and Diepold, the burgrave, said, " Our business is with you. We wish to know if you are responsible for the answer returned to us by the king."

" That," one of them replied, " is a secret of state which we are not bound to reveal."

" Let us follow," exclaimed the Protestant chief, " the ancient custom of Bohemia, and hurl them from the window."

They were in a room in the tower of the castle, and it was eighty feet to the water of the moat. The Catholic lords were instantly seized, dragged to the window and thrust out. Al most incredible as it may seem, the water and the mud of the moat so broke their fall, that neither of them was killed. They all recovered from the effects of their fall. Having per. formed this deed, Count Thurn and his companions returned to the delegates, informed them of what they had done, and urged them that the only hope of safety now, for any Protes- tant, was for all to unite in open and desperate resistance. Then mounting his horse, and protected by a strong body-guard, he rode through the streets of Prague, stopping at every cor- ner to harangue the Protestant populace. The city was thronged on the occasion by Protestants from all parts of the kingdom.

"I do not," he exclaimed, " propose myself as your chief, but as your companion, in that peril which will lead us to happy freedom or to glorious death. The die is thrown. It is too late to recall what is past. Your safety depends alone on unanimity and courage, and if you hesitate to burst asun- der your chains, you have no alternative but to perish by the hands of the executioner."

He was everywhere greeted with shouts of enthusiasm, and the whole Protestant population were united as one man in the cause. Even many of the moderate Catholics, disgusted with the despotism of the newly elected king, which embraced civil as well as religious affairs, joined the Protestants, for they feared the loss of their civil rights more than they dreaded the inroads of heresy.

With amazing celerity they now organized to repel the force which they knew that the emperor would immediately send to crush them. Within three days their plans were all matured and an organization effected which made the king tremble in his palace. Count Thurn was appointed their com- mander, an executive committee of thirty very efficient men was chosen, which committee immediately issued orders for the levy of troops all over the kingdom. Envoys were sent to

Moravia, Silesia, Lusatia, and Hungary, and to the Protestants all over the German empire. The Archbishop of Prague was expelled from the city, and the Jesuits were also banished. They then issued a proclamation in defense of their conduct, which they sent to the king with a firm but respectful letter.

One can not but be amused in reading their defense of the outrage against the council of regency. "We have thrown from the windows," they said, "the two ministers who have been the enemies of the State, together with their creature and flatterer, in conformity with an ancient custom prevalent throughout all Bohemia, as well as in the capital. This custom is justified by the example of Jezebel in holy Writ, who was thrown from a window for persecuting the people of God; and it was common among the Romans, and all other nations of antiquity, who hurled the disturbers of the public peace from rocks and precipices."

Matthias had very reluctantly sent his insulting and defiant answer to the reasonable complaints of the Protestants, and he was thunderstruck in contemplating the storm which had thus been raised—a storm which apparently no human wisdom could now allay. There are no energies so potent as those which are aroused by religious convictions. Matthias well knew the ascendency of the Protestants all over Bohemia, and that their spirit, once thoroughly aroused, could not be easily quelled by any opposing force he could array. He was also aware that Ferdinand was thoroughly detested by the Protestant leaders, and that it was by no means improbable that this revolt would thwart all his plans in securing his succession.

As the Protestants had not renounced their allegiance, Matthias was strongly disposed to measures of conciliation, and several of the most influential, yet fair-minded Catholics supported him in these views. The Protestants were too numerous to be annihilated, and too strong in their desperation

K

to be crushed. But Ferdinand, guided by the Jesuits, was implacable. He issued a manifesto, which was but a transcript
of his own soul, and which is really sublime in the sincerity
and fervor of its intolerance.

" All attempts," said he, " to bring to reason a people whom
God has struck with judicial blindness will be in vain. Since
the introduction of heresy into Bohemia, we have seen nothing
but tumults, disobedience and rebellion. While the Catholics
and the sovereign have displayed only lenity and moderation,
these sects have become stronger, more violent and more insolent; having gained all their objects in religious affairs, they
turn their arms against the civil government, and attack the
supreme authority under the pretense of conscience; not content with confederating themselves against their sovereign,
they have usurped the power of taxation, and have made alliances with foreign States, particularly with the Protestant
princes of Germany, in order to deprive him of the very means
of reducing them to obedience. They have left nothing to the
sovereign but his palaces and the convents; and after their recent outrages against his ministers, and the usurpation of the
regal revenues, no object remains for their vengeance and rapacity but the persons of the sovereign and his successor, and
the whole house of Austria.

" If sovereign power emanates from God, these atrocious
deeds must proceed from the devil, and therefore must draw
down divine punishment. Neither can God be pleased with
the conduct of the sovereign, in conniving at or acquiescing in
all the demands of the disobedient. Nothing now remains for
him, but to submit to be lorded by his subjects, or to free himself from this disgraceful slavery before his territories are
formed into a republic. The rebels have at length deprived
themselves of the only plausible argument which their preachers have incessantly thundered from the pulpit, that they were
contending for religious freedom; and the emperor and the
nouse of Austria have now the fairest opportunity to convince

the world that their sole object is only to deliver themselves from slavery and restore their legal authority. They are secure of divine support, and they have only the alternative of a war by which they may regain their power, or a peace which is far more dishonorable and dangerous than war. If successful, the forfeited property of the rebels will defray the expense of their armaments; if the event of hostilities be unfortunate, they can only lose, with honor, and with arms in their hands, the rights and prerogatives which are and will be wrested from them with shame and dishonor. It is better not to reign than to be the slave of subjects. It is far more desirable and glorious to shed our blood at the foot of the throne than to be driven from it like criminals and malefactors."

Matthias endeavored to unite his own peace policy with the energetic warlike measures urged by Ferdinand. He attempted to overawe by a great demonstration of physical force, while at the same time he made very pacific proposals. Applying to Spain for aid, the Spanish court sent him eight thousand troops from the Netherlands; he also raised, in his own dominions, ten thousand men. Having assembled this force he sent word to the Protestants, that if they would disband their force he would do the same, and that he would confirm the royal edict, and give full security for the maintenance of their civil and religious privileges. The Protestants refused to disband, knowing that they could place no reliance upon the word of the unstable monarch who was crowded by the rising power of the energetic Ferdinand. The ambitious naturally deserted the court of the sovereign whose days were declining, to enlist in the service of one who was just entering upon the kingly power.

Ferdinand was enraged at what he considered the pusillanimity of the king. Maximilian, the younger brother of Matthias, cordially espoused the cause of Ferdinand. Cardinal Kleses, a Catholic of commanding influence and of enlightened, liberal views, was the counselor of the king. Ferdinand

and Maximilian resolved that he should no longer have access to the ear of the pliant monarch, but he could be removed from the court only by violence. With an armed band they entered the palace at Vienna, seized the cardinal in the midst of the court, stripped him of his robes, hurried him into a carriage, and conveyed him to a strong castle in the midst of the mountains of the Tyrol, where they held him a close prisoner. The emperor was at the time confined to his bed with the gout. As soon as they had sent off the cardinal, Ferdinand and Maximilian repaired to the royal chamber, informed the emperor of what they had done, and attempted to justify the deed on the plea that the cardinal was a weak and wicked minister whose policy would certainly divide and ruin the house of Austria.

The emperor was in his bed as he received this insulting announcement of a still more insulting outrage. For a moment he was speechless with rage. But he was old, sick and powerless. This act revealed to him that the scepter had fallen from his hands. In a paroxysm of excitement, to prevent himself from speaking he thrust the bed-clothes into his mouth, nearly suffocating himself. Resistance was in vain. He feared that should he manifest any, he also might be torn from his palace, a captive, to share the prison of the cardinal. In sullen indignation he submitted to the outrage.

Ferdinand and Maximilian now pursued their energetic measures of hostility unopposed. They immediately put the army in motion to invade Bohemia, and boasted that the Protestants should soon be punished with severity which would teach them a lesson they would never forget. But the Protestants were on the alert. Every town in the kingdom had joined in the confederacy, and in a few weeks Count Thurn found himself at the head of ten thousand men inspired with the most determined spirit. The Silesians and Lusatians marched to help them, and the Protestant league of Germany sent them timely supplies. The troops of Ferdinand found opponents in every pass and in every defile, and in their endeavor to force their way through the fastnesses of the mountains, were frequently driven back with great loss. At length the troops of Ferdinand, defeated at every point, were compelled to retreat in shame back to Austria, leaving all Bohemia in the hands of the Protestants.

Ferdinand was now in trouble and disgrace. His plans had signally failed. The Protestants all over Germany were in arms, and their spirits roused to the highest pitch ; many of the moderate Catholics refused to march against them, declaring that the Protestants were right in resisting such oppression. They feared Ferdinand, and were apprehensive that his despotic temper, commencing with religious intolerance, would terminate in civil tyranny. It was evident to all that the Protestants could not be put down by force of arms, and even Ferdinand was so intensely humiliated that he was constrained to assent to the proposal which Matthias made to refer their difficulty to arbitration. Four princes were selected as the referees—the Electors of Mentz, Bavaria, Saxony and Palatine They were to meet at Egra the 14th of April, 1619.

But Matthias, the victim of disappointment and grief, was now rapidly approaching his end. The palace at Vienna was shrouded in gloom, and no smiles were seen there, and no sounds of joy were heard in those regal saloons. The wife of Matthias, whom he tenderly loved, oppressed by the humiliation and anguish which she saw her husband enduring, died of a broken heart. Matthias was inconsolable under this irretrievable loss. Lying upon his bed tortured with the pain of the gout, sinking under incurable disease, with no pleasant memories of the past to cheer him, with disgrace and disaster accumulating, and with no bright hopes beyond the grave, he loathed life and dreaded death. The emperor in his palace was perhaps the most pitiable object which could be found in all his realms. He tossed upon his pillow, the victim of remorse and despair, now condemning himself for his cruel treatment of his brother Rhodolph, now inveighing bitterly against the inhumanity and arrogance of Ferdinand and Maximilian.   On the 20th of March, 1619, the despairing spirit of the emperor passed away to the tribunal of the " King of kings and the Lord of lords.'

CHAPTER XVI.

FERDINAND II.

FROM 1619 TO 1621.

Possessions of the Emperor.—Power of the Protestants of Bohemia.—General Spirit of Insurrection.—Anxiety of Ferdinand.—Insurrection led by Count Thurn.—Unpopularity of the Emperor.—Affecting Declaration of the Emperor.—Insurrection in Vienna.—The Arrival of Succor.—Ferdinand seeks the Imperial Throne.—Repudiated by Bohemia.—The Palatinate.—Frederic offered the Crown of Bohemia.—Frederic crowned.—Revolt in Hungary.—Desperate Condition of the Emperor.—Catholic League.—The Calvinists and the Puritans.—Duplicity of the Emperor.—Foreign Combinations.—Truce between the Catholics and the Protestants.—The Attack upon Bohemia.—Battle of the White Mountain.

FERDINAND, who now ascended the throne by right of the coronation he had already received, was in the prime of life, being but forty-one years of age, and was in possession of a rare accumulation of dignities. He was Archduke of Austria, King of Hungary and of Bohemia, Duke of Styria, Carinthia and Carniola, and held joint possession, with his two brothers, of the spacious territory of the Tyrol. Thus all these wide-spread and powerful territories, with different languages, different laws, and diverse manners and customs, were united under the Austrian monarchy, which was now undeniably one of the leading powers of Europe. In addition to all these titles and possessions, he was a prominent candidate for the imperial crown of Germany. To secure this additional dignity he could rely upon his own family influence, which was very powerful, and also upon the aid of the Spanish monarchy. When we contemplate his accession in this light, he appears as one of the most powerful monarchs who ever ascended a throne.

But there is another side to the picture. The spirit of rebellion against his authority had spread through nearly all his territories, and he had neither State nor kingdom where his power seemed stable. In whatever direction he turned his eyes, he saw either the gleam of hostile arms or the people in a tumult just ready to combine against him.

The Protestants of Bohemia had much to encourage them. All the kingdom, excepting one fortress, was in their possession. All the Protestants of the German empire had espoused their cause. The Silesians, Lusatians and Moravians were in open revolt. The Hungarian Protestants, animated by the success of the Bohemians, were eager to follow their example and throw off the yoke of Ferdinand. With iron tyranny he had silenced every Protestant voice in the Styrian provinces, and had crushed every semblance of religious liberty. But the successful example of the Bohemians had roused the Styrians, and they also were on the eve of making a bold move in defense of their rights. Even in Austria itself, and beneath the very shadow of the palaces of Vienna, conspiracies were rife, and insurrection was only checked by the presence of the army which had been driven out of Bohemia.

Even Ferdinand could not be blind to the difficulties which were accumulating upon him, and to the precarious tenure of his power. He saw the necessity of persevering in the attempt at conciliation which he had so reluctantly commenced. And yet, with strange infatuation, he proposed an accommodation in a manner which was deemed insulting, and which tended only to exasperate. The very day of his accession to the throne, he sent a commission to Prague, to propose a truce; but, instead of conferring with the Protestant leaders, he seemed to treat them with intentional contempt, by address ing his proposal to that very council of regency which had become so obnoxious. The Protestants, justly regarding this as an indication of the implacable state of his mind, and conscious that the proposed truce would only enable him more effectually to rally his forces, made no reply whatever to his pro-

posals. Ferdinand, perceiving that he had made a great mistake, and that he had not rightly appreciated the spirit of his
foes, humbled himself a little more, and made still another
attempt at conciliation. But the Protestants had now resolved
that Ferdinand should never be King of Bohemia. It had
become an established tenet of the Catholic church that it is
not necessary to keep faith with heretics. Whatever solemn
promises Ferdinand might make, the pope would absolve him
from all sin in violating them.

Count Thurn, with sixteen thousand men, marched into
Moravia. The people rose simultaneously to greet him. He
entered Brunn, the capital, in triumph. The revolution was
immediate and entire. They abolished the Austrian government, established the Protestant worship, and organized a
new government similar to that which they had instituted in
Bohemia. Crossing the frontier, Count Thurn boldly entered
Austria and, meeting no foe capable of retarding his steps, he
pushed vigorously on even to the very gates of Vienna. As
he had no heavy artillery capable of battering down the walls,
and as he knew that he had many partisans within the walls
of the city, he took possession of the suburbs, blockaded the
town, and waited for the slow operation of a siege, hoping
thus to be able to take the capital and the person of the sovereign without bloodshed.

Ferdinand had brought such trouble upon the country, that
he was now almost as unpopular with the Catholics as with the
Protestants, and all his appeals to them for aid were of but
little avail. The sudden approach of Count Thurn had amazed
and discomfited him, and he knew not in what direction to
look for aid. Cooped up in his capital, he could hold no communication with foreign powers, and his own subjects manifested no disposition to come to his rescue. The evidences
of popular discontent, even in the city, were every hour becoming more manifest, and the unhappy sovereign was in
hourly expectation of an insurrection in the streets.

The surrender of Vienna involved the loss of Austria. With the loss of Austria vanished all hopes of the imperial crown. Bohemia, Austria, and the German scepter gone, Hungary would soon follow; and then, his own Styrian' ter ritories, sustained and aided by their successful neighbors, would speedily discard his sway. Ferdinand saw it all clearly, and was in an agony of despair. He has confided to his confessor the emotions which, in those terrible hours, agitated his soul. It is affecting to read the declaration, indicative as it is that the most cruel and perfidious man may be sincere and even conscientious in his cruelty and crime. To his Jesuitical confessor, Bartholomew Valerius, he said,

"I have reflected on the dangers which threaten me and my family, both at home and abroad. With an enemy in the suburbs, sensible that the Protestants are plotting my ruin, I implore that help from God which I can not expect from man. I had recourse to my Saviour, and said, 'Lord Jesus Christ, Thou Redeemer of mankind, Thou to whom all hearts are opened, Thou knowest that I seek Thy honor, not my own. If it be Thy will, that, in this extremity, I should be overcome by my enemies, and be made the sport and contempt of the world, I will drink of the bitter cup. Thy will be done.' I had hardly spoken these words before I was inspired with new hope, and felt a full conviction that God would frustrate the designs of my enemies."

Nerved by such a spirit, Ferdinand was prepared to endure all things rather than yield the slightest point. Hour after hour his situation became more desperate, and still he remained inflexible. Balls from the batteries of Count Thurn struck even the walls of his palace; murmurs filled the streets, and menaces rose to his ears from beneath his windows. "Let us put his evil counselors to the sword," the disaffected exclaimed; "shut him up in a convent; and educate his children a the Protestant religion."

At length the crisis had apparently arrived. Insurrection

was organized. Clamorous bands surged through the streets, and there was a state of tumult which no police force could quell. A band of armed men burst into the palace, forced their way into the presence of Ferdinand, and demanded the surrender of the city. At that moment, when Ferdinand might well have been in despair, the unexpected sound of trumpets was heard in the streets, and the tramp of a squadron of cavalry. The king was as much amazed as were the insurgents. The deputies, not knowing what it meant, in great alarm retreated from the palace. The squadron swept the streets, and surrounded the palace. They had been sent to the city by the general who had command of the Austrian forces, and, arriving at full speed, had entered unexpectedly at the only gate which the besiegers had not guarded.

Their arrival, as if by heavenly commission, and the tidings they brought of other succor near at hand, reanimated the king and his partisans, and instantly the whole aspect of things within the city was changed. Six hundred students in the Roman Catholic institutions of the city flew to arms, and organized themselves as a body-guard of the king. All the zealous Catholics formed themselves into military bands, and this encouraged that numerous neutral party, always existing in such seasons of uncertainty, ready to join those who shall prove to be the strongest. The Protestants fled from the city, and sought protection under the banners of Count Thurn.

In the meantime the Catholics in Bohemia, taking advantage of the absence of Count Thurn with his troops, had surrounded Prague, and were demanding its capitulation. This rendered it necessary for the Bohemian army immediately to strike their tents and return to Bohemia. Never was there a more sudden and perfect deliverance. It was, however, deliverance only from the momentary peril. The great elements of discontent and conflict remained unchanged.

It was very evident that the difficulties which Ferdinand had to encounter in his Austrian dominions, were so immense

that he could not hope to surmount them without foreign aid
He consequently deemed it a matter important above all oth
ers to secure the imperial throne. Without this strength the
loss of all his Austrian possessions was inevitable. With the
influence and the power which the crown of Germany would
confer upon him he could hope to gain all. Ferdinand immediately left Vienna and visited the most influential of the German princes to secure their support for his election. The
Catholics all over Germany, alarmed by the vigor and energy
which had been displayed by the Protestants, laid aside their
several preferences, and gradually all united upon Ferdinand.
The Protestants, foolishly allowing their Lutheran and Calvin-
istic differences to disunite them, could not agree in their candidate. Consequently Ferdinand was elected, and immediately crowned emperor, the 9th of September, 1619.

The Bohemians, however, remained firm in their resolve
to repudiate him utterly as their king. They summoned a
diet of the States of Bohemia, Moravia, Silesia and Lusatia
to meet at Prague. Delegates also attended the diet from
Upper and Lower Austria, as also many nobles from distant
Hungary. The diet drew up a very formidable list of grievances, and declared, in view of them, that Ferdinand had forfeited all right to the crown of Bohemia, and that consequent
ly it was their duty, in accordance with the ancient usages, to
proceed to the election of a sovereign. The Catholics were
now so entirely in the minority in Bohemia that the Protestants held the undisputed control. They first chose the Elect-
or of Saxony. He, conscious that he could maintain his post
only by a long and uncertain war, declined the perilous dignity.
They then with great unanimity elected Frederic, the Elector
of Palatine.

The Palatinate was a territory bordering on Bohemia, of
over four thousand square miles, and contained nearly seven
hundred thousand inhabitants. The elector, Frederic V., was
thus a prince of no small power in his own right. He had mar

ried a daughter of James I. of England, and had many powerful relatives. Frederic was an affable, accomplished, kind-
hearted man, quite ambitious, and with but little force of
character. He was much pleased at the idea of being elevated
to the dignity of a king, and was yet not a little appalled in
contemplating the dangers which it was manifest he must encounter. His mother, with maternal solicitude, trembling for
her son, intreated him not to accept the perilous crown. His
father-in-law, James, remonstrated against it, sternly declaring
that he would never patronize subjects in rebellion against
their sovereign, that he would never acknowledge Frederic's
title as king, or render him, under any circumstances, either
sympathy or support. On the other hand the members of the
Protestant league urged his acceptance; his uncles united
strongly with them in recommending it, and above all, his fascinating wife, whom he dotingly loved, and who, delighted at
the idea of being a queen, threw herself into his arms, and
plead in those persuasive tones which the pliant heart of Frederic could not resist. The Protestant clergy, also, in a strong
delegation waited upon him, and intreated him in the name of
that Providence which had apparently proffered to him the
crown, to accept it in fidelity to himself, to his country and to
the true religion.

The trembling hand and the tearful eye with which Frederic accepted the crown, proved his incapacity to bear the burden in those stormy days. Placing the government of the
Palatinate in the hands of the Duke of Deux Ponts, he repaired,
with his family, to Prague. A rejoicing multitude met him at
several leagues from the capital, and escorted him to the city
with an unwonted display of popular enthusiasm. He was
crowned with splendor such as Bohemia had never witnessed
before.

For a time the Bohemians surrendered themselves to the
most extravagant joy. Frederic was exceedingly amiable, and
just the prince to win, in calm and sunny days, the enthusias

tic admiration of his subjects. They were highly gratified in having the King of Bohemia dwell in his own capital at Prague, a privilege and honor which they had seldom enjoyed. Many of the German princes acknowledged Frederic's title, as did also Sweden, Denmark, Holland and Vienna. The revolution in Bohemia was apparently consummated, and to the ordinary observer no cloud could be seen darkening the horizon.

The Bohemians were strengthened in their sense of security by a similar revolution which was taking place in Hungary. As soon as Ferdinand left Vienna, to seek the crown of Germany, the Protestants of Hungary threw off their allegiance to Austria, and rallied around the banners of their bold, indomitable leader, Gabriel Bethlehem. They fell upon the imperial forces with resistless fury and speedily dispersed them. Having captured several of the most important fortresses, and having many troops to spare, Gabriel Bethlehem sent eighteen thousand men into Moravia to aid Count Thurn to disperse the imperial forces there. He then marched triumphantly to Presburg, the renowned capital of Hungary, within thirty miles of Vienna, where he was received by the majority of the inhabitants with open arms. He took possession of the sacred crown and of the crown jewels, called an assembly of the nobles from the various States of Hungary and Transylvania, and united them in a firm band against Ferdinand. He now marched up the banks of the Danube into Austria. Count Thurn advanced from Moravia to meet him. The junction of their forces placed the two leaders in command of sixty thousand men. They followed along the left bank of the majestic Danube until they arrived opposite Vienna. Here they found eighteen thousand troops posted to oppose. After a short conflict, the imperial troops retreated from behind their intrenchments across the river, and blew up the bridge.

In such a deplorable condition did the Emperor Ferdinand find his affairs, as he returned from Germany to Austria. He was apparently in a desperate position, and no human sagacity could foresee how he could retrieve his fallen fortunes. Apparently, could his despotic arm then have been broken, Europe might have been spared many years of war and woe. But the designs of Providence are inscrutable. Again there was apparently almost miraculous interposition. The imperial troops were rapidly concentrated in the vicinity of Vienna, to prevent the passage of the broad, deep and rapid river by the allied army. A strong force was dispatched down the right bank of the Danube, which attacked and dispersed a force left to protect the communication with Hungary. The season was far advanced, and it was intensely cold in those northern latitudes. The allied army had been collected so suddenly, that no suitable provision had been made for feeding so vast a host. Famine added its terrors to the cold blasts which menacingly swept the plains, and as there was imminent danger that the imperial army might cut off entirely the communication of the allies with Hungary, Gabriel Bethlehem decided to relinquish the enterprise of taking Vienna, and retired unimpeded to Presburg. Almost every fortress in Hungary was now in the possession of the Hungarians, and Ferdinand, though his capital was released, saw that Hungary as well as Bohemia had escaped from his hands. At Presburg Gabriel was, with imposing ceremonies, proclaimed King of Hungary, and a decree of proscription and banishment was issued against all the adherents of Ferdinand.

Germany was now divided into two great leagues, the Catholic and the Protestant. Though nominally religious parties, they were political as well as religious, and subject to all the fluctuations and corruptions attending such combinations. The Protestant league, composed of princes of every degree of dignity, who came from all parts of Germany, proudly mounted and armed, and attended by armed retainers, from a few score to many hundreds or even thousands, met at Nuremburg. It was one of the most influential and imposing assemblages which had ever gathered in Europe.

The Catholics, with no less display of pomp and power, for their league embraced many of the haughtiest sovereigns in Europe, met at Wurtzburg. There were, of course, not a few who were entirely indifferent as to the religious questions involved, and who were Catholics or Protestants, in subserviency to the dictates of interest or ambition. Both parties contended with the arts of diplomacy as well as with those of war. The Spanish court was preparing a powerful armament to send from the Netherlands to the help of Ferdinand. The Protestants sent an army to Ulm to watch their movements, and to cut them off.

Ferdinand was as energetic as he had previously proved himself inflexible and persevering. In person he visited Munich, the capital of Bavaria, that he might more warmly interest in his favor Maximilian, the illustrious and warlike duke. The emperor made him brilliant promises, and secured his cordial coöperation. The Duke of Bavaria, and the Elector of the Palatinate, were neighbors and rivals; and the emperor offered Maximilian the spoils of the Palatinate, if they should be successful in their warfare against the newly elected Bohemian king. Maximilian, thus persuaded, placed all his force at the disposal of the emperor.

The Elector of Saxony was a Lutheran; the Elector Palatine a Calvinist. The Lutherans believed, that after the consecration of the bread and wine at the sacramental table, the body and blood of Christ were spiritually present with that bread and wine. This doctrine, which they called *consubstantiation*, they adopted in antagonism to the papal doctrine of *transubstantiation*, which was that the bread and wine were actually transformed into, and became the real body and blood of Christ.

The difference between the Calvinists and the Lutherans, as we have before mentioned, was that, while the former considered the bread and wine in the sacraments as *representing* the body and the blood of Christ, the latter considered the body and the blood as spiritually present in the consecrated elements. This trivial difference divided brethren who were agreed upon all the great points of Christian faith, duty and obligation. It is melancholy, and yet instructive to observe, through the course of history, how large a proportion of the energies of Christians have been absorbed in contentions against each other upon shadowy points of doctrine, while a world has been perishing in wickedness. The most efficient men in the Church on earth, have had about one half of their energies paralyzed by contentions with their own Christian brethren. It is so now. The most energetic men, in pleading the cause of Christ, are often assailed even more unrelentingly by brethren who differ with them upon some small point of doctrine, than by a hostile world.

Human nature, even when partially sanctified, is frail indeed. The Elector of Saxony was perhaps a good man, but he was a weak one. He was a zealous Lutheran, and was shocked that a Calvinist, a man who held the destructive error that the bread and wine only *represented* the body and the blood of Christ, should be raised to the throne of Bohemia, and thus become the leader of the Protestant party. The Elector of Saxony and the Elector of the Palatine had also been naturally rivals, as neighbors, and possessors of about equal rank and power. Though the Calvinists, to conciliate the Lutherans, had offered the throne to the Elector of Saxony, and he had declined it, as too perilous a post for him to occupy, still he was weakly jealous of his rival who had assumed that post, and was thus elevated above him to the kingly dignity.

Ferdinand understood all this, and shrewdly availed himself of it. He plied the elector with arguments and promises, assuring him that the points in dispute were political merely and not religious; that he had no intention of opposing the Protestant religion, and that if the elector would abandon the Protestant league, he would reward him with a large accession of territory. It seems incredible that the Elector of Saxony could have been influenced by such representations. But so it was. Averring that he could not in conscience uphold a man who did not embrace the vital doctrine of the spiritual presence, he abandoned his Protestant brethren, and drew with him the Landgrave of Hesse, and several other Lutheran princes. This was a very serious defection, which disheartened the Protestants as much as it encouraged Ferdinand.

The wily emperor having succeeded so admirably with the Protestant elector, now turned to the Roman Catholic court of France—that infamous court, still crimsoned with the blood of the St. Bartholomew massacre. Then, with diplomatic tergiversation, he represented that the conflict was not a political one, but purely religious, involving the interests of the Church. He urged that the peace of France and of Europe required that the Protestant heresy should be utterly effaced; and he provoked the resentment of the court by showing how much aid the Protestants in Europe had ever received from the Palatinate family. Here again he was completely successful, and the young king, Louis XIII., who was controlled by his bigoted yet powerful minister, the Duke of Luines, cordially espoused his cause.

Spain, intolerant, despotic, hating Protestantism with perfect hatred, was eager with its aid. A well furnished army of twenty-four thousand men was sent from the Netherlands, and also a large sum of money was placed in the treasury of Ferdinand. Even the British monarch, notwithstanding the clamors of the nation, was maneuvered into neutrality. And most surprising of all, Ferdinand was successful in securing a truce with Gabriel Bethlehem, which, though it conferred peace upon Hungary, deprived the Bohemians of their powerful support.

The Protestants were strong in their combination; but still it was a power of fearful strength now arrayed against them. It was evident that Europe was on the eve of a long and terrible struggle. The two forces began to assemble. The Protestants rendezvoused at Ulm, under the command of the Margrave of Anspach. The Catholic troops, from their wide dispersion, were concentrating at Guntzburg, to be led by the Duke of Bavaria. The attention of all Europe was arrested by these immense gatherings. All hearts were oppressed with solicitude, for the parties were very equally matched, and results of most momentous importance were dependent upon the issue.

In this state of affairs the Protestant league, which extended through Europe, entered into a truce with the Catholic league, which also extended through Europe, that they should both withdraw from the contest, leaving Ferdinand and the Bohemians to settle the dispute as they best could. This seemed very much to narrow the field of strife, but the measure, in its practical results, was far more favorable to Ferdinand than to the Bohemians. The emperor thus disembarrassed, by important concessions, and by menaces, brought the Protestants of Lower Austria into submission. The masses, overawed by a show of power which they could not resist, yielded; the few who refused to bow in homage to the emperor were punished as guilty of treason.

Ferdinand, by these cautious steps, was now prepared to concentrate his energies upon Bohemia. He first attacked the dependent provinces of Bohemia, one by one, sending an army of twenty-five thousand men to take them unprepared. Having subjected all of Upper Austria to his sway, with fifty thousand men he entered Bohemia. Their march was energetic and sanguinary. With such an overpowering force they took fortress after fortress, scaling ramparts, mercilessly cutting down garrisons, plundering and burning towns, and massacreing the inhabitants. Neither sex nor age was spared, and a brutal soldiery gratified their passions in the perpetration of indescribable horrors. Even the Duke of Bavaria was shocked at such barbarities, and entered his remonstrances against them. Many large towns, terrified by the atrocities perpetrated upon those who resisted the imperial arms, threw open their gates, hoping thus, by submission, to appease the vengeance of the conqueror.

Frederic was a weak man, not at all capable of encountering such a storm, and the Bohemians had consequently no one to rally and to guide them with efficiency. His situation was now alarming in the extreme. He was abandoned by the Protestant league, hemmed in on every side by the imperial troops, and his hereditary domains of the Palatinate were overrun by twenty thousand Spaniards. His subjects, alarmed at his utter inefficiency, and terrified by the calamities which were falling, like avalanche after avalanche upon them, became dissatisfied with him, and despairing respecting their own fate. He was a Calvinist, and the Lutherans, had never warmly received him. The impotent monarch, instead of establishing himself in the affections of his subjects, by vigorously driving the invaders from his realms, with almost inconceivable silliness endeavored to win their popularity by balls and smiles, pleasant words and masquerades. In fact, Frederic, by his utter inefficiency, was a foe more to be dreaded by Bohemia than Ferdinand.

The armies of the emperor pressed on, throwing the whole kingdom into a state of consternation and dismay. The army of Frederic, which dared not emerge from its intrenchments at Pritznitz, about fifty miles south of Prague, consisted of but twenty-two thousand men, poorly armed, badly clothed, wretchedly supplied with military stores, and almost in a state of mutiny from arrears of pay. The generals were in perplexity and disagreement. Some, in the recklessness of despair, were for marching to meet the foe and to risk a battle; others were for avoiding a conflict, and thus protracting the war till the severity of winter should drive their enemies from the field, when they would have some time to prepare for another year's campaign. These difficulties led Frederic to apply for a truce. But Ferdinand was too wise to lose by wasting time in negotiations, vantage ground he had already gained. He refused to listen to any word except the unequivocal declaration that Frederic relinquished all right to the crown. Pressing his forces onward, he drove the Bohemians from behind their ramparts at Pritznitz, and pursued them down the Moldau even to the walls of Prague.

Upon a magnificent eminence called the White Mountain, which commanded the city and its most important approaches, the disheartened army of Frederic stopped in its flight, and made its last stand. The enemy were in hot pursuit. The Bohemians in breathless haste began to throw up intrenchments along the ravines, and to plant their batteries on the hills, when the banners of Ferdinand were seen approaching. The emperor was too energetic a warrior to allow his panic-stricken foes time to regain their courage. Without an hour's delay he urged his victorious columns to the charge. The Bohemians fought desperately, with far more spirit than could have been expected. But they were overpowered by numbers, and in one short hour the army of Frederic was annihilated. Four thousand were left dead upon the field, one thousand were drowned in the frantic attempt to swim the Moldau, and the rest were either dispersed as fugitives over hill and valley or taken captive. The victory of the emperor was complete, the hopes of Frederic crushed, and the fate of Bohemia sealed.

The contemptible Frederic, while this fierce battle was raging beneath the very walls of his capital, instead of placing himself at the head of his troops, was in the heart of the city, in the banqueting-hall of his palace, bowing and smiling and feasting his friends. The Prince of Anhalt, who was in command of the Bohemian army, had sent a most urgent message to the king, intreating him to dispatch immediately to his aid all the troops in the city, and especially to repair himself to the camp to encourage the troops by his presence. Frederic was at the table when he received this message, and sent word back that he could not come until after dinner. As soon as the combat commenced, another still more urgent message was sent, to which he returned the same reply. *After dinner* he mounted his horse and rode to the gate which led to the White Mountain. The thunders of the terrible battle filled the air ; the whole city was in the wildest state of terror and confusion ; the gates barred and barricaded. Even the king could not get out. He climbed one of the towers of the wall and looked out upon the gory field, strewn with corpses, where his army *had been*, but was no more. He returned hastily to his palace, and met there the Prince of Anhalt, who, with a few fugitives, had succeeded in entering the city by one of the gates.

The city now could not defend itself for an hour. The batteries of Ferdinand were beginning to play upon the walls, when Frederic sent out a flag of truce soliciting a cessation of hostilities for twenty-four hours, that they might negotiate respecting peace. The peremptory reply returned was, that there should not be truce for a single moment, unless Frederic would renounce all pretension to the crown of Bohemia. With such a renunciation truce would be granted for eight hours. Frederic acceded to the demand, and the noise of war was hushed.

CHAPTER XVII.

FERDINAND II.

FROM 1621 TO 1629.

THE citizens of Prague were indignant at the pusillanimity of Frederic. In a body they repaired to the palace and tried to rouse his feeble spirits. They urged him to adopt a manly resistance, and offered to mount the ramparts and beat off the foe until succor could arrive. But Frederic told them that he had resolved to leave Prague, that he should escape during the darkness of the night, and advised them to capitulate on the most favorable terms they could obtain. The inhabitants of the city were in despair. They knew that they had nothing to hope from the clemency of the conqueror, and that there was no salvation for them from irretrievable ruin but in the most desperate warfare. Even now, though the enemy was at their gates, their situation was by no means hopeless with a leader of any energy.

"We have still," they urged, "sufficient strength to withstand a siege. The city is not invested on every side, and reinforcements can enter by some of the gates. We have ample means in the city to support all the troops which can

be assembled within its walls.   The soldiers who have escaped
from the disastrous battle need but to see the Bohemian banners again unfurled and to hear the blast of the bugle, to return to their ranks.   Eight thousand troops are within a few
hours' march of us.   There is another strong band in the rear
of the enemy, prepared to cut off their communications.
Several strong fortresses, filled with arms and ammunition,
are still in our possession, and the Bohemians, animated by the
remembrance of the heroic deeds of their ancestors, are eager
to retrieve their fortunes."

Had Frederic possessed a tithe of the perseverance and
energy of Ferdinand, with these resources he might soon have
arrested the steps of the conqueror.   Never was the characteristic remark of Napoleon to Ney better verified, that " an
army of deer led by a lion is better than an army of lions led
by a deer."   Frederic was panic-stricken for fear he might
fall into the hands of Ferdinand, from whom he well knew that
he was to expect no mercy.   With ignominious haste, abandoning every thing, even the coronation regalia, at midnight,
surrounded by a few friends, he stole out at one of the gates
of the city, and putting spurs to his horse, allowed himself no
rest until he was safe within the walls of Berlin, two hundred
miles from Prague.

The despairing citizens, thus deserted by their sovereign,
and with a victorious foe at their very walls, had no alternative but to throw open their gates and submit to the mercy of
the conqueror.   The next day the whole imperial army, under
the Duke of Bavaria, with floating banners and exultant music, entered the streets of the capital, and took possession of the
palaces.   The tyrant Ferdinand was as vengeful and venomous
as he was vigorous and unyielding.   The city was immediately
disarmed, and the government intrusted to a vigorous Roman
Catholic prince, Charles of Lichtenstein.   A strong garrison
was left in the city to crush, with a bloody hand, any indications of insurrection, and then the Duke of Bavaria returned

with most of his army to Munich, his capital, tottering beneath the burden of plunder.

There was a moment's lull before the tempest of imperial
wrath burst upon doomed Bohemia. Ferdinand seemed to
deliberate, and gather his strength, that he might strike a
blow which would be felt forever. He did strike such a blow
—one which has been remembered for two hundred years, and
which will not be forgotten for ages to come—one which
doomed parents and children to weary years of vagabondage,
penury and woe which must have made life a burden.

On the night of the 21st of January, three months after
the capitulation, and when the inhabitants of Prague had begun to hope that there might, after all, be some mercy in the
bosom of Ferdinand, forty of the leading citizens of the place
were simultaneously arrested. They were torn from their families and thrown into dungeons where they were kept in terrific
suspense for four months. They were then brought before an
imperial commission and condemned as guilty of high treason.
All their property was confiscated, nothing whatever being
left for their helpless families. Twenty-three were immediately executed upon the scaffold, and all the rest were either consigned to life-long imprisonment, or driven into banishment.
Twenty-seven other nobles, who had escaped from the kingdom, were declared traitors. Their castles were seized, their
property confiscated and presented as rewards to Roman Catholic nobles who were the friends of Ferdinand. An order
was then issued for all the nobles and landholders throughout
the kingdom to send in a confession of whatever aid they had
rendered, or encouragement they had given to the insurrection. And the most terrible vengeance was threatened against
any one who should afterward be proved guilty of any act
whatever of which he had not made confession. The consternation which this decree excited was so great, that not only
was every one anxious to confess the slightest act which could
be construed as unfriendly to the emperor, but many, in their

L

terror, were driven to accuse themselves of guilt, who had taken no share in the movement. Seven hundred nobles, and the whole body of Protestant landholders, placed their names on the list of those who confessed guilt and implored pardon.

The fiend-like emperor, then, in the mockery of mercy, declared that in view of his great clemency and their humble confession, he would spare their forfeited lives, and would only punish them by depriving them of their estates. He took their mansions, their estates, their property, and turned them adrift upon the world, with their wives and their children, fugitives and penniless. Thus between one and two thousand of the most ancient and noble families of the kingdom were rendered houseless and utterly beggared. Their friends, involved with them in the same woe, could render no assistance. They were denounced as traitors; no one dared befriend them, and their possessions were given to those who had rallied beneath the banners of the emperor. "To the victors belong the spoils." No pen can describe the ruin of these ancient families. No imagination can follow them in their steps of starvation and despair, until death came to their relief.

Ferdinand considered Protestantism and rebellion as synonymous terms. And well he might, for Protestantism has ever been arrayed as firmly against civil as against religious despotism. The doctrines of the reformers, from the days of Luther and Calvin, have always been associated with political liberty. Ferdinand was determined to crush Protestantism. The punishment of the Elector Palatine was to be a signal and an appalling warning to all who in future should think of disputing the imperial sway. The elector himself, having renounced the throne, had escaped beyond the emperor's reach. But Ferdinand took possession of his ancestral territories and divided them among his Roman Catholic allies. The electoral vote which he held in the diet of the empire, Ferdinand transferred to the Duke of Bavaria, thus reducing the Protestant vote to two, and securing an additional Catholic suffrage. The ban of the empire was also published against the Prince of Anhalt, the Count of Hohenloe, and the Duke Jaegendorf, who had been supporters of Frederic. This ban of the empire deprived them of their territories, of their rank, and of their possessions.

The Protestants throughout the empire were terrified by these fierce acts of vengeance, and were fearful of sharing the same fate. They now regretted bitterly that they had dis banded their organization. They dared not make any move against the emperor, who was flushed with pride and power, lest he should pounce at once upon them. The emperor consequently marched unimpeded in his stern chastisements. Frederic was thus deserted entirely by the Protestant union ; and his father-in-law, James of England, in accordance with his threat, refused to lend him any aid. Various most heroic efforts were made by a few intrepid nobles, but one after another they were crushed by the iron hand of the emperor.

Ferdinand, having thus triumphed over all his foes, and having divided their domains among his own followers, called a meeting of the electors who were devoted to his cause, at Ratisbon, on the 25th of February, 1623, to confirm what he had done. In every portion of the empire, where the arm of the emperor could reach them, the Protestants were receiving heavy blows. They were now thoroughly alarmed and aroused. The Catholics all over Europe were renewing their league ; all the Catholic powers were banded together, and Protestantism seemed on the eve of being destroyed by the sword of persecution.

Other parts of Europe also began to look with alarm upon the vast power acquired by Austria. There was but little of conciliation in the character of Ferdinand, and his unbounded success, while it rendered him more haughty, excited also the jealousy of the neighboring powers. In Lower Saxony, nearly all the nobles and men of influence were Protestants. The principal portion of the ecclesiastical property was in their hands. It was very evident that unless the despotism of Ferdinand was checked, he would soon wrest from them their titles and possessions, and none the less readily because he had succeeded in bribing the Elector of Saxony to remain neutral while he tore the crown of Bohemia from the Elector of the Palatine, and despoiled him of his wide-spread ancestral territories.

James I. of England had been negotiating a marriage of his son, the Prince of Wales, subsequently Charles I., with the daughter of the King of Spain. This would have been, in that day, a brilliant match for his son; and as the Spanish monarch was a member of the house of Austria, and a coöperator with his cousin, the Emperor Ferdinand, in all his measures in Germany, it was an additional reason why James should not interfere in defense of his son-in-law, Frederic of the Palatine. But now this match was broken off by the influence of the haughty English minister Buckingham, who had the complete control of the feeble mind of the British monarch. A treaty of marriage was soon concluded between the Prince of Wales and Henrietta, a princess of France. There was hereditary hostility between France and Spain, and both England and France were now quite willing to humble the house of Austria. The nobles of Lower Saxony availed themselves of this new turn in the posture of affairs, and obtained promises of aid from them both, and, through their intercession, aid also from Denmark and Sweden.

Richelieu, the imperious French minister, was embarrassed by two antagonistic passions. He was eager to humble the house of Austria; and this he could only do by lending aid to the Protestants. On the other hand, it was the great object of his ambition to restore the royal authority to unlimited power, and this he could only accomplish by aiding the house of Austria to crush the Protestants, whose love of freedom all despots have abhorred. Impelled by these conflicting passions, he did all in his power to extirpate Protest-

antism from France, while he omitted neither lures nor intrigues to urge the Protestants in Germany to rise against the
despotism of Austria. Gustavus Adolphus, of Sweden, was
personally inimical to Ferdinand, in consequence of injuries
he had received at his hands.   Christian IV. of Denmark was
cousin to Elizabeth, the mother of Frederic, and, in addition
to this interest in the conflict which relationship gave him, he
was also trembling lest some of his own possessions should
soon be wrested from him by the all-grasping emperor.   A
year was employed, the year 1624, in innumerable secret in
trigues, and plans of combination, for a general rising of the
Protestant powers.   It was necessary that the utmost secrecy
should be observed in forming the coalition, and that all
should be ready, at the same moment, to coöperate against a
foe so able, so determined and so powerful.

Matters being thus essentially arranged, the States of Lower
Saxony, who were to take the lead, held a meeting at Sege-
berg on the 25th of March, 1625. They formed a league for
the preservation of their religion and liberties, settled the
amount of money and men which each of the contracting parties was to furnish, and chose Christian IV., King of Denmark,
their leader.   The emperor had for some time suspected that
a confederacy was in the process of formation, and had kept a
watchful eye upon every movement. The vail was now laid
aside, and Christian IV. issued a proclamation, stating the
reasons why they had taken up arms against the emperor.
This was the signal for a blaze of war, which wrapped all
northern Europe in a wide conflagration.   Victory ebbed
and flowed. Bohemia, Hungary, Denmark, Austria—all the
States of the empire, were swept and devastated by pursuing
and retreating armies. But gradually the emperor gained.
First he overwhelmed all opposition in Lower Saxony, and
riveting anew the shackles of despotism, rewarded his followers with the spoils of the vanquished. Then he silenced every
murmur in Austria, so that no foe dared lift up the voice or

peep. Then he poured his legions into Hungary, swept back
the tide of victory which had been following the Hungarian
banners, and struck blow after blow, until Gabriel Bethlehem
was compelled to cry for peace and mercy. Bohemia, previously disarmed and impoverished, was speedily struck down.

And now the emperor turned his energies against the
panic-stricken King of Denmark. He pursued him from fortress to fortress; attacked him in the open field, and beat
him; attacked him behind his intrenchments, and drove him
from them through the valleys, and over the hills, across
rivers, and into forests; bombarded his cities, plundered his
provinces, shot down his subjects, till the king, reduced almost
to the last extremity, implored peace. The emperor repelled
his advances with scorn, demanding conditions of debasement
more to be dreaded than death. The King of Denmark fled
to the isles of the Baltic. Ferdinand took possession of the
shores of this northern sea, and immediately commenced with
vigor creating a fleet, that he might have sea as well as land
forces, that he might pursue the Danish monarch over the
water, and that he might more effectually punish Gustavus
Adolphus of Sweden. He had determined to dethrone this
monarch, and to transfer the crown of Sweden to Sigismond,
his brother-in-law, King of Poland, who was almost as zealous
a Roman Catholic as was the emperor himself.

He drove the two Dukes of Mecklenburg from their territory, and gave the rich and beautiful duchy, extending along
the south-eastern shore of the Baltic, to his renowned general,
Wallenstein. This fierce, ambitious warrior was made generalissimo of all the imperial troops by land, and admiral of
the Baltic sea. Ferdinand took possession of all the ports,
from the mouth of the Keil, to Kolberg, at the mouth of the
Persante. Wismar, on the magnificent bay bearing the same
name, was made the great naval depot; and, by building,
buying, hiring and robbing, the emperor soon collected quite
a formidable fleet. The immense duchy of Pomerania was

just north-east of Mecklenburg, extending along the eastern shore of the Baltic sea some hundred and eighty miles, and about sixty miles in breadth. Though the duke had in no way displeased Ferdinand, the emperor grasped the magnificent duchy, and held it by the power of his resistless armies. Crossing a narrow arm of the sea, he took the rich and populous islands of Rugen and Usedom, and laid siege to the city of Stralsund, which almost commanded the Baltic sea.

The kings of Sweden and Denmark, appalled by the rapid strides of the imperial general, united all their strength to resist him. They threw a strong garrison into Stralsund, and sent the fleets of both kingdoms to aid in repelling the attack, and succeeded in baffling all the attempts of Wallenstein, and finally in driving him off, though he had boasted that " he would reduce Stralsund, even if it were bound to heaven with chains of adamant." Though frustrated in this attempt, the armies of Ferdinand had swept along so resistlessly, that the King of Denmark was ready to make almost any sacrifice fo. peace. A congress was accordingly held at Lubec in May, 1629, when peace was made ; Ferdinand retaining a large portion of his conquests, and the King of Denmark engaging no longer to interfere in the affairs of the empire.

Ferdinand was now triumphant over all his foes. The Protestants throughout the empire were crushed, and all their allies vanquished. He now deemed himself omnipotent, and with wild ambition contemplated the utter extirpation of Protestantism, and the subjugation of nearly all of Europe to his sway. He formed the most intimate alliance with the branch of his house ruling over Spain, hoping that thus the house of Austria might be the arbiter of the fate of Europe. The condition of Europe at that time was peculiarly favorable for the designs of the emperor. Charles I. of England was struggling against that Parliament which soon deprived him both of his crown and his head. France was agitated, from the Rhine to the Pyrenees, by civil war, the Catholics striving to exterminate the Protestants. Insurrections in Turkey absorbed all the energies of the Ottoman court, leaving them no time to think of interfering with the affairs of Europe. The King of Denmark was humiliated and prostrate. Sweden was .oo far distant and too feeble to excite alarm. Sigismond of Poland was in intimate alliance with the emperor. Gabriel Bethlehem of Hungary was, languishing on a bed of disease and pain, and only asked permission to die in peace.

The first step which the emperor now took was to revoke all the concessions which had been granted to the Protestants. In Upper Austria, where he felt especially strong, he abolished the Protestant worship utterly. In Lower Austria he was slightly embarrassed by engagements which he had so solemnly made, and dared not trample upon them without some little show of moderation. First he prohibited the circulation of all Protestant books; he then annulled all baptisms and marriages performed by Protestants; then all Protestants were excluded from holding any civil or military office; then he issued a decree that all the children, without exception, should be educated by Catholic priests, and that every individual should attend Catholic worship. Thus coil by coil he wound around his subjects the chain of unrelenting intolerance.

In Bohemia he was especially severe, apparently delighting to punish those who had made a struggle for civil and religious liberty. Every school teacher, university professor and Christian minister, was ejected from office, and their places in schools, universities and churches were supplied by Catholic monks. No person was allowed to exercise any mechanical trade whatever, unless he professed the Roman Catholic faith. A very severe fine was inflicted upon any one who should be detected worshiping at any time, even in family prayer, according to the doctrines and customs of the Protestant church. Protestant marriages were pronounced illegal, their children illegitimate, their wills invalid. The Protestant poor were driven from the hospitals and the alms-houses. No Protestant was allowed to reside in the capital city of Prague, but, whatever his wealth or rank, he was driven ignominiously from the metropolis.

In the smaller towns and remote provinces of the kingdom, a military force, accompanied by Jesuits and Capuchin friars, sought out the Protestants, and they were exposed to every conceivable insult and indignity. Their houses were pillaged, their wives and children surrendered to all the outrages of a cruel soldiery; many were massacred; many, hunted like wild beasts, were driven into the forest; many were put to the torture, and as their bones were crushed and quivering nerves were torn, they were required to give in their adhesion to the Catholic faith. The persecution to which the Bohemians were subjected has perhaps never been exceeded in severity.

While Bohemia was writhing beneath these woes, the emperor, to secure the succession, repaired in regal pomp to Prague, and crowned his son King of Bohemia. He then issued a decree abolishing the right which the Bohemians had claimed, to elect their king, forbade the use of the Bohemian language in the court and in all public transactions, and annulled all past edicts of toleration. He proclaimed that no religion but the Roman Catholic should henceforth be tolerated in Bohemia, and that all who did not immediately return to the bosom of the Church should be banished from the kingdom. This cruel edict drove into banishment thirty thousand families. These Protestant families composed the best portion of the community, including the most illustrious in rank, the most intelligent, the most industrious and the most virtuous. No State could meet with such a loss without feeling it deeply, and Bohemia has never yet recovered from the blow. One of the Bohemian historians, himself a Roman Catholic, thus describes the change which persecution wrought in Bohemia:

"The records of history scarcely furnish a similar example of such a change as Bohemia underwent during the reign of Ferdinand II. In 1620, the monks and a few of the nobility only excepted, the whole country was entirely Protestant. At the death of Ferdinand it was, in appearance at least, Catholic. Till the battle of the White Mountain the States enjoyed more exclusive privileges than the Parliament of England. They enacted laws, imposed taxes, contracted alliances, declared war and peace, and chose or confirmed their kings. But all these they now lost.

"Till this fatal period the Bohemians were daring, un-daunted, enterprising, emulous of fame; now they have lost all their courage, their national pride, their enterprising spirit. Their courage lay buried in the White Mountain. Individuals still possessed personal valor, military ardor and a thirst of glory, but, blended with other nations, they resembled the waters of the Moldau which join those of the Elbe. These united streams bear ships, overflow lands and overturn rocks; yet the Elbe is only mentioned, and the Moldau forgotten.

"The Bohemian language, which had been used in all the courts of justice, and which was in high estimation among the nobles, fell into contempt. The German was introduced, be-came the general language among the nobles and citizens, and was used by the monks in their sermons. The inhabitants of the towns began to be ashamed of their native tongue, which was confined to the villages and called the language of peas-ants. The arts and sciences, so highly cultivated and esteemed under Rhodolph, sunk beyond recovery. During the period which immediately followed the banishment of the Protestants, Bohemia scarcely produced one man who became eminent in any branch of learning. The greater part of the schools were conducted by Jesuits and other monkish orders, and nothing taught therein but bad Latin.

"It can not be denied that several of the Jesuits were men of great learning and science; but their system was to keep the people in ignorance. Agreeably to this principle they gave their scholars only the rind, and kept to themselves the pulp of literature. With this view they traveled from town to

town as missionaries, and went from house to house, examin·
ing all books, which the landlord was compelled under pain of
eternal damnation to produce. The greater part they confiscated and burnt. They thus endeavored to extinguish the
ancient literature of the country, labored to persuade the students that before the introduction of their order into Bohemia nothing but ignorance prevailed, and carefully concealed
the learned labors and even the names of our ancestors."

Ferdinand, having thus bound Bohemia hand and foot, and
having accomplished all his purpose in that kingdom, now en·
deavored, by cautious but very decisive steps, to expel Prot·
estant doctrines from all parts of the German empire. Decree
succeeded decree, depriving Protestants of their rights and
conferring upon the Roman Catholics wealth and station. He
had a powerful and triumphant standing army at his control,
under the energetic and bigoted Wallenstein, ready and able
to enforce his ordinances. No Protestant prince dared to
make any show of resistance. All the church property was
torn from the Protestants, and this vast sum, together with
the confiscated territories of those Protestant princes or nobles who had ventured to resist the emperor, placed at his disposal a large fund from which to reward his followers. The
emperor kept, however, a large portion of the spoils in his own
hands for the enriching of his own family.

This state of things soon alarmed even the Catholics. The
emperor was growing too powerful, and his power was bear·
ing profusely its natural fruit of pride and arrogance. The
army was insolent, trampling alike upon friend and foe. As
there was no longer any war, the army had become merely
the sword of the emperor to maintain his despotism. Wallenstein had become so essential to the emperor, and possessed
such power at the head of the army, that he assumed all the
air and state of a sovereign, and insulted the highest nobles
and the most powerful bishops by his assumptions of superior·
ity. The electors of the empire perceiving that the emperor

was centroliaing power in his own hands. and that they would
soon become merely provincial governors, compelled to obey
his laws and subject to his appointment and removal, began to
whisper to each other their alarm.

The Duke of Bavaria was one of the most powerful princes
of the German empire. He had been the rival of Count Wal
enstein, and was now exceedingly annoyed by the arrogance of
this haughty military chief. Wallenstein was the emperor's
right arm of strength. Inflamed by as intense an ambition as
ever burned in a human bosom, every thought and energy
was devoted to self-aggrandizement. He had been educated
a Protestant, but abandoned those views for the Catholic faith
which opened a more alluring field to ambition. Sacrificing
the passions of youth he married a widow, infirm and of advanced age, but of great wealth. The death of his wrinkled
bride soon left him the vast property without incumbrance.
He then entered into a matrimonial alliance which favored
his political prospects, marrying Isabella, the daughter of
Count Harruch, who was one of the emperor's greatest favorites.

When Ferdinand's fortunes were at a low ebb, and he knew
not in which way to find either money or an army, Wallenstein offered to raise fifty thousand men at his own expense,
to pay their wages, supply them with arms and all the munitions of war, and to call upon the emperor for no pecuniary
assistance whatever, if the emperor would allow him to retain
the plunder he could extort from the conquered. Upon this
majestic scale Wallenstein planned to act the part of a highwayman. Ferdinand's necessities were so great that he gladly availed himself of this infamous offer. Wallenstein made
money by the bargain. Wherever he marched he compelled
the people to support his army, and to support it luxuriously.
The emperor had now constituted him admiral of the Baltic
fleet, and had conferred upon him the title of duke, with the
splendid duchy of Mecklenburg, and the principality of Sagan

in Silesia. His overbearing conduct and his enormous extor-
tions—he having, in seven years, wrested from the German
princes more than four hundred million of dollars—excited a
general feeling of discontent, in which the powerful Duke of
Bavaria took the lead.

Envy is a stronger passion than political religion. Zealous
as the Duke of Bavaria had been in the cause of the papal
church, he now forgot that church in his zeal to abase an arrogant and insulting rival. Richelieu, the prime minister of
France, was eagerly watching for opportunities to humiliate
the house of Austria, and he, with alacrity, met the advances
of the Duke of Bavaria, and conspired with him to form a Catholic league, to check the ambition of Wallenstein, and to arrest
the enormous strides of the emperor. With this object in view,
a large number of the most powerful Catholic princes met at
Heidelberg, in March, 1629, and passed resolutions soliciting
Ferdinand to summon a diet of the German empire to take
into consideration the evils occasioned by the army of Wallenstein, and to propose a remedy. The emperor had, in his
arrogance, commanded the princes of the various States in
the departments of Suabia and Franconia, to disband their
troops. To this demand they returned the bold and spirited
reply,

"Till we have received an indemnification, or a pledge for
the payment of our expenses, we will neither disband a single
soldier, nor relinquish a foot of territory, ecclesiastical or secular, *demand it who will.*"

The emperor did not venture to disregard the request for
him to summon a diet. Indeed he was anxious, on his own
account, to convene the electors, for he wished to secure the
election of his son to the throne of the empire, and he needed
succors to aid him in the ambitious wars which he was waging
in various and distant parts of Europe. The diet was assembled at Ratisbon : the emperor presided in person. As he had
important favors to solicit, he assumed a very conciliatory tone

He expressed his regret that the troops had been guilty of such disorders, and promised immediate redress. He then, supposing that his promise would be an ample satisfaction, very graciously solicited of them the succession of the imperial throne for his son, and supplies for his army.

But the electors were not at all in a pliant mood. Some were resolved that, at all hazards, the imperial army, which threatened Germany, should be reduced, and that Wallenstein should be dismissed from the command. Others were equally determined that the crown of the empire should not descend to the son of Ferdinand. The Duke of Bavaria headed the party who would debase Wallenstein; and Cardinal Richelieu, with all the potent influences of intrigue and bribery at the command of the French court, was the soul of the party resolved to wrest the crown of the empire from the house of Austria. Richelieu sent two of the most accomplished diplomatists France could furnish, as ambassadors to the diet, who, while maintaining, as far as possible, the guise of friendship, were to do every thing in their power to thwart the election of Ferdinand's son. These were supplied with inexhaustible means for the purchase of votes, and were authorized to make any promises, however extravagant, which should be deemed essential for the attainment of their object.

Ferdinand, long accustomed to have his own way, was not anticipating any serious resistance. He was therefore amazed and confounded, when the diet returned to him, instead of their humble submission and congratulations, a long, detailed, emphatic remonstrance against the enormities perpetrated by the imperial army, and demanding the immediate reduction of the army, now one hundred and fifty thousand strong, and the dismission of Wallenstein, before they could proceed to any other business whatever. This bold stand animated the Protestant princes of the empire, and they began to be clamorous for their rights. Some of the Catholics even, espoused their cause, warning Ferdinand that, unless he granted the

Protestants some degree of toleration, they would seek redress by joining the enemies of the empire.

It would have been impossible to frame three demands more obnoxious to the emperor. To crush the Protestants had absorbed the energies of his life; and now that they were utterly prostrate, to lift them up and place them on their feet again, was an idea he could not endure. The imperial army had been his supple tool. By its instrumentality he had gained all his power, and by its energies alone he retained that power. To disband the army was to leave himself defenseless. Wallenstein had been every thing to the emperor, and Ferdinand still needed the support of his inflexible and unscrupulous energies. Wallenstein was in the cabinet of the emperor advising him in this hour of perplexity. His counsel was characteristic of his impetuous, headlong spirit. He advised the emperor to pour his army into the territory of the Duke of Bavaria; chastise him and all his associates for their insolence, and thus overawe the rest. But the Duke of Bavaria was in favor of electing the emperor's son as his successor on the throne of the empire; and Ferdinand's heart was fixed upon this object.

"Dismiss Wallenstein, and reduce the army," said the Duke of Bavaria, "and the Catholic electors will vote for your son; grant the required toleration to the Protestants, and they will vote for him likewise."

The emperor yielded, deciding in his own mind, aided by the Jesuitical suggestions of a monk, that he could afterwards recall Wallenstein, and assemble anew his dispersed battalions. He dismissed sixteen thousand of his best cavalry; suspended some of the most obnoxious edicts against the Protestants, and *implored* Wallenstein to resign his post. The emperor was terribly afraid that this proud general would refuse, and would lead the army to mutiny. The emperor accordingly accompanied his request with every expression of gratitude and regret, and assured the general of his continued favor. Wallenstein, well aware that the disgrace would be but temporary, quietly yielded. He dismissed the envoys of the emperor with presents, wrote a very submissive letter, and, with much ostentation of obedience, retired to private life.

CHAPTER XVIII.

THE hand of France was conspicuous in wresting all these sacrifices from the emperor, and was then still more conspicuous in thwarting his plans for the election of his son. The ambassadors of Richelieu, with diplomatic adroitness, urged upon the diet the Duke of Bavaria as candidate for the imperial crown. This tempting offer silenced the duke, and he could make no more efforts for the emperor. The Protestants greatly preferred the duke to any one of the race of the bigoted Ferdinand. The emperor was excessively chagrined by this aspect of affairs, and abruptly dissolved the diet. He felt that he had been duped by France; that a cunning monk, Richelieu's ambassador, had outwitted him. In his vexation he exclaimed, "A Capuchin friar has disarmed me with his rosary, and covered six electoral caps with his cowl."

The emperor was meditating vengeance—the recall of Wallenstein, the reconstruction of the army, the annulling of the edict of toleration, the march of an invading force into the territories of the Duke of Bavaria, and the chastisement of

all, Catholics as well as Protestants, who had aided in thwarting his plans—when suddenly a new enemy appeared. Gustavus Adolphus, King of Sweden, reigning over his remote
realms on the western shores of the Baltic, though a zealous
Protestant, was regarded by Ferdinand as a foe too distant
and too feeble to be either respected or feared. But Gustavus, a man of exalted abilities, and of vast energy, was
watching with intense interest the despotic strides of the emperor. In his endeavors to mediate in behalf of the Protestants of Germany, he had encountered repeated insults on the
part of Ferdinand. The imperial troops were now approaching his own kingdom. They had driven Christian IV., King
of Denmark, from his continental territories on the eastern
shore of the Baltic, had already taken possession of several of
the islands, and were constructing a fleet which threatened
the command of that important sea. Gustavus was alarmed,
and roused himself to assume the championship of the civil
and religious liberties of Europe. He conferred with all the
leading Protestant princes, formed alliances, secured funds,
stationed troops to protect his own frontiers, and then, assembling the States of his kingdom, entailed the succession
of the crown on his only child Christiana, explained to them
his plans of war against the emperor, and concluded a dignified and truly pathetic harangue with the following words.

"The enterprise in which I am about to engage is not
one dictated by the love of conquest or by personal ambition.
Our honor, our religion and our independence are imperiled.
I am to encounter great dangers, and may fall upon the field
of battle. If it be God's will that I should die in the defense
of liberty, of my country and of mankind, I cheerfully surrender myself to the sacrifice. It is my duty as a sovereign to
obey the King of kings without murmuring, and to resign the
power I have received from His hands whenever it shall suit
His all-wise purposes. I shall yield up my last breath with the
firm persuasion that Providence will support my subjects be-

cause they are faithful and virtuous, and that my ministers, generals and senators will punctually discharge their duty to my child because they love justice, respect me, and feel for their country."

The king himself was affected as he uttered these words, and tears moistened the eyes of many of the stern warriors who surrounded him.   With general acclaim they approved of his plan, voted him all the succors he required, and enthusiastically offered their own fortunes and lives to his service. Gustavus assembled a fleet at Elfsnaben, crossed the Baltic sea, and in June, 1630, landed thirty thousand troops in Pomerania, which Wallenstein had overrun.   The imperial army, unprepared for such an assault, fled before the Swedish king.   Marching rapidly, Gustavus took Stettin, the capital of the duchy, situated at the mouth of the Oder, and commanding that stream.   Driving the imperial troops everywhere before him from Pomerania, and pursuing them into the adjoining Mark of Brandenburg, he took possession of a large part of that territory.   He issued a proclamation to the inhabitants of Germany, recapitulating the arbitrary and despotic acts of the emperor, and calling upon all Protestants to aid in an enterprise, in the success of which the very existence of Protestantism in Germany seemed to be involved.   But so utterly had the emperor crushed the spirits of the Protestants by his fiend-like severity, that but few ventured to respond to his appeal.   The rulers, however, of many of the Protestant States met at Leipsic, and without venturing to espouse the cause of Gustavus, and without even alluding to his invasion, they addressed a letter to the emperor demanding a redress of grievances, and informing him that they had decided to establish a permanent council for the direction of their own affairs, and to raise an army of forty thousand men for their own protection.

Most of these events had occurred while the emperor, with Wallenstein, was at Ratisbon, intriguing to secure the succession of the imperial crown for his son. They both looked upon the march of the King of Sweden into the heart of Germany as the fool-hardy act of a mad adventurer. The courtiers ridiculed his transient conquests, saying, "Gustavus Adolphus is a king of snow. Like a snowball he will melt in a southern clime." Wallenstein was particularly contemptuous. "I will whip him back to his country," said he, "like a truant school-boy, with rods." Ferdinand was for a time deceived by these representations, and was by no means aware of the real peril which threatened him. The diet which the emperor had assembled made a proclamation of war against Gustavus, but adopted no measures of energy adequate to the occasion. The emperor sent a silly message to Gustavus that if he did not retire immediately from Germany he would attack him with his whole force. To this folly Gustavus returned a contemptuous reply.

A few of the minor Protestant princes now ventured to take arms and join the standard of Gustavus. The important city of Magdeburg, in Saxony, on the Elbe, espoused his cause. This city, with its bastions and outworks completely commanding the Elbe, formed one of the strongest fortresses of Europe. It contained, exclusive of its strong garrison, thirty thousand inhabitants. It was now evident to Ferdinand that vigorous action was called for. He could not, consistently with his dignity, recall Wallenstein in the same breath with which he had dismissed him. He accordingly concentrated his troops and placed them under the command of Count Tilly. The imperial troops were dispatched to Magdeburg. They surrounded the doomed city, assailed it furiously, and proclaimed their intention of making it a signal mark of imperial vengeance. Notwithstanding the utmost efforts of Gustavus to hasten to their relief, he was foiled in his endeavors, and the town was carried by assault on the 10th of May. Never, perhaps, did earth witness a more cruel exhibition of the horrors of war. The soul sickens in the contem

plation of outrages so fiend-like. We prefer to give the narrative of these deeds, which it is the duty of history to record,
in the language of another.

"All the horrors ever exercised against a captured place
were repeated and almost surpassed, on this dreadful event,
which, notwithstanding all the subsequent disorders and the
lapse of time, is still fresh in the recollection of its inhabitants
and of Germany. Neither age, beauty nor innocence, neither
infancy nor decrepitude, found refuge or compassion from the
fury of the licentious soldiery. No retreat was sufficiently secure to escape their rapacity and vengeance; no sanctuary
sufficiently sacred to repress their lust and cruelty. Infants
were murdered before the eyes of their parents, daughters
and wives violated in the arms of their fathers and husbands.
Some of the imperial officers, recoiling from this terrible scene,
flew to Count Tilly and supplicated him to put a stop to the
carnage. 'Stay yet an hour,' was his barbarous reply; 'let
the soldier have some compensation for his dangers and fatigues.'

"The troops, left to themselves, after sating their passions,
and almost exhausting their cruelty in three hours of pillage
and massacre, set fire to the town, and the flames were in an
instant spread by the wind to every quarter of the place.
Then opened a scene which surpassed all the former horrors.
Those who had hitherto escaped, or who were forced by the
flames from their hiding-places, experienced a more dreadful
fate. Numbers were driven into the Elbe, others massacred
with every species of savage barbarity—the wombs of preg-
nant women ripped up, and infants thrown into the fire or
impaled on pikes and suspended over the flames. History has
no terms, poetry no language, painting no colors to depict
all the horrors of the scene. In less than ten hours the most
rich, the most flourishing and the most populous town in Germany was reduced to ashes. The cathedral, a single convent
and a few miserable huts, were all that were left of its numer

ous buildings, and scarcely more than a thousand souls all that remained of more than thirty thousand inhabitants.

"After an interval of two days, when the soldiers were fatigued, if not sated, with devastation and slaughter, and when the flames had begun to subside, Tilly entered the town in triumph. To make room for his passage the streets were cleared and six thousand carcasses thrown into the Elbe. He ordered the pillage to cease, pardoned the scanty remnant of the inhabitants, who had taken refuge in the cathedral, and, surrounded by flames and carnage, had remained three days without food or refreshment, under all the terrors of impending fate. After hearing a *Te Deum* in the midst of military pomp, he paraded the streets; and even though his unfeeling heart seemed touched with the horrors of the scene, he could not refrain from the savage exultation of boasting to the emperor, and comparing the assault of Magdeburg to the sack of Troy and of Jerusalem."

This terrible display of vengeance struck the Protestants with consternation. The extreme Catholic party were exultant, and their chiefs met in a general assembly and passed resolutions approving the course of the emperor and pledging him their support. Ferdinand was much encouraged by this change in his favor, and declared his intention of silencing all Protestant voices. He recalled an army of twenty-four thousand men from Italy. They crossed the Alps, and, as they marched through the frontier States of the empire, they spread devastation and ruin through all the Protestant territories, exacting enormous contributions, compelling the Protestant princes, on oath, to renounce the Protestant league, and to unite with the Catholic confederacy against the King of Sweden.

In the meantime, Gustavus pressed forward into the duchy of Mecklenburg, driving the imperial troops before him. Tilly retired into the territory of the Elector of Saxony, robbing, burning and destroying everywhere. Uniting his force with the army from Italy he ravaged the country, resistlessly advancing even to Leipsic, and capturing the city. The elector, quite unable to cope with so powerful a foe, retired with his troops to the Swedish camp, where he entered into an offensive and defensive alliance with Gustavus. The Swedish army, thus reinforced, hastened to the relief of Leipsic, and arrived before its walls the very day on which the city surrendered.

Tilly, with the pride of a conqueror, advanced to meet them. The two armies, about equal in numbers, and commanded by their renowned captains, met but a few miles from the city. Neither of the commanders had ever before suffered a defeat. It was a duel, in which one or the other must fall. Every soldier in the ranks felt the sublimity of the hour. For some time there was marching and countermarching—the planting of batteries, and the gathering of squadrons and solid columns, each one hesitating to strike the first blow. At last the signal was given by the discharge of three pieces of cannon from one of the batteries of Tilly. Instantly a thunder peal rolled along the extended lines from wing to wing. The awful work of death was begun. Hour after hour the fierce and bloody fight continued, as the surges of victory and defeat swept to and fro upon the plain. But the ever uncertain fortune of battle decided in favor of the Swedes. As the darkness of evening came prematurely on, deepened by the clouds of smoke which canopied the field, the imperialists were everywhere flying in dismay. Tilly, having been struck by three balls, was conveyed from the field in excruciating pain to a retreat in Halle. Seven thousand of his troops lay dead upon the field. Five thousand were taken prisoners. All the imperial artillery and baggage fell into the hands of the conqueror. The rest of the army was so dispersed that but two thousand could be rallied under the imperial banners.

Gustavus, thus triumphant, dispatched a portion of his army, under the Elector of Saxony, to rescue Bohemia from the tyrant grasp of the emperor. Gustavus himself, with another portion, marched in various directions to cut off the resources of the enemy and to combine the scattered parts of the Protestant confederacy. His progress was like the tranquil march of a sovereign in his own dominions, greeted by the enthusiasm of his subjects. He descended the Maine to the Rhine, and then ascending the Rhine, took every fortress from Maine to Strasbourg. While Gustavus was thus extending his conquests through the very heart of Germany, the Elector of Saxony reclaimed all of Bohemia from the imperial arms. Prague itself capitulated to the Saxon troops. Count Thurn led the Saxon troops in triumph over the same bridge which he, but a few months before, had traversed a fugitive. He found, impaled upon the bridge, the shriveled heads of twelve of his companions, which he enveloped in black satin and buried with funeral honors.

The Protestants of Bohemia rose enthusiastically to greet their deliverers. Their churches, schools and universities were reëstablished. Their preachers resumed their functions. Many returned from exile and rejoiced in the restoration of their confiscated property. The Elector of Saxony retaliated upon the Catholics the cruel wrongs which they had inflicted upon the Protestants. Their castles were plundered, their nobles driven into exile, and the conquerors loaded themselves with the spoils of the vanquished.

But Ferdinand, as firm and inexorable in adversity as in prosperity, bowed not before disaster. He roused the Catholics to a sense of their danger, organized new coalitions, raised new armies. Tilly, with recruited forces, was urged on to arrest the march of the conqueror. Burning under the sense of shame for his defeat at Leipsic, he placed himself at the head of his veterans, fell, struck by a musket-ball, and died, after a few days of intense suffering, at the age of seventy-three. The vast Austrian empire, composed of so many heterogeneous States, bound together only by the iron energy of Ferdinand, seemed now upon the eve of its dissolution. The Protestants, who composed, in most of the States a majority, were cordially rallying beneath the banners of Gustavus. They had been in a state of despair. They now rose in exalted hope. Many of the minor princes who had been nominally Catholics, but whose Christian creeds were merely political dogmas, threw themselves into the arms of Gustavus. Even the Elector of Bavaria was so helpless in his isolation, that, champion as he had been of the Catholic party, there seemed to be no salvation for him but in abandoning the cause of Ferdinand. Gustavus was now, with a victorious army, in the heart of Germany. He was in possession of the whole western country from the Baltic to the frontiers of France, and apparently a majority of the population were in sympathy with him.

Ferdinand at first resolved, in this dire extremity, to assume himself the command of his armies, and in person to enter the field. This was heroic madness, and his friends soon convinced him of the folly of one so inexperienced in the arts of war undertaking to cope with Gustavus Adolphus, now the most experienced and renowned captain in Europe. He then thought of appointing his son, the Archduke Ferdinand, commander-in-chief. But Ferdinand was but twenty-three years of age, and though a young man of decided abilities, was by no means able to encounter on the field the skill and heroism of the Swedish warrior. In this extremity, Ferdinand was compelled to turn his eyes to his discarded general Wallenstein.

This extraordinary man, in renouncing, at the command of his sovereign, his military supremacy, retired with boundless wealth, and assumed a style of living surpassing even regal splendor. His gorgeous palace at Prague was patrolled by sentinels. A body-guard of fifty halberdiers, in sumptuous uniform, ever waited in his ante-chamber. Twelve nobles attended his person, and four gentlemen ushers introduced to his presence those whom he condescended to favor with an audience. Sixty pages, taken from the most illustrious families, embellished his courts. His steward was a baron of the highest rank; and even the chamberlain of the emperor had left Ferdinand's court, that he might serve in the more princely palace of this haughty subject. A hundred guests dined daily at his table. His gardens and parks were embellished with more than oriental magnificence. Even his stables were furnished with marble mangers, and supplied with water from an ever-living fountain. Upon his journeys he was accompanied by a suite of twelve coaches of state and fifty carriages. A large retinue of wagons conveyed his plate and equipage. Fifty mounted grooms followed with fifty led horses richly caparisoned.*

Wallenstein watched the difficulties gathering around the emperor with satisfaction which he could not easily disguise. Though intensely eager to be restored to the command of the armies, he affected an air of great indifference, and when the emperor suggested his restoration, he very adroitly played the coquette. The emperor at first proposed that his son, the Archduke Ferdinand, should nominally have the command, while Wallenstein should be his executive and advisory general. " I would not serve," said the impious captain, " as second in command under God Himself."

After long negotiation, Wallenstein, with well-feigned reluctance, consented to relinquish for a few weeks the sweets of private life, and to recruit an army, and bring it under suitable discipline. He, however, limited the time of his command to three months. With his boundless wealth and amazing energy, he immediately set all springs in motion. Adventurers from all parts of Europe, lured by the splendor of his past achievements, crowded his ranks. In addition to his own vast opulence, the pope and the court of Spain opened freely to him their purses. As by magic he was in a few weeks at the head of forty thousand men. In companies, regiments and battalions they were incessantly drilled, and by the close of three months this splendid army, thoroughly

* Coxe's "House of Austria," ii., 254.

furnished, and in the highest state of discipline, was presented to the emperor. Every step he had taken had convinced, and was intended to convince Ferdinand that his salvation depended upon the energies of Wallenstein. Gustavus was now, in the full tide of victory, marching from the Rhine to the Danube, threatening to press his conquests even to Vienna. Ferdinand was compelled to assume the attitude of a suppliant, and to implore his proud general to accept the command of which he had so recently been deprived. Wallenstein exacted terms so humiliating as in reality to divest the emperor of his imperial power. He was to be declared generalissimo of all the forces of the empire, and to be invested with unlimited authority. The emperor pledged himself that neither he nor his son would ever enter the camp. Wallenstein was to appoint all his officers, distribute all rewards, and the emperor was not allowed to grant either a pardon or a safe-conduct without the confirmation of Wallenstein. The general was to levy what contribution he pleased upon the vanquished enemy, confiscate property, and no peace or truce was to be made with the enemy without his consent. Finally, he was to receive, either from the spoils of the enemy, or from the hereditary States of the empire, princely remuneration for his services.

Armed with such enormous power, Wallenstein consented to place himself at the head of the army. He marched to Prague, and without difficulty took the city. Gradually he drove the Saxon troops from all their fortresses in Bohemia. Then advancing to Bavaria, he effected a junction with Bavarian troops, and found himself sufficiently strong to attempt to arrest the march of Gustavus. The imperial force now amounted to sixty thousand men. Wallenstein was so sanguine of success, that he boasted that in a few days he would decide the question, whether Gustavus Adolphus or Wallenstein was to be master of the world. The Swedish king was at Nuremberg with but twenty thousand men, when he heard of the approach of the imperial army, three times outnumbering his own. Disdaining to retreat, he threw up redoubts, and prepared for a desperate defense. As Wallenstein brought up his heavy battalions, he was so much overawed by the military genius which Gustavus had displayed in his strong intrenchments, and by the bold front which the Swedes presented, that notwithstanding his boast, he did not dare to hazard an attack. He accordingly threw up intrenchments opposite the works of the Swedes, and there the two armies remained, looking each other in the face for eight weeks, neither daring to withdraw from behind their intrenchments, and each hoping to starve the other party out. Gustavus did every thing in his power to provoke Wallenstein to the attack, but the wary general, notwithstanding the importunities of his officers, and the clamors of his soldiers, refused to risk an engagement. Both parties were all the time strengthening their intrenchments and gathering reinforcements.

At last Gustavus resolved upon an attack. He led his troops against the intrenchments of Wallenstein, which resembled a fortress rather than a camp. The Swedes clambered over the intrenchments, and assailed the imperialists with as much valor and energy as mortals ever exhibited. They were however, with equal fury repelled, and after a long conflict were compelled to retire again behind their fortifications with the loss of three thousand of their best troops. For another fortnight the two armies remained watching each other, and then Gustavus, leaving a strong garrison in Nuremberg, slowly and defiantly retired. Wallenstein stood so much in fear of the tactics of Gustavus that he did not even venture to molest his retreat. During this singular struggle of patient endurance, both armies suffered fearfully from sickness and famine. In the city of Nuremberg ten thousand perished. Gustavus buried twenty thousand of his men beneath his intrenchments. And in the imperial army, after the retreat of Gustavus, but thirty thousand troops were left to answer the roll-call.

Wallenstein claimed, and with justice, the merit of having arrested the steps of Gustavus, though he could not boast of any very chivalrous exploits. After various maneuvering, and desolating marches, the two armies, with large reinforcements, met at Lutzen, about thirty miles from Leipsic. It was in the edge of the evening when they arrived within sight of each other's banners. Both parties passed an anxious night, preparing for the decisive battle which the dawn of the morning would usher in.

Wallenstein was fearfully alarmed. He had not willingly met his dreaded antagonist, and would now gladly escape the issues of battle. He called a council of war, and even suggested a retreat. But it was decided that such an attempt in the night, and while watched by so able and vigilant a foe, would probably involve the army in irretrievable ruin, besides exposing his own name to deep disgrace. The imperial troops, thirty thousand strong, quite outnumbered the army of Gustavus, and the officers of Wallenstein unanimously advised to give battle. Wallenstein was a superstitious man and deeply devoted to astrological science. He consulted his astrologers, and they declared the stars to be unpropitious to Gustavus. This at once decided him. He resolved, however, to act on the defensive, and through the night employed the energies of his army in throwing up intrenchments. In the earliest dawn of the morning mass was celebrated throughout the whole camp, and Wallenstein on horseback rode along behind the redoubts, urging his troops, by every consideration, to fight valiantly for their emperor and their religion.

The morning was dark and lowering, and such an impenetrable fog enveloped the armies that they were not visible to each other. It was near noon ere the fog arose, and the two armies, in the full blaze of an unclouded sun, gazed, awestricken, upon each other. The imperial troops and the Swedish troops were alike renowned ; and Gustavus Adolphus and Wallenstein were, by universal admission, the two ablest cap-

tains in Europe. Neither force could even affect to despise
the other. The scene unfolded, as the vapor swept away, was
one which even war has seldom presented. The vast plain
of Lutzen extended many miles, almost as smooth, level and
treeless as a western prairie. Through the center of this plain
ran a nearly straight and wide road. On one side of this
road, in long line, extending one or two miles, was the army
of Wallenstein. His whole front was protected by a ditch and
redoubts bristling with bayonets. Behind these intrenchments
his army was extended ; the numerous and well-mounted cavalry at the wings, the artillery, in ponderous batteries, at the
center, with here and there solid squares of infantry to meet
the rush of the assailing columns. On the other side of the
road, and within musket-shot, were drawn up in a parallel line
the troops of Gustavus. He had interspersed along his double
line bands of cavalry, with artillery and platoons of musket-
eers, that he might be prepared from any point to make or
repel assault. The whole host stood reverently, with uncovered
heads, as a public prayer was offered. The Psalm which Watts
has so majestically versified was read—

> "God is the refuge of his saints,
>   When storms of dark distress invade;
> Ere we can offer our complaints,
>   Behold him present with his aid.
>
> "Let mountains from their seats be hurled
>   Down to the deep, and buried there,
> Convulsions shake the solid world;
>   Our faith shall never yield to fear."

From twenty thousand voices the solemn hymn arose and
floated over the field—celestial songs, to be succeeded by demoniac clangor. Both parties appealed to the God of battle ; both parties seemed to feel that their cause was just.
Alas for man !

Gustavus now ordered the attack. A solid column emerged
from his ranks, crossed the road, in breathless silence approached the trenches, while both armies looked on. They

were received with a volcanic sheet of flame which prostrated half of them bleeding upon the sod. Gustavus ordered column after column to follow on to support the assailants, and to pierce the enemy's center. In his zeal he threw
himself from his horse, seized a pike, and rushed to head the
attack. Wallenstein energetically ordered up cavalry and artillery to strengthen the point so fiercely assailed. And now
the storm of war blazed along the whole lines. A sulphureous
canopy settled down over the contending hosts, and thunderings, shrieks, clangor as of Pandemonium, filled the air. The
king, as reckless of life as if he had been the meanest soldier,
rushed to every spot where the battle raged the fiercest.
Learning that his troops upon the left were yielding to the
imperial fire, he mounted his horse and was galloping across
the field swept by the storm of war, when a bullet struck his
arm and shattered the bone. Almost at the same moment
another bullet struck his breast, and he fell mortally wounded
from his horse, exclaiming, " My God ! my God !"

The command now devolved upon the Duke of Saxe Wei
mar. The horse of Gustavus, galloping along the lines, conveyed to the whole army the dispiriting intelligence that their
beloved chieftain had fallen. The duke spread the report that
he was not killed, but taken prisoner, and summoned all to the
rescue. This roused the Swedes to superhuman exertions.
They rushed over the ramparts, driving the infantry back upon
the cavalry, and the whole imperial line was thrown into confusion. Just at that moment, when both parties were in the
extreme of exhaustion, when the Swedes were shouting victory and the imperialists were flying in dismay, General
Pappenheim, with eight fresh regiments of imperial cavalry,
came galloping upon the field. This seemed at once to restore
the battle to the imperialists, and the Swedes were apparently
undone. But just then a chance bullet struck Pappenheim
and he fell, mortally wounded, from his horse. The cry ran
through the imperia. ranks, "Pappenheim is killed and the

battle is lost." No further efforts of Wallenstein were of any avail to arrest the confusion. His whole host turned and fled. Fortunately for them, the darkness of the approaching night, and a dense fog settling upon the plain, concealed them from their pursuers. During the night the imperialists retired, and in the morning the Swedes found themselves in possession of the field with no foe in sight. But the Swedes had no heart to exult over their victory. The loss of their beloved king was a greater calamity than any defeat could have been. His mangled body was found, covered with blood, in the midst of heaps of the slain, and so much mutilated with the tramplings of cavalry as to be with difficulty recognized.

CHAPTER XIX.

FERDINAND II., FERDINAND III. AND LEOPOLD I

FROM 1632 TO 1662.

CHARACTER OF GUSTAVUS ADOLPHUS.—EXULTATION OF THE IMPERIALISTS.—DISGRACE OF WALLENSTEIN.—HE OFFERS TO SURRENDER TO THE SWEDISH GENERAL.—HIS ASSASSINATION.—FERDINAND'S SON ELECTED AS HIS SUCCESSOR.—DEATH OF FERDINAND,—CLOSE OF THE WAR.—ABDICATION OF CHRISTINA.—CHARLES GUSTAVUS. —PREPARATIONS FOR WAR.—DEATH OF FERDINAND III.—LEOPOLD ELECTED EMPEROR.—HOSTILITIES RENEWED.—DEATH OF CHARLES GUSTAVUS.—DIET CONVENED. —INVASION OF THE TURKS.

THE battle of Lutzen was fought on the 16th of November, 1632. It is generally estimated that the imperial troops were forty thousand, while there were but twenty-seven thousand in the Swedish army. Gustavus was then thirty-eight years of age. A plain stone still marks the spot where he fell. A few poplars surround it, and it has become a shrine visited by strangers from all parts of the world. Traces of his blood are still shown in the town-house of Lutzen, where his body was transported from the fatal field. The buff waistcoat he wore in the engagement, pierced by the bullet which took his life, is preserved as a trophy in the arsenal at Vienna.

Both as a monarch and a man, this illustrious sovereign stands in the highest ranks. He possessed the peculiar power of winning the ardent attachment of all who approached him. Every soldier in the army was devoted to him, for he shared all their toils and perils. "Cities," he said, "are not taken by keeping in tents; as scholars, in the absence of the master, shut their books, so my troops, without my presence, would slacken their blows."

In very many traits of character he resembled Napoleon,

combining in his genius the highest attributes of the statesman and the soldier. Like Napoleon he was a predestinarian, believing himself the child of Providence, raised for the accomplishment of great purposes, and that the decrees of his destiny no foresight could thwart. When urged to spare his person in the peril of battle, he replied,

"My hour is written in heaven, and can not be reversed."

Frederic, the unhappy Elector of the Palatine, and King of Bohemia, who had been driven from his realms by Ferdinand, and who, for some years, had been wandering from court to court in Europe, seeking an asylum, was waiting at Mentz, trusting that the success of the armies of Gustavus would soon restore him to his throne. The death of the king shattered all his hopes. Disappointment and chagrin threw him into a fever of which he died, in the thirty-ninth year of his age. The death of Gustavus was considered by the Catholics such a singular interposition of Providence in their behalf, that, regardless of the disaster of Lutzen, they surrendered themselves to the most enthusiastic joy. Even in Spain bells were rung, and the streets of Madrid blazed with bonfires and illuminations. At Vienna it was regarded as a victory, and *Te Deums* were chanted in the cathedral. Ferdinand, however, conducted with a decorum which should be recorded to his honor. He expressed the fullest appreciation of the grand qualities of his opponent, and in graceful words regretted his untimely death. When the bloody waistcoat, perforated by the bullet, was shown him, he turned from it with utterances of sadness and regret. Even if this were all feigned, it shows a sense of external propriety worthy of record.

It was the genius of Gustavus alone which had held together the Protestant confederacy. No more aid of any efficiency could be anticipated from Sweden. Christina, the daughter and heiress of Gustavus, was in her seventh year. The crown was claimed by her cousin Ladislaus, the King of Poland, and this disputed succession threatened the kingdom with the calamities of civil war. The Senate of Sweden in this emergence conducted with great prudence. That they might secure an honorable peace they presented a bold front of war. A council of regency was appointed, abundant succors in men and money voted, and the Chancellor Oxenstiern, a man of commanding civil and military talents, was intrusted with the sole conduct of the war. The Senate declared the young queen the legitimate successor to the throne, and forbade all allusion to the claims of Ladislaus, under the penalty of high treason.

Oxenstiern proved himself worthy to be the successor of Gustavus. He vigorously renewed alliances with the German princes, and endeavored to follow out the able plans sketched by the departed monarch. Wallenstein, humiliated by his defeat, had fallen back into Bohemia, and now, with moderation strangely inconsistent with his previous career, urged the emperor to conciliate the Protestants by publishing a decree of general amnesty, and by proposing peace on favorable terms. But the iron will of Ferdinand was inflexible. In heart, exulting that his most formidable foe was removed, he resolved with unrelenting vigor to prosecute the war. The storm of battle raged anew; and to the surprise of Ferdinand, Oxenstiern moved forward with strides of victory as signal as those of his illustrious predecessor. Wallenstein meanly attempted to throw the blame of the disaster at Lutzen upon the alleged cowardice of his officers. Seventeen of them he hanged, and consigned fifty others to infamy by inscribing their names upon the gallows.

So haughty a man could not but have many enemies at court. They combined, and easily persuaded Ferdinand, who had also been insulted by his arrogance, again to degrade him. Wallenstein, informed of their machinations, endeavored to rally the army to a mutiny in his favor. Ferdinand, alarmed by this intelligence, which even threatened his own dethronement, immediately dismissed Wallenstein from the command, and dispatched officers from Vienna to seize his person, dead or alive. This roused Wallenstein to desperation. Having secured the coöperation of his leading officers, he dispatched envoys to the Swedish camp, offering to surrender important fortresses to Oxenstiern, and to join him against the emperor. It was an atrocious act of treason, and so marvellous in its aspect, that Oxenstiern regarded it as mere duplicity on the part of Wallenstein, intended to lead him into a trap. He therefore dismissed the envoy, rejecting the offer. His officers now abandoned him, and Gallas, who was appointed as his successor, took command of the army.

With a few devoted adherents, and one regiment of troops, he took refuge in the strong fortress of Egra, hoping to maintain himself there until he could enter into some arrangement with the Swedes. The officers around him, whom he had elevated and enriched by his iniquitous bounty, entered into a conspiracy to purchase the favor of the emperor by the assassination of their doomed general. It was a very difficult enterprise, and one which exposed the conspirators to the most imminent peril.

On the 25th of February, 1634, the conspirators gave a magnificent entertainment in the castle. They sat long at the table, wine flowed freely, and as the darkness of night enveloped the castle, fourteen men, armed to the teeth, rushed into the banqueting hall from two opposite doors, and fell upon the friends of Wallenstein. Though thus taken by surprise, they fought fiercely, and killed several of their assailants before they were cut down. They all, however, were soon dispatched. The conspirators, fifty in number, then ascended the stairs of the castle to the chamber of Wallenstein. They cut down the sentinel at his door, and broke into the room. Wallenstein had retired to his bed, but alarmed by the clamor, he arose, and was standing at the window in his shirt, shouting from it to the soldiers for assistance.

"Are you," exclaimed one of the conspirators, "the traitor

who is going to deliver the imperial troops to the enemy, and tear the crown from the head of the emperor?"

Wallenstein was perfectly helpless. He looked around, and deigned no reply. "You must die," continued the conspirator, advancing with his halberd. Wallenstein, in silence, opened his arms to receive the blow. The sharp blade pierced his body, and he fell dead upon the floor. The alarm now spread through the town. The soldiers seized their arms, and flocked to avenge their general. But the leading friends of Wallenstein were slain; and the other officers easily satisfied the fickle soldiery that their general was a traitor, and with rather a languid cry of "Long live Ferdinand," they returned to duty.

Two of the leading assassins hastened to Vienna to inform the emperor of the deed they had perpetrated. It was welcome intelligence to Ferdinand, and he finished the work they had thus commenced by hanging and beheading the adherents of Wallenstein without mercy. The assassins were abundantly rewarded. The emperor still prosecuted the war with perseverance, which no disasters could check. Gradually the imperial arms gained the ascendency. The Protestant princes became divided and jealous of each other. The emperor succeeded in detaching from the alliance, and negotiating a separate peace with the powerful Electors of Saxony and Brandenburg. He then assembled a diet at Ratisbon on the 15th of September, 1639, and without much difficulty secured the election of his son Ferdinand to succeed him on the imperial throne. The emperor presided at this diet in person. He was overjoyed in the attainment of this great object of his ambition. He was now fifty-nine years of age, in very feeble health, and quite worn out by a life of incessant anxiety and toil. He returned to Vienna, and in four months, on the 15th of February, 1637, breathed his last.

For eighteen years Germany had now been distracted by war. The contending parties were so exasperated against each other, that no human wisdom could, at once, allay the strife. The new king and emperor, Ferdinand III., wished for peace, but he could not obtain it on terms which he thought honorable to the memory of his father. The Swedish army was still in Germany, aided by the Protestant princes of the empire, and especially by the armies and the treasury of France. The thunders of battle were daily heard, and the paths of these hostile bands were ever marked by smoldering ruins and blood. Vials of woe were emptied, unsurpassed in apocalyptic vision. In the siege of Brisac, the wretched inhabitants were reduced to such a condition of starvation, that a guard was stationed at the burying-ground to prevent them from devouring the putrid carcasses of the dead.

For eleven years history gives us nothing but a dismal record of weary marches, sieges, battles, bombardments, conflagrations, and all the unimaginable brutalities and miseries of war. The war had now raged for thirty years. Hundreds of thousands of lives had been lost. Millions of property had been destroyed, and other millions squandered in the arts of destruction. Nearly all Europe had been drawn into this vortex of fury and misery. All parties were now weary. And yet seven years of negotiation had been employed before they could consent to meet to consult upon a general peace. At length congresses of the belligerent powers were assembled in two important towns of Westphalia, Osnabruck and Munster. Ridiculous disputes upon etiquette rendered this division of the congress necessary. The ministers of *electors* enjoyed the title of *excellency*. The ministers of *princes* claimed the same title. Months were employed in settling that question. Then a difficulty arose as to the seats at table, who were entitled to the positions of honor. After long debate, this point was settled by having a large round table made, to which there could be no head and no foot.

For four years the great questions of European policy were discussed by this assembly. The all-important treaty, known in history as the peace of Westphalia, and which established the general condition of Europe for one hundred and fifty years, was signed on the 24th of October, 1648. The contracting parties included all the great and nearly all the minor powers of Europe. The articles of this renowned treaty are vastly too voluminous to be recorded here. The family of Frederic received back the Palatinate of which he had been deprived. The Protestants were restored to nearly all the rights which they had enjoyed under the beneficent reign of Maximilian II. The princes of the German empire, kings, dukes, electors, marquises, princes, of whatever name, pledged themselves not to oppress those of their subjects who differed from them in religious faith. The pope protested against this toleration, but his protest was disregarded. The German empire lost its unity, and became a conglomeration of three hundred independent sovereignties. Each petty prince or duke, though possessing but a few square miles of territory, was recognized as a sovereign power, entitled to its court, its army, and its foreign alliances. The emperor thus lost much of that power which he had inherited from his ancestors; as those princes, whom he had previously regarded as vassals, now shared with him sovereign dignity.

Ferdinand III., however, weary of the war which for so many years had allowed him not an hour of repose, gladly acceded to these terms of peace, and in good faith employed himself in carrying out the terms of the treaty. After the exchange of ratifications another congress was assembled at Nuremburg to settle some of the minute details, which continued in session two years, when at length, in 1651, the armies were disbanded, and Germany was released from the presence of a foreign foe.

Internal peace being thus secured, Ferdinand was anxious, before his death, to secure the succession of the imperial crown to his son who bore his own name. He accordingly assembled a meeting of the electors at Prague, and by the free use of bribes and diplomatic intrigue, obtained their engagement to support his son. He accomplished his purpose, and Ferdinand, quite to the astonishment of Germany, was chosen unanimously, King of the Romans—the title assumed by the emperor elect. In June, 1653, the young prince was crowned at Ratisbon. The joy of his father, however, was of short duration. In one year from that time the small-pox, in its most loathsome form, seized the prince, and after a few days of anguish he died. His father was almost inconsolable with grief. As soon as he had partially recovered from the blow, he brought forward his second son, Leopold, and with but little difficulty secured for him the crowns of Hungary and Bohemia, but was disappointed in his attempts to secure the suffrages of the German electors.

With energy, moderation and sagacity, the peacefully disposed Ferdinand so administered the government as to allay for seven years all the menaces of war which were continually arising. For so long a period had Germany been devastated by this most direful of earthly calamities, which is indeed the accumulation of all conceivable woes, ever leading in its train pestilence and famine, that peace seemed to the people a heavenly boon. The fields were again cultivated, the cities and villages repaired, and comfort began again gradually to make its appearance in homes long desolate. It is one of the deepest mysteries of the divine government that the destinies of millions should be so entirely placed in the hands of a single man. Had Ferdinand II. been an enlightened, good man, millions would have been saved from life-long ruin and misery.

One pert young king, in the search of glory, kindled again the lurid flames of war   Christina, Queen of Sweden, daughter of Gustavus Adolphus, influenced by romantic dreams, abdicated the throne and retired to the seclusion of the cloister Her cousin, Charles Gustavus, succeeded her. He thought it a fine thing to play the soldier, and to win renown by consigning the homes of thousands to blood and misery. He was a king, and the power was in his hands. Merely to gratify this fiend-like ambition, he laid claim to the crown of Poland, and

raised an army for the invasion of that kingdom. A portion
of Poland was then n a state of insurrection, the Ukraine
Cossacks having risen against John Cassimar, the king. Charles
Gustavus thought that this presented him an opportunity to
obtain celebrity as a warrior, with but little danger of failure.
He marched into the doomed country, leaving behind him a
wake of fire and blood. Cities and villages were burned; the
soil was drenched with the blood of fathers and sons, his bugle
blasts were echoed by the agonizing groans of widows and or-
phans, until at last, in an awful battle of three days, under the
walls of Warsaw, the Polish army, struggling in self-defense,
was cut to pieces, and Charles Gustavus was crowned a conqueror. Elated by this infernal deed, the most infernal which
mortal man can commit, he began to look around to decide
in what direction to extend his conquests.

Ferdinand III., anxious as he was to preserve peace, could
not but look with alarm upon the movements which now
threatened the States of the empire. It was necessary to present a barrier to the inroads of such a ruffian. He accordingly assembled a diet at Frankfort and demanded succors to oppose the threatened invasion on the north. He raised an army,
entered into an alliance with the defeated and prostrate, yet
still struggling Poles, and was just commencing his march,
when he was seized with sudden illness and died, on the 3d of
March, 1657. Ferdinand was a good man. He was not responsible for the wars which desolated the empire during the
first years of his reign, for he was doing every thing in his
power to bring those wars to a close. His administration was
a blessing to millions. Just before his death he said, and with
truth which no one will controvert, "During my whole reign
no one can reproach me with a single act which I knew to be
unjust." Happy is the monarch who can go into the presence
of the King of kings with such a conscience.

The death of the emperor was caused by a singular accident. He was not very well, and was lying upon a couch in

one of the chambers of his palace. He had an infant son, but
a few weeks old, lying in a cradle in the nursery. A fire broke
out in the apartment of the young prince. The whole palace
was instantly in clamor and confusion. Some attendants seized
the cradle of the young prince, and rushed with it to the chamber of the emperor. In their haste and terror they struck the
cradle with such violence against the wall that it was broken
to pieces and the child fell, screaming, upon the floor. The cry
of fire, the tumult, the bursting into the room, the dashing of
the cradle and the shrieks of the child, so shocked the debili-
tated king that he died within an hour.

Leopold was but eighteen years of age when he succeeded
to the sovereignty of all the Austrian dominions, including the
crowns of Hungary and Bohemia. It was the first great object of his ambition to secure the imperial throne also, which
his father had failed to obtain for him. Louis XIV. was now
the youthful sovereign of France. He, through his ambitious
and able minister, Mazarin, did every thing in his power to
thwart the endeavors of Ferdinand, and to obtain the brilliant
prize for himself. The King of Sweden united with the French
court in the endeavor to abase the pride of the house of Austria. But notwithstanding all their efforts, Leopold carried
his point, and was unanimously elected emperor, and crowned
on the 31st of July, 1657. The princes of the empire, however, greatly strengthened in their independence by the articles of the peace of Westphalia, increasingly jealous of their
rights, attached forty-five conditions to their acceptance of
Leopold as emperor. Thus, notwithstanding the imperial title,
Leopold had as little power over the States of the empire as
the President of the United States has over the internal concerns of Maine or Louisiana. In all such cases there is ever a
conflict between two parties, the one seeking the centralization
of power, and the other advocating its dispersion into various
distant central points.

The flames of war which Charles Gustavus had kindled

were still blazing. Leopold continued the alliance which his father had formed with the Poles, and sent an army of sixteen thousand men into Poland, hoping to cut off the retreat of Charles Gustavus, and take him and all his army prisoners But the Swedish monarch was as sagacious and energetic as he was unscrupulous and ambitious. Both parties formed alliances. State after State was drawn into the conflict. The flame spread like a conflagration. Fleets met in deadly conflict on the Baltic, and crimsoned its waves with blood. The thunders of war were soon again echoing over all the plains of northern and western Germany—and all this because a proud, unprincipled young man, who chanced to be a king, wished to be called a *hero*.

He accomplished his object. Through burning homes and bleeding hearts and crushed hopes he marched to his renown. The forces of the empire were allied with Denmark and Poland against him. With skill and energy which can hardly find a parallel in the tales of romance, he baffled all the combinations of his foes. Energy is a noble quality, and we may admire its exhibition even though we detest the cause which has called it forth. The Swedish fleet had been sunk by the Danes, and Charles Gustavus was driven from the waters of the Baltic. With a few transports he secretly conveyed an army across the Cattegat to the northern coast of Jutland, marched rapidly down those inhospitable shores until he came to the narrow strait, called the Little Belt, which separates Jutland from the large island of Fyen. He crossed this strait on the ice, dispersed a corps of Danes posted to arrest him, traversed the island, exposed to all the storms of mid-winter, some sixty miles to its eastern shore. A series of islands, with intervening straits clogged with ice, bridged by a long and circuitous way his passage across the Great Belt. A march of ten miles across the hummocks, rising and falling with the tides, landed him upon the almost pathless snows of Langeland. Crossing that dreary waste diagonally some dozen miles

to another arm of the sea ten miles wide, which the ices of a
winter of almost unprecedented severity had also bridged,
pushing boldly on, with a recklessness which nothing but success redeems from stupendous infatuation, he crossed this fragile surface, which any storm might crumble beneath his feet,
and landed upon the western coast of Laaland. A march of
thirty-five miles over a treeless, shelterless and almost uninhabited expanse, brought him to the eastern shore. Easily
crossing a narrow strait about a mile in width, he plunged into
the forests of the island of Falster. A dreary march of twenty-
seven miles conducted him to the last remaining arm of the
sea which separated him from Zealand. This strait, from
twelve to fifteen miles in breadth, was also closed by ice.
Charles Gustavus led his hardy soldiers across it, and then,
with accelerated steps, pressed on some sixty miles to Copen-
hagen, the capital of Denmark. In sixteen days after landing
in Jutland, his troops were encamped in Zealand before the
gates of the capital.

The King of Denmark was appalled at such a sudden apparition. His allies were too remote to render him any assistance. Never dreaming of such an attack, his capital was
quite defenseless in that quarter. Overwhelmed with terror
and despondency, he was compelled to submit to such terms
as the conqueror might dictate. The conqueror was inexorable in his demands. Sweden was aggrandized, and Denmark
humiliated.

Leopold was greatly chagrined by this sudden prostration
of his faithful ally. In the midst of these scenes of ambition
and of conquest, the " king of terrors" came with his summons
to Charles Gustavus. The passage of this blood-stained warrior to the world of spirits reminds us of the sublime vision
of Isaiah when the King of Babylon sank into the grave:

" Hell from beneath is moved for thee, to meet thee at thy
coming ; it stirreth up the dead for thee, even all the chief
ones of the earth ; it hath raised up from their thrones all

the kings of the nations. All they shall speak and say unto thee,

"'Art thou also become weak as we? Art thou become like unto us? Thy pomp is brought down to the grave, and the noise of thy viols; the worm is spread under thee, and the worms cover thee. How art thou fallen from heaven, O Lucifer, son of the morning! How art thou cut down to the ground which didst weaken the nations!'

"They that see thee shall narrowly look upon thee and consider thee, saying, ' Is this the man that made the earth to tremble, and didst shake kingdoms; that made the world as a wilderness and destroyed the cities thereof, that opened not the house of his prisoners?'"

The death of Charles Gustavus was the signal for the strife of war to cease, and the belligerent nations soon came to terms of accommodation. But scarcely was peace proclaimed ere new troubles arose in Hungary. The barbarian Turks, with their head-quarters at Constantinople, lived in a state of continual anarchy. The cimeter was their only law. The palace of the sultan was the scene of incessant assassinations. Nothing ever prevented them from assailing their neighbors but incessant quarrels among themselves. The life of the Turkish empire was composed of bloody insurrections at home, and still more bloody wars abroad. Mahomet IV. was now sultan. He was but twenty years of age. A quarrel for ascendency among the beauties of his harem had involved the empire in a civil war. The sultan, after a long conflict, crushed the insurrection with a blood-red hand. Having restored internal tranquillity, he prepared as usual for foreign war. By intrigue and the force of arms they took possession of most of the fortresses of Transylvania, and crossing the frontier, entered Hungary, and laid siege to Great Wardein.

Leopold immediately dispatched ten thousand men to succor the besieged town and to garrison other important fortresses. His succors arrived too late. Great Wardein fell into the hands of the Turks, and they commenced their merciless ravages. Hungary was in a wretched condition. The king, residing in Vienna, was merely a nominal sovereign. Chosen by nobles proud of their independence, and jealous of each other and of their feudal rights, they were unwilling to delegate to the sovereign any efficient power. They would crown him with great splendor of gold and jewelry, and crowd his court in their magnificent display, but they would not grant him the prerogative to make war or peace, to levy taxes, or to exercise any other of the peculiar attributes of sovereignty. The king, with all his sounding titles and gorgeous parade, was in reality but the chairman of a committee of nobles. The real power was with the Hungarian diet.

This diet, or congress, was a peculiar body. Originally it consisted of the whole body of nobles, who assembled annually on horseback on the vast plain of Rakoz, near Buda. Eighty thousand nobles, many of them with powerful revenues, were frequently convened at these tumultuous gatherings. The people were thought to have no rights which a noble was bound to respect. They lived in hovels, hardly superior to those which a humane farmer now prepares for his swine. The only function they fulfilled was, by a life of exhausting toil and suffering, to raise the funds which the nobles expended in their wars and their pleasure; and to march to the field of blood when summoned by the bugle. In fact history has hardly condescended to allude to the people. We have minutely detailed the intrigues and the conflicts of kings and nobles, when generation after generation of the masses of the people have passed away, as little thought of as billows upon the beach.

These immense gatherings of the nobles were found to be so unwieldy, and so inconvenient for the transaction of any efficient business, that Sigismond, at the commencement of the fifteenth century, introduced a limited kind of representation The bishops, who stood first in wealth, power and rank, and the highest dukes attended in person. The nobles of less exalted rank sent their delegates, and the assembly, much diminished in number, was transferred from the open plain to the city of Presburg. The diet, at the time of which we write, was assembled once in three years, and at such other times as the sovereign thought it necessary to convene it. The diet controlled the king, unless he chanced to be a man of such commanding character, that by moral power he could bring the diet to his feet. A clause had been inserted in the coronation oath, that the nobles, without guilt, could oppose the authority of the king, whenever he transgressed their privileges; it was also declared that no foreign troops could be introduced into the kingdom without the consent of the diet.

Under such a government, it was inevitable that the king should be involved in a continued conflict with the nobles. The nobles wished for aid to repel the Turks; and yet they were unwilling that an Austrian army should be introduced into Hungary, lest it should enable the king to enlarge those prerogatives which he was ever seeking to extend, and which they were ever endeavoring to curtail.

Leopold convened the diet at Presburg. They had a stormy session. Leopold had commenced some persecution of the Protestants in the States of Austria. This excited the alarm of the Protestant nobles of Hungary; and they had reason to dread the intolerance of the Roman Catholics, more than the cimeter of the Turk. They openly accused Leopold of commencing persecution, and declared that it was his intention to reduce Hungary to the state to which Ferdinand II. had reduced Bohemia. They met all the suggestions of Leopold, for decisive action, with so many provisos and precautions, that nothing could be done. It is dangerous to surrender one's arms to a highway robber, or one whom we fear may prove such, even if he does promise with them to aid in repelling a foe. The Catholics and the Protestants became involved in altercation, and the diet was abruptly dissolved.

The Turks eagerly watched their movements, and, encouraged by these dissensions, soon burst into Hungary with
an army of one hundred thousand men. They crossed the
Drave at Esseg, and, ascending the valley of the Danube,
directly north one hundred and fifty miles, crossed that stream
unopposed at Buda. Still ascending the stream, which here
flows from the west, they spread devastation everywhere
around them, until they arrived nearly within sight of the
steeples of Vienna. The capital was in consternation. To
add to their terror and their peril, the emperor was danger-
ously sick of the small-pox, a disease which had so often
proved fatal to members of the royal family. One of the imperial generals, near Presburg, in a strong position, held the
invading army in check a few days. The ministry, in their
consternation, appealed to all the powers of Christendom to
hasten to the rescue of the cross, now so seriously imperiled
by the crescent. Forces flowed in, which for a time arrested
the further advance of the Moslem banners, and afforded time
to prepare for more efficient action.

CHAPTER XX.

LEOPOLD I.

From 1662 to 1697.

WHILE Europe was rousing itself to repel this invasion of the Turks, the grand vizier, leaving garrisons in the strong fortresses of the Danube, withdrew the remainder of his army to prepare for a still more formidable invasion the ensuing year. Most of the European powers seemed disposed to render the emperor some aid. The pope transmitted to him about two hundred thousand dollars. France sent a detachment of six thousand men. Spain, Venice, Genoa, Tuscany and Mantua, forwarded important contributions of money and military stores. Early in the summer the Turks, in a powerful and well provided army, commenced their march anew. Ascending the valley of the Save, where they encountered no opposition, they traversed Styria, that they might penetrate to the seat of war through a defenseless frontier. The troops assembled by Leopold, sixty thousand in number, under the renowned Prince Montecuculi, stationed themselves in a very strong position at St. Gothard, behind the river Raab, which flows into the Danube about one hundred miles below Vienna. Here they threw up their intrenchments and prepared to resist the progress of the invader.

The Turks soon arrived and spread themselves out in military array upon the opposite side of the narrow but rapid stream. As the hostile armies were preparing for an engagement, a young Turk, magnificently mounted, and in gorgeous uniform, having crossed the stream with a party of cavalry, rode in advance of the troop, upon the plain, and in the spirit of ancient chivalry challenged any Christian knight to meet him in single combat. The Chevalier of Lorraine accepted the challenge, and rode forth to the encounter. Both armies looked silently on to witness the issue of the duel. It was of but a few moments' duration. Lorraine, warding off every blow of his antagonist, soon passed his sword through the body of the Turk, and he fell dead from his horse. The victor returned to the Christian camp, leading in triumph the splendid steed of his antagonist.

And now the signal was given for the general battle. The Turks impetuously crossing the narrow stream, assailed the Christian camp in all directions, with their characteristic physical bravery, the most common, cheap and vulgar of all earthy virtues. A few months of military discipline will make fearless soldiers of the most ignominious wretches who can be raked from the gutters of Christian or heathen lands. The battle was waged with intense fierceness on both sides, and was long continued with varying success. At last the Turks were routed on every portion of the field, and leaving nearly twenty thousand of their number either dead upon the plain or drowned in the Raab, they commenced a precipitate flight.

Leopold was, for many reasons, very anxious for peace, and immediately proposed terms very favorable to the Turks. The sultan was so disheartened by this signal reverse that he readily listened to the propositions of the emperor, and within nine days after the battle of St. Gothard, to the astonishment of all Europe, a truce was concluded for twenty years. The Hungarians were much displeased with the terms of this treaty; for in the first place, it was contrary to the laws of the kingdom

for the king to make peace without the consent of the diet,
and in the second place, the conditions he offered the Turks
were humiliating to the Hungarians. Leopold confirmed to
the Turks their ascendency in Transylvania, and allowed them
to retain Great Wardein, and two other important fortresses
in Hungary. It was with no little difficulty that the emperor
persuaded the diet to ratify these terms.

Leopold is to be considered under the twofold light of sov
ereign of Austria and Emperor of Germany. We have seen
that his power as emperor was quite limited. His power as
sovereign of Austria, also varied greatly in the different States
of his widely extended realms. In the Austrian duchies proper, upon the Danube, of which he was, by long hereditary descent, archduke, his sway was almost omnipotent. In Bohemia he was powerful, though much less so than in Austria, and
it was necessary for him to move with caution there, and not
to disturb the ancient usages of the realm lest he should excite
insurrection. In Hungary, where the laws and customs were
entirely different, Leopold held merely a nominal, hardly a
recognized sway. The bold Hungarian barons, always steel-
clad and mounted for war, in their tumultuous diets, governed
the kingdom. There were other remote duchies and principalities, too feeble to stand by themselves, and ever changing
masters, as they were conquered or sought the protection of
other powers, which, under the reign of Leopold, were portions of wide extended Austria. Another large and vastly
important accession was now made to his realms. The Tyrol,
which, in its natural features, may be considered but an extension of Switzerland, is a territory of about one hundred miles
square, traversed through its whole extent by the Alps. Lying just south of Austria it is the key to Italy, opening through
its defiles a passage to the sunny plains of the Peninsula; and
through those fastnesses, guarded by frowning castles, no foe
could force his way, into the valleys of the Tyrol. The most
sublime road in Europe is that over Mount Brenner, along the

banks of the Adige. This province had long been in the hands
of members of the Austrian family

On the 15th of June, 1665, Sigismond Francis, Duke of
Tyrol, and cousin of Leopold, died, leaving no issue, and the
province escheated with its million of inhabitants to Leopold,
as the next heir. This brought a large accession of revenue
and of military force, to the kingdom. Austria was now the
leading power in Europe, and Leopold, in rank and position,
the most illustrious sovereign. Louis XIV. had recently married Maria Theresa, eldest daughter of Philip IV., King of
Spain. Philip, who was anxious to retain the crown of Spain
in his own family, extorted from Maria Theresa, and from her
husband, Louis XIV., the renunciation of all right of succession, in favor of his second daughter, Margaret, whom he betrothed to Leopold. Philip died in September, 1665, leaving
these two daughters, one of whom was married to the King of
France, and leaving also an infant son, who succeeded to the
throne under the regency of his mother, Ann, daughter of Ferdinand III., of Austria. Margaret was then too young to be
married, but in a year from this time, in September, 1666, her
nuptials were celebrated with great splendor at Madrid. The
ambitious French monarch, taking advantage of the minority
of the King of Spain, and of the feeble regency, and in defiance of the solemn renunciation made at his marriage, resolved
to annex the Spanish provinces of the Low Countries to France,
and invaded the kingdom, leading himself an army of thirty
thousand men. The Spanish court immediately appealed to
Leopold for assistance. But Leopold was so embarrassed by
troubles in Hungary, and by discontents in the empire that he
could render no efficient aid. England, however, and other
powers of Europe, jealous of the aggrandizement of Louis
XIV. combined, and compelled him to abandon a large portion of the Netherlands, though he still retained several for
tresses. The ambition of Louis XIV. was inflamed, not checked
by this reverse, and all Europe was involved again in bloody

wars. The aggressions of France, and the devastations of
Turenne in the Palatinate, roused Germany to listen to the
appeals of Leopold, and the empire declared war against
France. Months of desolating war rolled on, decisive of no
results, except universal misery. The fierce conflict continued
with unintermitted fury until 1679, when the haughty monarch of France, who was as sagacious in diplomacy as he was
able in war, by bribes and threats succeeded in detaching one
after another from the coalition against him, until Leopold, deserted by nearly all his allies, was also compelled to accede to
peace.

France, under Louis XIV., was now the dominant power
in Europe. Every court seemed to be agitated by the intrigues of this haughty sovereign, and one becomes weary of
describing the incessant fluctuations of the warfare. The arrogance of Louis, his unblushing perfidy and his insulting assumptions of superiority over all other powers, exasperated
the emperor to the highest pitch. But the French monarch,
by secret missions and abounding bribes, kept Hungary in
continued commotion, and excited such jealousy in the different States of the empire, that Leopold was compelled to submit in silent indignation to wrongs almost too grievous for
human nature to bear.

At length Leopold succeeded in organizing another coalition to resist the aggressions of Louis XIV. The Prince of
Orange, the King of Sweden and the Elector of Brandenburg
were the principal parties united with the emperor in this confederacy, which was concluded, under the name of the "League
of Augsburg," on the 21st of June, 1686. An army of sixty
thousand men was immediately raised. From all parts of
Germany troops were now hurrying towards the Rhine. Louis,
alarmed, retired from the Palatinate, which he had overrun,
and, to place a barrier between himself and his foes, ordered
the utter devastation of the unhappy country. The diabolical
order was executed by Turenne. The whole of the Palatinate

was surrendered to pillage and conflagration. The elector from the towers of his castle at Mannheim, saw at one time two cities and twenty-five villages in flames. He had no force sufficient to warrant him to leave the walls of his fortress to oppose the foe. He was, however, so moved to despair by the sight, that he sent a challenge to Turenne to meet him in single combat. Turenne, by command of the king, declined accepting the challenge. More than forty large towns, besides innumerable villages, were given up to the flames. It was mid-winter. The fields were covered with snow, and swept by freezing blasts. The wretched inhabitants, parents and children, driven into the bleak plains without food or clothing or shelter, perished miserably by thousands. The devastation of the Palatinate is one of the most cruel deeds which war has ever perpetrated. For these woes, which no imagination can guage, Louis XIV. is responsible. He has escaped any adequate earthly penalty for the crime, but the instinctive sense of justice implanted in every breast, demands that he should not escape the retributions of a righteous God. " After death cometh the judgment."

This horrible deed roused Germany. All Europe now combined against France, except Portugal, Russia and a few of the Italian States. The tide now turned in favor of the house of Austria. Germany was so alarmed by the arrogance of France, that, to strengthen the power of the emperor, the diet with almost perfect unanimity elected his son Joseph, though a lad but eleven years of age, to succeed to the imperial throne. Indeed, Leopold presented his son in a manner which seemed to claim the crown for him as his hereditary right, and the diet did not resist that claim. France, rich and powerful, with marvelous energy breasted her host of foes. All Europe was in a blaze. The war raged on the ocean, over the marshes of Holland, along the banks of the Rhine, upon the plains of Italy, through the defiles of the Alps and far away on the steppes of Hungary and the shores of the Euxine. To all these points the emperor was compelled to send his troops. Year after year of carnage and woe rolled on, during which hardly a happy family could be found in all Europe.

> "Man's inhumanity to man
> Made countless millions mourn."

At last all parties became weary of the war, and none of the powers having gained any thing of any importance by these long years of crime and misery, for which Louis XIV., as the aggressor, is mainly responsible, peace was signed on the 30th of October, 1697. One important thing, indeed, had been accomplished. The rapacious Louis XIV. had been checked in his career of spoliation. But his insatiate ambition was by no means subdued. He desired peace only that he might more successfully prosecute his plans of aggrandizement. He soon, by his system of robbery, involved Europe again in war. Perhaps no man has ever lived who has caused more bloody deaths and more wide-spread destruction of human happiness than Louis XIV. We wonder not that in the French Revolution an exasperated people should have rifled his sepulcher and spurned his skull over the pavements as a foot-ball.

Leopold, during the progress of these wars, by the aid of the armies which the empire furnished him, recovered all of Hungary and Transylvania, driving the Turks beyond the Danube. But the proud Hungarian nobles were about as much opposed to the rule of the Austrian king as to that of the Turkish sultan. The Protestants gained but little by the change, for the Mohammedan was about as tolerant as the papist. They all suspected Leopold of the design of establishing over them despotic power, and they formed a secret confederacy for their own protection. Leopold, released from his warfare against France and the Turks, was now anxious to consolidate his power in Hungary, and justly regarding the Roman Catholic religion as the great bulwark against liberty encouraged the Catholics to persecute the Protestants.

Leopold took advantage of this conspiracy to march an army into Hungary, and attacking the discontented nobles, who had raised an army, he crushed them with terrible severity. No mercy was shown. He exhausted the energies of confiscation, exile and the scaffold upon his foes; and then, having intimidated all so that no one dared to murmur, declared the monarchy of Hungary no longer elective but hereditary, like that of Bohemia. He even had the assurance to summon a diet of the nobles to confirm this decree which defrauded them of their time-honored rights. The nobles who were summoned, terrified, instead of obeying, fled into Transylvania. The despot then issued an insulting and menacing proclamation, declaring that the power he exercised he received from God, and calling upon all to manifest implicit submission under peril of his vengeance. He then extorted a large contribution of money from the kingdom, and quartered upon the inhabitants thirty thousand troops to awe them into subjection.

This proclamation was immediately followed by another, changing the whole form of government of the kingdom, and establishing an unlimited despotism. He then moved vigorously for the extirpation of the Protestant religion. The Protestant pastors were silenced; courts were instituted for the suppression of heresy; two hundred and fifty Protestant ministers were sentenced to be burned at the stake, and then, as an act of extraordinary clemency, on the part of the despot, their punishment was commuted to hard labor in the galleys for life. All the nameless horrors of inquisitorial cruelty desolated the land.

Catholics and Protestants were alike driven to despair by these civil and religious outrages. They combined, and were aided both by France and Turkey; not that France and Turkey loved justice and humanity, but they hated the house of Austria, and wished to weaken its power, that they might enrich themselves by the spoils. A noble chief, Emeric Te-

keli, who had fled from Hungary to Poland, and who hated
Austria as Hannibal hated Rome, was in/ested with the command of the Hungarian patriots. Victory followed his standard, until the emperor, threatened with entire expulsion from
the kingdom, offered to reëstablish the ancient laws which he
had abrogated, and to restore to the Hungarians all those
civil and religious privileges of which he had so ruthlessly
defrauded them.

But the Hungarians were no longer to be deceived by his
perfidious promises. They continued the war ; and the sultan
sent an army of two hundred thousand men to coöperate with
Tekeli. The emperor, unable to meet so formidable an army,
abandoned his garrisons, and, retiring from the distant parts
of the kingdom, concentrated his troops at Presburg. But
with all his efforts, he was able to raise an army of only forty
thousand men. The Duke of Lorraine, who was intrusted
with the command of the imperial troops, was compelled to
retreat precipitately before outnumbering foes, and he fled
upon the Danube, pursued by the combined Hungarians and
Turks, until he found refuge within the walls of Vienna. The
city was quite unprepared for resistance, its fortifications being
dilapidated, and its garrison feeble. Universal consternation
seized the inhabitants. All along the valley of the Danube
the population fled in terror before the advance of the Turks.
Leopold, with his family, at midnight, departed ingloriously
from the city, to seek a distant refuge. The citizens followed
the example of their sovereign, and all the roads leading west-
ward and northward from the city were crowded with fugitives, in carriages, on horseback and on foot, and with all
kinds of vehicles laden with the treasures of the metropolis.
The churches were filled with the sick and the aged, pathetically imploring the protection of Heaven.

The Duke of Lorraine conducted with great energy, re-
pairing the dilapidated fortifications, stationing in posts of
peril the veteran troops, and marshaling the citizens and the

students to coöperate with the garrison. On the 14th of July, 1682, the banners of the advance guard of the Turkish army were seen from the walls of Vienna. Soon the whole mighty host, like an inundation, came surging on, and, surrounding the city, invested it on all sides. The terrific assault from innumerable batteries immediately commenced. The besieged were soon reduced to the last extremity for want of provisions, and famine and pestilence rioting within the walls, destroyed more than the shot of the enemy. The suburbs were destroyed, the principal outworks taken, several breaches were battered in the walls, and the terrified inhabitants were hourly in expectation that the city would be taken by storm. There can not be, this side of the world of woe, any thing more terrible than such an event.

The emperor, in his terror, had dispatched envoys all over Germany to rally troops for the defense of Vienna and the empire. He himself had hastened to Poland, where, with frantic intreaties, he pressed the king, the renowned John Sobieski, whose very name was a terror, to rush to his relief. Sobieski left orders for a powerful army immediately to commence their march. But, without waiting for their comparatively slow movements, he placed himself at the head of three thousand Polish horsemen, and, without incumbering himself with luggage, like the sweep of the whirlwind traversed Silesia and Moravia, and reached Tulen, on the banks of the Danube, about twenty miles above Vienna. He had been told by the emperor that here he would find an army awaiting him, and a bridge constructed, by which he could cross the stream. But, to his bitter disappointment, he found no army, and the bridge unfinished. Indignantly he exclaimed,

"What does the emperor mean? Does he think me a mere adventurer? I left my own army that I might take command of his. It is not for myself that I fight, but for him."

Notwithstanding this disappointment, he called into requisitioɪ all his energies to meet the crisis. The bridge was pushed forward to its completion. The loitering German troops were hurried on to the rendezvous. After a few days the Polish troops, by forced marches, arrived, and Sobieski found himself at the head of sixty thousand men, experienced soldiers, and well supplied with all the munitions of war. On the 11th of September the inhabitants of the city were over-joyed, in descrying from the towers of the city, in the dis-tance, the approaching banners of the Polish and German army. Sobieski ascended an elevation, and long and carefully scrutinized the position of the besieging host. He then calmly remarked,

"The grand vizier has selected a bad position. I under-stand him. He is ignorant of the arts of war, and yet thinks that he has military genius. It will be so easy to conquer him, that we shall obtain no honor from the victory."

Early the next morning, the 12th of September, the Polish and German troops rushed to the assault, with such amazing impetuosity, and guided by such military skill, that the Turks were swept before them as by a torrent. The army of the grand vizier, seized by a panic, fled so precipitately, that they left baggage, tents, ammunition and provisions behind. The garrison emerged from the city, and coöperated with the victors, and booty of indescribable value fell into their hands. As Sobieski took possession of the abandoned camp, stored with all the wealth and luxuries of the East, he wrote, in a tone of pleasantry to his wife,

"The grand vizier has left me his heir, and I inherit mil-lions of ducats. When I return home I shall not be met with the reproach of the Tartar wives, 'You are not a man, be cause you have come back without booty.'"

The inhabitants of Vienna flocked out from the city to greet the king as an angel deliverer sent from heaven. The next morning the gates of the city were thrown open, the streets were garlanded with flowers, and the King of Poland had a triumphal reception in the streets of the metropolis. The enthusiasm and gratitude of the people passed all ordinary bounds. The bells rang their merriest peals; files of maidens lined his path, and acclamations, bursting from the heart, greeted him every step of his way. They called him their father and deliverer. They struggled to kiss his feet and even to touch his garments. With difficulty he pressed through the grateful crowd to the cathedral, where he prostrated himself before the altar, and returned thanks to God for the signal victory. As he returned, after a public dinner, to his camp, he said, "This is the happiest day of my life."

Two days after this, Leopold returned, trembling and humiliated to his capital. He was received in silence, and with undisguised contempt. His mortification was intense, and he could not endure to hear the praises which were everywhere lavished upon Sobieski. Jealousy rankled in his heart, and he vented his spite upon all around him. It was necessary that he should have an interview with the heroic king who had so nobly come to his rescue. But instead of meeting him with a warm and grateful heart, he began to study the punctilios of etiquette, that the dreaded interview might be rendered as cold and formal as possible.

Sobieski was merely an elective monarch. Leopold was a hereditary king and an emperor. Leopold even expressed some doubt whether it were consistent with his exalted dignity to grant the Polish king the honor of an audience. He inquired whether an *elected monarch* had ever been admitted to the presence of an *emperor;* and if so, with what forms, in the present case, the king should be received. The Duke of Lorraine, of whom he made the inquiry, disgusted with the mean spirit of the emperor, nobly replied, "With open arms."

But the soulless Leopold had every movement punctiliously arranged according to the dictates of his ignoble spirit. The Polish and Austrian armies were drawn up in opposite lines upon the plain before the city. At a concerted signal the emperor and the king emerged from their respective ranks, and rode out upon the open plain to meet each other. Sobieski, a man of splendid bearing, magnificently mounted, and dressed in the brilliant uniform of a Polish warrior, attracted all eyes and the admiration of all hearts. His war steed pranced proudly as if conscious of the royal burden he bore, and of the victories he had achieved. Leopold was an ungainly man at the best. Conscious of his inability to vie with the hero, in his personal presence, he affected the utmost simplicity of dress and equipage. Humiliated also by the cold reception he had met and by the consciousness of extreme unpopularity in both armies, he was embarrassed and dejected. The contrast was very striking, adding to the renown of Sobieski, and sinking Leopold still deeper in contempt.

The two sovereigns advanced, formally saluted each other with bows, dismounted and embraced. A few cold words were exchanged, when they again embraced and remounted to review the troops. But Sobieski, frank, cordial, impulsive, was so disgusted with this reception, so different from what he had a right to expect, that he excused himself, and rode to his tent, leaving his chancellor Zaluski to accompany the emperor on the review. As Leopold rode along the lines he was received in contemptuous silence, and he returned to his palace in Vienna, tortured by wounded pride and chagrin.

The treasure abandoned by the Turks was so abundant that five days were spent in gathering it up. The victorious army then commenced the pursuit of the retreating foe. About one hundred and fifty miles below Vienna, where the majestic Danube turns suddenly from its eastern course and flows toward the south, is situated the imperial city of Gran. Upon a high precipitous rock, overlooking both the town and the river, there had stood for centuries one of the most imposing fortresses which mortal hands have ever reared. For seventy years this post had been in the hands of the Turks, and strongly garrisoned by four thousand troops, had bid defiance to every assault. Here the thinned and bleeding battalions of the grand vizier sought refuge. Sobieski and the Duke of Lorraine, flushed with victory, hurled their masses upon the disheartened foe, and the Turks were routed with enormous slaughter. Seven thousand gory corpses of the dead strewed the plain. Many thousands were driven into the river and drowned. The fortress was taken, sword in hand; and the remnant of the Moslem army, in utter discomfiture, fled down the Danube, hardly resting, by night or by day, till they were safe behind the ramparts of Belgrade.

Both the German and the Polish troops were disgusted with Leopold. Having reconquered Hungary for the emperor, they were not disposed to remain longer in his service. Most of the German auxiliaries, disbanding, returned to their own countries. Sobieski, declaring that he was willing to fight against the Turks, but not against Tekeli and his Christian confederates, led back his troops to Poland. The Duke of Lorraine was now left with the Austrian troops to struggle against Tekeli with the Hungarian patriots. The Turks, exasperated by the defeat, accused Tekeli of being the cause. By stratagem he was seized and sent in chains to Constantinople. The chief who succeeded him turned traitor and joined the imperialists. The cause of the patriots was ruined. Victory now kept pace with the march of the Duke of Lorraine. The Turks were driven from all their fortresses, and Leopold again had Hungary at his feet. His vengeance was such as might have been expected from such a man.

Far away, in the wilds of northern Hungary, at the base of the Carpathian, mountains, on the river Tarcza, one of the tributaries of the Theiss, is the strongly fortified town of Eperies. At this remote spot the diabolical emperor established his revolutionary tribunal, as if he thought that the shrieks of his victims, there echoing through the savage defiles of the mountains, could not awaken the horror of civil-

ized Europe. His armed bands scoured the country and transported to Eperies every individual, man, woman and child,
who was even suspected of sympathizing with the insurgents.
There was hardly a man of wealth or influence in the kingdom who was not dragged before this horrible tribunal, composed of ignorant, brutal, sanguinary officers of the king. Their
summary trial, without any forms of justice, was an awful tragedy. They were thrown into dungeons; their property confiscated; they were exposed to the most direful tortures which
human ingenuity could devise, to extort confession and to compel them to criminate friends. By scores they were daily consigned to the scaffold. Thirty executioners, with their assist-
ants, found constant employment in beheading the condemned.
In the middle of the town, the scaffold was raised for this
butchery. The spot is still called "The Bloody Theater of
Eperies."

Leopold, having thus glutted his vengeance, defiantly convoked a diet and crowned his son Joseph, a boy twelve years
of age, as King of Hungary, practically saying to the nobles,
"Dispute his hereditary right now, if you dare." The emperor had been too often instructed in the vicissitudes of war
to feel that even in this hour of triumph he was perfectly safe.
He knew that other days might come; that other foes might
rise; and that Hungary could never forget the rights of which
she had been defrauded. He therefore exhausted all the arts
of threats and bribes to induce the diet to pass a decree that
the crown was no longer elective but hereditary. It is marvelous that in such an hour there could have been any energy
left to resist his will. But with all his terrors he could only
extort from the diet their consent that the succession to the
crown should be confirmed in the males, but that upon the
extinction of the *male* line the crown, instead of being hereditary in the female line, should revert to the nation, who should
again confer it by the right of election.

Leopold reluctantly yielded to this, as the most he could

then hope to accomplish. The emperor, elated by success, assumed such imperious airs as to repel from him all his former allies. For several years Hungary was but a battle-field where Austrians and Turks met in incessant and bloody conflicts. But Leopold, in possession of all the fortresses, succeeded in repelling each successive invasion.

Both parties became weary of war. In November, 1697, negotiations were opened at Carlovitz, and a truce was concluded for twenty-five years. The Turks abandoned both Hungary and Transylvania, and these two important provinces became more firmly than ever before, integral portions of the Austrian empire. By the peace of Carlovitz the sultan lost one half of his possessions in Europe. Austria, in the grandeur of her territory, was never more powerful than at this hour: extending across the whole breadth of Europe, from the valley of the Rhine to the Euxine sea, and from the Carpathian mountains to the plains of Italy. A more heterogeneous conglomeration of States never existed, consisting of kingdoms, archduchies, duchies, principalities, counties, margraves, landgraves and imperial cities, nearly all with their hereditary rulers subordinate to the emperor, and with their local customs and laws.

Leopold, though a weak and bad man, in addition to all this power, swayed also the imperial scepter over all the States of Germany. Though his empire over all was frail, and his vast dominions were liable at any moment to crumble to pieces, he still was not content with consolidating the realms he held, but was anxiously grasping for more. Spain was the prize now to be won. Louis XIV., with the concentrated energies of the French kingdom, was claiming it by virtue of his marriage with the eldest daughter of the deceased monarch, notwithstanding his solemn renunciation of all right at his marriage in favor of the second daughter. Leopold, as the husband of the second daughter, claimed the crown, in the event, then impending, of the death of the imbecile and childless

king. This quarrel agitated Europe to its center, and deluged her fields with blood. If the *elective* franchise is at
times the source of agitation, the law of *hereditary* succession most certainly does not always confer tranquillity and
peace.

CHAPTER XXI.

LEOPOLD I. AND THE SPANISH SUCCESSION.

FROM 1697 TO 1710.

THE SPANISH SUCCESSION.—THE IMPOTENCE OF CHARLES II.—APPEAL TO THE POPE.—HIS
DECISION.—DEATH OF CHARLES II.—ACCESSION OF PHILIP V.—INDIGNATION OF AUS-
TRIA.—THE OUTBREAK OF WAR.—CHARLES III. CROWNED.—INSURRECTION IN HUN-
GARY.—DEFECTION OF BAVARIA.—THE BATTLE OF BLENHEIM.—DEATH OF LEOPOLD
I.—ELEONORA.—ACCESSION OF JOSEPH I.—CHARLES XII. OF SWEDEN.—CHARLES III·
IN SPAIN.—BATTLE OF MALPLAQUET.—CHARLES AT BARCELONA.—CHARLES AT MA-
DRID.

CHARLES II., King of Spain, was one of the most impotent of men, in both body and mind. The law of hereditary descent had placed this semi-idiot upon the throne of
Spain to control the destinies of twenty millions of people.
The same law, in the event of his death without heirs, would
carry the crown across the Pyrenees to a little boy in the palace of Versailles, or two thousand miles, to the banks of the
Danube, to another little boy in the gardens of Vienna.
Louis XIV. claimed the Spanish scepter in behalf of his wife,
the Spanish princess Maria Theresa, and her son. Leopold
claimed it in behalf of his deceased wife, Margaret, and her
child. For many years before the death of Philip II. the envoys of France and Austria crowded the court of Spain, employing all the arts of intrigue and bribery to forward the interests of their several sovereigns. The different courts of
Europe espoused the claims of the one party or the other.
accordingly as their interests would be promoted by the aggrandizement of the house of Bourbon or the house of Hapsburg.

Louis XIV. prepared to strike a sudden blow by gathering

an army of one hundred thousand men in his fortresses near the Spanish frontier, in establishing immense magazines of military stores, and in filling the adjacent harbors with ships of war. The sagacious French monarch had secured the coöperation of the pope, and of some of the most influential Jesuits who surrounded the sick and dying monarch.   Charles II. had long been harassed by the importunities of both parties that he should give the influence of his voice in the decision.   Tortured by the incessant vacillations of his own mind, he was at last influenced, by the suggestions of his spiritual advisers, to refer the question to the pope.   He accordingly sent an embassage to the pontiff with a letter soliciting counsel.

"Having no children," he observed, "and being obliged to appoint an heir to the Spanish crown from a foreign family, we find such great obscurity in the law of succession, that we are unable to form a settled determination.   Strict justice is our aim ; and, to be able to decide with that justice, we have offered up constant prayers to God.   We are anxious to act rightly, and we have recourse to your holiness, as to an infallible guide, intreating you to consult with the cardinals and divines, and, after having attentively examined the testaments of our ancestors, to decide according to the rules of right and equity."

Pope Innocent XII. was already prepared for this appeal, and was engaged to act as the agent of the French court. The hoary-headed pontiff, with one foot in the grave, affected the character of great honesty and impartiality.   He required forty days to examine the important case, and to seek divine assistance.   He then returned the following answer, admirably adapted to influence a weak and superstitious prince :

"Being myself," he wrote, "in a situation similar to that of his Catholic majesty, the King of Spain, on the point of appearing at the judgment-seat of Christ, and rendering an account to the sovereign pastor of the flock which has been intrusted to my care, I am bound to give such advice as will not reproach my conscience on the day of judgment. Your majesty ought not to put the interests of the house of Austria in competition with those of eternity. Neither should you be ignorant that the French claimants are the rightful heirs of the crown, and no member of the Austrian family has the smallest legitimate pretension. It is therefore your duty to omit no precaution, which your wisdom can suggest, to render justice where justice is due, and to secure, by every means in your power, the undivided succession of the Spanish monarchy to the French claimants."

Charles, as fickle as the wind, still remained undecided, and his anxieties preying upon his feeble frame, already exhausted by disease, caused him rapidly to decline. He was now confined to his chamber and his bed, and his death was hourly expected. He hated the French, and all his sympathies were with Austria. Some priests entered his chamber, professedly to perform the pompous and sepulchral service of the church of Rome for the dying. In this hour of languor, and in the prospect of immediate death, they assailed the imbecile monarch with all the terrors of superstition. They depicted the responsibility which he would incur should he entail on the kingdom the woes of a disputed succession; they assured him that he could not, without unpardonable guilt, reject the decision of the holy father of the Church; and growing more eager and excited, they denounced upon him the vengeance of Almighty God, if he did not bequeath the crown, now falling from his brow, to the Bourbons of France.

The dying, half-delirious king, appalled by the terrors of eternal damnation, yielded helplessly to their demands. A will was already prepared awaiting his signature. With a hand trembling in death, the king attached to it his name; but as he did so, he burst into tears, exclaiming, "I am already nothing." It was supposed that he could then survive but a few hours. Contrary to all expectation he revived, and expressed the keenest indignation and anguish that he had been thus beguiled to decide against Austria, and in favor of France. He even sent a courier to the emperor, announcing his determination to decide in favor of the Austrian claimant. The flickering flame of life, thus revived for a moment, glimmered again in the socket and expired. The wretched king died the 1st of November, 1699, in the fortieth year of his age, and the thirty-sixth of his reign.

On the day of his death a council of State was convened, and the will, the very existence of which was generally unknown, was read. It declared the Dauphin of France, son of the Spanish princess Maria Theresa, to be the successor to all the Spanish dominions; and required all subjects and vassals of Spain to acknowledge him. The Austrian party were astounded at this revelation. The French party were prepared to receive it without any surprise. The son of Maria Theresa was dead, and the crown consequently passed to her grandson Philip. Louis XIV. immediately acknowledged his title, when he was proclaimed king, and took quiet possession of the throne of Spain on the 24th of November, 1700, as Philip V.

It was by such fraud that the Bourbons of France attained the succession to the Spanish crown; a fraud as palpable as was ever committed; for Maria Theresa had renounced all her rights to the throne; this renunciation had been confirmed by the will of her father Philip IV., sanctioned by the Cortes of Spain, and solemnly ratified by her husband, Louis XIV. Such is "legitimacy—the divine right of kings." All the great powers of Europe, excepting the emperor, promptly acknowledged the title of Philip V.

Leopold, enraged beyond measure, dispatched envoys to rouse the empire, and made the most formidable preparations for war. A force of eighty thousand men was soon assembled. The war commenced in Italy. Leopold sent down his German troops through the defiles of the Tyrol, and, in the valley of the Adige, they encountered the combined armies of France, Spain and Italy. Prince Eugene, who had

already acquired great renown in the wars against the Turks
though by birth a French noble, had long been in the Austrian
service, and led the Austrian troops. William, of England,
jealous of the encroachments of Louis XIV., and leading with
him the States of Holland, formed an alliance with Austria.
This was pretty equally dividing the military power of Europe,
and a war of course ensued, almost unparalleled in its sanguinary ferocity. The English nation supported the monarch;
the House of Lords, in an address to the king, declared that
" his majesty, his subjects and his allies, could never be secure
till the house of Austria should be restored to its rights, and
the invader of the Spanish monarchy brought to reason."
Forty thousand sailors and forty thousand land troops were
promptly voted for the war.

William died on the 16th of March, in consequence of a
fall from his horse, and was succeeded by Anne, daughter of
James II. She was, however, but nominally the sovereign.
The infamously renowned Duke of Marlborough became the
real monarch, and with great skill and energy prosecuted the
eleven years' war which ensued, which is known in history as
the War of the Spanish Succession. For many months the
conflict raged with the usual fluctuations, the Austrian forces
being commanded on the Rhine by the Duke of Marlborough,
and in Italy by Prince Eugene. Portugal soon joined the
Austrian alliance, and Philip V. and the French becoming unpopular in Spain, a small party rose there, advocating the
claims of the house of Austria. Thus supported, Leopold, at
Vienna, declared his son Charles King of Spain, and crowned
him as such in Vienna. By the aid of the English fleet he
passed from Holland to England, and thence to Lisbon, where
a powerful army was assembled to invade Spain, wrest the
crown from Philip, and place it upon the brow of Charles
III.

And now Leopold began to reap the bitter consequences
of his atrocious conduct in Hungary. The Hungarian nobles

embraced this opportunity, when the imperial armies were fully engaged, to rise in a new and formidable invasion. Francis Ragotsky, a Transylvanian prince, led in the heroic enterprise. He was of one of the noblest and wealthiest families of the realm, and was goaded to action by the bitterest wrongs. His grandfather and uncle had been beheaded; his father robbed of his property and his rank; his cousin doomed to perpetual imprisonment; his father-in-law proscribed, and his mother driven into exile. The French court immediately opened a secret correspondence with Ragotsky, promising him large supplies of men and money, and encouraging him with hopes of the coöperation of the Turks. Ragotsky secretly assembled a band of determined followers, in the savage solitudes of the Carpathian mountains, and suddenly descended into the plains of Hungary, at the head of his wild followers, calling upon his countrymen to rise and shake off the yoke of the detested Austrian. Adherents rapidly gathered around his standard; several fortresses fell into his hands, and he soon found himself at the head of twenty thousand well armed troops. The flame of insurrection spread, with electric rapidity, through all Hungary and Transylvania.

The tyrant Leopold, as he heard these unexpected tidings, was struck with consternation. He sent all the troops he could collect to oppose the patriots, but they could make no impression upon an indignant nation in arms. He then, in his panic, attempted negotiation. But the Hungarians demanded terms both reasonable and honorable, and to neither of these could the emperor possibly submit. They required that the monarchy should no longer be hereditary, but elective, according to immemorial usage; that the Hungarians should have the right to resist *illegal* power without the charge of treason; that foreign officers and garrisons should be removed from the kingdom; that the Protestants should be reëstablished in the free exercise of their religion, and that their confiscated estates should be restored. The despot could not listen for one

moment to requirements so just; and appalled by the advance
of the patriots toward Vienna, he recalled the troops from
Italy.

About the same time the Duke of Bavaria, disgusted with
the arrogance and the despotism of Leopold, renounced alle
giance to the emperor, entered into an alliance with the
French, and at the head of forty thousand troops, French and
Bavarians, commenced the invasion of Austria from the west.
Both Eugene and Marlborough hastened to the rescue of the
emperor. Combining their forces, with awful slaughter they
mowed down the French and Bavarians at Blenheim, and then
overran all Bavaria. The elector fled with the mutilated remnants of his army to France. The conquerors seized all the
fortresses, all the guns and ammunition; disbanded the Bavarian troops, took possession of the revenues of the kingdom,
and assigned to the heart-broken wife of the duke a humble
residence in the dismantled capital of the duchy.

The signal victory of Blenheim enabled Leopold to concentrate his energies upon Hungary. It was now winter, and
the belligerents, during these stormy months, were active in
making preparations for the campaign of the spring. But Leopold's hour was now tolled. That summons came which prince
and peasant must alike obey, and the emperor, after a few
months of languor and pain, on the 5th of May, 1705, passed
away to that tribunal where each must answer for every deed
done in the body. He was sixty-five years of age, and had
occupied the throne forty-six years. This is the longest reign
recorded in the Austrian annals, excepting that of Frederic III.

The reign of Leopold was eventful and woeful. It was almost one continued scene of carnage. In his character there
was a singular blending of the good and the bad. In what is
usually called moral character he was irreproachable. He was
a faithful husband, a kind father, and had no taste for any sensual pleasures. In his natural disposition he was melancholy,
and so exceedingly reserved, that he lived in his palace almost

the life of a recluse. Though he was called the most learned prince of his age, a Jesuitical education had so poisoned and debauched his mind, that while perpetrating the most griev-ous crimes of perfidy and cruelty, he seemed sincerely to feel that he was doing God service. His persecution of the Prot-estants was persistent, relentless and horrible; while at the same time he was scrupulous in his devotions, never allowing the cares of business to interfere with the prescribed duties of the Church. *The Church*, the human church of popes, cardi-nals, bishops and priests, was his guide, not the *divine Bible.* . Hence his darkness of mind and his crimes. Pope Innocent XI. deemed him worthy of canonization. But an indignant world must in justice inscribe upon his tomb, "Tyrant and Persecutor."

He was three times married; first, to Margaret, daughter of Philip IV. of Spain; again, to Claudia, daughter of Ferdi-nand of Tyrol; and a third time, to Eleonora, daughter of Philip, Elector Palatine. The character and history of his third wife are peculiarly illustrative of the kind of religion in-culcated in that day, and of the beautiful spirit of piety often exemplified in the midst of melancholy errors.

In the castle of her father, Eleonora was taught, by priests and nuns, that God was only acceptably worshiped by self-sacrifice and mortification. The devout child longed for the love of God more than for any thing else. Guided by the teachings of those who, however sincere, certainly misunder-stood the spirit of the gospel, she deprived herself of every innocent gratification, and practiced upon her fragile frame all the severities of an anchorite. She had been taught that celibacy was a virtue peculiarly acceptable to God, and reso-lutely declined all solicitations for her hand.

The emperor, after the death of his first wife, sought Eleo-nora as his bride. It was the most brilliant match Europe could offer. Eleonora, from religious scruples, rejected the offer, notwithstanding all the importunities of her parents, who could not feel reconciled to the loss of so splendid an alliance. The devout maiden, in the conflict, exposed herself, bonnet-less, to sun and wind, that she might render herself unat-tractive, tanned, sun-burnt, and freckled, so that the emperor might not desire her. She succeeded in repelling the suit, and the emperor married Claudia of the Tyrol. The court of the Elector Palatine was brilliant in opulence and gayety. Eleonora was compelled to mingle with the festive throng in the scenes of pomp and splendor; but her thoughts, her affections, were elsewhere, and all the vanities of princely life had no in-fluence in leading her heart from God. She passed several hours, every day, in devotional reading and prayer. She kept a very careful register of her thoughts and actions, scrutiniz-ing and condemning with unsparing severity every question-able emotion. Every sick bed of the poor peasants around, she visited with sympathy and as a tender nurse. She groped her way into the glooms of prison dungeons to convey solace to the prisoner. She wrought ornaments for the Church, and toiled, even to weariness and exhaustion, in making garments for the poor.

Claudia in three years died, and the emperor again was left a widower. Again he applied for the hand of Eleonora. Her spiritual advisers now urged that it was clearly the will of God that she should fill the first throne of the universe, as the patroness and protectress of the Catholic church. For such an object she would have been willing to sweep the streets or to die in a dungeon. Yielding to these persuasions she mar-ried the emperor, and was conveyed, as in a triumphal march, to the gorgeous palaces of Vienna. But her character and her mode of life were not changed. Though she sat at the impe-rial table, which was loaded with every conceivable luxury, she condemned herself to fare as humble and abstemious as could be found in the hut of the most impoverished peasant. It was needful for her at times to appear in the rich garb of an empress, but to prevent any possible indulgence of pride,

FRANZ JOSEPH

Austria.

she had her bracelets and jewelry so arranged with sharp brads as to keep her in continued suffering by the laceration of the flesh.

She was, notwithstanding these austerities, which she practiced with the utmost secrecy, indefatigable in the discharge of her duties as a wife and an empress. She often attended the opera with the emperor, but always took with her the Psalms of David, bound to resemble the books of the performance, and while the tragic or the comic scenes of the stage were transpiring before her, she was studying the devout lyrics of the Psalmist of Israel. She translated all the Psalms into German verse ; and also translated from the French, and had printed for the benefit of her subjects, a devotional work entitled, " Pious Reflections for every Day of the Month." During the last sickness of her husband she watched with unwearied assiduity at his bed-side, shrinking from no amount of exhaustion or toil, She survived her husband fifteen years, devoting all this time to austerities, self-mortification and deeds of charity. She died in 1720 ; and at her express request was buried without any parade, and with no other inscription upon her tomb than—

ELEONORA,

A POOR SINNER,

Died, January 17, 1720.

Joseph, the eldest son of Leopold, was twenty-five years of age when, by the death of his father, he was called to the throne as both king and emperor, He immediately and cordially coöperated with the alliance his father had formed, and pressed the war against France, Spain and Italy. Louis XIV was not a man, however, to be disheartened by disaster. Though thousands of his choicest troops had found a grave at Blenheim, he immediately collected another army of one hundred and sixty thousand men, and pushed them forward to the seat of war on the Rhine and the Danube. Marlborough

and Eugene led Austrian forces to the field still more power
ful. The whole summer was spent in marches, countermarches
and bloody battles on both sides of the Rhine. Winter came,
and its storms and snows drove the exhausted, bleeding combatants from the bleak plains to shelter and the fireside. All
Europe, through the winter months, resounded with preparations for another campaign. There was hardly a petty prince
on the continent who was not drawn into the strife—to decide
whether Philip of Bourbon or Charles of Hapsburg, was entitled by hereditary descent to the throne of Spain.

And now suddenly Charles XII. of Sweden burst in upon
the scene, like a meteor amidst the stars of midnight. A
more bloody apparition never emerged from the sulphureous
canopy of war. Having perfect contempt for all enervating
pleasures, with an iron frame and the abstemious habits of a
Spartan, he rushed through a career which has excited the
wonder of the world. He joined the Austrian party; struck
down Denmark at a blow; penetrated Russia in mid-winter,
driving the Russian troops before him as dogs scatter wolves;
pressed on triumphantly to Poland, through an interminable
series of battles; drove the king from the country, and placed
a new sovereign of his own selection upon the throne; and
then, proudly assuming to hold the balance between the rival
powers of France and Austria, made demands of Joseph I., as
if the emperor were but the vassal of the King of Sweden.
France and Austria were alike anxious to gain the coöperation
of this energetic arm.

Early in May, 1706, the armies of Austria and France, each
about seventy thousand strong, met in the Netherlands. Marlborough led the allied Austrian troops; the Duke of Bavaria
was in command of the French. The French were again
routed, almost as disastrously as at Blenheim, losing thirteen
thousand men and fifty pieces of artillery. On the Rhine and
in Italy the French arms were also in disgrace. Throughout
the summer battle succeeded battle, and siege followed siege.

When the snows of another winter whitened the plains of Eu
rope, the armies again retired to winter quarters, the Austriar
party having made very decided progress as the result of .he
campaign. Marlborough was in possession of most of the
Netherlands, and was threatening France with invasion. Eugene had driven the French out of Italy, and had brought
many of the Italian provinces under the dominion of Austria.

In Spain, also, the warfare was fiercely raging. Charles III.,
who had been crowned in Vienna King of Spain, and who, as
we have mentioned, had been conveyed to Lisbon by a British
fleet, joined by the King of Portugal, and at the head of an
allied army, marched towards the frontiers of Spain. The
Spaniards, though they disliked the French, hated virulently
the English and the Dutch, both of whom they considered
heretics. Their national pride was roused in seeing England,
Holland and Portugal marching upon them to place over Spain
an Austrian king. The populace rose, and after a few sanguinary conflicts drove the invaders from their borders. December's storms separated the two armies, compelling them to
seek winter quarters, with only the frontier line between them.
It was in one of the campaigns of this war, in 1704, that the
English took the rock of Gibraltar, which they have held from
that day till this.

The British people began to remonstrate bitterly against
this boundless expenditure of blood and treasure merely to remove a Bourbon prince, and place a Hapsburg prince upon
the throne of Spain. Both were alike despotic in character,
and Europe had as much to fear from the aggressions of the
house of Austria as from the ambition of the King of France.
The Emperor Joseph was very apprehensive that the English
court might be induced to withdraw from the alliance, and
fearing that they might sacrifice, as the price of accommodation, his conquests in Italy, he privately concluded with France
a treaty of neutrality for Italy. This secured to him what he

had already acquired there, and saved France and Spain from the danger of losing any more Italian States.

Though the allies were indignant, and remonstrated against this transaction, they did not see fit to abandon the war. Immense preparations were made to invade France from the Netherlands and from Piedmont, in the opening of the spring of 1707. Both efforts were only successful in spreading far and wide conflagration and blood. The invaders were driven from the kingdom with heavy loss. The campaign in Spain, this year, was also exceedingly disastrous to the Austrian arms. The heterogeneous army of Charles III., composed of Germans, English, Dutch, Portuguese, and a few Spanish refugees, were routed, and with the loss of thirteen thousand men were driven from the kingdom. Joseph, however, who stood in great dread of so terrible an enemy as Charles XII., succeeded in purchasing his neutrality, and this fiery warrior marched off with his battalions, forty-three thousand strong, to drive Peter I. from the throne of Russia.

Joseph I., with exhausted resources, and embarrassed by the claims of so wide-spread a war, was able to do but little for the subjugation of Hungary. As the campaign of 1708 opened, two immense armies, each about eighty thousand strong, were maneuvering near Brussels. After a long series of marches and combinations a general engagement ensued, in which the Austrian party, under Marlborough and Eugene, were decisively triumphant. The French were routed with the loss of fifteen thousand in killed, wounded and prisoners. During the whole summer the war raged throughout the Low Countries with unabated violence. In Spain, Austria was not able to make any progress against Philip and his forces.

Another winter came, and again the wearied combatants, all of whom had received about as many blows as they had given, sought repose. The winter was passed in fruitless negotiations, and as soon as the buds of another spring began to swell, the thunders of war were again pealing over nearly all the hills and valleys of Europe. The Austrian party had resolved, by a gigantic effort, to send an army of one hundred thousand men to the gates of Paris, there to dictate terms to the French monarch. On the 11th of September, 1709, the Austrian force, eighty thousand strong, with eighty pieces of cannon, encountered the French, seventy thousand in number, with eighty pieces of cannon, on the field of Malplaquet. The bloodiest battle of the Spanish succession was then fought. The Austrian party, guided by Marlborough and Eugene, justly claimed the victory, as they held the field. But they lost twenty thousand in killed and wounded, and took neither prisoners nor guns. The loss of the French was but ten thousand. All this slaughter seemed to be accomplishing nothing. Philip still stood firm upon the Spanish throne, and Charles could scarcely gain the slightest foothold in the kingdom which he claimed. On the side of the Rhine and of Italy, though blood flowed like water, nothing was accomplished; the plan of invading France had totally failed, and again the combatants were compelled to retire to winter quarters.

For nine years this bloody war had now desolated Europe. It is not easy to defend the cause of Austria and her allies in this cruel conflict. The Spaniards undeniably preferred Philip as their king. Louis XIV. had repeatedly expressed his readiness to withdraw entirely from the conflict. But the Austrian allies demanded that he should either by force or persuasion remove Philip from Spain, and place the kingdom in the hands of the Austrian prince. But Philip was now an independent sovereign who for ten years had occupied the throne. He was resolved not to abdicate, and his subjects were resolved to support him. Louis XIV. said that he could not wage warfare against his own grandson. The wretched old monarch, now feeble, childless, and woe crushed, whose soul was already crimsoned with the blood of countless thousands, was so dispirited by defeat, and so weary of the war, that though he still refused to send his armies against his grandson, he even offered to pay a monthly subsidy of two hundred thousand dollars (one million livres) to the allied Austrian party, to be employed in the expulsion of Philip, if they would cease to make war upon him. Even to these terms, after blood had been flowing in torrents for ten years, Austria, England and Holland would not accede. "If I must fight either Austria and her allies," said Louis XIV., " or the Spaniards, led by their king, my own grandson, I prefer to fight the Austrians."

The returning sun of the summer of 1710, found the hostile armies again in the field. The allies of Austria, early in April, hoping to surprise the French, assembled, ninety thousand in number, on the Flemish frontiers of France, trusting that by an unexpected attack they might break down the fortresses which had hitherto impeded their way. But the French were on the alert to resist them, and the whole summer was again expended in fruitless battles. These fierce conflicts so concentrated the energies of war in the Netherlands, that but little was attempted in the way of invading Spain. The Spanish nobles rallied around Philip, melted their plate to replenish his treasury, and led their vassals to fight his battles. The ecclesiastics, as a body, supported his cause. Philip was a zealous Catholic, and the priests considered him as the defender of the Church, while they had no confidence in Charles of Austria, whose cause was advocated by heretical England and Holland.

Charles III. was now in Catalonia, on the Mediterranean coast of Spain. He had landed at Barcelona, with a strong force of English and Germans. He was a man of but little character, and his military operations were conducted entirely by the English general Stanhope and the German general Staremberg. The English general was haughty and domineering; the German proud and stubborn. They were in a continued quarrel contesting the preëminence. The two rival monarchs, with forces about equal, met in Catalonia a few miles from Saragossa, on the 24th of July, 1710. Though the inefficient Charles was very reluctant to hazard a battle, the generals insisted upon it. The Spaniards were speedily and totally routed. Philip fled with a small body-guard to Lerida. His army was thoroughly dispersed. The conquerors pressed on toward Madrid, crossed the Ebro at Saragossa, where they again encountered, but a short distance from the city, an army strongly posted upon some heights. Philip was already there. The conflict was short but bloody, and the generals of Charles were again victorious. Philip, with a disheartened remnant of his troops, retreated to Madrid. The generals dragged the timid and reluctant Charles on to Madrid, where they arrived on the 28th of September. There was no force at the capital to oppose them. They were received, however, by the citizens of the metropolis as foreign conquerors. Charles rode through the deserted streets, meeting only with sullen silence. A few who were hired to shout, were pelted, by the populace, with mud, as traitors to their lawful king. None flocked to his standard. Nobles, clergy, populace, all alike stood aloof from him. Charles and his generals were embarrassed and perplexed. They could not compel the nation to receive the Austrian king.

Philip, in the meantime, who had much energy and popularity of character, was rapidly retrieving his losses, and troops were flocking to his camp from all parts of Spain. He established his court at Valladolid, about one hundred and fifty miles north-east from Madrid. His troops, dispersed by the two disastrous battles, were reassembled at Lerida. The peasants rose in large numbers and joined them, and cut off all communication between Charles at Madrid and his ships at Barcelona. The Spanish grandees sent urgent messages to France for succors. General Vendome, at the head of three thousand horse, swept through the defiles of the Pyrenees, and, with exultant music and waving banners, joined Philip at Valladolid. Universal enthusiasm was excited. Soon thirty

thousand infantry entered the camp, and then took positions
on the Tagus, where they could cut off any reinforcements
which might attempt to march from Portugal to aid the invaders.

Charles was apparently in a desperate situation. Famine
and consequent sickness were in his camp. His army was
daily dwindling away. He was emphatically in an enemy's
country. Not a soldier could stray from the ranks without
danger of assassination. **He had taken Madrid, and Madrid
was his prison.**

CHAPTER XXII.

JOSEPH I. AND CHARLES VI.

FROM 1710 TO 1717.

PERPLEXITIES IN MADRID.—FLIGHT OF CHARLES.—RETREAT OF THE AUSTRIAN ARMY.—STANHOPE'S DIVISION CUT OFF.—CAPTURE OF STANHOPE.—STAREMBERG ASSAILED.—RETREAT TO BARCELONA.—ATTEMPT TO PACIFY HUNGARY.—THE HUNGARIAN DIET.—BARONIAL CROWNING OF RAGOTSKY.—RENEWAL OF THE HUNGARIAN WAR.—ENTERPRISE OF HERBEVILLE.—THE HUNGARIANS CRUSHED.—LENITY OF JOSEPH.—DEATH OF JOSEPH.—ACCESSION OF CHARLES VI.—HIS CAREER IN SPAIN.—CAPTURE OF BARCELONA.—THE SIEGE.—THE RESCUE.—CHARACTER OF CHARLES.—CLOISTERS OF MONTSERRAT.—INCREASED EFFORTS FOR THE SPANISH CROWN.—CHARLES CROWNED EMPEROR OF AUSTRIA AND HUNGARY.—BOHEMIA.—DEPLORABLE CONDITION OF LOUIS XIV.

GENERALS Stanhope and Staremberg, who managed the affairs of Charles, with but little respect for his judgment, and none for his administrative qualities, were in great perplexity respecting the course to be pursued. Some recommended the transference of the court from Madrid to Saragossa, where they would be nearer to their supplies. Others urged removal to Barcelona, where they would be under the protection of the British fleet. It was necessary to watch over Charles with the utmost care, as he was in constant danger of assassination. While in this state of uncertainty, tidings reached Madrid that the Duke of Noailles was on the march, with fifteen thousand men, to cut off the retreat of the Austrians, and at the same time Philip was advancing with a powerful army from Valladolid. This intelligence rendered instant action necessary. The Austrian party precipitately evacuated Madrid, followed by the execrations of the people As soon as the last battalions had left the city, the ringing of bells, the firing of artillery, and the shouts of the people, an

nounced the popular exultation in view of the departure of
Charles, and the cordial greeting they were giving to his rival
Philip. The complications of politics are very curious. The
British government was here, through years of war and blood,
endeavoring to drive from his throne the acknowledged King
of Spain. In less than a hundred years we find this same
government again deluging Europe in blood, to reseat upon
the throne the miserable Ferdinand, the lineal descendant of
this Bourbon prince.

Charles put spurs to his horse, and accompanied by a glittering cavalcade of two thousand cavaliers, galloped over the
mountains to Barcelona. His army, under the leadership of
his efficient English general, followed rapidly but cautiously
on, hoping to press through the defiles of the mountains which
separated them from Arragon before their passage could be
obstructed by the foe. The troops were chagrined and dispirited; the generals in that state of ill humor which want of
success generally engenders. The roads were bad, provisions
scarce, the inhabitants of the country bitterly hostile. It was
the middle of November, and cold blasts swept through the
mountains. Staremberg led the van, and Stanhope, with four
thousand English troops, occupied the post of peril in a retreat,
the rear. As the people of the country would furnish them
with no supplies, the pillage of towns and villages became a
necessity; but it none the less added to the exasperation of
the Spaniards.

A hurried march of about eighty miles brought the troops
to the banks of the Tagus. As General Staremberg, at the
head of the advance guard, pressed eagerly on, he left Stanhope at quite a distance behind. They encamped for a night,
the advance at Cifuentes, the rear at Brihuega. The hostility
of the natives was such that almost all communication was
cut off between the two sections of the army. In the confusion of the hasty retreat, and as no enemy was apprehended
in that portion of the way, the importance of hourly commu-

nication was forgotten. In the morning, as Stanhope put his troops again in motion, he was surprised and alarmed in seeing upon the hills before him the banners of an opposing host, far outnumbering his own, and strongly intrenched. The Earl of Stanhope at once appreciated the nearly utter hopelessness of his position. He was cut off from the rest of the army, had no artillery, but little ammunition, and was almost entirely destitute of provision. Still he scorned to surrender. He threw his troops behind a stone wall, and vigorously commenced fortifying his position, hoping to be able to hold out until Staremberg, hearing of his situation, should come to his release.

During the whole day he beat back the assaults of the Spanish army. In the meantime Staremberg was pressing on to Barcelona. In the evening of that day he heard of the peril of his rear guard. His troops were exhausted ; the night of pitchy blackness, and the miry roads, cut to pieces by the heavy artillery and baggage wagons, were horrible. Through the night he made preparations to turn back to aid his beleaguered friends. It was, however, midday before he could collect his scattered troops, from their straggling march, and commence retracing his steps. In a few hours the low sun of a November day sunk below the hills. The troops, overtaken by darkness, stumbling through the gloom, and apprehensive of a midnight attack, rested upon their arms, waiting, through the weary hours, for the dawn of the morning. The second day came, and the weary troops toiled through the mire, while Stanhope, from behind his slight parapet, baffled all the efforts of his foes.

The third morning dawned. Staremberg was within some fifteen miles of Briehuga. Stanhope had now exhausted all his ammunition. The inhabitants of the town rose against him and attacked him in the rear, while the foe pressed him in front. A large number of his troops had already fallen, and no longer resistance was possible. Stanhope and the remnant of his band were taken captive and conducted into the town of Briehuga. Staremberg, unaware of the surrender, pushed on until he came within a league of Briehuga. Anxiously he threw up signals, but could obtain no response. His fears of the worst were soon confirmed by seeing the Spanish army, in brilliant battle array, approaching to assail him. Philip himself was there to animate them by his presence; and the heroic French general, the Duke of Vendome, a descendant of Henry IV., led the charging columns.

Though the troops of Staremberg were inferior in number to those of the Spanish monarch, and greatly fatigued by their forced marches, a retreat at that moment, in the face of so active an enemy, was not to be thought of. The battle immediately commenced, with its rushing squadrons and its thunder peals. The Spaniards, sanguine of success, and inspired with the intensest hatred of their *heretical* foes, charged with irresistible fury. The left wing of Staremberg was speedily cut to pieces, and the baggage taken. The center and the right maintained their ground until night came to their protection. Staremberg's army was now reduced to nine thousand. His horses were either slain or worn out by fatigue. He was consequently compelled to abandon all his artillery and most of his baggage, as he again commenced a rapid retreat towards Barcelona. The enemy pressed him every step of the way. But with great heroism and military skill he baffled their endeavors to destroy him, and after one of the most arduous marches on record, reached Barcelona with a feeble remnant of but seven thousand men, ragged, emaciated and bleeding. Behind the walls of this fortified city, and protected by the fleet of England, they found repose.

We must now turn back a few years, to trace the progress of events in Hungary and Austria. Joseph, the emperor, had sufficient intelligence to understand that the rebellious and anarchical state of Hungary was owing to the cruelty and intolerance of his father. He saw, also, that there could be no

hope of permanent tranquillity but in paying some respect to
the aspirations for civil and religious liberty. The troubles in
Hungary distracted his attention, exhausted the energies of
his troops, and deprived him of a large portion of his political
and military power. He now resolved to try the effect of con
cessions. The opportunity was propitious, as he could throw
upon his father the blame of all past decrees. He accordingly
sent a messenger to the Hungarian nobles with the declaration
that during his father's lifetime he had never interfered in the
government, and that consequently he was in no respect responsible for the persecution of which they complained. And
he promised, on the honor of a king, that instead of attempting the enforcement of those rigorous decrees, he would faithfully fulfill all the articles he had sworn to observe at his coronation ; and that he accordingly summoned a diet for the redress of their grievances and the confirmation of all their
ancient privileges. As proof of his sincerity, he dismissed those
ministers who had advised the intolerant decrees enacted by
Leopold, and appointed in their place men of more mild and
lenient character.

But the Hungarians, deeming themselves now in a position
to enforce their claims by the energies of their army, feared
to trust to the promises of a court so often perjured. Without
openly renouncing allegiance to Austria, and declaring independence, they, through Ragotsky, summoned a diet to meet
at Stetzim, where their session would be protected by the Hungarian army. There was a large gathering of all the first nobility of the realm. A spacious tent was spread for the imposing assembly, and the army encircled it as with a sheltering
embrace. The session was opened with prayer and the administration of the sacrament of the Lord's Supper. Will the
time ever come when the members of the United States Congress will meet as Christian brethren, at the table of our Saviour, as they commence their annual deliberations for the welfare of this republic ? The nobles formed a confederacy for

the government of the country. The legislative power was committed to a senate of twenty-four nobles. Ragotsky was chosen military chief, with the title of Dux, or leader. Four of the most illustrious nobles raised Ragotsky upon a buckler on their shoulders, when he took the oath of fidelity to the government thus provisionally established, and then administered the oath to his confederates. They all bound themselves solemnly not to conclude any peace with the emperor, until their ancient rights, both civil and religious, were fully restored.

In reply to the advances made by the emperor, they returned the very reasonable and moderate demands that their chief, Ragotsky, should be reinstated in his ancestral realms of Transylvania, that the claim of *hereditary* sovereignty should be relinquished, and that there should be the restoration of those ancient civil and religious immunities of which Leopold had defrauded them. Upon these conditions they promised to recognize Joseph as their sovereign during his lifetime; claiming at his death their time-honored right of choosing his successor. Joseph would not listen for one moment to these terms, and the war was renewed with fury.

The Hungarian patriots had seventy-five thousand men under arms. The spirit of the whole nation was with them, and the Austrian troops were driven from almost every fortress in the kingdom. The affairs of Joseph seemed to be almost desperate, his armies struggling against overpowering foes all over Europe, from the remotest borders of Transylvania to the frontiers of Portugal. The vicissitudes of war are proverbial. An energetic, sagacious general, Herbeville, with great military sagacity, and aided by a peculiar series of fortunate events, marched down the valley of the Danube to Buda; crossed the stream to Pesth; pushed boldly on through the heart of Hungary to Great Waradin, forced the defiles of the mountains, and entered Transylvania. Through a series of brilliant victories he took fortress after fortress, until he subjugated the whole of Transylvania, and brought it again into subjection to the Austrian crown. This was in November, 1705.

But the Hungarians, instead of being intimidated by the success of the imperial arms, summoned another diet. It was held in the open field in accordance with ancient custom, and was thronged by thousands from all parts of the kingdom. With great enthusiasm and public acclaim the resolution was passed that Joseph was a tyrant and a usurper, animated by the hereditary despotism of the Austrian family. This truthful utterance roused anew the ire of the emperor. He resolved upon a desperate effort to bring Hungary into subjection. Leaving his English and Dutch allies to meet the brunt of the battle on the Rhine and in the Netherlands, he recalled his best troops, and made forced levies in Austria until he had created an army sufficiently strong, as he thought, to sweep down all opposition. These troops he placed under the most experienced generals, and sent them into Hungary in the summer of 1708. France, weakened by repeated defeats, could send the Hungarians no aid, and the imperial troops, through bloody battles, victoriously traversed the kingdom. Everywhere the Hungarians were routed and dispersed, until no semblance of an army was left to oppose the victors. It seems that life in those days, to the masses of the people, swept incessantly by these fiery surges of war, could only have been a scene, from the cradle to the grave, of blood and agony. For two years this dismal storm of battle howled over all the Hungarian plains, and then the kingdom, like a victim exhausted, prostrate and bleeding, was taken captive and firmly bound.

Ragotsky, denounced with the penalty of high treason, escaped to Poland. The emperor, anxious no longer to exasperate, proposed measures of unusual moderation. He assembled a convention; promised a general amnesty for all political offenses, the restitution of confiscated property, the liberation of prisoners, and the confirmation of all the rights which he had promised at his coronation. Some important points were not touched upon; others were passed over in vague and general terms. The Hungarians, helpless as a babe, had nothing to do but to submit, whatever the terms might be. They were surprised at the unprecedented lenity of the conqueror, and the treaty of peace and subjection was signed in January, 1711.

In three months after the signing of this treaty, Joseph I. died of the small-pox, in his palace of Vienna. He was but thirty-three years of age. For a sovereign educated from the cradle to despotic rule, and instructed by one of the most bigoted of fathers, he was an unusually good man, and must be regarded as one of the best sovereigns who have swayed the scepter of Austrian despotism.

The law of hereditary descent is frequently involved in great embarrassment. Leopold, to obviate disputes which he foresaw were likely to arise, had assigned Hungary, Bohemia, and his other hereditary estates, to Joseph. To Charles he had assigned the vast Spanish inheritance. In case Joseph should die without male issue he had decreed that the crown of the Austrian dominions should also pass to Charles. In case Charles should also die without issue male, the crown should then revert to the daughters of Joseph in preference to those of Charles. Joseph left no son. He had two daughters, the eldest of whom was but twelve years of age. Charles, who was now in Barcelona, claiming the crown of Spain as Charles III., had no Spanish blood in his veins. He was the son of Leopold, and of his third wife, the devout and lovely Eleonora, daughter of the Elector Palatine. He was now but twenty-eight years of age. For ten years he had been struggling for the crown which his father Leopold had claimed, as succeeding to the rights of his first wife Margaret, daughter of Philip IV.

Charles was a genteel, accomplished young man of eighteen when he left his father's palace at Vienna, for England, where a British fleet was to convey him to Portugal, and, by the energy of its fleet and army, place him upon the throne of Spain. He was received at Portsmouth in England, when he landed from Holland, with much parade, and was conducted by the Dukes of Marlborough and Somerset to Windsor castle, where he had an interview with Queen Anne. His appearance at that time is thus described by his partial chroniclers:

"The court was very splendid and much thronged. The queen's behavior toward him was very noble and obliging. The young king charmed all who were present. He had a gravity beyond his age, tempered with much modesty. His behavior in all points was so exact, that there was not a circumstance in his whole deportment which was liable to censure. He paid an extraordinary respect to the queen, and yet maintained a due greatness in it. He had the art of seeming well pleased with every thing, without so much as smiling once all the while he was at court, which was only three days. He spoke but little, and all he said was judicious and obliging."

Young Charles was engaged to the daughter of the King of Portugal; but the young lady died just before his arrival at Lisbon. As he had never seen the infanta, his grief could not have been very deep, however great his disappointment might have been. He made several attempts to penetrate Spain by the Portuguese frontier, but being repelled in every effort, by the troops of Philip, he again embarked, and with twelve thousand troops in an English fleet, sailed around the Peninsula, entered the Mediterranean and landed on the shores of Catalonia, where he had been led to believe that the inhabitants in a body would rally around him. But he was bitterly disappointed. The Earl of Peterborough, who was intrusted with the command of this expedition, in a letter home gave free utterance to his disappointment and chagrin.

"Instead of ten thousand men, and in arms," he wrote, "to cover our landing and strengthen our camp, we found only so many higglers and sutlers flocking into it. Instead of finding Barcelona in a weak condition, and ready to surrender upon the first appearance of our troops, we found a strong garrison to oppose us, and a hostile army almost equal to our own."

In this dilemma a council of war was held, and though many were in favor of abandoning the enterprise and returning to Portugal, it was at last determined, through the urgency of Charles, to remain and lay siege to the city. Barcelona, the capital of Catalonia, was then the principal sea-port of the Spanish peninsula on the Mediterranean. It contained a population of about one hundred and forty thousand. It was strongly fortified. West of the city there was a mountain called Montjoy, upon which there was a strong fort which commanded the harbor and the town. After a short siege this fort was taken by storm, and the city was then forced to surrender.

Philip soon advanced with an army of French and Spaniards to retake the city. The English fleet had retired. Twenty-eight French ships of war blockaded the harbor, which they could not enter, as it was commanded by the guns of Montjoy. The siege was very desperate both in the assault and the defense. The young king, Charles, was in the most imminent danger of falling into the hands of his foes. There was no possibility of escape, and it seemed inevitable that the city must either surrender, or be taken by storm. The French and Spanish army numbered twenty thousand men. They first attempted to storm Montjoy, but were repulsed with great slaughter. They then besieged it, and by regular approaches compelled its capitulation in three weeks.

This noble resistance enabled the troops in the city greatly to multiply and increase their defenses. They thus succeeded in protracting the siege of the town five weeks longer. Every day the beleagured troops from the crumbling ram-

parts watched the blue expanse of the Mediterranean, hoping
to see the sails of an English fleet coming to their rescue.
Two breaches were already effected in the walls. The garrison, reduced to two thousand, and exhausted by superhuman
exertions by day and by night, were almost in the last stages
of despair, when, in the distant horizon, the long looked-for
fleet appeared. The French ships, by no means able to cope
with such a force, spread their sails, and sought safety in
flight.

The English fleet, amounting to fifty sail of the line, and
transporting a large number of land troops, triumphantly
entered the harbor on the 3rd of May, 1706. The fresh
soldiers were speedily landed, and marched to the ramparts
and the breaches. This strong reinforcement annihilated the
hopes of the besiegers. Apprehensive of an immediate sally,
they retreated with such precipitation that they left behind
them in the hospitals their sick and wounded; they also
abandoned their heavy artillery, and an immense quantity of
military stores.

Whatever energy Charles might have shown during the
siege, all seemed now to evaporate. When the shot of the foe
were crumbling the walls of Barcelona, he was in danger of
the terrible doom of being taken a captive, which would have
been the annihilation of all his hopes. Despair nerved him to
effort. But now his person was no longer in danger; and
his natural inefficiency and dilatoriness returned. Notwithstanding the urgent intreaties of the Earl of Peterborough
to pursue the foe, he insisted upon first making a pilgrimage
to the shrine of the holy Virgin at Montserrat, twenty-four
miles from Barcelona.

This curious monastery consists of but a succession of
cloisters or hermitages hewn out of the solid rock. They are
only accessible by steps as steep as a ladder, which are also
hewn upon the face of the almost precipitous mountain. The
highest of these cells, and which are occupied by the youngest

monks, are at an elevation of three or four thousand feet above the level of the Mediterranean. Soon after Charles's pilgrimage to Montserrat, he made a triumphal march to Madrid, entered the city, and caused himself to be proclaimed king under the title of Charles III. But Philip soon came upon him with such force that he was compelled to retreat back to Barcelona. Again, in 1710, he succeeded in reaching Madrid, and, as we have described, he was driven back, with accumulated disaster, to Catalonia.

Three months after this defeat, when his affairs in Spain were assuming the gloomiest aspect, a courier arrived at Barcelona, and informed him that his brother Joseph was dead; that he had already been proclaimed King of Hungary and Bohemia, and Archduke of Austria; and that it was a matter of the most urgent necessity that he should immediately return to Germany. Charles immediately embarked at Barcelona, and landed near Genoa on the 27th of September. Rapidly pressing on through the Italian States, he entered Milan on the 16th of October, where he was greeted with the joyful intelligence that a diet had been convened under the influence of Prince Eugene, and that by its unanimous vote he was invested with the imperial throne. He immediately proceeded through the Tyrol to Frankfort, where he was crowned on the 22d of December. He was now more than ever determined that the diadem of Spain should be added to the other crowns which had been placed upon his brow.

In the incessant wars which for centuries had been waged between the princes and States of Germany and the emperor, the States had acquired virtually a constitution, which they called a capitulation. When Charles was crowned as Charles VI., he was obliged to promise that he would never assemble a diet or council without convening all the princes and States of the empire; that he would never wage war, or conclude peace, or enter into alliance with any nation without the consent of the States; that he would not, of his own authority,

put any prince under the ban of the empire ; that confiscated
territory should never be conferred upon any members of his
own family, and that no successor to the imperial crown should
be chosen during his lifetime, unless absence from Germany
or the infirmities of age rendered him incapable of administering the affairs of the empire.

The emperor, invested with the imperial crown, hastened
to Vienna, and, with unexpected energy, entered upon the
administration of the complicated interests of his wide-spread
realms.   After passing a few weeks in Vienna, he repaired to
Prague, where, in May, he was, with much pomp, crowned
King of Hungary.   He then returned to Vienna, and prepared to press with new vigor the war of the Spanish succession.

Louis XIV. was now suffering the earthly retribution for
his ill-spent life.   The finances of the realm were in a state of
hopeless embarrassment; famine was filling the kingdom with
misery ; his armies were everywhere defeated ; the impreca-
tions of a beggared people were rising around his throne;
his palace was the scene of incessant feuds and intrigues.   His
children were dead ; he was old, infirm, sick, the victim of insupportable melancholy—utterly weary of life, and yet awfully
afraid to die.   France, in the person of Louis XIV., who
could justly say, " I am the State," was humbled.

The accession of Charles to the throne of the empire, and
to that of Austria, Hungary and Bohemia, while at the same
time he claimed sovereignty over the vast realms of the Spanish kingdom, invested him with such enormous power, that
England, which had combined Europe against the colossal
growth of France, having humbled that power, was disposed
to form a combination against Austria.   There was in consequence an immediate relaxation of hostilities just at the time
when the French batteries on the frontiers were battered down,
and when the allied army had apparently an unobstructed way
opened to the gates of Paris.   In this state of affairs the Brit

ish ministry pressed negotiations for peace. The preliminaries were settled in London on the 8th of October, 1711. By
this treaty Louis XIV. agreed to make such a change in the
law of hereditary descent, as to render it impossible for any
king to wear at the same time the crowns of France and of
Spain, and made various other important concessions.

Charles, whose ambition was roused by his sudden and un
expected elevation, exerted all his energies to thwart the prog
ress of negotiations, and bitterly complained that the allies
were dishonorably deserting the cause which they had espoused. The emperor dispatched circular letters to all the
courts of Europe, and sent Prince Eugene as a special ambassador to London, to influence Queen Anne, if possible, to persevere in the grand alliance. But he was entirely unsuccessful.
The Duke of Marlborough was disgraced, and dismissed from
office. The peace party rendered Eugene so unpopular that
he was insulted in the streets of London. The Austrian party
in England was utterly defeated, and a congress was appointed
to meet at Utrecht to settle the terms of peace. But Charles
was now so powerful that he resolved to prosecute the war
even though abandoned by England. He accordingly sent an
ambassador to Utrecht to embarrass the proceedings as much
as possible, and, in case the grand alliance should be broken
up, to secure as many powers as possible in fidelity to Austria.

The States of the Netherlands were still warmly with Austria, as they dreaded so formidable a power as France directly upon their frontier. The other minor powers of the alliance
were also rather inclined to remain with Austria. The war
continued while the terms of peace were under discussion.
England, however, entered into a private understanding with
France, and the Duke of Ormond, who had succeeded Marlborough, received secret orders not to take part in any battle
or siege. The developments, upon fields of battle, of this dishonorable arrangement, caused great indignation on the part

of the allies. The British forces withdrew, and the French
armies, taking advantage of the great embarrassments thus
caused, were again gaining the ascendency. Portugal soon
followed the example of England and abandoned the alliance.
The Duke of Savoy was the next to leave. The alliance
was evidently crumbling to pieces, and on the 11th of April,
1713, all the belligerents, excepting the emperor, signed the
treaty of peace. Philip of Spain also acceded to the same
articles.

Charles was very indignant in being thus abandoned; and
unduly estimating his strength, resolved alone, with the resources which the empire afforded him, to prosecute the war
against France and Spain. Having nothing to fear from a
Spanish invasion, he for a time relinquished his attempts upon
Spain, and concentrating his armies upon the Rhine, prepared
for a desperate onset upon France. For two years the war
raged between Austria and France with war's usual vicissitudes of defeat and victory on either side. It was soon evident that the combatants were too equally matched for either
party to hope to gain any decisive advantage over the other.
On the 7th of September, 1714, France and Austria agreed to
sheathe the sword. The war had raged for fourteen years,
with an expenditure of blood and treasure, and an accumulation of misery which never can be guaged. Every party had
lost fourfold more than it had gained. "A war," says Marshal Villers, "which had desolated the greater part of Europe,
was concluded almost on the very terms which might have
been procured at the commencement of hostilities."

By this treaty of peace, which was signed at Baden, in
Switzerland, the States of the Netherlands were left in the
hands of Austria; and also the Italian States of Naples, Milan,
Mantua and Sardinia. The thunders of artillery had hardly
ceased to reverberate over the marshes of Holland and along
the banks of the Rhine, ere the "blast of war's loud organ"
and the tramp of charging squadrons were heard rising anew

from the distant mountains of Sclavonia. The Turks, in violation of their treaty of peace, were again on the march, ascending the Danube along its southern banks, through the defiles of the Sclavonian mountains. In a motley mass of one hundred and fifty thousand men they had passed Belgrade, crossed the Save, and were approaching Peterwarden.

Eugene was instantly dispatched with an efficient, compact army, disciplined by twelve years of warfare, to resist the Moslem invaders. The hostile battalions met at Karlowitz, but a few miles from Peterwarden, on the 5th of August, 1716. The tempest blazed with terrific fury for a few hours, when the Turkish host turned and fled. Thirty thousand of their number, including the grand vizier who led the host, were left dead upon the field. In their utter discomfiture they abandoned two hundred and fifty pieces of heavy artillery, and baggage, tents and military stores to an immense amount. Fifty Turkish banners embellished the camp of the victors.

And now Eugene led his triumphant troops, sixty thousand in number, down the river to lay siege to Belgrade. This fortress, which the labor of ages had strengthened, was garrisoned by thirty thousand troops, and was deemed almost impregnable. Eugene invested the place and commenced the slow and tedious operations of a siege. The sultan immediately dispatched an army of two hundred thousand men to the relief of his beleaguered fortress. The Turks, arriving at the scene of action, did not venture an assault upon their intrenched foes, but intrenched themselves on heights, outside of the besieging camp, in a semicircle extending from the Danube to the Save. They thus shut up the besiegers in the miasmatic marshes which surrounded the city, cut off their supplies of provisions, and from their advancing batteries threw shot into the Austrian camp. "A man," said Napoleon, "is not a soldier." The Turks had two hundred thousand *men* in their camp, raw recruits. Eugene had sixty thousand veteran *soldiers*. He decided to drive off the Turks who annoyed him. It was necessary for him to detach twenty thousand to hold in check the garrison of Belgrade, who might sally to the relief of their companions. This left him but forty thousand troops with whom to assail two hundred thousand **strongly intrenched.** **He did not hesitate in the undertaking.**

CHAPTER XXIII.

CHARLES VI.

FROM 1716 TO 1727.

HEROIC DECISION OF EUGENE.—BATTLE OF BELGRADE.—UTTER ROUT OF THE TURKS.—POSSESSIONS OF CHARLES VI.—THE ELECTOR OF HANOVER SUCCEEDS TO THE ENGLISH THRONE.—PREPARATIONS FOR WAR.—STATE OF ITALY.—PHILIP V. OF SPAIN.—DIPLOMATIC AGITATIONS.—PALACE OF ST. ILDEFONSO.—ORDER OF THE GOLDEN FLEECE.—REJECTION OF MARIA ANNE.—CONTEST FOR THE ROCK OF GIBRALTAR.—DISMISSAL OF RIPPERDA.—TREATY OF VIENNA.—PEACE CONCLUDED.

THE enterprise upon which Eugene had resolved was bold in the extreme. It could only be accomplished by consummate bravery aided by equal military skill. The foe they were to attack were five to one, and were protected by well-constructed redoubts, armed with the most formidable batteries. They were also abundantly supplied with cavalry, and the Turkish cavalry were esteemed the finest horsemen in the world. There was but one circumstance in favor of Eugene. The Turks did not dream that he would have the audacity to march from the protection of his intrenchments and assail them behind their own strong ramparts. There was consequently but little difficulty in effecting a surprise.

All the arrangements were made with the utmost precision and secrecy for a midnight attack. The favorable hour came. The sun went down in clouds, and a night of Egyptian darkness enveloped the armies. The glimmer of innumerable camp-fires only pointed out the position of the foe, without throwing any illumination upon the field. Eugene visited all the posts of the army, ordered abundant refreshment to be distributed to the troops, addressed them in encouraging words, to impress upon them the importance of the enterprise, and minutely assigned to each battalion, regiment, brigade and division its duty, that there might be no confusion. The whole plan was carefully arranged in all its details and in all its grand combination. As the bells of Belgrade tolled the hour of twelve at midnight, three bombs, simultaneously discharged, put the whole Austrian army in rapid and noiseless motion.

A dense fog had now descended, through which they could with difficulty discern the twinkling lights of the Turkish camp. Rapidly they traversed the intervening space, and in dense, solid columns, rushed over the ramparts of the foe. Bombs, cannon, musketry, bayonets, cavalry, all were employed, amidst the thunderings and the lightnings of that midnight storm of war, in the work of destruction. The Turks, roused from their slumber, amazed, bewildered, fought for a short time with maniacal fury, often pouring volleys of bullets into the bosoms of their friends, and with bloody cimeters smiting indiscriminately on the right hand and the left, till, in the midst of a scene of confusion and horror which no imagination can conceive, they broke and fled. Two hundred thousand men, lighted only by the flash of guns which mowed their ranks, with thousands of panic-stricken cavalry trampling over them, while the crash of musketry, the explosions of artillery, the shouts of the assailants and the fugitives, and the shrieks of the dying, blended in a roar more appalling than heaven's heaviest thunders, presented a scene which has few parallels even in the horrid annals of war.

The morning dawned upon a field of blood and death. The victory of the Austrians was most decisive. The flower of the Turkish army was cut to pieces, and the remnant was utterly dispersed. The Turkish camp, with all its abundant booty of tents, provisions, ammunition and artillery, fell into the hands of the conqueror. So signal was the victory, that the disheartened Turks made no attempt to retrieve their loss. Belgrade was surrendered to the Austrians, and the sultan im-plored peace. The articles were signed in Passarovitz, a small town of Servia, in July, 1718. By this treaty the emperor added Belgrade to his dominions, and also a large part of Wallachia and Servia.

Austria and Spain were still in heart at war, as the em-peror claimed the crown of Spain, and was only delaying act-ive hostilities until he could dispose of his more immediate foes. Charles, soon after the death of his cousin, the Portuguese princess, with whom he had formed a matrimonial engagement, married Elizabeth Christina, a princess of Brunswick. The imperial family now consisted of three daughters, Maria The-resa, Maria Anne and Maria Amelia. It will be remembered that by the family compact established by Leopold, the suc-cession was entailed upon Charles in preference to the daugh-ters of Joseph, in case Joseph should die without male issue. But should Charles die without male issue, the crown was to revert to the daughters of Joseph in preference to those of Charles. The emperor, having three daughters and no sons, with natural parental partiality, but unjustly, and with great want of magnanimity, was anxious to deprive the daughters of Joseph of their rights, that he might secure the crown for his own daughters. He accordingly issued a decree reversing this con-tract, and settling the right of succession first upon his daugh-ters, should he die without sons, then upon the daughters of Joseph, one of whom had married the Elector of Saxony and the other the Elector of Bavaria. After them he declared his sister, who had married the King of Portugal, and then his other sisters, the daughters of Leopold, to be in the line of succession. This new law of succession Charles issued under the name of the Pragmatic Sanction. He compelled his nieces, the daughters of Joseph, to give their assent to this Sanction, and then, for the remainder of his reign, made the greatest ef-forts to induce all the powers of Europe to acknowledge its validity.

Charles VI. was now, as to the extent of territory over which he reigned and the population subject to his sway, decidedly the most powerful monarch in Christendom. Three hundred princes of the German empire acknowledged him as their elected sovereign. By hereditary right he claimed dominion over Bohemia, Hungary, Transylvania, Wallachia, Servia, Styria, Carinthia, Carniola, the Tyrol, and all the rich and populous States of the Netherlands. Naples, Sicily, Mantua and Milan in Italy, also recognized his sovereignty. To enlightened reason nothing can seem more absurd than that one man, of very moderate capacities, luxuriating in his palace at Vienna, should pretend to hold dominion over so many millions so widely dispersed. But the progress of the world towards intelligent liberty has been very slow. When we contrast the constitution of the United States with such a political condition, all our evils and difficulties dwindle to utter insignificance.

Still the power of the emperor was in many respects apparent rather than real. Each of these States had its own customs and laws. The nobles were tumultuary, and ever ready, if their privileges were infringed, to rise in insurrection. Military force alone could hold these turbulent realms in awe; and the old feudal servitude which crushed the millions, was but another name for anarchy. The peace establishment of the emperor amounted to one hundred thousand men, and every one of these was necessary simply to garrison his fortresses. The enormous expense of the support of such an army, with all the outlays for the materiel of war, the cavalry, and the structure of vast fortresses, exhausted the revenues of a kingdom in which the masses of the people were so miserably poor that they were scarcely elevated above the beasts of the field, and where the finances had long been in almost irreparable disorder. The years of peace, however, were very few. War, a maelstrom which ingulfs uncounted millions, seems to have been the normal state of Ger many. But the treasury of Charles was so constantly drained that he could never, even in his greatest straits, raise more than one hundred and sixty thousand men; and he was often compelled to call upon the aid of a foreign purse to meet the expense which that number involved. Within a hundred years the nations have made vast strides in wealth, and in the consequent ability to throw away millions in war.

Charles VI. commenced his reign with intense devotion to business. He resolved to be an illustrious emperor, vigorously superintending all the interests of the empire, legislative, judicial and executive. For a few weeks he was busy night and day, buried in a hopeless mass of diplomatic papers. But he soon became weary of this, and leaving all the ordinary affairs of the State in the hands of agents, amused himself with his violin and in chasing rabbits. As more serious employment, he gave pompous receptions, and enveloped himself in imperial ceremony and the most approved courtly etiquette. He still, however, insisted upon giving his approval to all measures adopted by his ministers, before they were carried into execution. But as he was too busy with his entertainments, his music and the chase, to devote much time to the dry details of government, papers were accumulating in a mountainous heap in his cabinet, and the most important business was neglected.

Charles XII. was now King of Sweden; Peter the Great, Emperor of Russia; George I., King of England; and the shameful regency had succeeded, in France, the reign of Louis XIV. For eighteen years a bloody war had been sweeping the plains of Poland, Russia and Sweden. Thousands had been torn to pieces by the enginery of war, and trampled beneath iron hoofs. Millions of women and children had been impoverished, beggared, and turned out houseless into the fields to moan and starve and die. The claims of humanity must ever yield to the requisitions of war. This fierce battle of eighteen years was fought to decide which of three men, Peter of Russia, Charles of Sweden, or Augustus of Poland, should have the right to exact tribute from Livonia. This province was a vast pasture on the Baltic, containing about seventeen thousand square miles, and inhabited by about five hundred thousand poor herdsmen and tillers of the soil.

Peter the Great was in the end victorious in this long conflict; and having attached large portions of Sweden to his territory, with a navy upon the Baltic, and a disciplined army, began to be regarded as a European power, and was quite disposed to make his voice heard in the diplomacy of Europe. Queen Anne having died, leaving no children, the law of hereditary descent carried the crown of England to Germany, and placed it upon the brow of the Elector of Hanover, who, as grandson of James I., was the nearest heir, but who could not speak a word of English, who knew nothing of constitutional law, and who was about as well qualified to govern England as a Patagonian or Esquimaux would have been. But obedience to this law of hereditary descent was a political necessity. There were thousands of able men in England who could have administered the government with honor to themselves and to the country. But it is said in reply that the people of England, as a body, were not then, and probably are not even now, sufficiently enlightened to be intrusted with the choice of their own rulers. Respect for the ballot-box is one of the last and highest attainments of civilization. Recent developments in our own land have led many to fear that barbarism is gaining upon the people. If the *ballot-box* be overturned, the *cartridge-box* must take its place. The great battle we have to fight is the battle against popular ignorance. The great army we are to support is the army of teachers in the schools and in the pulpit, elevating the mind to the highest possible intelligence, and guiding the heart by the pure spirit of the gospel.

The emperor was so crowded with affairs of immediate

urgency, and it was so evident that he could not drive Philip
from the throne, now that he was recognized by all Europe,
that he postponed the attempt for a season, while he still
adopted the title of King of Spain. His troops had hardly
returned from the brilliant campaign of Belgrade, ere the emperor saw a cloud gathering in the north, which excited his
most serious apprehension. Russia and Sweden, irritated by
some of the acts of the emperor, formed an alliance for the
invasion of the German empire. The fierce warriors of the
north, led by such captains as Charles XII. and Peter the
Great, were foes not to be despised. This threatened invasion
not only alarmed the emperor, but alarmed George I. of
England, as his electorate of Hanover was imperiled; and
also excited the fears of Augustus, the Elector of Saxony, who
had regained the throne of Poland. England and Poland
consequently united with the emperor, and formidable preparations were in progress for a terrible war, when one single
chance bullet, upon the field of Pultowa, struck Charles XII.,
as he was looking over the parapet, and dispersed this cloud
which threatened the desolation of all Europe.

Austria was now the preponderating power in degenerate
Italy. Even those States which were not in subjection to the
emperor, were overawed by his imperious spirit. Genoa was
nominally independent. The Genoese arrested one of the
imperial officers for some violation of the laws of the republic.
The emperor sent an army to the gates of the city, threatening it with bombardment and utter destruction. They were
thus compelled immediately to liberate the officer, to pay a
fine of three hundred thousand dollars, and to send a senator
to Vienna with humble expressions of contrition, and to im
plore pardon.

The kingdom of Sardinia was at this time the most powerful State in Italy, if we except those united Italian States
which now composed an integral part of the Austrian empire
Victor Asmedeus, the energetic king, had a small but vigor

ous army, and held himself ready, with this army, for a suit
able remuneration, to engage in the service of any sovereign
without asking any troublesome questions as to the righteous-
ness of the expedition in which he was to serve. The Sardinian king was growing rich, and consequently ambitious.
He wished to rise from the rank of a secondary to that of a
primary power in Europe. There was but one direction in
which he could hope to extend his territories, and that was by
pressing into Lombardy. He had made the remark, which
was repeated to the emperor, "I must acquire Lombardy
piece by piece, as I eat an artichoke." Charles, consequently,
watched Victor with a suspicious eye.

The four great powers of middle and southern Europe
were Austria, England, France, and Spain. All the other
minor States, innumerable in name as well as number, were
compelled to take refuge, openly or secretly, beneath one or
another of these great monarchies.

In France, the Duke of Orleans, the regent during the minority of Louis XV., whose court, in the enormous expenditures of vice, exhausted the yearly earnings of a population of
twenty millions, was anxious to unite the Bourbon branches of
France and Spain in more intimate alliance. He accordingly
affianced the young sovereign of France to Mary Anne, daughter of Philip V. of Spain. At the same time he married his
own daughter to the king's oldest son, the Prince of Asturias,
who was heir to the throne. Mary Anne, to whom the young
king was affianced, was only four years of age.

The personal history of the monarchs of Europe is, almost
without exception, a melancholy history. By their ambition
and their wars they whelmed the cottages in misery, and by a
righteous retribution misery also inundated the palace. Philip
V. became the victim of the most insupportable melancholy.
Earth had no joy which could lift the cloud of gloom from his
soul. For months he was never known to smile. Imprisoning
himself in his palace he refused to see any company, and left

all the cares of government in the hands of his wife, Elizabeth Farnese.

Germany was still agitated by the great religious contest between the Catholics and the Protestants, which divided the empire into two nearly equal parties, bitterly hostile to each other. Various fruitless attempts had been made to bring the parties together, into *unity of faith*, by compromise. Neither party were reconciled to cordial *toleration*, free and full, in which alone harmony can be obtained. In all the States of the empire the Catholics and the Protestants were coming continually into collision. Charles, though a very decided Catholic, was not disposed to persecute the Protestants, as most of his predecessors had done, for he feared to rouse them to despair.

England, France, Austria and Spain, were now involved in an inextricable maze of diplomacy. Congresses were assembled and dissolved ; treaties made and violated ; alliances formed and broken. Weary of the conflict of arms, they were engaged in the more harmless squabbles of intrigue, each seeking its own aggrandizement. Philip V., who had fought so many bloody battles to acquire the crown of Spain, now, disgusted with the cares which that crown involved, overwhelmed with melancholy, and trembling in view of the final judgment of God, suddenly abdicated the throne in favor of his son Louis, and took a solemn oath that he would never resume it again. This event, which surprised Europe, took place on the 10th of February, 1724. Philip retired to St. Ildefonso.

The celebrated palace of St. Ildefonso, which became the retreat of the monarch, was about forty miles north of Madrid, in an elevated ravine among the mountains of Gaudarruma. It was an enormous pile, nearly four thousand feet above the level of the sea, and reared by the Spanish monarchs at an expense exceeding thirty millions of dollars. The palace, two stories high, and occupying three sides of a square, presents a front five hundred and thirty feet in length. In this front alone there are, upon each story, twelve gorgeous apartments in a suite. The interior is decorated in the richest style of art, with frescoed ceilings, and splendid mirrors, and tesselated floors of variegated marble. The furniture was embellished with gorgeous carvings, and enriched with marble, jasper and verd-antique. The galleries were filled with the most costly productions of the chisel and the pencil. The spacious garden, spread out before the palace, was cultivated with the utmost care, and ornamented with fountains surpassing even those of Versailles.

To this magnificent retreat Philip V. retired with his imperious, ambitious wife. She was the step-mother of his son who had succeeded to the throne. For a long time, by the vigor of her mind, she had dominated over her husband, and had in reality been the sovereign of Spain. In the magnificent palace of St. Ildefonso, she was by no means inclined to relinquish her power. Gathering a brilliant court around her, she still issued her decrees, and exerted a powerful influence over the kingdom. The young Louis, who was but a boy, was not disposed to engage in a quarrel with his mother, and for a time submitted to this interference; but gradually he was roused by his adherents, to emancipate himself from these shackles, and to assume the authority of a soveregn. This led to very serious trouble. The abdicated king, in his moping melancholy, was entirely in subjection to his wife. There were now two rival courts. Parties were organizing. Some were for deposing the son; others for imprisoning the father. The kingdom was on the eve of a civil war, when death kindly came to settle the difficulty.

The young King Louis, but eighteen years of age, after a nominal reign of but eight months, was seized with that awful scourge the small-pox, and, after a few days of suffering and delirium, was consigned to the tomb. Philip, notwithstanding his vow, was constrained by his wife to resume the crown, she probably promising to relieve him of all care. Such are the vicissitudes cf a hereditary government. Elizabeth, with woman's spirit, now commanded the emperor to renounce the title of King of Spain, which he still claimed. Charles, with the spirit of an emperor, declared that he would do no such thing.

There was another serious source of difficulty between the two monarchs, which has descended, generation after generation, to our own time, and to this day is only settled by each party quietly persisting in his own claim.

In the year 1430 Philip III., Duke of Burgundy, instituted a new order of knighthood for the protection of the Catholic church, to be called the order of the Golden Fleece. But twenty-four members were to be admitted, and Philip himself was the grand master. Annual meetings were held to fill vacancies. Charles V., as grand master, increased the number of knights to fifty-one. After his death, as the Burgundian provinces and the Netherlands passed under the dominion of Spain, the Spanish monarchs exercised the office of grand master, and conferred the dignity, which was now regarded the highest order of knighthood in Europe, according to their pleasure. But Charles VI., now in admitted possession of the Netherlands, by virtue of that possession claimed the office of grand master of the Golden Fleece. Philip also claimed it as the inheritance of the kings of Spain. The dispute has never been settled. Both parties still claim it, and the order is still conferred both at Vienna and Madrid.

Other powers interfered, in the endeavor to promote reconciliation between the hostile courts, but, as usual, only increased the acrimony of the two parties. The young Spanish princess Mary Anne, who was affianced to the Dauphin of France, was sent to Paris for her education, and that she might become familiar with the etiquette of a court over which she was to preside as queen. For a time she was treated with great attention, and child as she was, received all the homage which the courtiers were accustomed to pay to the Queen of

France. But amidst the intrigues of the times a change arose, and it was deemed a matter of state policy to marry the boy-king to another princess. The French court consequently rejected Maria Anne and sent her back to Spain, and married Louis, then but fifteen years of age, to Maria Lebrinsky, daughter of the King of Poland. The rejected child was too young fully to appreciate the mortification. Her parents, however, felt the insult most keenly. The whole Spanish court was roused to resent it as a national outrage. The queen was so indignant that she tore from her arm a bracelet which she wore, containing a portrait of Louis XV., and dashing it upon the floor, trampled it beneath her feet. Even the king was roused from his gloom by the humiliation of his child, and declared that no amount of blood could atone for such an indignity.

Under the influence of this exasperation, the queen resolved to seek reconciliation with Austria, that all friendly relations might be abandoned with France, and that Spain and Austria might be brought into intimate alliance to operate against their common foe. A renowned Spanish diplomatist, the Baron of Ripperda, had been for some time a secret agent of the queen at the court of Vienna, watching the progress of events there. He resided in the suburbs under a fictitious name, and eluding the vigilance of the ministry, had held by night several secret interviews with the emperor, proposing to him, in the name of the queen, plans of reconciliation. Letters were immediately dispatched to Ripperda urging him to come to an accommodation with the emperor upon almost any terms.

A treaty was soon concluded, early in the spring of 1725. The emperor renounced all claim to the Spanish crown, entered into an alliance, both offensive and defensive, with Philip, and promised to aid, both with men and money, to help recover Gibraltar from the English, which fortress they had held since they seized upon it in the war of the Spanish succession.

In consideration of these great concessions Philip agreed to recognize the right of the emperor to the Netherlands and to his acquisitions in Italy. He opened all the ports of Spain to the subjects of the emperor, and pledged himself to support the Pragmatic Sanction, which wrested the crown of Austria from the daughters of Joseph, and transmitted it to the daughters of Charles. It was this last clause which influenced the emperor, for his whole heart was set upon the accomplishment of this important result, and he was willing to make almost any sacrifice to attain it. There were also some secret articles attached which have never been divulged.

The immediate demand of Spain for the surrender of the rock of Gibraltar was the signal for all Europe to marshal itself for war—a war which threatened the destruction of hundreds of thousands of lives, millions of property, and which was sure to spread far and wide over populous cities and extended provinces, carnage, conflagration, and unspeakable woe. The question was, whether England or Spain should have possession of a rock seven miles long and one mile broad, which was supposed, but very erroneously, to command the Mediterranean. To the rest of Europe it was hardly a matter of the slightest moment whether the flag of England or Spain waved over those granite cliffs. It seems incredible that beings endowed with reason could be guilty of such madness.

England, with great vigor, immediately rallied on her side France, Hanover, Holland, Denmark and Sweden. On the other side were Spain, Austria, Russia, Prussia and a large number of the minor States of Germany. Many months were occupied in consolidating these coalitions, and in raising the armies and gathering the materials for the war.

In the meantime Ripperda, having so successfully, as he supposed, concluded his negotiations at Vienna, in a high state of exultation commenced his journey back to Spain. Passing down through the Tyrol and traversing Italy he embarked at

Genoa and landed at Barcelona. Here he boasted loudly of what he had accomplished.

"Spain and the emperor now united," he said, "will give the law to Europe. The emperor has one hundred and fifty thousand troops under arms, and in six months can bring as many more into the field. France shall be pillaged. George I. shall be driven both from his German and his British territories."

From Barcelona Ripperda traveled rapidly to Madrid, where he was received with almost regal honors by the queen, who was now in reality the sovereign. She immediately appointed him Secretary of State, and transferred to him the reins of government which she had taken from the unresisting hands of her moping husband. Thus Ripperda became, in all but title, the King of Spain. He was a weak man, of just those traits of character which would make him a haughty woman's favorite. He was so elated with this success, became so insufferably vain, and assumed such imperious airs as to disgust all parties. He made the most extravagant promises of the subsidies the emperor was to furnish, and of the powers which were to combine to trample England and France beneath their feet. It was soon seen that these promises were merely the vain-glorious boasts of his own heated brain. Even the imperial ambassador at Madrid was so repelled by his arrogance, that he avoided as far as possible all social and even diplomatic intercourse with him. There was a general combination of the courtiers to crush the favorite. The queen, who, with all her ambition, had a good share of sagacity, soon saw the mistake she had made, and in four months after Ripperda's return to Madrid, he was dismissed in disgrace.

A general storm of contempt and indignation pursued the discarded minister. His rage was now inflamed as much as his vanity had been. Fearful of arrest and imprisonment, and burning with that spirit of revenge which is ever strongest in weakest minds, he took refuge in the house of the British ambassador, Mr. Stanhope. Hostilities had not yet commenced Indeed there had been no declaration of war, and diplomatic relations still continued undisturbed. Each party was acting secretly, and watching the movements of the other with a jealous eye.

Ripperda sought protection beneath the flag of England, and with the characteristic ignominy of deserters and traitors, endeavored to ingratiate himself with his new friends by disclosing all the secrets of his negotiations at Vienna. Under these circumstances full confidence can not be placed in his declarations, for he had already proved himself to be quite unscrupulous in regard to truth. The indignant queen sent an armed force, arrested the duke in the house of the British ambassador, and sent him, in close imprisonment, to the castle of Segovia. He, however, soon escaped from there and fled to England, where he reiterated his declarations respecting the secret articles of the treaty of Vienna. The most important of these declarations was, that Spain and the emperor had agreed to drive George I. from England and to place the Pretender, who had still many adherents, upon the British throne. It was also asserted that marriage contracts were entered into which, by uniting the daughters of the emperor with the sons of the Spanish monarch, would eventually place the crowns of Austria and Spain upon the same brow. The thought of such a vast accumulation of power in the hands of any one monarch, alarmed all the rest of Europe. Both Spain and the emperor denied many of the statements made by Ripperda. But as *truth* has not been esteemed a diplomatic virtue, and as both Ripperda and the sovereigns he had served were equally tempted to falsehood, and were equally destitute of any character for truth, it is not easy to decide which party to believe.

England and France took occasion, through these disclosures, to rouse the alarm of Europe. So much apprehension was excited in Prussia, Bavaria, and with other princes of the

empire, who were appalled at the thought of having another
Spanish prince upon the imperial throne, that the emperor
sent ambassadors to these courts to appease their anxiety, and
issued a public declaration denying that any such marriages
were in contemplation; while at the same time he was promising the Queen of Spain these marriages, to secure her support. England and France accuse the emperor of deliberate,
persistent, unblushing falsehood.

The emperor seems now to have become involved in an
inextricable maze of prevarication and duplicity, striving in
one court to accomplish purposes which in other courts he was
denying that he wished to accomplish. His embarrassment
at length became so great, the greater part of Europe being
roused and jealous, that he was compelled to abandon Spain,
and reluctantly to sign a treaty of amity with France and England. A general armistice was agreed upon for seven years.
The King of Spain, thus abandoned by the emperor, was also
compelled to smother his indignation and to roll back his artillery into the arsenals. Thus this black cloud of war, which
threatened all Europe with desolation, was apparently dispelled.
This treaty, which seemed to restore peace to Europe, was
signed in June, 1727. It was, however, a hollow peace. The
spirit of ambition and aggression animated every court; and
each one was ready, in defiance of treaties and in defiance of
the misery of the world, again to unsheath the sword as soon
as any opportunity should offer for the increase of territory
or power.

CHAPTER XXIV.

CHARLES VI. AND THE POLISH WAR.

FROM 1727 TO 1735.

THE young King of France, Louis XV., from amidst the
orgies of his court which rivaled Babylon in corruption,
was now seventeen years of age, and was beginning to shake
off the trammels of guardianship and to take some ambitious
part in government. The infamous regent, the Duke of Orleans, died suddenly of apoplexy in 1723. Gradually the king's
preceptor, Fleury, obtained the entire ascendency over the
mind of his pupil, and became the chief director of affairs.
He saw the policy of reuniting the Bourbons of France and
Spain for the support of each other. The policy was consequently adopted of cultivating friendly relations between the
two kingdoms. Cardinal Fleury was much disposed to thwart
the plans of the emperor. A congress of the leading powers
had been assembled at Soissons in June, 1728, to settle some
diplomatic questions. The favorite object of the emperor now
was, to obtain from the European powers the formal guarantee
to support his decree of succession which conveyed the crown
of Austria to his daughters, in preference to those of his brother
Joseph.

The emperor urged the Pragmatic Sanction strongly upon the congress, as the basis upon which he would enter into friendly relations with all the powers.   Fleury opposed it, and with such influence over the other plenipotentiaries as to se- cure its rejection.   The emperor was much irritated, and inti- mated war.   France and England retorted defiance.   Spain was becoming alienated from the emperor, who had abandoned her cause, and was again entering into alliance with France The emperor had promised his eldest daughter, Maria Theresa, to Carlos, son of the Queen of Spain, and a second daughter to the next son, Philip.   These were as brilliant matches as an ambitious mother could desire.   But while the emperor was making secret and solemn promises to the Queen of Spain, that these marriages should be consummated, which would secure to the son of the queen the Austrian, as well as the Spanish crown, he was declaring to the courts of Europe that he had no such plans in contemplation.

The Spanish queen, at length, annoyed, and goaded on by France and England, sent an ambassador to Vienna, and de- manded of the emperor a written promise that Maria Theresa was to be the bride of Carlos.   The emperor was now brought to the end of his intrigues.   He had been careful heretofore to give only verbal promises, through his ministers.   After his reiterated public denials that any such alliance was anticipated, he did not dare commit himself by giving the required docu- ment.   An apologetic, equivocal answer was returned which so roused the ire of the queen, that, breaking off from Austria, she at once entered into a treaty of cordial union with En- gland and France.

It will readily be seen that all these wars and intrigues had but little reference to the welfare of the masses of the people.   They were hardly more thought of than the cattle and the poultry.   The only purpose they served was, by uninter- mitted toil, to raise the wealth which supported the castle and the palace, and to march to the field to fight battles, in which

they had no earthly interest.   The written history of Europe
is only the history of kings and nobles—their ambitions, intrigues and war.   The unwritten history of the dumb, toil-
ing millions, defrauded of their rights, doomed to poverty and
ignorance, is only recorded in the book of God's remembrance.
When that page shall be read, every ear that hears it will
tingle.

The frail connection between Austria and Spain was now terminated.   England, France and Spain entered into an alliance
to make vigorous war against Charles VI. if he manifested any
hostility to any of the articles of the treaty into which they
had entered.   The Queen of Spain, in her spite, forbade the
subjects of the emperor from trading at all with Spain, and
granted to her new allies the exclusive right to the Spanish
trade.   She went so far in her reconciliation with England as
to assure the king that he was quite welcome to retain the
rock of Gibraltar which he held with so tenacious a grasp.

In this treaty, with studied neglect, even the name of the
emperor was not mentioned; and yet the allies, as if to provoke a quarrel, sent Charles VI. a copy, peremptorily demanding assent to the treaty without his having taken any
part whatever in the negotiation.

This insulting demand fell like a bomb-shell in the palace
at Vienna.   Emperor, ministers, courtiers, all were aroused to
a frenzy of indignation.   " So insulting a message," said Count
Zinzendorf, " is unparalleled, even in the annals of savages."
The emperor condescended to make no reply, but very spirit-
edly issued orders to all parts of the empire, for his troops to
hold themselves in readiness for war.

And yet Charles was overwhelmed with anxiety, and was
almost in despair.   It was a terrible humiliation for the emperor to be compelled to submit, unavenged, to such an insult.
But how could the emperor alone, venture to meet in battle
England, France, Spain and all the other powers whom three
such kingdoms could, either by persuasion or compulsion,

bring into their alliance ? He plead with his natural allies. Russia had not been insulted, and was unwilling to engage in so distant a war. Prussia had no hope of gaining any thing, and declined the contest. Sardinia sent a polite message to the emperor that it was more for her interest to enter into an alliance with her nearer neighbors, France, Spain and England, and that she had accordingly done so. The treasury of Charles was exhausted ; his States were impoverished by constant and desolating wars. And his troops manifested but little zeal to enter the field against so fearful a superiority of force. The emperor, tortured almost beyond endurance by chagrin, was yet compelled to submit.

The allies were quite willing to provoke a war with the emperor; but as he received their insults so meekly, and made no movement against them, they were rather disposed to march against him. Spain wanted Parma and Tuscany, but France was not willing to have Spain make so great an accession to her Italian power. France wished to extend her area north, through the States of the Netherlands. But England was unwilling to see the French power thus aggrandized. England had her aspirations, to which both France and Spain were opposed. Thus the allies operated as a check upon each other.

The emperor found some little consolation in this growing disunion, and did all in his power to foment it. Wishing to humble the Bourbons of France and Spain, he made secret overtures to England. The offers of the emperor were of such a nature, that England eagerly accepted them, returned to friendly relations with the emperor, and, to his extreme joy, pledged herself to support the Pragmatic Sanction.

It seems to have been the great object of the emperor's life to secure the crown of Austria for his daughters. It was an exceedingly disgraceful act. There was no single respectable reason to be brought forward why his daughters should crowd from the throne the daughters of his elder deceased brother, the Emperor Joseph. Charles was so aware of the gross injustice of the deed, and that the ordinary integrity of humanity would rise against him, that he felt the necessity of exhausting all the arts of diplomacy to secure for his daughters the pledged support of the surrounding thrones. He had now by intrigues of many years obtained the guarantee of the Pragmatic Sanction from Russia, Prussia, Holland, Spain and England. France still refused her pledge, as did also many of the minor States of the empire. The emperor, encouraged by the success he had thus far met with, pushed his efforts with renewed vigor, and in January, 1732, exulted that he had gained the guarantee of the Pragmatic Sanction from all the Germanic body, with the exception of Bavaria, Palatine and Saxony.

And now a new difficulty arose to embroil Europe in trouble. When Charles XII., like a thunderbolt of war, burst upon Poland, he drove Augustus II. from the throne, and placed upon it Stanislaus Leczinski, a Polish noble, whom he had picked up by the way, and whose heroic character secured the admiration of this semi-insane monarch. Augustus, utterly crushed, was compelled by his eccentric victor to send the crown jewels and the archives, with a letter of congratulation, to Stanislaus. This was in the year 1706. Three years after this, in 1709, Charles XII. suffered a memorable defeat at Pultowa. Augustus II., then at the head of an army, regained his kingdom, and Stanislaus fled in disguise. After numerous adventures and fearful afflictions, the court of France offered him a retreat in Wissembourg in Alsace. Here the ex-king remained for six years, when his beautiful daughter Mary was selected to take the place of the rejected Mary of Spain, as the wife of the young dauphin, Louis XV.

In the year 1733 Augustus II. died. In anticipation of this event Austria had been very busy, hoping to secure the elective crown of Poland for the son of Augustus who had inherited his father's name, and who had promised to support the

Pragmatic Sanction. France was equally busy in the endeavor to place the scepter of Poland in the hand of Stanislaus, father of the queen. From the time of the marriage of his daughter with Louis XV., Stanislaus received a handsome pension from the French treasury, maintained a court of regal splendor, and received all the honors due to a sovereign. All the energies of the French court were now aroused to secure the crown for Stanislaus. Russia, Prussia and Austria were in natural sympathy. They wished to secure the alliance of Poland, and were also both anxious to destroy the republican principle of *electing* rulers, and to introduce hereditary descent of the crown in all the kingdoms of Europe. But an election by the nobles was now indispensable, and the rival powers were, with all the arts known in courts, pushing the claims of their several candidates. It was an important question, for upon it depended whether warlike Poland was to be the ally of the Austrian or of the French party. Poland was also becoming quite republican in its tendencies, and had adopted a constitution which greatly limited the power of the crown. Augustus would be but a tool in the hands of Russia, Prussia and Austria, and would coöperate with them in crushing the spirit of liberty in Poland. These three great northern powers became so roused upon the subject, that they put their troops in motion, threatening to exclude Stanislaus by force.

This language of menace and display of arms roused France. The king, while inundating Poland with agents, and lavishing the treasure of France in bribes to secure the election of Stanislaus, assumed an air of virtuous indignation in view of the interference of the Austrian party, and declared that no foreign power should interfere in any way with the freedom of the election. This led the emperor to issue a counter-memorial inveighing against the intermeddling of France.

In the midst of these turmoils the congress of Polish nobles met to choose their king. It was immediately apparent that there was a very powerful party organized in favor of Stanis-

laus. The emperor was for marching directly into the kingdom with an army which he had already assembled in Silesia
for this purpose, and with the bayonet make up for any de-
ficiency which his party might want in votes. Though Prussia demurred, he put his troops in motion, and the imperial and
Russian ambassadors at Warsaw informed the marshal of the
diet that Catharine, who was now Empress of Russia, and
Charles, had decided to exclude Stanislaus from Poland by
force.

These threats produced their natural effect upon the bold
warrior barons of Poland. Exasperated rather than intimi
dated, they assembled, many thousands in number, on the
great plain of Wola, but a few miles from Warsaw, and with
great unanimity chose Stanislaus their king. This was the
12th of September, 1733. Stanislaus, anticipating the result,
had left France in disguise, accompanied by a single attendant, to undertake the bold enterprise of traversing the heart
of Germany, eluding all the vigilance of the emperor, and of
entering Poland notwithstanding all the efforts of Austria,
Russia and Prussia to keep him away. It was a very hazard-
ous adventure, for his arrest would have proved his ruin.
Though he encountered innumerable dangers, with marvelous
sagacity and heroism he succeeded, and reached Warsaw on
the 9th of September, just three days before the election. In
regal splendor he rode, as soon as informed of his election, to
the tented field where the nobles were convened. He was received with the clashing of weapons, the explosions of artillery, and the acclamations of thousands.

But the Poles were not sufficiently enlightened fully to
comprehend the virtue and the sacredness of the ballot-box.
The Russian army was now hastening to the gates of Warsaw. The small minority of Polish nobles opposed to the election of Stanislaus seceded from the diet, mounted their horses,
crossed the Vistula, and joined the invading army to make war
upon the sovereign whom the majority had chosen. The rot

ribution for such folly and wickedness has come.   There is no longer any Poland.   They who despise the authority of the ballot-box inevitably usher in the bayonets of despotism.   Under the protection of this army the minority held another diet at Kamien (on the 5th of October), a village just outside the suburbs of Warsaw, and chose as the sovereign of Poland Augustus, son of the deceased king.   The minority, aided by the Russian and imperial armies, were too strong for the majority. They took possession of Warsaw, and crowned their candidate king, with the title of Augustus III.   Stanislaus, pressed by an overpowering force, retreated to Dantzic, at the mouth of the Vistula, about two hundred miles from Warsaw.   Here he was surrounded by the Russian troops and held in close siege, while Augustus III. took possession of Poland.   France could do nothing.   A weary march of more than a thousand miles separated Paris from Warsaw, and the French troops would be compelled to fight their way through the very heart of the German empire, and at the end of the journey to meet the united armies of Russia, Prussia, Austria and Poland under her king, now in possession of all the fortresses.

Though Louis XV. could make no effectual resistance, it was not in human nature but that he should seek revenge. When shepherds quarrel, they kill each other's flocks.   When kings quarrel, they kill the poor peasants in each other's territories, and burn their homes.   France succeeded in enlisting in her behalf Spain and Sardinia.   Austria and Russia were upon the other side.   Prussia, jealous of the emperor's greatness, declined any active participation.   Most of the other powers of Europe also remained neutral.   France had now no hope of placing Stanislaus upon the throne; she only sought revenge, determined to humble the house of Austria.   The mercenary King of Sardinia, Charles Emanuel, was willing to serve the one who would pay the most.   He first offered himself to the emperor, but upon terms too exorbitant to be accepted.   France and Spain immediately offered him terms even

more advantageous than those he had demanded of the emperor. The contract was settled, and the Sardinian army marched
into the allied camp.

The King of Sardinia, who was as ready to employ guile
as force in warfare, so thoroughly deceived the emperor as to
lead him to believe that he had accepted the emperor's terms,
and that Sardinia was to be allied with Austria, even when the
whole contract was settled with France and Spain, and the
plan of the campaign was matured. So utterly was the emperor deluded by a fraud so contemptible, in the view of every
honorable mind, that he sent great convoys of grain, and a
large supply of shot, shells and artillery from the arsenals of
Milan into the Sardinian camp. Charles Emanuel, dead to all
sense of magnanimity, rubbed his hands with delight in the
successful perpetration of such fraud, exclaiming, "*An virtus
an dolos, quis ab hoste requirat.*"

So cunningly was this stratagem carried on, that the emperor was not undeceived until his own artillery, which he had
sent to Charles Emanuel, were thundering at the gates of the
city of Milan, and the shot and shells which he had so unsus-
pectingly furnished were mowing down the imperial troops.
So sudden was the attack, so unprepared was Austrian Lombardy to meet it, that in twelve weeks the Sardinian troops
overran the whole territory, seized every city and magazine,
with all their treasures, leaving the fortress of Mantua alone
in the possession of the imperial troops. It was the policy of
Louis XV. to attack Austria in the remote portions of her widely-
extended dominions, and to cut off province by province. He
also made special and successful efforts to detach the interests
of the German empire from those of Austria, so that the
princes of the empire might claim neutrality. It was against
the possessions of Charles VI., not against the independent
States of the empire, that Louis XV. urged war.

The storms of winter were now at hand, and both parties
were compelled to abandon the field until spring. But during

the winter every nerve was strained by the combatants in preparation for the strife which the returning sun would introduce. The emperor established strong defenses along the banks of the Rhine to prevent the passage of the French; he also sent agents to all the princes of the empire to enlist them in his cause, and succeeded, notwithstanding the remonstrances of many who claimed neutrality, in obtaining a vote from a diet which he assembled, for a large sum of money, and for an army of one hundred and twenty thousand men.

The loss of Lombardy troubled Charles exceedingly, for it threatened the loss of all his Italian possessions. Notwithstanding the severity of the winter he sent to Mantua all the troops he could raise from his hereditary domains; and ordered every possible effort to be made to be prepared to undertake the offensive in the spring, and to drive the Sardinians from Lombardy. In the beginning of May the emperor had assembled within and around Mantua, sixty thousand men, under the command of Count Merci. The hostile forces soon met, and battle after battle thundered over the Italian plains. On the 29th of June the two armies encountered each other in the vicinity of Parma, in such numbers as to give promise of a decisive battle. For ten hours the demoniac storm raged unintermitted. Ten thousand of the dead covered the ground. Neither party had taken a single standard or a single prisoner, an event almost unparalleled in the history of battles. From the utter exhaustion of both parties the strife ceased. The Sardinians and French, mangled and bleeding, retired within the walls of Parma. The Austrians, equally bruised and bloody, having lost their leader, retired to Reggio. Three hundred and forty of the Austrian officers were either killed or wounded.

The King of Sardinia was absent during this engagement, having gone to Turin to visit his wife, who was sick. The morning after the battle, however, he joined the army, and succeeded in cutting off an Austrian division of twelve hundred men, whom he took prisoners. Both parties now waited

for a time to heal their wounds, repair their shattered weap
ons, get rested and receive reinforcements. Ten thousand pooɪ
peasants, who had not the slightest interest in the quarrel, had
now met with a bloody death, and other thousands were now
to be brought forward and offered as victims on this altar of
kingly ambition. By the middle of July they were again prepared to take the field. Both parties struggled with almost
superhuman energies in the work of mutual destruction; villages were burned, cities stormed, fields crimsoned with blood
and strewn with the slain, while no decisive advantage was
gained. In the desperation of the strife the hostile battalions
were hurled against each other until the beginning of January.
They waded morasses, slept in drenching storms, and were
swept by freezing blasts. Sickness entered the camp, and was
even more fatal than the bullet of the foe. Thousands moaned
and died in their misery, upon pallets of straw, where no sister, wife or mother could soothe the dying anguish. Another
winter only afforded the combatants opportunity to nurse
their strength that they might deal still heavier blows in
another campaign.

While the imperial troops were struggling against Sardinia and France on the plains of Lombardy, a Spanish squadron landed a strong military force of French and Spaniards
upon the peninsula of southern Italy, and meeting with no
force sufficiently powerful to oppose them, speedily overran
Naples and Sicily. The Spanish troops silenced the forts which
defended the city of Naples, and taking the garrison prisoners,
entered the metropolis in triumphal array, greeted by the acclamations of the populace, who hated the Austrians. After
many battles, in which thousands were slain, the Austrians were
driven out of all the Neapolitan States, and Carlos, the oldest
son of Philip V. of Spain, was crowned King of Naples, with
the title of Charles III. The island of Sicily was speedily subjugated and also attached to the Neapolitan crown.

These losses the emperor felt most keenly. Upon the

Rhine he had made great preparations, strengthening fortresses and collecting troops, which he placed under the command of his veteran general, Prince Eugene. He was quite sanguine that here he would be abundantly able to repel the assaults of his foes. But here again he was doomed to bitter disappointment. The emperor found a vast disproportion between promise and performance. The diet had voted him one hundred and twenty thousand troops; they furnished twelve thousand. They voted abundant supplies; they furnished almost none at all.

The campaign opened the 9th of April, 1734, the French crossing the Rhine near Truerbuch, in three strong columns, notwithstanding all the efforts of the Austrians to resist them. Prince Eugene, by birth a Frenchman, reluctantly assumed the command. He had remonstrated with the emperor against any forcible interference in the Polish election, assuring him that he would thus expose himself, almost without allies, to all the power of France. Eugene did not hesitate openly to express his disapprobation of the war. " I can take no interest in this war," he said; " the question at issue is not important enough to authorize the death of a chicken."

Eugene, upon his arrival from Vienna, at the Austrian camp, found but twenty-five thousand men. They were composed of a motley assemblage from different States, undisciplined, unaccustomed to act together and with no confidence in each other. The commanders of the various corps were quarreling for the precedence in rank, and there was no unity or subordination in the army. They were retreating before the French, who, in numbers, in discipline, and in the materiel of war, were vastly in the superiority. Eugene saw at once that it would be folly to risk a battle, and that all he could hope to accomplish was to throw such embarrassments as he might in the path of the victors.

The young officers, ignorant, impetuous and reckless, were for giving battle, which would inevitably have resulted in the

destruction of the army. They were so vexed by the wise cau
tion of Eugene, which they regarded as pusillanimity, that they
complained to the emperor that the veteran general was in his
dotage, that he was broken both in body and mind, and quite
unfit to command the army. These representations induced
the emperor to send a spy to watch the conduct of Eugene.
Though deeply wounded by these suspicions, the experienced
general could not be provoked to hazard an engagement. He
retreated from post to post, merely checking the progress of
the enemy, till the campaign was over, and the ice and snow of
a German winter drove all to winter quarters.

While recruiting for the campaign of 1735, Prince Eugene
wrote a series of most earnest letters to his confidential agent
in London, which letters were laid before George II., urging
England to come to the help of the emperor in his great extremity. Though George was eager to put the fleet and army
of England in motion, the British cabinet wisely refused to
plunge the nation into war for such a cause, and the emperor
was left to reap the bitter fruit of his despotism and folly.
The emperor endeavored to frighten England by saying that
he was reduced to such an extremity that if the British cabinet did not give him aid, he should be compelled to seek peace
by giving his daughter, with Austria in her hand as her dowry, to Carlos, now King of Naples and heir apparent to the
crown of Spain. He well knew that to prevent such an acquisition of power on the part of the Spanish monarch, who was
also in intimate alliance with France, England would be ready
to expend any amount of blood and treasure.

Charles VI. waited with great impatience to see the result
of this menace, hardly doubting that it would bring England
immediately to terms. Bitter was his disappointment and his
despair when he received from the court of St. James the calm
reply, that England could not possibly take a part in this war,
and that in view of the great embarrassments in which the
emperor was involved, England would take no offense in case

of the marriage of the emperor's second daughter to Carlos. England then advised the emperor to make peace by surrendering the Netherlands.

The emperor was now greatly enraged, and inveighed bitterly against England as guilty of the grossest perfidy. He declared that England had been as deeply interested as he was in excluding Stanislaus from the throne of Poland; that it was more important for England than for Austria to curb the exhorbitant power of France; that in every step he had taken against Stanislaus, he had consulted England, and had acted in accordance with her counsel; that England was reaping the benefit of having the father-in-law of the French king expelled from the Polish throne; that England had solemnly promised to support him in these measures, and now having derived all the advantage, basely abandoned him. There were bitter charges, and it has never been denied that they were mainly true. The emperor, in his indignation, threatened to tell the whole story to the *people* of England. It is strange that the emperor had found out that there were *people* in England. In no other part of Europe was there any thing but *nobles* and *peasants*.

In this extraordinary letter, addressed to Count Kinsky, the imperial ambassador in London, the emperor wrote:

"On the death of Augustus II., King of Poland, my first care was to communicate to the King of England the principles on which I acted. I followed, in every instance, his advice. * * * England has never failed to give me promises, both before and since the commencement of the war, but instead of fulfilling those promises, she has even favored my enemies. * * * Let the king know that I never will consent to the plan of pacification now in agitation; that I had rather suffer the worst of extremities than accede to such disadvantageous proposals, and that even if I should not be able to prevent them, I will justify my honor and my dignity, by publishing a circumstantial account of all the transaction, together with all the documents which I have now in possession. * * * If these representations fail, means must be taken to publish and circulate throughout England our answer to the proposal of good offices which was not made till after the expiration of nine months. Should the court of London proceed so far as to make such propositions of peace as are supposed to be in agitation, you will not delay a moment to circulate throughout England a memorial, containing a recapitulation of all negotiations which have taken place since 1710, together with the authentic documents, detailing my just complaints, and reclaiming, in the most solemn manner, the execution of the guaranties."

One more effort the emperor made, and it was indeed a desperate one. He dispatched a secret agent, an English Roman Catholic, by the name of Strickland, to London, to endeavor to overthrow the ministry and bring in a cabinet in favor of him. In this, of course, he failed entirely. Nothing now remained for him but to submit, with the best grace he could, to the terms exacted by his foes. In the general pacification great interests were at stake, and all the leading powers of Europe demanded a voice in the proceedings. For many months the negotiations were protracted. England and France became involved in an angry dispute. Each power was endeavoring to grasp all it could, while at the same time it was striving to check the rapacity of every other power. There was a general armistice while these negotiations were pending. It was, however, found exceedingly difficult to reconcile all conflicting interests. New parties were formed; new combinations entered into, and all parties began to aim for a renewal of the strife. England, exasperated against France, in menace made an imposing display of her fleet and navy. The emperor was delighted, and, trusting to gain new allies, exerted his skill of diplomacy to involve the contracting parties in confusion and discord.

Thus encouraged, the emperor refused to accede to the

terms demanded. He was required to give up the Nether-lands, and all his foreign possessions, and to retire to his hered-itary dominions. " What a severe sentence," exclaimed Count Zinzendorf, the emperor's ambassador, " have you passed on the emperor. No malefactor was ever carried with so hard a doom to the gibbet."

The armies again took the field. Eugene, again, though with great reluctance, assumed the command of the imperial forces. France had assembled one hundred thousand men upon the Rhine. Eugene had but thirty thousand men to meet them. He assured the emperor that with such a force he could not successfully carry on the war. Jealous of his reputation, he said, sadly, " to find myself in the same condi-tion as last year, will be only exposing myself to the censure of the world, which judges by appearancs, as if I were less capable, in my old age, to support the reputation of my former successes." With consummate generalship, this small force held the whole French army in check.

CHAPTER XXV.

CHARLES VI. AND THE TURKISH WAR RENEWED.

FROM 1735 TO 1739.

THE emperor being quite unable, either on the Rhine or in
Italy, successfully to compete with his foes, received blow
after blow, which exceedingly disheartened him. His affairs
were in a desperate condition, and, to add to his grief, dissensions filled his cabinet; his counsellors mutually accusing
each other of being the cause of the impending ruin. The
Italian possessions of the emperor had been thronged with
Austrian nobles, filling all the posts of office and of honor, and
receiving rich salaries. A change of administration, in the
transference of these States to the dominion of Spain and
Sardinia, " reformed" all these Austrian office-holders out of
their places, and conferred these posts upon Spaniards and
Sardinians. The ejected Austrian nobles crowded the court
of the emperor, with the most passionate importunities that
he would enter into a separate accommodation with Spain,
and secure the restoration of the Italian provinces by giving
his eldest daughter, Maria Theresa, to the Spanish prince,
Carlos. This would seem to be a very simple arrangement,

especially since the Queen of Spain so earnestly desired this match, that she was willing to make almost any sacrifice for its accomplishment. But there was an inseparable obstacle in the way of any such arrangement.

Maria Theresa had just attained her eighteenth year. She was a young lady of extraordinary force of character, and of an imperial spirit; and she had not the slightest idea of having her person disposed of as a mere make-weight in the diplomacy of Europe. She knew that the crown of Austria was soon to be hers; she understood the weakness of her father, and was well aware that she was far more capable of wearing that crown than he had ever been; and she was already far more disposed to take the reins of government from her father's hand, than she was to submit herself to his control. With such a character, and such anticipations, she had become passionately attached to the young Duke of Lorraine, who was eight years her senior, and who had for some years been one of the most brilliant ornaments of her father's court.

The duchy of Lorraine was one of the most extensive and opulent of the minor States of the German empire. Admirably situated upon the Rhine and the Meuse, and extending to the sea, it embraced over ten thousand square miles, and contained a population of over a million and a half. The duke, Francis Stephen, was the heir of an illustrious line, whose lineage could be traced for many centuries. Germany, France and Spain, united, had not sufficient power to induce Maria Theresa to reject Francis Stephen, the grandson of her father's sister, the playmate of her childhood, and now her devoted lover, heroic and fascinating, for the Spanish Carlos, of whom she knew little, and for whom she cared less. Ambition also powerfully operated on the very peculiar mind of Maria Theresa. She had much of the exacting spirit of Elizabeth, England's maiden queen, and was emulous of supremacy which no one would share. She, in her own right, was to inherit the crown of Austria, and Francis Stephen, high-born and noble as he was, and her recognized husband, would still be her subject. She could confer upon him dignity and power, retaining a supremacy which even he could never reach.

The emperor was fully aware of the attachment of his daughter to Francis, of her inflexible character; and even when pretending to negotiate for her marriage with Carlos, he was conscious that it was all a mere pretense, and that the union could never be effected. The British minister at Vienna saw very clearly the true state of affairs, and when the emperor was endeavoring to intimidate England by the menace that he would unite the crowns of Spain and Austria by uniting Maria and Carlos, the minister wrote to his home government as follows:

"Maria Theresa is a princess of the highest spirit; her father's losses are her own. She reasons already; she enters into affairs; she admires his virtues, but condemns his mismanagement; and is of a temper so formed for rule and ambition, as to look upon him as little more than her administrator. Notwithstanding this lofty humor by day, she sighs and pines all night for her Duke of Lorraine. If she sleeps, it is only to dream of him; if she wakes, it is but to talk of him to the lady in waiting; so that there is no more probability of her forgetting the very individual government, and the very individual husband which she thinks herself born to, than of her forgiving the authors of her losing either."

The empress was cordially coöperating with her daughter. The emperor was in a state of utter distraction. His affairs were fast going to ruin; he was harassed by counter intreaties; he knew not which way to turn, or what to do. Insupportable gloom oppressed his spirit. Pale and haggard, he wandered through the rooms of his palace, the image of woe. At night he tossed sleepless upon his bed, moaning in anguish which he then did not attempt to conceal, and giving free utterance to all the mental tortures which were goading him to madness. The queen became seriously alarmed lest his reason should break down beneath such a weight of woe. It was clear that neither reason nor life could long withstand such a struggle.

Thus in despair, the emperor made proposals for a secret and separate accommodation with France. Louis XV. promptly listened, and offered terms, appallingly definite, and cruel enough to extort the last drop of blood from the emperor's sinking heart. "Give me," said the French king, "the duchy of Lorraine, and I will withdraw my armies, and leave Austria to make the best terms she can with Spain."

How could the emperor wrest from his prospective son-in-law his magnificent ancestral inheritance? The duke could not hold his realms for an hour against the armies of France, should the emperor consent to their surrender; and conscious of the desperation to which the emperor was driven, and of his helplessness, he was himself plunged into the deepest dismay and anguish. He held an interview with the British minister to see if it were not possible that England might interpose her aid in his behalf. In frantic grief he lost his self control, and, throwing himself into a chair, pressed his brow convulsively, and exclaimed, "Great God! will not England help me? Has not his majesty with his own lips, over and over again, promised to stand by me?"

The French armies were advancing; shot and shell were falling upon village and city; fortress after fortress was surrendering. "Give me Lorraine," repeated Louis XV., persistently, "or I will take all Austria." There was no alternative but for the emperor to drink to the dregs the bitter cup which his own hand had mingled. He surrendered Lorraine to France. He, however, succeeded in obtaining some slight compensation for the defrauded duke. The French court allowed him a pension of ninety thousand dollars a year, until the death of the aged Duke of Tuscany, who was the last of the Medici line, promising that then Tuscany, one of the most important duchies of central Italy, should pass into the hands of Francis. Should Sardinia offer any opposition, the King of France promised to unite with the emperor in maintaining Francis in his possession by force of arms. Peace was thus obtained with France. Peace was then made with Spain and Sardinia, by surrendering to Spain Naples and Sicily, and to Sardinia most of the other Austrian provinces in Italy. Thus scourged and despoiled, the emperor, a humbled, woe-stricken man, retreated to the seclusion of his palace.

While these affairs were in progress, Francis Stephen derived very considerable solace by his marriage with Maria Theresa. Their nuptials took place at Vienna on the 12th of February, 1736. The emperor made the consent of the duke to the cession of Lorraine to France, a condition of the marriage. As the duke struggled against the surrender of his paternal domains, Cartenstein, the emperor's confidential minister, insultingly said to him, " Monseigneur, point de cession, point d'archiduchesse." *My lord, no cession, no archduchess.* Fortunately for Francis, in about a year after his marriage the Duke of Tuscany died, and Francis, with his bride, hastened to his new home in the palaces of Leghorn. Though the duke mourned bitterly over the loss of his ancestral domains, Tuscany was no mean inheritance. The duke was absolute monarch of the duchy, which contained about eight thousand square miles and a population of a million. The revenues of the archduchy were some four millions of dollars. The army consisted of six thousand troops.

Two months after the marriage of Maria Theresa, Prince Eugene died quietly in his bed at the age of seventy-three. He had passed his whole lifetime riding over fields of battle swept by bullets and plowed by shot. He had always exposed his own person with utter recklessness, leading the charge, and being the first to enter the breach or climb the rampart. Though often wounded, he escaped all these perils, and breathed his last in peace upon his pillow in Vienna.

His funeral was attended with regal honors. For three

days the corpse lay in state, with the coat of mail, the helmet and the gauntlets which the warrior had worn in so many fierce battles, suspended over his lifeless remains. His heart was sent in an urn to be deposited in the royal tomb where his ancestors slumbered. His embalmed body was interred in the metropolitan church in Vienna. The emperor and all the court attended the funeral, and his remains were borne to the grave with honors rarely conferred upon any but crowned heads.

The Ottoman power had now passed its culminating point, and was evidently on the wane. The Russian empire was beginning to arrest the attention of Europe, and was ambitious of making its voice heard in the diplomacy of the European monarchies. Being destitute of any sea coast, it was excluded from all commercial intercourse with foreign nations, and in its cold, northern realm, " leaning," as Napoleon once said, " against the North Pole," seemed to be shut up to barbarism. It had been a leading object of the ambition of Peter the Great to secure a maritime port for his kingdom. He at first attempted a naval depot on his extreme southern border, at the mouth of the Don, on the sea of Azof. This would open to him the commerce of the Mediterranean through the Azof, the Euxine and the Marmora. But the assailing Turks drove him from these shores, and he was compelled to surrender the fortresses he had commenced to their arms. He then turned to his western frontier, and, with an incredible expenditure of money and sacrifice of life, reared upon the marshes of the Baltic the imperial city of St. Petersburg. Peter I. died in 1725, leaving the crown to his wife Catharine. She, however, survived him but two years, when she died, in 1727, leaving two daughters. The crown then passed to the grandson of Peter I., a boy of thirteen. In three years he died of the small-pox. Anna, the daughter of the oldest brother of Peter I., now ascended the throne, and reigned, through her favorites, with relentless rigor.

It was one of the first objects of Anna's ambition to secure a harbor for maritime commerce in the more sunny climes of southern Europe. St. Petersburg, far away upon the frozen shores of the Baltic, where the harbor was shut up with ice for five months in the year, presented but a cheerless prospect for the formation of a merchant marine. She accordingly revived the original project of Peter the Great, and waged war with the Turks to recover the lost province on the shores of the Euxine. Russia had been mainly instrumental in placing Augustus II. on the throne of Poland; Anna was consequently sure of his sympathy and coöperation. She also sent to Austria to secure the alliance of the emperor. Charles VI., though his army was in a state of decay and his treasury empty, eagerly embarked in the enterprise. He was in a continued state of apprehension from the threatened invasion of the Turks. He hoped also, aided by the powerful arm of Russia, to be able to gain territories in the east which would afford some compensation for his enormous losses in the south and in the west.

While negotiations were pending, the Russian armies were already on the march. They took Azof after a siege of but a fortnight, and then overran and took possession of the whole Crimea, driving the Turks before them. Charles VI. was a very scrupulous Roman Catholic, and was animated to the strife by the declaration of his confessor that it was his duty, as a Christian prince, to aid in extirpating the enemies of the Church of Christ. The Turks were greatly alarmed by these successes of the Russians, and by the formidable preparations of the other powers allied against them.

The emperor hoped that fortune, so long adverse, was now turning in his favor. He collected a large force on the frontiers of Turkey, and intrusted the command to General Seckendorf. The general hastened into Hungary to the rendezvous of the troops. He found the army in a deplorable condition. The treasury being exhausted, they were but poorly supplied with the necessaries of war, and the generals and contractors nad contrived to appropriate to themselves most of the funds which had been furnished. The general wrote to the emperor, presenting a lamentable picture of the destitution of the army.

"I can not," he said, " consistently with my duty to God and the emperor, conceal the miserable condition of the barracks and the hospitals. The troops, crowded together without sufficient bedding to cover them, are a prey to innumerable disorders, and are exposed to the rain, and other inclemencies of the weather, from the dilapidated state of the caserns, the roofs of which are in perpetual danger of being overthrown by the wind. All the frontier fortresses, and even Belgrade, are incapable of the smallest resistance, as well from the dilapidated state of the fortifications as from a total want of artillery, ammunition and other requisites. The naval armament is in a state of irreparable disorder. Some companies of my regiment of Belgrade are thrust into holes where a man would not put even his favorite hounds ; and I can not see the situation of these miserable and half-starved wretches without tears. These melancholy circumstances portend the loss of these fine kingdoms with the same rapidity as that of the States of Italy."

The bold commander-in-chief also declared that many of the generals were so utterly incapable of discharging their duties, that nothing could be anticipated, under their guidance, but defeat and ruin. He complained that the governors of those distant provinces, quite neglecting the responsibilities of their offices, were spending their time in hunting and other trivial amusements. These remonstrances roused the emperor, and decisive reforms were undertaken. The main plan of the campaign was for the Russians, who were already on the shores of the Black sea, to press on to the mouth of the Danube, and then to march up the stream. The Austrians were to follow down the Danube to the Turkish province of Wallachia, and then, marching through the heart of that province, either effect a junction with the Russians, or inclose the Turks between the two armies. At the same time a large Austrian force, marching through Bosnia and Servia, and driving the Turks out, were to take military possession of those countries and join the main army in its union on the lower Danube.

Matters being thus arranged, General Seckendorf took the command of the Austrian troops, with the assurance that he should be furnished with one hundred and twenty-six thousand men, provided with all the implements of war, and that he should receive a monthly remittance of one million two hundred thousand dollars for the pay of the troops. The emperor, however, found it much easier to make promises than to fulfill them. The month of August had already arrived and Seckendorf, notwithstanding his most strenuous exertions, had assembled at Belgrade but thirty thousand infantry and fifteen thousand cavalry. The Turks, with extraordinary energy, had raised a much more formidable and a better equipped army. Just as Seckendorf was commencing his march, having minutely arranged all the stages of the campaign, to his surprise and indignation he received orders to leave the valley of the Danube and march directly south about one hundred and fifty miles into the heart of Servia, and lay siege to the fortress of Nissa. The whole plan of the campaign was thus frustrated. Magazines, at great expense, had been established, and arrangements made for floating the heavy baggage down the stream. Now the troops were to march through morasses and over mountains, without suitable baggage wagons, and with no means of supplying themselves with provisions in so hostile and inhospitable a country.

But the command of the emperor was not to be disobeyed. For twenty-eight days they toiled along, encountering innumerable impediments, many perishing by the way, until they arrived, in a state of extreme exhaustion and destitution, before the walls of Nissa. Fortunately the city was entirely unprepared for an attack, which had not been at all anticipated, and the garrison speedily surrendered. Here Seckendorf, having dispatched parties to seize the neighboring fortress, and the passes of the mountains, waited for further orders from Vienna. The army were so dissatisfied with their position and their hardships, that they at last almost rose in mutiny, and Seckendorf, having accomplished nothing of any moment, was compelled to retrace his steps to the banks of the Danube, where he arrived on the 16th of October. Thus the campaign was a total failure.

Bitter complaints were uttered both by the army and the nation. The emperor, with the characteristic injustice of an ignoble mind, attributed the unfortunate campaign to the incapacity of Seckendorf, whose judicious plans he had so ruthlessly thwarted. The heroic general was immediately disgraced and recalled, and the command of the army given to General Philippi. The friends of General Seckendorf, aware of his peril, urged him to seek safety in flight. But he, emboldened by conscious innocence, obeyed the imperial commands and repaired to Vienna. Seckendorf was a Protestant. His appointment to the supreme command gave great offense to the Catholics, and the priests, from their pulpits, inveighed loudly against him as a heretic, whom God could not bless. They arraigned his appointment as impious, and declared that, in consequence, nothing was to be expected but divine indignation. Immediately upon his arrival in Vienna the emperor ordered his arrest. A strong guard was placed over him, in his own house, and articles of impeachment were drawn up against him. His doom was sealed. Every misadventure was attributed to negligence, cupidity or treachery. He could offer no defense which would be of any avail, for he was not permitted to exhibit the orders he had received from the emperor, lest the emperor himself should be proved guilty of those disasters which he was thus dishonorably endeavoring to throw upon another. The unhappy Seckendorf, thus made the victim of the faults of others, was condemned to the dungeon. He was sent to imprisonment in the castle of Glatz, where he lingered in captivity for many years until the death of the emperor.

Charles now, in accordance with the clamor of the priests, removed all Protestants from command in the army and supplied their places with Catholics. The Duke of Lorraine, who had recently married Maria Theresa, was appointed generalissimo. But as the duke was young, inexperienced in war, and, as yet, had displayed none of that peculiar talent requisite for the guidance of armies, the emperor placed next to him, as the acting commander, Marshal Konigsegg. The emperor also gave orders that every important movement should be directed by a council of war, and that in case of a tie the casting vote should be given, not by the Duke of Lorraine, but by the veteran commander Konigsegg. The duke was an exceedingly amiable man, of very courtly manners and winning address. He was scholarly in his tastes, and not at all fond of the hardships of war, with its exposure, fatigue and butchery. Though a man of perhaps more than ordinary intellectual power, he was easily depressed by adversity, and not calculated to brave the fierce storms of disaster.

Early in March the Turks opened the campaign by sending an army of twenty thousand men to besiege Orsova, an important fortress on an island of the Danube, about one hundred miles below Belgrade. They planted their batteries upon both the northern and the southern banks of the Danube, and opened a storm of shot and shell upon the fortress. The Duke of Lorraine hastened to the relief of the important post, which quite commanded that portion of the stream. The imperial troops pressed on until they arrived within a few miles of the fortress. The Turks marched to meet them, and plunged into their camp with great fierceness. After a short but desperate conflict, the Turks were repulsed, and retreating in a panic, they broke up their camp before the walls of Orsova and retired.

This slight success, after so many disasters, caused im

mense exultation. The Duke of Lorraine was lauded as one
of the greatest generals of the age. The pulpits rang with
his praises, and it was announced that now, that the troops
were placed under a true child of the Church, Providence
might be expected to smile. Soon, however, the imperial
army, while incautiously passing through a defile, was assailed by a strong force of the Turks, and compelled to retreat, having lost three thousand men. The Turks resumed
the siege of Orsova; and the Duke of Lorraine, quite disheartened, returned to Vienna, leaving the command of the
army to Konigsegg. The Turks soon captured the fortress,
and then, ascending the river, drove the imperial troops before
them to Belgrade. The Turks invested the city, and the
beleaguered troops were rapidly swept away by famine and
pestilence. The imperial cavalry, crossing the Save, rapidly
continued their retreat. Konigsegg was now recalled in disgrace, as incapable of conducting the war, and the command
was given to General Kevenhuller. He was equally unsuccessful in resisting the foe; and, after a series of indecisive
battles, the storms of November drove both parties to winter
quarters, and another campaign was finished. The Russians
had also fought some fierce battles; but their campaign was
as ineffective as that of the Austrians.

The court of Vienna was now in a state of utter confusion.
There was no leading mind to assume any authority, and there
was irremediable discordance of counsel. The Duke of Lorraine was in hopeless disgrace; even the emperor assenting to
the universal cry against him. In a state almost of distraction the emperor exclaimed, "Is the fortune of my empire
departed with Eugene?" The disgraceful retreat to Belgrade
seemed to haunt him day and night; and he repeated again
and again to himself, as he paced the floor of his apartment,
"that unfortunate, that fatal retreat." Disasters had been so
rapidly accumulating upon him, that he feared for every thing.
He expressed the greatest anxiety lest his daughter, Maria

Theresa, who was to succeed him upon the throne, might be intercepted, in the case of his sudden death, from returning to Austria, and excluded from the throne. The emperor was in a state of mind nearly bordering upon insanity.

At length the sun of another spring returned, the spring of 1739, and the recruited armies were prepared again to take the field. The emperor placed a new commander, Marshal Wallis, in command of the Austrian troops. He was a man of ability, but overbearing and morose, being described by a contemporary as one who hated everybody, and who was hated by everybody in return. Fifty miles north of Belgrade, on the south bank of the Danube, is the fortified town of Peterwardein, so called as the rendezvous where Peter the Hermit marshaled the soldiers of the first crusade. This fortress had long been esteemed one of the strongest of the Austrian empire. It was appointed as the rendezvous of the imperial troops, and all the energies of the now exhausted empire were expended in gathering there as large a force as possible. But, notwithstanding the utmost efforts, in May but thirty thousand men were assembled, and these but very poorly provided with the costly necessaries of war. Another auxiliary force of ten thousand men was collected at Temeswar, a strong fortress twenty-five miles north of Peterwardein. With these forces Wallis was making preparations to attempt to recover Orsova from the Turks, when he received positive orders to engage the enemy with his whole force on the first opportunity.

The army marched down the banks of the river, conveying its baggage and heavy artillery in a flotilla to Belgrade, where it arrived on the 11th of June. Here they were informed that the Turkish army was about twenty miles below on the river at Crotzka. The imperial army was immediately pressed forward, in accordance with the emperor's orders, to attack the foe. The Turks were strongly posted, and far exceeded the Austrians in number. At five o'clock on the

morning of the 21st of July the battle commenced, and blazed
fiercely through all the hours of the day until the sun went
down. Seven thousand Austrians were then dead upon the
plain. The Turks were preparing to renew the conflict in the
morning, when Wallis ordered a retreat, which was securely
effected during the darkness of the night. On the ensuing
day the Turks pursued them to the walls of Belgrade, and,
driving them across the river, opened the fire of their batteries upon the city. The Turks commenced the siege in
form, and were so powerful, that Wallis could do nothing to
retard their operations. A breach was ere long made in one
of the bastions; an assault was hourly expected which the
garrison was in no condition to repel. Wallis sent word to
the emperor that the surrender of Belgrade was inevitable;
that it was necessary immediately to retreat to Peterwardein,
and that the Turks, flushed with victory, might soon be at
the gates of Vienna.

Great was the consternation which pervaded the court and
the capital upon the reception of these tidings. The ministers
all began to criminate each other. The general voice clamored
for peace upon almost any terms. The emperor alone remained firm. He dispatched another officer, General Schmettan, to hasten with all expedition to the imperial camp, and
prevent, if possible, the impending disaster. He earnestly
pressed the hand of the general as he took his leave, and said—

"Use the utmost diligence to arrive before the retreat of
the army; assume the defense of Belgrade, and save it, if not
too late, from falling into the hands of the enemy."

The energy of Schmettan arrested the retreat of Wallis,
and revived the desponding hopes of the garrison of Belgrade.
Bastion after bastion was recovered. The Turks were driven
back from the advance posts they had occupied. A new spirit
animated the whole Austrian army, and from the depths of
despair they were rising to sanguine hopes of victory, when
the stunning news arrived that the emperor had sent an envoy

to the Turkish camp, and had obtained peace by the surrender
of Belgrade. Count Neuperg having received full powers
from the emperor to treat, very imprudently entered the
camp of the barbaric Turk, without requiring any hostages for
his safety. The barbarians, regardless of the flag of truce, and
of all the rules of civilized warfare, arrested Count Neuperg,
and put him under guard. He was then conducted into the
presence of the grand vizier, who was arrayed in state, surrounded by his bashaws. The grand vizier haughtily demanded the terms Neuperg was authorized to offer.

"The emperor, my master," said Neuperg, "has intrusted
me with full powers to negotiate a peace, and is willing, for
the sake of peace, to cede the province of Wallachia to Turkey provided the fortress of Orsova be dismantled."

The grand vizier rose, came forward, and deliberately spit
in the face of the Count Neuperg, and exclaimed,

"Infidel dog! thou provest thyself a spy, with all thy
powers. Since thou hast brought no letter from the Vizier
Wallis, and hast concealed his offer to surrender Belgrade,
thou shalt be sent to Constantinople to receive the punishment
thou deservest."

Count Neuperg, after this insult, was conducted into close
confinement. The French ambassador, Villeneuve, now arrived. He had adopted the precaution of obtaining hostages
before intrusting himself in the hands of the Turks. The
grand vizier would not listen to any terms of accommodation
but upon the basis of the surrender of Belgrade. The Turks
carried their point in every thing. The emperor surrendered
Belgrade, relinquished to them Orsova, agreed to demolish all
the fortresses of his own province of Media, and ceded to Turkey Servia and various other contiguous districts. It was a
humiliating treaty for Austria. Already despoiled in Italy and
on the Rhine, the emperor was now compelled to abandon to
the Turks extensive territories and important fortresses upon
the lower Danube.

General Schmettan, totally unconscious of these proceedings, was conducting the defense of Belgrade with great vigor and with great success, when he was astounded by the arrival of a courier in his camp, presenting to him the following laconic note from Count Neuperg:

"Peace was signed this morning between the emperor, our master, and the Porte. Let hostilities cease, therefore, on the receipt of this. In half an hour I shall follow, and announce the particulars myself."

General Schmettan could hardly repress his indignation, and, when Count Neuperg arrived, intreated that the surrender of Belgrade might be postponed until the terms had been sent to the emperor for his ratification. But Neuperg would listen to no such suggestions, and, indignant that any obstacle should be thrown in the way of the fulfillment of the treaty, menacingly said,

"If you choose to disobey the orders of the emperor, and to delay the execution of the article relative to Belgrade, I will instantly dispatch a courier to Vienna, and charge you with all the misfortunes which may result. I had great difficulty in diverting the grand vizier from the demand of Sirmia, Sclavonia and the bannat of Temeswar; and when I have dispatched a courier, I will return into the Turkish camp and protest against this violation of the treaty."

General Schmettan was compelled to yield. Eight hundred janissaries took possession of one of the gates of the city; and the Turkish officers rode triumphantly into the streets, waving before them in defiance the banners they had taken at Crotzka. The new fortifications were blown up, and the imperial army, in grief and shame, retired up the river to Peterwardein. They had hardly evacuated the city ere Count Neuperg, to his inexpressible mortification, received a letter from the emperor stating that nothing could reconcile him to the idea of surrendering Belgrade but the conviction that its defense was utterly hopeless; but that learning that this was

by no means the case, he intreated him on no account to think
of the surrender of the city. To add to the chagrin of the
count, he also ascertained, at the same time, that the Turks
were in such a deplorable condition that they were just on the
point of retreating, and would gladly have purchased peace at
almost any sacrifice. A little more diplomatic skill might have
wrested from the Turks even a larger extent of territory than
the emperor had so foolishly surrendered to them.

CHAPTER XXVI.

MARIA THERESA.

FROM 1739 TO 1741.

ANGUISH OF THE KING.—LETTER TO THE QUEEN OF RUSSIA.—THE IMPERIAL CIRCULAR.
—DEPLORABLE CONDITION OF AUSTRIA.—DEATH OF CHARLES VI.—ACCESSION OF
MARIA THERESA.—VIGOROUS MEASURES OF THE QUEEN.—CLAIM OF THE DUKE OF
BAVARIA.—RESPONSES FROM THE COURTS.—COLDNESS OF THE FRENCH COURT.—FRED-
ERIC OF PRUSSIA.—HIS INVASION OF SILESIA.—MARCH OF THE AUSTRIANS.—BATTLE
OF MOLNITZ.—FIRMNESS OF MARIA THERESA.—PROPOSED DIVISION OF PLUNDER.—
VILLAINY OF FREDERIC.—INTERVIEW WITH THE KING.—CHARACTER OF FREDERIC.—
COMMENCEMENT OF THE GENERAL INVASION.

EVERY intelligent man in Austria felt degraded by the
peace which had been made with the Turks. The tidings were received throughout the ranks of the army with a
general outburst of grief and indignation. The troops intreated
their officers to lead them against the foe, declaring that they
would speedily drive the Turks from Belgrade, which had
been so ignominiously surrendered. The populace of Vienna
rose in insurrection, and would have torn down the houses of
the ministers who had recommended the peace but for the interposition of the military. The emperor was almost beside
himself with anguish. He could not appease the clamors of
the nation. He was also in alliance with Russia, and knew not
how to meet the reproaches of the court of St. Petersburg for
having so needlessly surrendered the most important fortress
on the Turkish frontier. In an interview which he held with
the Russian ambassador his embarrassment was painful to witness. To the Queen of Russia he wrote in terms expressive
of the extreme agony of his mind, and, with characteristic
want of magnanimity cast the blame of the very measures he

had ordered upon the agents who had merely executed his will.

"While I am writing this letter," he said, "to your imperial majesty, my heart is filled with the most excessive grief. I was much less touched with the advantages gained by the enemy and the news of the siege of Belgrade, than with the advice I have received concerning the shameful preliminary articles concluded by Count Neuperg.

"The history of past ages exhibits no vestiges of such an event. I was on the point of preventing the fatal and too hasty execution of these preliminaries, when I heard that they were already partly executed, even before the design had been communicated to me. Thus I see my hands tied by those who ought to glory in obeying me. All who have approached me since that fatal day, are so many witnesses of the excess of my grief. Although I have many times experienced adversity, I never was so much afflicted as by this event. Your majesty has a right to complain of some who ought to have obeyed my orders; but I had no part in what they have done. Though all the forces of the Ottoman empire were turned against me I was not disheartened, but still did all in my power for the common cause. I shall not, however, fail to perform in due time what avenging justice requires. In this dismal series of misfortunes I have still one comfort left, which is that the fault can not be thrown upon me. It lies entirely on such of my officers as ratified the disgraceful preliminaries without my knowledge, against my consent, and even contrary to my express orders."

This apologetic letter was followed by a circular to all the imperial ambassadors in the various courts of Europe, which circular was filled with the bitterest denunciation of Count Neuperg and Marshal Wallis. It declared that the emperor was not in any way implicated in the shameful surrender of Belgrade. The marshal and the count, thus assailed and held up to the scorn and execration of Europe, ventured to reply that they had strictly conformed to their instructions. The common sense of the community taught them that, in so rigorous and punctilious a court as that of Vienna, no agent of the emperor would dare to act contrary to his received instructions. Thus the infamous attempts of Charles to brand his officers with ignominy did but rebound upon himself. The almost universal voice condemned the emperor and acquitted the plenipotentiaries.

While the emperor was thus filling all the courts of Europe with his clamor against Count Neuperg, declaring that he had exceeded his powers and that he deserved to be hung, he at the same time, with almost idiotic fatuity, sent the same Count Neuperg back to the Turkish camp to settle some items which yet required adjustment. This proved, to every mind, the insincerity of Charles. The Russians, thus forsaken by Austria, also made peace with the Turks. They consented to demolish their fortress of Azof, to relinquish all pretensions to the right of navigating the Black sea, and to allow a vast extent of territory upon its northern shores to remain an uninhabited desert, as a barrier between Russia and Turkey. The treaty being definitively settled, both Marshal Wallis and Count Neuperg were arrested and sent to prison, where they were detained until the death of Charles VI.

Care and sorrow were now hurrying the emperor to the grave. Wan and haggard he moved about his palace, mourning his doom, and complaining that it was his destiny to be disappointed in every cherished plan of his life. All his affairs were in inextricable confusion, and his empire seemed crumbling to decay. A cotemporary writer thus describes the situation of the court and the nation:

"Every thing in this court is running into the last confusion and ruin; where there are as visible signs of folly and madness, as ever were inflicted upon a people whom Heaven is determined to destroy, no less by domestic divisions, than by the more public calamities of repeated defeats, defenselessness, poverty and plagues."

Early in October, 1740, the emperor, restless, and feverish in body and mind, repaired to one of his country palaces a few miles distant from Vienna. The season was prematurely cold and gloomy, with frost and storms of sleet. In consequence of a chill the enfeebled monarch was seized with an attack of the gout, which was followed by a very severe fit of the colic. The night of the 10th of October he writhed in pain upon his bed, while repeated vomitings weakened his already exhausted frame. The next day he was conveyed to Vienna, but in such extreme debility that he fainted several times in his carriage by the way. Almost in a state of insensibility he was carried to the retired palace of La Favourite in the vicinity of Vienna, and placed in his bed. It was soon evident that his stormy life was now drawing near to its close. Patiently he bore his severe sufferings, and as his physicians were unable to agree respecting the nature of his disease, he said to them, calmly,

"Cease your disputes. I shall soon be dead. You can then open my body and ascertain the cause of my death."

Priests were admitted to his chamber who performed the last offices of the Church for the dying. With perfect composure, he made all the arrangements relative to the succession to the throne. One after another the members of his family were introduced, and he affectionately bade them adieu, giving to each appropriate words of counsel. To his daughter, Maria Theresa, who was not present, and who was to succeed him, he sent his earnest blessing. With the Duke of Lorraine, her husband, he had a private interview of two hours. On the 20th of October, 1740, at two o'clock in the morning, he died, in the fifty-sixth year of his age, and the thirtieth of his reign. Weary of the world, he willingly retired to the anticipated repose of the grave.

> "To die,—to sleep ;—
> To sleep ! perchance to dream ;—ay, there's the rub ;
> For in that sleep of death what dreams may come,
> When we have shuffled off this mortal coil,
> Must give us pause."

By the death of Charles VI. the male line of the house of
Hapsburg became extinct, after having continued in uninter
rupted succession for over four hundred years. His eldest
daughter, Maria Theresa, who now succeeded to the crown of
Austria, was twenty-four years of age. Her figure was tall,
graceful and commanding. Her features were beautiful, and
her smile sweet and winning. She was born to command,
combining in her character woman's power of fascination with
man's energy. Though so far advanced in pregnancy that she
was not permitted to see her dying father, the very day after
his death she so rallied her energies as to give an audience to
the minister of state, and to assume the government with that
marvelous vigor which characterized her whole reign.

Seldom has a kingdom been in a more deplorable condition
than was Austria on the morning when the scepter passed into
the hands of Maria Theresa. There were not forty thousand
dollars in the treasury; the state was enormously in debt; the
whole army did not amount to more than thirty thousand men,
widely dispersed, clamoring for want of pay, and almost entirely destitute of the materials for war. The vintage had
been cut off by the frost, producing great distress in the country. There was a famine in Vienna, and many were starving
for want of food. The peasants, in the neighborhood of the
metropolis, were rising in insurrection, ravaging the fields in
search of game; while rumors were industriously circulated
that the government was dissolved, that the succession was
disputed, and that the Duke of Bavaria was on the march,
with an army, to claim the crown. The distant provinces were
anxious to shake off the Austrian yoke. Bohemia was agitated; and the restless barons of Hungary were upon the
point of grasping their arms, and, under the protection of Turkey, of claiming their ancestral hereditary rights. Notwithstanding the untiring endeavors of the emperor to obtain the
assent of Europe to the Pragmatic Sanction, many influential
courts refused to recognize the right of Maria Theresa to the

crown. The ministers were desponding, irresolute and incapable. Maria Theresa was young, quite inexperienced and in
delicate health, being upon the eve of her confinement. The
English ambassador, describing the state of affairs in Vienna
as they appeared to him at this time, wrote:

"To the ministers, the Turks seem to be already in Hungary; the Hungarians in insurrection; the Bohemians in open
revolt; the Duke of Bavaria, with his army, at the gates of
Vienna; and France the soul of all these movements. The
ministers were not only in despair, but that despair even was
not capable of rousing them to any desperate exertions."

Maria Theresa immediately dispatched couriers to inform
the northern powers of her accession to the crown, and troops
were forwarded to the frontiers to prevent any hostile invasion
from Bavaria. The Duke of Bavaria claimed the Austrian
crown in virtue of the will of Ferdinand I., which, he affirmed,
devised the crown to his daughters and their descendants in
case of the failure of the male line. As the male line was now
extinct, by this decree the scepter would pass to the Duke of
Bavaria. Charles VI. had foreseen this claim, and endeavored
to set it aside by the declaration that the clause referred to
in the will of Ferdinand I. had reference to *legitimate heirs*,
not *male* merely, and that, consequently, it did not set aside
female descendants. In proof of this, Maria Theresa had the
will exhibited to all the leading officers of state, and to the
foreign ambassadors. It appeared that *legitimate heirs* was
the phrase. And now the question hinged upon the point,
whether females were *legitimate heirs*. In some kingdoms
of Europe they were; in others they were not. In Austria
the custom had been variable. Here was a nicely-balanced
question, sufficiently momentous to divide Europe, and which
might put all the armies of the continent in motion. There
were also other claimants for the crown, but none who could
present so plausible a plea as that of the Duke of Bavaria.

Maria Theresa now waited with great anxiety for the reply

she should receive from the foreign powers whom she had notified of her accession. The Duke of Bavaria was equally active and solicitous, and it was quite uncertain whose claim would be supported by the surrounding courts. The first response came from Prussia. The king sent his congratulations, and acknowledged the title of Maria Theresa. This was followed by a letter from Augustus of Poland, containing the same friendly recognition. Russia then sent in assurances of cordial support. The King of England returned a friendly answer, promising coöperation. All this was cheering. But France was then the great power on the continent, and could carry with her one half of Europe in almost any cause. The response was looked for from France with great anxiety. Day after day, week after week passed, and no response came. At length the French Secretary of State gave a cautious and merely verbal declaration of the friendly disposition of the French court. Cardinal Fleury, the illustrious French Secretary of State, was cold, formal and excessively polite. Maria Theresa at once inferred that France withheld her acknowledgment, merely waiting for a favorable opportunity to recognize the claims of the Duke of Bavaria.

While matters were in this state, to the surprise of all, Frederic, King of Prussia, drew his sword, and demanded large and indefinite portions of Austria to be annexed to his territories. Disdaining all appeal to any documentary evidence, and scorning to reply to any questionings as to his right, he demanded vast provinces, as a highwayman demands one's purse, with the pistol at his breast. This fiery young prince, inheriting the most magnificent army in Europe, considering its discipline and equipments, was determined to display his gallantry as a fighter, with Europe for the arena. As he was looking about to find some suitable foe against which he could hurl his seventy-five thousand men, the defenseless yet large and opulent duchy of Silesia presented itself as a glittering prize worth the claiming by a royal highwayman.

The Austrian province of Silesia bordered a portion of Prussia While treacherously professing friendship with the court of Vienna, with great secrecy and sagacity Frederic assembled a large force of his best troops in the vicinity of Berlin, and in mid-winter, when the snow lay deep upon the plains, made a sudden rush into Silesia, and, crushing at a blow all opposition, took possession of the whole duchy.   Having accomplished this feat, he still pretended great friendship for Maria Theresa, and sent an ambassador to inform her that he was afraid that some of the foreign powers, now conspiring against her, might seize the duchy, and thus wrest it from her; that he had accordingly taken it to hold it in safety; and that since it was so very important, for the tranquillity of nis kingdom, that Silesia should not fall into the hands of an enemy, he hoped that Maria Theresa would allow him to retain the duchy as an indemnity for the expense he had been at in taking it."

This most extraordinary and impertinent message was accompanied by a threat.   The ambassador of the Prussian king, a man haughty and semi-barbaric in his demeanor, gave his message in a private interview with the queen's husband, Francis, the Duke of Lorraine. In conclusion, the ambassador added, "No one is more firm in his resolutions than the King of Prussia. He must and will take Silesia. If not secured by the immediate cession of that province, his troops and money will be offered to the Duke of Bavaria."

"Go tell your master," the Duke of Lorraine replied with dignity, "that while he has a single soldier in Silesia, we will rather perish than enter into any discussion. If he will evacuate the duchy, we will treat with him at Berlin. For my part, not for the imperial crown, nor even for the whole world, will I sacrifice one inch of the queen's lawful possessions."

While these negotiations were pending, the king himself made an ostentatious entry into Silesia. The majority of the

Silesians were Protestants. The King of Prussia, who had discarded religion of all kinds, had of course discarded that of Rome, and was thus nominally a Protestant. The Protestants, who had suffered so much from the persecutions of the Catholic church, had less to fear from the infidelity of Berlin than from the fanaticism of Rome. Frederic was consequently generally received with rejoicings. The duchy of Silesia was indeed a desirable prize. Spreading over a region of more than fifteen thousand square miles, and containing a population of more than a million and a half, it presented to its feudal lord an ample revenue and the means of raising a large army. Breslau, the capital of the duchy, upon the Oder, contained a population of over eighty thousand. Built upon several islands of that beautiful stream, its situation was attractive, while in its palaces and its ornamental squares, it vied with the finest capitals of Europe.

Frederic entered the city in triumph in January, 1741. The small Austrian garrison, consisting of but three thousand men, retired before him into Moravia. The Prussian monarch took possession of the revenues of the duchy, organized the government under his own officers, garrisoned the fortresses and returned to Berlin. Maria Theresa appealed to friendly courts for aid. Most of them were lavish in promises, but she waited in vain for any fulfillment. Neither money, arms nor men were sent to her. Maria Theresa, thus abandoned and thrown upon her own unaided energies, collected a small army in Moravia, on the confines of Silesia, and intrusted the command to Count Neuperg, whom she liberated from the prison to which her father had so unjustly consigned him. But it was mid-winter. The roads were almost impassable. The treasury of the Austrian court was so empty that but meager supplies could be provided for the troops. A ridge of mountains, whose defiles were blocked up with snow, spread between Silesia and Moravia.

It was not until the close of March that Marshal Neuperg

was able to force his way through these defiles and enter Silesia. The Prussians, not aware of their danger, were reposing
in their cantonments.   Neuperg hoped to take them by surprise and cut them off in detail.   Indeed Frederic, who, by
chance, was at Jagerndorf inspecting a fortress, was nearly
surrounded by a party of Austrian hussars, and very narrowly
escaped capture.   The ground was still covered with snow as
the Austrian troops toiled painfully through the mountains to
penetrate the Silesian plains.   Frederic rapidly concentrated
his scattered troops to meet the foe.   The warlike character
of the Prussian king was as yet undeveloped, and Neuperg,
unconscious of the tremendous energies he was to encounter,
and supposing that the Prussian garrisons would fly in dismay
before him, was giving his troops, after their exhausting march,
a few days of repose in the vicinity of Molnitz.

On the 8th of April there was a thick fall of snow, filling
the air and covering the fields.   Frederic availed himself of
the storm, which curtained him from all observation, to urge
forward his troops, that he might overwhelm the Austrians by
a fierce surprise.   While Neuperg was thus resting, all unconscious of danger, twenty-seven battalions, consisting of sixteen
thousand men, and twenty-nine squadrons of horse, amounting
to six thousand, were, in the smothering snow, taking their
positions for battle.   On the morning of the 10th the snow
ceased to fall, the clouds broke, and the sun came out clear
and bright, when Neuperg saw that another and a far more
fearful storm had gathered, and that its thunderbolts were
about to be hurled into the midst of his camp.

The Prussian batteries opened their fire, spreading death
through the ranks of the Austrians, even while they were hastily forming in line of battle.   Still the Austrian veterans, accustomed to all the vicissitudes of war, undismayed, rapidly
threw themselves into columns and rushed upon the foe.
Fiercely the battle raged hour after hour until the middle of
the afternoon, when the field was covered with the dead and

crimsoned with blood. The Austrians, having lost three thou
sand in slain and two thousand in prisoners, retired in confu
sion, surrendering the field, with several guns and banners, to
the victors. This memorable battle gave Silesia to Prussia,
and opened the war of the Austrian succession.

The Duke of Lorraine was greatly alarmed by the threatening attitude which affairs now assumed. It was evident that
France, Prussia, Bavaria and many other powers were combining against Austria, to rob her of her provinces, and perhaps to dismember the kingdom entirely. Not a single court
as yet had manifested any disposition to assist Maria Theresa.
England urged the Austrian court to buy the peace of Prussia
at almost any price. Francis, Duke of Lorraine, was earnestly
for yielding, and intreated his wife to surrender a part for
the sake of retaining the rest. "We had better," he said,
"surrender Silesia to Prussia, and thus purchase peace with
Frederic, than meet the chances of so general a war as now
threatens Austria."

But Maria Theresa was as imperial in character and as indomitable in spirit as Frederic of Prussia. With indignation
she rejected all such counsel, declaring that she would never
cede one inch of her territories to any claimant, and that, even
if her allies all abandoned her, she would throw herself upon
her subjects and upon her armies, and perish, if need be, in
defense of the integrity of Austria.

Frederic now established his court and cabinet at the camp
of Molnitz. Couriers were ever coming and going. Envoys
from France and Bavaria were in constant secret conference
with him. France, jealous of the power of Austria, was plotting its dismemberment, even while protesting friendship.
Bavaria was willing to unite with Prussia in seizing the empire and in dividing the spoil. These courts seemed to lay no
claim to any higher morality than that of ordinary highwaymen. The doom of Maria Theresa was apparently sealed.
Austria was to be plundered. Other parties now began to

rush in with their claims, that they might share in the booty.
Philip V. of Spain put in his claim for the Austrian crown as
the lineal descendant of the Emperor Charles V. Augustus,
King of Poland, urged the right of his wife Maria, eldest
daughter of Joseph. And even Charles Emanuel, King of
Sardinia, hunted up an obsolete claim, through the line of the
second daughter of Philip II.

At the camp of Molnitz the plan was matured of giving
Bohemia and Upper Austria to the Duke of Bavaria. Frederic of Prussia was to receive Upper Silesia and Glatz. Augustus of Poland was to annex to his kingdom Moravia and
Upper Silesia. Lombardy was assigned to Spain. Sardinia
was to receive some compensation not yet fully decided upon.
The whole transaction was a piece of as unmitigated villainy
as ever transpired. One can not but feel a little sympathy for
Austria which had thus fallen among thieves, and was stripped
and bleeding. Our sympathies are, however, somewhat alle-
viated by the reflection that Austria was just as eager as any
of the other powers for any such piratic expedition, and that,
soon after, she united with Russia and Prussia in plundering
Poland. And when Poland was dismembered by a trio of regal robbers, she only incurred the same doom which she was
now eager to inflict upon Austria. When pirates and robbers
plunder each other, the victims are not entitled to much sympathy. To the masses of the people it made but little difference whether their life's blood was wrung from them by Russian, Prussian or Austrian despots. Under whatever rule they
lived, they were alike doomed to toil as beasts of burden in
the field, or to perish amidst the hardships and the carnage of
the camp.

These plans were all revealed to Maria Theresa, and with
such a combination of foes so powerful, it seemed as if no
earthly wisdom could avert her doom. But her lofty spirit
remained unyielding, and she refused all offers of accommodation based upon the surrender of any portion of her territo-

ries. England endeavored to induce Frederic to consent to take the duchy of Glogau alone, suggesting that thus his Prussian majesty had it in his power to conclude an honorable peace, and to show his magnanimity by restoring tranquillity to Europe.

"At the beginning of the war," Frederic replied, "I might perhaps have been contented with this proposal. At present I must have four duchies. But do not," he exclaimed, impatiently, "talk to me of *magnanimity*. A prince must consult his own interests. I am not averse to peace; but I want four duchies, and I will have them."

Frederic of Prussia was no hypocrite. He was a highway robber and did not profess to be any thing else. His power was such that instead of demanding of the helpless traveler his watch, he could demand of powerful nations their revenues. If they did not yield to his demands he shot them down without compunction, and left them in their blood. The British minister ventured to ask what four duchies Frederic intended to take. No reply could be obtained to this question. By the four duchies he simply meant that he intended to extend the area of Prussia over every inch of territory he could possibly acquire, either by fair means or by foul.

England, alarmed by these combinations, which it was evident that France was sagaciously forming and guiding, and from the successful prosecution of which plans it was certain that France would secure some immense accession of power, granted to Austria a subsidy of one million five hundred thousand dollars, to aid her in repelling her foes. Still the danger from the grand confederacy became so imminent, that the Duke of Lorraine and all the Austrian ministry united with the British ambassador, in entreating Maria Theresa to try to break up the confederacy and purchase peace with Prussia by offering Frederic the duchy of Glogau. With extreme reluctance the queen at length yielded to these importunities, and consented that an envoy should take the proposal to the Prussian camp at Molnitz. As the envoy was about to leave he expressed some apprehension that the Prussian king might reject the proffer.

"I wish he may reject it," exclaimed the queen, passionately. "It would be a relief to my conscience. God only knows how I can answer to my subjects for the cession of the duchy, having sworn to them never to alienate any part of our country."

Mr. Robinson, the British ambassador, as mediator, took these terms to the Prussian camp. In the endeavor to make as good a bargain as possible, he was first to offer Austrian Guelderland. If that failed he was then to offer Limburg, a province of the Netherlands, containing sixteen hundred square miles, and if this was not accepted, he was authorized, as the ultimatum, to consent to the cession of the duchy of Glogau. The Prussian king received the ambassadors, on the 5th of August, in a large tent, in his camp at Molanitz. The king was a blunt, uncourtly man, and the interview was attended with none of the amenities of polished life. After a few desultory remarks, the British ambassador opened the business by saying that he was authorized by the Queen of Austria to offer, as the basis of peace, the cession to Prussia of Austrian Guelderland.

"What a beggarly offer," exclaimed the king. "This is extremely impertinent. "What! nothing but a paltry town for all my just pretensions in Silesia!"

In this tirade of passion, either affected or real, he continued for some time. Mr. Robinson waited patiently until this outburst was exhausted, and then hesitatingly remarked that the queen was so anxious to secure the peace of Europe, that if tranquillity could not be restored on other terms she was even willing to cede to Prussia, in addition, the province of Limburg.

"Indeed !" said the ill-bred, clownish king, contemptuously. "And how can the queen think of violating her solemn

oath which renders every inch of the Low Countries inalienable.
I have no desire to obtain distant territory which will be useless to me; much less do I wish to expend money in new fortification. Neither the French nor the Dutch have offended
me; and I do not wish to offend them, by acquiring territory in the vicinity of their realms. If I should accept Limburg,
what security could I have that I should be permitted to retain it ?"

The ambassador replied, "England, Russia and Saxony,
will give their guaranty."

"Guaranties," rejoined the king, sneeringly. "Who, in
these times, pays any regard to pledges? Have not both England and France pledged themselves to support the Pragmatic Sanction? Why do they not keep their promises?
The conduct of these powers is ridiculous. They only do what
is for their own interests. As for me, I am at the head of an
invincible army. I want Silesia. I have taken it, and I intend
to keep it. What kind of a reputation should I have if I
should abandon the first enterprise of my reign? No! I will
sooner be crushed with my whole army, than renounce my
rights in Silesia. Let those who want peace grant me my demands. If they prefer to fight again, they can do so, and
again be beaten."

Mr. Robinson ventured to offer a few soothing words to
calm the ferocious brute, and then proposed to give to him
Glogau, a small but rich duchy of about six hundred square
miles, near the frontiers of Prussia.

Frederic rose in a rage, and with loud voice and threatening gestures, exclaimed,

"If the queen does not, within six weeks, yield to my
demands, I will double them. Return with this answer to
Vienna. They who want peace with me, will not oppose my
wishes. I am sick of ultimatums; I will hear no more of them.
I demand Silesia. This is my final answer. I will give no
other."

Then turning upon his heel, with an air of towering indignation, he retired behind the inner curtain of his tent. Such was the man to whom Providence, in its inscrutable wisdom, had assigned a throne, and a highly disciplined army of seventy-five thousand men. To northern Europe he proved an awful scourge, inflicting woes, which no tongue can adequately tell.

And now the storm of war seemed to commence in earnest. The Duke of Bavaria issued a manifesto, declaring his right to the whole Austrian inheritance, and pronouncing Maria Theresa a usurper. He immediately marched an army into one of the provinces of Austria. At the same time, two French armies were preparing to cross the Rhine to coöperate with the Bavarian troops. The King of Prussia was also on the march, extending his conquests. Still Maria Theresa remained inflexible, refusing to purchase peace with Prussia by the surrender of Silesia.

"The resolution of the queen is taken," she said. "If the House of Austria must perish, it is indifferent whether it perishes by an Elector of Bavaria, or by an Elector of Brandenburg."

While these all important matters were under discussion, the queen, on the 13th of March, gave birth to a son, the Archduke Joseph. This event strengthened the queen's resolution, to preserve, not only for herself, but for her son and heir, the Austrian empire in its integrity. From her infancy she had imbibed the most exalted ideas of the dignity and grandeur of the house of Hapsburg. She had also been taught that her inheritance was a solemn trust which she was religiously bound to preserve. Thus religious principle, family pride and maternal love all now combined to increase the inflexibility of a will which by nature was indomitable.

CHAPTER XXVII.

MARIA THERESA.

FROM 1741 TO 1743.

MARIA Theresa, as imperial in spirit as in position, was unwilling to share the crown, even with her husband. Francis officiated as her chief minister, giving audience to foreign ambassadors, and attending to many of the details of government, yet he had but little influence in the direction of affairs. Though a very handsome man, of polished address, and well cultivated understanding, he was not a man of either brilliant or commanding intellect. Maria Theresa, as a woman, could not aspire to the imperial throne; but all the energies of her ambitious nature were roused to secure that dignity for her husband. Francis was very anxious to secure for himself the electoral vote of Prussia, and he, consequently, was accused of being willing to cede Austrian territory to Frederic to purchase his support. This deprived him of all influence whenever he avowed sentiments contrary to those of the queen.

England, jealous of the vast continental power of France, was anxious to strengthen Austria, as a means of holding

France in check. Seldom, in any of these courts, was the question of right or wrong considered, in any transaction. Each court sought only its own aggrandizement and the humiliation of its foes. The British cabinet, now, with very considerable zeal, espoused the cause of Maria Theresa. Pamphlets were circulated to rouse the enthusiasm of the nation, by depicting the wrongs of a young and beautiful queen, so unchivalrously assailed by bearded monarchs in overwhelming combination. The national ardor was thus easily kindled. On the 8th of August the King of England, in an animated speech from the throne, urged Parliament to support Maria Theresa, thus to maintain the *balance of power* in Europe. One million five hundred thousand dollars were immediately voted, with strong resolutions in favor of the queen. The Austrian ambassador, in transmitting this money and these resolutions to the queen, urged that no sacrifice should be made to purchase peace with Prussia; affirming that the king, the Parliament, and the people of England were all roused to enthusiasm in behalf of Austria; and that England would spend its last penny, and shed its last drop of blood, in defense of the cause of Maria Theresa. This encouraged the queen exceedingly, for she was sanguine that Holland, the natural ally of England, would follow the example of that nation. She also cherished strong hopes that Russia might come to her aid.

It was the plan of France to rob Maria Theresa of all her possessions excepting Hungary, to which distant kingdom she was to be driven, and where she was to be left undisturbed to defend herself as she best could against the Turks. Thus the confederates would have, to divide among themselves, the States of the Netherlands, the kingdom of Bohemia, the Tyrol, the duchies of Austria, Silesia, Moravia, Carinthia, Servia and various other duchies opulent and populous, over which the vast empire of Austria had extended its sway.

The French armies crossed the Rhine and united with the Bavarian troops. The combined battalions marched, sweeping all opposition before them, to Lintz, the capital of upper Austria. This city, containing about thirty thousand inhabitants, is within a hundred miles of Vienna, and is one of the most beautiful in Germany. Here, with much military and civic pomp, the Duke of Bavaria was inaugurated Archduke of the Austrian duchies. A detachment of the army was then dispatched down the river to Polten, within twenty-four miles of Vienna; from whence a summons was sent to the capital to surrender. At the same time a powerful army turned its steps north, and pressing on a hundred and fifty miles, over the mountains and through the plains of Bohemia, laid siege to Prague, which was filled with magazines, and weakly garrisoned. Frederic, now in possession of all Silesia, was leading his troops to coöperate with those of France and Bavaria.

The cause of Maria Theresa was now, to human vision, desperate. Immense armies were invading her realms. Prague was invested; Vienna threatened with immediate siege; her treasury was empty; her little army defeated and scattered; she was abandoned by her allies, and nothing seemed to remain for her but to submit to her conquerors. Hungary still clung firmly to the queen, and she had been crowned at Presburg with boundless enthusiasm. An eye-witness has thus described this scene :—

"The coronation was magnificent. The queen was all charm. She rode gallantly up the Royal Mount, a hillock in the vicinity of Presburg, which the new sovereign ascends on horseback, and waving a drawn sword, defied the four corners of the world, in a manner to show that she had no occasion for that weapon to conquer all who saw her. The antiquated crown received new graces from her head; and the old tattered robe of St. Stephen became her as well as her own rich habit, if diamonds, pearls and all sorts of precious stones can be called clothes."

She had but recently risen from the bed of confinement and the delicacy of her appearance added to her attractions. A table was spread for a public entertainment, around which all the dignitaries of the realm were assembled—dukes who could lead thousands of troops into the field, bold barons, with their bronzed followers, whose iron sinews had been toughened in innumerable wars. It was a warm summer day, and the cheek of the youthful queen glowed with the warmth and with the excitement of the hour. Her beautiful hair fell in ringlets upon her shoulders and over her full bosom. She sat at the head of the table all queenly in loveliness, and imperial in character. The bold, high-spirited nobles, who surrounded her, could appreciate her position, assailed by half the monarchies of Europe, and left alone to combat them all. Their chivalrous enthusiasm was thus aroused.

The statesmen of Vienna had endeavored to dissuade the queen from making any appeal to the Hungarians. When Charles VI. made an effort to secure their assent to the Pragmatic Sanction, the war-worn barons replied haughtily, "We are accustomed to be governed by men, not by women." The ministers at Vienna feared, therefore, that the very sight of the queen, youthful, frail and powerless, would stir these barons to immediate insurrection, and that they would scorn such a sovereign to guide them in the fierce wars which her crown involved. But Maria Theresa better understood human nature. She believed that the same barons, who would resist the demands of the Emperor Charles VI., would rally with enthusiasm around a defenseless woman, appealing to them for aid. The cordiality and ever-increasing glow of ardor with which she was greeted at the coronation and at the dinner encouraged her hopes.

She summoned all the nobles to meet her in the great hall of the castle. The hall was crowded with as brilliant an assemblage of rank and power as Hungary could furnish. The queen entered, accompanied by her retinue. She was dressed in deep mourning, in the Hungarian costume, with the crown of St. Stephen upon her brow, and the regal cimiter at her side. With a majestic step she traversed the apartment, and ascended the platform or tribune from whence the Kings of Hungary were accustomed to address their congregated lords. All eyes were fixed upon her, and the most solemn silence pervaded the assemblage.

The Latin language was then, in Hungary, the language of diplomacy and of the court. All the records of the kingdom were preserved in that language, and no one spoke, in the deliberations of the diet, but in the majestic tongue of ancient Rome. The queen, after a pause of a few moments, during which she carefully scanned the assemblage, addressing them in Latin, said :—

" The disastrous situation of our affairs has moved us to lay before our dear and faithful States of Hungary, the recent invasion of Austria, the danger now impending over this kingdom, and a proposal for the consideration of a remedy. The very existence of the kingdom of Hungary, of our own person, of our children and our crown, is now at stake. Forsaken by all, we place our sole resource in the fidelity, arms and long tried valor of the Hungarians; exhorting you, the states and orders, to deliberate without delay in this extreme danger, on the most effectual measures for the security of our person, of our children and of our crown, and to carry them into immediate execution. In regard to ourself, the faithful states and orders of Hungary shall experience our hearty coöperation in all things which may promote the pristine happiness of this ancient kingdom, and the honor of the people." *

* Some may feel interested in reading this speech in the original Latin, as it is now found recorded in the archives of Hungary. It is as follows :
" Allocutio Reginæ Hungariæ Mariæ Theresiæ, anno 1741. Afflictus rerum nostrarum status nos movit, ut fidelibus perchari regni Hungariæ statibus de hostili provinciæ nostrae hereditariæ, Austriæ invasione, et imminente

The response was instantaneous and emphatic. A thousand warriors drew their sabers half out of their scabbards, and then thrust them back to the hilt, with a clangor like the clash of swords on the field of battle. Then with one voice they shouted, " Moriamur pro nostra rege, Maria Theresa"—— *We will die for our sovereign, Maria Theresa.*

The queen, until now, had preserved a perfectly calm and composed demeanor. But this outburst of enthusiasm overpowered her, and forgetting the queen, she pressed her handkerchief to her eyes and burst into a flood of tears. No manly heart could stand this unmoved. Every eye was moistened, every heart throbbed with admiration and devo-tion, and a scene of indescribable enthusiasm ensued. Hun-gary was now effectually roused, and Maria Theresa was queen of all hearts. Every noble was ready to march his vassals and to open his purse at her bidding. All through the wide extended realm, the enthusiasm rolled like an in-undation. The remote tribes on the banks of the Save, the Theiss, the Drave, and the lower Danube flocked to her standards. They came, semi-savage bands, in uncouth garb, and speaking unintelligible tongues—Croats, Pandours, Scla-vonians, Warusdinians and Tolpaches. Germany was as-tounded at the spectacle of these wild, fierce men, apparently as tameless and as fearless as wolves. The enthusiasm spread rapidly all over the States of Austria. The young men, and especially the students in the universities, espoused the cause of the queen with deathless fervor. Vienna was strongly for

regno huic periculo, adeoque de considerando remedio propositionem scripto faciamus. Agitur de regno Hungaria, de personâ nostrâ, prolibus nostris, et coronâ, ab omnibus derelicti, unice ad inclytorum statuum fidelitatem, arma, et Hungarorum priscam virtutem confugimus, impense hortantes, velint status et ordines in hoc maximo periculo de securitate personæ nostræ, prolium, coronæ, et regni quanto ocius consulere, et ea in effectum etiam deducere. Quantum ex parte nostra est, quæcunque pro pristina regni hujus felicitate, et gentis decore forent, in iis omnibus benignitatem et clementiam nostram regiam fideles status et ordines regni experturi sunt."

tified, all hands engaging in the work. So wonderful was this movement, that the allies were alarmed. They had already become involved in quarrels about the division of the anticipated booty.

Frederic of Prussia was the first to implore peace. The Elector of Bavaria was a rival sovereign, and Frederic preferred seeing Austria in the hands of the queen, rather than in the hands of the elector. He was, therefore, anxious to withdraw from the confederacy, and to oppose the allies. The queen, as anxious as Frederic to come to an accommodation, sent an ambassador to ascertain his terms. In laconic phrase, characteristic of this singular man, he returned the following answer:—

"All lower Silesia; the river Neiss for the boundary. The town of Neiss as well as Glatz. Beyond the Oder the ancient limits to continue between the duchies of Brieg and Oppelon. Breslau for us. The affairs of religion in *statu quo.* No dependence on Bohemia; a cession forever. In return we will proceed no further. We will besiege Neiss for form. The commandant shall surrender and depart. We will pass quietly into winter quarters, and the Austrian army may go where they will. Let the whole be concluded in twelve days."

These terms were assented to. The king promised never to ask any further territory from the queen, and not to act offensively against the queen or any of her allies. Though the queen placed not the slightest confidence in the integrity of the Prussian monarch, she rejoiced in this treaty, which enabled her to turn all her attention to her other foes. The allies were now in possession of nearly all of Bohemia and were menacing Prague.

The Duke of Lorraine hastened with sixty thousand men to the relief of the capital. He had arrived within nine miles of the city, when he learned, to his extreme chagrin, that the preceding night Prague had been taken by surprise. That very day the Elector of Bavaria made a triumphal entry into the town, and was soon crowned King of Bohemia. And now the electoral diet of Germany met, and, to the extreme disappointment of Maria Theresa, chose, as Emperor of Germany, instead of her husband, the Elector of Bavaria, whom they also acknowledged King of Bohemia. He received the imperial crown at Frankfort on the 12th of February, 1742, with the title of Charles VII.

The Duke of Lorraine having been thus thwarted in his plan of relieving Prague, and not being prepared to assail the allied army in possession of the citadel, and behind the ramparts of the city, detached a part of his army to keep the enemy in check, and sent General Kevenhuller, with thirty thousand men, to invade and take possession of Bavaria, now nearly emptied of its troops. By very sagacious movements the general soon became master of all the defiles of the Bavarian mountains. He then pressed forward, overcoming all opposition, and in triumph entered Munich, the capital of Bavaria, the very day Charles was chosen emperor. Thus the elector, as he received the imperial crown, dropped his own hereditary estates from his hand.

This triumph of the queen's arms alarmed Frederic of Prussia. He reposed as little confidence in the honesty of the Austrian court as they reposed in him. He was afraid that the queen, thus victorious, would march her triumphant battalions into Silesia and regain the lost duchy. He consequently, in total disregard of his treaty, and without troubling himself to make any declaration of war, resumed hostilities. He entered into a treaty with his old rival, the Elector of Bavaria, now King of Bohemia, and Emperor of Germany. Receiving from the emperor large accessions of territory, Frederic devoted his purse and army to the allies. His armies were immediately in motion. They overran Moravia, and were soon in possession of all of its most important fortresses. All the energies of Frederic were consecrated to any cause in which he enlisted. He was indefatigable in his activity. With no sense of dishonor in violating a solemn treaty, with no sense of shame in conspiring with banded despots against a youthful queen, of whose youth, and feebleness and feminine nature they wished to take advantage that they might rob her of her possessions, Frederic rode from camp to camp, from capital to capital, to infuse new vigor into the alliance. He visited the Elector of Saxony at Dresden, then galloped to Prague, then returned through Moravia, and placed himself at the head of his army. Marching vigorously onward, he entered upper Austria. His hussars spread terror in all directions, even to the gates of Vienna.

The Hungarian troops pressed forward in defense of the queen. Wide leagues of country were desolated by war, as all over Germany the hostile battalions swept to and fro. The Duke of Lorraine hastened from Moravia for the defense of Vienna, while detached portions of the Austrian army were on the rapid march, in all directions, to join him. On the 16th of May, 1742, the Austrian army, under the Duke of Lorraine, and the Prussian army under Frederic, encountered each other, in about equal numbers, at Chazleau. Equal in numbers, equal in skill, equal in bravery, they fought with equal success. After several hours of awful carnage, fourteen thousand corpses strewed the ground. Seven thousand were Austrians, seven thousand Prussians. The Duke of Lorraine retired first, leaving a thousand prisoners, eighteen pieces of artillery and two standards, with the foe; but he took with him, captured from the Prussians, a thousand prisoners, fourteen cannon, and two standards. As the duke left Frederic in possession of the field, it was considered a Prussian victory. But it was a victory decisive of no results, as each party was alike crippled. Frederic was much disappointed. He had anticipated the annihilation of the Austrian army, and a triumphant march to Vienna, where, in the palaces of

the Austrian kings, he intended to dictate terms to the pros
trate monarchy.

The queen had effectually checked his progress, new levies
were crowding to her aid, and it was in vain for Frederic,
with his diminished and exhausted regiments, to undertake
an assault upon the ramparts of Vienna. Again he proposed
terms of peace. He demanded all of upper as well as lower
Silesia, and the county of Glatz, containing nearly seven
hundred square miles, and a population of a little over sixty
thousand. Maria Theresa, crowded by her other enemies,
was exceedingly anxious to detach a foe so powerful and
active, and she accordingly assented to the hard terms. This
new treaty was signed at Breslau, on the 11th of June, and
was soon ratified by both sovereigns. The Elector of Saxony
was also included in this treaty and retired from the contest.

The withdrawal of these forces seemed to turn the tide of
battle in favor of the Austrians. The troops from Hungary
fought with the most romantic devotion. A band of Croats
in the night swam across a river, with their sabers in their
mouths, and climbing on each other's shoulders, scaled the
walls of the fortress of Piseck, and made the garrison prisoners of war. The Austrians, dispersing the allied French and
Bavarians in many successful skirmishes, advanced to the
walls of Prague. With seventy thousand men, the Duke of
Lorraine commenced the siege of this capital, so renowned in
the melancholy annals of war. The sympathies of Europe
began to turn in favor of Maria Theresa. It became a
general impression, that the preservation of the Austrian
monarchy was essential to hold France in check, which colossal power seemed to threaten the liberties of Europe. The
cabinet of England was especially animated by this sentiment,
and a change in the ministry being effected, the court of St.
James sent assurances to Vienna of their readiness to support
the queen with the whole power of the British empire.
Large supplies of men and money were immediately voted.

Sixteen thousand men were landed in Flanders to coöperate with the Austrian troops. Holland, instigated by the example of England, granted Maria Theresa a subsidy of eight hundred and forty thousand florins. The new Queen of Russia, also, Elizabeth, daughter of Peter the Great, adopted measures highly favorable to Austria.

In Italy affairs took a singular turn in favor of the Austrian queen. The King of Sardinia, ever ready to embark his troops in any enterprise which gave him promise of booty, alarmed by the grasping ambition of France and Spain, who were ever seizing the lion's share in all plunder, seeing that he could not hope for much advantage in his alliance with them, proposed to the queen that if she would cede to him certain of the Milanese provinces, he would march his troops into her camp. This was a great gain for Maria Theresa. The Sardinian troops guarding the passes of the Alps, shut out the French, during the whole campaign, from entering Italy. At the same time the Sardinian king, with another portion of his army, aided by the Austrian troops, overran the whole duchy of Modena, and drove out the Spaniards. The English fleet in the Mediterranean coöperated in this important measure. By the threat of a bombardment they compelled the King of Naples to withdraw from the French and Spanish alliance. Thus Austria again planted her foot in Italy. This extraordinary and unanticipated success created the utmost joy and exultation in Vienna. The despondency of the French court was correspondingly great. A few months had totally changed the aspect of affairs. The allied troops were rapidly melting away, with none to fill up the dwindling ranks. The proud army which had swept over Germany, defying all opposition, was now cooped up within the walls of Prague, beleaguered by a foe whom victcry had rendered sanguine. The new emperor, claiming the crown of Austria, had lost his own territory of Bavaria; and tne capital of Bohemia, where he had so recently been enthroned, was hourly in peril of falling into the hands of his foes.

Under these circumstances the hopes of the Duke of Bavaria sank rapidly into despair. The hour of disaster revealed a meanness of spirit which prosperity had not developed. He sued for peace, writing a dishonorable and cringing letter, in which he protested that he was not to blame for the war, but that the whole guilt rested upon the French court, which had inveigled him to present his claim and commence hostilities. Maria Theresa made no other reply to this humiliating epistle than to publish it, and give it a wide circulation throughout Europe. Cardinal Fleury, the French minister of state, indignant at this breach of confidence, sent to the cabinet of Vienna a remonstrance and a counter statement. This paper also the queen gave to the public.

Marshal Belleisle was in command of the French and Bavarian troops, which were besieged in Prague. The force rapidly gathering around him was such as to render retreat impossible. The city was unprepared for a siege, and famine soon began to stare the citizens and garrison in the face. The marshal, reduced to the last extremity, offered to evacuate the city and march out of Bohemia, if he could be permitted to retire unmolested, with arms, artillery and baggage. The Duke of Lorraine, to avoid a battle which would be rendered sanguinary through despair, was ready and even anxious to assent to these terms. His leading generals were of the same opinion, as they wished to avoid a needless effusion of blood.

The offered terms of capitulation were sent to Maria Theresa. She rejected them with disdain. She displayed a revengeful spirit, natural, perhaps, under the circumstances, but which reflects but little honor upon her character.

"I will not," she replied, in the presence of the whole court; "I will not grant any capitulation to the French army. I will listen to no terms, to no proposition from Car-

dinal Fleury. I am astonished that he should come to me
now with proposals for peace; *he* who endeavored to excite
all the princes of Germany to crush me. I have acted with
too much condescension to the court of France. Compelled
by the necessities of my situation I debased my royal dignity
by writing to the cardinal in terms which would have softened the most obdurate rock. He insolently rejected my
entreaties; and the only answer I obtained was that his most
Christian majesty had contracted engagements which he
could not violate. I can prove, by documents now in my
possession, that the French endeavored to excite sedition
even in the heart of my dominions; that they attempted to
overturn the fundamental laws of the empire, and to set all
Germany in a flame. I will transmit these proofs to posterity
as a warning to the empire."

The ambition of Maria Theresa was now greatly roused.
She resolved to retain the whole of Bavaria which she had
taken from the elector. The duchy of Lorraine, which had
been wrested from her husband, was immediately to be invaded and restored to the empire. The dominions which had
been torn from her father in Italy were to be reannexed to
the Austrian crown, and Alsace upon the Rhine was to be reclaimed. Thus, far from being now satisfied with the possessions she had inherited from her father, her whole soul was
roused, in these hours of triumph, to conquer vast accessions
for her domains. She dreamed only of conquest, and in her
elation parceled out the dominions of France and Bavaria
as liberally and as unscrupulously as they had divided among
themselves the domain of the house of Austria.

The French, alarmed, made a great effort to relieve
Prague. An army, which on its march was increased to
sixty thousand men, was sent six hundred miles to cross
rivers, to penetrate defiles of mountains crowded with hostile
troops, that they might rescue Prague and its garrison from
the besiegers. With consummate skill and energy this criti-

cal movement was directed by General Mallebois. The garrison of the city were in a state of great distress. The trenches were open and the siege was pushed with great vigilance. All within the walls of the beleaguered city were reduced to extreme suffering. Horse flesh was considered a delicacy which was reserved for the sick. The French made sally after sally to spike the guns which were battering down the walls. As Mallebois, with his powerful reënforcement, drew near, their courage rose. The Duke of Lorraine became increasingly anxious to secure the capitulation before the arrival of the army of relief, and proposed a conference to decide upon terms, which should be transmitted for approval to the courts of Vienna and of Paris. But the imperious Austrian queen, as soon as she heard of this movement, quite regardless of the feelings of her husband, whom she censured as severely as she would any corporal in the army, issued orders prohibiting, peremptorily, any such conference.

" I will not suffer," she said " any council to be held in the army. From Vienna alone are orders to be received. I disavow and forbid all such proceedings, *let the blame fall where it may.*"

She knew full well that it was her husband who had proposed this plan; and he knew, and all Austria knew, that it was the Duke of Lorraine who was thus severely and publicly reprimanded. But the husband of Maria Theresa was often reminded that he was but the subject of the queen. So peremptory a mandate admitted of no compromise. The Austrians plied their batteries with new vigor, the wan and skeleton soldiers fought perseveringly at their embrasures; and the battalions of Mallebois, by forced marches, pressed on through the mountains of Bohemia, to the eventful arena. A division of the Austrian army was dispatched to the passes of Satz and Caden, which it would be necessary for the French to thread, in approaching Prague. The troops of

Mallebois, when they arrived at these defiles, were so exhausted by their long and forced marches, that they were incapable of forcing their way against the opposition they encountered in the passes of the mountains. After a severe
struggle, Mallebois was compelled to relinquish the design of
relieving Prague, and storms of snow beginning to incumber
his path, he retired across the Danube, and throwing up an
intrenched camp, established himself in winter quarters. The
Austrian division, thus successful, returned to Prague, and the
blockade was resumed. There seemed to be now no hope
for the French, and their unconditional surrender was hourly
expected. Affairs were in this state, when Europe was
astounded by the report that the French general, Belleisle,
with a force of eleven thousand foot and three thousand
horse, had effected his escape from the battered walls of the
city and was in successful retreat.

It was the depth of winter. The ground was covered with
snow, and freezing blasts swept the fields. The besiegers
were compelled to retreat to the protection of their huts.
Taking advantage of a cold and stormy night, Belleisle formed
his whole force into a single column, and, leaving behind him
his sick and wounded, and every unnecessary incumbrance,
marched noiselessly but rapidly from one of the gates of the
city. He took with him but thirty cannon and provisions for
twelve days. It was a heroic but an awful retreat. The
army, already exhausted and emaciate by famine, toiled on
over morasses, through forests, over mountains, facing frost
and wind and snow, and occasionally fighting their way
against their foes, until on the twelfth day they reached Egra
on the frontiers of Bavaria, about one hundred and twenty
miles east from Prague.

Their sufferings were fearful. They had nothing to eat
but frozen bread, and at night they sought repose, tentless,
and upon the drifted snow. The whole distance was strewed
with the bodies of the dead. Each morning mounds of frozen

corpses indicated the places of the night's bivouac. Twelve hundred perished during this dreadful march. Of those who survived, many, at Egra, were obliged to undergo the ampu tation of their frozen limbs. General Belleisle himself, during the whole retreat, was suffering from such a severe attack ot rheumatism, that he was unable either to walk or ride. His mind, however, was full of vigor and his energies unabated. Carried in a sedan chair he reconnoitred the way, pointed out the roads, visited every part of the extended line of march, encouraged the fainting troops, and superintended all the minutest details of the retreat. "Notwithstanding the losses of his army," it is recorded, "he had the satisfaction of preserving the flower of the French forces, of saving every cannon which bore the arms of his master, and of not leaving the smallest trophy to grace the triumph of the enemy."

In the citadel of Prague, Belleisle had left six thousand troops, to prevent the eager pursuit of the Austrians. The Prince Sobcuitz, now in command of the besieging force, mortified and irritated by the escape, sent a summons to the garrison demanding its immediate and unconditional surren-der. Chevert, the gallant commander, replied to the officer who brought the summons,—

"Tell the prince that if he will not grant me the honors of war, I will set fire to the four corners of Prague, and bury myself under its ruins."

The destruction of Prague, with all its treasures of architecture and art, was too serious a calamity to be hazarded. Chevert was permitted to retire with the honors of war, and with his division he soon rejoined the army at Egra. Maria Theresa was exceedingly chagrined by the escape of the French, and in the seclusion of her palace she gave vent to the bitterness of her anguish. In public, however, she assumed an attitude of triumph and great exultation in view of the recovery of Prague. She celebrated the event by magnificent entertainments. In imitation of the Olympic games, she established chariot races, in which ladies alone were the competitors, and even condescended herself, with her sister, to enter the lists.

All Bohemia, excepting Egra, was now reclaimed. Early in the spring Maria Theresa visited Prague, where, on the 12th of May, 1743, with great splendor she was crowned Queen of Bohemia. General Belleisle, leaving a small garrison at Egra, with the remnant of his force crossed the Rhine and returned to France. He had entered Germany a few months before, a conqueror at the head of forty thousand men. He retired a fugitive with eight thousand men in his train, ragged, emaciate and mutilated.

CHAPTER XXVIII.

MARIA THERESA.

FROM 1743 TO 1748.

THE cause of Maria Theresa, at the commencement of the year 1743, was triumphant all over her widely extended domains. Russia was cordial in friendship. Holland, in token of hostility to France, sent the queen an efficient loan of six thousand men, thoroughly equipped for the field. The King of Sardinia, grateful for his share in the plunder of the French and Spanish provinces in Italy, and conscious that he could retain those spoils only by the aid of Austria, sent to the queen, in addition to the coöperation of his armies, a gift of a million of dollars. England, also, still anxious to check the growth of France, continued her subsidy of a million and a half, and also with both fleet and army contributed very efficient military aid. The whole force of Austria was now turned against France. The French were speedily driven from Bavaria; and Munich, the capital, fell into the hands of the Austrians. The emperor, in extreme dejection, unable to present any front of resistance, sent to the queen entreating a treaty of neutrality, offering to withdraw all claims to the

Austrian succession, and consenting to leave his Bavarian
realm in the hands of Maria Theresa until a general peace.
The emperor, thus humiliated and stripped of all his territories, retired to Frankfort.

On the 7th of September Egra was captured, and the
queen was placed in possession of all her hereditary domains.
The wonderful firmness and energy which she had displayed,
and the consummate wisdom with which she had conceived
and executed her measures, excited the admiration of Europe.
In Vienna, and throughout all the States of Austria, her popularity was unbounded. After the battle of Dettingen, in which
her troops gained a decisive victory, as the queen was returning to Vienna from a water excursion, she found the banks of
the Danube, for nine miles, crowded with her rejoicing subjects. In triumph she was escorted into the capital, greeted
by every demonstration of the most enthusiastic joy.

Austria and England were now prepared to mature their
plans for the dismemberment of France. The commissioners
met at Hanau, a small fortified town, a few miles east of
Frankfort. They met, however, only to quarrel fiercely.
Austrian and English pride clashed in instant collision. Lord
Stair, imperious and irritable, regarded the Austrians as outside barbarians whom England was feeding, clothing and protecting. The Austrian officers regarded the English as remote islanders from whom they had hired money and men.
The Austrians were amazed at the impudence of the English
in assuming the direction of affairs. The British officers were
equally astounded that the Austrians should presume to take
the lead. No plan of coöperation could be agreed upon, and
the conference broke up in confusion.

The queen, whose heart was still fixed upon the elevation
of her husband to the throne of the empire, was anxious to
depose the emperor. But England was no more willing to
see Austria dominant over Europe than to see France thus
powerful. Maria Theresa was now in possession of all her

vast ancestral domains, and England judged that it would endanger the balance of power to place upon the brow ol her husband the imperial crown. The British cabinet con· sequently espoused the cause of the Elector of Bavaria, and entered into a private arrangement with him, agreeing to ac knowledge him as emperor, and to give him an annual pen· sion that he might suitably support the dignity of his station, The wealth of England seems to have been inexhaustible, for half the monarchs of Europe have, at one time or other, been fed and clothed from her treasury. George II. contracted to pay the emperor, within forty days, three hundred thousand dollars, and to do all in his power to constrain the queen of Austria to acknowledge his title.

Maria Theresa had promised the King of Sardinia large ac cessions of territory in Italy, as the price for his coöperation. But now, having acquired those Italian territories, she was ex ceedingly reluctant to part with any one of them, and very dishonorably evaded, by every possible pretense, the fulfill· ment of her agreement. The queen considered herself now so strong that she was not anxious to preserve the alliance of Sardinia. She thought her Italian possessions secure, even in case of the defection of the Sardinian king. Sardinia ap pealed to England, as one of the allies, to interpose for the execution of the treaty. To the remonstrance of England the queen peevishly replied,

"It is the policy of England to lead me from one sacri fice to another. I am expected to expose my troops for no other end than voluntarily to strip myself of my possessions. Should the cession of the Italian provinces, which the King of Sardinia claims, be extorted from me, what remains in Italy will not be worth defending, and the only alternative left is that of being stripped either by England or France."

While the queen was not willing to give as much as she had agreed to bestow, the greedy King of Sardinia was grasp ing at more than she had promised. At last the king, in a rage threatened, that if she did not immediately comply with his demands, he would unite with France and Spain and the emperor against Austria. This angry menace brought the queen to terms, and articles of agreement satisfactory to Sardinia were signed. During the whole of this summer of 1743, though large armies were continually in motion, and there were many sanguinary battles, and all the arts of peace were destroyed, and conflagration, death and woe were sent to ten thousand homes, nothing effectual was accomplished by either party. The strife did not cease until winter drove the weary combatants to their retreats.

For the protection of the Austrian possessions against the French and Spanish, the queen agreed to maintain in Italy an army of thirty thousand men, to be placed under the command of the King of Sardinia, who was to add to them an army of forty-five thousand. England, with characteristic prodigality, voted a million of dollars annually, to aid in the payment of these troops. It was the object of England, to prevent France from strengthening herself by Italian possessions. The cabinet of St. James took such an interest in this treaty that, to secure its enactment, one million five hundred thousand dollars were paid down, in addition to the annual subsidy. England also agreed to maintain a strong squadron in the Mediterranean to coöperate with Sardinia and Austria.

Amidst these scenes of war, the usual dramas of domestic life moved on. Prince Charles of Lorraine, had long been ardently attached to Mary Anne, younger sister of Maria Theresa. The young prince had greatly signalized himself on the field of battle. Their nuptials were attended in Vienna with great splendor and rejoicings. It was a union of loving hearts. Charles was appointed to the government of the Austrian Netherlands. One short and happy year passed away, when Mary Anne, in the sorrows of child-birth, breathed her last.

The winter was passed by all parties in making the most

vigorous preparations for a new campaign. England and France were now thoroughly aroused, and bitterly irritated against each other. Hitherto they had acted as auxiliaries for other parties. Now they summoned all their energies, and became principals in the conflict. France issued a formal declaration of war against England and Austria, raised an army of one hundred thousand men, and the debauched king himself, Louis XV., left his *Parc Aux Cerfs* and placed himself at the head of the army. Marshal Saxe was the active commander. He was provided with a train of artillery superior to any which had ever before appeared on any field. Entering the Netherlands he swept all opposition before him.

The French department of Alsace, upon the Rhine, embraced over forty thousand square miles of territory, and contained a population of about a million. While Marshal Saxe was ravaging the Netherlands, an Austrian army, sixty thousand strong, crossed the Rhine, like a torrent burst into Alsace, and spread equal ravages through the cities and villages of France. Bombardment echoed to bombardment; conflagration blazed in response to conflagration; and the shrieks of the widow, and the moans of the orphan which rose from the marshes of Burgundy, were reëchoed in an undying wail along the valleys of the Rhine.

The King of France, alarmed by the progress which the Austrians were making in his own territories, ordered thirty thousand troops, from the army in the Netherlands, to be dispatched to the protection of Alsace. Again the tide was turning against Maria Theresa. She had become so arrogant and exacting, that she had excited the displeasure of nearly all the empire. She persistently refused to acknowledge the emperor, who, beyond all dispute, was legally elected; she treated the diet contemptuously; she did not disguise her determination to hold Bavaria by the right of conquest, and to annex it to Austria; she had compelled the Bavarians to take the oath of allegiance to her; she was avowedly meditating gigantic projects in the conquest of France and Italy; and it was very evident that she was maturing her plans for the re-conquest of Silesia. Such inordinate ambition alarmed all the neighboring courts. Frederic of Prussia was particularly alarmed lest he should lose Silesia. With his accustomed energy he again drew his sword against the queen, and became the soul of a new confederacy which combined many of the princes of the empire whom the haughty queen had treated with so much indignity. In this new league, formed by Frederic, the Elector Palatine and the King of Sweden were brought into the field against Maria Theresa. All this was effected with the utmost secrecy, and the queen had no in-timation of her danger until the troops were in motion. Frederic published a manifesto in which he declared that he took up arms " to restore to the German empire its liberty, to the emperor his dignity, and to Europe repose."

With his strong army he burst into Bohemia, now drained of its troops to meet the war in the Netherlands and on the Rhine. With a lion's tread, brushing all opposition away, he advanced to Prague. The capital was compelled to surrender, and the garrison of fifteen thousand troops became prisoners of war. Nearly all the fortresses of the kingdom fell into his hands. Establishing garrisons at Tabor, Budweiss, Frauen-berg, and other important posts, he then made an irruption into Bavaria, scattered the Austrian troops in all directions, entered Munich in triumph, and reinstated the emperor in the possession of his capital and his duchy. Such are the fortunes of war. The queen heard these tidings of accumulated dis-aster in dismay. In a few weeks of a summer's campaign, when she supposed that Europe was almost a suppliant at her feet, she found herself deprived of the Netherlands, of the whole kingdom of Bohemia, the brightest jewel in her crown, and of the electorate of Bavaria.

But the resolution and energy of the queen remained indomitable. Maria Theresa and Frederic were fairly pitted against each other. It was Greek meeting Greek. The queen immediately recalled the army from Alsace, and in person repaired to Presburg, where she summoned a diet of the Hungarian nobles. In accordance with an ancient custom, a blood-red flag waved from all the castles in the kingdom, summoning the people to a levy *en masse*, or, as it was then called, to a general insurrection. An army of nearly eighty thousand men was almost instantly raised. A cotemporary historian, speaking of this event, says:

"This amazing unanimity of a people so divided amongst themselves as the Hungarians, especially in point of religion, could only be effected by the address of Maria Theresa, who seemed to possess one part of the character of Elizabeth of England, that of making every man about her a hero."

Prince Charles re-crossed the Rhine, and, by a vigorous march through Suabia, returned to Bohemia. By surprise, with a vastly superior force, he assailed the fortresses garrisoned by the Prussian troops, gradually took one after another, and ere long drove the Prussians, with vast slaughter, out of the whole kingdom. Though disaster, in this campaign, followed the banners of Maria Theresa in the Netherlands and in Italy, she forgot those reverses in exultation at the discomfiture of her great rival Frederic. She had recovered Bohemia, and was now sanguine that she soon would regain Silesia, the loss of which province ever weighed heavily upon her heart. But in her character woman's weakness was allied with woman's determination. She imagined that she could rouse the chivalry of her allies as easily as that of the Hungarian barons and that foreign courts, forgetful of their own grasping ambition, would place themselves as pliant instruments in her hands.

In this posture of affairs, the hand of Providence was again interposed, in an event which removed from the path of the queen a serious obstacle, and opened to her aspiring mind new visions of grandeur. The Emperor Charles VII., an amiable man, of moderate abilities, was quite crushed in spirit by the calamities accumulating upon him. Though he had regained his capital, he was in hourly peril of being driven from it again. Anguish so preyed upon his mind, that, pale and wan, he was thrown upon a sick bed. While in this state he was very injudiciously informed of a great defeat which his troops had encountered. It was a death-blow to the emperor. He moaned, turned over in his bed, and died, on the 20th of January, 1745.

The imperial crown was thus thrown down among the combatants, and a scramble ensued for its possession such as Europe had never witnessed before. Every court was agitated, and the combinations of intrigue were as innumerable as were the aspirants for the crown. The spring of 1745 opened with clouds of war darkening every quarter of the horizon. England opened the campaign in Italy and the Netherlands, her whole object now being to humble France. Maria Theresa remained uncompromising in her disposition to relinquish nothing and to grasp every thing. The cabinet of England, with far higher views of policy, were anxious to detach some of the numerous foes combined against Austria; but it was almost impossible to induce the queen to make the slightest abatement of her desires. She had set her heart upon annexing all of Bavaria to her realms. That immense duchy, now a kingdom, was about the size of the State of South Carolina, containing over thirty thousand square miles. Its population amounted to about four millions. The death of the Emperor Charles VII., who was Elector of Bavaria, transmitted the sovereignty of this realm to his son, Maximilian Joseph.

Maximilian was anxious to withdraw from the strife. He agreed to renounce all claim to the Austrian succession, to acknowledge the validity of the queen's title, to dismiss the auxiliary troops, and to give his electoral vote to the Duke of Lorraine for emperor. But so eager was the queen to grasp the Bavarian dominions, that it was with the utmost difficulty that England could induce her to accede even to these terms.

It is humiliating to record the readiness of these old monarchies to sell themselves and their armies to any cause which would pay the price demanded. For seven hundred and fifty thousand dollars England purchased the alliance of Poland, and her army of thirty thousand men. Before the treaty was formally ratified, the Emperor Charles VII. died, and there were indications that Bavaria would withdraw from the French alliance. This alarmed the French ministry, and they immediately offered Poland a larger sum than England had proffered, to send her army to the French camp. The bargain was on the point of being settled, when England and Austria again rushed in, and whispered in the ear of Augustus that they intended to chastise the King of Prussia thoroughly, and that if Poland would help them, Poland should be rewarded with generous slices of the Prussian territory. This was a resistless bribe, and the Polish banners were borne in the train of the Austrian alliance.

The Duke of Lorraine was much annoyed by the imperial assumption of his wife. She was anxious to secure for him the crown of Germany, as adding to her power and grandeur. But Francis was still more anxious to attain that dignity, as his position in the court, as merely the docile subject of his wife, the queen, was exceedingly humiliating. The spring of 1745 found all parties prepared for the renewal of the fight. The drama was opened by the terrible battle of Fontenoy in the Netherlands. On the 11th of May eighty thousand French met the Austrian allied army of fifty thousand. After a few hours of terrific slaughter the allies retreated, leaving the French in possession of the field. In Italy, also, the tide of war set against the queen. The French and Spaniards poured an army of seventy thousand men over the Alps into Italy. The queen, even with the aid of Sardinia, had no force capable of resisting them. The allies swept the country.

The King of Sardinia was driven behind the walls of his capital. In this one short campaign Tortona, Placentia, Parma,
Pavia, Cazale and Aste were wrested from the Austrians, and
the citadels of Alexandria and Milan were blockaded.

The queen had weakened her armies both in the Netherlands and Itály that she migh accumulate a force sufficient to
recover Silesia, and to crush, if possible, her great antagonist
Frederic. Maria Theresa was greatly elated by her success
in driving the Prussians from Bavaria, and Frederic was
mortified and irritated by this first defeat of his arms. Thus
animated, the one by hope, the other by vengeance, Maria and
Frederic gathered all their resources for a trial of strength
on the plains of Silesia. France, fully occupied in the Netherlands and in Italy, could render Frederic no assistance. His
prospects began to look dark. War had made sad ravages in
his army, and he found much difficulty in filling up his wasted
battalions. His treasury was exhausted. Still the indomitable monarch indulged in no emotions of dejection.

Each party was fully aware of the vigilance and energy
of its antagonist. Their forces were early in the field. The
month of April was passed in stratagems and skirmishes, each
endeavoring in vain to obtain some advantage over the other
in position or combinations. Early in May there was a pretty
severe conflict, in which the Prussians gained the advantage.
They feigned, however, dejection and alarm, and apparently
commenced a retreat. The Austrians, emboldened by this
subterfuge, pursued them with indiscreet haste. Prince
Charles pressed the retiring hosts, and followed closely after
them through the passes of the mountains to Landshut and
Friedburg. Frederic fled as if in a panic, throwing no obstacle in the path of his pursuers, seeming only anxious to
gain the ramparts of Breslau. Suddenly the Prussians
turned—the whole army being concentrated in columns of
enormous strength. They had chosen their ground and their
hour. It was before the break of day on the 3d of June,

among the hills of Hohenfriedberg. The Austrians were taken utterly by surprise. For seven hours they repelled the impetuous onset of their foes. But when four thousand of their number were mangled corpses, seven thousand captives in the hands of the enemy, seventy-six standards and sixty-six pieces of artillery wrested from them, the broken bands of the Austrians turned and fled, pursued and incessantly pelted by Frederic through the defiles of the mountains back to Bohemia. The Austrians found no rest till they had escaped beyond the Riesengeberg, and placed the waves of the Elbe between themselves and their pursuers. The Prussians followed to the opposite bank, and there the two armies remained for three months looking each other in the face.

Frederic, having gained so signal a victory, again proposed peace. England, exceedingly desirous to detach from the allies so energetic a foe, urged the queen, in the strongest terms, to accede to the overtures. The queen, however, never dismayed by adversity, still adhered to her resolve to reconquer Silesia. The English cabinet, finding Maria Theresa deaf to all their remonstrances and entreaties, endeavored to intimidate her by the threat of withdrawing their subsidies

The English ambassador, Sir Thomas Robinson, with this object in view, demanded an audience with the queen. The interview, as he has recorded it, is worthy of preservation.

"England," said the ambassador to the queen, "has this year furnished five million, three hundred and ninety-three thousand seven hundred and sixty-five dollars. The nation is not in a condition to maintain a superiority over the allies in the Netherlands, Italy and Silesia. It is, therefore, indispensable to diminish the force of the enemy. France can not be detached from the alliance. Prussia can be and must be. This concession England expects from Austria. What is to be done must be done immediately. The King of Prussia can not be driven from Bohemia this campaign. By making peace with him, and thus securing his voluntary withdrawal, your majesty can send troops to the Netherlands, and check the rapid progress of the French, who now threaten the very existence of England and Holland. If they fall, Austria must inevitably fall also. If peace can be made with Prussia France can be checked, and the Duke of Lorraine can be chosen emperor."

"I feel exceedingly grateful," the queen replied, "to the king and the English nation, and am ready to show it in every way in my power. Upon this matter I will consult my ministers and acquaint you with my answer. But whatever may be the decision, I can not spare a man from the neighborhood of the King of Prussia. In peace, as well as in war, I need them all for the defense of my person and family."

"It is affirmed," Sir Thomas Robinson replied, "that seventy thousand men are employed against Prussia. From such a force enough might be spared to render efficient aid in Italy and in the Netherlands."

"I can not spare a man," the queen abruptly replied.

Sir Thomas was a little touched, and with some spirit rejoined, "If your majesty can not spare her troops for the general cause, England will soon find it necessary to withdraw her armies also, to be employed at home."

This was a home thrust, and the queen felt it, and replied, "But why may we not as well detach France from the alliance, as Prussia?"

"Because Prussia," was the reply, "can be more easily induced to accede to peace, by allowing her to retain what she now has, than France can be induced to yield, by surrendering, as she must, large portions of her present acquisitions."

"I must have an opportunity," Maria Theresa continued, "to strike Prussia another blow. Prince Charles has still enough men to give battle."

"But should he be the victor in the battle," Sir Thomas replied, "Silesia is not conquered. And if the battle be lost, your majesty is well nigh ruined."

T

"If I had determined," said the queen, "to make peace with Frederic to-morrow, I would give him battle to-night. But why in such a hurry? Why this interruption of operations which are by no means to be despaired of? Give me only to October, and then you may do as you please."

"October will close this campaign," was the answer. "Our affairs are going so disastrously, that unless we can detach Prussia, by that time France and Prussia will be able to dictate terms to which we shall be compelled to accede."

"That might be true," the queen replied, tartly, "if I were to waste my time, as you are urging me to do, in marching my troops from Bohemia to the Rhine, and from the Rhine to the Netherlands. But as for my troops, I have not a single general who would condescend to command such merely *machinery* armies. As for the Duke of Lorraine, and my brother, Prince Charles, they shall not thus degrade themselves. The great duke is not so ambitious of an empty honor, much less to enjoy it under the patronage of Prussia. You speak of the imperial dignity! Is it compatible with the loss of Silesia? Great God! give me only till October. I shall then at least be able to secure better conditions."

The English ambassador now ventured, in guarded phrase, but very decisively, to inform the queen that unless she could accede to these views, England would be constrained to withdraw her assistance, and, making the best terms she could for herself with the enemy, leave Austria to fight her own battles; and that England requested an immediate and a specific answer. Even this serious menace did not move the inflexible will of the queen. She, with much calmness, replied,

"It is that I might, with the utmost promptness, attend to this business, that I have given you so expeditious an audience, and that I have summoned my council to meet so early. I see, however, very clearly, that whatever may be my decisions, they will have but little influence upon measures which are to be adopted elsewhere."

The queen convened her council, and then informed England, in most courteous phrase, that she could not accede to the proposition. The British cabinet immediately entered into a private arrangement with Prussia, guaranteeing to Frederic the possession of Silesia, in consideration of Prussia's agreement not to molest England's Hanoverian possessions.

Maria Theresa was exceedingly indignant when she became acquainted with this treaty. She sent peremptory orders to Prince Charles to prosecute hostilities with the utmost vigor, and with great energy dispatched reёnforcements to his camp. The Hungarians, with their accustomed enthusiasm, flocked to the aid of the queen; and Frederic, pressed by superior numbers, retreated from Bohemia back to Silesia, pursued and pelted in his turn by the artillery of Prince Charles. But Frederic soon turned upon his foes, who almost surrounded him with double his own number of men. His army was compact and in the highest state of discipline. A scene of terrible carnage ensued, in which the Austrians, having lost four thousand in killed and two thousand taken prisoners, were utterly routed and scattered. The proud victor, gathering up his weakened battalions, one fourth of whom had been either killed or wounded in this short, fierce storm of war, continued his retreat unmolested.

While Maria Theresa, with such almost superhuman inflexibility, was pressing her own plans, the electoral diet of Germany was assembled at Frankfort, and Francis, Duke of Lorraine, was chosen emperor, with the title of Francis I. The queen was at Frankfort when the diet had assembled, and was plying all her energies in favor of her husband, while awaiting, with intense solicitude, the result of the election. When the choice was announced to her, she stepped out upon the balcony of the palace, and was the first to shout, " Long live the emperor, Francis I." The immense concourse assembled in the streets caught and reёchoed the cry. This result was exceedingly gratifying to the queen; she regarded it as a noble triumph, adding to the power and the luster of her house.

The duke, now the emperor, was at Heidelberg, with an army of sixty thousand men. The queen hastened to him with her congratulations. The emperor, no longer a submissive subject, received his queenly spouse with great dignity at the head of his army. The whole host was drawn up in two lines, and the queen rode between, bowing to the regiments on the right hand and the left, with majesty and grace which all admired.

Though the queen's treasury was so exhausted that she had been compelled to melt the church plate to pay her troops, she was now so elated that, regardless of the storms of winter, she resolved to send an army to Berlin, to chastise Frederic in his own capital, and there recover long lost Silesia. But Frederic was not thus to be caught napping. Informed of the plan, he succeeded in surprising the Austrian army, and dispersed them after the slaughter of five thousand men. The queen's troops, who had entered Silesia, were thus driven pell-mell back to Bohemia. The Prussian king then invaded Saxony, driving all before him. He took possession of the whole electorate, and entered Dresden, its capital, in triumph. This was a terrible defeat for the queen. Though she had often said that she would part with her last garment before she would consent to the surrender of Silesia, she felt now compelled to yield. Accepting the proffered mediation of England, on the 25th of December, 1745, she signed the treaty of Dresden, by which she left Silesia in the hands of Frederic. He agreed to withdraw his troops from Saxony, and to acknowledge the imperial title of Francis I.

England, in consequence of rebellion at home, had been compelled to withdraw her troops from the Netherlands; and France, advancing with great vigor, took fortress after fortress, until nearly all of the Low Countries had fallen into her hands. In Italy, however, the Austrians were successful, and

Maria Theresa, having dispatched thirty thousand troops to their aid, cherished sanguine hopes that she might recover Milan and Naples. All the belligerent powers, excepting Maria Theresa, weary of the long war, were anxious for peace. She, however, still clung, with deathless tenacity, to her determination to recover Silesia, and to win provinces in Italy. England and France were equally desirous to sheathe the sword. France could only attack England in the Netherlands; England could only assail France in her marine. They were both successful. France drove England from the continent; England drove France from the ocean.

Notwithstanding the most earnest endeavors of the allies, Maria Theresa refused to listen to any terms of peace, and succeeded in preventing the other powers from coming to any accommodation. All parties, consequently, prepared for another campaign. Prussia entered into an alliance with Austria, by which she agreed to furnish her with thirty thousand troops. The queen made gigantic efforts to drive the French from the Netherlands. England and Holland voted an army of forty thousand each. The queen furnished sixty thousand; making an army of one hundred and forty thousand to operate in the Netherlands. At the same time the queen sent sixty thousand men to Italy, to be joined by forty-five thousand Sardinians. All the energies of the English fleet were also combined with these formidable preparations. Though never before during the war had such forces been brought into the field, the campaign was quite disastrous to Austria and her allies. Many bloody battles were fought, and many thousands perished in agony; but nothing of any importance was gained by either party. When winter separated the combatants, they retired exhausted and bleeding.

Again France made overtures for a general pacification, on terms which were eminently honorable. England was disposed to listen to those terms. But the queen had not yet accomplished her purposes, and she succeeded in securing the rejection of the proposals. Again the belligerents gathered their resources, with still increasing vigor, for another campaign. The British cabinet seemed now to be out of all patience with Maria Theresa. They accused her of not supplying the contingents she had promised, they threatened to withhold their subsidies, many bitter recriminations passed, but still the queen, undismayed by the contentions, urged forward her preparations for the new campaign, till she was thunderstruck with the tidings that the preliminaries of peace were already signed by England, France and Holland.

Maria Theresa received the first formal notification of the terms agreed to by the three contracting powers, from the English minister, Sir Thomas Robinson, who urged her concurrence in the treaty. The indignant queen could not refrain from giving free vent to her displeasure. Listening for a moment impatiently to his words, she overwhelmed him with a torrent of reproaches.

"You, sir," she exclaimed, "who had such a share in the sacrifice of Silesia; you, who contributed more than any one in procuring the cessions to Sardinia, do you still think to persuade me? No! I am neither a child nor a fool! If you will have an instant peace, make it. I can negotiate for myself. Why am I always to be excluded from transacting my own business? My enemies will give me better conditions than my friends. Place me where I was in Italy before the war; but *your King of Sardinia* must have all, without one thought for me. This treaty was not made for me, but for him, for him singly. Great God, how have I been used by that court! There is *your King of Prussia!* Indeed these circumstances tear open too many old wounds and create too many new ones. Agree to such a treaty as this!" she exclaimed indignantly, "No, no, I will rather lose my head"

CHAPTER XXIX.

MARIA THERESA.

FROM 1748 TO 1759.

TREATY OF PEACE.—DISSATISFACTION OF MARIA THERESA.—PREPARATION FOR WAR.—RUPTURE BETWEEN ENGLAND AND AUSTRIA.—MARIA THERESA.—ALLIANCE WITH FRANCE.—INFLUENCE OF MARCHIONESS OF POMPADOUR.—BITTER REPROACHES BETWEEN AUSTRIA AND ENGLAND.—COMMENCEMENT OF THE SEVEN YEARS' WAR.—ENERGY OF FREDERIC OF PRUSSIA.—SANGUINARY BATTLES.—VICISSITUDES OF WAR.—DESPERATE SITUATION OF FREDERIC.—ELATION OF MARIA THERESA.—HER AMBITIOUS PLANS.—AWFUL DEFEAT OF THE PRUSSIANS AT BERLIN.

NOTWITHSTANDING the bitter opposition of Maria Theresa to peace, the definitive treaty was signed at Aix-la-Chapelle on the 18th of October, 1748, by France, England and Holland. Spain and Sardinia soon also gave in their adhesion. The queen, finding it impossible to resist the determination of the other powers, at length reluctantly yielded, and accepted the terms, which they were ready unitedly to enforce should she refuse to accede to them. By this treaty all the contracting powers gave their assent to the Pragmatic Sanction. The queen was required to surrender her conquests in Italy, and to confirm her cessions of Silesia to Prussia. Thus terminated this long and cruel war. Though at the commencement the queen was threatened with utter destruction, and she had come out from the contests with signal honor, retaining all her vast possessions, excepting Silesia and the Italian provinces, still she could not repress her chagrin. Her complaints were loud and reiterated. When the British minister requested an audience to congratulate her upon the return of peace, she snappishly replied,

A visit of condolence would be more proper, under these circumstances, than one of congratulation. The British minister will oblige me by making no allusion whatever to so disagreeable a topic."

The queen was not only well aware that this peace could not long continue, but was fully resolved that it should not be permanent. Her great rival, Frederic, had wrested from her Silesia, and she was determined that there should be no stable peace until she had regained it. With wonderful energy she availed herself of this short respite in replenishing her treasury and in recruiting her armies. Frederic himself has recorded the masculine vigor with which she prepared herself for the renewal of war.

"Maria Theresa," he says, "in the secrecy of her cabinet, arranged those great projects which she afterwards carried into execution. She introduced an order and economy into the finances unknown to her ancestors; and her revenues far exceeded those of her father, even when he was master of Naples, Parma, Silesia and Servia. Having learned the necessity of introducing into her army a better discipline, she annually formed camps in the provinces, which she visited herself that she might animate the troops by her presence and bounty. She established a military academy at Vienna, and collected the most skillful professors of all the sciences and exercises which tend to elucidate or improve the art of war. By these institutions the army acquired, under Maria Theresa, such a degree of perfection as it had never attained under any of her predecessors; and a woman accomplished designs worthy of a great man."

The queen immediately organized a standing army of one hundred and eight thousand men, who were brought under the highest state of discipline, and were encamped in such positions that they could, at any day, be concentrated ready for combined action. The one great object which now seemed to engross her mind was the recovery of Silesia. It was, of course, a subject not to be spoken of openly; but in secret conference with her ministers she unfolded her plans and sought counsel. Her intense devotion to political affairs, united to a mind of great activity and native strength, soon placed her above her ministers in intelligence and sagacity; and conscious of superior powers, she leaned less upon them, and relied upon her own resources. With a judgment thus matured she became convinced of the incapacity of her cabinet, and with great skill in the discernment of character, chose Count Kaunitz, who was then her ambassador at Paris, prime minister. Kaunitz, son of the governor of Moravia, had given signal proof of his diplomatic abilities, in Rome and in Paris. For nearly forty years he remained at the head of foreign affairs, and, in conjunction with the queen, administered the government of Austria.

Policy had for some time allied Austria and England, but there had never been any real friendship between the two cabinets. The high tone of superiority ever assumed by the court of St. James; its offensive declaration that the arm of England alone had saved the house of Austria from utter ruin, and the imperious demand for corresponding gratitude, annoyed and exasperated the proud court of Vienna. The British cabinet were frequently remonstrated with against the assumption of such airs, and the employment of language so haughty in their diplomatic intercourse. But the British government has never been celebrated for courtesy in its intercourse with weaker powers. The chancellor Kaunitz entreated them, in their communications, to respect the sex and temper of the queen, and not to irritate her by demeanor so overbearing. The emperor himself entered a remonstrance against the discourtesy which characterized their intercourse. Even the queen, unwilling to break off friendly relations with her unpolished allies, complained to the British ambassador of the arrogant style of the English documents.

"They do not," said the queen, "disturb me, but they give great offense to others, and endanger the amity existing between the two nations. I would wish that more courtesy might mark our intercourse."

But the amenities of polished life, the rude islanders despised. The British ambassador at Vienna, Sir Robert Keith, a gentlemanly man, was often mortified at the messages he was compelled to communicate to the queen. Occasionally the messages were couched in terms so peremptory and offensive that he could not summon resolution to deliver them, and thus he more than once incurred the censure of the king and cabinet, for his sense of propriety and delicacy. These remonstrances were all unavailing, and at length the Austrian cabinet began to reply with equal rancor.

This state of things led the Austrian cabinet to turn to France, and seek the establishment of friendly relations with that court. Louis XV., the most miserable of debauchees, was nominally king. His mistress, Jeanette Poisson, who was as thoroughly polluted as her regal paramour, governed the monarch, and through him France. The king had ennobled her with the title of Marchioness of Pompadour. Her power was so boundless and indisputable that the most illustrious ladies of the French court were happy to serve as her waiting women. Whenever she walked out, one of the highest nobles of the realm accompanied her as her attendant, obsequiously bearing her shawl upon his arm, to spread it over her shoulders in case it should be needed. Ambassadors and ministers she summoned before her, assuming that air of royalty which she had purchased with her merchantable charms. Voltaire, Diderot, Montesquieu, waited in her ante-chambers, and implored her patronage. The haughty mistress became even weary of their adulation.

"Not only," said she one day, to the Abbé de Bernis, "have I all the nobility at my feet, but even my lap-dog is weary of their fawning."

With many apologies for requiring of the high-minded Maria Theresa a sacrifice, Kaunitz suggested to her the expediency of cultivating the friendship of Pompadour. Silesia was engraved upon the heart of the queen, and she was prepared to do any thing which could aid her in the reconquest of that duchy. She stooped so low as to write a letter with her own hand to the marchioness, addressing her as " our dear friend and cousin."

This was a new triumph for Pompadour, and it delighted her beyond measure. To have the most illustrious sovereign of Europe, combining in her person the titles of Queen of Austria and Empress of Germany, solicit her friendship and her good offices, so excited the vanity of the mistress, that she became immediately the warm friend of Maria Theresa, and her all powerful advocate in the court of Versailles. England was now becoming embroiled with France in reference to the possessions upon the St. Lawrence and Ohio in North America. In case of war, France would immediately make an attack upon Hanover. England was anxious to secure the Austrian alliance, that the armies of the queen might aid in the protection of Hanover. But Austria, being now in secret conference with France, was very reserved. England coaxed and threatened, but could get no definite or satisfactory answer. Quite enraged, the British cabinet sent a final declaration that, " should the empress decline fulfilling the conditions required, the king can not take any measures in coöperation with Austria, and the present system of European policy must be dissolved."

The reply of the empress queen develops the feelings of irritation and bitterness which at that time existed between the two cabinets of Austria and England.

" The queen," Maria Theresa replied, " has never had the satisfaction of seeing England do justice to her principles. If the army of Austria were merely the hired soldiers of England, the British cabinet could not more decisively assume the control of their movements than it now does, by requiring their removal from the center of Austria, for the defense of England and Hanover. We are reproached with the great efforts England has made in behalf of the house of Austria. But to these efforts England owes its present greatness. If Austria has derived useful succors from England, she has purchased those succors with the blood and ruin of her subjects; while England has been opening to herself new sources of wealth and power. We regret the necessity of uttering these truths in reply to unjust and unceasing reproaches. Could any consideration diminish our gratitude towards England, it would be thus diminished by her constant endeavor to represent the aid she has furnished us as entirely gratuitous, when this aid has always been and always will be dictated by her own interests."

Such goading as this brought back a roar. The British envoy was ordered to demand an explicit and categorical reply to the following questions:

1. If the French attack Hanover, will the queen render England assistance?

2. What number of troops will she send; and how soon will they be in motion to join the British and Hanoverian troops?

The Austrian minister, Kaunitz, evaded a reply, coldly answering, "Our ultimatum has been given. The queen deems those declarations as ample as can be expected in the present posture of affairs; nor can she give any further reply till England shall have more fully explained her intentions."

Thus repulsed, England turned to Prussia, and sought alliance with the most inveterate enemy of Austria. Frederic, fearing an assault from united Russia and Austria eagerly entered into friendly relations with England, and on the 16th of January, 1756, entered into a treaty with the cabinet of Great Britain for the defense of Hanover.

Maria Theresa was quite delighted with this arrangement, for affairs were moving much to her satisfaction at Versailles. Her "dear friend and cousin" Jeanette Poisson, had dismissed all the ministers who were unfriendly to Austria, and had replaced them with her own creatures who were in favor of the Austrian alliance. A double motive influenced the Marchioness of Pompadour. Her vanity was gratified by the advances of Maria Theresa, and revenge roused her soul against Frederic of Prussia, who had indulged in a cutting witticism upon her position and character.

The marchioness, with one of her favorites, Cardinal Bernis, met the Austrian ambassador in one of the private apartments of the palace of the Luxembourg, and arranged the plan of the alliance between France and Austria. Maria Theresa, without the knowledge of her ministers, or even of her husband the emperor, privately conducted these negotiations with the Marchioness du Pompadour. M. Kaunitz was the agent employed by the queen in this transaction. Louis XV., sunk in the lowest depths of debauchery, consented to any arrangements his mistress might propose. But when the treaty was all matured it became necessary to present it to the Council of State. The queen, knowing how astounded her husband would be to learn what she had been doing, and aware of the shock it would give the ministry to think of an alliance with France, pretended to entire ignorance of the measures she had been so energetically prosecuting.

In very guarded and apologetic phrase, Kaunitz introduced the delicate subject. The announcement of the unexpected alliance with France struck all with astonishment and indignation. Francis, vehemently moved, rose, and smiting the table with his hand, exclaimed, "Such an alliance is unnatural and impracticable—it never shall take place." The empress, by nods and winks, encouraged her minister, and he went on detailing the great advantages to result from the French alliance. Maria Theresa listened with great attention to his arguments, and was apparently convinced by them. She then gave her approbation so decisively as to silence all debate. She said that such a treaty was so manifestly for the interest of Austria, that she was fearful that France would not accede to it. Since she knew that the matter was already arranged and settled with the French court, this was a downright lie, though the queen probably regarded it as a venial fib, or as diplomacy.

Thus curiously England and Austria had changed their allies. George II. and Frederic II., from being rancorous foes became friends, and Maria Theresa and Louis XV. unfurled their flags together. England was indignant with Austria for the French alliance, Austria was indignant with England for the Prussian alliance. Each accused the other of being the first to abandon the ancient treaty. As the British ambassador reproached the queen with this abandonment, she replied,

"I have not abandoned the old system, but Great Britain has abandoned me and that system, by concluding the Prussian treaty, the first intelligence of which struck me like a fit of apoplexy. I and the King of Prussia are incompatible. No consideration on earth shall induce me to enter into any engagement to which he is a party. Why should you be surprised if, following your example in concluding a treaty with Prussia, I should enter into an engagement with France ?"

"I have but two enemies," Maria Theresa said again, "whom I have to dread—the King of Prussia and the Turks. And while I and the Empress of Russia continue on the same good terms as now subsist between us, we shall, I trust, be able to convince Europe that we are in a condition to defend ourselves against those adversaries, however formidable."

The queen still kept her eye anxiously fixed upon Silesia, and in secret combination with the Empress of Russia made preparation for a sudden invasion. With as much secrecy as was possible, large armies were congregated in the vicinity of

Prague, while Russia was cautiously concentrating her troops upon the frontiers of Livonia. But Frederic was on the alert, and immediately demanded of the empress queen the signifi cance of these military movements.

"In the present crisis," the queen replied, "I deem it necessary to take measures for the security of myself and my allies, which tend to the prejudice of no one."

So vague an answer was of course unsatisfactory, and the haughty Prussian king reiterated his demand in very imperious tones.

"I wish," said he, "for an immediate and categorical answer, not delivered in an oracular style, ambiguous and inconclusive, respecting the armaments in Bohemia, and I demand a positive assurance that the queen will not attack me either during this or the following year."

The answer returned by the queen to this demand was equally unsatisfactory with the first, and the energetic Prussian monarch, wasting no more words, instantly invaded Saxony with a powerful army, overran the duchy, and took possession of Dresden, its capital. Then wheeling his troops, with twenty-four thousand men he marched boldly into Bohemia. The queen dispatched an army of forty thousand to meet him. The fierce encounter took place at Lowositz, near the banks of the Elbe. The military genius of Frederic prevailed, and the Austrians were repulsed, though the slaughter was about equal on each side, six thousand men, three thousand upon each side, being left in their blood. Frederic took possession of Saxony as a conquered province. Seventeen thousand soldiers, whom he made prisoners, he forced into his own service. Eighty pieces of cannon were added to his artillery train, and the revenues of Saxony replenished his purse.

The anger of Maria Theresa, at this humiliation of her ally was roused to the highest pitch, and she spent the winter in the most vigorous preparations for the campaign of the spring

She took advantage of religious fanaticism, and represented, through all the Catholic courts of Europe, that there was a league of the two heretical powers, England and Prussia, against the faithful children of the Church. Jeanette Poisson, Marchioness of Pompadour, who now controlled the destinies of France, raised, for the service of Maria Theresa, an army of one hundred and five thousand men, paid all the expenses of ten thousand Bavarian troops, and promised the queen an annual subsidy of twelve millions of imperial florins. The emperor, regarding the invasion of Saxony as an insult to the empire, roused the States of Germany to coöperate with the queen. Europe was again ablaze with war.

It was indeed a fearful combination now prepared to make a rush upon the King of Prussia. France had assembled eighty thousand men on the Rhine. The Swedes were rally· ing in great numbers on the frontiers of Pomerania. The Russians had concentrated an army sixty thousand strong on the borders of Livonia. And the Queen of Austria had one hundred and fifty thousand men on the march, through Hungary and Bohemia, to the frontiers of Silesia. Frederic, with an eagle eye, was watching all these movements, and was employing all his amazing energies to meet the crisis. He resolved to have the advantage of striking the first blow, and adopted the bold measure of marching directly into the heart of the Austrian States. To deceive the allies he pretended to be very much frightened, and by breaking down bridges and establishing fortresses seemed intent upon merely presenting a desperate defense behind his ramparts.

Suddenly, in three strong, dense columns, Frederic burst into Bohemia and advanced, with rapid and resistless strides, towards Prague. The unprepared Austrian bands were driven before these impetuous assailants as chaff is dispersed by the whirlwind. With great precipitation the Austrian troops, from all quarters, fled to the city of Prague and rallied beneath its walls. Seventy thousand men were soon collected strongly intrenched behind ramparts, thrown up outside of the city, from which ramparts, in case of disaster, they could retire behind the walls and into the citadel.

The king, with his army, came rushing on like the sweep of the tornado, and plunged, as a thunderbolt of war, into the camp of the Austrians. For a few hours the battle blazed as if it were a strife of demons—hell in high carnival. Eighteen thousand Prussians were mowed down by the Austrian bat teries, before the fierce assailants could scale the ramparts Then, with cimeter and bayonet, they took a bloody revenge Eight thousand Austrians were speedily weltering in blood The shriek of the battle penetrated all the dwellings in Prague, appalling every ear, like a wail from the world of woe. The routed Austrians, leaving nine thousand prisoners in the hands of Frederic, rushed through the gates into the city, while a storm of shot from the batteries on the walls drove back the pursuing Prussians.

Prague, with the broken army thus driven within its walls, now contained one hundred thousand inhabitants. The city was totally unprepared for a siege. All supplies of food being cut off, the inhabitants were soon reduced to extreme suffer- ing. The queen was exceedingly anxious that the city should hold out until she could hasten to its relief. She succeeded in sending a message to the besieged army, by a captain of grenadiers, who contrived to evade the vigilance of the be- siegers and to gain entrance to the city.

"I am concerned," said the empress, "that so many gen- erals, with so considerable a force, must remain besieged in Prague, but I augur favorably for the event. I can not too strongly impress upon your minds that the troops will incur everlasting disgrace should they not effect what the French in the last war performed with far inferior numbers. The honor of the whole nation, as well as that of the imperial arms, is interested in their present behavior. The security of Bohemia, of my other hereditary dominions, and of the Ger man empire itself, depends on a gallant defense and the preservation of Prague.

"The army under the command of Marshal Daun is daily strengthening, and will soon be in a condition to raise the siege. The French are approaching with all diligence. The Swedes are marching to my assistance. In a short space of time affairs will, under divine Providence, wear a better aspect."

The scene in Prague was awful. Famine strode through all the streets, covering the pavements with the emaciate corpses of the dead. An incessant bombardment was kept up from the Prussian batteries, and shot and shell were falling incessantly, by day and by night, in every portion of the city. Conflagrations were continually blazing; there was no possible place of safety; shells exploded in parlors, in chambers, in cellars, tearing limb from limb, and burying the mutilated dead beneath the ruins of their dwellings. The booming of the cannon, from the distant batteries, was answered by the thunder of the guns from the citadel and the walls, and blended with all this uproar rose the uninterrupted shrieks of the wounded and the dying. The cannonade from the Prussian batteries was so destructive, that in a few days one quarter of the entire city was demolished.

Count Daun, with sixty thousand men, was soon advancing rapidly towards Prague. Frederic, leaving a small force to continue the blockade of the city, marched with the remainder of his troops to assail the Austrian general. They soon met, and fought for some hours as fiercely as mortals can fight. The slaughter on both sides was awful. At length the fortune of war turned in favor of the Austrians, though they laid down nine thousand husbands, fathers, sons, in bloody death, as the price of the victory. Frederic was almost frantic with grief and rage as he saw his proud battalions melting away before the batteries of the foe. Six times his cavalry charged with the utmost impetuosity, and six times they were as fiercely repulsed. Frederic was finally compelled to withdraw, leaving fourteen thousand of his troops either slain or prisoners. Twenty-two Prussian standards and forty-three pieces of artillery were taken by the Austrians.

The tidings of this victory elated Maria Theresa almost to delirium. Feasts were given, medals struck, presents given, and the whole empire blazed with illuminations, and rang with all the voices of joy. The queen even condescended to call in person upon the Countess Daun to congratulate her upon the great victory attained by her husband. She instituted, on the occasion, a new military order of merit, called the order of Maria Theresa. Count Daun and his most illustrious officers were honored with the first positions in this new order of knighthood.

The Prussians were compelled to raise the siege of Prague, and to retreat with precipitation. Bohemia was speedily evacuated by the Prussian troops. The queen was now determined to crush Frederic entirely, so that he might never rise again. His kingdom was to be taken from him, carved up, and apportioned out between Austria, Sweden, Poland and Russia.

The Prussians retreated, in a broken band of but twenty-five thousand men, into the heart of Silesia, to Breslau, its beautiful and strongly fortified capital. This city, situated upon the Oder, at its junction with the Ohlau, contained a population of nearly eighty thousand. The fugitive troops sought refuge behind its walls, protected as they were by batteries of the heaviest artillery. The Austrians, strengthened by the French, with an army now amounting to ninety thousand, followed closely on, and with their siege artillery commenced the cannonade of the city. An awful scene of carnage ensued, in which the Austrians lost eight thousand men and the Prussians five thousand, when the remnant of the Prussian garrison, retreating by night through a remote gate, left the city in the hands of the Austrians.

It was now mid-winter. But the iron-nerved Frederic, undismayed by these terrible reverses, collected the scattered fragments of his army, and, finding himself at the head of thirty thousand men, advanced to Breslau in the desperate attempt to regain his capital. His force was so inconsidera‑ ble as to excite the ridicule of the Austrians. Upon the ap‑ proach of Frederic, Prince Charles, disdaining to hide behind the ramparts of the city on the defensive, against a foe thus insulting him with inferior numbers, marched to meet the Prussians. The interview between Prince Charles and Fred‑ eric was short but very decisive, lasting only from the hour of dinner to the going down of a December's sun. The twilight of the wintry day had not yet come when seven thousand Austrians were lying mangled in death on the blood-stained snow. Twenty thousand were made prisoners. All the bag‑ gage of the Austrian army, the military chest, one hundred and thirty-four pieces of cannon, and fifty-nine standards fell into the hands of the victors. For this victory Fred‑ eric paid the price of five thousand lives ; but *life* to the poor Prussian soldier must have been a joyless scene, and death must have been a relief.

Frederic now, with triumphant banners, approached the city. It immediately capitulated, surrendering nearly eighteen thousand soldiers, six hundred and eighty-six officers and thir‑ teen generals as prisoners of war. In this one storm of battle, protracted through but a few days, Maria Theresa lost fifty thousand men. Frederic then turned upon the Russians, and drove them out of Silesia. The same doom awaited the Swedes, and they fled precipitately to winter quarters behind the cannon of Stralsund. Thus terminated the memorable campaign of 1757, the most memorable of the Seven Years' War. The Austrian army was almost annihilated; but the spirit of the strife was not subdued in any breast.

The returning sun of spring was but the harbinger of new woes for war-stricken Europe. England, being essentially a

maritime power, could render Frederic but little assistance
in troops; but the cabinet of St. James was lavish in voting
money Encouraged by the vigor Frederic had shown, the
British cabinet, with enthusiasm, voted him an annual subsidy
of three million two hundred and fifty thousand dollars.

Austria was so exhausted in means and in men, that notwithstanding the most herculean efforts of the queen, it was
not until April of the year 1758 that she was able to concentrate fifty thousand men in the field, with the expensive equipments which war demands. Frederic, aided by the gold of
England, was early on the move, and had already opened the
campaign by the invasion of Moravia, and by besieging Ol-
mutz.

The summer was passed in a series of incessant battles,
sweeping all over Germany, with the usual vicissitudes of war.
In the great battle of Hockkirchen Frederic encountered a
woful defeat. The battle took place on the 14th of October,
and lasted five hours. Eight thousand Austrians and nine
thousand Prussians were stretched lifeless upon the plain.
Frederic was at last compelled to retreat, abandoning his
tents, his baggage, one hundred and one cannon, and thirty
standards. Nearly every Prussian general was wounded.
The king himself was grazed by a ball; his horse was shot
from under him, and two pages were killed at his side.

Again Vienna blazed with illuminations and rang with rejoicing, and the queen liberally dispensed her gifts and her
congratulations. Still nothing effectual was accomplished by
all this enormous expenditure of treasure, this carnage and
woe; and again the exhausted combatants retired to seek
shelter from the storms of winter. Thus terminated the third
year of this cruel and wasting war.

The spring of 1759 opened brightly for Maria Theresa.
Her army, flushed by the victory of the last autumn, was in
high health and spirits. All the allies of Austria redoubled
their exertions; and the Catholic States of Germany with re

ligious zeal rallied against the two heretical kingdoms of
Prussia and England. The armies of France, Austria, Sweden and Russia were now marching upon Prussia, and it
seemed impossible that the king could withstand such adversaries. More fiercely than ever the storm of war raged,
Frederic, at the head of forty thousand men, early in June
met eighty thousand Russians and Austrians upon the banks
of the Oder, near Frankfort. For seven hours the action
lasted, and the allies were routed with enormous slaughter;
but the king, pursuing his victory too far with his exhausted
troops, was turned upon by the foe, and was routed himself
in turn, with the slaughter of one half of his whole army.
Twenty-four thousand of the allies and twenty thousand Prussians perished on that bloody day.

Frederic exposed his person with the utmost recklessness.
Two horses were shot beneath him; several musket balls
pierced his clothes; he was slightly wounded, and was rescued
from the foe only by the almost superhuman exertions of his
hussars. In the darkness of the night the Prussians secured
their retreat.

We have mentioned that at first Frederic seemed to have
gained the victory. So sanguine was he then of success that
he dispatched a courier from the field, with the following bil-
let to the queen at Berlin:—

"We have driven the enemy from their intrenchments;
in two hours expect to hear of a glorious victory."

Hardly two hours had elapsed ere another courier was sent
to the queen with the following appalling message:—

"Remove from Berlin with the royal family. Let the
archives be carried to Potsdam, and the capital make conditions with the enemy."

In this terrible battle the enemy lost so fearfully that no
effort was made to pursue Frederic. Disaster never disheartened the Prussian king. It seemed but to rouse anew his
energies. With amazing vigor he rallied his scattered forces,

and called in reёnforcements. The gold of England was at his disposal; he dismantled distant fortresses and brought their cannon into the field, and in a few days was at the head of twenty-eight thousand men, beneath the walls of his capital, ready again to face the foe.

The thunderings of battle continued week after week, in unintermitted roar throughout nearly all of Germany. Winter again came. Frederic had suffered awfully during the campaign, but was still unsubdued. The warfare was protracted even into the middle of the winter. The soldiers, in the fields, wading through snow a foot deep, suffered more from famine, frost and sickness than from the bullet of the foe. In the Austrian army four thousand died, in sixteen days of December, from the inclemency of the weather. Thus terminated the campaign of 1759.

CHAPTER XXX.

MARIA THERESA.

FROM 1759 to 1780.

DESOLATIONS OF WAR.—DISASTERS OF PRUSSIA.—DESPONDENCY OF FREDERIC.—DEATH OF THE EMPRESS ELIZABETH.—ACCESSION OF PAUL III.—ASSASSINATION OF PAUL III.—ACCESSION OF CATHARINE.—DISCOMFITURE OF THE AUSTRIANS.—TREATY OF PEACE.—ELECTION OF JOSEPH TO THE THRONE OF THE EMPIRE.—DEATH OF FRANCIS, —CHARACTER OF FRANCIS.—ANECDOTES.—ENERGY OF MARIA THERESA.—PONIATOW-SKI.—PARTITION OF POLAND.—MARIA THERESA AS A MOTHER.—WAR WITH BAVA-RIA.—PEACE.—DEATH OF MARIA THERESA.—FAMILY OF THE EMPRESS.—ACCESSSION OF JOSEPH II.—HIS CHARACTER.

THE spring of 1760 found all parties eager for the renewal of the strife, but none more so than Maria Theresa. The King of Prussia was, however, in a deplorable condition. The veteran army, in which he had taken so much pride, was now annihilated. With despotic power he had assembled a new army; but it was composed of peasants, raw recruits, but poorly prepared to encounter the horrors of war. The allies were marching against him with two hundred and fifty thousand men. Frederic, with his utmost efforts, could muster but seventy-five thousand, who, to use his own language, " were half peasants, half deserters from the enemy, soldiers no longer fit for service, but only for show."

Month after month passed away, during which the whole of Prussia presented the aspect of one wide field of battle. Frederic fought with the energies of desperation. Villages were everywhere blazing, squadrons charging, and the thunders of an incessant cannonade deafened the ear by night and by day. On the whole the campaign terminated in favor of Frederic the allies being thwarted in all their endeavors to crush him. In one battle Maria Theresa lost twenty thousand men.

During the ensuing winter all the continental powers were again preparing for the resumption of hostilities in the spring, when the British people, weary of the enormous expenditures of the war, began to be clamorous for peace. The French treasury was also utterly exhausted. France made overtures to England for a cessation of hostilities; and these two powers, with peaceful overtures, addressed Maria Theresa. The queen, though fully resolved to prosecute the war until she should attain her object, thought it not prudent to reject outright such proposals, but consented to the assembling of a congress at Augsburg. Hostilities were not suspended during the meeting of the congress, and the Austrian queen was sanguine in the hope of being speedily able to crush her Prussian rival. Every general in the field had experienced such terrible disasters, and the fortune of war seemed so fickle, now lighting upon one banner and now upon another, that all parties were wary, practicing the extreme of caution, and disposed rather to act upon the defensive. Though not a single pitched battle was fought, the allies, outnumbering the Prussians, three to one, continually gained fortresses, intrenchments and positions, until the spirit even of Frederic was broken by calamities, and he yielded to despair. He no longer hoped to be able to preserve his empire, but proudly resolved to bury himself beneath its ruins. His despondency could not be concealed from his army, and his bravest troops declared that they could fight no longer.

Maria Theresa was elated beyond measure. England was withdrawing from Prussia. Frederic was utterly exhausted both as to money and men; one campaign more would finish the work, and Prussia would lie helpless at the feet of Maria Theresa, and her most sanguine anticipations would be realized. But the deepest laid plans of man are often thwarted by apparently the most trivial events. One single individual chanced to be taken sick and die. That individual was Elizabeth, the Empress of Russia. On the 5th of January, 1762,

U

she was lying upon her bed an emaciate suffering woman, gasping in death. The departure of her last breath changed the fate of Europe.

Paul III., her nephew, who succeeded the empress, detested Maria Theresa, and often inveighed bitterly against her haughtiness and her ambition. On the contrary, he admired the King of Prussia. He had visited the court of Berlin, where he had been received with marked attention; and Frederic was his model of a hero. He had watched with enthusiastic admiration the fortitude and military prowess of the Prussian king, and had even sent to him many messages of sympathy, and had communicated to him secrets of the cabinet and their plans of operation. Now, enthroned as Emperor of Russia, without reserve he avowed his attachment to Frederic, and ordered his troops to abstain from hostilities, and to quit the Austrian army. At the same time he sent a minister to Berlin to conclude an alliance with the hero he so greatly admired. He even asked for himself a position in the Prussian army as lieutenant under Frederic.

The Swedish court was so intimately allied with that of St. Petersburg, that the cabinet of Stockholm also withdrew from the Austrian alliance, and thus Maria Theresa, at a blow, lost two of her most efficient allies. The King of Prussia rose immediately from his despondency, and the whole kingdom shared in his exultation and his joy. The Prussian troops, in conjunction with the Russians, were now superior to the Austrians, and were prepared to assume the offensive. But again Providence interposed. A conspiracy was formed against the Russian emperor, headed by his wife whom he had treated with great brutality, and Paul III. lost both his crown and his life, in July 1762, after a reign of less than six months.

Catharine II., wife of Paul III., with a bloody hand took the crown from the brow of her murdered husband and placed it upon her own head. She immediately dissolved the

ELIZABETH BRIDGE

Prussian alliance, declared Frederic an enemy to the Prussian name, and ordered her troops, in coöperation with those of Austria, to resume hostilities against Frederic. It was an instantaneous change, confounding all the projects of man. The energetic Prussian king, before the Russian troops had time so to change their positions as to coöperate with the Austrians, assailed the troops of Maria Theresa with such impetuosity as to drive them out of Silesia. Pursuing his advantage Frederic overran Saxony, and then turning into Bohemia, drove the Austrians before him to the walls of Prague. Influenced by these disasters and other considerations, Catharine decided to retire from the contest. At the same time the Turks, excited by Frederic, commenced anew their invasion of Hungary. Maria Theresa was in dismay Her money was gone. Her allies were dropping from her. The Turks were advancing triumphantly up the Danube, and Frederic was enriching himself with the spoils of Saxony and Bohemia. Influenced by these considerations she made overtures for peace, consenting to renounce Silesia, for the recovery of which province she had in vain caused Europe to be desolated with blood for so many years. A treaty of peace was soon signed, Frederic agreeing to evacuate Saxony; and thus terminated the bloody Seven Years' War.

Maria Theresa's eldest son Joseph was now twenty-three years of age. Her influence and that of the Emperor Francis was such, that they secured his election to succeed to the throne of the empire upon the death of his father. The emperor elect received the title of King of the Romans. The important election took place at Frankfort, on the 27th of May, 1764. The health of the Emperor Francis I., had for some time been precarious, he being threatened with apoplexy. Three months after the election of his son to succeed him upon the imperial throne, Francis was at Inspruck in the Tyrol, to attend the nuptials of his second son Leopold, with Maria Louisa, infanta of Spain. He was feeble and dejected, and longed to return to his home in Vienna. He imagined that the bracing air of the Tyrol did not agree with his health, and looking out upon the summits which tower around Inspruck exclaimed,

"Oh! if I could but once quit these mountains of the Tyrol."

On the morning of the 18th of August, his symptoms assumed so threatening a form, that his friends urged him to be bled. The emperor declined, saying,

"I am engaged this evening to sup with Joseph, and I will not disappoint him; but I will be blooded to-morrow."

The evening came, and as he was preparing to go and sup with his son, he dropped instantly dead upon the floor. Fifty-eight years was his allotted pilgrimage—a pilgimage of care and toil and sorrow. Even when elevated to the imperial throne, his position was humiliating, being ever overshadowed by the grandeur of his wife. At times he felt this most keenly, and could not refrain from giving imprudent utterance to his mortification. Being at one time present at a levee, which the empress was giving to her subjects, he retired, in chagrin, from the imperial circle into a corner of the saloon, and took his seat near two ladies of the court. They immediately, in accordance with regal etiquettè, rose.

"Do not regard me," said the emperor bitterly, and yet with an attempt at playfulness, "for I shall remain here until the *court* has retired, and shall then amuse myself in contemplating the crowd."

One of the ladies replied, "As long as your imperial majesty is present the court will be here."

"You are mistaken," rejoined the emperor, with a forced smile; "the empress and my children are the court. I am here only as a private individual."

Francis I., though an impotent emperor, would have made a very good exchange broker. He seemed to be fond of mercantile life, establishing manufactories, and letting out money on bond and mortgage. When the queen was greatly pressed for funds he would sometimes accept her paper, always taking care to obtain the most unexceptionable security. He engaged in a partnership with two very efficient men for farming the revenues of Saxony. He even entered into a contract to supply the *Prussian* army with forage, when that army was expending all its energies, during the Seven Years' War, against the troops of Maria Theresa. He judged that his wife was capable of taking care of herself. And she was. Notwithstanding these traits of character, he was an exceedingly amiable and charitable man, distributing annually five hundred thousand dollars for the relief of distress. Many anecdotes are related illustrative of the emperor's utter fearlessness of danger, and of the kindness of his heart. There was a terrible conflagration in Vienna. A saltpeter magazine was in flames, and the operatives exposed to great danger. An explosion was momentarily expected, and the firemen, in dismay, ventured but little aid. The emperor, regardless of peril, approached near the fire to give directions. His attendants urged him not thus to expose his person.

"Do not be alarmed for me," said the emperor, "think only of those poor creatures who are in such danger of perishing."

At another time a fearful inundation swept the valley of the Danube. Many houses were submerged in isolated positions, all but their roofs. In several cases the families had taken refuge on the tops of the houses, and had remained three days and three nights without food. Immense blocks of ice, swept down by the flood, seemed to render it impossible to convey relief to the sufferers. The most intrepid boatmen of the Danube dared not venture into the boiling surge. The emperor threw himself into a boat, seized the oars, and saying, "My example may at least influence others," pushed out into the flood and successfully rowed to one of the houses. The boatmen were shamed into heroism, and the imperiled people were saved.

Maria Theresa does not appear to have been very deeply afflicted by the death of her husband; or we should, perhaps, rather say that her grief assumed the character which one would anticipate from a person of her peculiar frame of mind. The emperor had not been faithful to his kingly spouse, and she was well acquainted with his numerous infidelities. Still she seems affectionately to have cherished the memory of his gentle virtues. With her own hands she prepared his shroud, and she never after laid aside her weeds of mourning. She often descended into the vault where his remains were deposited, and passed hours in prayer by the side of his coffin

Joseph, of course, having been preëlected, immediately assumed the imperial crown. Maria Theresa had but little time to devote to grief. She had lost Silesia, and that was a calamity apparently far heavier than the death of her husband. Millions of treasure, and countless thousands of lives had been expended, and all in vain, for the recovery of that province. She now began to look around for territory she could grasp in compensation for her loss. Poland was surrounded by Austria, Russia and Prussia. The population consisted of two classes—the nobles who possessed all the power, and the *people* who were in a state of the most abject feudal vassalage. By the laws of Poland every person was a noble who was not engaged in any industrial occupation and who owned any land, or who had descended from those who ever had held any land. The government was what may perhaps be called an aristocratic republic. The masses were mere slaves. The nobles were in a state of political equality. They chose a chieftain whom they called *king*, but whose power was a mere shadow. At this time Poland was in a state of anarchy. Civil war desolated the kingdom, the nobles being divided into numerous factions, and fighting fiercely against each other. Catharine, the Empress of Russia, espoused the cause of her favorite, Count Poniatowski, who was one of the candidates for the crown of Poland, and by the influence of her money

and her armies placed him upon the throne and maintained
him there. Poland thus, under the influence of the Russian
queen, became, as it were, a mere province of the Russian
empire.

Poniatowski, a proud man, soon felt galled by the chains
which Catharine threw around him. Frederic of Prussia
united with Catharine in the endeavor to make Poniatowski
subservient to their wishes. Maria Theresa eagerly put in
her claim for influence in Poland. Thus the whole realm
became a confused scene of bloodshed and devastation.
Frederic of Prussia, the great regal highwayman, now proposed to Austria and Russia that they should settle all the
difficulty by just dividing Poland between them. To their
united armies Poland could present no resistance. Maria
Theresa sent her dutiful son Joseph, the emperor, to Silesia,
to confer with Frederic upon this subject. The interview
took place at Neiss, on the 25th of August, 1769. The two
sovereigns vied with each other in the interchange of courte-
sies, and parted most excellent friends. Soon after, they held
another interview at Neustadt, in Moravia, when the long
rivalry between the houses of Hapsburg and Brandenburg
seemed to melt down into most cordial union. The map of
Poland was placed before the two sovereigns, and they
marked out the portion of booty to be assigned to each of the
three imperial highwaymen. The troops of Russia, Austria
and Prussia were already in Poland. The matter being thus
settled between Prussia and Austria, the Prussian king immediately conferred with Catharine at St. Petersburg. This
ambitious and unprincipled woman snatched at the bait presented, and the infamous partition was agreed to. Maria
Theresa was very greedy, and demanded nearly half of Poland
as her share. This exorbitant claim, which she with much
pertinacity adhered to, so offended the two other sovereigns
that they came near fighting about the division of the spoil.
The queen was at length compelled to lower her pretensions,

The final treaty was signed between the three powers on the 5th of August, 1772.

The three armies were immediately put in motion, and each took possession of that portion of the Polish territory which was assigned to its sovereign. In a few days the deed was done. By this act Austria received an accession of twenty-seven thousand square miles of the richest of the Polish territory, containing a population of two million five hundred thousand souls. Russia received a more inhospitable region, embracing forty-two thousand square miles, and a population of one million five hundred thousand. The share of Frederic amounted to thirteen thousand three hundred and seventy-five square miles, and eight hundred and sixty thousand souls.

Notwithstanding this cruel dismemberment, there was still a feeble Poland left, upon which the three powers were continually gnawing, each watching the others, and snarling at them lest they should get more than their share. After twenty years of jealous watchings the three powers decided to finish their infamous work, and Poland was blotted from the map of Europe. In the two divisions Austria received forty-five thousand square miles and five million of inhabitants. Maria Theresa was now upon the highest pinnacle of her glory and her power. She had a highly disciplined army of two hundred thousand men; her treasury was replenished, and her wide-spread realms were in the enjoyment of peace. Life had been to her, thus far, but a stormy sea, and weary of toil and care, she now hoped to close her days in tranquillity.

The queen was a stern and stately mother. While pressed by all these cares of state, sufficient to have crushed any ordinary mind, she had given birth to sixteen children. But as each child was born it was placed in the hands of careful nurses, and received but little of parental caressings. It was seldom that she saw her children more than once a week

Absorbed by high political interests, she contented herself with receiving a daily report from the nursery. Every morning her physician, Van Swieter, visited the young imperial family, and then presented a formal statement of their condition to the strong-minded mother. Yet the empress was very desirous of having it understood that she was the most faithful of parents. Whenever any foreign ambassador arrived at Vienna, the empress would contrive to have an interview, as it were by accident, when she had collected around her her interesting family. As the illustrious stranger retired the children also retired to their nursery.

One of the daughters, Josepha, was betrothed to the King of Naples. A few days before she was to leave Vienna the queen required her, in obedience to long established etiquette, to descend into the tomb of her ancestors and offer up a prayer. The sister-in-law, the Emperor Joseph's wife, had just died of the small-pox, and her remains, disfigured by that awful disease, had but recently been deposited in the tomb. The timid maiden was horror-stricken at the requirement, and regarded it as her death doom. But an order from Maria Theresa no one was to disobey. With tears filling her eyes, she took her younger sister, Maria Antoinette, upon her knee, and said,

"I am about to leave you, Maria, not for Naples, but to die. I must visit the tomb of our ancestors, and I am sure that I shall take the small-pox, and shall soon be buried there." Her fears were verified. The disease, in its most virulent form, seized her, and in a few days her remains were also consigned to the tomb.

In May, 1770, Maria Antoinette, then but fifteen years of age, and marvelously beautiful, was married to the young dauphin of France, subsequently the unhappy Louis XVI. As she left Vienna, for that throne from which she was to descend to the guillotine, her mother sent by her hand the following letter to her husband:

"Your bride, dear dauphin, is separated from me. As she has ever been my delight so will she be your happiness. For this purpose have I educated her; for I have long been aware that she was to be the companion of your life. I have enjoined upon her, as among her highest duties, the most tender attachment to your person, the greatest attention to every thing that can please or make you happy. Above all, I have recommended to her humility towards God, because I am convinced that it is impossible for us to contribute to the happiness of the subjects confided to us, without love to Him who breaks the scepters and crushes the thrones of kings according to His own will."

In December, 1777, the Duke of Bavaria died without male issue. Many claimants instantly rose, ambitious of so princely an inheritance. Maria Theresa could not resist the temptation to put in her claim. With her accustomed promptness, she immediately ordered her troops in motion, and, descending from Bohemia, entered the electorate. Maria Theresa had no one to fear but Frederic of Prussia, who vehemently remonstrated against such an accession of power to the empire of Austria. After an earnest correspondence the queen proposed that Bavaria should be divided between them as they had partitioned Poland. Still they could not agree, and the question was submitted to the cruel arbitrament of battle. The young Emperor Joseph was much pleased with this issue, for he was thirsting for military fame, and was proud to contend with so renowned an antagonist. The death of hundreds of thousands of men in the game of war, was of little more moment to him than the loss of a few pieces in a game of chess.

The Emperor Joseph was soon at the head of one hundred thousand men. The King of Prussia, with nearly an equal force, marched to meet him. Both commanders were exceedingly wary, and the whole campaign was passed in maneuvers and marchings, with a few unimportant battles. The queen was weary of war, and often spoke, with tears in her eyes, of the commencement of hostilities. Without the knowledge of her son, who rejoiced in the opening strife, she entered into a private correspondence with Frederic, in which she wrote, by her secret messenger, M. Thugut:

"I regret exceedingly that the King of Prussia and myself, in our advanced years, are about to tear the gray hairs from each other's heads. My age, and my earnest desire to maintain peace are well known. My maternal heart is alarmed for the safety of my sons who are in the army. I take this step without the knowledge of my son the emperor, and I entreat that you will not divulge it. I conjure you to unite your efforts with mine to reëstablish harmony."

The reply of Frederic was courteous and beautiful. "Baron Thugut," he wrote, "has delivered me your majesty's letter, and no one is, or shall be acquainted with his arrival. It was worthy of your majesty to give such proofs of moderation, after having so heroically maintained the inheritance of your ancestors. The tender attachment you display for your son the emperor, and the princes of your blood, deserves the applause of every heart, and augments, if possible, the high consideration I entertain for your majesty. I have added some articles to the propositions of M. Thugut, most of which have been allowed, and others which, I hope, will meet with little difficulty. He will immediately depart for Vienna, and will be able to return in five or six days, during which time I will act with such caution that your imperial majesty may have no cause of apprehension for the safety of any part of your family, and particularly of the emperor, whom I love and esteem, although our opinions differ in regard to the affairs of Germany."

But the Emperor Joseph was bitterly opposed to peace, and thwarted his mother's benevolent intentions in every possible way. Still the empress succeeded, and the articles were signed at Teschen, the 13th day of May, 1779. The queen was overjoyed at the result, and was often heard to say that no act of her administration had given her such heartfelt joy. When she received the news she exclaimed,

" My happiness is full. I am not partial to Frederic, but I must do him the justice to confess that he has acted nobly and honorably. He promised me to make peace on reasonable terms, and he has kept his word. I am inexpressibly happy to spare the effusion of so much blood."

The hour was now approaching when Maria Theresa was to die. She had for some time been failing from a disease of the lungs, and she was now rapidly declining. Her sufferings, as she took her chamber and her bed, became very severe; but the stoicism of her character remained unshaken. In one of her seasons of acute agony she exclaimed,

" God grant that these sufferings may soon terminate, for, otherwise, I know not if I can much longer endure them."

Her son Maximilian stood by her bed-side. She raised her eyes to him and said,

" I have been enabled thus far to bear these pangs with firmness and constancy. Pray to God, my son, that I may preserve my tranquillity to the last."

The dying hour, long sighed for, came. She partook of the sacrament of the Lord's Supper, and then, assembling her family around her, addressed to them her last words.

" I have received the sacraments," said she, " and feel that I am now to die." Then addressing the emperor, she continued, " My son, all my possessions after my death revert to you. To your care I commend my children. Be to them a father. I shall die contented, you giving me that promise." Then looking to the other children she added, " Regard the emperor as your sovereign. Obey him, respect him, confide in him, and follow his advice in all things, and you will secure his friendship and protection."

Her mind continued active and intensely occupied with the affairs of her family and of her kingdom, until the very last moment. During the night succeeding her final interview with her children, though suffering frcm repeated fits of suffo- cation, she held a long interview with the emperor upon affairs of state. Her son, distressed by her evident exhaustion, en- treated her to take some repose; but she replied,

" In a few hours I shall appear before the judgment-seat of God ; and would you have me lose my time in sleep?"

Expressing solicitude in behalf of the numerous persons dependent upon her, who, after her death, might be left friend- less, she remarked,

"I could wish for immortality on earth, for no other reason than for the power of relieving the distressed."

She died on the 29th of November, 1780, in the sixty- fourth year of her age and the forty-first of her reign.

This illustrious woman had given birth to six sons and ten daughters. Nine of these children survived her. Joseph already emperor, succeeded her upon the throne of Austria and dying childless, surrendered the crown to his next brother Leopold. Ferdinand, the third son, became governor of Aus- trian Lombardy. Upon Maximilian was conferred the elec- torate of Cologne. Mary Anne became abbess of a nunnery. Christina married the Duke of Sa¿ony. Elizabeth entered a convent and became abbess. Caroline married the King of Naples, and was an infamous woman. Her sister Joanna, was first betrothed to the king, but she died of small-pox; Josepha was then destined to supply her place ; but she also fell a victim to that terrible disease. Thus the situation was vacant for Caroline. Maria Antoinette married Louis the dauphin, and the story of her woes has filled the world.

The Emperor Joseph II., who now inherited the crown of Austria, was forty years of age, a man of strong mind, edu- cated by observation and travel, rather than by books. He was anxious to elevate and educate his subjects, declaring that it was his great ambition to rule over freemen. He had many noble traits of character, and innumerable anecdotes are re lated illustrative of his energy and humanity. In war he was ambitious of taking his full share of hardship, sleeping on the bare ground and partaking of the soldiers' homely fare. He was exceedingly popular at the time of his accession to the throne, and great anticipations were cherished of a golden age about to dawn upon Austria. "His toilet," writes one of his eulogists, "is that of a common soldier, his wardrobe that of a sergeant, business his recreation, and his life perpetual motion."

The Austrian monarchy now embraced one hundred and eighty thousand square miles, containing twenty-four millions of inhabitants. It was indeed a heterogeneous realm, composed of a vast number of distinct nations and provinces, differing in language, religion, government, laws, customs and civilization. In most of these countries the feudal system existed in all its direful oppression. Many of the provinces of the Austrian empire, like the Netherlands, Lombardy and Suabia, were separated by many leagues from the great central empire. The Roman Catholic religion was dominant in nearly all the States, and the clergy possessed enormous wealth and power. The masses of the people were sunk in the lowest depths of poverty and ignorance. The aristocratic few rejoiced in luxury and splendor.

CHAPTER XXXI.

JOSEPH II. AND LEOPOLD, II.

FROM 1780 TO 1792.

ACCESSION OF JOSEPH II.—HIS PLANS OF REFORM.—PIUS VI.—EMANCIPATION OF THE SERFS.—JOSEPH'S VISIT TO HIS SISTER, MARIA ANTOINETTE.—AMBITIOUS DESIGNS. —THE IMPERIAL SLEIGH RIDE.—BARGES ON THE DNEISTER.—EXCURSION TO THE CRIMEA.—WAR WITH TURKEY.—DEFEAT OF THE AUSTRIANS.—GREAT SUCCESSES.— DEATH OF JOSEPH.—HIS CHARACTER.—ACCESSION OF LEOPOLD II.—HIS EFFORTS TO CONFIRM DESPOTISM.—THE FRENCH REVOLUTION.—EUROPEAN COALITION.— DEATH OF LEOPOLD.—HIS PROFLIGACY.—ACCESSION OF FRANCIS II.—PRESENT EXTENT AND POWER OF AUSTRIA.—ITS ARMY.—POLICY OF THE GOVERNMENT.

WHEN Joseph ascended the throne there were ten languages, besides several dialects, spoken in Austria—the German, Hungarian, Sclavonian, Latin, Wallachian, Turkish, modern Greek, Italian, Flemish and French. The new king formed the desperate resolve to fuse the discordant kingdom into one homogeneous mass, obliterating all distinctions of laws, religion, language and manners. It was a benevolent design, but one which far surpassed the power of man to execute. He first attempted to obliterate all the old national landmarks, and divided the kingdom into thirteen States, in each of which he instituted the same code of laws. He ordered the German language alone to be used in public documents and offices; declared the Roman Catholic religion to be dominant. There were two thousand convents in Austria. He reduced them to seven hundred, and cut down the number of thirty-two thousand idle monks to twenty-seven hundred; and nobly issued an edict of toleration, granting to all members of Protestant churches the free exercise of their religion All Christians, of every denomination, were declared to be equally eligible to any offices in the State.

These enlightened innovations roused the terror and rage of bigoted Rome. Pope Pius VI. was so much alarmed that he took a journey to Vienna, that he might personally remonstrate with the emperor. But Joseph was inflexible, and the Pope returned to Rome chagrined and humiliated that he had acted the part of a suppliant in vain.

The serfs were all emancipated from feudal vassalage, and thus, in an hour, the slavery under which the peasants had groaned for ages was abolished. He established universities, academies and public schools ; encouraged literature and science in every way, and took from the priests their office of censorship of the press, an office which they had long held. To encourage domestic manufactures he imposed a very heavy duty upon all articles of foreign manufacture. New roads were constructed at what was called enormous expense, and yet at expense which was as nothing compared with the cost of a single battle.

Joseph, soon after his coronation, made a visit to his sister Maria Antoinette in France, where he was received with the most profuse hospitality, and the bonds of friendship between the two courts were much strengthened. The ambition for territorial aggrandizement seems to have been an hereditary disease of the Austrian monarchs. Joseph was very anxious to attach Bavaria to his realms. Proceeding with great caution he first secured, by diplomatic skill, the non-intervention of France and Russia. England was too much engaged in the war of the American Revolution to interfere. He raised an army of eighty thousand men to crush any opposition, and then informed the Duke of Bavaria that he must exchange his dominions for the Austrian Netherlands. He requested the duke to give him an answer in eight days, but declared peremptorily that in case he manifested any reluctance, the

emperor would be under the painful necessity of compelling
him to make the exchange.

The duke appealed to Russia, France and Prussia for aid.
The emperor had bought over Russia and France. Frederic
of Prussia, though seventy-four years of age, encouraged the
duke to reject the proposal, and promised his support. The
King of Prussia issued a remonstrance against this despotic
act of Austria, which remonstrance was sent to all the courts
of Europe. Joseph, on encountering this unexpected obstacle, and finding Europe combining against him, renounced
his plan and published a declaration that he had never intended to effect the exchange by force. This disavowal, however, deceived no one. A confederacy was soon formed,
under the auspices of Frederic of Prussia, to check the encroachments of the house of Austria. This Germanic League
was almost the last act of Frederic. He died August 17,
1786, after a reign of forty-seven years, in the seventy-fifth
year of his age.

The ambitious Empress of Russia, having already obtained
the Crimea, was intent upon the subversion of the Ottoman
empire, that she might acquire Constantinople as her maritime metropolis in the sunny south. Joseph was willing to
allow her to proceed unobstructed in the dismemberment of
Turkey, if she would not interfere with his plans of reform
and aggrandizement in Germany.

In January, 1787, the Empress of Russia set out on a pleasure excursion of two thousand miles to the Crimea; perhaps
the most magnificent pleasure excursion that was ever attempted. She was accompanied by all the court, by the
French, English and Austrian ministers, and by a very gorgeous retinue. It was mid-winter, when the imperial party,
wrapped in furs, and in large sledges richly decorated, and
prepared expressly for the journey, commenced their sleigh
ride of a thousand miles. Music greeted them all along the
way; bonfires blazed on every hill; palaces, brilliant with

illuminations and profusely supplied with every luxury, wel
comed them at each stage where they stopped for refreshment or repose. The roads were put in perfect order; and
relays of fresh horses every few miles being harnessed to the
sledges, they swept like the wind over the hills and through
the valleys.

The drive of a few weeks, with many loiterings for pleasure in the cities on the way, took them to Kief on the Dnie-
per. This ancient city, the residence of the grand dukes of
Russia, contained a population of about twenty-six thousand.
Here the imperial court established itself in the ducal palaces,
and with music, songs and dances beguiled the days until,
with the returning spring, the river opened. In the meantime an immense flotilla of imperial barges had been prepared
to drift down the stream, a thousand miles, to its mouth at
Kherson, where the river flows into the Black sea. These
barges were of magnificent dimensions, floating palaces, containing gorgeous saloons and spacious sleeping apartments.
As they were constructed merely to float upon the rapid current of the stream, impelled by sails when the breeze should
favor, they could easily be provided with all the appliances of
luxury. It is difficult to conceive of a jaunt which would
present more of the attractions of pleasure, than thus to glide
in saloons of elegance, with imperial resources and surrounded
by youth, beauty, genius and rank, for a thousand miles down
the current of one of the wildest and most romantic streams
of Europe.

It was a beautiful sunny morning of May, when the regal
party, accompanied by the music of military bands, and with
floating banners, entered the barges. The river, broad and
deep, rolls on with majestic flow, now through dense forests,
black and gloomy, where the barking of the bear is heard and
wolves hold their nightly carousals; now it winds through
vast prairies hundreds of miles in extent; again it bursts
through mountain barriers where cliffs and crags rise sub

limely thousands of feet in the air; here with precipitous sides
of granite, bleak and scathed by the storms of centuries, and
there with gloomy firs and pines rising to the clouds, where
eagles soar and scream and rear their young. Flocks and
herds now graze upon the banks; here lies the scattered
village, and its whole population, half civilized men, and
matrons and maidens in antique, grotesque attire, crowd the
shores. Now the pinnacles and the battlements of a great
city rise to view. Armies were gathered at several points to
entertain the imperial pleasure-party with all the pomp and
pageantry of war. At Pultowa they witnessed the maneuver-
ings of a battle, with its thunderings and uproar and apparent
carnage—the exact representation of the celebrated battle of
Pultowa, which Peter the Great gained on the spot over
Charles XII. of Sweden.

The Emperor Joseph had been invited to join this party,
and, with his court and retinue, was to meet them at Kherson,
near the mouth of the Dneister, and accompany the empress
to the Crimea. But, perhaps attracted by the splendor of the
water excursion, he struck across the country in a north-east
direction, by the way of Lemberg, some six hundred miles, to
intercept the flotilla and join the party on the river. But the
water of the river suddenly fell, and some hundred miles
above Kherson, the flotilla ran upon a sand bar and could not
be forced over. The empress, who was apprised of the approach of the emperor, too proud to be found in such a
situation, hastily abandoned the flotilla, and taking the carriages which they had with them, drove to meet Joseph.
The two imperial suites were soon united, and they swept on,
a glittering cavalcade, to Kherson. Joseph and Catharine
rode in a carriage together, where they had ample opportunity of talking over all their plans of mutual aggrandizement.
As no one was permitted to listen to their conversations, their
decisions can only be guessed at.

They entered the city of Kherson, then containing about

sixty thousand inhabitants, surrounded by all the magnificence which Russian and Austrian opulence could exhibit. A triumphal arch spanned the gate, upon which was inscribed in letters of gold, "The road to Byzantium." Four days were passed here in revelry. The party then entered the Crimea, and continued their journey as far as Sevastopol, where the empress was delighted to find, within its capacious harbor, many Russian frigates at anchor. Immense sums were expended in furnishing entertainments by the way. At Batcheseria, where the two sovereigns occupied the ancient palace of the khans, they looked out upon a mountain in a blaze of illumination, and apparently pouring lava floods from its artificial volcanic crater.

Joseph returned to Vienna, and immediately there was war—Austria and Russia against Turkey. Joseph was anxious to secure the provinces of Bosnia, Servia, Moldavia and Wallachia, and to extend his empire to the Dneister. With great vigor he made his preparations, and an army of two hundred thousand men, with two thousand pieces of artillery, were speedily on the march down the Danube. Catharine was equally energetic in her preparations, and all the north of Europe seemed to be on the march for the overthrow of the Ottoman empire.

Proverbially fickle are the fortunes of war. Joseph commenced the siege of Belgrade with high hopes. He was ignominiously defeated, and his troops were driven, utterly routed, into Hungary, pursued by the Turks, who spread ruin and devastation widely around them. Disaster followed disaster. Disease entered the Austrian ranks, and the proud army melted away. The emperor himself, with about forty thousand men, was nearly surrounded by the enemy. He attempted a retreat by night. A false alarm threw the troops into confusion and terror. The soldiers, in their bewilderment fired upon each other, and an awful scene of tumult ensued. The emperor, on horseback, endeavored to rally the fugitives, but he was swept away by the crowd, and in the midnight darkness was separated from his suite. Four thousand men perished in this defeat, and much of tne baggage and several guns were lost. The emperor reproached his aides-de-camp with having deserted him. One of them sarcastically replied,

"We used our utmost endeavors to keep up with your imperial majesty, but our horses were not so fleet as yours."

Seventy thousand Austrians perished in this one campaign. The next year, 1789, was, however, as prosperous as this had been adverse. The Turks at Rimnik were routed with enormous slaughter, and their whole camp, with all its treasures, fell into the hands of the victors. Belgrade was fiercely assailed and was soon compelled to capitulate. But Joseph was now upon his dying bed. The tidings of these successes revived him for a few hours, and leaving his sick chamber he was conveyed to the church of St. Stephen, where thanksgivings were offered to God. A festival of three days in Vienna gave expression to the public rejoicing.

England was now alarmed in view of the rapid strides of Austria and Russia, and the cabinet of St. James formed a coalition with Holland and Prussia to assist the Turks. France, now in the midst of her revolutionary struggle, could take no part in these foreign questions. These successes were, however, but a momentary gleam of sunshine which penetrated the chamber of the dying monarch. Griefs innumerable clustered around him. The inhabitants of- the Netherlands rose in successful rebellion and threw off the Austrian yoke. Prussia was making immense preparations for the invasion of Austria. The Hungarians were rising and demanding emancipation from the court of Vienna. These calamities crushed the emperor. He moaned, and wept and died. In his last hours he found much solace in religious observances, devoutly receiving the sacrament of the Lord's Supper, and passing much of his time in prayer. He died on the 20th of February, 1790, in the forty-ninth year of his age, and the tenth of his reign.

Joseph had been sincerely desirous of promoting the best interests of his realms; but had been bitterly disappointed in the result of most of his efforts at reform. Just before he died, he said, "I would have engraven on my tomb, 'Here lies the sovereign who, with the best intentions, never carried a single project into execution.'" He was married twice, but both of his wives, in the prime of youth, fell victims to the small-pox, that awful disease which seems to have been a special scourge in the Austrian royal family. As Joseph II. died without children, the crown passed to his next brother, Leopold, who was then Grand Duke of Tuscany.

Leopold II., at his accession to the throne, was forty-three years of age. He hastened to Vienna, and assumed the government. By prudent acts of conciliation he succeeded in appeasing discontents, and soon accomplished the great object of his desire in securing the election to the imperial throne. He was crowned at Frankfort, October 9, 1790. With frankness very unusual in the diplomacy of kings, he sought friendly relations with all the neighboring powers. To Frederic William, who was now King of Prussia, he wrote:

"In future, I solemnly protest, no views of aggrandizement will ever enter into my political system. I shall doubtless employ all the means in my possession to defend my country, should I unfortunately be driven to such measures; but I will endeavor to give no umbrage. To your majesty in particular, I will act as you act towards me, and will spare no efforts to preserve perfect harmony."

To these friendly overtures, Frederic William responded in a similar spirit; but still there were unsettled points of dispute between the two kingdoms which threatened war, and large armies were gathered on their respective frontiers in preparation for the commencement of hostilities. In 1790, after much correspondence, they came to terms, and articles of peace were signed. At the same time an armistice was concluded with the Turks.

The spirit of liberty which had emancipated the colonies of North America from the aristocratic sway of England, shivering the scepter of feudal tyranny in France, had penetrated Hungary. Leopold was endeavoring to rivet anew the shackles of despotism, when he received a manly remonstrance from an assembly of Hungarians which had been convened as Pest. In the following noble terms they addressed the king.

" The fame, august sovereign, which has preceded you, has declared you a just and gracious prince. It says that you forget not that you are a man ; that you are sensible that the king was made for the people, not the people for the king. From the rights of nations and of man, and from that social compact whence states arose, it is incontestable that the sovereignty originates from the people. This axiom, our parent Nature has impressed on the hearts of all. It is one of those which a just prince (and such we trust your majesty ever will be) can not dispute. It is one of those inalienable imprescriptible rights which the people can not forfeit by neglect or disuse. Our constitution places the sovereignty jointly in the king and people, in such a manner that the remedies necessary to be applied according to the ends of social life, for the security of persons and property, are in the power of the people.

" We are sure, therefore, that at the meeting of the ensuing diet, your majesty will not confine yourself to the objects mentioned in your rescript, but will also restore our freedom to us, in like manner as to the Belgians, who have conquered theirs with the sword. It would be an example big with danger, to teach the world that a people can only protect or regain their liberties by the sword and not by obedience."

But Leopold, trembling at the progress which freedom was making in France, determined to crush this spirit with an iron heel. Their petition was rejected with scorn and menace

With great splendor Leopold entered Presburg, and was crowned King of Hungary on the 10th of November, 1790. Having thus silenced the murmurs in Hungary, and established his authority there, he next turned his attention to the recovery of the Netherlands. The people there, breathing the spirit of French liberty, had, by a simultaneous rising, thrown off the detestable Austrian yoke. Forty-five thousand men were sent to effect their subjugation. On the 20th of November, the army appeared before Brussels. In less than one year all the provinces were again brought under subjection to the Austrian power.

Leopold, thus successful, now turned his attention to France. Maria Antoinette was his sister. He had another sister in the infamous Queen Caroline of Naples. The complaints which came incessantly from Versailles and the Tuilleries filled his ear, touched his affections, and roused his indignation. Twenty-five millions of people had ventured to assert their rights against the intolerable arrogance of the French court. Leopold now gathered his armies to trample those people down, and to replace the scepter of unlimited despotism in the hands of the Bourbons. With sleepless zeal Leopold coöperated with nearly all the monarchs in Europe, in combining a resistless force to crush out from the continent of Europe the spirit of popular liberty. An army of ninety thousand men was raised to coöperate with the French emigrants and all the royalists in France. The king was to escape from Paris, place himself at the head of the emigrants, amounting to more than twenty thousand, rally around his banners all the advocates of the old regime, and then, supported by all the powers of combined Europe, was to march upon Paris, and take a bloody vengeance upon a people who dared to wish to be free. The arrest of Louis XVI. at Varennes deranged this plan. Leopold, alarmed not only by the impending fate of his sister, but lest the principles of

popular liberty, extending from France, should undermine his own throne, wrote as follows to the King of England:

"I am persuaded that your majesty is not unacquainted with the unheard of outrage committed by the arrest of the King of France, the queen my sister and the royal family, and that your sentiments accord with mine on an event which, threatening more atrocious consequences, and fixing the seal of illegality on the preceding excesses, concerns the honor and safety of all governments. Resolved to fulfill what I owe to these considerations, and to my duty as chief of the German empire, and sovereign of the Austrian dominions, I propose to your majesty, in the same manner as I have proposed to the Kings of Spain, Prussia and Naples, as well as to the Empress of Russia, to unite with them, in a concert of measures for obtaining the liberty of the king and his family, and setting bounds to the dangerous excesses of the French Revolution."

The British *people* nobly sympathized with the French in their efforts at emancipation, and the British government dared not *then* shock the public conscience by assailing the patriots in France. Leopold consequently turned to Frederic William of Prussia, and held a private conference with him at Pilnitz, near Dresden, in Saxony, on the 27th of August, 1791. The Count d'Artois, brother of Louis XVI., and who subsequently ascended the French throne as Charles X., joined them in this conference. In the midst of these agitations and schemes Leopold II. was seized with a malignant dysentery, which was aggravated by a life of shameless debauchery, and died on the 1st of March, 1792, in the forty-fifth year of his age, and after a reign of but two years.

Leopold has the reputation of having been, on the whole, a kind-hearted man, but his court was a harem of unblushing profligacy. His broken-hearted wife was compelled to submit to the degradation of daily intimacy with the mistress of her husband. Upon one only of these mistresses the king lavished two hundred thousand dollars in drafts on the bank of Vienna. The sums thus infamously squandered were wrested from the laboring poor. His son, Francis II., who succeeded him upon the throne, was twenty-two years of age. In most affecting terms the widowed queen entreated her son to avoid those vices of his father which had disgraced the monarchy and embittered her whole life.

CHAPTER XXXII.

AUSTRIA AND THE FRENCH REVOLUTIONS.

FROM 1792 TO 1860.

ONE of the first measures of the young monarch, Francis II., was to make the insolent demand of regenerated France, that the old Bourbon monarchy should be restored with all its execrable domination of despotism. This insult to thirty millions of freemen, ordering them to bow the neck again to the yoke of slavery, and to hold out their free hands and free feet that the manacles and the gyves might again be riveted, roused intense indignation. France repelled the insolence with scorn. To enforce this mandate, the Austrian monarch accumulated vast armies, and entered into negotiations with Louis XVI., with the French emigrants, and with the surrounding despotisms. The spirit of the French nation was so roused by these atrocities, that Louis XVI. himself, pallid and woe-stricken, was compelled to declare war against those his friends, with whom he was secretly conferring, that he might by their aid remount his ancient throne of absolutism.

An allied army of Austrians, a hundred and fifty thousand strong, together with twenty thousand French emigrants,

was soon on the march to overthrow the constitutional
monarchy of France, and to restore again to the king the
sceptre of despotism. The British Government, restrained
by popular opinion in England, did not venture openly
to join the allies, but supplied them abundantly with money.
The Duke of Brunswick, who was appointed commander-
in-chief of the allied army, issued a manifesto, dated Cob-
lentz, July 15, 1792, in which the French nation were commanded to restore the Bourbons immediately to their former
absolute power, and to punish all who had taken any part
in the movement for constitutional liberty. At the same
time the duke threatened to hang every Frenchman who
should resist the invaders, and to burn every city or village
which should present any opposition to his march.

Austria, Russia, Prussia, and England were in heart united
to enforce this proclamation. France, in unspeakable peril,
was stung to desperation. The king, who was known to be
in co-operation with the invaders, was dethroned and imprisoned, and finally executed. . The aristocrats, who were waiting
to join the enemy, were massacred. England now openly
joined the allies, placed herself at their head, and declared
war against France. The exultant battalions of the foe
crossed the French frontiers, and, sweeping resistlessly on
with sword and flame, arrived within a few days' march of
Paris. The consternation in the capital was terrible. The
whole French people rose *en masse*, and rushed, like wolves at
bay, upon the enemy; and they were driven, broken, bleeding,
and breathless, from the kingdom.

At the same time in which these scenes were transpiring,
Austria, dominant in Italy, had gathered large armies in
Venetia, Lombardy, and Piedmont, and, in alliance with
Naples and Switzerland, was preparing to invade France on
her Alpine frontier.

All the States of Northern Italy were completely overawed by the imperial court at Vienna, and were compelled
to put their troops on the march at the summons of the
Austrian bugles. All despotic Europe was now combined

against republican France. Month after month the terrible conflict raged, crimsoning the waves of the Rhine with blood, and waking the clangor of war amidst the solitudes of the Alps. The strife was prosecuted with unparalleled ferocity; for the most deadly passions of the human heart were called into action.

At length the young general, Napoleon Bonaparte, was intrusted with the defence of France on the Alpine frontier. His movement was like the sweep of the mountain whirlwind. The storm of war gathered blackness for a moment among the cliffs of the Alps, and then burst with flash and peal upon the plains of Piedmont. The Austrians were scattered like autumnal leaves; and the victor, master of Piedmont, unfurled his banners over the battlements of Turin. Not a moment was allowed for repose. The broken bands of the Austrians rallied with recruited strength on the plains of Lombardy. Terrific and awfully sanguinary was the strife. But again the imperial legions of despotism were trampled down by the heroic patriots struggling for liberty. The Austrians, in dismay, fled into Venetia. Napoleon pursued them. In terror they crossed the Tagliamento, and retreated from Italy. Still Napoleon, with fearlessness which amazed Europe, followed on, chasing the multitudinous foe through defiles and forests, over rivers and plains and mountain-ranges, pelting them with artillery, charging them with cavalry, and scattering bullets like hailstones through their panting ranks. The Archduke Charles, brother of the Emperor of Austria, was in command of the retreating army. Napoleon, who was fighting only for peace, anxious to arrest the flow of blood in this hour of triumph, ventured to take the initiative in imploring a cessation of hostilities. He addressed the following letter to the archduke : —

"GENERAL-IN-CHIEF, — Have we not slain enough of our fellow-men? Have we not inflicted a sufficiency of woes upon humanity? Europe, which took up arms against the French Republic, has laid them aside. Your nation alone remains hostile; and blood is about to flow more copiously than

ever. Whatever may be the result of this campaign, many
thousand men must perish; and, after all, we must come to
an accommodation. If the overture which I have the honor
to make shall be the means of saving a single life, I shall be
more proud of the civic crown, which I shall be conscious of
having deserved, than of all the melancholy glory which military success can confer."

The Austrian archduke replied, "In the duty assigned to
me, there is no power either to scrutinize the causes, or to terminate the duration, of the war. I am not invested with
any authority in that respect, and therefore cannot enter into
any negotiation for peace."

> "The war, that for a space did fail,
> Now trebly thundering swelled the gale."

The pursuers and the pursued rushed on with hot haste
amidst all the uproar, confusion, and carnage of war, until
Napoleon, from the heights around Leoben, with his glass,
could discern the towers of Vienna. All was consternation
in the Austrian capital. The emperor and his court fled, like
deer, to the wilds of Hungary, at the same time despatching
ambassadors to Napoleon imploring peace. It was all France
wanted. The preliminaries were soon settled. By the treaty
of Campo Formio, which ensued, France extended her frontier
to the Rhine as a safeguard against future attacks; and Austria
recognized the Cisalpine republic which Napoleon had established in Italy, consisting of Lombardy, Modena, and several
smaller States. Napoleon was anxious to liberate Venice from
Austria; but he could not accomplish this without perpetuat-
ing a cruel war for an object in which France had no especial
interest, and during which he might lose all that he had thus
far gained.

England, the undisputed mistress of the sea, still continued
the conflict against republican France. The expedition to
Egypt was organized; and Napoleon was placed at the head
of it to attack England in India, the only vulnerable point
then presented. Napoleon had hardly left France ere England

succeeded in forming a new coalition against the infant republic. Austria joined it eagerly, sent vast armies into Italy, and soon recovered the provinces which Napoleon had liberated. Again the combined armies of Austria and of the re-enslaved States of Italy were climbing the Alps to pour down upon the plains of France, while the veteran battalions of all Northern Europe were crowding to the Rhine. England was energetic with both fleet and army in co-operating in this most iniquitous crusade which was ever waged.

"The English fleet," says the British "Westminster Review," "was ordered to Genoa to support the enemies of France; but it was in defiance of English public opinion. There is no fact in our history more easy of proof than that the voice of universal England was raised in protest against being dragged into war with France. The lord mayor and corporation of London petitioned against the war. At Islington fifty thousand persons met to demand neutrality. Thus, while the British fleet was covering Austrian movements against Bonaparte on the shores of Genoa, the English people at home were praying and petitioning in vain against the war with the French Republic."

Napoleon, having suddenly returned from Egypt and assumed the consular command, sent the flower of the French army, under General Moreau, to beat off the foes of France upon the Rhine. With amazing celerity and secrecy he assembled another army of sixty thousand raw recruits at Dijon, near the foot of the Alps. Before putting his armies in motion he wrote to both the King of England and the Emperor of Austria, imploring peace. A contemptuous and insulting refusal was the only reply.

Napoleon crossed the Alps, fell upon the Austrians at Marengo; and they bit the dust. On the gory field, surrounded by the dead and the dying and all the melancholy wrecks of war, the victor thus again addressed the Emperor of Austria, —

"SIRE, — It is on the field of battle, amid the sufferings of a multitude of wounded, and surrounded by fifteen thousand corpses, that I beseech your Majesty to listen to the voice of humanity, and not to suffer two brave nations to cut each other's throats for interests not their own. It is my part to press this upon your Majesty, being upon the very theatre of war. Your Majesty's heart cannot feel it so keenly as does mine."

The Austrian army, utterly routed, was at the mercy of the conqueror. Generously Napoleon permitted them to return unmolested to their homes, upon the sole condition that they would quietly withdraw from Italy. Austria now desired peace; but she was so entangled with her alliance with England, that she could not enter into a treaty with France without the consent of the court of St. James. That consent could not be obtained; and the Austrian troops, in obedience to the coalition which England had organized, accumulated her troops in powerful array upon the Rhine. On the 3d of December, 1800, in a dark and stormy night, General Moreau, with sixty thousand Frenchmen, encountered the Archduke John, at the head of seventy thousand Austrians, in the forest of Hohenlinden. A terrible battle ensued.

When the morning dawned, twenty thousand mutilated bodies were left upon the field, with gory locks frozen to the snow. The Austrians, utterly routed, fled down the valley of the Danube towards Vienna. Moreau followed them like an avenging spirit, sweeping them down with war's fierce blasts. He had arrived within thirty miles of the panic-stricken capital, when the emperor, trembling for his crown, sent commissioners imploring peace. "It is for that alone," Moreau replied, "that we are fighting."

Austria was thus compelled to sheathe the sword without consulting England. Joseph Bonaparte as the ambassador of Napoleon, and Count Cobentzel as the plenipotentiary of Austria, met at Lunéville. It was in February, 1801. Again Austria acknowledged the Rhine as the boundary of France, and recognized the independence of the Batavian, Helvetic, Cisalpine, and Ligurian Republics, consenting that they should be permitted to choose whatever form of government they might prefer. These free governments had been gradually established during the progress of the war.

But England, sweeping all seas with her invincible fleet, still continued the strife. Not a fishing-boat could in safety leave a French cove. Every port in France was liable to bombardment. At length the clamor of the English *people* compelled the government to the peace of Amiens. But the ministry were eager to renew the war, and in eighteen months did so without any proclamation of hostilities, seizing two hundred French ships, containing fifteen millions of dollars, which were floating, unsuspicious of danger, in English ports. War was resumed with redoubled ferocity. Napoleon now resolved to transport his army to London, that in the British capital he might compel his inflexible foes to grant peace to Europe.

The British Government, alarmed in view of the preparations Napoleon was making at Boulogne, through the influence of enormous bribes organized a new coalition. Austria, Russia, and Sweden were thus induced to raise an army of five hundred thousand men to embarrass Napoleon by suddenly attacking him in the rear. England agreed to pay annually six million of dollars for every hundred thousand men the allies raised. Austria, without any declaration of war, leading an immense army, followed by the solid battalions of Russia and Sweden, for the third time commenced her march upon Paris, hoping stealthily to plunge the dagger into Napoleon's back. But Napoleon was not caught sleeping. Twenty thousand carriages were instantly in motion, transporting his army from the shores of the channel to the banks of the Rhine. In a brief address to the senate, as Napoleon left Paris, he said, —

" Senators, I am about to leave Paris to place myself at the head of the army. The wishes of the eternal enemies of the continent are accomplished. Hostilities have commenced in the midst of Germany. Austria and Russia have united with England, and our generation is involved anew in the calamities of war. A few days ago I cherished the hope that peace would not be disturbed. But the Austrian army has passed the Inn. All my hopes of peace are vanished."

The world-renowned campaign of Ulm and Austerlitz

ensued. In twenty days the Austrian army was annihilated.
As thirty-six thousand Austrian troops at Ulm laid down
their arms before the conqueror, Napoleon said to the dejected
officers, —

"Gentlemen, your master wages against me an unjust war.
I say it candidly, I know not for what I am fighting : I know
not what he requires of me."

Without allowing his foes one hour to recover from their
panic, Napoleon pressed on to Vienna. Like a torrent he
swept the valley of the Danube; and in forty days from the
time he left Boulogne, his army was encamped in the squares
of the Austrian capital, and Napoleon was occupying the
palaces of the emperor. Francis, with the fragments of his
army, had fled to join the Russians, who were hurrying to his
relief. The situation of Napoleon was now perilous in the
extreme. He was nearly a thousand miles from Paris. Four
hundred and fifty thousand men, from the various points of
the compass, were on the march to crush him. The Emperor
of Russia was at the distance of but a few days' march in the
north, at the head of one hundred thousand men, hurrying to
join other vast bodies of men in their advance upon Vienna.
The blasts of winter were already sweeping the whitened hills.

Napoleon, urging his troops to forced marches, to prevent
the junction of the foe, met the Russians and the broken
bands of the Austrians, with the two emperors, Alexander and
Francis, at their head, upon the field of Austerlitz. It was
the 1st of December, 1805. In one short terrific tempest of
war, the allied army was destroyed. Alexander, with the
bleeding, shattered remnants of his bands, commenced a precipitate retreat toward Russia. The Emperor Francis was
hopelessly ruined, and had nowhere to retreat to, unless he
abandoned his realms. Thus humiliated, he sought an interview with Napoleon, and met him, at the fire of his bivouac,
on the side of a bleak hill. Conscious of guilt, and deeply
dejected, he attempted an ignoble apology for his crime by
saying, —

"The English are a nation of merchants. In order to

secure for themselves the commerce of the world, they are willing to set the continent in flames."

Napoleon, anxious for peace, was exceedingly moderate in his terms. He allowed the Emperor of Russia to retire unmolested, simply exacting from him the promise no longer to prosecute hostile movements against France. From Austria, also, he took for himself not one foot of territory. Francis paid the expenses of the war, and consented that the electors of Bavaria and Wurtemberg, who were friends and allies of Napoleon, should be elevated to the rank of kings. The republican kingdom of Italy was also enlarged, and rendered more powerful by the annexation of Venice, Austria receiving in exchange the electorate of Salzburg.

Napoleon thus rewarded his friends, and strengthened the barriers which were to protect France from those great northern despotisms, Russia, Prussia, and Austria, which were instinctively hostile to the establishment of any free institutions on the soil of Europe.

The Emperor of France had hardly returned to Paris from this campaign, when England formed another coalition against him, uniting Russia and Prussia in the alliance. This coalition led to the campaigns of Jena and Eylau. Notwithstanding the solemn treaties into which Austria had entered, Francis was eager to join the foes of France, when he thought Napoleon was crippled beyond redemption on the distant banks of the Vistula. Elated with the hope that Napoleon was so crowded by his foes, that he could not resent the outrage, Austria began to arm, preparing to cut off the retreat of the French. To meet this peril, Napoleon immediately ordered another army of a hundred thousand men to be raised in France, and thoroughly equipped for war. He then sent, through his minister, the following wonderfully frank communication to the Emperor Francis, —

"France understands perfectly the intentions of Austria. To save Austria from calamity, I explain myself with frankness. France is abundantly prepared to meet any force Austria can raise against her. If the emperor wishes to send officers to ascertain our strength, we engage to show them the depots, the camps of reserve, and the divisions on the march. They shall see, that, independently of the hundred thousand French already in Germany, a second army of one hundred thousand is preparing to cross the Rhine to check any hostile movement on the part of Vienna."

This unexpected revelation of the ability of France to punish the contemplated perfidy caused Austria to drop her arms. The peace of Tilsit detached Russia and Prussia from the coalition with England, and the British cabinet was again left to struggle alone in the attempt to restore the Bourbons to their despotic throne. Still Austria, chagrined by reiterated defeats, and humiliated by the loss of Italy, was eager for some favorable opportunity to renew the strife with France, hoping to regain lost honor and lost territory. The wished-for opportunity soon occurred. Napoleon was embroiled in the Spanish war, when Austria again listened to England, and again entered into a coalition against France. Napoleon was driving the army of Sir John Moore out of the Spanish peninsula, when he received the tidings that Austria was preparing for another assault.

"It seems," said he, "that the waters of oblivion flow past Vienna. They have forgotten the lessons of experience. They want new ones: they shall have them; and this time they shall be terrible. I do not desire war. I have no interest in it."

"Napoleon," says Thiers, "was sincere, and spoke the truth, in asserting that he did not desire war, but that he would wage it tremendously if forced into it."

With an army of two hundred thousand men, Austria commenced the conflict by crossing the Inn, and invading the territory of Napoleon's ally, the King of Bavaria. As usual, the Austrian emperor conducted with the utmost perfidy, commencing hostilities without any declaration of war. Napoleon was not taken by surprise. At midnight, in Paris, he received intelligence of the movements of the foe. He immediately took carriage to place himself at the head of his army, saying to his friends as he bade them adieu, —

"Very well. Behold us once more at Vienna. Since they force me to it, they shall have war to their hearts' content."

The Austrians had five hundred thousand troops in the field, two hundred thousand of whom had crossed the Inn. Napoleon met the foe at Echmul, and scattered them in dismay before his impetuous charges. As they fled, Napoleon pursued them, and, overtaking them at Ratisbon, chastised them again with a dripping sword. He then chased them down the Danube to Vienna. For ten hours he bombarded the doomed city, throwing into it three thousand shells, until it capitulated. The Austrian emperor and his army fled across the Danube. Napoleon pursued them closely, and, after the sanguinary conflicts of Essling and Aspern, again brought Austria upon her knees on the field of Wagram. At the close of this decisive battle, when the Austrian empire was again at the mercy of Napoleon, all the French marshals were assembled in his tent to consider the proposal Austria had presented for an armistice. The question was earnestly discussed.

"Austria," said one party, "is the irreconcilable enemy of the popular government in France. Unless deprived of the power of again injuring us, she will never cease to violate the most solemn treaties, whenever there is a prospect of advantage. It is indispensable to put an end to these coalitions perpetually springing up against us, by dividing Austria, which is the centre of them all."

"Should the Austrian emperor," replied the other party, "retreat to the Bohemian mountains, Russia and Prussia will probably join the coalition. A great and final conflict is evidently approaching between the North and the South. It is of the utmost importance to conciliate Austria, that she may be detached from the coalition."

Napoleon listened thoughtfully, and then said, "Gentlemen, enough blood has been shed. I accept the armistice."

Francis resorted to every species of trickery to prolong the negotiations, hoping for aid from the English, who had landed in great strength at the mouth of the Scheldt; but at length the treaty was signed on the 14th of October, 1809. It was the fourth treaty Austria had made with France within sixteen years. In this treaty of Vienna, which Napoleon negotiated while occupying the palaces of the Austrian emperor, the frontiers of Bavaria were strengthened and extended, so that this ally of France might not be again so defencelessly exposed to Austrian invasion. Saxony received an additional population, amounting to a million five hundred thousand. The kingdom of Italy also received important accessions of territory, that it might present a more impregnable front to its despotic and gigantic neighbor. France strengthened her allies, but added not a rood of ground to her own domain.

"When compared," says Lockhart, "with the signal triumphs of the campaign of Wagram, the terms on which Napoleon signed the peace were universally looked upon as remarkable for moderation."

Soon after this, Austria became intimately allied with France by the marriage of Maria Louisa, the daughter of the emperor, with Napoleon. It was supposed that this measure of State policy would secure the peace of Europe by preventing any further acts of hostility on the part of Austria. The divorce of Josephine was the great mistake, and, in the sight of God, the great sin, of Napoleon's life. Savary, the Duke of Rovego, who was familiar with all the details, thus describes the motives which led to this sublime tragedy : —

"Nothing can be more true," says he, "than that the sacrifice of the object of his affections was the most painful that Napoleon experienced throughout his life. A feeling of personal ambition was supposed to be the mainspring of all his actions. This was a very mistaken impression. With great reluctance he had altered the form of government; and, if he had not been apprehensive that the State would again fall a prey to those dissensions which are inseparable from an elective form of government, he would not have changed an order of things which permanently secured those principles. He desired to hand his work down to posterity. He could not be blind to the fact that the perpetual warfare into which a jealousy of his strength had plunged him had in reality no other object than his own downfall, because with him must necessarily crumble that gigantic power which was no longer upheld by the revolutionary energy he had himself repressed.

"The emperor had no children. He dismissed the idea of appointing Eugene his heir, because he had nearer relations; and it would have given rise to dissensions which it was his principal object to avoid. He also considered the necessity in which he was placed of forming an alliance sufficiently powerful, in order that, in the event of his system being at any time threatened, that alliance might be a resting-point, and save it from total ruin. He likewise hoped that it would be the means of putting an end to that series of wars, of which he was desirous, above all things, of avoiding a recurrence. These were the motives which determined him to break a union so long contracted. He wished it less for himself than for the purpose of interesting a powerful State in the maintenance of an order of things established in France."

The marriage-ceremony of Napoleon and Maria Louisa was celebrated in Vienna on the 11th of May, 1810. The Archduke Charles, brother of the Emperor Francis, stood as proxy for Napoleon. A little more than two years from this time occurred the dreadful disaster of the campaign of Russia. A French army of nearly half a million was buried beneath the snows of the North. Europe again sprang to arms to crush, in the person of Napoleon, free institutions. With almost supernatural energy the French emperor raised another army, and, with fearful odds against him, was holding at bay the armies of England, Russia, and Prussia upon the plains of Dresden. Austria seized upon this occasion again to join the allies, that she might recover what she had lost. Francis raised an army of two hundred thousand men; and with the ringing of bells, the explosion of artillery, and the flight of rockets, on the 12th of August, 1813, this proud army joined the ranks of Napoleon's already outnumbering foes. Napoleon was on the banks of the Elbe with but two hundred and sixty thousand troops. The allies surrounded him five hundred thousand strong. The battles of Dresden and Leipsic en-

sued. Napoleon fought with heroism which amazed the world
but finally, overwhelmed with numbers, fell.

The allies marched to Paris, leading the Bourbons behind
their guns, and replaced them upon the throne of France.
Napoleon was sent to Elba; and Maria Louisa, with her son,
taken captive by her own father, was conveyed by a guard of
soldiers to Vienna. The sublime drama of "The Hundred
Days" soon ensued, followed by the disaster of Waterloo.
Napoleon was entombed in the glooms of St. Helena; and
despotism was re-established all over Europe.

The victorious despots met in congress at Vienna in September, 1814, to divide the spoil. There were present at this
congress the Emperors of Austria and Russia, the Kings of
Prussia, Denmark, Bavaria, and Wurtemberg, and also a large
number of princes and dukes. The Pope was represented by
Cardinal Consalvi. England sent as her representatives Lord
Castlereagh, the Duke of Wellington, Lords Cathcart, Clan-
carty, and Stuart. The Bourbons of France were represented
by Prince Talleyrand, and several others of the most illustrious of the *ancienne noblesse*. Ambassadors from Spain, Portugal, and Sweden, were also admitted to the deliberations.
Prince Metternich, who has been justly styled, "The incarna-
tion of Austrian despotism," presided. The result of the long
deliberations was summed up in one hundred and twenty-one
articles, which were signed on the 9th of June, 1815. By
these treaties the Austrian despotism received vast accessions
of strength. The constitutional kingdoms of Italy were annihilated; and the woe-stricken Italians, bound hand and foot,
were surrendered again to their former masters. Austria received Venetia, Lombardy, Tuscany, Modena, Parma, and
various other minor States. Naples was restored, re-enslaved,
to the infamous Ferdinand. Austria constructed Venetia and
Lombardy into a kingdom, over which she placed one of her
archdukes as viceroy. The remaining States she parcelled out
among her dukes and princes. Again the repose of the slave-
plantation was spread over Europe. In reference to the acts
of this congress of the allies, "The British Quarterly" says, —

"The treaties of Vienna, though the most desperate efforts have been made by the English diplomatists to embalm them as monuments of political wisdom, are fast becoming as dead as those of Westphalia. In fact, they should be got under ground with all possible despatch; for no compacts, so worthless, so wicked, so utterly subversive of the rights of humanity, are to be found in the annals of nations."

After the perpetration of this great crime, Austria remained comparatively quiet, with occasional outbreaks but no great change, until the year 1836. On the 8th of March of this year, the Emperor Francis died. Regarding his throne as the great bulwark of absolutism, he ever manifested the most relentless hostility to constitutional freedom. It is reported, that when his physician, Baron Stifft, in a congratulatory address upon his health, remarked, —

"There is nothing, sire, like a good physical constitution," the emperor nervously interrupted him, exclaiming, —

"What do you say? Let me never hear that word again! Say my *robust health, strong bodily system,* but never say my *constitution.* I have no constitution; and I never will have one."

The death of Francis produced no change in the national policy. He died at the age of sixty-seven, having outlived three of his four wives, and having manifested, it is said, at the death of each, about as much concern as "old Bluebeard himself." Ferdinand I. succeeded Francis, and governed his vast and discordant estates with ordinary ability until the revolution in Paris of 1848, which overthrew Louis Philippe, and introduced to France first the republic, and then the empire under Louis Napoleon.

This immense revolution, overthrowing a despotism wielded for the benefit of the aristocracy, and introducing in its stead a despotism which maintained the cause of the people, shook all the realms of Austria like an earthquake. The significance of this revolution in France has not generally been understood in the United States. It has been generally regarded merely as a change of masters, France exchanging the despotic

Bourbons for the equal despotism of Louis Napoleon.   Instead
of this, it was a radical change of administration, overthrowing
the reign of aristocratic privilege, and introducing the reign
of republican equality.   In the present state of France, it is
said that no government can stand which is not upheld by the
energies of despotism.   The people have, then, only to choose
between a despotism upholding the assumptions of the aristocracy, and a despotism maintaining popular rights.   Of course,
they choose the latter.

Thus the empire in France was re-established by the masses
of the people.   They drove aristocratic absolutism from the
throne, and placed Louis Napoleon, the representative of de-
mocracy, upon it; and they cheerfully gave into his hands
enough of despotic power to enable him to maintain their
rights against the immense pressure of all the nobles of France,
combined with the sympathies of all the monarchies of Europe.
With skill and fidelity never surpassed, Louis Napoleon has
proved himself equal to the trust.   Had his government been
less decisive and energetic, long ago popular rights would have
been trampled in the mire.   Under his sway, France has risen
to be at the head of all the European monarchies.

A few years ago Louis Napoleon needed money.   He appealed to the people for a loan of one hundred and fifty millions of dollars.   In crowds they rushed to his treasury, bringing with them the almost incredible sum of nearly eight hundred millions of dollars, — five times as much as he asked for,
or could consent to receive.   This one fact sufficiently illus-
trates how differently the people regard the dictatorial power
they have placed, for their own defence, in the hands of Napoleon, from the despotic power swayed by the Bourbons.

A revolution of so marked a character taking place in
France, of course, agitated Europe to its centre.   The Austrian provinces in Italy immediately arose to strike for freedom.
By the treaty of Vienna, Sardinia had been constituted nominally an independent kingdom, embracing the Island of Sardinia, and the continental provinces of Piedmont, Savoy, and
Nice.   This feeble kingdom was not allowed to retain the free

institutions which it had enjoyed as a part of the kingdom of Italy under the protection of Napoleon; but it was watched with an eagle eye, and was overawed by Austrian despotism on the one side, and by the re-established Bourbon despotism on the other. As the Italian provinces of Lombardy and Venetia rose to break from their Austrian masters, the Piedmontese, sympathizing with them, and also wishing to escape from the despotism ever brooding over their realm, marched to the aid of their brethren.

The Austrians were driven out of Lombardy, and across the Mincio. Venetia threw off the hated yoke, and declared for independence. Hungary rose, almost as one man, demanding the restoration of their ancient constitutional rights. The doom of the hoary despotism seemed to be sealed; but the sympathies of all the courts of Europe, excepting that of France, and even including England, were hostile to these peoples struggling for constitutional rights. In the pages of Sir Archibald Alison, the court historian, we meet with the most painful demonstration of this fact.

"It is," says "The Edinburgh Review," "utterly repugnant to the first principles of our own policy and to every page in our own history, to lend encouragement to the separation of nationalities from other empires, which we fiercely resist when it threatens to dismember our own."

Thus frowned upon by all Europe, and swept by the disciplined armies which Austria poured down through all the passes of the Tyrolese Alps, Italy was again subdued. Radetzky, in command of these forces, with tiger-like ferocity desolated the land with fire and sword. Sardinia was compelled to make a humiliating peace. The unhappy Italians were punished as slaves are punished who attempt an insurrection with partial success, but with final defeat.

The conflict in Hungary, and around the very throne of the Austrian emperor, demands a more particular notice. The intelligence of the revolution in Paris reached Vienna on the 1st of March, 1848. The whole population of the city was thrown into a state of the most intense excitement. The professors of the University of Vienna, with the students, two thousand in number, accompanied by an immense concourse of the people, crowded the imperial palace, presenting a petition to the emperor, respectfully but firmly demanding that the government should "introduce measures of reform tempered by wisdom." They implored a constitution which should confer religious liberty, freedom of the press, and a national legislature, in which the people should be represented.

Prince Metternich, who had ever been the great bulwark of despotism, was the especial object of popular hatred. In terror he fled from his palace, scarcely venturing to lay aside his disguise, or to look behind him, until he found refuge in London. Ferdinand, paralyzed and overpowered by the popular feeling, which in such resistless billows was dashing against his throne, granted all the patriots asked. The ministry was changed, a national guard organized, and despotic Austria seemed on the eve of regeneration. The people, demanding only a *constitutional* instead of an *absolute* monarchy, had no disposition to dethrone the emperor, and least of all did they desire to run the risk of attempting to exchange the monarchy for a republic. Gratified at the compliance of the emperor with their reasonable requests, they rallied around him with enthusiasm, greeting him with applause whenever he appeared. This event, so animating to every lover of human freedom, Sir Archibald Alison describes: —

"As a convulsion which brought Austria to the brink of ruin, all but swept it from the book of nations, and reduced it to the humiliation of invoking the perilous intervention of a foreign power."

The intelligence of the revolution in Paris reached Presburg, the capital of Hungary, when the diet of that kingdom was in session. Kossuth and the leading advocates of reform immediately sent an address to the Emperor Ferdinand, petitioning for a redress of grievances in Hungary. The Hungarian patriots were willing that Hungary should remain under the executive of the Austrian emperor: they only demanded that they should have a legislature or parliament of their own, with freedom of the press and of religious worship. Such a request was reasonable and moderate in the extreme.

Kossuth, accompanied by one hundred and fifty Hungarian gentlemen, repaired to Vienna, and presented this petition to the emperor. Immense crowds in Vienna greeted this delegation with shouts of " Long live Kossuth ! " The emperor, conscious of his powerlessness, promised to grant their just demands. A constitution was adopted in Hungary, abolishing all aristocratic privileges, and making both prince and peasant equal in the eye of the law. The peasants in Hungary had long been feudal slaves, attached to the soil, and transferred with the estates, and deprived of all political rights. Kossuth and his friends carried in the Hungarian diet a decree of absolute and universal emancipation.

" This sudden transition," it is recorded, " of the peasantry from servitude to civil and political liberty, was nowhere stained in Hungary by riots or disorder, as was feared, or perhaps hoped, by the court party : on the contrary, on most of the estates the peasantry contributed, by their own free will, to the work of the landlords during the time of mowing and harvesting, that the crops might not be damaged through any difficulty in securing hired laborers for those agricultural operations."

This beneficent revolution introduced the sclavonic races to all the constitutional rights and privileges which had been so long withheld from them. The Magyars were consistent; and, in acquiring liberty for themselves, they conferred the same inestimable boon upon the enslaved races.

But Ferdinand, while making these forced concessions, and assuming content, was perfidiously preparing for resistance. An army was raised and sent into Hungary, and it endeavored to take possession of Prague. The Hungarians resisted. The Austrians planted their batteries on some neighboring heights, and for forty-eight hours bombarded the wretched city, until it presented the most awful aspect of smouldering ruins and blood. The patriots for a time were crushed ; but the cry of indignation was so loud and fierce, not only throughout Hun gary, but through all the streets of Vienna, that Ferdinand, in terror and disguise, escaped from his capital, and fled to Innspruck, a strong fortress in the Tyrol, three hundred miles south-west from Vienna.

The flight of the emperor created throughout Austria a sensation hardly exceeded by that excited in France by the flight of Louis XVI. It was a declaration of war against the people, and against all popular reform. The standing army of Austria, ever the pliant tool of despotism, was now called into requisition. The imperial troops commenced, in Hungary, a war of devastation such as earth has not often witnessed. The sky through the wide horizon was illumined by night with the fires of burning villages, and was obscured by day by the smoke of these vast conflagrations.

As we have before mentioned, there were two principal races in Hungary, — the Sclaves and the Magyars, descendants of ancient Gothic tribes. The Magyar race had been decidedly in the ascendency, the superior race, in the possession of all the political power; while the Sclaves, greatly depressed, occupied the position of a servile peasantry. Nearly all the imperial troops drafted from Hungary were taken from the Sclaves, who composed about one-third of the Hungarian population. With the most atrocious perfidy, Austrian gold was lavished to incite the Sclaves to rise against the Magyars, though there was no shadow of a plea for such action, the Sclavonic races having been reinstated in all the rights and privileges of manhood. Many of the Sclaves, ignorant and debased, were induced to enlist in the army of the emperor.

The emperor now returned to Vienna, and, with his troops ravaging Hungary, he issued an edict demanding the expulsion of Kossuth, the leader of the patriots, from the Hungarian ministry. Kossuth was thus compelled to resign, and his post was assigned to a partisan of the emperor. But the people rallied around Kossuth, who had been sacrificed for his love for them; and the cabinet at Vienna resolved with all the horrors of war to bring Hungary again into abject submission to its sway.

On the 11th of September, 1848, an army of thirty thousand men, under the Austrian general Jellachich, crossed the Drave, the frontier river of Hungary, and marched upon Pesth. With singular unanimity, nearly all Hungary sprang to arms in self-defence. The troops were placed under the command of Georgey, a Hungarian noble, who had espoused the popular cause. But Kossuth was the intellectual head of the nation, and the soul of the war which now ensued. His genius inspired every movement; and the Hungarians rallied at his call with enthusiasm which perhaps has never been equalled. One hundred thousand men were speedily enrolled, and on the march to repel the invaders.

The heads of the two armies came together in many bloody conflicts; and the Austrians, routed again and again, were compelled to sue for an armistice. The popular party in Vienna were in strong sympathy with the Hungarians; and it was with manifest reluctance that the Austrian troops could be brought to fight against those who asked only for constitutional liberty. Under these circumstances, a new revolution swept the streets of Vienna; and in one day of frenzied uproar and carnage the monarchy was again laid prostrate at the feet of the people. But though the populace, in their just and wild wrath, could destroy an execrable despotism, they had not sufficient intelligence and virtue to construct a stable government upon its ruins.

A "committee of public safety" was appointed, at whose demand the emperor was compelled to dismiss his aristocratic ministry, and appoint a popular one in its stead. The emperor also recalled his proclamation against Hungary, removed the detested Jellachich from the command of the army, and granted a general amnesty for all political offences. Again the emperor sought refuge in flight. All the troops who could be relied upon were speedily assembled around the emperor, from their wide dispersion throughout the empire, and were ordered to march upon Vienna. From the steeples of the city the dismayed inhabitants soon beheld an army of sixty thousand men — infantry, artillery, and cavalry — approaching to wreak upon them merciless vengeance. In a state of indescribable consternation the whole city sprang to arms. On the morning of the 20th of October, 1848, the bombardment commenced. The roar of artillery, the shouts of battle, the bursting of shells, the shrieks of the terrified, the cry of the wounded, the frenzy of women and children, ruin, conflagration, blood, all presented a spectacle which the most vivid imagination cannot conceive.

All the day and all the night the horrible storm continued. The city was now on fire in twenty places. The streets were clogged with the mangled bodies of the dead. The flames, spreading rapidly, and flashing to the skies, threatened to consume the whole city and all its inmates. Shells, like hailstones, were falling everywhere, and there was no place of safety. The city could no longer be defended, and was compelled to capitulate. The imperial army, composed mostly of mercenary troops, marched in ferociously, and took military possession of the city. All hopes of popular reform were now at an end; and the old despotism was reconstructed, and cemented in the blood of the people.

But Ferdinand I. was now weary of his crown, which to him had proved truly a crown of thorns. He resolved to abdicate; and as he had no children, and as his brother Charles refused the perilous gift of sovereignty, the sceptre was transferred to Francis Joseph, the son of Charles, a young man eighteen years of age. It was the 2d of December, 1848. The young emperor, hoping to quiet the restlessness of his re-enslaved people, promised to confer upon them a liberal constitution, — a promise which it became subsequently manifest that he had no intention of performing. The inhabitants of Vienna, exhausted by war, in submission, accepted the promise.

But the inhabitants of Hungary, while willing to acknowledge the sovereignty of the emperor, still demanded a parliament of their own. The kingdom of Hungary contained one hundred and thirty-three thousand square miles, being one-tenth larger than England and Ireland united, and numbered a population of about thirteen million. They firmly claimed, that, while they cordially accepted the executive authority of the Emperor of Austria, they should enjoy a Hungarian legislature. But the young emperor, Francis Joseph, flushed with the subjugation of his subjects in Austria proper, treated the demand as insolence. He abolished the Hungarian constitution, dissolved the legislative bodies, and threw into prison the Hungarian commissioners sent to confer with him. At the same time the imperial army, which by a bombardment had so successfully chastised Vienna into subjection, was sent into Hungary to inflict the same doom upon Pesth, then the Hungarian capital.

All the horrors of civil war now desolated Hungary. Jellachich, the Austrian commander-in-chief, issued a proclamation, in whieh he threatened to shoot every Hungarian taken with arms in his hands, and to demolish every town which should present the least resistance. As the imperial army with its veteran soldiers approached the capital, the Hungarian Government, with Kossuth at its head, retired to Debreczin, about two hundred miles east of Pesth. It was on the 5th of January, 1849, when this retreat commenced; and the Hungarian army, encumbered with thousands of citizens, women and children, suffered all that mortals can endure, multitudes perishing of cold, starvation, and misery. The Austrians took possession of Pesth; but, with the mercury only five degrees above zero, they did not venture to pursue the retiring Hungarians.

In this dark hour a speech from Kossuth seemed to electrify all Hungary; and the nation, as one man, sprang to arms. Month after month the war raged all over the kingdom with varied success. But gradually the Hungarians were gaining ground. In battle after battle they were driving back their invaders; and Austria found that her mercenary troops were not able to crush a heroic nation roused to despair. Francis Joseph then appealed to Russia for help. The great northern autocrat listened eagerly to the appeal; for Nicholas feared, that, should the Hungarians secure constitutional liberty, the **Polanders might demand the same boon. There was not a**

W

single nation in Europe in sympathy with the Hungarians, excepting France; and France was then menaced with a coalition of all Europe to restore that aristocratic *régime* which for a fourth time she had rejected. Even the British Government, through Lord Palmerston, sanctioned the intervention of Russia in this cruel war against Hungary, assuming that the Hungarians were subjects in revolt against their lawful sovereign.

The serried battalions of Russia were instantly on the march, a hundred and sixty-two thousand strong, to join the vast armies which Austria had raised, the two most powerful despotisms on the globe combining against a heroic people, demanding only a constitutional monarchy. Still Hungary bore up bravely, without one thought of yielding even to Russia and Austria in coalition. By a stupendous effort an army was raised of one hundred and forty thousand men. Renowned battles ensued, and victories were won, which struck the allies with dismay, and which caused every Hungarian heart to throb with rapture. There were many deeds of valor and magnanimity performed by the Hungarians which merit immortal renown. But, unfortunately, there now arose a serious division among the Hungarian chiefs. Kossuth, the intellectual guide and head of the Hungarian struggle, was for declaring independence. Georgey, who was commander-in-chief of the army, was in favor of still remaining under the Austrian monarchy, seeking only the reform of abuses. The counsels of Kossuth triumphed; and on the 14th of April, 1849, Hungary issued her declaration of independence, and Kossuth was by acclamation elected governor. There was extraordinary unanimity throughout the nation in these measures; but Georgey, whose counsels had been rejected, was exceedingly chagrined and indignant.

Austria and Russia now roused themselves to redoubled efforts. They raised a united army of two hundred and forty thousand men, and with this enormous force again marched upon Hungary. But there was no longer confidence between the governor of the republic and the commander-in-chief of the army. Georgey openly proclaimed his disapproval of the declaration of independence, and Kossuth watched him with an anxious eye. A series of unfortunate battles ensued, in which the Hungarians, though they fought with bravery never surpassed, were generally worsted. Treason was bitterly suspected as the Hungarians were again and again overpowered. At last it became evident that Hungary must fall. These reverses, seeming to confirm the judgment of Georgey, strengthened his influence, and roused his party to more decisive action.

Under these circumstances Kossuth resigned his office of governor, and Georgey was invested with dictatorial power. The other leading generals of the army, with Kossuth, felt that they had been betrayed. General Bem, in an interview with Georgey, was so impressed with the conviction of his treachery, that he refused to accept, in parting, his proffered hand. Mounting his horse, he galloped to meet at an appointed rendezvous, in the ancient forest of Lugos, several hundred of his fellow-soldiers, chiefly officers.

"Hungary," said he, "has fallen, betrayed rather than conquered. To-morrow it will be proclaimed that 'order reigns in Pesth,' — the order of the executioner. I have no wish to influence others; but so long as I have an inch of steel in my hand, or a brave man at my side, I will defend the cause to which I have devoted my body, my soul, my blood, and my life."

Nearly the whole band received these words with acclamation, and, conscious of their inability any longer to maintain the struggle, retreated to the mountains of Transylvania. Georgey made an unconditional surrender of his whole army of nearly thirty thousand men, with one hundred and forty guns, to the Russians. The scene of surrender was made by the proud victor one of great military pomp and triumph, and to the vanquished it was as melancholy and humiliating as can well be imagined. This event took place at two o'clock in the afternoon of the 14th of August, 1849, at Szollos, which spot has thus been rendered forever memorable.

At the same time, by the order of Georgey, all the fortresses in his possession, and the dispersed corps of the army, were surrendered to the allies, and Hungary was again a shackled slave at the feet of her conquerors. Confiscations, imprisonments, and executions ensued, which extorted a wail of anguish so loud and prolonged, that it thrilled upon the ears of all Christendom. Georgey was pardoned; but fourteen of his highest officers, men whose virtues and heroism had secured the admiration of Europe, perished upon the scaffold. Kossuth, accompanied by about five thousand Hungarians, escaped into the Turkish territory, and took refuge in Orsova, where they were nobly protected by the Sultan from their foes, clamorous for their blood. From Turkey they finally secured a passage to England, and thence to America, and were scattered all over the world, the martyrs of liberty.

Kossuth, after pleading in America the cause of his country in strains of eloquence never surpassed in Ancient Greece or Rome, returned to England, where he has since remained, almost the idol of every generous heart, despairingly awaiting the dawn of a brighter day. The infamous Haynau, who by his atrocities in sending the most illustrious men to the scaffold, and in causing ladies of the highest rank to be scourged, has acquired the nickname of the " Hangman " and the " Hyena," was appointed the Austrian governor of Hungary ; and he ruled the subjugated realm with a rod of iron. The constitution was annulled, trial by jury abolished, the censorship of the press established, and freedom of religious worship prohibited. The Jesuits were again restored to power.

Austria, having been thus effectually aided by Russia, could not join England, France, and Turkey against the Czar in the campaign of Sevastopol. Francis Joseph assumed neutrality. But Nicholas was highly indignant that the Emperor of Austria did not fly to his aid. Consequently, at the close of the war, the Emperor of Russia, rejecting friendly intercourse with Austria, sought friendship and alliance with France. Still it was manifest that the interests of Russia and Austria were so identical, as the two leading aristocratic despotisms of Europe, that, to resist the people struggling for liberty, they would be compelled to unite.

The rapid advance which Sardinia has recently been making in the path of constitutional liberty was exciting the Austrian dominions in Italy to strike for the same progress. Austria, alarmed, sent an army of two hundred thousand men into Sardinia. France immediately sent an army, which the emperor led in person, to aid the Sardinians to repel the invaders. In every battle the Austrians were routed. They were driven out of Piedmont and of Lombardy; and, after the dreadful carnage of Magenta and Solferino, the French and Sardinians were about to drive the Austrians from Venetia, and thus entirely from Italy, when Russia, Prussia, and England interposed their remonstrances. Their threat to unite with Austria against France, Sardinia, and all Italy, then rising in arms, which would have introduced, probably, the most desolating war earth has ever known, compelled France and Sardinia to assent to the treaty of peace called the Treaty of Villafranca.

By this treaty Lombardy was wrested from Austria, and, to the inexpressible joy of its inhabitants, united with the Italian kingdom of Sardinia. The Duchies of Tuscany, Parma, and Modena also drove off their Austrian masters, and, protected by France against Austrian invasion, joined also the Sardinian kingdom. The Venetians, from the highest elations of hope, were again plunged into unutterable despair, as they were left helpless in the hands of their detested masters. Hungary, also, was on the eve of a new struggle for liberty, elated by the fact that the Austrian army was fully engrossed by the struggle with France and Sardinia. New gleams of joy began to penetrate the despairing mind of Kossuth. He repaired to Italy, issued a proclamation to his countrymen, and in a few weeks would have been at the head of all Hungary in arms, when the peace of Villafranca blighted all their prospects, liberating a veteran army of two hundred thousand Austrian troops to crush the slightest movement of the Hungarian people.

But again Venetia and Hungary are grasping their arms,

preparing to strike simultaneously and desperately for freedom. The wonderful success of Garibaldi, in emancipating
Sicily and Naples from intolerable despotism, and annexing
them to the Sardinian kingdom, thus forming a kingdom of
Italy consisting of nearly twenty million of inhabitants, probably secures the emancipation of the Papal States, also, from the
detested sway of the Pope. This will unite all Italy, excepting Venetia, in the Kingdom of Italy. This will certainly be
followed by a rising of the Venetians to break the Austrian
yoke, and unite with their Italian brethren. Austria will
pour her armies into Venetia; and Hungary will instantly
rise. Russia, it is said, is even now preparing to march to the
help of Austria. France, it is said, is prepared to march to
the help of Italy. What will the British Government do?

The last arrivals from Europe announce the following as
the substance of an important telegram recently received from
Vienna : —

"The Emperor Alexander and his government desire sincerely a perfect reconciliation with Austria. The good understanding between Austria and Russia ought never to have
been interrupted. The necessary arrangement for a meeting
between the two emperors will be made without delay; and
measures will be taken to put an end to the present state of
things, which is no longer tolerable."

Such is the attitude of Austria, and of these great questions
of reform, as the autumnal leaves of 1860 are falling to the
ground.

This powerful empire, as at present constituted, embraces : —

1. The hereditary States of Austria, containing 76,199 square miles, 9,843,490 inhabitants.						
2. The duchy of Styria	"	8,454	"	"	780,100	"
3. Tyrol	"	11,569	"	"	738,000	"
4. Bohemia	"	20,172	"	"	3,380,000	"
5. Moravia	"	10,192	"	"	1,805,500	"
6. The duchy of Auschnitz in Galicia	"	1,843	"	"	335,190	"
7. Illyria.............................	"	9,132	"	"	897,000	"
8. Hungary	"	125,105	"	"	10,628,500	"
9. Dalmatia	"	5,827	"	"	320,000	"
10. Venetia...........................	"	8,270	"	"	2,000,000	"
11. Galicia...............	"	82,272	"	"	4,075,000	"

Thus the whole Austrian monarchy contains 256,399 square

miles, and a population which now probably exceeds forty millions. The standing army of this immense monarchy in time of peace consists of 271,400 men, which includes 39,000 horse and 17,790 artillery. In time of war this force can be increased to almost any conceivable amount.

Thus slumbers this vast despotism, in the heart of central Europe, the China of the Christian world. The utmost vigilance is practised by the government to seclude its subjects, as far as possible, from all intercourse with more free and enlightened nations. The government is in continual dread lest the kingdom should be invaded by those liberal opinions which are circulating in other parts of Europe. The young men are prohibited, by an imperial decree, from leaving Austria to prosecute their studies in foreign universities. "Be careful," said Francis II. to the professors in the university at Labach, "not to teach too much. I do not want learned men in my kingdom : I want good subjects, who will do as I bid them." Some of the wealthy families, anxious to give their children an elevated education, and prohibited from sending them abroad, engaged private tutors from France and England. The government took tne alarm, and forbade the employment of any but native teachers. The Bible, the great chart of human liberty, all despots fear and hate. In 1822 a decree was issued by the emperor, prohibiting the distribution of the Bible in any part of the Austrian dominions.

The censorship of the press is rigorous in the extreme. No printer in Austria would dare to issue the sheet we now write; and no traveller would be permitted to take this book across the frontier. Twelve public censors are established at Vienna, to whom every book published within the empire, whether original or reprinted, must be referred. No newspaper or magazine is tolerated which does not advocate despotism. Only those items of foreign intelligence are admitted into those papers which the emperor is willing his subjects should know. The *freedom* of republican America is carefully excluded. The slavery which disgraces our land is ostentatiously exhibited in harrowing descriptions and appalling engravings as a specimen of the degradation to which republican ınstıtu tions doom the laboring class.

A few years ago an English gentleman dined with Prince Metternich, the illustrious prime minister of Austria, in his beautiful castle upon the Rhine. As they stood, after dinner, at one of the windows of the palace, looking out upon the peasants laboring in the vineyards, Metternich, in the following words, developed his theory of social order : —

"Our policy is to extend all possible *material* happiness to the whole population; to administer the laws patriarchally; to prevent their tranquillity from being disturbed. Is it not delightful to see those people looking so contented, so much in the possession of what makes them comfortable, so well fed, so well clad, so quiet, and so religiously observant of order? If they are injured in persons or property, they have immediate and unexpensive redress before our tribunals; and, in that respect, neither I nor any nobleman in the land has the smallest advantage over a peasant."

APPENDIX.

THE NEW CONSTITUTION, AND SEPARATION FROM GERMANY.

THE REICHSRATH TRANSFORMED INTO A NATIONAL LEGISLATURE. — THE "PATH OF CONSTITUTIONALISM." — JEALOUSY BETWEEN AUSTRIA AND PRUSSIA. — WAR WITH DENMARK. — QUARREL BETWEEN AUSTRIA AND PRUSSIA ABOUT SCHLESWIG-HOLSTEIN. — ALLIANCE BETWEEN PRUSSIA AND ITALY. — THE SIX WEEKS' WAR AND SADOWA. — ITALY GAINS VENETIA. — AUSTRIA LOSES HER PLACE IN GERMANY. — THE PATH OF CONSTITUTIONALISM ONCE MORE. — RECONCILIATION OF HUNGARY. — BOSNIA AND HERZEGOVINIA.

THERE is an old proverb which says, "It is always darkest just before daylight." This seems often to be the case, not only in the lives of individual men, but also in the history of the great advances in reform and freedom which have been made among nations. The history of Austria is a good illustration. As was said in the last chapter, the year 1860 found Austria sunk in the darkest night of despotism. The heroic struggle of the Hungarians for freedom had failed. Their chains seemed to be more firmly riveted than ever. The constitution, which had been wrung from the emperor by the agitation which the Hungarian uprising had produced, after a languid existence of a few years, was withdrawn. Except Venetia, the Italian provinces had indeed gained their independence; but poor Venetia seemed to be held in a grasp as cruel and hopeless as ever.

The tranquillity of repression and despair reigned, but already the sun of a more hopeful day was rising. The year 1860 saw the beginning of a new era for Austria. Her wisest statesmen saw that she could no longer stem the rapidly rising tide of liberal influences, and keep her place among the nations.

Without warning, — apparently by a sudden impulse, — really, doubtless, because he had the wisdom to see that he could no longer do otherwise safely, the Emperor Francis Joseph entered "on the path of constitutionalism."

The numbers and the power of the Reichsrath, or council of the empire, were enlarged by a patent issued in March; and on the 21st of October a new constitution was promulgated, in which the emperor expressly renounced the despotic powers which he and his predecessors had so long and so earnestly cherished, and declared that hereafter the right to issue, alter, and abolish laws was to be exercised by him and his successors only with the co-operation of the lawfully assembled diets and of the Reichsrath.

This was followed by propositions in regard to similar changes in Hungary; and on the 27th of February, 1861, a decree was issued, that Hungary, Croatia, Sclavonia, and Transylvania should have the constitutions restored which formerly belonged to them respectively.

At the same time a "fundamental law" was established, which decreed representative institutions for the empire. By this law the Reichsrath was converted into a constitutional legislature composed of two bodies; viz., peers and deputies. That is, an upper and a lower house, similar to the Lords and Commons of England, or the Senate and Representatives of our own country. And this fundamental law declared the constitution and duties of each body. On the 1st of May the new Reichsrath was formally opened by the emperor at Vienna. He then declared his conviction, that "liberal institutions, with the conscientious introduction and maintenance of the principles of equal rights of all the nationalities of his empire: of the equality of all his subjects in the eye of the law; of the participation of the represent-

atives of the people in the legislature, — would lead to the
salutary transformation of the whole monarchy."

Hungary, Croatia, Sclavonia, and Transylvania declined
to send representatives to this Reichsrath. They claimed
that they had constitutions of their own, and rights distinct
from those of the empire at large.

But although all the details of the reform could not be
carried out at once, although all the conflicting claims of
the many and varied nationalities which compose the Austrian empire could not be satisfied and adjusted in a moment,
the "path of constitutionalism," which had seemed so
dreadful heretofore to the Emperors of Austria, was now
fairly entered upon ; and, with a few exceptions, up to the
present time it has not been departed from.   Indeed, Austria
has gone so far and so long in this path now, that it would
be difficult if not impossible for her to turn aside from it
into the old ways of autocratic repression.   The spirit of
the age has fairly lifted this old despotism off its feet, and
set it on a higher plane of freedom ; and this has been done
by an apparently bloodless revolution.   But not really so ;
for the revolts of 1848, and the apparently disastrous struggle of the Hungarians for freedom, have borne late fruit in
the reformation of Austrian government.   Not only that,
but the events which we are now about to describe have
helped on the cause of constitutionalism by changing entirely the position of Austria in Germany.

Austria had for centuries held the leading place in the
German Confederation ; but, since the days of Frederick the
Great, Prussia had been rising in power and influence.   The
smaller States of Germany grouped themselves about these
two great powers.   Between them there had naturally arisen
a great and growing jealousy.   The North of Germany,
represented by Prussia, was commercial in its interests.
The South, represented by Austria, was agricultural.   In
the North, there was industry, progress, education.   In the

South, there had been more repression and conservatism. The North was Protestant, and had experienced all the awakening tendencies which Protestantism has always carried with it. The South had remained under the blighting influence of popery. Since the days of the Reformation, North and South Germany, Prussia, and Austria had more than once been at war with each other; and these conflicts were not forgotten. Now a new tide of popular impulse was rising, which was destined to renew the conflict. Since the days of the wars of Napoleon, a great desire had arisen for the union of the German people under one government. German patriots felt that it was a great loss and damage to this great people — one 'in language and in interests — to go on longer weakened by petty political divisions, split up in a crowd of discordant kingdoms and principalities, only loosely held together in a confederation when they might be one great nation. The Prussian Government, guided now by Bismarck, the keenest, most daring, and most able of modern statesmen, constituted itself the champion of this national aspiration. It was natural that German patriots should look to Prussia rather than Austria as their leader, because, although Prussia was far from being liberal in government, she was purely German; while the Austrian empire was made up of many nationalities, and only a small part of it was German at all. Bohemians and Hungarians and Croats could have little interest in a united German fatherland.

The first step toward the realization of this long-cherished dream was now to be taken. The means which were used to further this noble end were, we must admit, unworthy of so great a cause.

Three small German duchies, Schleswig, Holstein, and Lauenburg, had been attached to Denmark. By a treaty called the Treaty of London, made in 1852, the succession to the government of these duchies was fixed in the Danish crown. Austria and Prussia had signed this treaty. On the 15th of November, 1863, Ferdinand VII., King of Denmark, died; and there was a general ferment of opinion throughout Germany on the subject of these duchies. There was a doubt as to the right of the new Danish king, Christian IX., to the succession. It seemed possible now to do something toward uniting Germany. Austria and Prussia denied the right of Denmark. The matter came before the diet. The duchies were claimed as part of Germany, and a decree of execution was put forth against Christian IX. by the diet of the German Confederation.

It was intended that this decree should be carried out by detachments of such troops of all the States included in the Confederation as might be determined upon by the diet; and, in accordance with this, troops from Hanover and Saxony marched into Holstein, and the Danes retired into Schleswig.

But this did not suit the purpose of Prussia. She artfully proposed that Austria and Prussia alone, as the leading powers in Germany, should execute the decree. To this Austria assented; and hostilities began Feb. 1, 1864. There could be but one result of such a war. It was the strong against the weak. On whichever side the right was, the might was not with the Danes. Perhaps they ought to have had the assistance of England. She was one of the parties to the Treaty of London. But England was not prepared to go to war with Austria and Prussia. The Danes got only an empty sympathy from England; and after a heroic stand, in which they proved themselves worthy foes of their powerful antagonists, they were conquered. On Oct. 30, 1864, the Treaty of Vienna was signed, making over the duchies to Germany.

Now the question was, how to dispose of them. Prussia laid claim to Holstein. She said it was hers by inheritance; that annexation to Prussia would be very advantageous to the interests of Germany in general and not antagonistic to Austria in particular; that the geographical position of the two countries would make it necessary for Prussia to guard Holstein.

Austria said No! to all this. She had been intrusted by the diet with the carrying out of this matter, and could make no such arrangement as Prussia proposed. At any rate, Austria could not allow Prussia to have this increase of territory without a corresponding increase on her part.

And so the quarrel about the dividing of poor little Denmark's spoils went on, as doubtless Bismarck expected it would. For really it was more than a quarrel about which should get a small slice more of territory than the other. It was the beginning of strife between the old order of things and the new spirit of German unity. It was becoming evident that a united fatherland would exalt Prussia and injure Austria. And so the policy of Austria was to keep the small German States separate. She made herself the champion of the Confederation and the diet which had designed making Holstein an independent state under the auspices of the diet and governed by some popular prince.

It is a singular fact, that not only the conservative attitude of Austria as to German politics was getting her into trouble with Prussia, but her new departure toward constitutional freedom was actually a means of aggravating the difficulty. For Prussia and her great prime minister, Bismarck, although representing the patriotism of Germany as to the question of a united fatherland, came very far from representing popular liberty. The Prussian Government was a despotism more enlightened, but not less stern, than that from which Austria was just emerging. The liberals in the duchies, while they may have loved German unity, loved freedom more; and Austria with her new constitution began to seem like a great sun rising out of midnight darkness. They, therefore, turned to her, and preferred that she, rather than Prussia, should control their destinies; and others of the smaller German States sympathized with them. Particularly in Schleswig, which for the present was under the joint administration of Austria and Prussia, things were said and done which gave offense to Prussia. Her officials wanted to repress the expression of popular feeling. Austria, consistently with her new-fledged freedom, and, perhaps, because popular expression favored her side of the quarrel, encouraged it. Bitter recriminations passed between the courts of the two great powers.

At last the strife was quieted by a meeting of the Emperor Francis Joseph with King William at Gastein near Salzburg. An agreement was then made between them, by which the administration of the newly acquired territory was divided, Prussia taking charge of Schleswig, and Austria of Holstein.

The "Convention of Gastein" seemed to produce quiet, but there were other causes of disturbance. Italy, ever on the watch for an opportunity to redeem Venetia, was cultivating friendship with Prussia. Bismarck, seeing doubtless that the trouble with Austria was quieted only in appearance and for the moment, and knowing how valuable the aid of Italy might be in the near future, was meeting her advances in a way that could not but excite Austrian jealousy.

And then there was beside, the irrepressible though at present repressed contest for supremacy in Germany, — a contest which inevitably went on in spite of outward friendliness. There was nothing durable in the arrangement made at the meeting of King William with the Austrian emperor. Perhaps Bismarck, who was the master spirit in all the affair, did not mean that there should be.

On the 30th of January, 1866, he sent a note to Austria, protesting against the freedom of discussion which was allowed in Holstein, the discussion complained of being all against Prussia.

Soon after a second note was sent. This spoke of "the happy days of Gastein," but mourned that affairs were now assuming a very serious aspect; that the bearing of the government of Holstein must be regarded as directly aggressive. It said that Prussia had a right to request Austria to maintain Holstein *in statu quo*, as Prussia felt bound to do in regard to Schleswig. Austria was required to ponder and negotiate, and the note closed with a threat. It stated, that if a negative or evasive answer should be returned, painful as that would be, Prussia would be forced to believe Austria no longer friendly. If it should be impossible for her to act in concert with Austria, Prussia must contract closer alliances in other directions for the advancement of her own immediate interests.

This was supposed to refer to an alliance with Italy, Austria's mortal enemy. The note itself was considered almost a declaration of war. Austria did return a negative and evasive answer. The crisis was fast developing. A council of war was held at Vienna. As to Italy, detested as she was by the Austrians, war would be welcomed with her. If the war gave Italy a chance of gaining Venetia, it also might give Austria a chance to recover what she had lost by the battles of Magenta and Solferino. As to Prussia, it was thought that her army was neither large nor in good condition. It was thought that the German Confederation might be induced to demand decisive action on the Schleswig-Holstein affair. If, in response to this demand, Prussia yielded, her prestige would be destroyed. If she did not yield, she would have all the diet against her; and a decree of federal execution might be obtained against Prussia, and then she might be crushed with all the combined forces of the Confederation.

After the council of war, Austria began secretly to make preparations. The fortresses, especially Cracow, were strengthened: the troops in Bohemia, which lies near Prussia, were re-enforced.

The attention of Prussia was excited, and she began to ask the meaning of all these warlike preparations. Austria replied that the populace in Bohemia had broken out in riots against the Jews.

But the Jews of Bohemia almost all lived in Prague; and the Austrian anxiety for their welfare was bringing troops, as it seemed to Prussia, suspiciously near her frontier. Slowly and cautiously the Austrian army was mobilized. That is, the battalions were raised to their full strength, and supplied with the transportation and other material necessary for a campaign. Steps were taken to strengthen the fortresses in Italy. Military preparations were also made secretly in Saxony and Wurtemberg.

But this activity of preparation for war could not escape the observation of the Prussian Government. Prussia was not so weak or so unprepared as she was supposed to be. She had really been leading her rival on toward the conflict. Bismarck had outwitted the Austrian statesmen throughout the whole affair. He now began to show his purpose boldly. A decree was issued in the king's name, which declared that the authors of any attempt to subvert his authority or that of the Emperor of Austria in the duchies would be imprisoned. The Austrian ambassador protested. The reception of his protest was such that Austria told the States of the Confederation to arm themselves.

Then Bismarck declared, that, on account of the armaments of Austria, Prussia was at last compelled to take measures for the protection of Silesia, which lay near the Austrian frontier; and, moreover, that Prussia must seek guaranties for the future.

This forced from the other German States a declaration of their policy. They wanted to go to war for neither of the antagonists, but to refer the whole matter to the diet. But the days of the diet were numbered. Underneath and far more important than the question as to whether Prussia or Austria should get their way in Schleswig-Holstein, the real question now before Germany was, Shall the old Confedera-

tion be superseded by a new Germany united under the leadership of Prussia? That could be decided only by war, and
the time for decision had come.

Prussia now began openly to put her army on a war-foot-
ing. The battalions which garrisoned the places nearest the
Austrian frontier were increased, but not yet raised to the
full war standard. The field artillery was made completely
ready. The fortresses were garrisoned and provisioned.
Confident in the rapidity with which the whole of her forces
could be mobilized under the new system, which had been for
a long time silently perfected, Prussia delayed until the last
moment calling her men away from their workshops and
farms.

Now the two great rivals stood face to face. Before they
came to blows they argued with each other, as nations, no
less than individual men, who are quarreling, often do. An
English writer puts the debate in this way :—

AUSTRIA. "You must disarm. I really don't mean any
thing by the troops in Bohemia."

PRUSSIA. "Yes, you do. When you disarm, I will."

AUSTRIA. "Well, then, I will withdraw from Bohemia;
but I must take measures for the defense of Venetia against
Italy."

But the Prussians say, "This is just as much a threat
against us as the troops in Bohemia. When Italy is crushed,
then your whole force can be turned against us."

But an Austrian army was got ready against Italy; and
then Prussia took her new ally under her protection, and
demanded, not only disarmament in Bohemia, but also in
Venetia.

Austria answered by increasing her army still more, and
then proposed once more to submit the whole question about
Schleswig-Holstein to the diet. Prussia would have no more
of the diet. She began to mobilize her army; and, at the
end of fourteen days, four hundred and ninety thousand men

stood on parade, armed, clothed, equipped, provided with transportation trains, provisions, ammunition, and field hospitals.

It is doubtful whether a great army has ever been put in the field with such marvelous rapidity. The new Prussian system was now for the first time displayed in its full practical power. And along with this system, by which all the able-bodied men of the nation had been made efficient and well-trained soldiers, ready to be called into the ranks at a few days' notice, a new weapon was now to be brought into use, which was destined to revolutionize warfare.

Breech-loading rifles had been tried before on a limited scale; but, though they had been found far more deadly than other arms, they were considered too complicated for the use of ordinary soldiers.

But a breech-loading weapon invented by a humble mechanic had been adopted by the Prussian Government. It was called the "needle-gun," from the peculiar mechanism used to explode the cartridge. A large portion of the Prussian troops were armed with this now historic needle-gun, with what result we shall see.

The war may be said to have begun on June 16, 1866, when the Prussians entered Saxony, which sided with Austria, and marched upon Dresden, its capital. A strong force also occupied Hanover and Hesse-Cassel, thus protecting the Prussian rear. The Saxon army retired as the Prussians approached, and marched to join the Austrians. The Prussians then occupied Dresden, and thus secured in Saxony a good basis for offensive operations.

The Prussians were divided into three armies. The first was under command of Prince Frederick Charles, who afterward became popularly known among the soldiers as "Our Fritz." The second was commanded by the Crown Prince; and the third, or "army of the Elbe," by Gen. Herwarth. In all, they had about two hundred and twenty-five thousand men in the field, with seven hundred and seventy-four cannon.

The Austrian force was composed of two armies. One under Count Clam Gallas, the other and largest under Gen. Benedek. In all, they numbered over two hundred and sixty thousand men, with seven hundred and sixteen cannon.

The Prussians now marched through the mountain-defiles into Bohemia. To their surprise, and that of every one else, they passed these easily defended defiles without opposition. The reputation of Gen. Benedek was so great, that every one suspected some deep-laid plan by which the Prussians were to be enticed into the heart of the enemy's country and overwhelmed. But no plan at all seems to have been formed. With all her long preparation, the crisis found her unready, her army ill-organized, poorly equipped and provisioned. Benedek had announced to the soldiers, that he was going "to lead the brave and faithful Austrian army against the unjust and wanton foes of the empire." But, instead, the Prussian army was being led against him. It was from the start, and all the way through, a defensive war on the part of Austria. Though brave enough, the Austrians lacked the spirit which animated the Prussians.

The Austrians expected the attack to come from behind the mountains of Eastern Bohemia, and had massed their largest army there. And so, when the advance of Frederick Karl's army crossed the Erzgebirge, it was opposed only by the outlying brigades of Clam Gallas. There were several unimportant engagements, and then a severe fight at Podol, which cost the Austrians a loss of twenty-four hundred men, while the Prussians lost only one hundred and twenty-four.

Two of the Prussian armies now advanced leisurely, driving the enemy before them toward Munchengratz, where Clam Gallas was intrenched. On the 28th of June he was attacked; and, after a short but sharp fight, he was forced to retreat in haste.

The Prussian armies continued to advance by several routes. They took Gitschin after a severe battle, in which they lost two thousand men, and the Austrians twice as many, and encamped the next morning near Horzitz, having established communication with the forces of the Crown Prince: while Clam Gallas retired to join the main army under Benedek. He had proved himself a skillful commander. For with only half as many men as the Prussians, and less than half as many guns, he had compelled his enemies to spend six days in advancing forty miles.

Meanwhile the third Prussian army had crossed the defiles with but little trouble. Gen. Steinmetz alone met with opposition, and was once driven back into the pass. But he persevered, and by six-hours' fighting he got through with a loss of nearly two thousand men. The Austrians lost six thousand. On the 28th he had another battle at Skalitz. He was again successful, causing a loss to the Austrians of over eleven thousand. The Prussian right wing also had a hard fight in coming through the mountains. After coming through one of these defiles, they were driven back. The Austrian general, Gablentz, obtained re-enforcements; and a corps of the Prussian guards was sent to re-enforce the right wing and attack Gablentz. There was a series of battles; and the Austrians were again defeated with a loss of four thousand, while the Prussians lost only eight hundred and thirty-four.

The great preponderance of Austrian loss in these battles was owing, not only to the superior fighting qualities of the Prussian army, but also to the fact that the needle-gun vastly increased the effectiveness of each Prussian soldier.

The deadly power of breech-loading arms was being conclusively proved.[1]

The three Prussian armies were now all in Bohemia, and

---

[1] It is said, that, in one of the first of these engagements, " an entire battalion of Austrians was struck down almost to a man."

moving steadily forward in lines converging toward a point
north of the Austrian army, which was now concentrated
between Josephstadt and Königgrätz.

The two armies were now face to face, and the decisive
battle of the war was to be fought.

On the 1st of July the King of Prussia arrived at the head-
quarters of the army. He had heard that Gen. Benedek
intended to attack the Prussians before the Crown Prince
and the army under his command could come up. The
Crown Prince was approaching, but he was still fifteen miles
away. King William resolved not to wait, either for his
arrival or for Benedek's onset, but to attack at once, and
thus anticipate his enemies.

A message was sent to the Crown Prince, ordering him to
hasten his advance; and on July 3, at eight o'clock in the
morning, the Prussians began to move upon the Austrian
position. They would have been less hasty, it may be, had
they known the true state of affairs. They supposed they
had only part of the Austrian army before them. They were
soon undeceived.

At the foot of the slope, on the crest of which was the
Austrian position, were several villages, occupied by outposts.
The Prussians carried these easily enough, and advanced up
the slope. But now they were met by a withering fire from
their enemy's artillery. Their progress was checked. They
could not advance in the face of the storm of shot and shell
which burst upon them. They were compelled to halt. Benedek, seeing the Prussians hesitate, now hurled his reserves
against their left wing, intending to cut it off, and crush it
before the Crown Prince could have time to come up to its
help. But the Prussians stood their ground with true German stubbornness. All efforts to drive them from their posi
tion were in vain; though at times the left wing wavered,
and seemed on the point of giving way before the overwhelm
ing weight of the Austrian assault. Thus the battle con-

tinued, the artillery on both sides keeping up an incessant and tremendous fire, until, as the day wore on, the Austrian right showed signs of wavering. It was evident that help was coming to the sorely pressed Prussians.

The advance of the army of the Crown Prince was attacking the flank of the Austrian right wing. The Prussians began to cheer. The unseen assailant of the Austrians was evidently becoming more and more formidable every minute. The Crown Prince had come. The Austrian right wing was giving way. It was being rolled up and crushed. The Prussians advanced, and, by partially enclosing the Austrians between two fires, threw them into confusion. The battle was decided. The Austrians were hopelessly and terribly defeated. Their army was speedily broken up, and the soldiers fled in confusion. Many perished in the waters of the Elbe, or were crushed under the wheels of the fleeing baggage-wagons. All that saved the Austrians from the extremest horrors and miseries of such a terrible defeat, was their splendid cavalry, which with undaunted courage stood between the flying host and their foes, — that, and the further fact, that the Prussians were deficient in cavalry.

This great battle is sometimes called Königgrätz, but more commonly Sadowa, from the small town of that name near the battle-field. The Prussian loss was 9,000 men, killed and wounded. The Austrians lost 16,235 killed and wounded, and 22,684 prisoners.

They asked for a truce. It was refused ; and the Prussians pushed forward for Vienna, whither Benedek had withdrawn the shattered remnant of his army. At the same time the Southern army, which had been employed against Italy, was brought to the capital. Every thing was done to strengthen the fortifications of the city ; and preparations were made for a last desperate stand, when the Emperor of the French intervened, and proposed a truce. This was accepted, and was soon followed by a treaty of peace.

Italy, the ally of Prussia in this war, though entering actively into the strife, did not greatly distinguish herself. She entered into the war with the enthusiasm which became her revived nationality, and with heroic determination to free Venetia from the hated Austrian yoke.

An army of two hundred thousand men was raised. Half of this number, under Gen. Della Marmora, were to cross the Mincio between Peschiera and Mantua. The other half were stationed around Bologna to operate on the lower Po.

The Austrian Archduke Albert opposed this force. He had ninety thousand men, beside the garrisons of the great fortresses which compose what is called " the Quadrilateral," and that of Venetia, which were not available for active service.

La Marmora crossed the Po with his army. He proceeded on his march in a careless manner. The Archduke Albert watched him closely ; and, when the Italian army became entangled between the river and the hills, the Austrians attacked them in full force.

The Italian left wing was broken, and would have been destroyed had not another division crossed the river, and, coming to their assistance, held the enemy at bay for the remainder of the day.

The Austrian attack on the Italian right was at first unsuccessful. In the center were the villages of Custoza and Monte Belvidere. These were the keys to the Italian position. There was an obstinate struggle on both sides for the possession of these villages ; but toward the close of the day the Austrians gained them, and victory was decided in their favor. The Italians fell back in fair order toward the Mincio, and were soon re-assembled on the right bank of the river. The loss to each side in this battle was about eight thousand.

The Italian generals now spent more than a week in discussing another plan for a campaign, since this first one had failed. In the mean time the news of Sadowa came, and with it the news that Austria had ceded Venetia to the French Emperor, Napoleon III. Although it was well understood that this was done simply to save Austria the humiliation of giving up Venetia directly to Italy, and that the French emperor would surely hand that much-desired province over, the Italians refused to make a separate treaty with Austria. They remained true to their ally, Prussia, and continued to prosecute the war vigorously. Gen. Garibaldi, with his volunteers, and Gen. Medeci, with a division of the Italian army, advanced into the Trentino, driving before them the small body of Austrians which had been left after the Archduke's army had been withdrawn from Italy to assist in the defense of Vienna. The Italians also made vigorous war by sea. In this, however, they were not very successful; the Austrian admiral, with his small fleet, proving more than a match for them, in spite of their great ironclads. At last Italy was content to sign an armistice. She laid claim to the Trentino, but it was thought that she was sufficiently rewarded and Austria sufficiently punished by the cession of Venetia to a now really united Italy.

By the treaty of Prague (Aug. 23, 1866) which now followed, Austria was completely bereft of her ancient place in Germany. The old Confederation was dissolved; and a new Germany, with Prussia at its head, appeared.

Austria was entirely excluded from participation in this new Germany, and had to consent formally to the surrender of Venetia to Italy, and to pay beside a war indemnity of forty million thalers, the Prussian troops to remain on her territory until it was paid.

It was bitter humiliation to Austria, but the peace purchased at such a heavy cost has brought its blessings. As soon as it was concluded, the emperor turned his attention to home affairs. We have seen how, when constitutional reforms were introduced into the Austrian empire before the

X

war with Prussia, Hungary was dissatisfied. She insisted on
her right to self-government, and refused to be put off with
any thing else.   There was no insurrection or revolution in
Hungary this time.   It was a purely passive resistance that
was now offered. The Hungarians refused to pay taxes : and
Austria, always in financial straits, was, in consequence of
the war, sorely pressed for money ; and this sort of resistance
on the part of Hungary was very effective.

On Dec. 14, 1865, the emperor opened the Hungarian
Diet in person at Pesth.   He then declared, that, so far as
it did not affect the unity of the empire and the position of
Austria as a European power, he was willing to grant what
they demanded, and recognize their right to self-government.

In November, 1866, after the peace had been concluded,
an imperial rescript, signed by the emperor, was published,
in which he promised, by the appointment of a responsible
ministry and the restoration of municipal self-government, to
do justice to the constitutional demands of Hungary.

Not only was the cause of German unity advanced by the
humbling of Austria, but the renovation of the Austrian empire itself and the long-delayed liberation of Hungary was
promoted by it. Austria, having ceased to be a great German
power, was compelled to cherish the other nationalities committed to her care. Of these Hungary was the most important ; and she was now to assume the place which rightfully
belonged to her, — the leading place in the membership of
States which compose the Austrian empire.

The progress of Austria in liberal government has been
rapid since the war with Prussia.

In 1866 Baron Beust, a Saxon, and therefore a foreigner
in Austria, and a Protestant, became the minister of foreign
affairs. Afterward he was made prime minister and chancel
lor of the empire.

In 1867 the Reichsrath assembled at Vienna to deliberate
on amendments to the Hungarian Constitution, on the re-

sponsibility of the imperial ministers to the Reichsrath, on the extension of constitutional self-government in the different provinces, on the re-organization of the army, on the improvement of the administration of justice, and the promotion of the economical interests of the country.

In his speech at the opening of this meeting of the Reichsrath, the emperor said, "To-day we are about to establish a work of peace and concord. Let us throw a veil of forgetfulness over the immediate past, which has inflicted such deep wounds upon the empire. Let us lay to heart the lessons which it leaves behind ; but let us derive with unshaken courage new strength, and the resolve to seek the peace and prosperity of the empire."

On the 8th of June, 1867, the Emperor and Empress of Austria were crowned King and Queen of Hungary at Pesth.

On the 30th of July, 1870, the concordat with Rome, which had long been an incubus upon Austria, was suspended, on account of the proclamation of the infallibility of the pope. One beneficent result of this action was, the bringing about of a better state of feeling between Austria and Italy. A sympathy which had hitherto been wanting arose between these two countries. In the great war of 1870, between France and Prussia, Austria took no part. Nothing could more plainly show how entirely her connection with Germany had been severed ; and nothing could better prove how utterly her hope of regaining her position in Germany had gone out, than the fact that she remained a silent spectator of this great struggle, one result of which was, to consolidate Prussian power in Germany more firmly than ever. It was far better for Austria that she should remain at peace, and exert her strength in the task so new to her of perfecting the institutions of a constitutional state. To this task she applied herself.

In 1873 a reform bill was passed, taking the election of members of the Reichsrath out of the hands of the provincial diets, and transferring it to the body of electors in the several provinces. Almost every householder now has the right to vote.

In the autumn of 1873 an international exhibition of the world's industry, similar to those which had taken place at London and Paris, and afterward in our own country, was held at Vienna. It attracted visitors from all parts of the world.

In 1874 a bill for the abolition of the concordat with the pope was introduced by the government, and measures were taken for the restriction of the power of the Romish clergy. One by one the fetters and the props of despotism were falling, and Austria was entering more and more entirely into the progressive spirit of the age.

The emperor had not always maintained his course " in the path of constitutionalism.'' Between the years 1865 and 1867 he had been inclined to swerve from it. But the terrible lessons of Sadowa had made him sadder and wiser ; and now, in his speech at the opening of the Reichsrath on the 15th of November, 1874, he declared, that, " by the system of direct popular elections, the empire has obtained real independence.''

The treaty of Berlin, which resulted from the war between Russia and Turkey, placed the former Turkish provinces of Bosnia and Herzegovinia under the administration of Austria. It has proved a troublesome trust. But it has extended Austrian territory and influence in the direction of her now manifest destiny. Practically these provinces have been incorporated into the Austrian empire. The acquisition has increased her strength in Eastern Europe. " Austria, as a constitutional state, no longer enfeebled by the just discontent of the multitudinous races which she governs, enjoys abundantly the elements out of which a prosperous career may be fashioned.''

CHAPTER XXXIV.

HISTORY OF AUSTRIA-HUNGARY SINCE 1878.

HETEROGENEITY OF POPULATION.—EXTERNAL AND INTERNAL PROGRESS.—THE TRIPLE ALLIANCE.—FEARS OF A RUSSIAN WAR.—IMPROVEMENTS IN THE ARMY.—REFORMS IN CURRENCY AND IN THE FRANCHISE.—THE CIVIL MARRIAGE BILL.—LANGUAGE AND RACE ANTAGONISM.—ANTI-SEMITISM.—DEATH OF THE CROWN PRINCE: OF KOSSUTH.—THE MILLENNIAL EXPOSITION IN HUNGARY.—ASSASSINATION OF THE EMPRESS ELIZABETH.—THE FUTURE OF AUSTRIA-HUNGARY.

THE history of Austria-Hungary since the treaty of Berlin in 1878 has been, on the one hand, one of internal improvements, both material and constitutional, making for a higher order of civilization and adjustment of relations with foreign nations. This has been accomplished, on the other hand, not without much party strife, and friction between the several nationalities which the monarchy now embraces. This national emulation is the more to be expected when we consider the differences of customs, religion, and particularly of language, which exist within the comparatively small region covered by the Austria-Hungarian dominion. Not only Germans and Hungarians, but several Slavonic nationalities, such as Czechs and Poles, are represented within its borders to-day. In the imperial army eleven languages are spoken; and the strong religious antagonism which often breaks forth into violent expression between Catholics and Jews goes also to make the internal life of the nation at times very turbulent. A great part, however, of the political perturbation arises from the jealousy with which those speaking one language regard the political favors bestowed upon, or successes gained by, those speaking a different language.

It is to be noticed too that the parts out of which Austria-Hungary are formed are less homogeneous, politically, than those of any other European nation, and that consequently it has required much shrewd diplomacy on the part of the country and her advisers to refrain from falling into the horrors of a war with other nations, and thus, possibly, embroiling the whole of Europe.

An example of the heterogeneity just referred to is the peculiar relations of Austria to Bosnia and Herzegovina, whose fate was narrated in the last chapter. The Congress of Berlin ceded these two small countries to Austria, to be administered and occupied, while, strictly speaking, the title of them remained with, and to this day belongs to, Turkey, of which they are a province. Add to this that when occupied a dispute arose immediately between Austria and Hungary as to which of them should have the privileges which this occupation implied. This difference between the two parts of the Austria-Hungarian monarchy was settled only by agreeing that both should have the two new countries, and that the common imperial government should administer them.

Perhaps a still better example of the national heterogeneity is the great number of national and political parties in the houses of parliament. It will suffice to mention two of them. The German party of the Austrian lower house is anxious to return to the state of affairs which existed from 1806 to 1866; in other words, they desire to be united in some manner to Germany. This party represents the Germans, numerous in Bohemia, Moravia, Styria, Lower Austria, Silesia, and some in the Alps. On the other hand, Poles and Ruthenians wish to be united with Russia.

The progress made in the administration of the country since 1878, during which time she has had no serious wars and her material and national prosperity has ostensibly increased, falls naturally into two divisions. 1st. External progress, which will include the improvement of relations with foreign powers already referred to. 2d. Internal progress. To these will be added a short account of the party strife, in spite of which the monarchy has grown to be one of the great powers of Europe. Party strife is common enough in most nations, but has been more markedly spectacular in Austria-Hungary than in most of the other nations.

The most significant advance made in the direction of external progress by Austria-Hungary was when in 1879 she signed a defensive treaty of alliance with Germany. . This was, on Germany's part, a far-seeing policy of the late Prince Bismarck.   It resulted in added strength both to Germany and Austria, and the latter was once and for all excluded from all purely German affairs.   Both countries were thus a further protection to the peace of Europe, in that they constituted a formidable enemy with which, in case of any war, Russia would have to cope.   This was an important gain in the European politics of the time, for Russia had been making great strides in the direction of Constantinople. This alliance between Austria-Hungary and Germany tended to hold Russia back.

The alliance, still further strengthened in the autumn of 1881 by Italy's joining, thus forming the so-called *Dreibund* or Triple Alliance, gave to Austria-Hungary a still more powerful voice in the concert of European powers.

The subsequent history of the country is marked only

by the occasional disturbances in peaceful tranquillity caused by revolution and disorder in the smaller Balkan states—Servia, Roumania and Bulgaria.

A difference arose in 1883 between Austria and Roumania over the latter's refusal to accept the decisions of a conference which had met in London in February, and at which the representative of Austria had made concessions in the favor of Roumania. This disaffection, on the part of the smaller state, was patched up, however, by a friendly visit of the king, Charles, to the court of Vienna.

The year 1884 saw the end of a rivalry with Russia under the leadership of Count Kalnoky, who had been appointed three years before to the duties of Foreign Minister upon the death of Haymerle. An interview between the emperors of Austria, Germany and Russia was brought about, at which a more cordial *entente* between them was effected by the efforts of the foreign ministers. This marked the highest point of success in foreign relations since 1866; for it Austria had to thank a line of notable foreign ministers. Counts Beust and Andrassy had managed the felicitous alliance with Germany, under Count Haymerle Italy had been added to the alliance, and Kalnoky had effected the reconciliation of Russia. Austria was now more strongly protected against attack from foreign nations than she had been for several hundred years. Although not altogether approved by the Hungarian half of the monarchy, whose patriotism was somewhat hurt by the terms of the agreement, the understanding with Russia was shown to be in the direction of peace and not to have any ulterior motive; and the wholesome effects of the confidence in the balance of power in Europe which it gave rise to was of great material advantage not only to Austria-Hungary, but to the small states of the Balkan peninsula, and in-

spired the latter, together with Turkey, with a wish
to maintain the best relations possible with the dual
monarchy.

In the following year a temporary estrangement took
place between the peoples of Austria and Germany,
though it did not, of course, take the shape of open
rupture. Prince Bismarck had concluded an agreement with Spain by which the duties levied on rye
imported from that country were to be made lower
than those on rye brought into Germany from Austria.
This, though not in itself enough to cause any very
hard feeling, was only one of a number of changes
made in German tariffs which were not pleasing to
Austria. In addition to the injured sentiment regarding tariffs, Germany had still further irritated Austria
by expelling many Austria-Hungarian Poles who had
settled in Germany. This action, however, having
been satisfactorily explained by the German authorities, and measures having been taken by the home government to receive and give temporary shelter to the
refugees, the irritation was allayed and finally forgotten. Promises on the part of the government to make
a final customs arrangement with Germany further
quieted the dissatisfaction at this time.

The attention of Europe was now turned in the
direction of Bulgaria, where a revolution threatened to
terminate the balance begun by the Congress of Berlin
and to precipitate the powers into the former state of
conflict which was ended by that congress. The sympathies of Germany and Austria now tended to draw
them further apart, and, at the same time, to unite
England and Austria. The latter, however, wisely refrained from taking any active part in the eastern
question, and preserved its neutrality.

In 1887 the amicable relations with Russia were
brought to a state of great tension, resultant upon

the threatening attitude, position and mobilization of
the Russian army upon the Austrian frontier of Galicia.   Measures were quickly taken to protect Galicia,
which, on the northeastern boundary of Hungary, was
particularly open to attack from Russia on account of
its geographical nature.   Galicia is a plain separated
from Russian Poland on the north partially by the
river Vistula.   In addition to its easy access from
Russia, it is further unfortunate strategically, being
separated from Hungary by a great natural barrier,
the Krapacks or Western Carpathian Mountains.   The
threatening position occupied by large numbers of
the Russian army, which were gathering about the
Galician frontier, was the signal for a display of
great activity in the Austria-Hungarian army.   By
extraordinary work on the part of the gun factories,
the whole army was supplied with Mannlicher rifles,
and the cavalry and infantry were much increased in
numbers.

The following year saw closer relations established
between Austria and Turkey.   This was due merely
to material causes in the shape of two railways, one
to Salonica, opened May 18, and another to Constantinople, opened August 11.   This year, too, the Emperor
Francis Joseph celebrated the fortieth anniversary of
his succession to the throne, which he ascended December 3, 1848, and was gratified to observe that the international atmosphere of Europe was less clouded than
at any time for many years.

The continued peaceful foreign relations in the case
of Austria were and have been undisturbed to the present day, Austria having wisely refrained from doing
anything to subvert the pacific order of events.   In 1891
an appeal was made to her to give aid in restoring to
the Pope of Rome his temporal power in Italy, but this
was obviously impossible, in view of the nature of the

participation of King Humbert's government in the Triple Alliance.

The foreign relations of Austria-Hungary since that time, in the hands of Count Kalnoky, and after 1895 under the guidance of his successor, Count Goluchowsky, who closely follows the policy of Kalnoky, have been continually directed toward the peace of nations, though a proposition for general disarmament, made as early as 1893, was unfavorably received by the monarchy. Compacts, largely commercial in nature, were made with Servia in 1892, with Russia in 1894, and again in 1897, the latter excluding England from the advantages of the agreement.

The internal progress of the country has been most satisfactory on its material side, though the legislation necessary for its accomplishment has been carried on with the most unfortunately notorious partisan disagreements, which too often resulted in individual personal violence on the part of the legislators. The time, however, available for serious debate in the Austria-Hungarian parliaments has been devoted, after much consideration of the details of carrying out the provisions made by the Berlin Congress, to the preparation and passage of several laws important to the peaceful and prosperous administration of the interior.

The greatest attention next to the maintenance of the army was given to the legislation with respect to the reform of the currency, the franchise, and the civil regulation of marriages. In 1886 a bill was introduced creating a militia, to be composed of all men between the ages of nineteen and forty-two not belonging either to the regular army or the regular reserves. It was estimated that the strength of this militia would be about 330,000. This bill was passed in 1889, but not without demonstrations of much violence on the part of the Hungarians, who were obliged to see this measure permanently adopted instead of for ten years only, as before, which would have given them more voice in the matter. The strengthening of the army and the frontier defenses continued in 1891. The apparent intention on the part of Russia to station permanently a large force on the Galician frontier called for appropriations to be made for costly stone barracks to be built and extensive new fortifications at Brody, Tarnopol and Stanislau. This, together with increase of artillery, new rifles and tents and smokeless powder in 1891, was followed in 1893 by a reorganization and extension of the *landwehr* or regular militia. There was nothing in this, however, that would not be expected, as a natural increase of army, after the agreement between Germany and Austria; which agreement is understood to have stipulated a regular augmentation of the military forces in order to keep pace with the other European powers.

The reform of the currency was taken up in 1892, and after lengthy consideration and investigation concerning the position abroad of Austria-Hungarian State Funds, the two parliaments, at Vienna and at Buda-Pesth, simultaneously resolved in July to adopt a gold standard and to mint two new gold coins and two new silver coins, besides numerous nickel and bronze pieces as fractional currency, which took the place of the then existing coinage.* In 1894 the resumption of specie payments went into effect.

The electoral reform was accomplished in 1893, un-

---

* The gold coins are:
  20 kronen piece = $4.052   10 kronen piece = $2.026
  The silver coins are:
      1 krone = 100 heller = $0.20   ½ krone = $0.10
  The nickel are:
          20 heller = $0.04   10 heller = $0.02
  The bronze coins are of one and two-heller pieces.

der the new Windischgrätz ministry, by the extension
of the franchise so as to give a vote not only to lit-
erates, but to all who have contributed to a working-
man's fund for the space of two years. In order to
counterbalance the excessive power which might thus
be given to the new voters, they were put in a new
curia or voting class, whose delegates in the Reichsrath were limited to 43. This gives five *curiæ* to the
Reichsrath, the other four being: first, the great land-
owners, with 85 delegates; second, the towns, with 48
delegates; third, the chambers of commerce, with 21
delegates; and, fourth, the rural communities, with
129 delegates. This new adjustment in the franchise
gave to the large middle class a representation which
they had long coveted.

In spite, however, of the reforms of the franchise,
the abuse still maintains by which the emperor is allowed, in some cases obliged, to create peers for the
purpose of influencing the vote in parliament. As
late as 1895, he created, on the "recommendation" of
the premier, Baron Banffy, four new peers, which enabled him to pass through the House of Magnates bills
for freedom of worship, and to allow those not Jews to
be converted to Judaism.

Much of the interest in the internal progress of Austria has centered about the legislation with regard to
marriage. As early as 1883 a bill was announced
making legal the marriage of a Jew and a Christian.
Further legislation was resumed in 1892 in the shape
of a bill providing that all marriages should be performed with the civil ceremony first. This was neces-
sitated by the fact that it had long been the custom in
Hungary for the male children of mixed marriages to
be brought up in the faith of their fathers and the female
in that of their mothers. An attempt had been made
to compel the clergyman tending to the spiritual needs

of one parent, when he baptized an infant to his faith, to notify the pastor who attended to those of the other. To this order of things the Catholic clergy refused to agree, and all attempts to make them act in accordance with it, or to bring about any reconciliation, had been found useless. To remedy this state of affairs, even though indirectly, obligatory civil marriage was proposed. The bill was at first rejected, then sent back to the lower house for amendments, but returned to the House of Magnates unchanged, where it finally passed on June 21, 1894, by a very small majority. This was followed by a second bill concerning the religion of the children of mixed marriages, and a third, which provided that births, deaths and marriages should be registered by the government. These bills were the subject of much contention for several years, and were finally made laws only upon the most earnest desires of the emperor, who was known to have, in spite of this fact, a personal dislike for the bill. It had been a struggle between Roman Catholics and other religions, and terminated as it did in spite of the fact that Greek Catholic and Greek orthodox churches did not favor it. The orthodox Jews were also opposed to it.

Complicated with the question of civil marriage were two other politico-religious matters—one, that of the children of mixed marriages, being just noticed, and the other involving the free practice of all religions. Previous to 1892 the custom had been to divide the religious beliefs into two classes, one of which was "received" and the other merely "tolerated." The Jewish faith had been included under the latter head, and by the present bill it was proposed, among other things, to "receive" the Jewish religion. This bill, called the "Freedom of Worship" bill, granted the right to decline or profess any religion whatever.

To illustrate how the feelings of rivalry engendered

between the different nationalities of Austria-Hungary
continually came to the surface in the parliamentary
actions, we here notice the story of the repeated defeat
of the project to found a Czech university in Prague.
There was already a German university there; in fact,
the most ancient German university in Europe, having
been founded in 1348. There was also a good reason
for the establishment of a Czech university; for the
number of residents of Prague, speaking that language, was, at this time (1881), as great as that of
the German-speaking inhabitants. The bill for the
foundation of the university was read for the third
time on May 31, 1881, and the Germans in the Hungarian parliament, who were in the majority, all voted
against it. The bill was then dropped, and instruction
in the Czech language was taken up by a branch of
the German university. Certain German students of
the university, with their colors ostentatiously displayed, marched, on June 26 of the same year, sing-
ing German national songs as they went, to a little
village called Kuchelbad, where they celebrated the
founding of a new student society called *Austria*.
The Czechs were much enraged by this show of pride,
broke their way into the room where the students were
holding their meeting, and attacked them. This resulted in a serious riot, which was not put down for
several days. As an indication of the implacable
hatred between these two nationalities, this incident
caused great solicitude in Vienna for the stability of
the empire; so great, in fact, that General von Kraus
was appointed military governor of Bohemia, and the
civilian, Baron von Weber, was retired.

In 1886 a bill was introduced in parliament to remove
certain regulations concerning the use of the Czech language in Bohemia. These regulations had been bitterly opposed by the Germans there, and had caused

them much discomfort and irritation. The German members demanded that the Czech language should be used only in the purely Czechish localities. This movement was rejected, whereupon 73 German members left the diet at once and refused to take part in any of its doings. This had been done before in 1871, and the diet had been forced to make concessions to the seceding Germans; but this time the scheme did not work, and the example of the members at Prague was not, as they had hoped it would be, followed by their German brothers at Vienna.

In October, 1895, an unfortunate series of riots occurred at Agram, during a visit of the emperor. Agram is in Croatia, where the native population is Roman Catholic, but there is a proportion of Servians who are believers in the Greek Orthodox faith. The Servians have been permitted to use the Servian flag in their religious celebrations. The use of Servian flags and colors on the occasion of the festivities attending the presence of the emperor was so intensely irritating to their Croatian neighbors that the latter, chiefly students, stoned the windows of the church where the Servians were, entered it and carried off the flags there displayed. With the mob at their heels, the students then proceeded to disfigure other Servian buildings, and then exhibited in a similar manner their hatred toward the Hungarian insignia on a triumphal arch erected in honor of the emperor. The gendarmes succeeded in restoring the Hungarian colors, but did not dare to replace the Servian flag, as the disorder was becoming more general, and was directed particularly toward the Servians, than whom the Croatians are three times as numerous. Order was restored only after the arrest and punishment of the ringleaders.

The race feeling against the Jews in the empire has always been very strong, as is illustrated by the following incident which occurred in 1882, and absorbed public attention for a year. It was reported in Hungary that Esther Solyoszy, a Christian girl, had been murdered by a Jew in a small village near Tokay. It was further claimed that she was murdered so that her blood could be used in the rites attending the ordination of a Jew butcher, a superstition concerning the Jews current among the Magyar Protestants. Three months after the disappearance of Esther Solyoszy, a body of a girl was found near by drowned in the river Theiss, and alleged to be that of the murdered girl. It was subsequently proved that it was not, and that persons of anti-Semitic sympathies had hired men to place the body in the river and caused the accusation of murder to be preferred against the Jewish butcher. The matter was dragged into the debates of the Hungarian parliament and called forth violent language and action on the part of some of the deputies.

The sentiment of hatred against the Jews in the city of Vienna is shown by the speeches of several of the members of the Reichsrath on excluding the Jews from the benefits of the electoral reform of 1896. Said one: "Jews, whether baptized or not, are excluded from exercising the franchise, and are a menace to the whole community. There is no means of protection against their encroachments, unless it be the confiscation of their property. These insolent persons deserve nothing but the horsewhip"; and another affirmed: "I am of the opinion that the franchise can be exercised only by men in human society. I cannot concede to the Jews the right of humanity, and think we should make all intercourse between men and Jews punishable by criminal law, as an obscene act contrary to nature."

This perhaps will give, better than anything else,

in addition to the light it throws upon contemporary anti-Semite feeling in the monarchy, a glimpse of the manners of Austria-Hungarian legislation.

Certain events of public interest in Austria-Hungary, and indeed in the whole civilized world, have occurred during the time covered by this chapter.

In 1889 the Crown Prince Rudolph, then thirty-one years of age, shot himself through the head with a pistol—a sad incident, which was the more unfortunate owing to the circumstances of doubtful morality which surrounded the latter years of his life. The brother of the emperor then became the heir-apparent to the throne. He, in turn, transferred this prerogative to his son, the Archduke Francis Ferdinand, nephew of the present emperor.

In 1894 the Hungarian patriot, Louis Kossuth, died. His funeral at Buda-Pesth was a signal for national demonstrations of sorrow, and was publicly attended. Over two hundred thousand persons lined the route of his funeral procession. An oration was delivered by the famous writer, Mamus Jokai. Partisan feeling ran so high at the time that the Royal Opera and the National Theatre were seriously damaged by the onslaught of a mob led by university students.

The one thousandth year of the existence of Hungary as a nation was celebrated by the opening on May 2, 1896, of a millennial exposition at Buda-Pesth. The exposition was opened amid brilliant pageantry by the king in person. Features of the exhibition were a collection of historical relics displayed in buildings in the styles of various centuries and specially built for the occasion. The products of the country—industrial and agricultural—were given a full representation in the exhibition. A village was also constructed in the exposition grounds to illustrate the different nationalities which go to make up the Hungarian population. The

Asiatic origin of the Magyar race was shown by the works of an Arabian writer who affirms that they were originally a tribe of nomadic Turks, driven from their own country, who finally crossed the plains of the lower Danube, and, on the invitation of King Arnulph of Bavaria, settled in what is now Hungary. Christianity was introduced in the tenth century, and at the same time the different tribes which had hitherto remained nomadic warriors were united to form the nucleus of the present Hungarian nation. The Hungarians were a bulwark against the inroads of the eastern barbarians, and thus were of permanent use in the progress of western civilization. The development of the Hungarian people during the last hundred years was shown by the population which at the beginning of the nineteenth century was three millions and is now over eight millions.

In the same year, 1896, was consummated the work, intrusted to Austria-Hungary by the Congress of Berlin in 1878, of making a channel through what is called the Iron Gate of the Danube. The Iron Gate is really one of a series of rocks projecting out of the water between Orsova in Hungary and Gladova in Servia, which have made navigation there always very precarious. The rock known as the Iron Gate was cut through by a canal two miles long, over two hundred and fifty feet broad and ten feet deep. The work of excavating this enormous channel took several years to complete, and cost nearly $10,000,000. As a result of this the Danube was then for the first time navigable from the Black Sea the entire distance to Vienna. The completion of this work was signalized by the presence of the Emperor Francis Joseph, who formally opened the river to navigation with imposing ceremonies on September 27th.

In the following year, 1897, a remarkable agrarian

movement in the peasantry of Galicia and other portions of the country was headed by an excommunicated
priest, a socialist and a man of much eloquence. He
fired his hearers to riotous demonstration, as is so frequently the case in the annals of the Austria-Hungarian
monarchy, but with little result, the insurrection being
finally put down by the imperial troops.

The year 1898 was a turbulent one in Austria-Hungarian politics. The new cabinet of Baron von Sautsch
resigned and was replaced by one under the Count von
Thun Hohenstein.

On September 10th a man supposed to be an Italian
anarchist named Lucchesi assassinated the Empress
Elizabeth. Her body was taken to Vienna. The assassin declared he had done the deed on his own responsibility and not upon the instigation of others.
As a result of the information that he was an Italian,
anti-Italian outbreaks occurred in Austria and even in
France, where there was no great Austrian sympathy.
The funeral of the empress took place at Vienna on
September 17th amid marks of general sorrow and
sympathy for the bereaved emperor.

From the viewpoint of 1898, it would seem that the
present chapter might conclude once for all the history
as a separate nation of Austria-Hungary. The seeds
of disruption have been sown by the government and
must ere long be reaped. The many divergent tendencies, political, religious and linguistic, which make
Austria not a strongly centralized government but a
conglomeration of petty states with differing interests,
have caused this monarchy of to-day to be likened to a
barrel of gunpowder into which a spark is expected
any moment to fall. What these strongly centrifugal
tendencies point to is the partition of the empire by
Germany and Russia, the two gradually increasing
in strong centralized administration and in homogene-

ous character, and already attracting to themselves and absorbing the commercial and the sentimental interests of different parts of the Austria-Hungarian empire. The empire had in 1897 an army estimated on the basis of the grand war total of 1,700,000 men, but, as already noted, there are eleven different dialects spoken by these men, and it is predicted that they could hardly be held together against any one enemy of Austria in case of war.

INDEX.

A.

ADOLPHUS (of Nassau) election of over the Germanic empire, 36.

summoned to answer charges against him, 37.

deposed by the diet, 37.

death of, 37.

ADRIAN assumes the tiara, 114.

ÆNEAS SYLVIUS, remarks of, 72.

AGNES (daughter of Cunegunda) to marry Rhodolph's son, 31.

engaged in the massacre, 40.

enters a convent, 41.

AIX-LA-CHAPELLE, coronation of Albert I. at, 38.

coronation of Charles V. at, 107.

taken possession of by Rhodolph, 193.

peace of, 461.

ALBERT (fourth Count of Hapsburg), 17.

departure of for the holy war, 17.

address of to his sons, 18.

death of, 18.

the favorite captain of Frederic II., 19.

ALBERT I. succeeds his father, 35.

his character, 35.

elected Emperor of Germany, 37.

victor at Gelheim, 37.

assassination of, 40.

ALBERT III. rules with Otho, 46.

acquisitions of, 47.

ALBERT IV., succession of, 51.

improvements projected by, 58.

ALBERT V. declared of age, 59.

accepted King of Hungary, 62.

death of, 65.

ALBERT (of Bavaria) declines the throne of Hungary, 66.

ALBERT (Archduke) the candidate of the Catholics, 229.

ALLIANCE of barons to crush Rhodolph of Hapsburg, 21.

same dissolved, 22.

ALPHONSO (of Castile) candidate for crown of Germany, 23.

ALPHONSO (King of Naples), abdication of, 84.

AMURATH, conquests of, 64.

ANABAPTISTS, rise of the sect of, 115.

ANHALT (Prince of), dispatched with a list of grievances to the emperor, 211.

ANHALT (Prince of) (*continued*), address to the emperor, 212.

ban of the empire declared against, 265.

ANN (Princess of Hungary and Bohemia), marriage of to Ferdinand I., 145.

ANNA (of Russia), desire of to secure a harbor for Russia, 400.

ANECDOTES of Rhodolph, 33.

of Charles V., 144.

APOLOGY of Maximilian, 96.

ASCHHAUSEN, confederacy at, 194.

AUGSBURG, diet of, 24.

bold speech of the diet at, 102.

triumphal reception of Maurice at, 138.

Confession of, 118.

AUGUSTUS II. loses and regains his empire, 382.

death of, 382.

AULIC COUNCIL, establishment of the, 102.

AUSTRIA, a portion of given as dowry to Hedwige, 25.

nucleus of the empire of, 27.

invasion of by John of Bohemia, 49.

wonderful growth of, 52.

division of, 72.

accession of Ladislaus over, 81.

the house of invested with new dignity, 101.

becomes a part of Spain, 108.

the empire of apparently on the eve of dissolution, 286.

the leading power in Europe, 314.

dispute as to the succession to the crown of, 352.

treaty between Spain and, 373.

Maria Theresa ascends the throne of, 415.

deplorable state of at that time, 415.

defeat of by Frederic, 420.

the proposed division of, 422.

prosperity of, 444.

important territory wrested from, 458.

alliance of with Prussia, 459.

Joseph II. ascends the throne of, 491.

situation and character of, 492.

languages spoken in, 493.

Leopold ascends the throne of, 500.

Y

CHRISTIANA (*continued*) abdicates in favor of Charles Gustavus, 302.
CHRISTIAN IV. (of Denmark), leader of the Protestants, declares war, 267.
conquered by Ferdinand, 268.
CHURCH, exactions of the, 102.
CILLI, influence of Count over Ladislaus, 68.
driven from the empire, 68.
CLEMENT VII. succeeds Adrian as pope, 116.
CLEVES, duchy of put in sequestration, 213.
COLOGNE, the Archbishop of joins the Protestants, 124.
deposition of the Archbishop of, 126.
CONDUCT, Luther presented with a safe, 110.
CONFESSION OF AUGSBURG, 118.
reading of, 119.
CONGRESS at Rothenburg, 226.
at Hanau, 445.
at Prague, 1618, and letter of to Matthias, 236.
of electors at Frankfort, 35.
CONSPIRACY against Albert, 36.
formed by Albert against Adolphus, 37.
CONSTANTINOPLE, capture of by the Turks, 64.
CONSTITUTION, Charles V. required to sign a, 108.
COUNCIL of Trent, 124.
of Trent in 1562, 164.
of State convened in Spain, 331.
CREMNITZ, resistance of, 148.
CREMONIA to be disposed of as plunder, 89.
CROATIA invaded by the Turks, 195.
CROTZKA, battle of, 407.
CRUSADE against the Turks, 64.
CUNEGUNDA (wife of Ottocar), her taunts, 27.
offer of to place Bohemia under the protection of Rhodolph, 31.

D.

DANUBE, position of Austria on the, 25.
DAUN (Count), honors of at his victory, 478.
DENMARK, the King of obliged to yield to Charles Gustavus, 306.
DIEPOLD thrown from the palace by the mob, 328.
DIET, command of the of Augsburg to Ottocar, 14.
at Augsburg, 118.
at Augsburg, 130.
at Brussels, 139.
at Lubec, 269.
at Prague, in 1547, 158.
at Prague, 179.
the Protestant at Prague, 209.
decrees of the, 210.
at Passau, 137.
its agreement as to the rights of the Protestants, 188.
at Pilgram, 66.
at Presburg, accusation of Leopold by the, 309.
at Ratisbon, 179.
at Spires, 116.

DIET (*continued*) at Stetzim, 349.
demands of, 350.
at Worms, 86.
refusal of the at Worms to coöperate with Maximilian, 96.
at Znaim, 61.
power of the Hungarian, 308.
DOCTRINE of the three parties, 190.
ancient and modern, contention about shadowy points of, 255.
DRESDEN, treaty of, 458.

E.

ERNEST, death of, 202.
ELEONORA (wife of Leopold), her character, 335.
marriage of, 336.
her death, 337.
ELFSNABEN, a fleet assembled at by Gustavus Adolphus, 281.
ELIZABETH (wife of Philip V.), ambition of, 371.
demands of on Charles VI., 372.
ELIZABETH (of Russia), death of, 479.
EMERIC TEKELI invested with the Hungarian forces, 319.
ENGLAND, assistance of against the Turks, 94.
supports the house of Austria against France, 332.
curious contradictory conduct of, 346.
pledge of to support the Pragmatic Sanction, 380.
supports Austria to check France, 428.
determines to support Maria Theresa, 436.
prodigality of, 447.
war declared against by France, 448.
purchases the aid of Poland, 452.
private arrangement of with Prussia, 457.
remonstrated with for its treatment of the queen, 463.
alliance of with Prussia, 466.
a subsidy voted Prussia by, 475.
alarmed at the strides of Austria and Russia, 499.
EPERIES, tribunal at, 324.
ERNEST, conquests of, 59.
EUGENE (Prince) commands the Austrian army, 332.
his heroic capture of Belgrade, 363.
his disapproval of the war, 389.
death of, 398.
funeral honors of, 399.
EUROPE, condition of the different powers of, 269.
EXCOMMUNICATION of the Venetians, 97.

F.

FAMILY of Rhodolph, 25.
the three daughters of the imperial, 364.
FERDINAND (of Austria) invested with the government of the Austrian States, 113.

www.ingramcontent.com/pod-product-compliance
Lightning Source LLC
Chambersburg PA
CBHW032252020726
47495CB00001B/76